Hope Springs™

THE VIRTUE CHRONICLES

THE WARRIOR MAIDEN

Hope Springs™

THE VIRTUE CHRONICLES

THE WARRIOR MAIDEN

By Paul McCusker

AUGUSTINE INSTITUTE
Greenwood Village, CO

Augustine Institute
6160 S. Syracuse Way, Suite 310
Greenwood Village, CO 80111
Tel: (866) 767-3155
www.augustineinstitute.org

Cover design: Ben Dybas

© 2020 Paul McCusker
All rights reserved.

ISBN 978-1-950939-99-2

Printed in Canada

Dedicated to the Maiden herself.

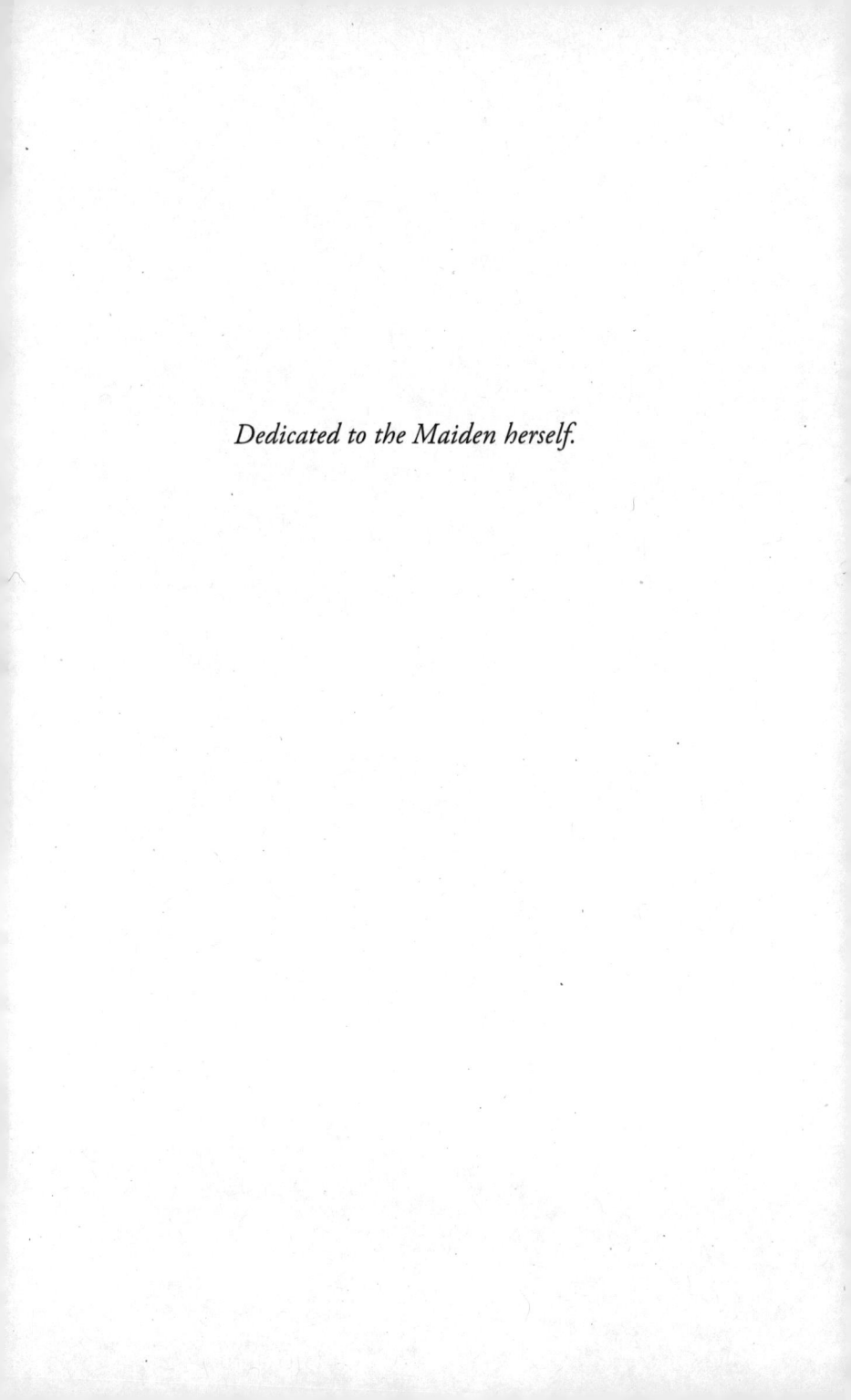

THE WARRIOR MAIDEN

CHAPTER 1	1
CHAPTER 2	13
CHAPTER 3	19
CHAPTER 4	39
CHAPTER 5	45
CHAPTER 6	53
CHAPTER 7	73
CHAPTER 8	85
CHAPTER 9	99
CHAPTER 10	105
CHAPTER 11	113
CHAPTER 12	123
CHAPTER 13	131
CHAPTER 14	143
CHAPTER 15	155
CHAPTER 16	161
CHAPTER 17	171
CHAPTER 18	177

CHAPTER 19	191
CHAPTER 20	203
CHAPTER 21	209
CHAPTER 22	223
CHAPTER 23	239
CHAPTER 24	251
CHAPTER 25	257
CHAPTER 26	263
CHAPTER 27	279
CHAPTER 28	301
CHAPTER 29	317
CHAPTER 30	337
CHAPTER 31	351
CHAPTER 32	363
CHAPTER 33	369
CHAPTER 34	377
CHAPTER 35	389
CHAPTER 36	415
CHAPTER 37	431
CHAPTER 38	445
CHAPTER 39	453
CHAPTER 40	459
CHAPTER 41	467
CHAPTER 42	479

1

Andrew Perry stood in the middle of a room full of clocks. There were clocks of all kinds hanging on the walls, sitting on shelves, standing like soldiers in perfect rows.

He rubbed his eyes. His legs were unsteady. He felt as if he'd just stepped off a moving train.

A loud and solemn chime began behind him, coming from a man-sized clock in the corner. The hands on its ornate face showed 3:20. Why was the clock chiming at 3:20?

It was odd. But then again, everything Andrew had just experienced was odd.

How am I going to explain this to my parents? he wondered.

The other clockfaces in the room peered at him. They announced a different time: 11:03.

He now remembered the clocks chiming eleven o'clock when he first entered the room to find Eve. The clocks had to be wrong.

His eye went to his coat draped across an antique chair nearby. When had he put it there? According to the clocks, it would have been only moments ago. That was before he'd followed Eve through the door of the giant clock and gone back in time.

It was crazy to think about now. *Back in time.* Not just a few minutes or a couple of years, but several *centuries* to England, to the time of Robin Hood. Andrew and Eve had spent days and days there.

He could still feel the humidity and heat of the forest. The smell of the damp green lingered in his nostrils. The chirping of the birds was like a distant song in his ears. It was a sharp contrast to the dry, crisp air and the street noise of Hope Springs, Colorado, just outside.

"Are you leaving?" Eve Virtue asked.

Lost in his thoughts, Andrew had forgotten she was there. He also hadn't realized he'd picked up his coat and now held it in his hands.

"I have to go home and talk to my parents," he said.

Eve looked at him with an anxious expression. Her cheeks were flushed, as if she'd been running. Her dark, short-cropped hair was disheveled. Her eyes were wide, and Andrew wondered yet again what color they really were. Were they blue, green, azure, hazel? Eve herself didn't know.

Those eyes, along with her hair and the shape of her face, reminded Andrew of a pixie.

"You're going home?" she asked.

CHAPTER ONE

"I was gone a long time. They'll be worried."

"You weren't gone a long time," she said. "Remember? Time moves differently in the past than it does here." To prove her point, she took hold of the back of his arm and guided him to the open doorway. "See?"

Andrew looked out at the vast main floor of the Virtue Curiosity Shoppe. It was filled end to end with tables, shelves, racks, and display cases overflowing with antiques, knickknacks, and collectibles.

Catherine Drake stood behind a counter near the front door of the shop. That was exactly where she had been when Andrew and Eve first went into the room of clocks. Mrs. Drake was Eve's aunt and the owner of the shop. She looked over at them and smiled. Then her attention went to a customer coming through the front door.

"Why does it feel like I just woke up?" Andrew asked.

"That can happen with time travel," Eve said.

She would know, Andrew thought. She had been jumping back and forth in time for a while.

"England, Robin Hood, the sword fights and battles ... weren't a dream?" Andrew asked, just to make sure.

"No. All of it really happened."

Andrew shook his head. "I have to go home and tell my parents."

"Let me show you something first," Eve said quickly. She wiggled a finger for him to follow her.

They made their way along the rear wall of the shop.

"Wait!" Catherine Drake called out to them.

"Oh no," Eve whispered as she froze in place.

"Eve, Andrew. Come here for a minute," Mrs. Drake said.

Eve rolled her eyes and groaned. "Let's get it over with."

"What? What's going on?" Andrew asked.

"You'll see."

Still clutching his coat, Andrew weaved his way around the tables and stands. The customer who had just entered stepped around the front counter to greet him.

"This is Dr. Vince Howard," Mrs. Drake said. "He teaches history in Denver."

Dr. Howard was tall, with a narrow, pleasant face marked by deep wrinkles on his forehead and the corners of his eyes. A salt-and-pepper-colored goatee adorned his mouth and chin, matching his shaggy gray hair. He wore a tan shirt and a brown waistcoat, jeans, and cowboy boots. All he was missing was a cowboy hat, and he would have looked as if he'd just come from a rodeo.

Dr. Howard shook Andrew's hand. Andrew noticed rough calluses on the man's palms.

"A pleasure to meet you, Andrew." Dr. Howard had a deep voice. "Catherine tells me you like history."

"Dr. Howard often comes to Hope Springs to shop for antiques," said Mrs. Drake. "He's interested in our local history. Just like you are."

Dr. Howard looked closely at Andrew. Then his eyes went up to an enormous painting hanging on the far

CHAPTER ONE

wall. Andrew's gaze followed along. In the painting, two men posed in front of a large bookcase. An oversized globe of the world stood between them. The men were Alfred Virtue and Theodore Perry, ancestors of Eve and Andrew.

Looking as they did in the 1920s, the men were dressed in suits with long jackets and vests, stiff collars, and dark ties. Alfred Virtue sported a moustache and wore gold wire-framed glasses. Theodore Perry was clean-shaven and had wavy sandy-colored hair. His lips were pressed into a slightly embarrassed smile. Each man had a hand on the oversized globe. Alfred Virtue and Theodore Perry were business partners and best friends.

"You could be twins," Dr. Howard said to Andrew, nodding to Theodore Perry.

Andrew nodded. "Everybody says that."

"We should compare notes about your family history," Dr. Howard said. "My great-grandfather lived here around the time of Alfred Virtue. I think they did business together. He probably knew Theodore Perry, too."

Andrew gave him another nod. "Okay."

Dr. Howard's gaze went to Eve, who was standing just behind Andrew. "Hello, Eve. Are you hiding?"

"Hi," Eve said in a flat tone. "We were just about to go downstairs," she added quickly and tugged at Andrew's sleeve. "Let's go." She began to back away.

"Good to meet you," Andrew said, moving in Eve's direction.

"Likewise," said Dr. Howard. Then he turned his attention back to Mrs. Drake. She leaned on the counter and smiled at him like a schoolgirl.

Eve picked up her pace. Andrew hustled alongside her and whispered, "What's wrong with you?"

"Nothing," Eve said sharply.

They reached the far corner of the shop and rounded a tall bookcase. Half hidden behind it was a short hallway with a water fountain, two public bathrooms, and a stairwell leading downstairs. A metal Employees Only sign hung on a thin chain that stretched across the entrance to the stairs.

Eve unhooked the chain from the sign. They rattled loudly. She stepped into the stairwell and gestured for Andrew to do the same. He moved past her and down a few stairs while she hooked the chain again.

"You don't like Dr. Howard?" Andrew asked as they walked down the stairs.

Eve shrugged.

Andrew came to a landing and stopped. "Does your aunt like him?" he asked.

Eve shot him an annoyed look, then continued down the next set of stairs.

"Where's your uncle?" Andrew asked as he followed her.

"He died before I was born."

"So she's allowed to have a boyfriend if she wants."

Eve frowned. "He's not her boyfriend."

CHAPTER ONE

"Then why don't you like him?"

"I never said I don't like him." She reached the bottom of the stairs and stopped. "I don't think he's right for her."

"Oh," Andrew said, still thinking there was more to it than that.

"I live with Aunt Catherine," Eve explained. "If she marries him, then ..." She didn't finish her sentence. Instead, she pushed through a fire door and into a wide, dimly lit hallway.

"Where are your parents?" Andrew asked.

"They're not around." Eve walked ahead of him.

"Where are they?"

"Somewhere that isn't here," she said, her tone sharp again. "Aunt Catherine is my legal guardian."

"Why?"

"Forget about it," she snapped. Her voice echoed down the hall.

"Okay, then how about telling me where we are," he said, aware that the hallway was lined with various doors.

"The old bank had offices down here. And two vaults." She stopped at a large square iron door that stood open against the wall. The mechanics of its locks were an elaborate system of rods, levers, and boxes. "This is the main vault."

To the left of the open door was the vault itself, with bars protecting a room filled with safety-deposit boxes. In the middle sat a metal table and chairs. All of them were covered with file boxes, stacks of ledgers, and small plastic containers. A rack of clothes stood off to the right.

"My aunt uses the vault for storage," Eve explained.

"Is there anything in the deposit boxes?" Andrew asked.

"They were cleaned out when the bank closed down," Eve said. "If there's any treasure, it'll be in *this* one."

They came to another vault door. Unlike the first, this one was closed and smaller. It was painted a shiny black, with a gold border around the edges. In the center of the door was a detailed painting of a forest and stream at the foot of the Rocky Mountains. Below the painting, cursive lettering said *Theobold Safe & Lock Co., Denver.* To the left was a combination dial. Next to that was a large handle with a lock for a key. A design of black and gold pedestals and flowers adorned the sides. Matching gold trimmings crowned the top.

"There's a treasure in there?" Andrew asked.

"Nobody knows. That's the mystery," Eve said. She grabbed the door handle and gave it a tug. "Alfred Virtue had this specially built. We haven't found the combination or the key."

"Why don't you get a locksmith to break in?" asked Andrew.

"The family has tried over and over. Years ago they brought Mr. Theobold down from Denver. He said Alfred Virtue designed it so the only way to break in is to blow the whole thing up, which would destroy whatever is inside."

"Nobody knows what's in it?"

CHAPTER ONE

Eve shook her head. "That's why no one wants to risk damaging it. Alfred Virtue could have all kinds of valuable stuff in there."

"What about all those X-ray, sonic, infrared, whatever-they're-called machines?"

"They don't work," Eve replied. "In fact, the whole building messes up tech equipment like that. Computers glitch up. Cell phones can't get signals ..."

"Why?"

"I have a theory. Come to the office and I'll show you." She moved away.

Andrew hesitated. He put his hand on the black iron door. It was smooth and cool to the touch. "I guess nobody has figured out the combination—or where the key is to get in," he said.

"No." Eve gave him a knowing smile. "Alfred Virtue only left a few clues."

"What kind of clues?"

"The kind no one has ever figured out," Eve said. "But *we* will."

"We?" Andrew asked, following her down the hallway.

Eve stopped at an open doorway. "You went back in time with me and met Robin Hood, and you don't want to help me find out more?"

Andrew gave a small shrug. "Yeah. But I—" He stopped. He wasn't sure how far he wanted to dig into the mysteries of Alfred Virtue and the Radiant Stone or this mysterious vault.

Eve put her hands on her hips and glared at him. "What do you want to do—go home? Tell your parents? Great. Go ahead. And you know what? They won't believe you. And if they do, they won't let you near the Radiant Stone ever again."

Andrew flinched at her sudden outburst. "What's wrong with you?" he asked. He felt annoyed that she was so annoyed.

"I'm tired of people being so flaky," she said. Her eyes were now a dark and stormy purple color.

"I'm not being flaky," Andrew countered. "*You* dragged me into this whole time-travel thing, remember? I haven't had any time to think about it."

"You had days and days in England!" Eve argued.

"How was I supposed to think *there* when we were running all over the country? And we've only been home for a little while! What do you want from me?"

"Nothing," she said with a grim look Andrew had come to know. "Go home. Tell your parents, if that's what you want."

Was that what he wanted? He wasn't sure. Changing tactics, he asked, "What did your Aunt Catherine say about you jumping around in time?"

"She knows about the stone," Eve said as a gotcha. "She says she likes my sense of adventure. She thinks traveling in time is kind of like going to school, but even better than learning algebra. She's Alfred Virtue's great-granddaughter, you know. She's a lot like him. What will your parents say?"

CHAPTER ONE

"How am I supposed to know?" Andrew replied. "Why are you so mad?"

She paused, then lowered her head. "Because I'm tired of doing this on my own." She turned away, then stepped through the doorway, disappearing into the darkness of the room behind her.

"You're not on your own," Andrew said. He lingered in the doorway. "I'm here now, aren't I?"

Her voice brightened. "Then come in."

"To where?"

"Alfred Virtue's private office."

There was a telltale click when Eve flipped a switch inside the dark room. Old bulbs hanging from wires in the ceiling flickered into a dull yellow and then brightened to a harsh white.

The room was crammed with tables and filing cabinets, metal and wooden shelves, and racks of glass beakers. Papers, books, and ledgers covered the surface spaces. A desk in the middle of the room held a microscope, various hammer-like tools, a pile of yellowed newspapers, and science magazines from the 1920s. Near the microscope was a stack of three notebooks.

"Those are Alfred Virtue's journals," Eve said. "I'm pretty sure there are more than those three, but I haven't found them. Maybe they're locked in that vault."

Andrew hooked his coat on a rack stand next to the door. A dusty gray smock draped down from one of the pegs. A black hat hung on another.

He turned back to the desk and picked up one of the notebooks. Flipping past the rough leather cover, he carefully touched the mass of scrawls handwritten in pencil and black ink. Some pages had drawings and diagrams of the Radiant Stone with arrows pointing to the various facets. Others had math equations and formulas. Still others had sketches of rocks and gems.

"You read all of this stuff?" Andrew asked.

"Over and over again," Eve said. She reached up to her neck and pulled out the silver necklace with the silver case that held the Radiant Stone.

She looped it over her head and placed it on the desk. "For some reason, this thing feels heavier in our time," she said.

The case always reminded Andrew of an oversized pocket watch. He pressed a stem on the top. The silver cover clicked open. Small clasps at the top and bottom of the case held the Radiant Stone in place. The stone glowed like a shiny jewel under the white electric light. The facets shimmered with different shades of blue, red, green, black, and even specks of yellow.

"What are you doing?" Eve asked.

"Just looking," Andrew said as he propped open the notebook he had picked up. A drawing of the stone covered most of a page. He leaned over to compare the drawing with the stone itself.

"Don't touch the stone," Eve said quickly.

"I *know*!" Andrew snapped. Touching any of the facets would send him back in time. *Where* he was sent depended on which facet he touched. Alfred Virtue had

CHAPTER TWO

spent months, maybe years, figuring out which facet linked to which time and place. The drawing had arrows with notes written in a neat cursive.

Andrew looked at the stone, then the drawing. Then a question came to his mind. "If all I have to do is touch a facet to go back in time, why did I have to follow you into the big clock?"

"Because that's what Alfred Virtue said to do."

"But *why*? Why did we need the clock?"

Eve said, "It gets our bodies ready."

Andrew was baffled. "How?"

Eve grabbed another journal and flipped through the pages, as if trying to find a particular entry. She finally gave up and tossed the journal back on the desk. "Radonite."

"What?"

"Radonite," she said again. "The numbers on the big clock and the pendulum and the frame are all made of a rock called *radonite*. It's the rock Alfred Virtue found around the Radiant Stone."

Andrew shook his head. "I don't understand."

"How can I explain it?" she muttered to herself. Then she said, "Okay, so you know how a diamond is usually found in a rock called *kimberlite*?"

"No."

"Well, I looked it up. Trust me, it is," she said. "The Radiant Stone is like that. It was found in a weird rock that looked like coal, but nobody'd ever seen it before. Alfred Virtue brought some to Hope Springs and showed it to a local rock expert. The expert said it was unknown and unnamed. So Alfred Virtue called it *radonite*. He later found out that it acts like a kind of stabilizer. It makes time travel easier on our bodies."

"Like travel medicine?" Andrew said.

"Kind of," said Eve. "Alfred Virtue brought in *a lot* of radonite and put some into parts of this building and the mystery vault and some of the clocks you saw in the Clock Room."

"What happens if we use the Radiant Stone and there isn't any radonite around?" Andrew asked.

"It'd be like dropping fast in an airplane, or going down into deep water pressure," she explained. "Our bodies won't have time to adjust. We'll feel really sick."

Andrew was worried. "What kind of sick? Is our hair going to fall out? Are we going to get cancer?"

"Nothing like that," said Eve. "Maybe an upset stomach. Sometimes headaches and dizziness. You feel achy like you have the flu."

Andrew picked up another notebook. It opened to a section where a few pages had been roughly torn out. He held it up to Eve. "What happened to these pages?"

"I don't know." She pointed to words written at the top of one of the tears: *Beware of* . . . .

"Beware of what?" Andrew asked.

"Look at the page right before."

Andrew turned the page. A sketch of the Radiant Stone took up most of the sheet. Alfred Virtue had drawn an arrow pointing to a facet just left of the center.

CHAPTER TWO

"Beware of this facet?" Andrew asked. "Where does it go?"

Eve looked closer. "It must be written on the missing pages."

Andrew turned his attention to the Radiant Stone, still lying in the open case. He leaned down to look at the facet. It flickered in the light, and he thought he saw an image. "Is that a *castle*?"

Eve bent down to look. "What?"

"There." Andrew pointed. His forefinger moved close to the facet.

"Don't touch it!" Eve snapped at him.

Later, the two of them would argue over what happened next. Andrew would claim that he didn't intend to touch the stone, but Eve reached over to grab his hand and pushed his finger against the facet. Eve would insist that he touched the facet with the tip of his finger just as her hand made contact with his.

Either way, Eve was touching Andrew's hand when his finger pressed against the facet of the Radiant Stone.

And that was that.

3

A brilliant flash of light caused Andrew to yelp. Eve gasped. They instinctively lifted their hands to cover their faces.

The musty smell of the office gave way to fresh, crisp air. Andrew heard the sound of trickling water nearby. Farther off came the voices of men and women and the low murmur of a crowd gathered somewhere.

Andrew lowered his hands. He blinked, trying to regain his sight. His senses told him that he was sitting on soft earth with his back against rough stones.

"Ouch," Eve said to his right.

Andrew glanced over. Eve was standing, stretching, blinking her eyes, and looking as confused as he felt.

They were on a riverbank of grass and mud. A river flowed past only a few feet away. Andrew turned to see that he was at the base of a stone bridge. Broad arches rose high above him. They stretched from one fat stone pillar to another, all the way across the river to another bank. On both sides of the bank, steep inclines led to the top of the bridge.

Andrew started to stand, but a dull ache rolled through his body. Every muscle hurt. Then a razor-sharp pain went through his head. "My head hurts," he said, pressing his temples.

"Mine, too," said Eve. She looked pale and swayed unsteadily.

Bracing himself against the closest stone pillar, he tried to get to his feet.

"Oh no," he said as a sudden wave of nausea hit him. He bent near the pillar and threw up. Not once, not twice, but three times.

Eve made a face. "Ew."

He staggered a few feet, then dropped to his knees in a patch of mud. "Is this—?" he started to ask, but he hurled one more time before he could finish the question.

"This is what happens when we touch the stone without the radonite," Eve said. She held out her hand to him. "Let's go back before we have any worse side effects."

He grabbed her hand. She pulled him to his feet. Another wave of nausea hit him, and he had to close his eyes until it passed. He took a deep breath.

"Hurry," she said, still holding his hand. "Use the Radiant Stone."

Andrew let go of her hand and looked at her, puzzled. He showed her both of his hands. They were empty. "I don't have it," he said. "Don't you?"

Her eyes widened. "No!" She touched her neck. The chain wasn't there. Frantically she checked her pockets.

CHAPTER THREE

Andrew spun one way, then another. He looked on the ground near his feet. Then they both scrambled back and forth, searching along the riverbank and the water's edge.

The Radiant Stone wasn't there.

"What does this mean?" Andrew asked. "We're here. It must be here too."

Eve shook her head. "You touched the stone, but you weren't holding it. It's still sitting on Alfred Virtue's desk."

Andrew's head throbbed. He couldn't think straight. "What does that mean?"

"It means we can't go back to our time," she said. Her wide eyes filled with tears.

"There has to be a way back," Andrew said.

"How? The Radiant Stone was our only way back!" she cried out.

Andrew sank onto the wet grass. He thought he might throw up again.

Eve sat down next to him. She lowered her head. Andrew could hear her whispering, along with an occasional sniffle. It sounded as if she was praying.

Andrew closed his eyes and joined her.

Suddenly she stood up and wiped the tears from her face in a decisive "I'm done crying about it" gesture. "Let's see where we are," she said.

They looked up. The bank on the opposite side of the river inclined to an open horizon. Behind them, the ground rose more gently to uneven ledges covered with bushes. At the top was a short wall of stone.

Andrew craned his neck. He thought he could see the peaks of various roofs. Above and beyond them was a high wall and what looked like the towers of a castle.

"Are we back in Robin Hood's time?" he asked.

"There's a path," Eve said, pointing to a break in the bushes.

Andrew stood up, but his head started spinning. He doubled over, sure he was going to vomit again.

"Wait here." Eve darted to the path, then disappeared into the bushes. He caught glimpses of her as she made her way to the top of the hill.

Andrew sat down again until the wave of nausea passed. He focused on the sounds coming from somewhere overhead. He could hear muttering voices mixed with the clip-clop of horses' hooves on what must have been a dirt road. There was also the familiar rattling and creaking of wooden carts. It was a sound he had come to know from his time with Robin Hood.

He lowered his head, hoping that the bad effects of time traveling had passed.

A few minutes later, Eve returned. "We're dressed all wrong," she said, grabbing fistfuls of mud and smearing it on her jeans and pullover. She did the same to her tennis shoes, almost covering the tops with the brown muck.

"What are you doing?" Andrew asked.

"We have to blend in with the people up there."

CHAPTER THREE

"What are they wearing?" he asked.

"Definitely *not* jeans, tennis shoes, and shirts with factory-made stitching." She scooped up a handful of mud and threw it at him. A big brown splotch hit the middle of his shirt.

"Hey!" he cried out.

Eve began to tear at the stitching on her sleeves. "We have to disguise ourselves to look like peasants."

"Peasants? Like the ones we saw in England?"

"They look almost the same," she said. She tore a small hole in the fabric near her shoulder. "But I think they're speaking French."

Andrew gasped. "French! But you said we can only go to places in history where the stone has been."

"It's not what *I* said. It's what Alfred Virtue said."

"I don't care who said it. The Radiant Stone was from England. How can we be in France?"

"How am I supposed to know?" Eve shrugged. "The stone must have been in France at this point in history."

"At what point? What year is it?"

She frowned at him. "It's not like I could go up and ask someone, 'Excuse me. What year is it?' All the clothes look alike to me. It might be the thirteen or fourteen hundreds."

She knelt down and started rubbing more dirt on Andrew's clothes. Then she stood up and said, "Let's go. Something is happening up there. People are crowding along the bridge."

Andrew rolled around on the ground. He was beginning to feel better. He got to his feet again and presented himself. "How do I look?"

"Disgusting. How about me?"

"Like you've been mud wrestling with pigs."

"Good," Eve said. "I think we'll fit in."

Together they ascended the bank on a narrow path through the thick bushes. On level ground, Andrew saw what Eve had seen: a crowd of people were pressed together on the long bridge. They didn't seem to be moving in any particular direction. It looked as if they were waiting for something to happen.

Andrew saw a tall arched gate to his left. The road from the bridge continued past guards and into a town. Stretching away in the other direction, beyond the bridge, were green fields and a forest.

The people on the bridge looked a lot like the peasants Andrew had known in the time of Robin Hood. They wore rough and ragged clothes in dull colors of browns, blues, and blacks. The men wore long-sleeved shirts, tunics, breeches, and leather shoes laced around their ankles. A few heads were covered with hoods that draped onto the men's shoulders.

Some of the women wore long dresses with V-shaped collars. Their waists were belted with thin straps. Other women wore wool skirts and plain tops under leather vests pulled together by leather laces. The women wore their hair long and braided or tucked their hair into funny heart-shaped headdresses.

CHAPTER THREE

"We could be almost anywhere at any time in the Middle Ages," Eve whispered to Andrew.

"I guess fashions didn't change a lot back then," he said. Cocking his head slightly, he listened to the crowd. Fragments of sentences and words came to his ears. He was pretty sure the peasants were speaking French, just as Eve had said.

"Which way should we go?" Andrew asked.

"Across the bridge to the woods," Eve said.

Andrew looked at the crowd on the bridge. "We won't make it through that," he said. He shot a glance through the gate. Guards inside were nudging the people to keep moving and stay off the main road. "Let's go that way. Maybe there's a way out if we follow the road through the town."

Just then an old woman near Eve turned slightly, just enough to see Eve's face. She suddenly gasped and spun around. "*Qui est-ce? La Pucelle? Jeanne? La Sainte Fille!*"

Eve backed up, shaking her head. "No. No. I am not," she said.

The woman became more excited. "*Jeanne! Jeanne!*" she shouted and pointed at Eve.

Heads turned. The crowd pushed in to see what the fuss was about.

"What's going on?" Andrew asked Eve, backing away with her.

She looked alarmed. "I think they're freaked because I'm a girl dressed like a boy."

Andrew heard words and exclamations like *pucelle!* and *fille habillée en garçon!* and *la Sainte Fille!* and *jeune fille du Christ* and *vierge de Domrémy*.

Slowly he began to understand what they were saying. "They're calling you a girl saint from a place called Domrémy," he said to her.

"No!" Eve shouted to the mob. She waved her hands and cried out, *"Je ne suis pas qui vous dites que je suis!"*

Andrew looked at her, shocked. "You spoke French!"

"I did?" Eve said, looking equally shocked.

"You said you're not who they say you are," Andrew repeated, then realized he knew what the French words meant in English. He gasped and put a hand over his mouth. *How do I know that?* he wondered.

The crowd surrounded Eve, pushing Andrew away. He was in danger of losing her. He began to shove and elbow everyone around him.

"Stop!" someone shouted from behind the mob. The voice was commanding enough to stifle the chaos. A tall old man plowed through the crowd. He waved a long staff, as if he might strike anyone who wouldn't yield. "Fools! Step aside!" he roared. "Go away!"

He wore a long cloak made of a rich scarlet-colored silk. The fringes of the cloak were lined with gold. White hair crowned the man's head, and his thick beard flew out in wisps like white cotton candy. His face was a web of wrinkles that framed dark circles under angry eyes.

CHAPTER THREE

The peasants scattered, muttering under-the-breath curses as they withdrew.

The old man towered over Eve and stabbed his staff into the dirt. "Now then," he said, eyeing her face. He fixed his gaze on her eyes, tilting his head one way and then the other.

Andrew knew he was trying to figure out her eye color. It's what everyone did.

A perplexed look crossed his face. "What are you?" he asked.

"My name is Eve," she replied.

The old man's eyes then moved to her clothes and on down to her shoes.

"What are *those*?" he asked, pointing to her shoes with the tip of his staff.

She looked down. "Shoes?" she said, as if it was a trick question.

Andrew realized that her sneakers, even covered with mud, looked unlike anything anyone would wear at that time.

The old man bent down to look more closely. Then he suddenly grabbed her foot. She fell onto her back.

"Stop it!" Eve said and kicked at him.

Andrew rushed forward, ready to leap at the old man. But the man was quick and jabbed at Andrew's shoulder with his staff, knocking him away.

"Let me go!" Eve shouted, kicking harder at the old man with her free foot.

"What goes on here?" another voice called out. A guard dressed in a gold helmet, chain mail, and boots stormed up. His hand rested on the hilt of the sword attached to his belt. "What are you doing?"

The old man let Eve go and stood up to his full height. He was a giant next to the guard.

The guard looked at him and went pale. "A thousand apologies, commander!" he said, saluting as he backed away.

The old man turned to Eve again. His eyes were sharp like an eagle's. "Where do you come from?" he asked.

"Far away," Eve said.

Andrew stepped forward again. "What is wrong with you?" he asked, rubbing his aching shoulder.

The old man gave him a once-over, grunted, and then addressed Eve again. He pointed at her with a bony finger. "Child of Satan, you do not belong here." He lifted his staff.

Fearing the man would strike Eve, Andrew threw himself between them. He held up his arms to protect her.

The old man lowered his staff again. "I know what you are," he said quietly, then turned quickly and marched away. The crowd parted for him once again.

"What was that all about?" Andrew asked as he helped Eve back to her feet.

Eve looked shaken and said softly, "We have to change our clothes."

CHAPTER THREE

"We'll never get across the bridge," Andrew said. "Put your head down. Let's go into the town and figure out where we are."

Eve agreed. Lowering her head, she came close to Andrew as they walked through the gate. The guard scowled at them as they went past.

"There," Andrew said, leading Eve alongside a rickety old cart being pulled slowly by a heavily bearded man.

The man glanced at them. "Try to steal anything and I'll cut your hands off," he said.

Andrew peered into the back of the cart. It was full of what looked like piles of manure. "You do not have to worry about that," he said and continued on.

The narrow streets were congested with people who seemed to be watching for someone or something, like spectators waiting for a parade.

What is going on here? Andrew wondered.

He looked up at buildings in various sizes and shapes made of wood and stone. Some were leaning as if they might tip over. Crude signs hung from doorways, announcing the presence of bakers, butchers, weavers, and cobblers. But many of the shop doors were closed and the windows shuttered.

Even though Eve tried to keep her face hidden, people still gawked at her. Andrew heard whispers behind their backs.

"Is it?"

"No, it isn't. It can't be. She wouldn't enter the town on foot, would she?"

"No! She is coming on horseback with her soldiers."

"This was a mistake," Eve said to Andrew from the side of her mouth. "We should have gone across the bridge to the woods."

"We won't find any clothes there," Andrew said.

"We won't find any here either," she countered. "Unless we plan to steal them."

Andrew hadn't thought of that. "There must be a way out of town if we keep going," he said.

He saw a heavyset man wearing a stained apron standing in a shop doorway. Andrew pulled Eve out of the flow of people and went over to him. The smell of rotten meat lingered in the air from the open door behind him. Andrew assumed the man was a butcher.

"Pardon me, sir."

"I am not open for business today," the man said.

"I do not want to buy anything. I want to know where we are," Andrew said.

Big bushy eyebrows lifted high on the man's forehead. "Are you an *imbecile*?" the butcher asked.

"We are strangers," Andrew explained. "We have come a long way."

Eve came closer and added, "We are lost. That is why we do not know the name of the town."

Andrew realized they were both talking to the butcher more formally.

CHAPTER THREE

The butcher gave them a wary look. Andrew noticed that his eyes paused on Eve's eyes and then on their clothes. Slowly he said, "This is Chinon, on the river Vienne." He gestured up at something behind them.

Andrew turned and saw the castle peering at them over a high ledge.

"That is the home of the Dauphin, our king. How could you not know?" the butcher asked.

"Is that why everyone is on the street? Is the dolphin coming?" Andrew asked.

"*Dauphin*," Eve corrected him, pronouncing it *doe-fan*. "It's the word they use for a prince."

Andrew gave her a "How do you know that?" look.

"My Aunt Catherine loves Shakespeare," she said with a shrug.

A puzzled look from the butcher. "What are you saying?"

"Why are the people in the street?" Eve asked him. "Who is coming?"

"*She* is coming. The Maiden of Domrémy." He gestured to Eve's hair and clothes. "The one you are dressed as. You are a girl wearing the clothes of a boy. You have done it for her, yes?"

Eve smiled without answering.

The butcher raised his grimy hands. "Be careful, child. There are those who say it is a sin for a girl to dress as a boy. They will box your ears."

"Someone already tried that," Eve said.

Andrew asked, "How do we get out of town?"

"That way is the bridge," the butcher said, pointing to the left.

"It is too crowded," Andrew said.

The man pointed to the right and said, "Then follow this road to the gate. But it, too, will be crowded. She will be coming from that direction."

"*Merci*," Eve said and pulled at Andrew's arm.

Andrew also thanked the butcher. Then they continued on.

"A girl dressed as a boy is a big deal, I guess," Andrew said.

"And a girl with short hair," Eve affirmed.

"They were calling you the Maiden of Christ and a saint, too. I don't get it," he said.

"They don't know me." She gave him a coy smile.

At last, the street led them to another arched gate. They passed through and found themselves jostled by a crowd that didn't seem to know which way it was going. A group of people spread out onto an open meadow to one side of the gate. A field led to the river on the other side. Violet and yellow wildflowers showed their colors in spite of being trampled by the feet of the many campers.

Eve nudged Andrew and pointed. A forest stood in the distance ahead. The sun shone brightly, a sharp contrast to the shadows inside the town. She picked up her pace. "Hurry."

CHAPTER THREE

"What's the rush?" Andrew asked, following her through the crush of people. He knew the answer even as he asked the question. The woods were like home to Eve. He had noticed it during their adventure with Robin Hood.

They walked against the traffic of merchants and pilgrims headed for the town. The glances and double takes continued. Then the crowds thinned, and Andrew and Eve eventually came to an open stretch of road.

Eve sped up to a jog. Then she sprinted toward the trees.

"Slow down," Andrew complained. He worried as much about rushing into the woods as he did about rushing into a strange building. They never knew what might be waiting for them. Robin had taught them that.

Several yards along the road that cut through the forest, Eve slowed down. She turned her head this way and that. Then she dashed away from the road into a denser part of the forest. A canopy of branches and budding leaves softened the morning light.

Andrew tried to keep up as she dodged brush and branches. Then she leapt over a fallen tree and disappeared from his sight. He scrambled onto the top of the log and found her sitting on a floor of old leaves. She had already eased her back against the log and closed her eyes.

"What are you doing?" Andrew asked. He stood over her.

"Resting for a minute. We have to think."

Andrew slid off the log and dropped down next to her. He caught his breath and then asked, "I want to know how we were speaking French."

"It's something the Radiant Stone does," Eve said. She looked at him out of the corner of her eye. "Didn't you wonder why we could understand what people were saying in Robin Hood's time?"

"I figured it was because they were speaking English," Andrew said.

Eve sighed like Andrew's mom sometimes did when he wasn't paying attention.

"Have you read any books in Old English at school?" she asked. "*Canterbury Tales* by Chaucer?"

"One of the nuns read us parts of it," he said. "The words were kind of like ours, but with a lot of 'eths' and extra 'esses' and 'foresooths' and stuff like that."

"That's how they talked when we were with Robin Hood."

"I remember some 'thees' and 'thous,' but..." Andrew's voice trailed off as he slowly remembered. "When we first got there, it sounded strange. But I figured I just got used to how they were talking. It made sense to me."

"It wasn't you. It was the Radiant Stone."

"I don't get it."

"Alfred Virtue wrote that somehow the Radiant Stone makes our brains work differently. It *translates*." She sat up and leaned on her elbows. "He figured out in

CHAPTER THREE

his time travels that people in the past were talking the way they always talked, but he heard them in a way he could understand. And when they heard him talk, they understood him as if he was speaking in their languages."

Andrew thought about it. "You mean like in the Bible on the day of Pentecost, when the disciples were talking in languages they didn't know?"

"Something like that," Eve said. "Alfred Virtue wondered if the Radiant Stone was a piece from the Tower of Babel. That's how everyone could speak in one language."

"That's crazy."

"It was just a theory," she said.

"It's still crazy."

She giggled. "All of it is crazy."

They sat in silence for a moment. Then Andrew stood up and checked their surroundings. It was another habit he'd picked up from his time with Robin Hood. He looked in every direction and listened for any sound of movement. A few birds called, but otherwise the forest was still. He breathed in the fragrance of the damp wood, decaying bark, and old smoke.

"I feel sick, and tired," Eve said without opening her eyes.

Picking up a broken branch, Andrew wondered if he could sharpen it into a weapon. He tested its thickness, but it snapped too easily to be useful. "We need a plan," he said.

Eve groaned. "How can we plan? We're stuck somewhere in time. We don't even know where. We have the wrong clothes and no money and..." She leaned back against the log again and draped her arm over her eyes. "What are we going to do?"

Andrew didn't say anything for a long time. He didn't know what to say. He couldn't imagine that they were really stuck back in time.

God won't leave us here, he thought. He struggled against a feeling of despair. He prayed, *Dear God, please get us back to our own time.*

A bird called from somewhere deeper in the forest. Andrew turned. A single shaft of golden light had broken through the trees. A deer stood in the middle of the brilliant shower of rays. It seemed to be watching him. Then, with a nod, it bounded away.

Eve stirred. "What are you looking at?"

He didn't see the point of trying to describe it. "What if God put us here for a reason?" he said. "What if there's something He wants us to do in this time and place?"

Eve sat up. She wrapped her arms around her knees. "Remember the number-one rule of time travel: *we don't belong here.*"

"That was Alfred Virtue's rule," Andrew countered. "But God is God, and He can do whatever He wants."

"You think God put us here?" she asked.

"I think we made a mistake, but God can use our mistake to do something good." Andrew had often heard his parents say that very thing.

CHAPTER THREE

"What's good about living and dying where we don't belong?"

"That's what we have to find out," Andrew said.

At that moment, a violent shout came from another part of the forest.

4

Andrew and Eve were on their feet in an instant. In her hand Eve held a tall branch that had the makings of a good long staff.

Surprised, Andrew asked, "Where did you get that?"

"It was on the ground next to me," she replied. She pounded the end of the branch against the ground. It gave a sturdy thud.

Another shout came from the direction of the road.

"Are we going to help?" Andrew asked, giving Eve a knowing look.

Based on their past experiences, their instincts were to help someone in need.

"You need a weapon," Eve said.

"I'll find one on the way."

The skills Andrew and Eve had learned from their time with Robin Hood in the English greenwood served them well. They navigated the forest easily, leaping over nature's obstacles.

They raced toward the road, deeper into the forest and farther away from the town.

They could see movement through the trees ahead. "Something is happening on the road," Eve said, slowing down.

Crouching behind the wide trunk of a gnarled tree, Andrew peered around one side while Eve checked the other.

A dozen men on foot, dressed as peasants, were blocking the passage of seven people on horseback. Some of the riders were wearing armor. Swords and spears were held high on both sides. It looked to Andrew like a standoff.

"Outlaws," Eve whispered.

"Whose side are we on?" Andrew asked. The outlaws were the good guys in Robin Hood's time.

"I'll bet the ones on foot are the bad guys," Eve said.

As if to prove her point, one of the men on the ground thrust a long staff at the horses. The horses reared up, but the riders held firm.

"We come on the king's business," a man on horseback said with a voice like a bass drum. He struggled to control his black stallion.

"What king?" came the response from a scrawny man with wild red hair. "The fool in the castle? He is no king."

"Traitor! He is your king and mine!" came a much lighter voice from the riders.

Eve turned to Andrew. "That sounds like a girl," she said.

CHAPTER FOUR

Andrew searched around the fat roots of the tree for any stones he might find. A couple of handfuls would do the trick. Even the smallest pebble hurt if thrown hard enough. He stuffed what he could find into his pockets.

"If you are going to the king, then you must have treasure," the red-headed outlaw said.

"Silver and gold we do not have," said the lighter voice. "Our treasure is word from God, to be delivered to the king alone."

The outlaw snorted. "Are you pilgrims?"

"Of a kind," the deep voice replied.

"We come from the court of Robert de Baudricourt in Vaucouleurs," another rider said. "Leave us in peace to go on our way."

Coarse laughter burst from the outlaws. "The business of any king, duke, or the pope himself is no matter to us. We will leave you, but not in peace."

"We know whose side we're on," Eve said. She lifted her makeshift staff. "I'll crawl to that bush by the road and cause a distraction. Can you get close enough to do what you need to do?"

Andrew nodded. "There's a tree overlooking the road. I'll climb that."

Eve dropped low to the ground and made her way forward. Andrew bent down and half crawled, half walked, ahead. They crept toward the road as silently as two bugs crawling on a leaf.

Eve reached a large holly bush that was positioned just behind the outlaws.

Andrew came up behind a fat tree. Well hidden from the road, he pulled himself to the lowest branch. Then he swung up to the next one and another higher than that. He reached a height overlooking the standoff. Circling around to the front of the tree, he crawled along a thick branch until he reached a good vantage point. The leaves were tiny, but the branches were full enough to give him cover. He perched there and began to take the stones from his pockets, lining them up on the flat surface of a nearby branch.

The band of thieves now brandished knives and spears. They slowly formed a half circle around the horseback riders.

Still crouching behind the bush, Eve was only a few feet from the outlaw closest to her. She held her staff with both hands. She looked up at Andrew and gave a small wave. Only then did he realize that he should have asked how she planned to cause a distraction. Whatever it was, she had to do it quickly. The outlaws were now in position to attack the riders.

At that moment, Eve stabbed her staff into the nearest outlaw's leg. She hit him hard enough to bring him down to one knee. He cried out angrily and twisted around to grab his leg. Eve jabbed quickly just under his ribs, knocking the wind out of him. He doubled over.

CHAPTER FOUR

The outlaws spun to their fallen comrade. Andrew used the moment to throw his first stone, striking one of them square in the forehead. The thief staggered backward from the blow. Andrew sent another stone rocketing to the red-headed outlaw who had turned to help the man Eve had brought down. The stone caught him near the temple. He staggered and fell to his knees.

Eve sprung up, shouting and swinging her branch. The outlaws who were still standing spun toward her. "Ha!" she cried out, then raced back into the woods.

Andrew let fly a third stone, catching another outlaw just above his ear. He reeled to one side.

The outlaws turned this way and that, as if they couldn't figure out which direction their attackers were coming from.

The horseback riders looked astonished at the chaos. Suddenly the light-voiced rider cried, "Forward!"

With shouts, the riders spurred their horses and plowed through the outlaws. The band of thieves scattered with profanities and cries of pain.

The party on horseback disappeared around a bend in the road. The sounds of galloping horses' hooves soon faded away.

Andrew scrambled down the tree. Eve was there, her staff still in hand. They pressed close together behind the trunk.

Two of the outlaws had left the road and were searching around the bush where Eve had hidden.

"Who attacked us?" one shouted. "Find them!"

"I cannot see anyone!" another yelled.

"Let's get out of here," Andrew whispered.

Crouching low, they made their way back into the deepest part of the forest as silently as they'd come.

5

"We should go back to the town," Andrew said to Eve when they'd stopped to catch their breath in a thick clump of bushes. "It'll be safer."

The two peered over the top of the bushes. Andrew heard shouts far away but saw no sign of the outlaws.

Eve tipped her head at Andrew. They sprinted on, staying parallel to the road while keeping a safe distance.

"I wonder where the riders went," Andrew said.

"To the castle gate, if they're smart," Eve replied.

She had barely finished speaking when Andrew heard the snort of a horse just ahead. He held up a hand to Eve. They crouched down.

"The riders?" Eve said.

The uneasy shuffle of hooves on the forest floor was unmistakable.

They carefully made their way forward.

"Why did the riders leave the road?" Andrew whispered.

They crept onward. Soon, the view through the trees answered Andrew's question. An armored rider was using a knife to scrape at one of his horse's hooves.

"If my horse has been crippled, those scoundrels will pay dearly," the rider growled.

He was short and burly, with a thick head of black hair and a full beard. He wore armor on his upper body and gray hose on his lower body. More armor was strapped around his knees, lower legs, and feet.

"We'll have to go around them," Eve whispered. "They might think we're the outlaws and attack."

"Or we can hide here until they move on," Andrew countered.

"Or you may join them," a man said from behind.

Startled, Andrew spun around. A hand caught his arm in a vicelike grip. He looked into the face of the second armored rider, a young man with a shock of brown hair on top of his shaved head. His beard was thin and his skin was a sunbaked brown. He looked at Andrew with lively brown eyes.

A set of arms quickly encircled Eve and lifted her from the ground. She cried out, kicking at her assailant.

"Be calm," the one clutching her said. "If you are the ones who gave us aid, then you need not fear. We are in your debt."

Andrew relaxed. Looking at Eve, he signaled with a nod.

Eve stopped struggling. The riders released them both.

"Come along," said the young man. "We have food and water, if those are of any interest to you."

CHAPTER FIVE

The man who had grabbed Eve was tall and clean-shaven with a shaggy head of hair that splayed out from under a green cap. He wore a dark-green tunic, brown hose, and leather boots strapped around his legs. He reminded Andrew of Robin Hood.

The two men kept Andrew and Eve between them as they walked to the other riders. Andrew casually reached into his pocket and took out one of the few stones he had left. He slipped it into his fist. He noticed that Eve held her staff with both hands. Just in case.

The rest of the party stood inside the circle of horses. Two men wearing blousy tunics and dark hose down to their leather shoes rubbed the horses' backs and flanks. Andrew assumed they were servants to the men in armor.

Another man stepped from behind a horse. He wore a red cap that flopped down the side of his head. His tunic matched the cap. A dull yellow cloak around his shoulders gave him the look of a servant from a royal court. Dark knee-high boots covered his legs.

"What have we here?" The question came from the rider with the light voice, who now stepped out from between the two servants. It was a young woman. She seemed small and frail compared to the rest of the group. Andrew figured she might be a little over five feet tall. She wore a black wool cap above her slender face and had a round nose and full red lips. She was dressed in the clothes of a squire: a gray tunic, a black shirt, dark hose and breeches, and riding boots. Her large, determined eyes rested on Andrew. He shuffled nervously.

A smile crept onto her lips. She pulled the cap from her head, revealing black cropped hair. "How is it that two children are alone in the forest?"

"And how is it that two children have the cunning to ward off highway robbers?" asked the burly man.

The young woman held up her hand. "We are being discourteous. First, tell us your names."

"I am Andrew," he said, giving a slight bow.

"I am Evangeline." Eve curtsied.

The young woman's eyes darted to Eve, then sharpened. "Come here. I want to see you more closely."

Eve stepped over to her. They stood facing each other. Andrew was astonished.

"Good Maiden," said the burly man with a laugh, "she could be your sister."

"Why is she dressed as a man?" asked the younger armor wearer in the group.

The young woman asked Eve with a playful tone, "Do you mock me?"

Eve shook her head. "I cannot mock someone I do not know."

The young woman peered closely at Eve's eyes. "You have the eyes of an angel," she said softly. "Perhaps God has sent you to help me with my mission."

"Who are you?" Eve asked.

"I am Jeanne d'Arc of Domrémy."

CHAPTER FIVE

Jeanne d'Arc? Andrew thought. *Why does that sound so familiar?*

"You are the one the townspeople are waiting to see," Eve said.

Now Andrew understood.

"The townspeople are waiting to see *me*?" asked Jeanne.

The red-capped man rolled his eyes. "Someone in the castle has spread the word."

"The entire countryside knows," said the burly man. "Did you truly believe our journey would be kept a secret?"

"There are crowds all over the town," Eve said.

Jeanne looked dismayed. "It is Laetare Sunday. I do not want to distract the people from their Lenten disciplines. They should be praying, not waiting for me."

"I fear no Lenten observances will thwart them from coming to see you," countered the man who looked like Robin Hood. He now had a longbow slung over his shoulder to complete the resemblance.

"Perhaps we should wait until tomorrow to enter the town," Jeanne said.

"You would keep the Dauphin waiting?" asked the red-capped man.

Jeanne smiled. "I cannot believe he is sitting idly on his throne waiting for me."

"Let us wait until noon, after the Mass has been celebrated," the burly man suggested.

Jeanne looked thoughtful, then said, "Back home the children will be celebrating Laetare Sunday with picnics at the miraculous Gooseberry Spring. They will hang wreaths on the Fairy Tree." A sad look crossed her face. "The fairies are no more. But to drink from the spring will keep the children free from fevers for an entire year."

Andrew heard in Jeanne's voice the tone of a young girl. *How old is she?* he wondered. *Fifteen? Sixteen?*

"Good Maiden," said the burly man, "it is well that you drank from the spring for so many years. Few women would have the strength to ride a horse for as many leagues as you have."

"My strength comes from the One who sent me," she said.

Suddenly she turned and waved to them all. "Let us not be inhospitable to our two angels. I have given my name; now you must each do the same. Declare yourselves."

The burly man gave a grand bow, his armor clanging as he did. "I am Bertrand de Poulengy, and this is my servant Julien."

Julien, in a red and blue tunic, also bowed.

The younger guard gave a quick nod. "I am Jean de Metz, squire to Robert de Baudricourt, with my servant Jean." The servant wore a dark-blue tunic and also bowed.

Too many Jeans, Andrew thought.

The man with the longbow stood up straight. "I am Richard l'Archer."

"And I am Colet de Vienne, a royal messenger," the man with the red cap said as he swept it off his head and gave a low, dramatic bow.

CHAPTER FIVE

"These good men have brought me safely from Vaucouleurs," Jeanne said. "Now we must share what food and drink we have before we enter the town. I know you are angels, but you must be hungry and thirsty."

They gathered in a small circle, and Jeanne prayed for them all. Then the servants passed around morsels of bread and cheese. Andrew noticed that Richard l'Archer and the two servants kept their eyes on the surrounding forest. Watching for the outlaws, he assumed.

Bertrand asked, "Tell me, children, why you are alone in the forest. Where are your parents? Are you beggars? Orphans?"

Andrew and Eve gave the simplest and most truthful answers they could. Their parents were not with them, they said. So they traveled alone as wayfarers who only came to Chinon that day.

"Then you must travel with us," Jeanne exclaimed happily. "By the grace of God, we will meet the gentle Dauphin."

"Is that your mission?" Eve asked.

Jeanne nodded. "I am to tell him that he must allow me to drive the English away. Only then will he be crowned as the true king of France."

Andrew and Eve looked at each other.

"Drive the English away?" Eve asked. "Are they here?"

Bertrand snorted. "Here? They are all over France as unwelcome invaders. How could you not know that?"

"It is for me to persuade them to go home," Jeanne said.

"You mean you are going to fight in a war?" asked Andrew, worried.

"Only if the English will not heed my warnings to depart on their own," came her reply.

"And if they do not?" asked Eve.

Jeanne's eyes were wide and innocent. She said earnestly, "Then I shall wage war. God has willed that it must be done. So I shall do it."

After they had all eaten, the riders prepared to enter the town. The men checked their weapons and inspected the condition of their clothes. Jeanne went off alone to pray.

Andrew sat down next to a nearby tree and nestled in where the roots clawed at the ground like bony fingers. One of the men said something about the wet spring they'd had. The damp mulch under Andrew's bottom proved it. He'd also learned that it was now early March—March 5th, in fact. Jeanne and her company had been traveling from some other part of France since February 23rd. It was a miracle that they had come safely through parts of enemy country, until they met the highway robbers.

"We are in no fit state to see the Dauphin," Colet de Vienne announced.

"Surely he will be forgiving, knowing how far we have traveled," said Jean de Metz.

"I suggest we go to an inn first to make ourselves presentable," Colet said.

A debate followed about whether to stay in the forest or at an inn. Finally the decision was made. They would stay at an inn. Bertrand's servant, Julien, climbed onto his horse and rode off to Chinon to make the arrangements.

Andrew looked at his own mud-covered clothes. He knew that if they were washed, he'd have a bigger problem explaining them. He shivered. Though the sky was blue, the air was cold and damp. He wished he'd brought his coat, strange as it would look. He thought of it now, hanging uselessly in Alfred Virtue's office.

Eve stepped over to him, a blanket pulled around her.

"Where did you get that?" he asked.

"One of the servants gave it to me." She sniffed. "It's a horse blanket."

"I wish I had one. It's cold," he said.

"Share?" She sat down next to him and shrugged a corner of the blanket from her nearest shoulder.

He hesitated. In spite of all they'd gone through in the time of Robin Hood, they still knew very little about each other.

Eve must have noticed his reluctance. "Or you can stay cold," she said simply.

He pulled the blanket around his shoulder. Side by side, they sat in silence for a moment.

"Do you know the story of Joan of Arc?" Eve asked.

"I remember a little from history class." He thought for a moment. "She was sent by God to make the Dauphin the rightful king of France."

"You're only saying that because *she* said it." Eve elbowed him.

He laughed, then asked, "Who is the king now?"

"Someone from England. One of the English Henrys, I think." She picked up a small stick and scraped at the mud on the side of her shoe. "I can't remember why an English king is ruling France."

"The two countries fought all the time," Andrew recalled. "Henry the Fifth invaded them and kicked their rear ends at a place called Agincourt."

Eve looked astonished.

Andrew smiled. "Your Aunt Catherine isn't the only one who likes Shakespeare. My parents love the movie about Henry the Fifth. Though I forgot the part about the Dauphin. He was an annoying little weasel."

Eve sighed. "I wish we'd gone back to England instead."

"We could have found Robin," Andrew said, brightening up.

Eve shook her head. "We're a couple of hundred years too late. He's dead by now."

Andrew groaned. "We just saw him this morning, and now he's been dead for a couple hundred years?"

Eve tossed her stick aside. "So what are we going to do?" she asked.

"About what?"

"About being stuck here."

"How am I supposed to know?" Andrew said. "You're the expert on time travel."

"And *you're* the one who said God put us here."

They fell into a quiet sulk. "Maybe we're here to help Jeanne," Andrew eventually suggested.

Eve glanced around as if to make sure no one was listening. "How can we help? Don't you remember?" She leaned in close and whispered, "They burn her at the stake. You think God put us here to light the match?"

"Maybe He wants us to blow it out."

"We can't change history," Eve stated. "If we try, time will mess us up."

"Then we'll have to figure it out as we go along," Andrew said hopefully.

"For the rest of our lives?" she asked.

Andrew shrugged. "We'll get home somehow. I don't believe God will leave us stranded here."

Eve turned to him. "What if He does?"

Andrew tried to think of an answer but couldn't come up with one. Then he noticed that Jeanne and her escorts were looking at them.

Jeanne nodded to Bertrand, then strode over to them. She knelt down. "What are we to do with you, my angels?" she asked. "Your clothes are..." She gestured to their jeans and sneakers. "Of what are these made?"

"Cotton," said Eve.

She pointed to their shoes. "What make of leather are these?"

"The plastic kind," said Andrew.

CHAPTER SIX

Jeanne looked confused, as if she hadn't heard correctly. "*Plass-teek*? From what country do they come?" she asked. "I have never seen such a thing in France."

Andrew said, "My clothes came from a shop. I cannot say how they were made."

Bertrand joined them. He said to Jeanne, "Dear Maiden, it is enough of an offense for you to be dressed in a man's clothes, but for this girl to do the same is sheer folly. Their clothes betray a foreign tailor. The court of the Dauphin will suspect a plot. They may believe we are in league with those who would do harm to him."

"This is easily remedied," Jeanne said. She went over to her horse and opened a worn satchel. From it she retrieved a red dress and, with further digging, a pair of leather shoes.

Jean de Metz saw the dress and cried out, "How is it possible? I gave orders to burn that dress!" He scowled at his servant.

The servant spread his hands. "She was unyielding, master! She refused to part with it."

"Just as well," said Jeanne. "It is good we have clothes for our angel." She handed the dress and shoes to Eve.

Eve stood up. The dress looked as if it might fit. She moved away to change.

"What of the boy?" Bertrand asked.

Jean de Metz pointed to his servant. "For his disobedience, he will find suitable clothes for the boy."

"Me?" the servant asked. "Where will I find them?"

"In Chinon."

"Master, the shops will be closed," the servant complained.

De Metz gave him a stern look. "That is a problem for you to solve."

With a pained expression, the servant bowed.

At midday, Jeanne and her guards walked their horses to the road, then mounted them. Andrew assumed that he and Eve would follow on foot, but Jeanne insisted that Eve ride with Richard l'Archer and Andrew ride with Jean de Metz.

The red dress and shoes were awkward for Eve. She had to ride sidesaddle.

With a commanding "Forward!" Jeanne spurred her horse on.

They rode at a slow but steady pace. Coming out of the forest, Andrew lifted a hand to shield his eyes from the bright sun overhead. As his eyes adjusted, he saw the town ahead. It sat like an obedient servant at the foot of the castle walls, towers, and turrets. The Vienne River curved like a blue ribbon to the left. Furrowed fields spread far away to the right.

"God's glory!" Jeanne cried out.

Chinon came alive as they approached. Word spread that *Jeanne la Pucelle* was coming.

CHAPTER SIX

A rider sped toward them from the town. It was Julien, Bertrand's servant. He reined in his horse alongside his master's. "I have found an inn for us," he announced.

"Then I shall go directly to the castle to inform the Dauphin of our arrival," Colet said.

"May God grant you speed," Jeanne called out.

Colet urged his horse on and galloped away.

As the riders came to the gate of Chinon, the townspeople called out much as they had earlier: *Jeanne of Domrémy, Maiden of Honor! Virgin Saint!* Some shouted out to her as the savior of France. A few shook fists and declared her to be a false prophetess. Andrew heard others complain that she was dressed as a man.

Jeanne seemed unconcerned. She rode with her shoulders erect and her head held high.

They followed Julien around a corner to a side street. Each rider dismounted in front of a ramshackle building made of dark wood and plaster. They eyed the place with concern.

"Sneeze and it will collapse," Bertrand said.

"With apologies, sir," said Julien. "It is the only inn that would have us. The madame seems like a good-hearted woman."

"We have not come this far to be fussy," Jeanne said. She pushed the wooden door. The rusty hinges squeaked loudly. The door listed as if it would fall off.

They stepped into a low-ceilinged room with a few tables and chairs. At the far end was a counter made of an old door and two sawhorses. It was covered with bottles and cups.

"Ah!" a woman exclaimed, bustling around the counter. She was thin, with a bony frame that resembled an assembly of matchsticks. Her tunic and skirt looked as if they'd swallowed everything but her head. "I am Marie de Loire. Welcome!"

"Greetings," said Bertrand.

The woman knelt in front of Jeanne and lowered her head. "Welcome, saintly Maiden."

Jeanne reached down and touched her shoulder. "None of that, dear mother. Stand up," she said.

The innkeeper smiled, then stood and waved for everyone to sit down. They made themselves as comfortable as they could on the rickety chairs. Cups of drink were quickly placed in front of them. Plates of bread, cheese, and suspicious-looking meat were delivered by a somewhat harried girl who looked like a younger version of the innkeeper.

Andrew ate slowly and carefully. Eve held up a piece of cheese, inspected it, then put it down again. Jeanne did not eat at all.

"I have rooms for you," Marie de Loire said.

"*Merci*, but no," protested Jeanne. "We need only clean ourselves up. The Dauphin will summon us soon."

The woman laughed. "You will not see him today, sweet girl. His advisers will not allow it. They must discuss and debate long before they will welcome you into their sacred company."

CHAPTER SIX

"But he summoned us," Jeanne said. "It was he who—"

"Trust me, child," the woman interrupted. "You will want the rooms. You, with your maidservant." She gestured to Eve. "The men will share the largest room I have."

"*Merci*," said Jean de Metz.

The woman added proudly, "I have prayed for my cats to drive away the rats, and by the grace of Saint Gertrude, they have. You will be undisturbed. But the rats up there"—she nodded toward the castle—"are another matter."

The other Jean, the servant of Jean de Metz, asked her where he might find a change of clothes for Andrew.

Marie de Loire gave Andrew a once-over, then said, "I have clothes that will fit him. They belonged to my son. He donned armor to fight for our country. Killed, he was, by the English murderers in Burgundy. Come!"

The innkeeper was right. The clothes fit Andrew perfectly—a wool tunic that draped down to his knees, wool hose, and leather boots that laced up the front. A leather belt cinched around his waist, with a loop to hold a knife.

"Perfect!" she said with a clap of her hands.

It bothered Andrew to wear the clothes of a dead person. It bothered him more when the harried servant took his clothes away to be washed.

Jean de Metz also gave the servant girl Eve's modern clothes to wash. Eve shot Andrew a worried glance.

Colet returned from the castle and delivered the disheartening news that the Dauphin would not grant an audience with Jeanne until he consulted with the wisest of his court.

Marie de Loire flashed a knowing smile at Jeanne. "You see?"

"I fear we have come for nothing," Colet complained. "The Dauphin is surrounded by men of doubtful intent."

"What men?" Jeanne asked.

"Georges de La Trémoille is a wily character. He will not readily serve your mission if it interferes with his own desires. The Archbishop of Reims plays one side against another, as it suits him."

"What are we to do?" Jeanne asked.

Colet said in a reassuring tone, "As a royal messenger, I must stay at the castle. There, I will discern who will aid your cause."

After Colet left, Jeanne said to her small group, "God desires to teach me patience."

Marie de Loire laughed. "I fear God has little to do with the goings-on in that castle."

"Mind your tongue, old woman," Bertrand warned her.

"I speak plainly," the innkeeper snapped back, her hands on her hips. "Was it not God's will for us to suffer defeat at the hands of the English again and again? Do you not remember the tales of the battle at Crécy, when the English King Edward's out-numbered soldiers defeated our French army with mere *arrows*? Or when Edward's

CHAPTER SIX

son, the Black Prince, destroyed the French army at Poitiers? It was not so long ago that King Henry the Fifth conquered us at Agincourt."

"What are you suggesting?" Bertrand asked sourly.

"These victories must have been the will of God. Why else would He allow the Dauphin to live as an exile in his own country? Why else does the Duke of Burgundy dance like a puppet for the English boy-king Henry, the sixth of that name? Why does He allow the English to rule us at all?"

"Perhaps it was the will of God for us to be humbled," said Jeanne. "Now it is His will for the true king of France to be crowned in Reims. It is time for France to be French again, without the foreign invaders."

"Reims!" the lady cried. "How will you dislodge the coward from Chinon to crown him in Reims? Have you forgotten that you must first pass poor Orléans to reach Reims? The English hold that city under siege."

"By God's power, I will free Orléans," Jeanne said.

The woman's jaw dropped. "*You*, dear child?"

"God has said it will be so," Jeanne replied.

Marie de Loire closed her mouth and said very little for the rest of the day.

Afternoon slipped away. Jeanne and her companions did not dare to go outside, fearing the crowds would mob Jeanne. Instead, they prowled around the inn. The men scrubbed their clothes and stitched any tears they found. Then they gave their weapons a detailed shine.

Evening chased the daylight from the inn. Lamps were lit in the various rooms. Jeanne led everyone in evening prayers, then said goodnight. Eve went with her into a small room at the back.

Andrew joined the five men in a large open room with two beds and a pile of thin straw mats. Bertrand and Jean de Metz claimed the two beds, since they were paying for everything from their own pockets. The two servants deferred to Richard l'Archer, allowing him to pile two of the mats on top of each other so he might sleep more comfortably. They gave "Andrew the Angel" the remaining mat, which was only slightly better than sleeping on the hardwood floor.

At dawn, Andrew awakened in time to see Bertrand hand Richard l'Archer a pouch of money. Richard saw that Andrew was awake. He gave a quick salute, then left.

"Where is he going?" Andrew asked.

"Home to Vaucouleurs," Bertrand said. "His work for us is finished."

The two servants busied themselves by bringing bowls of water so the men could wash and shave.

A little later, Andrew bumped into Eve in the narrow hallway between the rooms. She looked tired.

"You didn't sleep?" he asked.

CHAPTER SIX

"Jeanne prayed for part of the night. Sometimes out loud," Eve said, then smiled. "I tried to join her but kept falling asleep. See? I am not a holy maiden."

"Are you Jeanne's servant now?" Andrew asked.

Eve shrugged. "I'm following along to see what happens. Isn't that the plan?"

"I guess so," Andrew said. What else could they do?

Marie de Loire greeted them in the main room, then cautioned them about going outside. "The people are already crowding the lane to see the Maiden. If they know you are with her, they may mob you."

"We are getting used to it," Eve said.

Bertrand, Jean de Metz, and the servants sat down at a table. A few minutes later, Jeanne joined them.

Breakfast—if it could be considered breakfast—consisted of a watery kind of porridge and warm bread. Only Andrew, Eve, and the servants ate. Jeanne and the two soldiers refrained.

"Why will you not eat?" Andrew asked Bertrand and Jean de Metz.

"A meal first thing in the morning is for peasant workers, women, and children," Bertrand replied.

"I fit those categories," Eve said, then dipped a piece of bread into her bowl of porridge.

"Me, too." Andrew laughed and upended his bowl of porridge into his mouth.

The men looked at him, unimpressed.

Suddenly Jeanne put a hand over her mouth and giggled. Then she laughed outright. For a moment, Andrew saw the young peasant girl from a small village somewhere.

How did she wind up here? he wondered.

Later that morning, some men arrived from the castle. The innkeeper became very excited and dashed to a back room to find refreshments. The two servants, Jean and Julien, raced to tell their masters.

"Look," Eve whispered as three men came through the door.

Andrew was surprised to see that one of them was the white-haired old man who had assaulted Eve on the bridge the day before. "He's from the court?"

The old man went to a corner table away from the others. He sat down without speaking. The other two men invited Jeanne to be seated so they could talk.

One of the men was bald, but he sported a brown beard that hung down to the middle of his chest. The other was clean-shaven and had thin, curly white hair matted against his scalp. Both wore long cloaks. They introduced themselves with elaborate titles that went on so long, Andrew had lost interest by the time they reached their names.

CHAPTER SIX

Andrew noticed that the old man at the table wasn't looking at Jeanne. His eyes were on Eve. Slowly his gaze shifted to Andrew.

Andrew stared back at him. The old man's eyes were dark and showed no emotion. Andrew looked away.

Bertrand and Jean de Metz entered from the back of the inn. The two men gave them quick nods of greeting. The bald one held up his hand for them to stay back.

"The Dauphin has sent us to inquire about your mission here," the bald man said.

"My mission is for his ears only," said Jeanne.

"As we are here in his name, you should treat us as you would him," the curly-haired man said to Jeanne. "If not, then you will never be granted an audience with him."

Jeanne paused as if weighing her options. Then she said, "The King of Heaven has sent me to lift the siege of Orléans and to lead the Dauphin to Reims for his coronation."

The eyebrows of both men lifted up. The old man at the table leaned forward. His gaze shot from Andrew to Eve and then to Jeanne.

"You have come to inspire the Dauphin with these words?" the bald man asked. "You hope to entice him to attack Orléans?"

Jeanne shook her head. "It is not for him to attack Orléans. God has sent me to do it."

"*You?*" the curly-haired man asked, his eyebrows lifting.

"Who put this idea into your head?" the bald man asked.

"Messengers from God," said Jeanne.

"What messengers?" asked the bald man.

"Saint Michael and his angels," Jeanne replied.

The two men scooted back in their chairs, as if they feared a bolt of lightning might strike her. One exclaimed something that Andrew's mind couldn't translate, and the tone made him glad of it.

"We have heard rumors of this but dared not believe it," said the bald man.

The curly-haired man held up a thick finger. "How do you know it was Saint Michael and his angels? Perhaps it was a devil and its legions?"

"I would have recognized one from the other," Jeanne said. "Saint Michael would not allow me to be deceived."

The bald man snorted. "Arrogant child! Was it not a widow in Champagne who entertained both? Women are easy prey to the wiles of the devil."

"Some women, perhaps, but not I," Jeanne said calmly. "I can prove what I say."

The bald man waved his hand. "How? Will Saint Michael appear to us now?"

"That is his business, not mine," said Jeanne. "I have a message to deliver to the Dauphin. It is something only he can know, because it is from his prayers."

CHAPTER SIX

"You know what he prays?" the curly-haired man asked.

"The messengers told me," Jeanne replied.

"We shall see about that," the bald man said.

The curly-haired man turned his sights to Bertrand and Jean de Metz. "You are the two escorts from Robert de Baudricourt?"

"We are," Bertrand answered.

"The Dauphin wishes to speak with you," the bald one said.

"When?" asked Jean de Metz.

"Now." The bald man stood up. The curly-haired one did the same.

Jean de Metz and Bertrand looked at each other.

De Metz gave a quick bow to the men. "As you wish," he said.

"What of my audience with the Dauphin?" Jeanne asked, slowly rising.

"In time, if he desires it," the bald man said.

Out the door they went, with Bertrand asking the two men, "May we seek compensation from the Dauphin for bringing the girl safely to him?"

The old man slowly stood up, as if in pain. With stooped shoulders, he followed the others. He turned at the door as if to say something, but then he shook his head and walked on, latching the door behind him.

Marie rushed out from a back room. She fanned an apron at her flushed face. "By the saints!" she cried and collapsed into a chair. "Never have I entertained members of the royal court."

Jeanne frowned. "Why does the Dauphin delay? Is he playing games with me?"

"Dear child, he is a scared rabbit," Marie said. "He has been played the fool too often. He fears you have come to do the same."

"How can I assure him otherwise if he will not see me?" Jeanne lamented.

"How indeed?" Marie asked.

Jeanne attempted to disguise herself to attend Mass but was easily recognized. The crowd pressed in to touch her, pushing Andrew and Eve aside.

During the Mass, Andrew was distracted by all of the looks and whispering. Finally the priest shouted for the parishioners to cease their disrespect for God.

Back at the inn, Jeanne complained, "The people clamor to see me, but not the Dauphin."

So they sat and waited and prayed. To pass the time, Andrew and Eve played a game of stacking small sticks of wood to see how high they could go without toppling. The game ended when the innkeeper used the sticks as kindling for a fire.

Jeanne watched the sticks burn, with a somber expression on her face.

CHAPTER SIX

Supper included potatoes, bread, and another unidentifiable kind of meat.

"When did they invent french fries?" Andrew whispered to Eve.

"They didn't. French fries are American," she whispered back.

"Then why are they called French?" asked Andrew.

"It has something to do with cutting the potatoes in long strips, or something like that," Eve explained.

"Give me a knife and I'll invent them now," Andrew said.

Eve laughed. "They don't have deep fryers yet."

"I'll invent those, too," said Andrew.

In the middle of the meal, Bertrand and Jean de Metz returned from the castle.

Jeanne stood up as they came in. "Well? Tell me of your audience with the Dauphin."

"Please be seated, good Maiden," Bertrand said. He and Jean de Metz sat down. Their servants busied themselves setting food in front of the two men.

"The king asked us about our travels," de Metz explained. "He had heard rumors of miracles."

"It has been said that rivers parted for us," Bertrand said, smiling.

"He also heard that an ambush was foiled," said Jean de Metz.

Jeanne looked at Andrew and Eve. "And so it was."

Bertrand gulped down a tankard of ale, then wiped his mouth with the back of his hand. "The only miracle I saw was that we brought you safely through enemy lands, defying even the foul weather. That is miracle enough for me."

"It will be a greater miracle if we are compensated for our efforts," Jean de Metz added.

"When will the Dauphin see me?" Jeanne asked.

Bertrand gazed at her sadly. "In his own sweet time."

7

It didn't take as long as they feared.

Serving as the royal messenger, Colet arrived the next afternoon with three guards from the castle. With a wary smile, he bowed and said, "The Dauphin bids you come. He will see you, even against the advice of many in his court."

Jeanne lifted her hands and said, "Thanks be to God! Hurry! Gather your things. We must go."

"Not everyone," Colet said. "*You.*"

Jeanne froze. "What of my angels? I cannot go without them."

Colet waved a hand at Andrew and Eve. "Your two angels may go as your servants. The others must remain—or depart. It is up to them."

"Depart! We must be compensated," insisted Bertrand.

"I am assured you will be," Colet said. "However, our Maiden must be seen first."

Jeanne bid farewell to Bertrand de Poulengy and Jean de Metz, her guides and protectors. "God will reward you for what you have done," she said. "I hope we will see one another again."

De Metz came close to her and said, "If ever you are in need of help, send a messenger to us. We will come."

Bertrand gave her a reassuring nod.

"*Merci*," she said, touching their hands like a blessing.

The servants of Bertrand and Jean de Metz retrieved Jeanne's horse from the stable, saddling it for the short journey up to the castle. Jeanne thanked them for their dutiful service to her.

Getting to the castle gate up the steep and dusty hill was a slow process. The people of Chinon gathered around Jeanne's horse, reaching out to touch her leg or foot. Colet, also on horseback, shouted at them to get back. The three castle guards shoved them aside, demanding that they make way.

Andrew and Eve were given a horse of their own and trailed behind the others. The crowd pressed in again. Andrew hoped they wouldn't get knocked off or trampled.

The procession came to the main gate. Reaching a drawbridge, the crowds were forced to stay back or risk falling into the moat below.

"Tell me of the castle," Jeanne said to Colet, now that she was able to be heard.

"There are *three* castles behind these walls," Colet explained. "To the west are the towers of the Fort du Coudray. Then, in the middle, is the Château du Milieu. The Dauphin resides there, in the chamber of Saint Louis.

It is next to the Grande Salle, the great hall, where you will be received. The garrison is in the stronghold to the right."

"Is there a chapel?" Jeanne asked.

"Yes, dear Maiden. It is just beyond this gate. The second Henry of England built it, under the patronage of Saint George. You know of Saint George?"

"A valiant knight," Jeanne answered. "He slew a dragon and saved a king's daughter, though he was still martyred for his faith."

Colet nodded. "Bound to a wheel with terrible spikes, like Saint Catherine. But the wheel miraculously broke, so he was murdered with an axe."

Once inside the gate, they entered a courtyard. Soldiers and workers alike turned from their duties to see the young woman on horseback.

A coarse-looking man staggered toward them. He was half dressed in his guard uniform and reeked of alcohol. He leered up at Jeanne. "Give me time, and I will put you in a different condition than you are."

Jeanne slowed her horse and gazed down at him. "Why do you use your time to offend God, when you are so near to death?"

The man opened his mouth to respond, but he suddenly went pale. He pressed his lips together and stumbled back as if she had struck him.

"Clear the way!" Colet shouted. "Or the Dauphin shall hear of it."

With the sounds of shuffling feet and rattling armor, the men drew back. Suddenly, a robed friar pushed through the crowd and called out, "*Jesu Maria.*" He lifted his hands and blessed Jeanne as she went past.

They crossed a second drawbridge and came to yet another courtyard. Colet dismounted. Servants suddenly appeared and helped Jeanne do the same. She waved them away and climbed down herself.

A man in a lavish red robe with a fur-lined collar stepped forward. He bowed low. "I am the Count of Vendôme, Louis de Bourbon. I have been given the honor of escorting you to the king."

Jeanne curtsied, which looked strange for someone in a man's clothes. "*Merci*, good count."

Led by the count, Andrew and Eve followed the entourage through a set of large doors. Andrew felt lost as they trekked down various hallways. They climbed a broad staircase and finally reached a set of huge wooden doors.

"His Highness is inside," the count said.

The doors seemed to swing open on their own.

Andrew would always remember the sight of Jeanne framed in that massive arched doorway, a tiny figure facing a great giant. Beyond her was a long meeting hall that stretched to a gigantic fireplace. Hundreds of people were gathered, dressed in the colorful clothes of the wealthy, the clergy, and high-ranking soldiers. Tapestries covered the walls, separated by dozens of lit torches

CHAPTER SEVEN

hanging on iron rings. The room smelled of sweat, perfume, and burning oil.

The Count of Vendôme walked quickly ahead of the company and seemed to melt into the crowd. Jeanne slowly entered. Her black-and-gray clothes looked dull compared to all the colors around her. The assembly went silent.

Andrew and Eve stayed several feet behind Jeanne. Andrew searched the faces of the gawking crowd. Some looked at Jeanne with expressions of disdain. A few smirked. Most looked at her as if she were part of a freak show that had arrived to entertain them. Andrew then caught sight of a tall figure behind the others. It was the old man who had grabbed Eve on the bridge.

Jeanne's head turned slowly to the left and the right. She paused, stopping in front of a young man wearing robes far more royal than any of the others. He smiled at her.

The Dauphin, Andrew thought.

But rather than bow, as Andrew expected, Jeanne only nodded and walked past the young man.

Ahead was a large chair, the size of a throne. In it was a man sitting regally, his hands clasped in front of him as if waiting for her to come and pay homage. Surely that was the Dauphin.

Jeanne only glanced at the man, then turned toward a small cluster of men and women off to the side. A white-haired woman wearing a black, ornately jeweled dress was there. She smiled kindly at Jeanne.

"Pardon me," Jeanne said to the woman, then stepped past her. Andrew heard Jeanne say "Ah" to another young-looking man dressed in a modest tunic. He had a thin, pale face, with small eyes and a large nose. His thick lips hung like two sausages over a weak chin. Bony, hose-covered legs gave him the look of a stork.

Jeanne knelt at his feet.

The man on the throne stood up with an indignant expression. "What are you doing?" he called out.

Andrew and Eve looked at each other. *It has to be a mistake,* thought Andrew. *Poor Jeanne has come all this way and is kneeling in front of the wrong man.*

Then it got worse.

"Gentle Dauphin," Jeanne said, her head lowered. "May God give you a long life."

The pale stork of a man looked at her helplessly. His small eyes darted one way, then another, as if he wanted someone in the crowd to stop the embarrassment. He rubbed his nose nervously.

"Why do you speak to me?" he asked, then pointed to the man in the large chair. "There is your lord."

Jeanne did not bother to look toward the chair. "In God's name, noble Dauphin," she said, "it is you and none other."

A sound like a childish giggle came from the man's throat. Then the man relaxed. "I am your Dauphin," he said.

Jeanne smiled up at him. Laughter echoed around the hall.

CHAPTER SEVEN

"They tried to trick her," Eve whispered to Andrew.

"Pray, who are you?" the Dauphin asked. He reached down and gently lifted Jeanne to her feet. "Why have you come to me?"

Jeanne stood before him, her voice strong. "The King of Heaven sends me to you with this message: You shall be anointed and crowned in the city of Reims. You shall be the king of France, the lieutenant of the King of Heaven."

Whispers rolled through the crowd, followed by a stern look from the Dauphin. The gathering fell silent again.

"In my heart I yearn to believe you," he said. "Give me cause to do so."

"Sire, if I tell you things so secret that you and God alone know them, will you believe that He has sent me?" Jeanne asked.

"I will," said the Dauphin.

Jeanne looked at the assembly, all straining to hear her.

The Dauphin saw her expression and, taking her arm, led her to the far end of the hall near the massive hooded fireplace.

Andrew wasn't sure they should follow. Without looking to anyone for permission, Eve did. Andrew tagged along.

The Dauphin gave the two children a suspicious look as they approached.

Jeanne ignored them, a signal that the Dauphin should do the same.

"What, then, is the secret?" the Dauphin asked. "I have so few, with spies watching me at every turn."

Jeanne said softly, "Remember, sire, last All Saints' Day. You were alone in your oratory, in the chapel of the castle at Loches."

The Dauphin's small eyes widened. Andrew could see his mind working. He was trying to figure out how a peasant girl could know anything about his chapel in the castle at Loches or his whereabouts months before.

"I remember it well," he said, his voice a dry rasp.

"You asked three things of God," she told him.

The Dauphin's mouth fell open.

"Have you spoken of these things to a confessor or to anyone who might have betrayed them to me?" she asked.

"I have not," he said.

"Then hear me, gentle Dauphin. Your first request of God was that he should remove you from the throne if you are not France's true heir. You do not desire to be the cause of prolonging a war that brings so much suffering."

The Dauphin slowly nodded. "It is so. And the second?"

"The second was that you alone should be punished if your sins have caused the many troubles the people of France are forced to endure. You said you are willing to die, if God requires it."

Tears came to the Dauphin's eyes. "It is as you say. Speak to me of the third."

"The third request was that the people should be forgiven, and God's anger appeased, if their own sins are the cause of their misery."

CHAPTER SEVEN

The Dauphin lowered his head for a moment. Then lifting it up again, he said, "You have spoken the truth."

He wiped his eyes, then turned suddenly and marched to the center of the hall. All eyes were on him now, as the people anxiously awaited his verdict.

"God has sent her to me," he announced.

Andrew was sure the big moment would lead to Jeanne and the Dauphin going off somewhere to talk about what would happen next. It wasn't as easy as that.

With the Dauphin's announcement, a clamor rose from the crowd. Various men stepped forward, appealing to the Dauphin to be cautious and wise. They demanded that Jeanne be tested further to prove that she spoke for God.

The Dauphin looked conflicted. Finally he raised his hands to quiet them. "Please! Be still!" With an apologetic expression, he turned to Jeanne and said, "Dear Maiden, you will be taken to the Tower of Coudray."

Jeanne looked bewildered.

Andrew was shocked. *How could the Dauphin put her in a tower?* From his history lessons, he thought that being taken to a tower was the same as being put in prison.

An escort of servants and guards came forward and escorted the three of them to the western side of the grounds. At the base of a large tower, they were met by a man who introduced himself as Guillaume Bellier, the chief steward of the Dauphin. Next to him was his wife, Madame Bellier, an elf-like woman with a glowing smile.

"The tower is the royal residence for honored guests," said the steward.

Andrew was relieved.

Madame Bellier bowed to Jeanne. Then she looked at Eve and said, "Dear child, I have never seen eyes that color."

"She is my angel," Jeanne said, then gestured to Andrew. "This boy is her helper."

Andrew flinched. "I am not her helper," he said.

Eve shot him a grin.

A young man—maybe fourteen or fifteen years old—stepped forward. He had brown hair cut in the shape of a bowl, and a round face that was scarred with acne. He bowed his head.

"This is Louis de Coutes, our *Minguet*," Monsieur Bellier said to Jeanne. "He is to be your page during the day. My wife will see to you at night."

Wicks and torches were lit; then they entered the tower. Inside it looked exactly as it did outside: round. The staircase rose like a corkscrew around an edge of stony shadows. They passed various doors along the way.

"A round room is on every floor," Monsieur Bellier said.

"Dignitaries often stay here when visiting," Madame Bellier explained, then added cheerfully, "The king must think of you as a dignitary."

CHAPTER SEVEN

"Why am I to stay in this tower?" Jeanne asked with an impatient tone. "There is too much work to be done for me to be idle here."

Madame Bellier gave her a sympathetic smile. "Dear child, Saint Paul tells us to test the spirits that come our way. We must be discerning. Our prince would be a fool to follow the vision of every person who stands at the gate and claims to speak for God."

"I am not 'every person,'" Jeanne said. "*God* has sent me with this message."

"You ask too much of those who have not seen or heard what you have," Madame Bellier countered. "Allow us to prove your message."

"While you prove it, the English are spilling French blood," Jeanne said sharply.

"French blood has been spilled for a hundred years under the eyes of God. What is another day or month to Him?" Madame Bellier asked without losing her pleasant tone.

Jeanne frowned. For a moment, Andrew saw the face of a young girl sulking.

They stopped at a doorway. Monsieur Bellier said, "Minguet, you and the servant boy—"

"My name is Andrew," he cut in.

"Yes, *Andrew*," Bellier continued. "The two of you will stay in here. Jeanne will stay with her angel and Madame in the room above you."

Madame Bellier continued to lead the ladies upward. Monsieur Bellier followed them, explaining how King

Philip the Fourth held the Knights Templar captive in the castle one hundred years before. His voice faded away.

Louis stepped into the room. Andrew lingered at the doorway. He thought he heard a noise from somewhere down the stairs. He turned and, from the corner of his eye, saw movement just around the curve. The shadow of a man stood still against the wall. Then it slowly retreated until it was out of sight.

8

"I'm sure it was the old man from the bridge," Andrew said to Eve the next morning.

They were standing outside the chapel of Saint Martin. The Dauphin had commanded that it be reserved solely for Jeanne and her company.

"What does he want?" Eve asked. "I had a dream last night about that wild look he had in his eyes when he came after me. I think he's crazy."

"He's definitely creepy," said Andrew.

Eve stepped back and eyed him from head to foot. "You're wearing new clothes."

Andrew had on a dark-gray tunic with black leggings and shoes. A leather belt was buckled around his waist.

"Monsieur Bellier gave them to me this morning. He said I have to look appropriate for the court."

"And me?" Eve asked, spreading her arms and turning slowly. She was now adorned in a long white tunic with a dark-blue dress underneath.

"Pretty," he said.

She tugged at her dress. "I would rather wear my real clothes."

The door to the chapel opened, and Madame Bellier stepped through.

Jeanne came out a few seconds later. She was wearing the same black-and-gray outfit.

"Thanks be to God for the Dauphin's kindness in providing us with a private chapel," Jeanne said. She turned to Madame Bellier. "When may I see him again?"

"First, you must meet with Madame de Trèves and Madame de Gaucourt," said Madame Bellier.

"Who are they?" Jeanne asked.

Madame Bellier looked surprised. "How do you not know? Madame de Trèves is the wife of Robert Le Maçon of Trèves, the chancellor and one of the king's most trusted advisers. Madame de Gaucourt is the wife of Raoul de Gaucourt, the captain of Chinon and bailiff of Orléans."

Jeanne nodded. Andrew thought she was trying to look impressed but really didn't care.

Madame Bellier seemed to realize Jeanne's feelings and added, "The queen of Sicily has arranged everything."

Jeanne looked puzzled. "Of what interest am I to the queen of Sicily?"

"She is Yolande of Aragon, the Dauphin's mother-in-law. Surely you have heard of her. She certainly has a keen interest in you."

"Does she?"

"Oh yes. She greatly desires your success in God's mission. That is why she wants everything proven."

"How am I to be 'proven' by these good ladies?" Jeanne asked, bristling.

"Madame de Trèves and Madame de Gaucourt will get to know you. Then they will be able to assure the Dauphin that you are who and what you say you are."

Jeanne sighed. "If it will satisfy the Dauphin, I will comply. *Then* may I see him?"

"Of course you may," Madame Bellier assured her. "Once the council speaks with you."

Jeanne's shoulders slumped. "Is it necessary?" she asked.

"It is by the Dauphin's command," Madame Bellier said.

Jeanne nodded and straightened up. "Then let us begin."

"What would you like me to do?" Eve asked.

"You must stay by your lady's side," Madame Bellier replied. "Wait patiently, nearby, wherever she is. Louis, our Minguet, will be with you."

Louis suddenly appeared from around a corner and gave a quick bow.

"What am I supposed to do?" Andrew asked.

Madame Bellier turned to Andrew as if she had forgotten he was there. "What are your skills? Have you ever served in a royal court?"

"No," he said.

"As a page or a squire?"

"No."

She gave him the smile of a teacher who didn't know what to do with a misfit student. "I suggest you explore the castle and its grounds. Louis will train you in the ways of a page when he is not attending to Jeanne. Perhaps my husband will invent a purpose for you."

Andrew watched the four of them walk away. He felt annoyed. Why would God put him in this time and not give him anything to do?

He looked around and decided to take Madame Bellier's advice. How often would he have the chance to wander around a real castle without worrying about getting in trouble? Now was a very good time to explore.

He learned quickly that in many ways, a castle was like a busy city. Messengers raced in all directions. There were carpenters fixing wooden beams and masons chiseling on stone. Blacksmiths hammered on anvils, while groomsmen brushed the horses. Cooks chopped at vegetables on wooden tables and stirred the contents of large cauldrons with iron spoons.

Chickens got under Andrew's feet. The occasional cat meowed at him. Dogs chased each other. Children scampered and played in corners, out of the way of scowling soldiers. Guards stood at attention or strolled with their spears held like walking sticks, their hands on the hilts of their swords. Cadets sparred with one another using wooden swords or stood with their bows,

CHAPTER EIGHT

shooting arrows at targets tied to bales of hay. The air was filled with the smell of damp straw, smoke, animals, and sweat.

Suddenly, a peasant woman rushed from a doorway, her hands covering her face. She sobbed loudly as she passed Andrew. He watched her rush off, then turned to see a robed man just inside a nearby room. The man was standing over a dead body stretched out on a slab. Andrew was sure he'd seen the face of the dead man before. It was the guard who had been so rude to Jeanne when they arrived at the castle the day before.

The robed man saw Andrew staring. He stepped to the door and said, "Take heed and learn from this man. This is what happens when you drink too much."

"What happened to him?" Andrew asked.

"The fool fell into the river last night," the man said, then closed the door on Andrew.

As Andrew walked away, he remembered Jeanne's words to the drunken guard. She had rebuked him for disrespecting God when he was so close to death.

Had Jeanne known the man was going to die, or was the man punished for being abusive to her?

Bored of exploring the courtyards, Andrew found his way to the main castle, where the Dauphin lived and kept court. He hoped he would bump into Eve. He went to a doorway he thought they had used when they first arrived. A guard gave him a cautious look.

"I am a servant of Jeanne," Andrew said. "The Maiden?"

The guard pushed the door open. Andrew entered a passageway that ended in a set of stairs. He followed them up to a wide hallway where small groups of people stood chatting softly. Servants flitted here and there. They were better uniformed than the ones in the courtyard.

Women adorned in satin, velvet, and lace dresses seemed to float in and out of various doorways. Men in regal-looking tunics and robes walked with their heads close together in quiet consultation.

Andrew was hardly noticed. Only the guards saw him and gestured for him to move on or warned him not to go down a particular hallway. He heard doors opening and closing and voices echoing from other places. He wandered down one passage, then another. Soon he was lost.

Behind him, a gruff voice asked, "Who are you? What are you doing here?"

Andrew ignored the man and picked up his pace as if he hadn't heard. The footsteps behind him quickened. Andrew darted down a side corridor. He saw a door standing slightly ajar and slipped through. He pulled the door behind him and waited. The footsteps came rushing up, then past.

Andrew leaned against the door and caught his breath. He turned to see what kind of room he'd entered. It was

CHAPTER EIGHT

a narrow stairwell. Somewhere up above, men were talking. Then Andrew heard a girl's voice. It was Jeanne.

Creeping to the top of the stairs, Andrew found himself in the shadows of a low-ceilinged balcony. He went to a wooden rail and carefully peeked over. The room was a large rectangle with tall arched windows and banners. Men in brightly colored robes sat around an oversized table. At the far end of the table, Jeanne stood with her hands clasped in front of her. She looked like a prisoner in front of a panel of judges.

He took another step, and the floor creaked loudly beneath his foot. He backed up to make sure he wasn't seen. A hand fell on his shoulder and another clasped over his mouth.

"Shhh," a woman's voice said into his ear. "You must not give us away."

Andrew relaxed. The woman took her hands away. He turned and recognized her. She was the white-haired woman the Dauphin had hidden behind when he'd tried to trick Jeanne.

"I am Queen Yolande of Aragon," she whispered.

She reminded him of a queen. She wore a dress of white and gold with pearls sewn into the collar and sleeves. A white covering on her head framed her slender face. She had a petite nose and thin lips that were now pressed into a smile. Her eyes were sharp and alert, like a bird's.

Andrew remembered the name. "You are the Dauphin's mother-in-law."

"Indeed. And you are Andrew, one of the Maiden's angels."

"How do you know that?" Andrew asked.

"There are few things I do not know," she said. She leaned back, and Andrew saw that she was sitting in a small chair. She nodded to the proceedings below them. "The Maiden is doing well against the council. I have seen men quiver from fear when facing those men. She, however, has great courage."

"Do they believe her?" he asked.

"Does it matter what they believe?" Queen Yolande asked. "Men hold their petty positions of power, but women hold the most important positions of influence. They may tell the king what they think, but the king will listen to me."

"I was thirteen years old," Andrew heard Jeanne saying. He turned to the edge of the balcony.

"That was when you first heard a voice from God?" a man asked Jeanne.

"Yes. The first time made me fearful," she said.

Another man asked, "Was this at night? Were you sleeping?"

"No, sir. It was noon. I was in my father's garden. The Voice came from the direction of the church. A brightness came with it, a great light. The Voice was clear. I understood everything I was told."

"What did the Voice tell you?" asked the first man.

Jeanne said, "I was told to be virtuous and attend church as often as I may. Then the Voice told me that I must leave my home, in secret, because of my mission."

"Leave your home to go where?" the same man asked.

"To Robert de Baudricourt at the fortress of Vaucouleurs."

Another man asked, "For what purpose?"

"The Voice said that Robert de Baudricourt would provide me with the means to reach the Dauphin with a message from God."

"How did you know the voice—or the message—was from God?"

"Saint Michael gave me assurance."

"Saint Michael! How did you know it was Saint Michael?" asked the first man.

"By his voice. It was the voice of an angel. He spoke as an angel," Jeanne said, as if the answer should have been obvious.

"You are skilled in the languages of the angels?"

Jeanne gave a slight laugh. "No, sir. But I knew immediately when I heard him speak. He told me that Saint Catherine and Saint Margaret would come to me with advice, and I should take action on what they said."

"Did you speak to anyone about this?" asked yet another man.

"Only Robert de Baudricourt, to persuade him that I was not insane."

"Did he believe you?"

"No. He told me to go home. Later I returned, and he agreed to give me the men to lead me here."

"Tell us again, clearly, what mission the Voice gave you," asked the first man.

"I was told to raise the siege that has laid low the city of Orléans, so the Dauphin may be crowned king at Reims."

Jeanne's statement caused an immediate reaction. The men began talking all at once. The sounds of stomping and banging around the table shot through the rafters.

After everyone had calmed down, a different man asked, "Are you skilled with the sword? With leading men in battle?"

"No," Jeanne said calmly. "I told the Voice that I was a poor girl who knew nothing of these things. But I later thought of the unskilled peasant men and women our Lord uses for His purposes."

"You are thinking of our Holy Mother Mary?" a kindly voice asked.

"Yes."

"You dare to compare yourself to the Holy Mother?" a harsher voice exclaimed.

"No. I only compare myself as a poor peasant girl to other peasants who heard God and sought to serve Him."

"That is enough for today," the first man said.

"For today?" Jeanne asked.

"We will speak again," he replied.

CHAPTER EIGHT

"But sir—" Jeanne began to say.

The first man interrupted her and said firmly, "We will speak again."

Chairs were pushed back. Voices fell into low mumbles and whispers. The meeting was over.

Andrew heard a noise behind him and turned. Queen Yolande of Aragon was gone.

Andrew found his way back to the tower. Eve was sitting alone on the bottom step.

"What are you doing here?" he asked.

"Jeanne is meeting with the Dauphin now," she said. "I thought I'd come back and rescue you from your dull and dreary life. Where have you been?"

"Wandering the castle, like Madame Bellier said."

"Did you see anything interesting?"

"A few things." Andrew told her about the dead guard, and spying on the king's council meeting, and Queen Yolande of Aragon.

"I saw her too," said Eve. "When Jeanne met with Madame de Trèves and Madame de Gaucourt. I think the queen has a lot of power around here."

Andrew agreed.

Eve stood up. "Have you been to the top of the tower?"

"Not yet."

"Louis took me there earlier. The view is amazing."

"You went to the tower with Louis?" Andrew asked. "By yourselves?"

Eve nodded. "Did you know that Louis speaks French and English, and a little bit of Spanish?"

"No," Andrew said.

The two of them made the slow journey up the tower stairs. Eve chattered on about Louis's family and how they had been in the service of the House of Orléans for more than one hundred years. They were great warriors, she said, and Louis's mother was from a noble Scottish family. Sadly, Louis's father had died a year ago and left the family to fend for themselves. One of the sisters got married to the governor of a place called Châteaudun, which helped. Finally, the Duke of Orléans gave them the money to survive.

Andrew glanced out of a small window in the tower. He guessed they were only halfway to the top. His legs hurt, and he was tired of hearing about Louis.

He said, "Since we're stuck here, maybe you should *marry* Louis. Then you can hang around with all the rich people and not worry about being a peasant, like I'll probably be."

Eve stopped in her tracks and frowned at him. "You had to ruin it, didn't you?"

"Ruin what?" he asked, confused.

"Never mind," she growled. "I don't feel like going to the tower now. You go." She retreated a few steps.

"What did I do?"

CHAPTER EIGHT

"I made a friend," Eve said, retreating a few more steps. "But then you spoiled it by talking about being stuck here and getting married."

"I was joking!"

She picked up her speed and rounded the corner out of sight. He could hear her shoes padding against the stone steps and fading until the slam of a door cut them off.

He looked at the steps winding up and away from him. He had a long way to go.

He sighed. What else was there to do?

9

The view from the roof of the tower was amazing, just as Eve had said. The roofs of Chinon were directly below. The bridge over the river Vienne snaked from east to west. Green fields, forests, and vineyards stretched out in all directions. The lands to the north rolled away like waves. Roads leading to other towns and villages spread from the castle like roots from a tree.

Andrew leaned on the parapet and looked down. The sheer drop to the ground below made him dizzy. He stepped back.

"It would be easy to fall" came a low voice from behind him.

Andrew spun around. The white-haired old man from the bridge stood between Andrew and the door to the stairs. His sword was drawn.

"What do you want?" Andrew asked.

"Tell me how you think you will escape," the old man said. Drawing closer, he held the sword up to Andrew's chest.

Andrew swallowed hard.

"How will you escape?" the old man asked again. The point of the sword now touched the fabric of Andrew's tunic.

"I do not know," Andrew said.

"Then why did you put yourself at risk?" the old man asked.

"I did not know I was at risk. I came for the view," Andrew said feebly.

"You are always at risk in this world. You will not survive if you do not understand that." The old man grunted, then lowered his weapon. "Where is your sword? Do you have a sword?"

"No."

The old man snorted. "How do you *not* have a sword?" he yelled, raising a hand to the heavens. "How old are you? Eleven or twelve? And you have no sword?"

"Why are you yelling at me?" Andrew shouted.

"Because someone needs to," he snapped. "You must be prepared."

"Is that why you attacked my friend on the bridge? To prepare her?"

He shrugged. "What else am I to do with a sorceress?"

"She is not a sorceress!"

"She has the eyes of a sorceress."

"They are the eyes of a *girl*. She is only a girl!" Andrew said.

CHAPTER NINE

"And you are only a boy?" the old man said. "I think not."

"What else do you think I am?" Andrew asked.

The old man stepped closer. "I was looking from the bridge by the river. I saw no one. *No one.* And then I saw someone. *Two* someones. A boy. A girl. They appeared from nowhere. Out of nothing. They were not there, and then they were."

Andrew was speechless. *The old man saw us arrive from our time! No wonder he was spooked.*

"Do you think I am a lunatic?" the old man asked.

Andrew didn't dare answer.

"Some think so. I know what they call me behind my back. *La Démence*—demented, insane. *La Rage.*" He shrugged. "Maybe so. There are times when I think so myself. There are times when I remember things that cannot be part of my memory. Do you understand?"

No, Andrew thought. He stood frozen where he was.

"You and your friend are like bugs buzzing in my head," the old man continued. "You tease at my thoughts. You make me want to remember what I cannot call to mind."

Andrew swallowed hard. "Like what?"

"If I knew, I would not be wasting my time with you!" he said angrily. He suddenly grabbed Andrew's wrist and pulled him to the door. "Come. You must train."

"Train? To do what?" Andrew pulled back, digging his heels into the gravel of the tower roof.

"To fight."

Andrew struggled, but the old man's grip was too strong.

"I do not want to train you," he said. "But Madame Bellier has told me I must. She said you have no skill. I will give you skill."

"Ah!" Andrew said. *Madame Bellier arranged this.* "You should have said so. Now, please let go."

The old man looked down at his hand on Andrew's wrist as if he didn't know how it got there. He released his grip. "I am sorry. I am not doing it on purpose," he said.

Andrew rubbed his wrist.

Stepping back, the old man gave a curt bow. "I am Simon Le Fantôme."

Andrew bowed without taking his eyes off the man. "I am Andrew ... Le Perry."

"Well, Andrew Le Perry, we will find you a sword, and you will train to fight. Then when you are leaning over the side of a tower and someone sneaks up from behind to attack, you will be prepared."

"Does that happen a lot around here?" Andrew asked.

"Once is more than enough," the old man said. "Come. We have work to do."

They began the long descent down the stairs.

"Are you a royal trainer?" Andrew asked along the way.

"Not at all!" the old man said, as if the idea were preposterous. "Some believe I should never be allowed

CHAPTER NINE

to hold a weapon. One does not know what I will do with it."

Andrew took no comfort from that statement.

Simon gave Andrew a sideways glance. "In war, there is no better man to have by your side than me. I fought with the fifth Henry at Agincourt."

Andrew gasped. "You fought with Henry the Fifth *against* the French?"

"Of course I did! I am from England..." He hesitated, then frowned. "Or so I believe."

"But you sound French. And you are in the castle of the Dauphin who wants to get rid of the English."

Simon shrugged. "I go where there is work," he said.

"What work? Are you a soldier-for-hire?"

"I am a jeweler," he replied. "Have you seen the Dauphin's clothes? The jewels around his neck, on his sleeves, around his armor—they are my handiwork. But I am also a soldier. One must be to survive. You will learn."

10

Simon Le Fantôme took Andrew to the courtyard where soldiers were still training. Simon disappeared through a doorway, then returned a few minutes later with a sword about the length of Andrew's arm. It was surprisingly light.

"Now we begin," Simon said, drawing his sword. "Basic skills."

He showed Andrew how to position his feet, body, and arms while holding a sword. Then he guided Andrew through the movements of stepping back and forth and from side to side. Simon complained about the weakness of Andrew's wrists and the lack of muscle control in his arms and legs.

"The goal is simple," the old man said. "You must stop your enemy. To stop him means you must be prepared to kill. For that, you must aim here." He hit his chest with the flat of his palm.

"Can I not wound him in the arm or leg?" Andrew asked.

"Imbecile!" Simon cried out. "Arms and legs move about quickly. How will you hit them? You must strike at the largest part of his body." He slammed the palm of his hand against his chest again. It made a loud thud. "Do not talk. Listen to me. Watch."

Simon began to go through slow movements, showing Andrew the stances he must take and the different ways to thrust the sword.

Andrew lost track of the time. He thrashed at a bale of hay, lunged at a man of straw, and finally exchanged blows with Simon himself. All the while, Simon taunted him. "Not that way; *this* way" and "Again! Again!"

Later Andrew caught sight of Eve and Louis standing off to the side, watching him. The glance away from Simon cost him a jab to his arm.

"Foolish boy," Simon shouted. "Concentrate!"

Andrew scowled. Then, with a roar, he lunged at the old man with his sword held high. Simon knocked him on his backside.

"That is all for today," Simon announced.

Andrew sat on the muddy ground. His muscles ached and his head hurt.

Eve brought him a cup of water. He noticed that she was looking cautiously at Simon from the corner of her eye. Simon glanced at her, then turned to a nearby barrel and used his hands to splash water on his face.

"It *is* him," Eve whispered as she handed Andrew the cup.

CHAPTER TEN

"Simon Le Fantôme," Andrew said. He took a long drink, then added, "Madame Bellier asked him to train me."

She knelt next to Andrew. "Did he tell you why he attacked me on the bridge?"

"He saw us arrive from our time," Andrew whispered.

Eve's mouth fell open. "He *saw* it?"

"He thinks you're a sorceress." Andrew pointed to her eyes. "*Those* convinced him. I don't know what he thinks I am."

"Keep that sword with you at all times," Simon said loudly as he approached them.

She cringed.

He tossed a leather sheath at Andrew. "Put this around your waist. Get used to your sword's weight and where it is on your body. It must become to you like another limb."

Eve stood up and glared at the old man. "I am *not* a sorceress!"

Simon's hairy face twitched. He said, "Then what are you?"

"I am just a girl!" she shouted.

Andrew struggled to his feet, in case the old man did something crazy.

"Then how did you come here?" Simon's voice grew louder as he spoke. "Tell me how you appeared beneath the bridge! If you are not a sorceress, then what are you?"

"A guest of the Dauphin!" Guillaume Bellier yelled from a doorway.

Simon came to attention, then quickly bowed. "Monsieur," he said.

"All this time in the castle, and you still have the manners of a brute," Bellier said. "Go on. The Dauphin has need of you."

Simon stood to his full height, towering over Bellier. "In another time, you would not have spoken to me in such a tone."

Bellier did not move, but his eyes betrayed concern. "Do not keep the Dauphin waiting."

Simon pointed at Andrew. "Practice," he said, then marched away.

Andrew fumbled with the sheath for his sword.

Bellier snapped his fingers. Louis rushed forward. "Sir?"

"Show him," Bellier said, then walked off.

Louis fastened the sheath around Andrew's waist. Then he showed Andrew how to slide the sword into the sheath without hurting himself. "It will take time," he said.

Eve watched them, then asked, "What about me? When will I be trained?"

Louis chuckled. "You?"

"Yes, *me*," Eve snapped. "If I am to travel with Jeanne, then I should know how to defend myself."

Louis flinched. "You are right, of course," he said. "I would be delighted to teach you."

CHAPTER TEN

Andrew didn't like the idea of the two of them training together. "Maybe you should learn from Simon," he quickly suggested.

Eve shook her head. "He scares me."

"He scares everyone," said Louis.

"Then why is he here?" Eve asked. "What do you know about him?"

Louis held up his hands. "He is a mystery. The stories are told that he was once a jeweler to the royal court in London. One night he was attacked by someone seeking a precious stone he possessed. His wife was murdered in the fight. They say it unhinged his mind. He seeks revenge through battle."

"He told me he fought with Henry the Fifth at Agincourt," Andrew said.

"So the legends say," Louis agreed. "They also say that he fought with kings *before* Henry—in Scotland and England."

"Why is he now with the French?" Andrew asked.

Louis shrugged. "No one knows for certain. It is whispered that he is eyes and ears for Queen Yolande of Aragon. She trusts him."

"Should we be worried about him?" Andrew asked.

"Worried? No. But I would not trust him readily," Louis said, then added, "Trust *no one* readily. The Dauphin's court is a den of well-dressed vipers."

"Can we trust you?" Eve asked him.

He gave her a coy smile. "Trust *no one* readily," he said again.

That evening Jeanne and her cohorts were served dinner in a dining room near the tower. The Dauphin's kitchen offered a variety of meats: beef, lamb, chicken, mutton, pork sausage, heron, and bizarrely, peacock and swan. Andrew couldn't bring himself to eat the peacock or swan. Eve tried them, but only because Louis insisted. She smiled at Louis as if she liked the taste of both. When he turned away, she made a disgusted face at Andrew.

The meal also included leeks, onions, turnips, cabbage, and some kind of bean soup. Fresh bread and various kinds of cheeses were laid out. Madame Bellier made a fuss about the presence of salt for the table. Andrew didn't realize that salt was rare.

As they sat around the table, Andrew thought of his family back in Hope Springs. An ache touched his heart. *I might never see them again*, he thought. He took a deep breath and fought back a sudden feeling of panic.

"What's wrong?" Eve whispered to him.

He shook his head and pushed his plate away. He'd lost his appetite.

After the meal, they all went to the chapel. Jeanne led them in evening prayers. Andrew prayed that God would

CHAPTER TEN

help him not to worry or be afraid. *I'm here for a reason,* he told himself. *God will take care of us—and then He will show us how to get home.*

Jeanne remained in the chapel as everyone else filed out. Andrew was the last to leave. He glanced back and saw Jeanne kneeling with her hands clasped tightly in front of her. He was sure he heard her softly crying. He closed the door.

The room Andrew and Louis shared was windowless, though heavy curtains hung along the circular wall to block any drafts. There were two small beds of straw, small tables with small lamps, small pitchers with small cups, small chairs, and small rugs. Andrew felt cramped and wondered why the room was so small when the tower was so big. Compared to the width of the tower, the room seemed small. And there was no fireplace. The only means of warmth came from large fur blankets. Though it was now spring, the rains made everything feel damp.

Andrew sat on the edge of his bed and rubbed his aching legs.

Louis gave Andrew a stone.

"Why?" Andrew asked.

"Use it to sharpen your sword," Louis said. He sat down and began scraping a stone against his own sword. "The lunatic will look it over tomorrow and knock you on the head for not doing it."

Andrew watched Louis, then copied what he did.

It was a good thing.

The next day Simon Le Fantôme inspected the sword. He looked disappointed that he couldn't knock Andrew on the head.

11

In the days that followed, Jeanne met with various women the Dauphin had sent to examine her. They judged that she was a virtuous young maiden. She then submitted to more questions from the council and met privately with the Dauphin. Andrew was not told what they talked about.

Eve stayed by Jeanne's side. When Eve wasn't needed, Louis taught her how to use a sword. Andrew continued his training with Simon. Not only did they practice with the sword, but Simon taught him about history and politics and the culture of France.

"The river Vienne makes Chinon ideal for trade," Simon explained one afternoon while parrying with Andrew. "Centuries ago, the Romans built a camp here. Then Saint Mexme, a disciple of Saint Martin, established a monastery not far from here. The town was built after that. Then the English came and took it over for decades. Now the Dauphin is here. For how long, God alone knows."

Andrew grunted at him. He didn't know what to say.

"You think this is the prattling of an old man?" Simon asked. "Heed me, boy. The glory of man comes and goes. I have seen it for myself. In the span of time, we are great only in our own eyes."

"How old are you?" Andrew asked.

"I do not remember." Simon sheathed his sword, then walked over to a large barrel of water. Tugging at his shirt, he let it fall to his waist and began to splash water on his face and body.

Andrew's eyes widened. Simon's back was covered with scars.

The old man turned to him, scrubbing his face with his hands. Simon's chest was wide and muscular. It was the body of a younger man. But it was also scarred. Simon saw the boy's gaze.

"Battles," the old man explained. "A mere jeweler should never bear such scars."

"Why do you?" Andrew asked.

"A man must fight for what is right," the old man said.

"What is right?"

Simon paused, stroking his bushy beard. "If the English kings who claim this land would pay the same devotion to their own land, the people would not suffer as they do."

"Do you believe Jeanne will drive the English out of France?" asked Andrew.

"Jeanne has an important role to play." He pulled his shirt on again. "It will cost her everything," he said in a very dark tone.

CHAPTER ELEVEN

There was a commotion beyond the courtyard, at the main gate. A moment later a rider galloped in on a beautiful black steed. The rider was dressed all in red and leapt from his horse before it had come to a full stop.

"Where is she?" he called out. He had dark hair and a hero's face—slender, with a firm jaw and confident eyes. "The girl from God! Where is she?"

When none of the gathering crowd answered, Andrew stepped forward, "I believe she is with the Dauphin now."

The man gave Andrew a quick look-over; then his eyes went to Simon and narrowed. "Simon Le Fantôme," he said, scowling. "I thought you were dead."

"Thought or hoped, my lord duke?" Simon asked with a bow.

"It is all the same to me," the man said. He pointed at Andrew. "Take me to the Dauphin."

Andrew hesitated. "Me? But—"

Simon pushed Andrew forward. "Do not keep the Duke of Alençon waiting," he said. "No doubt he sacrificed a day of boar hunting to join us."

"It was quail, actually," the duke said with a wry smile.

Just then, two servants rode up, looking as if they'd just lost a race. They were covered in dust. Andrew guessed they had been trying to keep up with the duke's horse.

"Stable the horses," the duke said to the servants. To Andrew he said, "Lead on!"

Andrew prayed he would remember the way to the Dauphin's chambers. He had gone with Eve a couple of times but now worried he would take a wrong turn.

"Are you being tutored by Le Fantôme?" the duke asked as they walked.

"Yes, my lord," Andrew said.

"He is an untrustworthy scoundrel," said the duke. "He fought alongside our enemies at Agincourt. My father was killed there."

"I am sorry, my lord," said Andrew.

"Le Fantôme also fought for the Duke of Bedford at the Battle of Verneuil," the duke continued, his tone filled with venom. "I was taken prisoner then by the English. They held me for ransom for five years."

Unsure of what to say, Andrew repeated, "I am sorry, my lord."

The duke seemed to be fuming. "I would happily kill Le Fantôme if he were not under the protection of Queen Yolande—and the Dauphin, of course. They see his value in ways I do not."

They came to the hall of the Dauphin's private residence. Eve and Louis were sitting close together in chairs along the wall, talking in low voices. At the sight of the duke, they leapt to their feet. Eve gave Andrew a puzzled look.

"Announce me," the duke said to Andrew. "Tell the Dauphin that John the Second, the Duke of Alençon, has come for an audience."

Louis opened the door for Andrew. Andrew gave Eve a pained look before stepping through the doorway.

He realized now that he'd never actually been inside this room. First, he came to a curtained area. He moved the curtains this way and that until he found a door. He carefully pushed that open and entered a small chamber with a few pieces of furniture. No one was there. Then he heard laughter coming from the other side of another door. He slowly opened that door and was met by lush green curtains hanging just inside. Pushing through them, he entered an ornately decorated meeting room.

The Dauphin was sitting at a table with a book the size of a Bible open in front of him. Jeanne stood nearby, her hands clasped behind her, as if she had been waiting.

"My angel!" she cried out to Andrew.

The Dauphin looked up. "What is it you want?"

"Sire, the Duke of—"

Andrew didn't finish the sentence, since the duke himself now strode in. He winked at Andrew as he passed and gave a swift bow to the Dauphin. "God grant you peace, my king!"

The Dauphin rose quickly, arms outstretched. "John!"

Jeanne watched the two men embrace and asked, "Who is this?"

The Dauphin hooked an arm around the duke and led him to Jeanne. "This is John, the Duke of Alençon!" he announced grandly.

Jeanne bowed. "You are most welcome, my lord duke. The more we gather together the royal blood of France, the better it will be."

The duke took her hand and, bowing, kissed it lightly.

Seeing Andrew again, the Dauphin waved him away. "Go, child."

Andrew bowed and tried to leave. First, he got tangled in the green curtains and then had a near miss with the door. Eventually he returned to the hall.

Eve looked anxiously at him as he came out. "What was that all about?" she asked.

"He's a duke," Andrew said.

"Do you not know the Duke of Alençon?" Louis asked.

"Should I?" asked Andrew.

"He is one of the greatest men in France," Louis said. "There are those who would make him the king, if they could."

"The Dauphin might have a problem with that," Andrew said. He shot a look at Eve. "I am sorry for interrupting your *date*."

Eve looked at him aghast. Then she blushed.

Louis looked baffled. "Date? What is a date?"

Andrew gave a slight shrug, then walked away, hiding his grin.

The next morning, Andrew, Louis, and Eve were allowed to join Jeanne for the Dauphin's Mass in his private chapel. The Duke of Alençon was with them, along with Madame Bellier, and a man Andrew had seen before: Georges de La Trémoille. La Trémoille was the one who had sat in the royal chair when Jeanne first met the Dauphin. He was one of the Dauphin's closest counselors. He had a horse-like face with a small mouth, a long nose, and small eyes set too close together. Andrew was immediately struck with an uneasy feeling of distrust. La Trémoille joined the others in the Mass, kneeling and praying earnestly. Andrew felt guilty for judging him.

After the Mass, Jeanne told the Dauphin, "I have a message for you."

The Dauphin waved for the small group to depart. "Not you, my lord duke. Nor you, La Trémoille."

Madame Bellier shuffled out with a worried look on her face. Louis followed her.

Andrew and Eve hesitated.

Jeanne said, "My angels must stay."

The Dauphin nodded.

Andrew and Eve went to the chairs lining the back wall of the chapel and sat down.

"What is this message?" the Dauphin asked. "From whom does it come?"

"God," Jeanne said.

The Dauphin glanced at the duke and La Trémoille. "What has God told you?" he asked Jeanne.

"My gentle Dauphin," Jeanne said. "Give your kingdom into the hands of the King of Heaven, and the King of Heaven will return it as a gift to you, as He has often done for your predecessors. You and all that should be yours will be restored."

The Dauphin waited, but Jeanne said no more. He looked unsure of how to respond. "Ah. Well. *Merci.*"

Then, as if there was nothing more to say, he clapped his hands together. "Shall we eat?"

Andrew wasn't sure what to think. Did the Dauphin really believe Jeanne? Would he entrust his kingdom to the King of Heaven?

No answers came that day.

The Dauphin invited Jeanne, the duke, and La Trémoille into his royal chambers to talk. Eve and Louis waited outside the doors as usual. Andrew, with nothing to do, went off to find Simon Le Fantôme. He was not in his usual places around the courtyard. Finally, a guard pointed Andrew to a row of doors at the edge of the courtyard. They were the officers' quarters.

"Fifth from the right," the guard said.

Andrew walked over and knocked. He heard a muffled sound inside. Hoping it was a summons, he slowly opened the door.

The room was a mere cell, small and dark. There was a bed, a large trunk, a nightstand, a table covered with weapons, and a shelf holding papers and a few books. Simon sat on the side of the bed, his head in his hands. Next to him was a small wooden box with the lid open. A black cloth hid whatever was inside.

Simon's head snapped up. "What do you want?" His hand went to the box and closed the lid.

"Are we training today?" Andrew asked, stepping back through the doorway.

"No. Go away." Even in the dim light, Andrew saw that Simon's eyes were puffy and red-rimmed.

CHAPTER ELEVEN

Andrew hesitated. "Are you all right?"

"What is it to you?" Simon asked, sneering. "If I say yes, will you be satisfied? If I say no, will you be able to help me?"

Andrew shuffled his feet where he stood.

Simon began to pound his fists against his temples. "There is a pain here."

"I will find a doctor."

"No doctor can ease this pain," Simon said.

"I can find a priest."

"No!" Simon shouted. "I am beyond absolution. Not even God can help me."

"God can help anyone who asks Him," Andrew said.

Simon stood up and glared at him, his fists raised. Andrew backed up another step, then another, until he stumbled onto the pavement outside. Simon scowled at the boy, then slammed the door in his face.

12

"He must be crazy," Eve said quietly.

Andrew had found her in a meadow behind the castle. She was there with the Dauphin, the Duke of Alençon, and other members of the royal court. They were all watching Jeanne, in full armor, riding on the duke's black steed. She carried a long lance in her arms and rode back and forth in front of a straw man that had been fastened to a pole. She came at the straw man with the lance, hitting it squarely in its center.

It was an afternoon of clear blue skies and a warm springtime sun. Eve and Andrew stood with three other servants. They were several paces behind the Dauphin and the duke, who sat in high-backed chairs. Food and drink were spread out on a table in front of them.

"Maybe pain is making Simon crazy," Andrew suggested. He was beginning to feel sorry for the old man.

"He makes me nervous," Eve said. "I wish you did not have to go near him."

Jeanne called out with a loud *Ha!* She had knocked the head off the straw man. She laughed like a young girl at play.

Andrew noticed Louis standing at the far edge of the meadow, ready to run for the lance if Jeanne dropped it.

"She is both graceful and skilled," Andrew heard the duke say. "But she must have a proper horse if she is to go into battle." He leaned toward the Dauphin. "Will she go into battle?"

The Dauphin bit into an apple. "I await my council's report."

"Even so, she may have my horse. He is perfect for her," said the duke.

"You are generous," the Dauphin said.

The duke watched Jeanne for a moment, then said, "Sire, you must give her relief from all of the questioning. It is overwhelming for a peasant girl. Allow me to take her to meet my wife. It will be restful."

The Dauphin sighed. "It would be a relief to me, dear John. I know she is impatient. So yes, take her home with you."

"You are gracious, as always," said the duke.

The Dauphin snapped his fingers, and a servant rushed forward. "Bring her to me," he said.

The servant ran out into the meadow, waving his arms. Jeanne rode up to him, heard his message, then guided the horse toward the Dauphin. She took off her helmet. "Yes, my Dauphin?"

The prince told her about the duke's offer of the horse and the visit.

Jeanne's face lit up. "My lord duke! You are too kind to me."

The duke smiled. "It is a small gesture."

Louis ran up to Jeanne. She tossed him the lance, then dismounted. Louis pulled at her gloves and took her helmet. Jeanne said to the duke, "I would be most pleased to meet your wife. I know she is the daughter of the Duke of Orléans. He is still being held hostage in England?"

"I am sorry to say that he is," the duke replied. "You are well informed."

"He is a brave and courageous man." Jeanne's face was radiant. "My lord, I would have your wife know that God loves her father and will keep her father safe. If necessary, I will cross the English Channel myself to fetch him back to France. Please tell her."

"You may tell her yourself," said the duke.

Jeanne was insistent that she go alone to the duke's residence at the Abbey of Saint-Florent-lès-Saumur. "It would do us well," she explained to Eve. "For me, it will take my mind off the Dauphin's indecision. For you, it will ease the burden of watching me pace impatiently."

Andrew was relieved to learn that Louis would return to other duties while Jeanne was away. He said to Eve, "We'll have time to explore the castle."

"I *have* explored the castle." Eve was sulking.

Now what? he wondered. Was she sulking because she couldn't go with Jeanne, or because she wouldn't have time with Louis?

"Have you been to the secret balcony that overlooks the Dauphin's council?" he asked.

She lifted an eyebrow. "No."

"Come on. I'll show you."

Even before Andrew and Eve reached the top of the steps to the balcony, they could hear shouting from the council room below.

Eve paused. "Isn't this spying?"

Andrew continued on. "Trust me."

They came to the chair where he'd seen Queen Yolande before. It sat empty in a half shadow.

The two of them edged forward to the rail. They peeked over. Several men sat at the table below. Eve gave only the quickest look, then withdrew. "I've seen it. Let's go," she whispered.

CHAPTER TWELVE

"His Royal Highness wants a report about Jeanne!" Andrew recognized the sneering tone of Georges de La Trémoille.

Eve froze at the mention of Jeanne's name. She slowly approached the rail again.

"What excuses can we give for our delay?" La Trémoille demanded.

A fist slammed against the table. Then a different voice said, "We must be wise. She comes from a frontier town very near to our Burgundian enemies. They may have sent her to lure our lord into a trap."

"We have spoken to her again and again," La Trémoille said. "Do any of you truly believe she is a spy?

"The girl is without guile, innocent even in her determination," said another voice.

"Caution!" an older, raspy voice said. "Keep the girl at a proper distance. She is too close to the Dauphin. It is good she has gone away. That allows us more time."

"Time? We have had enough time!" cried one man.

The raspy-voiced man asked, "Are *you* convinced, my lord La Trémoille? If you were to give a report to our lord right now, what would you advise?"

La Trémoille was quiet.

"You see?" the voice said. "Still you cannot decide."

"I am not a learned theologian." La Trémoille's tone was silky smooth. "I may debate the prudence of the politics, or the military strategy. But the Dauphin's first question is one of spiritual trust."

"A question of this importance is beyond us as a council," another member said.

"Is that what we will say?" La Trémoille asked, then mocked them. "'Forgive us, sire, but after days of debate, we have concluded that we are fools who cannot decide.'"

There was silence for a moment. Then the raspy-voiced man said, "The greatest theological minds of our nation are refugees in Poitiers. Let *them* meet with her. Let *them* advise the Dauphin about what to do. Is that not their purpose? What else have they been doing since they were banished from Paris?"

Andrew could hear the shuffling of bodies and the creaking of various chairs.

"I see," said La Trémoille. "If they advise him to heed the girl, and she fails to save Orléans, then the blame rests with them. If they advise him to ignore the girl, then they take responsibility for better or worse. We are off the hook."

Murmurings followed that Andrew couldn't hear well. But the tone told him the council agreed.

"I shall tell the Dauphin," La Trémoille said. Then the meeting ended.

"Poitiers?" Eve whispered.

"*Fools!*" came a harsh whisper from behind them.

Eve gasped loudly. Andrew turned, already knowing who had spoken.

Queen Yolande of Aragon sat in the shadows.

CHAPTER TWELVE

How does she do that? Andrew wondered.

She leaned forward, part of her face in a half light. "They are no better than Pontius Pilate, washing their hands of the matter instead of making a proper decision. Have they asked themselves why God would send a peasant girl to us now? Have they considered that God is finally answering our prayers, as He once did for the Hebrew slaves? Might this be the rescue they have long desired, ever since God allowed Henry to bring down His judgment at Agincourt?"

"Is the Dauphin supposed to be Moses?" Andrew asked.

Queen Yolande slowly shook her head. "Love him as I do, I confess that he is not. He has been in a crisis of faith and purpose most of his life. Until the Maiden arrived." Her eyes went to Eve. "You must be Evangeline."

Eve curtsied.

The queen gave her a sharp look. "You are Jeanne's angel. What do you believe?"

"I believe she is a messenger from God," Eve said.

The queen turned to Andrew.

Andrew nodded. "So do I."

"As do I." Queen Yolande sighed. She knit her fingers together in her lap. "The members of the council hope to save their own skins. They would rather cower under the rule of the English than disturb their ease. So the girl must go to Poitiers for more questioning. God have mercy on her."

Andrew wondered how the queen got in and out of the balcony without being seen. He asked, "Is there a secret door behind the chair?"

Queen Yolande smiled at him. "Yes. Would you like to see it?"

13

The secret door was hidden in the wood paneling behind the chair. Andrew and Eve followed Queen Yolande into a cramped passage. The queen reached into a wooden box fixed to the wall. A moment later, she used a flint device to light a small lamp.

The queen whispered, "The castle is filled with hidden passages. One could easily become lost. It has taken me a long time to learn where they all go."

"Why are they here?" Eve asked.

"The kings of old wanted to move freely to meet privately with trusted advisers. Secret passageways have been used for less noble purposes as well," she said.

A narrow hall went off to the right and another to the left. They continued straight. Eventually they came to a set of creaky wooden stairs. Descending to another floor, they reached a landing with more steps that led downward.

"What is down there?" Andrew asked.

"A courtyard and the soldiers' quarters," Queen Yolande said. "The men-at-arms have used this passage to position themselves for battle."

"All of the soldiers know about this?" Andrew asked.

"A few of the officers. It would not be a secret passage otherwise," the queen replied. She guided them to the right, down a long passage with various corridors to other parts of the castle. Finally she stopped and lifted her candle. A small latch was attached to the wall in front of them.

"Where are we now?" Eve asked.

"Where you should be," she said. She carefully lifted the latch and slowly opened the door. Stepping back, she gestured for the children to go through.

Eve and Andrew stepped into a room that looked like a storage closet.

"Where is—?" Eve started to ask, but Queen Yolande had closed the door. It seemed to disappear into the plaster of the wall.

The storage room was filled with shelves of linens and various crates. Another door stood on the opposite side of the room. They slipped through and found themselves in a hall. From there, they made their way back to the courtyard and then the tower.

Later in the afternoon, Eve and Andrew walked along the castle wall overlooking Chinon.

"I want my clothes," Eve said suddenly. "I may be stuck here forever, but I want my clothes."

Andrew had forgotten all about them. "They're at the inn. We left them there to be washed."

"Can we get them back?" Eve asked.

"Sure."

They made their way to the main gate. The guard gave them a long look as they approached. "You are with the Maiden?" he said.

"Yes, sir," Andrew confirmed. "We have to go into the town to pick up some clothes."

"Be back before sunset," he told them.

It was as easy as that.

Marie de Loire, the innkeeper, greeted them happily when they arrived. "I thought I would never see you again," she exclaimed. "Sit! Tell me everything! I have made a fresh stew."

Andrew and Eve sat down while the innkeeper dished out large bowls of a stew with venison. She asked them endless questions about life in the castle.

When they'd finished telling her all they could, Andrew remembered why they had come. He asked the innkeeper, "Do you still have our clothes? You took them away to be washed when we arrived."

"Yes, of course," she said. "But they are not here. I gave them to the tall, hairy man from the castle. He came one day and asked oh so many questions about the two of you. As if I would know the answers! Then, seeing as he lived at the castle, I asked if he would please give you the bundle of your clean clothes. He promised he would."

Andrew and Eve shared a glance.

"Simon?" Andrew asked.

"He never said his name," she replied.

"He did not give them to us," Eve said.

"Ah!" Marie de Loire said. She looked worried.

"He is a busy man," Andrew suggested. "Maybe he has forgotten."

"Yes, yes, I am sure he is," Marie said with a nod.

As Andrew and Eve walked back to the castle, Eve asked, "Why would Simon take our clothes?"

Andrew shrugged.

Back inside the castle grounds, Andrew went to the door of Simon's room. Eve kept her distance.

Andrew pounded on the door. No answer. Another pounding. Nothing.

"Where is Simon Le Fantôme?" Andrew asked a soldier standing nearby.

The soldier held up his hands, like a shrug. "He comes and goes as he pleases."

Andrew decided to see if the door was locked. He lifted the latch and pushed. The door creaked open.

He glanced back at Eve. She gave him a "What are you doing?" look. Andrew held up his forefinger for her to wait; then he stepped into the room.

The room was much as it had looked before, though tidier. Weapons that had been on a table now hung from

CHAPTER THIRTEEN

hooks on the walls—a crossbow, a sword, and a plain silver shield, dented and scratched. Pieces of armor lay piled in a corner.

Where would he put our clothes? Andrew wondered.

His earlier tour of the secret passageway made Andrew look closely at the back wall. It was a combination of dark crossbeams and plaster. Toward the corner, he saw faint horizontal and vertical lines that looked like cracks—or the outline of a door. He pushed the panel. Nothing happened. He ran his hands along the rugged wood, wondering if there might be a hidden latch. Nothing.

Then he saw a bronze hook where two of the beams met. He pulled it down and then tried to turn it to one side and then the other. It didn't budge. He pushed it up. Suddenly it slid into the wall. There was a soft click. The panel cracked open slightly.

Andrew opened the door wider and peered into the darkness. A corridor ran to the left, directly behind the walls of the garrison. Thin shafts of light shone randomly through cracks in the walls of other rooms. Wooden shelving had been built from floor to ceiling just to the right of the entrance.

Adjusting his eyes to the darkness, he saw the shelves filled with dust-covered junk. There were old brown bottles and jugs, an oil lamp with flint next to it, frayed leather pouches, and a rusty knife. On the ground sat boxes of varying sizes, packed with rusted tools, chains, old spikes, and wooden posts. He noticed one crate with a clasp and lock on it. But there was no sign of their clothes. Satisfied, he pushed the secret door closed again.

He turned back to the room. *Maybe our clothes are under the bed*, he thought. Kneeling down, he gazed at the bed cover. It was uneven and lumpy. Something was underneath. Then he saw something sticking out from under the edge of the cover. Blue denim. Andrew pulled the cover back. There, spread on the bed, were their clothes.

It looked as if Simon had laid them out to examine each one. The stitching on the shoulders and sleeves of their shirts had been picked at. The rivets on their jeans were torn, along with sections of the seams. Their tennis shoes were there as well, sitting upside down. Deep lines were scratched in the soles and heels. It looked as if Simon had cut them with a knife in an attempt to figure out what they were made of.

Eve coughed loudly out in the courtyard. Then Andrew heard the deep sound of Simon's voice. He gasped.

"Monsieur Le Fantôme, I have come to ask you to train me with a sword," Eve said loudly.

Panicked, Andrew quickly threw the bed cover over the clothes. What was he going to do? Hide under the bed?

"I do not train girls," he heard Simon say gruffly. His voice was closer to the door now.

"I am a fast learner," Eve said. She was stalling him.

Thinking fast, Andrew grabbed the bronze hook and opened the secret panel again. He stepped inside the

CHAPTER THIRTEEN

passageway, then clawed at the inner wood to pull the panel closed. His fingers caught hold of a small ring. He used it to shut the door. The latch clicked.

He heard Simon throw open the door to the room. Eve was pleading with him to train her. Simon was adamant. *No girls!*

"Who has been in my room?" Simon shouted. The door slammed.

Andrew retreated into the corridor, nearly banging into the shelves. Dust billowed from the junk lying there. He stepped back, afraid he was going to sneeze. His heart raced.

Simon banged around in the room, muttering to himself.

Andrew moved a few feet farther along the wall, touching the shelves to guide him in the dim light. His hand brushed against smooth wood. Looking closer, he saw that it was the wooden box he had seen next to Simon on the bed. Andrew reached for it just as he heard the click of the latch on the other side of the wall.

Simon is coming! he thought.

Andrew tiptoed as fast as he could before the secret panel opened. He pressed himself against the wall at the far end of the shelves. He hoped it was enough to hide him. The light from Simon's room cast the old man's shadow onto the opposite wall. Andrew heard Simon step into the secret corridor. The shadow grew larger. Andrew held his breath.

The shadow turned toward the shelving. There was a soft grunt and something scraping against wood. Simon's shadow shrunk again as he returned to his room. From the outline, it looked as if the old man had retrieved the box from the shelf. The panel closed and the shadow disappeared.

Relieved, Andrew stepped out from the wall. He looked at the shelf. The box was gone. Squinting, he turned and slowly made his way down the secret passage. Thin shafts of light from the various rooms helped guide his way. He hoped that if he went far enough, he would find a way out.

The passageway seemed to go on and on. Muffled voices came from the other side of the wall, along with an occasional bump or bang. He reached a dead end. Fear rose up within him. Then he saw that the passage continued in deep darkness to the left. He would have to grope his way forward.

As he looked at the yawning black passageway, he thought he saw a flicker of light ahead. He decided to take the chance and walked carefully with his hands in front of him.

The flicker of light took shape as he got closer to it. It was a vertical line that shone through another secret door. He paused and listened. No sound came from the other side. He pushed on the door, but it wouldn't move. He ran his fingers around whatever edges he could feel. His hand brushed against something metal. Pushing up, he heard a familiar click, and the hidden door opened slightly. He nudged it farther and peeked out.

He stood behind a wall of stacked barrels. He followed them to an opening that led to a large room filled with tables and benches. It was empty of people now, but Andrew imagined it was a room for the soldiers to sit and drink. He crossed to a single door on the other side of the room and followed it through to an arched passage. To the left was a long alley leading to stone stairs. To the right was an entrance back to the courtyard.

"Thank God," he said.

Andrew found Eve waiting for him in the courtyard.

"You're covered with cobwebs," Eve said and dusted him off with her hand. "I was afraid Simon would catch you."

"He never saw me. I hid in a secret passage."

"Did you find our clothes?" she asked.

"Yes," Andrew said. "And it looked like he was trying to take them apart to figure out what they are. I'm worried. He's too curious about us." He went over to a barrel of water and splashed some on his face and neck.

"What if he takes our clothes to the Dauphin?" Eve asked. "Anyone who looks closely enough will know they're all wrong. The rubber on our shoes will give us away."

"It'll be worse if Simon tells them how we appeared out of nowhere. They'll burn *us* at the stake," Andrew said.

Eve plucked a strand of cobweb from Andrew's shoulder. "What should we do? Run away?"

"To where?" Andrew asked.

Simon Le Fantôme suddenly emerged from his room several yards away. "I have changed my mind." He was looking at Eve. "I will train you both."

Eve shuffled uneasily. "I am not sure if I—"

"Tomorrow at dawn," he commanded, then spun on his heels and disappeared from view.

Eve groaned to Andrew, "Great. That's the last thing I need."

"You asked."

"It was the only thing I could think of to stall him." She scowled. "I want my clothes back."

The next morning at dawn, Simon met them in the courtyard. He handed Eve a sack. "I am not here to be your errand boy," he said.

Eve opened the top and looked in. She opened it wider for Andrew to see. Their clothes were inside.

Simon handed Eve a small sword. "You will need time to catch up," he said, then added as a taunt, "Though it will not be hard. This boy is not very good."

CHAPTER THIRTEEN

Andrew rolled his eyes.

The training began. Andrew watched Eve move quickly with her thrusts and dodges. She was light on her feet. He remembered how skilled she was with a staff in their days with Robin Hood.

Simon looked impressed as well. Though grunts were the best he could manage as compliments.

The entire time, Andrew wondered if and when Simon would ask them about the clothes.

The training finished midmorning. Simon never asked.

Back in the tower, Andrew and Eve took their clothes out of the sack. The shoes were still scarred, but the clothes looked as if Simon had made a clumsy attempt to stitch the seams to look as they had. A few rivets were missing from the jeans.

"What should we do with them?" Andrew asked.

Eve shoved the clothes back into the sack and took it over to a battered trunk in the corner. "I'll keep them here until we can find a better hiding place," she said, then dropped the sack inside.

Andrew watched her close the lid. He wondered if they would ever wear those clothes again.

14

Jeanne returned from her visit with the Duke of Alençon and his wife a few days later. She was rosy cheeked and seemed happy. She told stories of quail hunting and long walks, meals full of conversation, and laughter and playfulness.

The Dauphin summoned the Maiden. Andrew and Eve went with her. They watched from the back of the royal chamber. Louis soon joined them and whispered, "Back to work."

With a thin smile, the Dauphin told Jeanne that he had made up his mind about allowing her to fight at Orléans. She was delighted. Then he crushed the moment by explaining that *first* she would have to travel to the city of Poitiers to meet with the professors and theologians there.

Andrew saw the look on her face. Her eyes glistened. He imagined the arguments she wanted to give against this delay. Instead, she stood up straight and said, "Then let us go at once."

The group of travelers quickly grew from just Jeanne and her company to the Dauphin himself, along with Regnault de Chartres, the Archbishop of Reims. Andrew recognized the Archbishop from the council meetings and an occasional glimpse of him in the halls of the castle.

The Archbishop had a lean face, with large eyes and a hooked nose. A gray beard spilled over the front of his collar. He was officially robed in white, with an embroidered gold cape and a white fur-lined collar. He often wore the traditional miter but traded it for a simpler skullcap for the journey.

The Dauphin and the Archbishop rode in separate carriages, surrounded by the royal guard. Though he was not an official member of the guard, Simon rode along with the caravan. Hardly anyone noticed him, though Andrew was watchful. The old man kept pace at the rear, wearing a hooded cloak over his armor. He looked more like a hermit than a soldier.

Andrew, Eve, and Louis settled in the back of a wagon, driven by one of the guards. Jeanne rode the black steed that the Duke of Alençon had given her. She refused to change into traditional women's clothes, wearing instead the garb of a page. Though she kept her head held high, she looked grim. Eve told Andrew that Jeanne had complained the night before about being forced to endure yet another round of questioning.

"What will it take for them to believe?" Jeanne had asked again and again.

CHAPTER FOURTEEN

Along the way, Andrew learned that the city of Poitiers had often been part of the tug-of-war between the English and the French. It was now the capital of the Dauphin's territory. He had installed his parliament there. Though, according to Louis, parliament had nothing to do, since there were no laws to pass or court cases to hear.

"For all of the glory of the buildings there, the counselors themselves are poor," Louis explained. "They say the families of those holding high positions wear rags and walk barefoot."

"Why will the Dauphin not help them?" Eve asked.

Louis looked around to make sure no one was listening. "How? The Dauphin has no money."

"But he is the ruler," Eve said.

"The ruler of what?" Louis growled. "He rules over the scraps that the English have left for him." He nodded to Jeanne. "But *she* will change all that. She will make him a true king."

The caravan moved at a slow and maddening pace, stopping in a field overnight and reaching Poitiers in the middle of the next day. At a distance, Poitiers looked like a magnificent city, dominated by the spires of a cathedral and the square towers of a castle.

Dignitaries from the town greeted them at the edge of the city. Andrew, Eve, and Louis were told to walk as part of a formal procession behind the Dauphin, the Archbishop, and Jeanne to the city center.

In the press of the procession, Andrew wound up next to Simon.

"A farce," the old man said sourly. "A dozen men will interrogate her—and then what? They might believe her or declare her a witch and have her burned at the stake."

"They will not burn her," said Andrew.

"That will come later," Simon said, his gaze on something far away.

Andrew was surprised. "How do you know that?"

Simon looked at him. "Know what?"

"That Jeanne will be burned at the stake," Andrew said, keeping his voice low.

Simon's bushy eyebrows lifted. "Will she?"

"You just said so."

Simon frowned. "Did I?" He shook his head violently as if trying to get rid of a bad thought.

Andrew was confused. Did Simon really say what he heard him say? Andrew replayed the conversation in his mind a few times later—and then gave up.

As the procession entered the city, lines of people gathered, raising their hands to welcome the dignitaries. Andrew saw that their clothes were little more than rags. Their faces were pinched, their eyes set in dark circles. He realized that many were lifting their hands not to honor the Dauphin but to beg for his help.

CHAPTER FOURTEEN

In contrast, the buildings looked majestic. There were churches with names like *Notre-Dame-la-Grande* and the *Saint-Pierre Cathedral*, which was still being built. Nearby was a rectangular-shaped church called *St. John the Baptist*, which Louis said was the oldest Christian building in France. And there was also the Saint-Hilaire-le-Grand church, built over the tomb of Saint Hilary.

The procession labored along the narrow streets and finally came to a stop in front of a mansion. Speeches were made. Then one of the city officials, a lawyer named Jean Rabateau, invited Jeanne and her company into the Hôtel de la Rose.

"We're staying at a hotel?" Andrew whispered to Eve.

Eve shook her head. "I think they use the word *hotel* for a house with a lot of rooms," she said.

The Dauphin, the Archbishop, and the royal guard continued on to their official residences.

Though the Hôtel de la Rose was impressive from the outside, Andrew thought it looked run-down inside. He later learned that Rabateau was a poor lawyer, in part because he refused to take bribes. Even the mansion was not his but was borrowed from another family.

Jean Rabateau's wife and a handful of meager-looking servants met Jeanne and her company in the large foyer. Jeanne was taken to a room with Eve. Andrew and Louis shared a room across the hall from them.

Jeanne asked if there was a private place where she might pray. Madame Rabateau directed her to a small chapel in another part of the mansion. It had a simple altar and benches.

"This will do perfectly," Jeanne said.

A large sitting room had been set up for Jeanne's interrogation. Jean Rabateau told her that the professors and clerics would arrive the next day. Jeanne looked anxious. She didn't eat that evening. Instead, she went to the chapel to pray.

When Andrew and Eve saw her a few hours later, she told them, "The blessed Saint Catherine came to comfort me and remind me that she had to defend the Gospel against more than fifty pagan doctors."

She explained that Saint Michael had also appeared to her. He said she would be "victorious in her trial and made worthy of 'our Lord Jesus Christ, the hope and crown of those who strive for him.'"

The next day, Andrew and Eve were allowed to sit in on the interrogation. The officials, clergy, and theologians assembled on one side of a long table, facing Jeanne. She sat in a chair opposite them, looking slight and pale.

A priest called Brother Jean Lombard began by saying, "We desire to know what led you to come to our king."

Jeanne sighed as she told yet again how a Voice had spoken to her when she was younger, saying, "God has great pity on the people of France. Jeanne, you must

CHAPTER FOURTEEN

go into France." She explained, "On hearing these words, I began to weep. Then the Voice told me to go to Vaucouleurs, where a captain would take me to the Dauphin."

Another brother asked, "The Voice told you that God will deliver the people of France from their distress. But if God will deliver them, why does He need soldiers?"

It sounded to Andrew like a silly question.

The Maiden looked frustrated but restrained herself. "In God's name," she said, "the soldiers will fight, and God will give the victory."

One theologian demanded to know why Jeanne insisted on calling the king her "gentle Dauphin" instead of by his true title. "He is Charles the Seventh, proclaimed king upon the death of his father, the beloved Charles the Sixth."

Her answer was straightforward. "I will not call him 'king' until he is anointed and crowned at Reims. To that city I intend to take him."

And on it went.

By the end of the first day, Jeanne looked worn out. She confided to Andrew and Eve that she despaired of the days to come, not knowing how long the examination would take or who would show up to ask her questions.

The days dragged into weeks.

None of the questioners were overtly rude to her, but they asked many of the same questions over and over. At times she became irritated and gave curt responses. Andrew sometimes winced but had to remind himself that Jeanne was a teenager being hammered by more than a dozen men who were two or three times her age.

Andrew noticed that Jeanne relaxed when she was in the chapel, or walking in the nearby fields. She also enjoyed hanging out with the soldiers and servants. They said they had faith in her. Andrew noticed that she told them stories about the Voices of Saint Michael, Saint Catherine, and Saint Margaret that she never mentioned to the officials.

When Andrew asked her why, Jeanne said simply, "I was not sent to them. They are not why I came. I came with a message for the Dauphin, not for them."

Again and again, Andrew heard Jeanne tell her interrogators, "I come from the King of Heaven to raise the siege of Orléans and take the Dauphin to be crowned and anointed at Reims." It was as simple as that.

Andrew sometimes stayed in the room after Jeanne had been dismissed. The officials did not notice him as they debated among themselves. A priest named Gérard Machet, the Dauphin's own confessor, stated that he believed Jeanne was the fulfillment of a prophecy about a maiden coming to help the king of France. A weighty discussion followed about the role of prophetic women in the Holy Scriptures and throughout history.

CHAPTER FOURTEEN

A few of the officials objected to Jeanne wearing men's clothes and cutting her hair short. They debated Old Testament verses about the sin of women wearing men's garments.

"They were an abomination to God," one old priest argued. "Saint Paul himself wrote against cutting a woman's hair."

Others countered that Jeanne was acting from pure motives out of modesty and not to defy God or the Scriptures.

"Why will they not believe God?" Jeanne complained to Andrew and Eve privately. "They want proof, they want a sign, but the proof and the sign will be God's victory. How can I show them Saint Michael, Saint Catherine, or Saint Margaret unless they appear for themselves? They are not at my beck and call to summon as I wish."

It was as if it never occurred to her that others would doubt the revelations she had been given so freely, especially men who claimed to serve God.

Brother Séguin was one of those men. He told her, "God would not have us place faith in your words without a miracle to prove that you are acting by His command. Without that, how can we advise the king to turn over an army to you and risk the lives of so many soldiers on your claims?"

"In God's name," Jeanne cried out, "it was not to give a sign that I came to Poitiers. But take me to Orléans, and I will show you the signs I have been sent to give. Give me soldiers—it does not matter how many—and I will go to Orléans!"

During all of this, Andrew and Eve began to feel like prisoners in Poitiers. They could not go out, for fear of being mobbed by those who wanted to meet Jeanne. The only people they saw were the servants and soldiers around the hotel.

Andrew overheard one soldier talk about two men who had escaped from the English siege of Orléans. The men were told about Jeanne and her mission and raced back to tell the people of the city. Appeals were sent to the Dauphin. He had to make a decision.

Andrew also learned that the interrogators had sent priests to Domrémy to ask about the Maiden. They inquired about her birth, her life, her behavior, her purity, and her soundness of mind. The responses were consistent. Jeanne was a young woman of simplicity, faith, honesty, devotion, humility, and purity.

The day finally came when the officials presented their report to the Dauphin. They had determined that the prayers of the poor people of France and all who sought peace and justice might well be answered. The Dauphin should not reject Jeanne, they advised. Instead, they should allow that God had sent her to bring the people comfort. Though Jeanne had not provided a miraculous sign, her life and testimony were enough for them to trust her. "We find no evil in her," they proclaimed.

CHAPTER FOURTEEN

They concluded that the king should not hinder Jeanne from taking an army to Orléans. He should trust God to do as He had told her He would.

When the report was made public, shouts and celebrations filled the streets of Poitiers. Andrew imagined that the same would happen everywhere else once the news spread throughout France.

He thought, *If hope had a voice, this is what it would sound like.*

Jeanne was on her knees in the private chapel at the Hôtel de la Rose when a message came from the Dauphin. She must travel immediately to the cities of Tours and Blois.

"Why Tours and Blois?" Eve asked her.

The Maiden beamed. "Because that is where I'll find the commanders, troops, and supplies for my army. Finally I can do what God has sent me to do."

15

The next day, Andrew and Eve sped with Jeanne and the entire company back to Chinon. There, they both learned what it meant to be servants. Eve worked long hours assembling uniforms, sewing buttons, and packing various crates and trunks. Andrew often ran from one end of the castle to the other as a messenger. When he wasn't doing that, he gathered weapons and whatever provisions of food he could find and carried them to the transport wagons.

In the midst of it all, Simon either ignored Andrew or exhausted him with sword training. There were no odd moments, nor any questions about the clothes. The old man maintained a fierce look as he stayed focused on the battle ahead.

A contingency of soldiers was assembled in Chinon to escort the long procession to Tours. The Dauphin had two-wheeled and four-wheeled wagons loaded with everything from wine, clothes, and armor to bedding, a mattress, kitchen utensils, and chapel furnishings. The horses were saddled for the higher-ranking members of the court.

Andrew discovered that Queen Yolande actually *owned* the city of Tours. In fact, it was only one of many towns and lands in France that rightfully belonged to her. Few knew how rich she really was, but it was rumored that the Dauphin would have been penniless without her help. It was also rumored that she was funding Jeanne's mission with her own money.

Jeanne was to ride next to the Dauphin at the front of the convoy. Eve was invited into the queen's carriage. Andrew made his way to a wagon at the rear. He would ride with Louis and a handful of soldiers.

"Have you seen Evangeline?" Louis asked.

"She is with Queen Yolande."

Louis shook his head. "A servant from the queen was just here asking for her."

Andrew was concerned. When and where had he last seen Eve?

"I last saw her in the tower," Louis said.

Andrew dashed to the tower. He took the steps two at a time to Jeanne's quarters. The door was open, but no one was there. He wasn't sure where to check next. He made a snap decision to check the very top of the tower.

With a sharp stitch in his side, he pushed through the door to the tower roof. Eve wasn't there. *Where did she go?* He fought to catch his breath as he leaned on the parapet.

He held on to the stones as he tried to think of where she might have gone. He glanced at the town below and

CHAPTER FIFTEEN

then at the surrounding fields. *This might be the last time I enjoy this view*, he thought.

His gaze drifted over to the bridge. He stood up straight. There, on the side closest to the town, he saw a figure pacing along the bridge. A figure in a red dress.

It must be Eve, he thought. He took a deep breath and gathered his strength to rush down the stairs.

"Do not leave without us," he shouted to Louis as he raced past the caravan and through the main gate.

"They will not wait!" Louis called after him.

Andrew's legs felt wobbly as he ran down the hill, through the town, and out to the bridge. Eve was not there. He groaned, leaning against the railing of the bridge. He looked down at the north bank, where they appeared when they had first arrived. Then he saw her.

"Eve!" he called out, but it was little more than a croak. Holding his side, he pushed himself around to the path that would take him down to the riverbank.

The water had risen since he was last there. The bank was only a narrow slip of rock, dirt, and grass. Eve stood near the water's edge with the sack of their clothes cradled in her arms.

"What are you doing?" Andrew wheezed as he stumbled from the bushes. "Everyone is about to leave."

Eve had a grim expression on her face. Her eyes were red. "What are we doing?" she asked.

"We're helping Jeanne," he wheezed in reply.

"We are about to go into a *war*," she said. "We could die."

"We're kids. No one expects us to fight," he countered.

"Look at some of the soldiers and the squires and the pages. They're only a little older than we are. *Jeanne* is only a little older than they are."

There was no point arguing. "Okay. Fine. What are you saying?"

Eve's lower lip trembled. "I want to go home."

"How?" he asked. He felt frustrated. "I don't get it. You weren't like this when we were running all over the place with Robin Hood."

"We had the Radiant Stone there," she said. "We could leave whenever we wanted. We can't do that now."

"You want to leave Jeanne?"

"They're going to burn her at the stake," she said. "What if they burn us, too?"

Andrew shook his head. "They won't."

"That's what *she* probably thinks."

"God will keep us safe."

"That's what she thinks too."

"It's her time, not ours. We don't belong here. The rules are different, remember?" he said.

"We don't know all the rules. We don't know how many people touched that stone, went off in time, and died," she said. She hugged the sack and shivered. "I'm afraid."

"We are *not* going to die here, Eve," he said firmly.

"Is that faith or stupidity?" Eve asked. She turned away and began to search along the bank.

"What are you doing?"

"I'm going to hide our clothes here," she said. "I put a message inside."

"What kind of message?"

"I'm asking for help." Eve moved close to the pillars that held up the bridge.

Andrew followed her. "Who is going to help us?"

"Alfred Virtue."

"*What?*" Andrew asked, dumbfounded. "How is he supposed to help us?"

She scrambled onto a ledge at the base of the nearest pillar. "We know he found the Radiant Stone, right? And it must have been connected to this spot, or we wouldn't have come here, right? So maybe if we hide our clothes and a message for help, he'll find it and come back to help us."

"But he is, like, *six hundred* years away from us," Andrew said.

Eve stepped along the large blocks of stone that shored up the bridge. The river coursed to her right.

Andrew carefully followed her, still unsure of what she was doing. "Do you have any idea what the chances are that he'll get your message?" he asked. "The river could wash the sack away. The weather might ruin it. It might turn into dust. Lots of people might find it in the meantime, and..."

Eve turned and glared at him. "Don't tell me all the reasons it won't work. I have to try. It gives me hope."

She looked up at the stonework. The underside of the bridge stretched out above them. Something flapped its wings in the darkness.

"Where are you going to put the sack?" he asked, coming close to her.

"There's a gap just a few feet up." She clenched the leather strap at the top of the sack between her teeth.

"Ew," said Andrew.

Finding footholds in the rough surface of the stonework, Eve climbed as high as she could go. With one hand, she grasped the jagged edge of a stone. Then with her other hand, she shoved the sack into a space out of Andrew's sight.

Andrew was sure she'd fall into the river. She didn't. She climbed back down, and they returned to the riverbank.

It won't work, Andrew thought. He actually felt sorry for her.

From somewhere on the bridge, a woman shouted, "You must hurry! The Maiden is about to leave."

"I am hurrying, I am hurrying!" an irritated man replied.

"We have to go," Andrew said. "Are you coming?"

Before she could answer, a voice said, "Of course she is coming."

The two of them spun around. Simon Le Fantôme stood by the path, his face twisted in rage.

16

Eve gasped and staggered back.

"What do you want?" Andrew asked.

Simon's eyes were wild, his face twisted into pure rage.

Andrew looked for a way to escape, but there was nowhere for him and Eve to go. Except into the river.

The old man took a few quick steps, then grabbed the collars of their tunics. He jerked the two kids up, half carrying them under his arms like a couple of small animals.

"Put us down!" Eve cried. She punched at him.

Simon squeezed harder and lurched back to the path. He slowly lumbered up to the bridge. Once there, he threw Andrew and Eve onto the ground, then quickly drew his sword.

"What is wrong with you?" Eve demanded.

Andrew half crawled a few feet away, then clambered to his feet. He clawed at the hilt of his sword, fumbling to get it out of its sheath. "Stop!" he shouted.

"I heard what you said," Simon snarled, his voice raw. "This is not your time. What do you mean? Whose time is it?"

"How am I supposed to know?" Eve asked, still sitting on the ground.

Simon raised his hands, ready to grab her. "Will we die at Orléans? Tell me, *witch*!"

"Back, old man," Louis said as he strode toward them from the bridge. He held up his sword.

Simon scowled at him. "Mind yourself, boy."

Louis took a fighting stance. "On guard," he said.

"What would the Maiden say if I were to kill her servant here?" Simon asked.

Louis smiled. "What *would* she say? I do not think she would look upon you kindly. Though no one would miss *you* should I strike you down."

The old man's face suddenly relaxed. The feverish look in his eyes softened. He grunted at Louis as he sheathed his sword. "See to your charges," he said, then pushed past the lad.

"What was that about?" Louis asked.

"How should I know? He is insane," Eve said. "*Merci*."

"The caravan is ready to depart," Louis said. He slid his sword into its sheath. "Jeanne said she will not depart without you. Everyone is angry. Are you coming?"

"I am," Andrew said. He looked at Eve for her answer.

CHAPTER SIXTEEN

Eve took a deep breath and stood up. "So am I. God help us."

The caravan reached the city of Tours that afternoon. Jeanne was mobbed yet again by crowds that wanted to touch her. They grabbed at her legs, wanting to kiss her feet in honor. It was slow going.

Andrew saw the castle, with its round, rocket-like tower. Then he gazed at the great cathedral, which dominated the other churches, houses, and shops around it.

Louis nudged him, gesturing toward the many buildings they passed. "It is no coincidence that we are here," he said. "Tours has some of the finest craftsmen in France. There are weavers of silk, craftsmen of silver and gold, forgers of coats of mail and armor. Our Maiden will be equipped with all she needs."

Jeanne and her company were taken to the house of Jean Dupuy. Dupuy was a friend of Queen Yolande, a member of her council, and a leader in the city. He lived in a great manor house and welcomed them warmly.

Later in the afternoon, the Duke of Alençon arrived in Tours. So did Jeanne's dear friends and escorts Jean de Metz and Bertrand de Poulengy. It seemed like one happy reunion after another.

That night, Andrew heard a commotion downstairs. He raced down to see Jeanne embracing and weeping over two men who had just arrived. The men were Pierre and Jean, her brothers from Domrémy.

"I thank God I may welcome you," she said to them. Jeanne feigned a serious expression. "Our father has not sent you to drown me, has he?"

Her brothers laughed.

Jeanne turned to Madame Dupuy, who had also been watching the scene. "My father said he would rather they drown me than allow me to leave home for this mission," Jeanne explained.

"He has since changed his mind," said Pierre. "He is thankful to God, and proud of you."

Jeanne looked touched and hugged him.

Andrew could see their resemblance to Jeanne. There was a light to their eyes, especially when they smiled, he thought.

Jeanne was surrounded by able-bodied men, each worthy to be called a military commander. Louis de Coutes was assigned to her for as long as she needed him, along with another fifteen-year-old boy named Raymond. Together they would serve as pages to the warrior Maiden. Two heralds named Guyenne and Ambleville also joined their ranks to deliver messages.

CHAPTER SIXTEEN

Jean d'Aulon would serve Jeanne as a proper squire to bear her shield and armor. D'Aulon was tall and muscular, with thinning brown hair and blue eyes. Andrew guessed he was around forty years old. Though he seemed friendly enough, he bore a look of hard determination that came from years of experience in battle.

With her military staff in place, Jeanne now had to decide about her weapons, clothes, and armor.

The Dauphin's master armorer brought craftsmen from the city to measure the Maiden for a breastplate and backplate. They would be made of wrought iron. Various models of helmets were tried on her head to see which size would fit. She was presented with different styles of armlets; elbow pieces; gloves that covered fingers, hands, and forearms; shoes; and steel protection for her thighs, knees, and shins. She was also shown fabric for the loose coat she would wear over it all.

Jeanne argued that she wanted nothing fancy. "The armor may be white and unadorned," she told them again and again.

The Dauphin also commanded that a banner be made for her out of a durable white cloth and silk fringe. The Dauphin's own artist, from Scotland, would design the banner according to Jeanne's instructions.

Jeanne prayed and then reported that the Voices had told her the banner should show the image of Our Lord sitting in judgment in the clouds of Heaven. Jesus was to be placed upon His throne, blessing with His right hand

and holding in His left a globe of the world. Jeanne also wanted angels on both sides of Jesus, the image of the *fleur-de-lis* and the names *Jhesus* and *Maria* at the top. The background was to be strewn with royal lilies in gold.

"I will carry the banner into battle myself," Jeanne announced.

Jean d'Aulon asked, "How will you fight with your sword if you carry a banner?"

"If I carry the banner, then I will not use my sword," she replied.

D'Aulon cocked an eyebrow. "Then you will not need a sword?"

"I must have a sword," she said. "Though the sword I bear must come from the hand of Saint Catherine herself."

"How am I to find a sword that Saint Catherine used?" d'Aulon asked. "She had many. Do you want the sword she brought from Alexandria in Egypt? The one the Prince of the Franks gave her?"

"I want the sword that has five crosses engraved on the blade."

Jean d'Aulon tossed up his hands in exasperation. "Where am I to find this sword?"

Jeanne looked as if she could not understand why d'Aulon was so upset. "It is at the Church of Saint Catherine's in Fierbois. Behind the altar. Saint Catherine has told me so herself."

The squire rolled his eyes and said, "Of course. That makes perfect sense."

CHAPTER SIXTEEN

Later, Andrew went with d'Aulon to seek advice from a master armorer named Espee.

With a face permanently darkened by soot and smoke, Espee merely shrugged. "I have heard of no such sword. But if it is battle worthy, then she should use it. Shall we go to Fierbois and see?"

So Master Espee, Jean d'Aulon, and Andrew went to the Church of Saint Catherine in Fierbois to find the sword.

Though Fierbois was only eighteen miles from Tours, the journey took longer than it should have because the armorer and Andrew were clumsy riding horses. The armorer complained that all the bouncing on the horse caused him a lot of pain.

Andrew had never ridden a horse at such a high speed. He clung to the reins with white-knuckled fists and lifted his backside to ease the pounding he got from the galloping. But then his legs ached and finally gave out. D'Aulon alone was the skilled rider and smiled patiently each time they had to stop.

They found two priests serving at the Church of Saint Catherine. Father Robert was short, with white hair. Brother Gilles was slender and had dark hair. Both wore black robes.

Alarmed by the arrival of the three strangers, the priests were even more alarmed by the letter Jean d'Aulon handed to them. Jeanne had given instructions about where to find the sword.

Father Robert read Jeanne's letter, then handed it to Brother Gilles.

"There has been a mistake," Father Robert said. "The Maiden describes a sword with five crosses engraved upon it. There is no sword of that kind here."

"Come inside," Brother Gilles said.

The five of them went into the church. Andrew gasped. Shields, armor, and swords adorned the entire length of the walls. "It looks more like an armory than a church," he said.

Father Robert spread his hands in a "What can we do?" fashion. "When the men of our country were faced with danger, they called to Saint Catherine for help. When she saved them, they would come here and offer their armor and weapons as a sign of thanks. We hang them for all to see."

"And sell the rest to feed the poor," Brother Gilles added. He tapped the letter. "The Maiden writes that Saint Catherine's sword is behind the altar."

"I can assure you, there is no sword behind the altar," Father Robert said.

"See for yourselves." Brother Gilles led them down the center aisle of the church. Andrew's eyes went from the weapons and shields to the beautiful stained-glass windows, then up to the arched roof far above him.

They reached the altar and searched the stone walls, the ledge beneath the stained-glass window, and then every inch of the altar itself.

CHAPTER SIXTEEN

"You see? No sword," said Father Robert.

Andrew thought about the secret passageway at Chinon and wondered if the sword was behind a hidden panel. The walls were solid. He knelt and rubbed his fingers along the stone tiles on the floor. "Why is this tile larger than the others?" he asked.

"I had not noticed it," Brother Gilles said. "Odd, since I have often scrubbed these floors."

D'Aulon drew a knife and shoved the point into a crack between the larger tile and the smaller ones around it. The knife pushed through to open space below. He worked the blade all the way around the edges. "Help me," he said.

The priests ran off and returned with thin pikes. It took a lot of effort to find the right angle without destroying the tile, but eventually they were able to lift it up. Beneath was a long, rectangular space no more than a foot deep. In the darkness, they saw a rough cloth.

"A rag?" Brother Gilles said, then reached into the space. "No, it is more."

He carefully brought out a moldy cloth that was wrapped around something long and thin. He laid it down and pulled the rag away.

Inside the cloth was a rusty sword with five crosses engraved on the blade.

Father Robert performed the Sign of the Cross. "Saint Catherine, save us," he said.

The armorer picked up the sword, using his fat thumb to scrape at the rust. Small brown flakes fell. "It is beautiful workmanship," he said and held the sword up. The blade caught the sunlight and glowed.

"How could the Maiden know?" Father Robert asked.

"Saint Catherine told her," said Jean d'Aulon.

The two priests decided they must journey back with d'Aulon, Andrew, and Master Espee to present the sword to Jeanne.

"Allow us time to prepare it," Father Robert said.

"Pray, stay the night," said Brother Gilles.

The three men were given a meal and places to rest in the small house next to the church. Meanwhile, the priests busied themselves preparing the sword. They also asked the townspeople to help with what needed to be done.

The next morning, Jean d'Aulon readied the horses for the journey back to Tours. The townspeople gathered around him. Brother Gilles carefully slid the sword into a sheath of red velvet with a fleur-de-lis symbol embroidered on the side. He then wrapped the sword and sheath in a sturdy black cloth.

"Let us say a Mass of Thanksgiving," Father Robert announced. "Then we will deliver the sword to its new owner."

17

The return to Tours took on its own kind of pageantry. Word about the "miracle of the sword" went ahead of the travelers. By the time they reached the city, people were clamoring to see the newly discovered Sword of Saint Catherine.

Jeanne received the sacred weapon at the castle. "This is the sword Saint Catherine said I should have," she announced and held it high for the Dauphin's court to see. Shouts of celebration went up.

"This is the sign the officials in Poitiers yearned to see," Queen Yolande said to Andrew with an ironic smile.

Walking back to the manor house of Dupuy, Jeanne said to Jean d'Aulon, "The sheath for this sword is too fancy. It is made for show, not for battle. Please find me a simple leather one to use."

The next day, Andrew found Jeanne pacing in the front hall of the house. Eve stood nearby, watching her mistress with a doleful expression.

"What is wrong?" Andrew asked quietly.

Eve shook her head. "Something is bothering her."

Jeanne stopped and looked at them. "Why do my angels whisper?"

"We whisper because we do not want to disturb you," Eve said.

"You whisper a lot," Jeanne said. "Why do you whisper now?"

"I asked why you are pacing," Andrew said.

"I am pacing because I desire to confess my sins to a priest I can trust," Jeanne said. She gazed at them eagerly. "Now tell me. What do you whisper about at other times? What weighs on your hearts?"

Andrew and Eve glanced at each other.

"Sometimes ..." Eve began, then hesitated.

"Go on," coaxed Jeanne.

Eve continued. "I want to go home, but I do not know how to get there."

Jeanne suddenly sat on the floor and leaned her back against the wall. "I know that feeling." She beckoned them to sit down next to her. "Two of my brothers have come, which should make me happy. Yet when I look at them, I think of Domrémy and the fields in which I ran, and the games I once played as a child. When I think of these things, I feel a quickening in my heart for those

CHAPTER SEVENTEEN

simpler days. I know I will never see them again. God may give me a year for this mission. But I fear I will have no more time than that."

Andrew was sitting cross-legged. He looked down at his hands, wanting to avoid eye contact with her. He feared she would see something there that betrayed what he knew about her future.

"Are you afraid?" he asked.

"I am not afraid. God is with me. I was born for this," Jeanne replied. She said to Eve, "Now, what do you think about?"

Eve said, "I think about our town and the beautiful mountains and the joy of discovering new things. I miss them."

"And you?" Jeanne asked Andrew.

"I think about my family," he said. "I wonder if I will ever see them again."

Jeanne smiled. "Are your parents good? Are they kind? Do they love Jesus and His Church?"

"Yes."

"Do you have brothers and sisters?"

"I have a sister named Elizabeth, a brother named Nicholas, and another sister named Samantha." Andrew took a deep breath. Talking about his family caused a swell of emotion in his chest. It threatened to slide up to his eyes and come out as tears.

"Do you love your sisters?" Jeanne asked.

Andrew nodded. "One of them is like you," he said.

Jeanne giggled. "You are in trouble, then."

Eve turned to Andrew. "What do you mean?"

Andrew thought for a moment, then said, "My sister Elizabeth has a ... I am not sure how to say it. She has a special relationship with God."

"Do Voices speak to her?" asked Jeanne.

"It would not surprise me," he said. Then he revealed something he had never told anyone. "She has seen her guardian angel."

Eve blinked as if she hadn't heard right. "Is that possible?"

"It is for her." Andrew quickly regretted saying anything. "You cannot tell anyone. Ever. It is a family secret."

Jeanne looked solemn. "As her brother, you must not mock or doubt her. If what you say is true, then she will suffer a pain few others will ever know."

"What pain?" Andrew asked.

Jeanne sighed. "Loneliness. The pain of separation. To see and know what others cannot see or know sets her apart. It makes her more different than any other kind of difference a man or woman may feel. She must find her consolation from God alone, and what morsels of comfort you may give her."

Andrew lowered his head as Jeanne spoke. His eyes burned. "If I ever see her again, I will remember what you said."

"Why will you not see her?" Jeanne asked. "Is she far away?"

CHAPTER SEVENTEEN

"Very far."

"We are stranded here," Eve added.

"Stranded?" Jeanne said the word as if contemplating its meaning. "As in a shipwreck? Marooned?"

"Something like that," Eve said. "I do not think we will ever see home again."

Jeanne reached out and took both of their hands in hers. "Oh, my angels. We feel as one. Never will I see Domrémy again. Yet our true home also awaits us."

The burning in Andrew's eyes wouldn't stop. He heard Eve sniffle.

"No matter how far away we may be," Jeanne said, "we are never abandoned. God is with us always. And He often sends someone to remind us it is true."

Just then, there was a loud pounding on the large front door. A maid appeared from a side room and pulled it open. A young man in a gray robe entered.

"What is it you want?" asked the maid.

The man looked around, as if lost. "I am seeking"—his eyes caught Jeanne, Andrew, and Eve sitting on the floor—"the Maiden and her two angels! Just as I expected to find them." He drifted past the puzzled maid and knelt before Jeanne.

Jeanne stood up. Andrew and Eve did the same.

The man continued. "God told me to come to this house. He said I would find the Maiden and her two angels sitting on the floor."

Jeanne laughed.

The gray-robed man looked up at her. He explained that he was a monk from the Augustinians, an order that had taken their rule from Saint Francis himself. "I have been traveling the countryside, and everyone I meet has said I must find you. I went to Chinon, but you had already left. I came to the abbey here in Tours, and it was while I prayed that I was told to come here."

She waved for him to stand up. "You are Brother Jean Pasquerel," Jeanne said.

The monk looked surprised as he stood.

"I have heard of you from those I trust," she explained. "They have told me I will like you when I know you."

"Who told you about me?" the monk asked.

Jeanne answered by gesturing to the sky, then said, "I would be honored for you to hear my confession."

He gave her a warm smile. "It is what I have come to do. Today, tomorrow, and to the end of our lives, if God wills it."

18

Jeanne and her company spent their remaining days in Tours assembling more supplies and weapons for the move to Blois. Jeanne became more excited. The city of Blois put them thirty miles closer to Orléans. At Blois, she would finally meet with the Dauphin's military commanders and troops.

The morning of their departure, Jeanne was again placed at the front of the procession, arrayed in the splendor of her new armor. The Sword of Saint Catherine was at her side. The gentle wind unfurled her beautiful new banner.

Outside of Blois, a sprawling military camp spread out across the green fields. Andrew saw white, red, and blue tents dotting the landscape. It looked as if hundreds or even thousands of soldiers were there. Some were gathered near the tents, tending to cauldrons and campfires. Some were on horseback, churning up the ground as they practiced their maneuvers. Some marched while others honed their skills in sword fighting or archery.

Andrew was surprised to see jugglers, jesters, and troubadours plying their trade for any coins the soldiers might throw their way. Women also moved freely around the camp. It looked almost like a carnival.

Monks were there to give the men spiritual counsel, hear confessions, or conduct Mass on makeshift altars.

The city of Blois itself sat sunbathed on the north side of the Loire River. Like Chinon, the streets threaded uphill, leading to a castle. Soldiers and wagons bearing provisions poured in and out of every gate.

Once inside the city, the procession had to stop more than once until a soldier scooted away a cow or a pig, a few sheep, or some wayward chickens. Animals seemed to run everywhere. The people saw them and came out of their homes with outstretched arms. Laughing children darted on and off the street.

The castle grounds were also overrun with troops. Most were officers who commanded underlings to put this barrel over here and that crate over there and those boxes on top of that one. It was then Andrew realized that the march to Orléans wasn't only to battle the English. It was a rescue mission to get food to the starving citizens under siege.

The members of the procession from Tours scattered in different directions. Andrew and Eve went with Louis to a meeting hall, where the Dauphin's military commanders had been assembled for Jeanne's arrival.

Andrew wondered, more than once, what these hardened men of battle thought about following a teenage peasant girl. What was she to them? Definitely not a professional soldier. She wasn't even a man, though she dressed like one. She was just an inexperienced peasant girl who might or might not have been sent by God to lead them in battle. How would she cope in battle, where a lot of the fighting would be hand to hand against men twice her size? How would she respond to the filth, sweat, and blood?

The commanders were watchful as they stood there waiting for Jeanne. Andrew followed Eve and Louis to one side of the hall, where they could see the meeting unfold.

"Who are all these men?" Eve asked softly.

"That is the Marshal of Sainte-Sévère," Louis said, pointing to a stout, ruddy-faced man in silver armor. "And that creepy-looking man next to Sainte-Sévère is Gilles, the Baron de Rais.

Andrew was amused. The Baron de Rais had long black hair and a trimmed beard dyed blue.

Louis nodded to another man who had close-cropped hair; a long, combed beard; and a face that looked more like it belonged to a librarian than a soldier.

"That's Ambroise de Loré," Louis said. "He is celebrated for destroying an English regiment not far from one of the English governors. Few have ever made it that close."

Andrew recognized the silver-haired and leather-faced Captain Raoul de Gaucourt from Chinon. It was his wife who had inspected Jeanne when she had first arrived there.

A crash came from the back of the room, followed by angry shouts. Heads turned. A man with a wolf-like face and lean body stood over a hapless young soldier who had dropped a tray of wine.

"Fool!" the man shouted, adding words that Andrew knew were bad at any time and in any language.

Louis chuckled. "That is Gascon Étienne de Vignolles, though everyone calls him 'La Hire.'"

"Why La Hire?" Andrew asked.

Louis shrugged. "I am not certain. Because he is prickly like a hedgehog?"

"What does La Hire have to do with a hedgehog?" Eve asked.

"It is a play with words," Louis said, as if no further explanation was needed.

La Hire was still ranting at the poor soldier when Jeanne strode into the hall, the Duke of Alençon at her side. Silence fell on the assembly, leaving only La Hire's voice and foul words shaking the rafters.

"Enough of that, sir," Jeanne said sharply to La Hire.

The old soldier spun to face her. He looked as if he might strike her for interrupting him. But when

CHAPTER EIGHTEEN

he saw Jeanne, his expression changed to one of open astonishment. His eyes, narrow from rage, grew wide.

To everyone's surprise, the man stammered as he bowed to the Maiden, "Forgive me, Holy Maiden."

Jeanne laughed lightly, touching his shoulder. "It is not for me to forgive," she said. "But I beg you ..." Here she turned and raised her voice to the entire assembly. "I beg all of you to go to confession. Cleanse yourselves with God's absolution. No more swearing or blasphemy, from the highest ranking commander to the lowliest soldier."

This announcement caused whispers and murmurs to roll through the men.

Jeanne continued. "Those who wish to join this fight must attend Mass twice daily. None will be forced against his will. However, anyone who refuses will be released from our service."

The Baron de Rais cried out, "Dear Maiden, you must be reasonable."

Jeanne gave him a steely look. "I would also have you release all women from the camp."

Gasps and loud protests came from the soldiers.

"Hear me, men of valor!" Jeanne called out, silencing them. "We go to Orléans as the army of God. The fate of France is in the hands of the pure."

Andrew expected at least one of the captains to complain further, but they all fell quiet and merely nodded as Jeanne passed among them. She took her position behind a large table covered with maps. Looking up, she calmly faced the men sent to help her.

"Good men, what must I know about Orléans?"

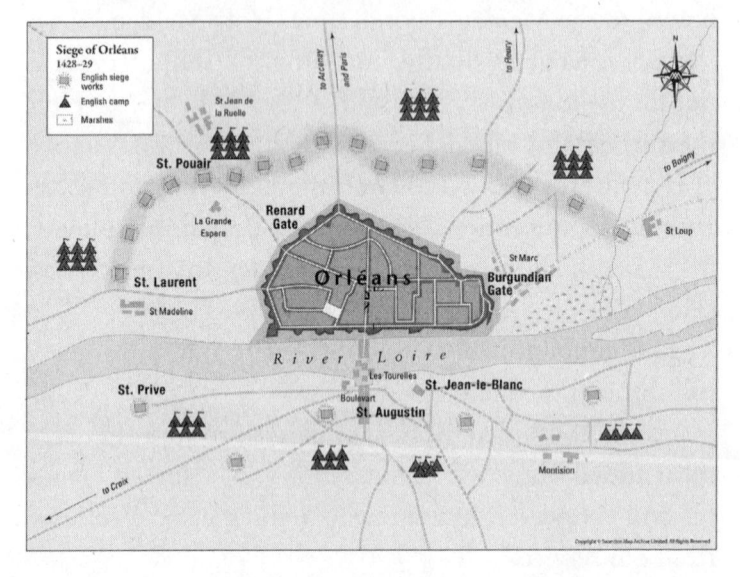

A barrage of reports and opinions followed. Orléans should never have been taken by the English while the duke was still a prisoner in England, the commanders told her. To take it was to defy the laws of war, which said that the land of a prisoner was protected so the prisoner could pay his ransom. Yet Orléans was besieged. The French protested. The English didn't care.

The Duke of Alençon explained that the English king's commander, the Earl of Salisbury, attacked Orléans because of its position on the river Loire. If the English captured the city, they would have control over the supply

CHAPTER EIGHTEEN

lines into France and a sure passage into the Dauphin's territory.

La Hire pointed to the map. "The Earl of Salisbury has attacked and claimed towns up and down the river from Orléans. But Orléans has its high walls and some thirty watchtowers. And it has a great stone bridge that serves as the single entrance across the river from the south, should the other gates be closed. That is how the city has escaped a complete capture."

Jeanne moved some of the papers around on the table and came to a sketch of Orléans. "I see it. The fortress at the end of the bridge. *Les Tourelles*, it is called."

"It is like a castle unto itself," said La Hire. "Salisbury was able to take the Tourelles, but the valiant men of Orléans damaged the bridge so the English could not cross to the gate. Taking Tourelles was the death of him."

At this point, Louis leaned over to Andrew and explained that Salisbury had been killed by a French cannonball while he was looking from the window of the tower to the city. Another English commander, the Earl of Suffolk, replaced Salisbury. Suffolk quickly realized he did not have the troops to surround the city completely, nor could he capture the bridge. So he settled down for a long and grueling siege, hoping to starve the people of Orléans into surrendering.

"So they are stuck?" Andrew asked.

"More or less," said Louis. "Suffolk has had to take over the surrounding buildings and construct small fortresses all around Orléans to watch for our army. He brought in Sir John Talbot to command the English forces in Tourelles."

"Have the French tried to attack them?" asked Eve.

Louis nodded. "The Dauphin sent his cousin Jean de Dunois and the ferocious La Hire to save Orléans. But alas, the two could not rally enough men to defeat the English in open battle. Instead, they looked for weaknesses on the English side by engaging in skirmishes. They also attacked the English supply lines from the north. Their efforts annoyed Suffolk but did not help Orléans."

Andrew's attention went back to Jeanne as he heard her say, "For months, forty thousand people have been trapped inside a city that was built to hold only fifteen thousand."

"It is true, Maiden," La Hire said. "And English arrows and cannon fire bombard them relentlessly. The stress of constant danger and the despair of death oppresses them."

The Duke of Alençon reminded everyone that his father-in-law, the Duke of Orléans, had written a well-known ballad explaining the misery of the French people. "Their suffering is a chastisement for their sins of pride, gluttony, laziness, dishonesty, and injustices. The people must renounce their sins, live holy lives, attend Mass, and appeal to Mary and the saints for help."

"Have they done this?" asked Jeanne.

"They have, dear Maiden," said the duke.

"And what do they believe God will do in response?" she asked.

The duke smiled at her. "They believe that a young maiden is coming with a fresh army to liberate them. They have heard that much-needed food and supplies are on the way. For the first time in months, the people have hope."

Jeanne had a steely-eyed look. "Now the people's suffering will end," she declared to her commanders.

Many of the men cheered. The Duke of Alençon gazed at her proudly.

"The English troops are spread thin," said La Hire. "They are weary and diseased. That great traitor, the Duke of Burgundy, has removed his soldiers from the siege and sent them to other parts. Yet the Duke of Suffolk does not dare give up his position, though they do not have the strength to attack. It is all they can do to maintain the siege. God has given us the right moment to strike."

Jeanne now turned her attention to the issue of supplies. She learned that wheat, sheep, pigs, cows, and other foodstuffs had been gathered. She assigned their safe delivery to Marshal Saint-Sévère and Gilles, the Baron de Rais. "Good men, how will you get the provisions to the people of Orléans?"

Gilles stepped forward. "The English are positioned on the north, west, and south of Orléans," he said, pointing to the map on the table. "Even now, the eastern gate of the city is open to merchants. They attempt to bring into the city whatever they can carry on their backs and on small wagons."

The Marshal of Sainte-Sévère said, "The English still have troops scattered in strongholds along the roads approaching from the east. They sometimes attack the merchants."

"What do you propose we do?" Jeanne asked. "How will we approach the city if the roads are open to attack?"

Gilles replied, "We will not use the road. We will use the river Loire itself. The officials of Orléans will send barges eastward on the river to the town of Crécy. We will meet them there and transport the provisions quickly back down the river to Orléans."

"Go immediately," Jeanne ordered. "Assure the city officials and their people that we are coming."

The rest of the meeting dealt with the battle itself. Jeanne and the commanders gathered around the table and marked the positions of seventy-one cannons along the walls of Orléans. They discussed the lack of master gunners to fire them. They debated the skill of the English archers and the need for more French shields to protect the soldiers from the arrows. The commanders finally settled on the grim reality that most of the battle would be fought hand to hand at Tourelles.

CHAPTER EIGHTEEN

"How can a woman fight against brute strength?" Louis asked Andrew and Eve. "There will be men with swords and lances, iron clubs and battle-axes. How can she enter such a battle?"

"By the grace of God," said Eve.

As the preparations for the march from Blois to Orléans were finalized, Jeanne spent more and more time in prayer. Eve joined her, while Andrew helped distribute supplies to the soldiers and load more provisions into wagons.

One afternoon, Andrew had a rare moment with Jeanne and Eve in Jeanne's quarters.

"The English must be given a chance to repent and depart peacefully," Jeanne announced. "I must now send a letter of terms."

Andrew and Eve sat with heart-pounding admiration as Jeanne, who could not read or write, dictated a stern letter to the king of England and all his commanders in France. She warned them that God had sent her to restore the royal blood of France to its rightful place on the throne. She told them to hand over the keys to the cities they had violated, confess their sins, and pay back what they had stolen or destroyed. In exchange, she would allow them to depart in peace. If not, she promised to bring about a great injury to them. She begged them not to bring about their own destruction.

It was clear to Andrew that Jeanne hoped to avoid war, if possible. But he suspected the English would only laugh at her.

Jeanne listened to her herald Guyenne read back the written appeal. Then she ordered him to carry the letter to Sir John Talbot, the English commander at Tourelles. "Our attack will affect him more than anyone," Jeanne reasoned.

Looking very worried, Guyenne bowed, then departed.

The next morning, Jeanne dressed in her full armor of white. Eve was at her side, wearing her red dress. Andrew thought they both looked calm, even peaceful.

La Hire approached the Maiden, suggesting they tour the camp. "The sight of you will encourage the men."

Jeanne agreed and went off with him.

Eve walked over to Andrew, who had been watching them from the back of a supply wagon.

"Are you okay?" Andrew asked as he leapt down.

"Yes," she said. "Jeanne and I were praying in the chapel, and I felt ... I'm not sure what I felt. It's too hard to explain. It was like God put His arms around me and held me close. Now I'm ready for the battle."

"You aren't going into battle," Andrew said.

"I'm not staying *here*," Eve said.

Andrew was stunned. "What? The commanders have said clearly that they don't want any inexperienced

CHAPTER EIGHTEEN

fighters tripping them up during the battle. We are to stay with the wagons behind the archers."

Eve nodded. "Then I'll stay with you and watch."

"You shouldn't be near the battlefield at all!" Andrew said. "What if the English break through? What if we get pulled into the battle itself?"

"Then we'll fight," Eve said firmly. "But I must be wherever Jeanne is. I will *not* hide here in Blois while she is fighting there."

Andrew knew it was better not to argue.

A Mass and prayers were offered that night. They would march to Orléans the next morning.

Andrew heard from Louis that La Hire himself had prayed, "Lord God, please do for La Hire what La Hire would do for you if you were captain and La Hire was God."

Some of the men laughed at the prayer, sure it was a joke. Andrew thought it was the sincere prayer of a man who prayed very little but prayed honestly when he did.

The Maiden slept in her armor that night—if she slept at all.

19

Veni, Creator Spiritus,
mentes tuorum visita,
imple superna gratia
quae tu creasti pectora.

Under the banner of the cross, priests and monks chanted, *"Come, Holy Spirit, Creator blest, and in our souls take up Thy rest; come with Thy grace and heavenly aid to fill the hearts which Thou hast made."*

A long line of horsemen followed, with Jeanne at the head, her banner held high. The Duke of Alençon rode with her, along with Jean de Metz and Bertrand de Poulengy. Jeanne's brothers, Pierre and Jean, rode behind them with various squires and pages. The assembly of commanders came next, looking fierce and determined.

The priests sang out,

Qui diceris Paraclitus,
altissimi donum Dei,

fons vivus, ignis, caritas,
et spiritalis unctio.

"O comforter, to Thee we cry, O heavenly gift of God Most High, O fount of life and fire of love, and sweet anointing from above."

They continued with ...

Tu, septiformis munere,
digitus paternae dexterae,
Tu rite promissum Patris,
sermone ditans guttura.

Andrew heard the words *"Thou in Thy sevenfold gifts are known; Thou, finger of God's hand we own; Thou, promise of the Father, Thou who dost the tongue with power imbue."*

More than five hundred soldiers marched behind the assembly, with spears pointed to the heavens. Bows and other weapons with leather straps were slung over shoulders or held firm in tight fists.

The priests chanted,

Kindle our sense from above,
and make our hearts o'erflow with love;
with patience firm and virtue high
the weakness of our flesh supply.

Andrew and Eve sat next to the driver of a horse-drawn wagon that was burdened with food and more weapons. More wagons followed, some pulled by horses and others by servants.

The priests continued,

Far from us drive the foe we dread,
and grant us Thy peace instead;
so shall we not, with Thee for guide,
turn from the path of life aside.

Oh, may Thy grace on us bestow
the Father and the Son to know;
and Thee, through endless times confessed,
of both the eternal Spirit blest.

Now to the Father and the Son,
Who rose from death, be glory given,
with Thou, O Holy Comforter,
henceforth by all in earth and heaven.
Amen.

The final *Amen* was now a distant sound, nearly lost in the tramping of feet and hooves and the rattle of wooden wagon wheels.

The day wore on. Dark clouds gathered overhead. The procession stopped for the night in a large field. Andrew didn't know where. Tents and campfires were quickly set up. Jeanne made sure they had an altar to celebrate Mass.

That night, Jeanne again slept in her armor, though the burden of it was beginning to show on her face. Her shoulders seemed slumped.

Eve wanted to unstrap sections of the armor to lessen the weight.

Jeanne shook her head. "It is my cross to bear for our Lord. Dare I refuse it?"

In the morning, with the sun rising over their shoulders, they marched on to the besieged city. Clouds rolled in, and an unhelpful rain fell heavily on the entire region.

Andrew understood from the wagon driver that they were circling wide around Orléans from the south side. The plan was to avoid any skirmishes with the English forces that manned the posts closer to the city.

"We will drive to the southeast of the city and assemble there," the man explained.

Andrew assumed it made sense to go that way. But as they ascended the rising lands around the town of Olivet, Jeanne seemed agitated. Andrew and Eve crested a hill with her. Even through the rain, they had a clear view of the belfries and towers of Orléans, just across the Loire River.

CHAPTER NINETEEN

The army was marching toward the river. Andrew watched as the livestock and carts of provisions split away from the main formation of troops and headed east.

"Why are we here and Orléans is over there?" Jeanne asked. "What were they thinking? I want to speak with my commanders *now*!" She stormed back down the hill.

La Hire barked at a handful of foot soldiers to put up a tent. They hastily erected a few poles and a large tarp in the middle of the field. The rain poured down. Jeanne went inside the tent and waited for her commanders to arrive.

Andrew joined Eve and Louis near the edge of the tent, just under the roof to get out of the rain. Brother Pasquerel stood next to them, his hands clasped as if in prayer. Andrew wondered what was about to happen. Jeanne was visibly upset.

Once she had their attention, Jeanne asked her commanders, "Why are we on the south side of the river? Why are we not on the north side?" She had to speak loudly to defeat the loud tapping of the rain on the tarp. "I see the walls and towers of Orléans over there, but we are here. Are we lost?"

Captain de Gaucourt spoke first. "No, good Maiden. We are not lost."

"No? Then what is this deception? Why have you tricked me?" she asked.

"It is no trick," La Hire offered, taking off his wet helmet and cradling it under his arm. "The English forces are stronger on the north side of the river. We are not ready to battle them. We came around the south and to the east—"

"Not ready to battle them? Why are we not ready to battle them?" Jeanne shouted angrily, cutting him off.

"We have only five hundred men," La Hire reminded her.

Jeanne looked at him in disbelief. "What of the three thousand I saw at Blois?"

"They remain in Blois," said the Duke of Alençon. "The Dauphin did not want his entire force to join us yet."

"Why are we here, if not to take Orléans?" Jeanne asked, her voice strained.

"We are delivering the provisions," said Marshal Sainte-Sévère. "That is our first act. Then comes the battle."

Andrew thought Jeanne might cry with rage.

Sainte-Sévère added in slow, measured words, "Dear Maiden, please remember that the provisions are to be transported from Crécy."

"Remind me, where is Crécy?"

"A few miles farther east along the river," said Gilles de Rais. "It places us safely out of the reach of Lord Talbot and his English army."

CHAPTER NINETEEN

"We have not come this far to be out of their reach!" Jeanne glared at the commanders. "You have known all along that you would come this way. You did this even though God Himself made it clear to me that we must march on the other side and attack the English. You have deceived me."

Andrew watched the faces of the commanders. At that moment, he realized they did not really believe Jeanne was in charge of this battle. What could a peasant girl know about war—God or no God?

La Hire was undaunted. "To fight now would be folly. Let us first engage the English as they have engaged Orléans—by siege."

"We came to defeat them in battle, not to wait until they grow old and die," Jeanne snapped.

"*Pucelle*," Marshal Sainte-Sévère said, "we understand your disappointment. But delivering the provisions from Crécy is vital to our success."

There was a blast of wet wind. The top of the tent strained at the poles, threatening to blow away.

Andrew heard the decisive sounds of a horse racing to the tent. Then a muddied page pushed open the tent flap and entered. With a bow, he announced that Jean de Dunois, the defender of Orléans, was even now at the river's edge with some of the city's officials. He had just landed in a small boat from Orléans and would soon join them.

"Was he part of your plan?" Jeanne asked.

"The plan was mostly his idea," said the Duke of Alençon. "He is the son of the Duke of Orléans, the defender of the city."

"He will send boats and barges from Orléans to Crécy to bring back the provisions," Marshal Saint-Sévère explained.

Jeanne fumed while they waited.

Jean de Dunois soon arrived. He was tall and broad shouldered and wore a simple cloak with a cap adorning his narrow, clean-shaven face. Even drenched with rain, he looked noble and dignified.

He smiled at Jeanne as he took off his dripping cap and bent low to greet her. "Sweet Maiden," he said, "I rejoice that you are here."

"You are the defender of Orléans?" she asked.

"I am." He looked up at her, rain sliding down his face.

"Was it by your order that I was brought to *this* side of the river rather than the side that would allow us to fight Lord Talbot's army?"

Dunois stood and looked kindly at the girl. "Our council deemed it the wisest decision."

"Would you not agree that our Lord is wiser than the wisest of your council?" she challenged him. "The King of Heaven has sent me to help you, and He is greater than any captain or army you hope to trust." Jeanne gave her commanders a sharp look. "You would all do well to heed me. Not for my sake, but for the sake of God Himself, who was moved to pity by the appeals of Saint Louis and Saint Charlemagne for your city."

Dunois made the Sign of the Cross and said, "I admit my mistake, kind Maiden."

Jeanne was clearly surprised by his admission. "Let us begin afresh. Tell me the plan so I may consider it properly," she said.

Dunois looked at the other commanders. When none of them spoke, he said, "Your provisions will be transported to Crécy, where our barges will meet them and then bring them back downriver to Orléans. It will be safer than the road, since the English have strongholds between us."

"How far is Crécy?" she asked.

"Five miles."

"The barges have departed?"

Dunois pursed his lips and looked slightly embarrassed. "The barges have not departed for Crécy yet." He gestured to the sky. "The wind is against us."

"Is it?" Jeanne asked. The tapping of the rain had all but stopped. She marched past her commanders out into the open air. Facing the river, she said, "The wind will change soon."

Dunois came to her side. He shook his head. "Dear Maiden, it has only just begun to blow from the east and will do so for several days."

"It will change," Jeanne said again. "God's mission will not be thwarted by the wind."

The commanders gathered around them. Andrew and Eve followed Brother Pasquerel to the edge of the crowd.

"We will meet your boats in Crécy today," Jeanne declared.

"But the wind—," said Dunois.

"It will change." Jeanne looked at him with eyes of fire.

Suddenly, it was as if the sky slowly exhaled its last breath. There was a strange stillness to the air. Then the wind gently resumed, touching their damp skin.

"The wind is coming from the west," Brother Pasquerel whispered to Andrew and Eve.

Jeanne raised her hand, feeling the breeze. "Sail your boats and barges to Crécy. We will meet you there," she said to Dunois.

Andrew watched the faces of the commanders. Some seemed astonished; others looked fearful. He imagined they were wondering, *Does Jeanne have the power to change the direction of the wind?* He wondered the same thing.

With a look of delight, Dunois gave another low bow and said, "Sail with us, Maiden. Then return with me and the provisions to Orléans."

"How will you prevent the English from setting upon us all when we return from Crécy? They could easily come around from the northwest side of your city," Jeanne asked Dunois, though the question went to her captains as well.

"A company of my men will feign an attack to distract them," Dunois replied.

Jeanne gave him an approving nod.

Dunois drew closer to Jeanne. "Come, dear lady, sail with us to Crécy. Bring a few of your captains. Then I would have us enter Orléans together, so the besieged citizens can see you. It will renew their hope."

"I must not leave my army," Jeanne said.

"Why not?" Dunois asked, nodding to the group of commanders. "Are they not enough to lead your men?"

"The soldiers are in a state of grace, ready for battle," she said. "I fear for their waywardness if I am not with them."

"Brother Pasquerel will represent you," Captain de Gaucourt said. "We will command the men to remain worthy of your banner and their duty to God."

Jeanne looked uneasy. A reassuring smile from Brother Pasquerel caused her to relax.

"As you wish," she said.

She summoned her brothers, her squire, and Andrew and Eve to come with her. Bertrand de Poulengy and Jean de Metz followed along. Louis carried her banner.

Once they gathered on the boat, Dunois commanded the sailors to make all good speed for Crécy.

Jeanne watched as they moved farther away from Orléans. She sighed. "I am delayed yet again."

Dunois arranged for Jeanne and her companions to stay the night in Crécy at the home of his fellow soldier and friend Guy de Cailly.

In spite of her frustration, Jeanne allowed herself to be freed from her armor, eat a proper meal, and even have a bath.

Eve told Andrew later that Jeanne still fretted about being away from the army. "She was like a worried mother who left her kids with a babysitter," Eve said.

Jeanne retreated to her room alone to pray.

Later, La Hire arrived at the house.

Jeanne rushed to the dining room, where La Hire sat at the dining table picking at a plate of pheasant. Eve followed Jeanne and quietly joined Andrew, who was standing by the wall. She rolled her eyes at him, as if she knew what was to come.

La Hire half stood to greet Jeanne, then sat down again.

"Why have you come? Why are you not with our soldiers?" she asked him.

"They have departed for Blois," he said, pushing small bones around the plate with his stubby fingers.

"Blois!" Jeanne cried, the blood rushing to her cheeks.

La Hire reached for a chalice, saw that it was empty, then put it down again. "Now that we know the strength of the English and their positions around Orléans, we decided it is time to bring the remainder of our forces to the city."

"*We* decided?" she said.

La Hire grunted. "We have kept enough soldiers to ensure that you and the provisions reach Orléans for your grand entrance."

Jeanne sat down in a large chair across from the commander. She clenched her hands tightly on the table. "Another plan without my consultation."

La Hire stayed focused on his plate of pheasant.

A servant entered carrying a jug. She poured wine into the empty chalice in front of La Hire. He quickly drained it.

Andrew saw Dunois slip through a doorway at the other end of the room and linger there, watching the scene play out.

Jeanne said, "You sent our troops all the way back to Blois, for no other purpose than to retrieve the soldiers who should have come with us to begin with?"

La Hire nodded.

"How will they cross the river when they arrive here?" she asked. "The defender of Orléans has said that his barges will be of no use for so many men."

"They will not cross here," La Hire said simply. "There is a bridge at Blois. They will cross there."

CHAPTER TWENTY

Jeanne spoke slowly, like a small child trying to work out a math problem. "So. The army will cross the river at Blois. They will then come to Orléans on the *north* side."

"Yes."

"That was my original plan," she reminded him.

La Hire eyed his plate. "So it was," he admitted. He lifted his gaze and smiled at her.

Jeanne cried out and dropped her face into her hands.

Dunois now stepped forward. "Dear Maiden, we wage a war that is as much of the mind as of might. To come from the north, we would have had to drive through the English army to reach Orléans. To come around from the south, as you have done, allows us to deliver you and the provisions to the people of Orléans, building their spirits. Let the English become aware of you. Let them wonder all the more about your mission. Let them believe their forces have us outnumbered. Let them see our forces march away, so they will think we have retreated. Let them feel confusion about our plans. Then let them see with great terror, the three thousand men returning, ready to fight for the French witch."

"*Witch!*" Jeanne said, lifting her head.

"It is what they believe you are," Dunois said. "Our spies tell us the English fear you. They are perplexed that our armies will follow you into battle. They think you have bewitched us."

Jeanne pounded her fist on the table. "I have appealed to them in the name of the saints! How can they think such a thing?"

La Hire laughed. "They are arrogant fools."

Jeanne rose from the table, her eyes darting from La Hire to Dunois. "Was it too bothersome for you to consult with me about your plan? Or have you just made this up, using your honey tongue to calm me?"

"We made a mistake," Dunois said. "I ask your forgiveness."

Jeanne glared at him. "Then here is *my* plan. I will not ride a barge back to Orléans. We will take the road."

Dunois shook his head. "Sweet Maiden, there are English strongholds along the way."

"So?" she asked like a dare, then walked out. Eve gave Andrew a wary look and then followed her.

Andrew stayed where he was and watched the two men.

La Hire chuckled. "She is unpredictable," he said.

Dunois leaned on the table. "Do you believe?"

"Believe what?" La Hire asked.

"That the Maiden has been sent to us by God?"

La Hire chewed on a small bone. "God has sent her to us, I am sure. But He also sent us to her to use our wits and skill to accomplish her mission."

Dunois remained calm. "We must give her our loyalty and faith, or we will *fail* as we failed before. Have you forgotten?"

La Hire looked away. "I have not forgotten," he said.

CHAPTER TWENTY

Jeanne spent the next morning watching the provisions being loaded onto barges. She urged the soldiers to work speedily. "The people of Orléans need us," she said.

At midday, fifty soldiers arrived from a garrison in another part of France. They had heard about Jeanne and had marched for two days from Gâtinais to fight with her. They carried unusual weapons made of long poles with spikes and iron tops bent like hooks. The handles on the sides were used to swing the poles like scythes in a field, except these scythes would cut down the enemy rather than wheat.

Jeanne welcomed the men and prayed for them.

Once the provisions were ready, Dunois signaled for the barges to depart. Jeanne wore her white armor and was given a white horse to ride, since her black steed had remained with the troops returning to Blois.

"You ride the steed of the great heralds and archangels," Dunois said.

The procession was small but impressive. Jeanne was again at its head, along with Jean de Dunois. Behind them was Jeanne's squire Jean d'Aulon, then her brothers Pierre and Jean, Louis, La Hire, Bertrand de Poulengy, and Jean de Metz, along with only a handful of soldiers and the men from Gâtinais. Andrew and Eve shared an old horse that Guy de Cailly had provided.

Night came as they marched, and torches were lit.

They passed the Bastille Saint-Loup, which contained a church and a convent. The English had turned the convent into an outpost.

All eyes in the procession were on the doors, windows, and tower of the bastille. Would the English soldiers launch an attack?

The answer proved to be no. Instead, dim lamps flickered inside the stronghold. Shadows moved. A face appeared quickly over the top of the tower, then disappeared again.

"It was shrewd to travel at night," La Hire said with a chuckle. "The English are too scared to fight the French demon."

Jeanne gave him a knowing smile.

21

The procession marched through the Burgundian Gate on the east side of Orléans. The crowds pressed in a fevered frenzy around Jeanne and her company. The faces of the townspeople were like flickering masks of shadow and yellow in the torchlight.

It was the same as every other city Jeanne entered: hands reaching out, the occasional rush forward to kiss her feet, screams for her attention, and tearful shouts of praise to God. Church bells rang, and from the distance came the muffled sounds of cannon fire.

Jeanne held high the Sword of Saint Catherine. The pole of her banner had been tied onto her saddle, so the banner waved freely at her side. She kept a look of resolve on her face, though Andrew was sure he'd seen a smile creep onto her lips from time to time.

As they approached the cathedral, a corner of the banner fell onto a lifted torch and caught fire. The crowd screamed and reared back. Jeanne calmly reached over and smothered the flame with her gloved hand. The applause for that small act was wild and enthusiastic, as if she'd performed a miracle.

Dunois ordered the soldiers to clear a path into the cathedral. There they could give thanks to God. The leading lords, nobles, and captains of Orléans met Jeanne on the steps, bowing and kissing her hand in welcome.

She strode down the long aisle to the altar, then knelt to perform the Sign of the Cross. She bowed her head in silent prayer. The others crowded inside and did the same.

Occasionally, Andrew heard the sounds of a battle raging outside the city as French forces distracted the English.

From the cathedral, the company marched to the Renard Gate, which faced the English forces to the west. The mansion of Jacques Boucher, the treasurer to the Duke of Orléans, was nearby. It was one of the largest and most beautiful mansions in the city, with enough rooms for Jeanne and her party.

Jacques Boucher bid his guests enter. According to tradition, Jeanne was given a room to share with her hostess, Madame Boucher, and her daughter, Charlotte. Eve would also stay with them. Andrew, on the other hand, was given a room nearby with Jean d'Aulon and Louis.

As they settled in, Andrew heard a servant say to Jeanne, "It is as if the siege has already ended."

CHAPTER TWENTY-ONE

"Only in our hearts," said Jeanne. "The real battle is now to come."

The hardest work for Jeanne was having patience.

Dunois had told her that the barges would reach Orléans quickly. The river was swollen from all of the rain, he explained, and would move them speedily. The English troops in Saint-Loup could not attack from the riverbank, since the banks were tree lined. And if the trees did not hide the barges, the night would.

Dunois was right. The barges arrived in the middle of the night. They were guided to the riverbank at the southeastern corner of the city, then moored in the moat closest to the Burgundian Gate.

The city became festive as the supplies were brought inside by the soldiers. The hard-pressed townspeople were delighted to see all of the livestock and the many crates of dried goods.

Many began to call it "the Maiden's bounty" and rushed to the mansion to thank Jeanne for saving them.

Jeanne spent most of the next day with Dunois at his residence. Andrew noticed that while she was there, the commanders met privately at Boucher's hotel.

What are they planning without her now? Andrew wondered.

He helped Jean d'Aulon clean Jeanne's armor. They sharpened her sword, then polished her horse's saddle. Andrew sensed that something was stirring in the city. Crowds began to surround the mansion.

"What is wrong with them?" he asked.

"The people of Orléans are restless," d'Aulon said. "Like Jeanne, they do not want to wait for days and weeks to drive out the English. They want to attack now."

Later, Jeanne returned to the Boucher mansion with Dunois. La Hire cornered them both and suggested they allow the people to release their pent-up anger.

"How?" asked Dunois.

"Let them attack the small stronghold of Saint-Pouair. It is a mere eight hundred yards from the city," La Hire replied.

Jeanne looked unsure. "We cannot attack the English until they have been given the chance to leave peacefully."

La Hire howled with laughter. "The English will not leave peacefully!"

"What of my letter to Lord Talbot?" Jeanne asked. "I sent Guyenne to deliver it. Did he not arrive? Did the English not receive it?"

"Ah, about that," Dunois said, clasping his hands together. He cleared his throat. "Dear Maiden, they received your letter and took your herald prisoner."

CHAPTER TWENTY-ONE

"What? That is not in keeping with the rules of engagement," she said.

"It is worse," Dunois continued. "They claim they will burn Guyenne at the stake, since he is in league with you, the French witch."

Jeanne cried out, "No! We must save him! Where is Ambleville? He serves as my second herald."

Ambleville was summoned and bowed low to Jeanne. "Yes, my lady."

Jeanne told him, "You must go to the English with a message. Tell their great commander, Lord Talbot, that he must free Guyenne to me immediately. Then he must take his army back to England."

Ambleville's eyes grew wide. He swallowed hard and said, with a loud gulp, "My lady?"

"Write down my words," she said.

With trembling hands, the herald recorded a new letter from Jeanne that restated what she had said in her first letter.

"Take the letter to Lord Talbot. And do not come back without Guyenne," she said.

With a fear-filled look, Ambleville bowed, then departed.

"It will not be as easy as that," Dunois said to Jeanne.

"We shall see."

It was a few hours before Ambleville returned. He was a sickly white. His clothes were dirty and torn. "They threatened to take me prisoner as well," he said and held out a response from the English.

Dunois grabbed the letter from Ambleville's hands before Jeanne could see it. After reading it to himself, he held it behind his back.

"There is no cause for you to read it, good Maiden," he said. "They have responded to your letter with contempt and abuse."

"What of my herald?" Jeanne asked.

"They will not release him, nor will they leave."

La Hire rubbed his hands together. "Now allow me to lead that skirmish at Saint-Pouair."

Jeanne grew more distressed and shook her head. "It is not enough. Where is the closest point to the English?"

"The Bridge Gate," La Hire said. He looked confused about what she was asking.

"I will speak to them myself," Jeanne said, then marched off.

Dunois and La Hire tried to stop her, but Jeanne would not listen. She went to the Bridge Gate and stepped out in full view of the English troops that held Tourelles at the far end. She didn't stop there but continued walking along the ruined bridge, navigating around deep cracks and holes from the earlier battle.

D'Aulon, Andrew, Louis, and Eve stayed on her heels.

CHAPTER TWENTY-ONE

On the bridge, they reached a rampart called *La Belle-Croix*. D'Aulon caught Jeanne's arm and said, "Good Maiden, go no farther. They can hear you from here."

Ahead, Andrew could see the English soldiers gathering in the windows of Tourelles.

Jeanne climbed the rampart and shouted in a voice louder than Andrew thought she was capable of: "Tell me! Who is there?"

A low voice shouted back, "I am Captain William Glasdale. Is that the witch of France?"

Jeanne ignored the insult. "Surrender in God's name, and I will grant you your lives!"

A barrage of blistering insults came from the captain, with his soldiers joining in.

Andrew blushed at their words. Eve put her hands over her ears.

Finally the captain said, "If ever I get my hands on you, I will burn you alive, witch that you are!"

Jeanne looked shaken, stepping back as if he had struck her. In a voice that once again reminded Andrew that she was only a teenage girl, Jeanne shouted "Liars!"

She climbed from the rampart and stormed back to the city gate. Her company followed her, walking backward. They were afraid that the English might rain arrows down on them.

La Hire looked amused when they returned. "Is that enough for you?" he asked Jeanne.

"Do what you must," she said, fuming.

As the afternoon waned, La Hire led a small company of citizens and soldiers from Orléans to dislodge the English from the fortress of Saint-Pouair just north of the city.

The company looked more like a mob of rioters than a coordinated army. They carried clubs and shovels and threw rocks at the wooden stronghold. The English inside seemed bewildered by this sudden random attack.

Soon the band of fighters was close enough to the fortress to set it on fire. Kindling was laid at the base of the wall. La Hire called for a lit torch.

Suddenly the English army gave a ferocious cry, "In the name of Saint George!"

The French reared back, stricken with fear. Invoking the name of Saint George had been the practice of the English before their greatest victories against the French. The small band from Orléans raced back to the safety of the city.

Once inside the gate, La Hire merely shrugged and said, "I hope they got that out of their systems."

The next day was Sunday. Combat was forbidden.

After the morning Mass, Dunois joined Jeanne at the Boucher mansion. He expressed his dismay that no word had come from Blois about the whereabouts of the troops. "Let us hope the Dauphin is not holding them back."

CHAPTER TWENTY-ONE

"Surely he would not restrain us," Jeanne said. "Not now."

"I will see for myself."

"I will go with you," Jeanne said.

Dunois shook his head. "Dear Maiden, you must stay here to command."

Jeanne laughed. "When have I ever been in command? What is to prevent you from taking the army into battle yourself, before I have been told of their arrival?"

He gave her his most charming smile. "In good faith, then, allow your squire to accompany me. Let him be your eyes and ears."

Jeanne nodded. "Go, then."

Within an hour, Dunois and d'Aulon left Orléans with a company of soldiers as an escort. La Hire rode with them until they were safely beyond the reach of the English.

When La Hire returned to Jeanne an hour later, he looked puzzled. "We have given the English many opportunities to attack, but they do not. Is it stupidity? Fear? Or do they have a plan?"

"Let us pray they are fearful of God, if not of us," said Jeanne.

Andrew began to feel besieged. The people of Orléans often surrounded the mansion, calling for Jeanne to come out. Mothers wanted her blessing on their children. Young girls wanted to hear words of inspiration. Men of all ages wanted to view this saint-in-the-making.

"They will break down the doors," Jacques Boucher complained.

"Saddle my horse," Jeanne said to Louis. "If they want to see me, then let them."

"They may tear you apart," warned Boucher.

"I will be safe enough," Jeanne said.

Mounted on her horse, she emerged from the stable and rounded the front of the mansion. The crowd saw her and cried out. Andrew expected them to mob her. Instead, they suddenly fell silent. A few of them dropped to their knees.

"Come, my friends." Jeanne spoke calmly as she slowly rode away from the mansion.

The people followed with puzzled expressions on their faces.

"What is she doing?" Andrew asked Eve as they walked along.

"I have no idea," Eve said.

"Will you lead us into battle now?" a man called out.

"A battle of a different kind," Jeanne said to him.

She led them to the cathedral. Remaining on her horse, she said, "I would ask you to enter this holy place and pray for me. For our battle is not only one of flesh and blood but of spirit. Seek out a priest and confess your sins. To some, I would ask that you go to the places

CHAPTER TWENTY-ONE

of the poor and give them comfort. Find the sick and infirm and pray for healing."

From there, Jeanne rode throughout the town, listening to the people and giving them words of encouragement and consolation. They emerged from their houses and shops to cheer her on, to touch her, and to receive her blessing.

Jeanne returned to the mansion, satisfied that the people would calm down. She retreated to the chapel Boucher had set up for her. Only a little time had passed when she emerged again with a fierce look of determination on her face.

"I want to speak with the English again," she announced as she strode to the front door.

"I will find La Hire," Louis said.

Jeanne spun to him. "No!"

Louis stepped back, his arms raised in surrender.

"La Hire has his secret plans, and I have mine," Jeanne said.

Andrew and Eve tagged along as Jeanne left the mansion and walked the short distance to the Renard Gate. The gate faced the English on the western side of the city. The guards stationed there were confused by her sudden arrival.

She demanded that they open the gate. Flustered, one captain insisted that they needed permission first from his commander. She argued that she was equal to any commander.

A crowd gathered as Jeanne demanded that she be allowed to pass through. One of the guards ran off to find someone in charge. The other guard gave the order to open the gates.

The growing crowd looked on as Jeanne thanked him, then walked through the gate. Peasants followed from the city, along with a few soldiers. They marched west along the main road. Andrew looked to the left and right as they passed the burnt shells of houses. He worried that English soldiers might be hiding there.

Jeanne marched decisively. She kept her eyes fixed ahead. They came close to one of the English forts. It was little more than a tall pile of rough-hewn logs. A wide trench had been dug around it to serve as a moat.

Andrew saw men with torches moving on the parapets. He imagined archers lining up to release a volley of arrows at them.

"My lady, do you want to die here?" an uneasy soldier asked.

"No one will die tonight," Jeanne replied firmly.

A door opened at the front of the fort. An advance guard of English soldiers marched out to the edge of the moat. "What is your business?" an armored man called out. He had a round face and bushy beard.

"I have come with a message for your commander," said Jeanne.

"I am the Duke of Granville, the commander here," he said. "Speak the message from where you stand."

"I beg you to retreat before the hosts of the Lord! Surrender, and your lives shall be spared," she shouted. "In God's name, go back to England. If you will not, I will make you suffer for it."

The duke laughed. The soldiers on the parapet joined him.

"Would you have us surrender to a woman?" asked the duke.

"You surrender to God Himself," Jeanne replied.

More derisive laughter came from the English soldiers, then rude insults telling the country girl to go home and tend to her cows. The French soldiers in the crowd moved forward, pulling at their swords.

Jeanne sternly waved them back.

"Since you have come as a messenger, we will not kill you," shouted Granville. Then he taunted the French soldiers. "Your witch may protect you tonight, but she will do you little good when we burn her."

"It is enough," Jeanne said. Then she signaled for everyone to return to the city.

When they had reached safety and closed the gate behind them, one of the soldiers asked Jeanne, "My lady, why did you go to them?"

She said sadly, "In God's name, I would have them willingly submit to peace before they are forced to submit to death."

That night, Eve and Andrew found themselves alone with Jeanne after prayers in the private chapel.

Eve asked, "Jeanne, how did you know the English would not kill you?"

Jeanne looked solemnly at Eve. "My angel, these things I know for certain from the Voices who guide me: I will break the siege of Orléans. I will be wounded in the battle, but not fatally. I will lead the Dauphin to Reims for his coronation."

"You will be wounded in battle?" Andrew asked. "You know that?"

"I have seen it as in a dream," Jeanne said. "I do not want you to be alarmed when it happens. Though I may cry from the pain, I will recover."

"Have the Voices told you anything else about your future?" Eve asked.

"They have not, nor have I asked them," Jeanne said. "The weight of the future is too much for any of us. Perhaps that is why God mercifully keeps it hidden from our eyes."

Jeanne bid them good night and went off to her room.

Eve remained with Andrew in the chapel. Her eyes were awash with tears. "The longer I'm with her, the more it breaks my heart to know what will happen to her."

Andrew sighed. "I wish I knew what will happen to *us*."

22

Another day of tense waiting came and went. No word had come about the expected troops from Blois.

Jeanne paced in her room, refusing to eat. Then she prowled around the mansion praying for a messenger to come from the Dauphin. When nothing happened by late afternoon, she announced to Louis that she wanted her horse saddled again. "I will not wait idly by."

"Where will you ride to?" Eve asked.

"I want to see the strength of the enemy."

Once again Jeanne went to the Renard Gate. Once again Andrew and Eve followed her as she trotted through its archway. A small crowd of townspeople followed the Maiden as well. No one seemed to care that they were moving within range of the English archers.

"God will preserve Jeanne, and He will preserve us," a woman said.

Jeanne stopped in the fields surrounding Orléans, gazing at the English fortresses and camps as if she was making mental notes of their positions.

The English watched her every move. Andrew could hardly imagine what they were thinking. Jeanne moved this way and that, with the small crowd tagging along.

It looks like she's giving a guided tour, he thought.

La Hire rushed out of the Renard Gate with a handful of soldiers. He positioned them along the walls of Orléans, weapons ready.

Then Jeanne suddenly turned and announced, "It is time for vespers. Let us go to the cathedral."

Just as the crowd had followed her out of the city, they now followed her back, collecting more of the townspeople along the way.

That evening the cathedral was overflowing.

Eve and Andrew stepped out of the cathedral after the Mass. Eve squeezed Andrew's arm.

Andrew looked at her. "What's wrong?"

She was staring openmouthed at the cathedral square.

Andrew followed her gaze. People were milling around as usual. Then he saw what had stopped Eve. Simon Le Fantôme stood in the middle of the crowd, with people flowing around him like water around a large rock. Simon's eyes were on Andrew and Eve. Then, as if satisfied that they had seen him, he turned and walked away.

Andrew watched as the old man strolled to the edge of the square. He glanced back at them again, then continued over to the doorway of a closed shop. He turned to face them, his expression like a dare.

"He wants us to follow him," Andrew said.

"So he can attack us again?" Eve shook her head. "Not a chance."

"Then *I'll* go," Andrew said. He made his way across the square, hoping it wasn't a mistake.

A half-lit torch hung on a nearby iron ring. It splashed yellow and red on Simon's shaggy face. Andrew tried to recognize from his expression if the old man was in his right mind.

"The girl does not want to speak with me?" Simon asked.

"Why would she? You attacked us the last time we saw you."

"Did I?" Simon gave Andrew a pained look. "I had hoped that was a dream."

"It was not a dream," Andrew said. "What do you want?"

"Sir."

"What do you want, *sir*?"

"Tell me, what will you do when the battle starts?" he asked. "Will you fight, or will you hide?"

"I will be wherever Jeanne tells me to be," Andrew said.

Simon looked around. "The English are preparing. Reinforcements and provisions are coming from the north to strengthen them. It will be a fierce fight on both sides." He stooped slightly to gaze at Andrew's face. "Have you ever been in battle?"

"Not like this one," Andrew replied.

He flinched as Simon put a heavy hand on his shoulder. "Remember, boy. Once you have seen a battle, you will never close your eyes without seeing it again."

Why is he giving me fatherly advice? Andrew wondered.

Simon added, "The English have summoned an assassin. I believe he is going to slay the Maiden."

Andrew was surprised. "How do you know that?"

"I see and hear what others do not." His hand went to the hilt of his sword. "Beware of strangers."

"I am surrounded by strangers," Andrew pointed out.

"You will know the assassin when you see him. He has a patch over his right eye."

"A patch," Andrew repeated. Didn't all of the villains he'd seen in movies look like that? "Why does he have a patch on his eye?"

"Because that is where I stabbed him," said Simon.

Andrew flinched. "You did?"

"He is known as Vincent the Ravager. Beware. Even to say his name is to invite death." With that cryptic warning, Simon nudged past Andrew and strode into the square.

Head and shoulders above everyone else, Simon was easy for Andrew to watch until the old man disappeared down a side street.

CHAPTER TWENTY-TWO

Eve didn't wait for Andrew at the cathedral. He found her later at the Boucher mansion.

"You want me to tell Jeanne that a crazy man thinks she's being hunted by an assassin?" Eve asked after Andrew told her what Simon had said.

"It could be true," he said. "Tell her, just in case. I'll tell La Hire."

"But if we say the name, we'll be killed," Eve teased.

Andrew rolled his eyes. "I know it sounds overdramatic, but we have to be careful."

Eve glanced around to make sure no one was listening. "She won't die from an assassin," she whispered.

"But someone else might," Andrew said.

"Did Simon tell you why he stabbed the man in the eye?" she asked.

"I didn't have time to ask," Andrew replied. He frowned. "I have a nagging feeling about him, but I can't explain why."

"I have a nagging feeling too," she said. "It's called *fear*."

The next morning, the head of worship at the Orléans cathedral organized a procession for the annual Feast of the Finding of the Holy Cross. Jeanne joined the procession, along with the city officials.

Andrew found himself searching the faces in the crowd for anyone with an eye patch.

Later that day, soldiers arrived from garrisons in Gien, Château-Renard, and Montargis to join the coming battle. Jeanne gratefully received them. But Andrew knew she was worried that the main army from Blois still hadn't come.

As the new soldiers marched through the Burgundian Gate, Andrew got La Hire's attention and repeated what Simon had told him.

La Hire looked grave. "If Simon has said so, then we would do well to believe him." The captain gave an occasional salute to the incoming troops. "Does he know who the assassin is?"

"It is someone called Vincent the Ravager."

La Hire jerked his head around quickly and muttered a few words that would have upset Jeanne. "The Ravager! I will alert our guards." He snorted. "The English must be desperate to summon that madman."

"Simon told me he stabbed the Ravager in the eye," Andrew added.

La Hire nodded. "A fight over a treasure, or some such thing. Simon lost his wife. Vincent lost his eye. That is as much as I know."

Later that evening, Andrew sensed an undercurrent of excitement in the city. Louis, who always knew what was being said, reported that rumors were spreading about the army from Blois. They were on their way and should arrive in the morning.

Shortly after dawn, the sentries in the watchtowers sent word that the lances and banners of the reinforcements could be seen. More word came from the watchtowers facing south that a caravan of provisions was making its way around to Crécy. Like the earlier supplies, they would be transported down the river on barges.

Jeanne and La Hire mounted their horses. They summoned as many soldiers as they could to ride out and meet their approaching army. Andrew and Eve went to the top of the wall to watch. Andrew noticed that the English did the same from their various bastions.

"Why will the English not attack them?" Eve asked.

Louis, who stood nearby, said, "It is rumored that the English are too frightened to attack Jeanne."

Ahead of the troops, Brother Pasquerel led a group of priests under a banner of the cross. The words of a psalm they were singing rose to the tops of the castle walls. Moments later, their singing was drowned out by the loud ringing of the cathedral bells.

Orléans was overcome with joy—and soon overwhelmed with soldiers. The new arrivals needed places to stay and food to eat. Already filled to capacity, the city looked as if it might burst at the seams. No one seemed to mind. The townspeople celebrated as if it was a holiday.

Jeanne looked pleased to see Jean d'Aulon again and brought him back to the Boucher mansion for a meal.

They talked privately, and by the time the plates were cleared away, Jeanne seemed annoyed. Andrew wondered if d'Aulon had raised her suspicions yet again that she was being left out of her commanders' decision-making.

All was made clearer when Dunois strode in with his usual swagger and bowed to Jeanne. She greeted him but seemed aloof to his charms.

"The provisions are coming on barges from Crécy, like before," he said. "However, we have received news that the notorious English captain John Fastolf is bringing reinforcements and provisions to the English as well."

"I want to know when he arrives," Jeanne said.

Dunois was hesitant. "My lady, is it so important for you to—"

"In God's name, I *command* you to tell me when he has arrived," she said angrily. "If you do not, I swear I will have your head."

Andrew was shocked.

Dunois's expression remained calm. "I assure you, I will let you know." He bowed, then walked out.

Jeanne slumped into a chair. Her face was flushed. "I am undone," she groaned.

D'Aulon admitted that he was exhausted from the journey.

"Then rest while you may," Jeanne advised.

"*Merci*," he said.

"You should rest as well," Eve suggested. Jeanne agreed, and they went up the stairs.

CHAPTER TWENTY-TWO

Andrew and Louis followed d'Aulon to his room and helped him out of his armor. At once, he dropped onto a couch and fell fast asleep. Louis sat on the floor, propping himself up in a corner. He closed his eyes. Andrew looked at them both, shrugged, then leaned back in a chair.

I'll close my eyes for just a minute, he thought.

Andrew was suddenly awakened by a commotion. Jeanne was in the room with them, shouting, "Where is my armor?"

Andrew leapt out of the chair. *How long have I been sleeping?* he wondered.

Jeanne was leaning over d'Aulon, shaking him roughly. "In God's name, my council has told me to go against the English, but are we fighting against their fortress or against Fastolf?"

"Dear Maiden," d'Aulon said, sitting up and rubbing his eyes. "Have you been dreaming?"

"My Voices have told me that a battle has begun! French blood is being spilled even now!" Jeanne cried out. "My armor! I must have it now!"

Two other servants appeared from the hallway and scrambled to Jeanne's room to help her into her armor. Eve looked at Andrew, mystified, then followed them.

D'Aulon was suited up again, looking bewildered as Andrew and Louis strapped his armor into place.

A short time later, the uproar moved downstairs as Jeanne now commanded for her horse to be saddled.

"Why did you not tell me that our blood is being spilled?" she asked Louis.

Louis stammered, "I did not know that it is." He dashed away.

Brother Pasquerel arrived in the midst of the chaos. "What goes on?" he asked.

"Cruel man! Why did you not tell me the blood of our people is soaking the ground?" she cried.

Brother Pasquerel looked as puzzled as everyone else. "What blood?"

"Where is my banner?" Jeanne shouted.

Brother Pasquerel put up his hands. "Jeanne, stop for a moment. Tell us what—"

Shouts in the street interrupted him.

Going to the doors, he threw them open. A crowd had gathered around a man lying on the steps. Blood covered the side of his head and had stained his tunic. Brother Pasquerel knelt next to him. Jeanne stood in the doorway, looking pale and shaken.

"There is a battle at Saint-Loup," the man said in a pained voice. "The English are killing us."

Louis rounded the corner with Jeanne's saddled horse. She raced along the steps and leapt upon its back, grabbing her banner from Louis's hands. She spurred the horse away. The crowds parted for her, and Andrew was sure he saw sparks flying from the horse's hooves on the stone street.

Jean d'Aulon, Louis, and Andrew hurried to find horses so they could follow her.

"What about me?" Eve called to Andrew.

"Help Brother Pasquerel!" Andrew shouted.

D'Aulon rode on alone. Louis found another horse that he shared with Andrew. They raced to the Burgundian Gate but were slowed by a solemn parade of wounded men being helped back inside the city.

Andrew saw Jeanne ahead. She, too, had been delayed. She turned on her saddle, looking at the injured soldiers. "Are they French?" she called out.

"Yes," came the reply.

"It makes my hair stand on end," she said, then spurred her horse forward.

Louis and Andrew galloped east on the main road to Saint-Loup, trailing d'Aulon and Jeanne. Andrew remembered passing the bastion there when they first came from Crécy. The English had been using it as an outpost.

Louis slowed their horse as they reached the rear guard of the French troops. The ground was covered with the wounded and the dead. Jeanne guided her horse among them. D'Aulon paused by the road.

"The English are slaughtering us!" someone cried to Jeanne.

"What is happening?" Jeanne asked.

"Our soldiers are preparing to retreat to Orléans," a man replied.

"No!" Jeanne shouted at the troops, her banner waving in the wind. "Boldly! Attack the English boldly!" She spun her horse around and bounded forward to the battle.

The soldiers who were still standing watched her go. They looked at one another and then raced after her with a warlike shout.

Andrew was astonished as the French soldiers rolled like a wave back into the field of battle.

Captain Raoul de Gaucourt was in the thick of the fight. At the sight of Jeanne and the return of so many of his men, he roared and raised his sword high. The soldiers around him did the same and threw themselves at the English with renewed strength.

With ferocious blows, the French forced the English soldiers back. Soon they were pressed against the fortress walls and had to withdraw inside. It was not enough protection. The French forces battered their way in.

"Preserve the church!" Jeanne shouted. "Take nothing for yourselves!"

Within an hour, the battle was won. Forced to surrender, the English lost their fortress and all their supplies inside.

The victorious French returned to a jubilant Orléans. The church bells rang. As one voice, the townspeople shouted praises to their heroes. It had been a very long time since they'd seen such courage, or the glory of such a triumph.

Jeanne did not celebrate. She walked among the French wounded, offering them words of comfort. She found Brother Pasquerel praying over the dead bodies of the English.

CHAPTER TWENTY-TWO

Kneeling and weeping, Jeanne said, "So many of the English men were killed without the benefit of confession. I beg you, dear brother, to remind our soldiers to confess their sins."

"They are drunk from their victory," Brother Pasquerel said. "They are not thinking about confession."

Jeanne stood up. "If they refuse, I will leave them to battle without me."

Brother Pasquerel bowed to her. "I will tell them so."

"Now, please hear *my* confession," she asked softly. "Then let us present this day to God in a Mass."

That night, Jeanne summoned the commanders to the mansion for a meeting. She demanded to know how the battle at Saint-Loup had started.

Dunois explained, "It was another diversion. We wanted to take the attention of the English away from the barges on the river."

"Why did you not tell me?" Jeanne asked.

Before Dunois could reply, La Hire burst into the room. He was in his full armor and dropped into a chair. He shouted for a drink.

"Where have you been?" asked Dunois.

"While you were seeking glory elsewhere, I was routing the English forces on the north side of the city," he said. "They had every intention of saving their fortress at Saint-Loup, but we stopped them. They turned back when they saw the smoke from the fire."

Jeanne asked, "What of the wounded and the dead?"

Dunois said, "Of the fifteen hundred French who went to battle, only one hundred have been wounded or killed."

"And the English?" she asked.

Captain de Gaucourt cleared his throat. "Most of the English were killed."

A shadow crossed Jeanne's face.

"It is the nature of war, dear Maiden," La Hire reminded her.

"This victory was greater than we could have hoped for," Dunois rushed to add. "We have not only reclaimed the abbey, but the English have abandoned their stronghold at Saint Jean-le-Blanc across the river to the southeast. And we have cut off their supply lines to the east. That side of the Loire River is ours."

"And yet you still could not be bothered to tell me of your plans," Jeanne said, her gaze falling on all of the commanders.

"Dear Maiden—" Dunois began to say.

Jeanne held up her hand. "It is better that you do not speak."

Dunois bowed, then took a few steps back.

"Tomorrow is the Feast of the Ascension of Our Lord," Jeanne said. "I will honor it by not wearing my armor. There will be no attack on the English. See to it that your soldiers make a good confession and stay pure. Otherwise, God may allow us to suffer defeat because of our sins."

"As you command," Dunois said.

Jeanne bid them good night, then left the room.

Some of the commanders raged against the girl.

"How dare she rebuke us for doing what we have come to do!" a sour-looking captain named Guillaume de Gamache said. "I despise her insolence against more experienced men! She is nothing more than a saucy child of low birth!"

La Hire called them to silence. "There are few things more wounding to old soldiers than to be embarrassed. You feel humiliated that you must yield to a mere girl."

The commanders agreed.

"Yet we are not dealing with a mere girl," he continued. "Will any of you deny that the battle for Saint-Loup was lost until she arrived? Will you argue the inspiration she is to our soldiers and the people of this city? Will you dispute that she confounds the English? Will you contest that her raw knowledge of military strategy is nothing less than remarkable?"

Somewhere in the muttering, the answer was a reluctant acceptance of what La Hire was suggesting to them.

"Then stop complaining! You dishonor yourselves," La Hire said. He caught Andrew's eye and winked at him.

Gilles de Rais stood. "We must seize the momentum of today's victory. We must meet tomorrow to discuss the battle against the English. How are we to do that when she has commanded us to take the day off?"

Dunois stood up. "She has not commanded that we all attend Mass," he reminded them. "Let us meet while she is there. *Then* we will submit to her our counsels for how and where to attack the English. I am sure she will approve."

They agreed.

Andrew was surprised that grown-ups could be so foolish.

As the meeting ended, La Hire caught Andrew by the arm. "You are not spying on us, are you?"

"No," Andrew said quickly.

"That is good," La Hire said. "If I thought you were, I would be forced to ban you from our meetings. Do you understand?"

Andrew swallowed hard. "Yes, sir."

23

Andrew decided not to tell Eve about the commanders' intentions. He knew she would have to tell Jeanne. Instead, he decided to watch everything play out, especially since Dunois was going to report to Jeanne anyway.

The next morning, Eve went with Jeanne to the Feast of Ascension Day Mass. Andrew followed La Hire to the town hall, where the commanders had planned to meet. As the defender of Orléans, Dunois led the meeting. The chancellor, Guillaume Cousinot, was there to represent the city officials.

Andrew overheard the chancellor say that his wife had invited Jeanne to lunch. It was not a coincidence. The chancellor's home adjoined the town hall. The idea was to make sure that Jeanne didn't accidentally find her captains having a meeting without her.

When the commanders finished their meeting, they sent Chancellor Cousinot and Dunois to inform Jeanne of what they had decided.

Andrew followed the two men to the chancellor's home.

Jeanne greeted them in the sitting room as if their arrival was a pleasant surprise. The two men sat down. The chancellor nodded to his wife, who stood up, curtsied, and left the room. Andrew found a chair next to Eve and sat down.

As soon as the men were comfortable, Jeanne asked, "Well? What news do you bring from your meeting?"

"Meeting, good Maiden?" Cousinot asked. "What meeting?"

"The meeting you had next door," Jeanne said, leveling her gaze at him.

He squirmed. "Well, yes, it is true. We met."

"To discuss the battle," Jeanne continued. Her gaze went to Dunois. "Without my presence."

"It seemed best to debate our plans and then present you with our suggestion," Dunois said, his tone dripping with charm.

"What is your suggestion?" Jeanne asked.

Cousinot signaled a servant to bring in a large parchment. He spread it out on a side table. Andrew saw that it was a map of the area around Orléans.

Cousinot explained how they planned to lure the English into a battle on the west side of the city—at the English fortress of Saint Laurent. "This will draw their troops from two of the fortresses on the south side of the river. If the English meet us at Saint Laurent to fight, it will leave Tourelles and the bridge without reinforcements. We shall then reclaim them."

Jeanne nodded. "Where will I be positioned?"

CHAPTER TWENTY-THREE

"You will join the troops and citizens at Saint Laurent," Cousinot said.

"I see." Jeanne stood up. She paced the room.

The two men watched her anxiously.

She stopped in front of them. "Now tell me what you have *really* decided to do. I assure you, I have kept far greater secrets than whatever you have schemed."

The chancellor's lips moved, but he didn't say anything.

Dunois stood quickly and said, "Dear Maiden, do not be angry with us."

"Why should I not be?" Jeanne countered, pointing at the map. "You would have me join a *ruse* battle at Saint Laurent when you know the *true* battle will be at Tourelles."

Dunois was undaunted. "We cannot fight at Tourelles if the English forces there have not been drawn away. Attacking Saint Laurent is the only way to do that."

"This is not a trick to keep me away from the real battle?" asked Jeanne.

"We would save you from battle if we could," Dunois said. "But we know you will not allow it."

"It is the best plan," added Cousinot.

"So it is," Jeanne agreed. "But I must give the English one more chance to leave."

Andrew and Eve listened as Jeanne dictated another letter to the English. She reminded them that they had no right to be in France. She warned them that the King of Heaven was now commanding them, through her, to depart. She said that if they failed to leave, she would make a war cry against them that they would never forget. She signed the letter *Jhesus Maria, Jeanne la Pucelle.*

Then, just as the newest herald prepared to leave, she added a postscript: "I would have sent you my letter in a more honorable manner, but you have imprisoned my herald Guyenne and detained and mistreated my other herald. Please send Guyenne back to me, and I will return the English soldiers we captured at Saint-Loup."

The herald looked concerned. "My lady, I beg you not to send me on this errand."

Jeanne gazed at him for a moment. Then she said, "We will try another means."

She wrapped the letter around an arrow, tied it with a thread, and had an archer with a crossbow shoot it into an English camp outside Orléans.

She watched from the city wall as the arrow fell to the ground. The English sent a soldier to grab it up. When he returned to his company, the soldiers began to shout abusive words and foul names at Jeanne.

Andrew watched to see what Jeanne would do. The Maiden endured the abuse as long as she could, then burst into tears and retreated from the wall. She went to her room, where she later said that God had given her comfort. She also summoned Brother Pasquerel to stay near so that he could hear her confession first thing in the morning.

CHAPTER TWENTY-THREE

"It is done," Jeanne said to her two angels at the end of the evening. "At long last, I will fulfill God's mission to drive the English from Orléans."

The city was awake at daybreak. Mass was sung for Jeanne, her company, and all of the men about to fight.

"Jeanne won't let me go with her," Eve said to Andrew after Mass.

"Did you want to go?" he asked.

Eve gave him a shy smile. "No. But I thought I should offer."

"La Hire has told me to stay in the city too," Andrew told her. "He said to watch from the southwest corner of the wall. I'll be able to see what is happening on the west side at Saint Laurent and then move around to watch the south side at Tourelles. Come there with me."

They were about to set off when they happened upon Louis. He was struggling to strap the sides of his armor in place.

"I am off to a bad start," he said while Eve fastened the straps for him.

"What is wrong?" Andrew asked.

"Captain de Gaucourt has locked the Burgundian Gate and placed guards there to keep the townspeople from joining the battle."

"Why would he stop them?" asked Eve.

"To keep them from getting in the way of his army. The people are ready to riot. Jeanne has gone to calm things down." He groaned. "I would not want to be Captain de Gaucourt right now. Jeanne believes the people should be allowed to fight for their city."

"Done," Eve said, inspecting Louis's armor.

Andrew gave him a once-over. "Your armor looks a lot like Jeanne's," he said.

Louis smiled. "Good."

Eve suddenly kissed him on the cheek. "Be careful."

Louis blushed. "*Merci.*" He hurried away.

Andrew rolled his eyes at Eve.

"What?" she asked.

"Nothing," he said. "Let's go!"

Andrew and Eve struggled to stay out of the way as the guards raced to their battle positions on the city wall.

Looking out at the fields bathed in the morning sunlight, Andrew wondered if he was in the wrong place. Maybe he should be on the field with everyone else.

"Which is which?" Eve asked, pointing to the various enemy strongholds around Orléans.

Andrew pointed to the west. "That little fortress is called Saint Laurent. That's the one Jeanne is supposed to attack from the Renard Gate."

CHAPTER TWENTY-THREE

He moved his finger, following the land to an island in the middle of the river. There sat another English-made fortress. "That one's called Charlemagne."

Then he pointed across the river back to the land and yet another fortress. "That one is called the Champ de Saint-Privé."

"We have to conquer all of those?" Eve asked.

"That's just the beginning," Andrew said. He led her around to the south wall. "Keep down," he said, "just in case the English in Tourelles shoot their arrows at us."

Eve crouched, her eyes just above the top of the wall.

Andrew pointed to the damaged bridge leading from the south gate of the city. The castle-like fortress with multiple towers sat at the other end. "That's Tourelles," Andrew said.

"I've seen it before, remember?" Eve said.

"But do you know what's beyond it?" Andrew asked. "That's where it gets tricky."

Andrew explained that to get to the main fortress of Tourelles from the south, the French first had to take back a monastery called *Saint Augustin*. The English had captured it when the siege started. He pointed to the monastery, with its church-like spire on top.

"That doesn't sound so bad," said Eve.

"That's only the beginning," Andrew corrected her. "Then our army has to get past an obstacle course of defenses."

"Like what?" Eve asked.

"Well, first, the soldiers have to get over a wall made of tree trunks."

"Nice."

"Then they have to cross a trench to a sort of ledge called a *boulevard*."

"Okay."

"Then there's a wide dry moat to get across."

"Uh-huh."

"Then they'll reach a forty-foot-high stone wall that leads to a small stronghold called a *bastion*."

"And that's Tourelles?" asked Eve.

"No, the stronghold is across a drawbridge from Tourelles," Andrew replied. "Once they take the stronghold, they'll have to fight to get to Tourelles."

"The whole thing sounds like a video game I once played," Eve said.

"I wish it was as easy as a video game," Andrew said. "The whole time our army is trying to get into Tourelles, the English troops will be shooting arrows or cannonballs at our soldiers or dropping hot tar on their heads."

Eve shook her head. "Do we really believe Jeanne and the army can do all that?"

"They hope to do that much today," said Andrew. "Then the English might surrender Tourelles."

"What if they refuse?" Eve asked.

"Then it will be a hard battle tomorrow."

They moved back along the wall to a vantage point on the west side of the city. A trumpet sounded, and they watched as Jeanne, on horseback, led a company of

CHAPTER TWENTY-THREE

soldiers and townspeople out of the Renard Gate. They crossed to the fortress of Saint Laurent.

"It looks like Jeanne won the argument about allowing the townspeople to fight," Andrew said.

"Something is wrong. Jeanne has forgotten her banner," Eve said, pointing.

Andrew looked. "That's strange."

As the French moved forward, the English in Saint Laurent gave a rousing cry and rushed out against them. Armor of gold, silver, and gray caught the morning light in bright flashes and dull flickers. The two sides looked evenly matched as they slammed together with a loud clashing of swords and shields. Andrew thought it sounded like cars crashing on an icy highway. A choking dust rose up and over them.

The battle for Orléans had officially begun.

Andrew lost track of time. Jeanne was waving her sword, but her company of soldiers held a solid circle around her to keep the English at a distance. For a while, the English forces prevailed, driving the French toward the Renard Gate. Then, for reasons Andrew could not figure out, the French got the upper hand and pushed the English back toward the stronghold of Saint Laurent.

All the while, Andrew remembered the plan. He gazed toward the Charlemagne fortress on the island, then checked the two fortresses on the south side of the river.

He watched to see if the English troops would come out to help their comrades at Saint Laurent. The soldiers were positioned on the walls, but the gates remained closed.

"They aren't taking the bait," Andrew said.

One of the guards on the wall behind him announced that Captain de Gaucourt had finally given the command to open the Burgundian Gate. The captain now led armored soldiers and plainly dressed citizens east around to the river. He had organized them onto anchored boats and barges that would ferry them across to the southern side of the Loire.

"Jeanne won that argument, too," Eve said, smiling.

"Come on," Andrew said, then moved east along the wall. But Eve didn't follow him.

"What's wrong?" he called back.

She pointed behind her. "I'm worried about Jeanne."

Andrew nodded, knowing he should do the same. But Jeanne was part of a ruse to distract the English from the main battle. The outcome of the day would happen in the south and southeast.

Andrew continued on, slipping through a line of archers who were preparing for their part in the battle. His eyes landed on the fortress called *Saint Jean-le-Blanc* that the English had abandoned. This didn't stop some of the townspeople from attacking it anyway. Axes and clubs in hand, they assaulted the main gate and cheered their victory when it opened easily.

Most of the army had now assembled on the south side of Orléans. There, they began their march to the Augustin monastery. The townspeople surged ahead of the troops, emboldened by their vain victory at Saint Jean-le-Blanc.

For several minutes, it looked as if the English had abandoned Augustin as well, but suddenly a terrifying roar came from inside the monastery. Then archers appeared along the top of the walls and unleashed swarms of arrows on the townspeople below.

Andrew raised his hands to his mouth in horror as the screams tore the air, and one man after another fell to the dirt. Panic overtook many of the townspeople. They turned and crashed into the seasoned soldiers, who were trying to move forward. Captain de Gaucourt shouted orders, but the cries of the wounded turned his words into whispers.

Volleys of arrows continued to rain down on the French. It was a blood-filled and chaotic scene.

Then came mind-numbing explosions. Cannons previously unseen now appeared at various portals. The stone balls smashed into the fleeing civilians and mowed down the soldiers.

Andrew pressed himself closer to the wall, terror-stricken by the slaughter. "Where are *our* cannons?" he cried out.

"The order has not been given," said a soldier next to him.

"Look at what's happening down there!" Andrew pointed at the battlefield. "That should be the order!"

The soldier raised a gloved fist to strike him, but held back. He turned away instead.

A fresh roar sounded amid a blast of trumpets. Andrew pressed against the edge of the wall to see the English troops now pouring through the gates of Augustin. They began to chase the scattered French forces. Clashing swords rang loudly, blades crashed against armor, clubs with spikes hammered against shields. The crude weapons of the heroic townspeople were no match for the real weapons wielded by the English soldiers. Men dropped to their knees; others fell lifeless underfoot. Arrows flew from all directions, and the pounding cannons sent stone balls mercilessly into the French warriors. Andrew felt sick at the unfolding slaughter.

He wasn't sure he could watch any more.

But then he caught sight of Jean d'Aulon. The squire had moved to the front of the retreating French line. He reached the fortress of Saint Jean-le-Blanc, along with a fighter Andrew didn't recognize. D'Aulon beckoned the scattered French soldiers to use the abandoned fortress as a base for the battle. French archers quickly took up positions and sent arrows flying back to the English. The English foot soldiers spun around to attack d'Aulon and his valiant company.

"The plan failed," Eve said at Andrew's side. Her cheeks were smeared with tears. "The English have captured Jeanne!"

24

"What? No!" Andrew shouted. "Where? How?"

"It was awful. The English surrounded her horse and pulled her to the ground," Eve cried.

"But that's wrong," Andrew said. "She can't be captured. Not today."

"I saw it," Eve said, her voice shaken by sobs. "The English broke through the circle of soldiers, yanked her from the horse, and dragged her back to their fortress at Saint Laurent."

Andrew stumbled along the castle wall to see for himself. She couldn't have been captured!

He looked to the southwest. The English troops on the island stronghold of Charlemagne were boating to land and circling around the western side of the city. The soldiers from the Saint-Privé fortress were dashing out to do the same.

"They are going to brag about their catch," Andrew said. *How could the battle go so wrong so fast?* he wondered. *Jeanne was supposed to win this battle!*

Horns blew to the southeast.

"What now?" Andrew asked. He moved along the wall and suddenly realized that Eve had taken hold of his hand. He held it tight as they returned to view the main battlefield. Together they peered over the wall.

Eve gasped.

It isn't possible, thought Andrew.

Galloping on their horses toward the English were La Hire and *Jeanne*—her banner flying high.

"How can she be *here* when I saw her captured *there*?" Eve asked, clearly baffled.

Andrew had an idea. "Louis dressed in armor that looked a lot like Jeanne's," he said.

"He was a decoy?" Eve asked. "They captured poor Louis?"

"He sacrificed himself for *that*," Andrew said, gesturing to the hundreds of soldiers who now joined Jeanne and La Hire in the battle below. They moved like a tidal wave behind the banners of Jeanne's commanders. French warriors seemed to be coming from everywhere.

The retreating French soldiers turned on their heels and rushed back into the battle. Even the wounded struggled to their feet and grabbed what weapons they could to fight.

The English troops stopped in their tracks. They nearly tripped over each other as they scrambled back toward the Augustin fortress.

"Fire!" Andrew heard from behind him. Before he knew what was happening, the cannons of Orléans

CHAPTER TWENTY-FOUR

erupted with deafening roars. He and Eve put their hands over their ears.

The cannonballs smashed the retreating English and cut off their escape to the fortress. The smell of gunpowder filled the air around Andrew and Eve.

Andrew now understood. The French had fooled the English on two fronts, scattering them to the west and the south. Not only were the English fooled, but the French retreat had lured them out of their fortresses so that Jeanne and her army could strike at them on the open field with superior numbers.

The surprise, as great as it was, did not make the fighting any less brutal. Andrew heard the din of pain and death. It was a grotesque clamor, dark and terrible.

Jeanne never drew her sword but sped on her horse from one part of the battlefield to another, urging the French to fight. The combat was slow going. It seemed as if this campaign was being won an inch at a time. The English shrunk in numbers as they fell. Some were able to retreat into the Augustin fortress.

Andrew feared this might be yet another turning point in the fight. Behind those walls, the English could regroup and begin a fresh attack. But the doors of the fortress were not strong enough to stop the oncoming French forces. They crashed through them as if the thick beams were made of mere sticks of wood.

It was impossible for Andrew to see what was happening inside the fortress. He caught glimpses of soldiers moving behind the windows and holes in the walls, through the open passages, and between the buildings of the monastery compound. Now and then, he saw English soldiers trying to escape through other doors and gates.

The English still held their fortresses at Saint-Privé and Saint Laurent to the west. It now looked as if they were not coming out to aid their comrades at Augustin.

Andrew and Eve were pushed aside as a company of French archers came to the wall. They let fly their arrows toward Tourelles, attempting to distract the English soldiers there from the main battle.

Andrew could no longer guess which way the fight was going. It seemed to surge in one direction, then another. There was a strange ebb and flow to it, like water splashing back and forth in a rocking tub.

"Look," Eve said, pointing to the middle of the field.

Simon Le Fantôme was in the thick of battle, his sword swinging and slashing at everyone around him.

"Do not stand there idle!" one of the archers shouted at Andrew. "Distribute arrows to the line of archers!" Then he turned to Eve. "*You!* Fetch drink and bread for these men."

"Yes, sir!" both children said, then went to work.

The evening darkness crept over Andrew and Eve almost before they knew it was there.

Andrew noticed that a fire had broken out inside the Augustin fortress.

CHAPTER TWENTY-FOUR

"Are they going to burn it down?" Eve asked.

"No," said one of the archers. "We are purging it."

Jeanne appeared at one of the pinnacles of the fortress and waved her banner at the English in Tourelles.

And so the first day of battle ended with a French victory. But Andrew knew that the harder fight was about to begin. No ruses or combat tricks would breach the obstacle course that protected Tourelles. He also knew the English would not yield it. Tomorrow would require raw nerve, brute strength, and the faith of a child.

25

The soldiers and citizens of Orléans took positions between the captured fortress of Augustin and Saint-Marceau, a town to the south. They guarded what they had painfully gained from the English. Priests and nurses set up camps to tend to the wounded and offer prayers for the dead.

The rest of the French fighting forces wearily made their way back to the city for a much-needed rest.

Eve ran ahead of Andrew to greet Jeanne. When he caught up, he saw Jeanne limping through the gate and leading her horse by the reins. They learned that she had been wounded in the foot by some kind of foreign weapon made of sharp spikes. She looked pale and admitted she was overcome with fatigue. La Hire came alongside her, lifted her in his strong arms, and carried her all the way back to the Boucher mansion.

Jeanne was placed in a chair in the dining room, where Madame Boucher nursed her foot. Soup and bread were offered, but Jeanne only sampled it, claiming she wasn't hungry.

Eve admitted to Andrew that she felt anxious about Louis. He had been captured, but she had no idea what the English would do to him.

Andrew put the question to La Hire.

The old soldier shook his head. "They will be angry that they were deceived. Pray they do not abuse him all the more for it. The lad had a lot of courage to do what he did."

Dunois arrived, his gallant face smeared with dirt and blood. He knelt next to Jeanne's chair and said, "You are indeed a valiant warrior. Never have I seen such a display of bravery."

Jeanne gave him a weak nod. "Will you see to it that food, drink, and all things necessary are delivered to those who stayed behind in Saint-Marceau?"

"I have ordered the barges and wagons to operate throughout the night," Dunois assured her.

A moment of silence passed. Then Jeanne eyed Dunois. "Is there something else?"

"The commanders have met," he said.

"Again? Without me?" she asked.

"Some of them believe our victory today has given us the advantage," he explained. "The town of Saint-Marceau is well supplied. They suggest we do not go into battle tomorrow."

"Why would we not press our advantage?" she asked.

CHAPTER TWENTY-FIVE

"To allow the Dauphin to send us more of his army before we fight again."

"Is that your suggestion?" Jeanne asked him.

He gave her a grim smile. "I suggest nothing. I am merely the council's messenger."

"They have their council, and I have mine," Jeanne said. "Mine will make good on His promise, whereas yours will come to nothing. Tomorrow we will rise even earlier than we did today. On the field of battle, we will do the best we can, by God's grace. There is much that remains to be done, and more to suffer."

Dunois nodded to her bandaged foot. "Is that not enough?"

"This is little more than a scratch," she said. "My blood will spill from a greater wound before this is finished."

"Surely not," said Dunois.

Jeanne gave him a grave look. "Bring me a map of Tourelles. Summon my captains. We must plan our attack."

Looking at the map, Andrew saw that the battle to capture Tourelles would be harder than he had described to Eve earlier. In fact, he thought it looked impossible.

The first obstacle was a wall made of tree trunks that stood over ten feet high. It was called a *palisade*. Jeanne's army would have to get past that to an initial drawbridge, which the English would raise. That would leave the French to deal with the first trench. It was at least ten feet wide and twenty feet deep. Worse, the sides of the trench were filled with soft earth so that any invaders would be unable to scale it.

At the top of the trench was the *boulevard*. It was twenty feet wide and circled around Tourelles like a horseshoe. But between the boulevard and Tourelles was a dry moat about twenty feet deep and more than thirty feet wide. The steep angle of the moat's walls made climbing difficult, even with ladders.

Then came the forty-foot-high stone wall of the outer stronghold, with a vast courtyard behind it. From there, the English could drop hot tar and oil onto the invaders.

On the other side of the courtyard was a moat filled with water from the Loire River. It was more than twenty feet wide and required a drawbridge to cross into Tourelles.

As Andrew had told Eve earlier, while the French army was attempting to get past all of these defenses, the English would be hitting them with arrows, spears, axes, and other kinds of sharp weapons.

Andrew looked from the map to Eve. She saw the same thing he'd seen and mouthed the word *How?*

"Can your Voices allow our soldiers to grow wings and fly over that?" La Hire asked.

"Perhaps they will, once we break down the palisade," said Jeanne.

"Our cannons will destroy the palisade," said Dunois hopefully.

"Then we will use the debris to fill the trench and cross over to the boulevard," Jeanne said. "Once we're there, we will use scaling ladders to climb the dry moat, all the way to the top of the first wall."

"The English will strike the first French head that appears at the top, or they will use poles to push the ladders away," said La Hire.

"Our archers on the walls of the captured fortresses will keep them too busy to succeed," Jeanne suggested.

"And then?" asked Gilles de Rais.

"We invade the stronghold, cross the courtyard, and fight to take Tourelles itself," she said. "That is the goal of our battle, is it not?"

The commanders nodded unhappily.

Jeanne gazed at each of their faces. "Sleep, men of stout hearts. Then rise to victory."

26

Andrew felt sluggish and thickheaded when the call to awaken came. It was still dark. The sun knew better than to get up so early.

He trudged down to the private chapel to join Jeanne and Eve for Mass with Brother Pasquerel. Eve looked as if she hadn't slept at all.

After Mass, they dressed for the battle ahead. Jeanne refused to eat any breakfast. As far as Andrew could tell, she hadn't eaten much at all since arriving in Orléans. Later, as they departed the Boucher mansion, a peasant woman brought Jeanne a fish and begged her to eat before she went into battle.

Jeanne smiled at her. "If God wills it, I will share this with an English prisoner when I return tonight. Bring it to me when I cross the bridge from Tourelles."

Captain La Hire gave Andrew new orders. "Put on a breastplate and come with us to the fortress of Augustin. You will hand out weapons, restock the ammunition, deliver water, and if necessary, bandage the wounded."

Andrew saluted and said, "Aye, aye, Captain."

Eve grabbed his arm. "If you are going, then I am going."

Andrew shook his head. "No."

"Why not?"

"Because you are—"

"A girl?" Eve was defiant. "So is Jeanne. I am going."

"But you said back at Chinon that you were afraid," Andrew reminded her.

"I am still afraid. But I am going anyway," Eve said.

They had to find breastplates and backplates that would fit the two of them. They struggled with each other's straps and buckles. Andrew felt as if someone had hung two heavy doors around his neck.

Eve tugged at one of the buckles. "How do they fight in these things?"

"I will be worn out before I even get to the fortress," Andrew complained.

The troops and townspeople marched to the Burgundian Gate with Jeanne in the lead. She waved her banner for them to follow. Once again, Captain de Gaucourt refused to open the gate.

"Why are you here?" he shouted at them. "Did you not learn your lesson yesterday? And you soldiers, go back. My orders were that there would be no fighting today."

Andrew wondered if the captains were conspiring against Jeanne. Were they trying to stop her from fighting a battle they didn't want to have?

Jeanne was furious. "You are siding with the devil against your own people."

De Gaucourt looked as if she'd slapped him. "Dear Maiden, I am here to serve."

"Then serve us now," she said. "I am commanding you to open the gate."

De Gaucort looked helpless. "Where is Captain La Hire? The defender of Orléans, Jean de Dunois? Allow me to send a messenger for clarification."

"While you do, we lose our advantage against the enemy," she said.

The townspeople roared against Captain de Gaucourt and his guards. They began to push and shove their way to the gate. The soldiers stepped aside, many of them looking defiantly at the captain. Andrew feared that a riot might break out.

Captain de Gaucourt considered the situation. "Open the gate!" he shouted.

By the time Jeanne and her initial company marched to the river to cross over, the other captains arrived with their various banners and troops.

Slowly the French forces made it to the south side of the river and joined the other companies still holding the land and fortresses they had captured the day before. Though everyone looked tired, they had been replenished by the food and provisions that were delivered throughout the night. Fresh arrows, hammers, axes, lead and powder for the cannons, and ladders had arrived. All eyes were on Tourelles.

Andrew heard a soldier say confidently that the battle should not take very long, since the French outnumbered the English inside the stronghold.

Captain La Hire said sharply, "Do not be a fool! The English commanders are shrewd. They know we cannot overwhelm Tourelles by our numbers. We must attack in smaller groups, making their numbers even greater than ours."

The soldier mumbled an apology, then skulked off.

La Hire shot a look at Andrew. "And what, pray tell, will the English to the west of us be doing? Will they renew their attack? Will they circle around to the Renard Gate and attempt to take the city while we are fighting for Tourelles?"

Andrew hadn't thought of that.

"May God grant us another trick," said La Hire. "If Louis has served us as we hope, the English may not know what to do."

"Louis?" Eve asked, perking up. "How is he serving you if he has been captured?"

La Hire gave her a roguish smile. "The English will question Louis about our plans. He is to tell them that we have soldiers hiding behind the Renard Gate. They will suspect that if they send reinforcements to the south of the city to fight for Tourelles, our hidden forces will rush out of the Renard Gate and attack their fortresses on the west."

Andrew understood. "Oh, but now they will think twice about attacking the Renard Gate to invade the city

CHAPTER TWENTY-SIX

on that side because they do not know how many soldiers are hidden there."

"Do we have soldiers at that gate?" Eve asked.

"Not very many," La Hire replied. "But the English do not know that."

"So you *wanted* them to capture Louis?" Eve asked.

La Hire nodded. "His bravery is greater than anyone realizes."

Andrew and Eve looked at one another, impressed.

La Hire put on his helmet and turned his gaze toward Tourelles. "The fortunes of war are a mix of plans, accidents, and the hand of God. Pray today that the hand of God determines our victory."

The horns blared for the Battle of Tourelles to begin.

Andrew did not have time to watch the battle. He raced from one point to another in the Augustin fortress and on the battlefield, carrying weapons or water. Eve was sent to help Brother Pasquerel with the wounded. Reports came to him in bits and pieces about how the battle was going.

He heard that Jeanne's plan was going as they had hoped. Though the English bombarded the French army with arrows and cannonballs from inside Tourelles, the French destroyed the palisade. That allowed them to deal with the next obstacle: the trench. Using the logs from the palisade, they began to build a makeshift bridge.

It was slow going, but by late morning, they reached the boulevard and captured the few English who tried to defend it.

This brought them to the next obstacle: the dry moat. Long ladders were used to climb into the moat, and then they were moved to the other side for the soldiers to climb. The English attacked from the high wall of the stronghold with rocks, hot oil and tar, and even stones they pried loose from the walls of the fortress. The French covered themselves with shields as they struggled to scale the wall. Many were wounded or slain. The few soldiers who made it to the top of the ladders were beaten back with axes and clubs. Some fell to their deaths.

The French soldiers began to despair. The victory that some thought would be so easy to achieve now seemed like a vain hope.

At noon, the captains withdrew their forces to the shelter of the Augustin fortress to regroup. Andrew slipped into the room to hear what they had to say.

"It is as we feared," Gilles de Rais complained. "We should have waited until the Dauphin sent us more men. Waging battle today was a mistake."

"No!" Jeanne argued. "Keep heart! The fortress will be ours!"

To the surprise of the commanders, Jeanne handed her banner to a page standing nearby—a boy named Mugot. Then she dashed from the room. She raced out of the fortress and made her way to the front line of the

CHAPTER TWENTY-SIX

battle. Mugot stumbled behind her but held the banner high.

Andrew watched, astonished, as Jeanne reached a handful of men carrying one of the scaling ladders. She shouted to them, "All who are with me, come now!"

Together, Jeanne and the soldiers carried the ladder to the dry moat. The French commanders were dumbfounded. La Hire and Dunois stepped forward, unsure of what to do. Captain de Gamache—the man who had called Jeanne a "saucy child of low birth"—was the only one to take action. He leapt on his horse and rode after her.

The English watched Jeanne from the stronghold wall. They loudly mocked and taunted her. Andrew expected them to attack, but they didn't. They seemed curious to see what this mere girl thought she was going to do.

With her soldiers, Jeanne disappeared from view into the dry moat. Captain de Gamache followed her.

The commanders still delayed, but Andrew joined a few other men in a mad dash to the boulevard. An eerie silence fell all around. It was as if both sides of the battle had stopped to see this wild act of bravery. The ladder was put in place against the wall, and Jeanne approached to make the climb.

Andrew looked up at the English. With growing fear, he saw a single archer lean over the parapet with his longbow.

"Watch out!" Andrew cried out.

But it was too late.

The archer released his arrow, and it flew straight at Jeanne, striking her in the chest. She spun backward, fell off the ladder, and crashed to the ground.

Captain de Gamache and the nearby soldiers surrounded her. They used their shields to protect her from anything else the English might send their way.

The English cheered. Some shouted praise that the witch was wounded. "Spilled blood will take her power away," they exclaimed.

French archers positioned themselves to provide cover while Jeanne was brought up from the dry moat. De Gamache and his soldiers carried her to the Augustin fortress. Andrew stayed with them. He couldn't tell if she was dead or alive.

Silence rolled like a wave through the ranks of the French forces. It was as if the entire battle had come to a halt.

Inside the Augustin fortress, they carefully placed Jeanne on the ground. The captains surrounded her.

Andrew saw that the arrow had struck her at an odd angle between her shoulder and right breast. Jeanne suddenly gasped and then began to weep from the pain. She reached with her left hand and grabbed the arrow. With a spine-tingling scream, she pulled the arrow out and threw it aside.

Captain de Gamache commanded that her armor be removed. Andrew pushed in to help, but two soldiers nudged him aside. They clumsily yanked her in one direction, then another as they loosened the various straps. Jeanne cried out.

"Be careful!" Andrew shouted.

One of the soldiers was muttering as he worked. Andrew realized he was speaking the words of some kind of spell.

"What are you doing?" Dunois asked the soldier.

"It will stop the bleeding," the soldier said.

"No," Jeanne said sharply to him. "I would rather die than save myself by sinning against God. Keep your charms to yourself."

Brother Pasquerel broke through the circle around her, with Eve hot on his heels. She looked at Jeanne and went pale. Andrew stepped over to her. She grabbed his arm to steady herself.

Brother Pasquerel knelt down, opened a small pouch, and took out a bottle of oil and a container of something that looked to Andrew like fat. He put both on the wound, then dressed it with a bandage. "This will do until we can get her back to the city," he said.

Jeanne closed her eyes. Her groans mixed with whispered prayers. Then she opened her eyes and proclaimed, "Saint Catherine and Saint Margaret have come, as I knew they would."

She relaxed.

Brother Pasquerel made the Sign of the Cross.

The commanders looked helplessly at one another. They began to move away, speaking in low tones. Andrew assumed the battle was finished.

Suddenly Jeanne sat up. "Help me with my armor," she said.

Brother Pasquerel laid a hand on her arm. "You must rest."

Dunois knelt next to her. "Hear your priest. We must stop now. Sound the retreat," he said.

"No! We have not finished what we came to do," Jeanne said. She used Brother Pasquerel as a brace to help her stand. "Where is my horse?"

Orders were given to the soldiers standing nearby to find Jeanne's horse.

"She can't go back into battle," Eve whispered to Andrew.

"Would you try to stop her?" Andrew asked. He moved into the gap and grabbed Jeanne's breastplate. It was smeared with blood. He struggled to put it in place and fix the straps on the sides.

Mugot, who had been carrying Jeanne's banner, helped with the other pieces of armor.

Captain de Gamache watched Jeanne, then bowed and said, "Maiden, I am sorry for my harsh words about you. Truly you are the bravest of captains."

"I bear no grudge," she said. "You are a brave and noble knight."

Dunois spread his arms in an appeal. "Dear Maiden, I beg you not to go. Rest. Eat. Drink."

CHAPTER TWENTY-SIX

"No," she said again. A shout came from outside. The soldiers had retrieved Jeanne's horse.

Andrew and Mugot came alongside Jeanne and helped her outside. With gasps of pain, she climbed onto her horse. Looking down at her bewildered commanders, she said, "Tell your men to take comfort and refresh themselves. We will take the English when I return."

"Return?" asked La Hire.

Jean d'Aulon ran up to Jeanne, carrying her banner. "I found this," he said. He looked at Jeanne sitting on her horse in her blood-stained armor. Then he noticed the befuddled looks on everyone's faces. "What have I missed?" he asked.

Jeanne smiled at him. "Hold on to my banner until I come back," she said. Spurring her horse, she turned and rode south, away from the Augustin fortress, Tourelles, and the battlefield.

"Where are you going?" Dunois called after her.

She did not answer but continued on to some nearby hills.

With a confused expression, d'Aulon looked at the banner and then at Dunois. "What is in those hills?" he asked.

Dunois shrugged. "Nothing but vineyards."

"Perhaps she is going to pray for us," Eve said.

Looking alarmed, Dunois said, "Let us hope so."

The French troops made a few half-hearted attempts to attack Tourelles during the afternoon, but without success. The worry on everyone's minds was if and when Jeanne would return.

As the afternoon waned, an impatient d'Aulon lifted Jeanne's banner and shouted, "Follow this blessed banner to victory!"

With the banner in one hand and his shield in the other, he ran for the stronghold wall. A group of soldiers saw the banner and shouted, following the squire.

Andrew watched from his position near the Augustin fortress. "What is this?" he heard Dunois ask. "Who gave the command to attack?"

The English in Tourelles let loose arrows and crossbow bolts at d'Aulon as he and the men entered the dry moat. Andrew expected the worst. He could not guess how d'Aulon and his brave men could protect themselves from the onslaught. Suddenly, Jeanne's banner came into view as d'Aulon climbed the ladder. He waved it at the French troops, trying to rally them.

The English archers turned their arrows on d'Aulon but could not seem to find the right position to strike him down. The French archers sent a slew of arrows buzzing at the top of the wall, driving the English back.

"They will kill him if we do not help," Andrew shouted. He was about to run for the stronghold when he heard a loud shout from somewhere behind him. He

CHAPTER TWENTY-SIX

spun around to see Jeanne riding onto the battlefield at a full gallop.

"In God's name, you will enter soon. Do not be afraid!" she shouted. "The English have no more power over you! To my banner! Bring more ladders!"

At the sight of her, the soldiers seemed to come alive. As one man, they threw themselves again at Tourelles.

The faces of the English men on the wall betrayed their shock and fear. They retreated from view as French archers let more arrows fly.

Andrew watched with awe as the French raised a dozen ladders against the wall. Men crawled like spiders up each one, rising higher and higher. The English came forward to drop stones onto the soldiers, but the French arrows drove them back again.

Jeanne rode back and forth along the boulevard, urging the French soldiers onward.

Then came a riotous shout from the city of Orléans. Andrew ran from the Augustin fortress and followed the brow of a hill to get a better view. He saw the city gate to the great bridge open. Soldiers and townspeople flooded out with giant planks of wood. Even with his limited view, Andrew could guess what they were doing: the planks would cover the massive holes in the bridge so they could cross from the city to the north side of Tourelles. The English would now be attacked from two sides.

Jeanne cried out to the English, "Surrender now! Receive mercy!"

A man Andrew remembered as William Glasdale, the English commander, appeared on the wall. He looked down at her.

Jeanne begged him, "Hear me! For the sake of your men and their souls, yield to the King of Heaven!"

Glasdale scowled at her, then disappeared again.

Fewer arrows flew from the English side. The men on the wall had retreated farther into the stronghold. French soldiers breached the wall, climbing over the top.

A French boat came into view on the river. It was pulling a second boat that had been lit on fire. Both boats were sailing toward Tourelles. Andrew angled around the battlefield to see what the French were trying to do.

The men in the first boat allowed the flaming boat to come alongside them. Then using long poles, they pushed the second boat into the moat that flowed between the stronghold and Tourelles itself. Soon, flames from the vessel engulfed the drawbridge that connected the two fortresses.

Andrew was alarmed to see the main gate to Tourelles open. A small group of armored English soldiers ran onto the burning drawbridge. He guessed they were trying to escape. Instead, they crashed through the weakened wood on the bridge. One or two fell into the flaming boat. Others splashed into the moat. The weight of their

CHAPTER TWENTY-SIX

armor ensured that they would never see the surface again. Andrew felt sick to his stomach.

"The commander has been killed!" came a cry from the stronghold. A captured English soldier stood there, pale-faced. He pointed to the water below. William Glasdale was one of the men who had just fallen to his death.

Upon hearing the news, Jeanne dismounted her horse and knelt down. Andrew learned later that she had prayed for the souls of the dead English.

The black of the night sky was stained red by the flames from the drawbridge. Soon, Tourelles itself was on fire. The remaining English soldiers attempted to fight their way onto the great bridge that led to the city, but the French forces caught them. Many of the English simply laid down their weapons and raised their arms in surrender.

The battle was over.

Later, the fires on the drawbridge and the fort itself were put out. The remaining English soldiers were rounded up. Andrew and Eve followed Jeanne and the weary French soldiers marching slowly through Tourelles and onto the great bridge back to Orléans.

Andrew remembered Jeanne telling a peasant woman that she would enter the city this way. He wondered if

Jeanne would share the peasant woman's fish with an English soldier, as she had said.

Otherwise, everything Jeanne had promised about the siege of Orléans had become reality.

The bells of the city began to ring. Somewhere, beautiful voices sang the "Te Deum."

Andrew and Eve looked at each other as they crossed the threshold of the gate.

"What next?" Eve asked.

27

Jeanne returned to the Boucher mansion to have her wounds treated properly. She was taken to her room, and the door was closed on the males in the house so Madame Boucher and Eve could undress her.

Eve asked a servant for some bread and wine. Andrew did not expect Jeanne to partake. As far as anyone knew, she had refused to eat for days. So he was surprised when Eve came back out to report that Jeanne had diluted the wine with water and dipped the bread into the mixture. She even asked for more.

A physician with a wrinkled face and a droopy moustache arrived later. As he came through the door, he announced that he would have to cleanse and cauterize the wound using burning rods. He sent servants to prepare the coals.

The physician went into Jeanne's room, then returned to the hall several minutes later with a mystified look on his face. "The wound does not need my services." He made the Sign of the Cross and added, "Someone with greater skill has already begun the healing."

Andrew learned later from Eve that Jeanne had gone into the hillside vineyards to pray. Her reappearance on the battlefield came after she'd been given renewed strength and comfort from her Voices.

That night, the ringing of the bells and celebrations in the city were not enough to keep Jeanne or her entire company from their sleep. Andrew fell onto his cot with a deep sense of joy.

Morning arrived sooner than Andrew expected. At dawn, d'Aulon shook him.

"Up, lad. The English are on the move," he said.

Andrew had forgotten that the army of the Duke of Granville and Captain John Talbot were still encamped on the west side of city. Were they planning to counterattack?

Andrew quickly dressed and rushed out of the room. He bumped into Eve on the stairs. Jeanne was ahead of them, along with her commanders. They all walked straight to the Renard Gate to see what the English were doing.

"We should attack *now*," said Captain La Hire.

The English army appeared to be very busy, but it was hard to discern whether they were preparing to attack or retreat.

"It is Sunday," Jeanne said to La Hire. "Bring an altar. We shall say Mass here."

"What if they attack?" La Hire asked.

"Surely they will not attack while we celebrate the Mass," Jeanne said. "If you are worried, then watch to see if they face us or turn their backs on us while we worship."

An altar was set up, and priests from the cathedral came out to celebrate the Mass. Jeanne would not look at the English troops. She kept her eyes on the chalice and paten, her face filled with a childlike anticipation at the sight of the Body and Blood of Jesus.

Andrew sneaked peeks at the English. They had paused in their work to watch the Mass. Then they turned their backs to Orléans.

"They're retreating," he whispered to Eve.

After the Mass concluded, Captain La Hire said unhappily. "I still think we should attack them now."

Jeanne said, "It is not the Lord's pleasure that we should fight them today. You will have the chance another time."

"By then, they may have the strength to kill us," La Hire grumbled.

Andrew later learned that more than four hundred English soldiers were slain in the battle for Tourelles. The French suffered the loss of over one hundred soldiers and civilians. He also heard that the English had left their sick and injured in the various strongholds they had abandoned. The French found food, ammunition, cannons, and mortars as well.

Guyenne, Jeanne's herald, was set free. So was Louis, who blushed when Eve gave him a long hug. The young page assured Captain La Hire that he had passed along the false information when the English questioned him. Together, they wondered if that was why Captain Talbot and the Duke of Granville did nothing to help their allies at Tourelles.

A formal procession with Jeanne, her commanders, and the city officials filed through Orléans. It stopped at the cathedral, where a service of thanksgiving was held. All there praised God for the end of the siege of Orléans.

All the same, Jeanne's commanders were nervous. Some of them believed the English would seek revenge against other French towns. Many of the men decided to leave Orléans and spread out in different directions to protect their territories.

In the evening, Andrew took time to explore the Boucher mansion. He found a small library with a selection of leather-bound books. He glanced at one after another and marveled that he could read the French and Latin words.

He had curled up in a chair to read an account of a woman called Eleanor of Aquitaine when Louis appeared at the door. "There you are! I have been looking everywhere for you."

CHAPTER TWENTY-SEVEN

Andrew laid the book on a side table. "Is something wrong?"

"Come with me," Louis said softly. "There is someone who needs to speak with you."

"Who?"

"Simon Le Fantôme," Louis replied.

Just hearing the name made Andrew feel anxious. "What does *he* want?"

"He was wounded."

"During the battle?" Andrew asked.

"During the battle but not *in* the battle," said Louis. "You should hurry."

They slipped out of the mansion and made their way through the city. Though Sunday was meant to be a day of rest, celebrations were still being held in some of the homes, public inns, and taverns.

"Simon was found near the vineyard behind Saint Jean-le-Blanc," Louis explained as they walked. "That is where Jeanne rode to after she was wounded."

"What was Simon doing there?" Andrew asked.

"Let him explain."

After turning onto one street and then another, they came to an alley. A single wooden door sat at the far end. Louis knocked. The door opened, then slanted to one side as if it would fall off its hinges. A man with dark, curly hair and equally dark eyes looked at the two boys. He recognized Louis and, with a grunt, bid them enter.

The place was one large shadow that smelled of rotten wood, sweat, and old vegetables. They walked down a short hall to a closet-sized room, where they found Simon Le Fantôme stretched out on a cot. His long legs hung off the end. A single lamp burned on a bedside table. But no amount of light could have put color into Simon's pale face.

As sick as the old man looked, his eyes darted to them as they entered. His hand went to his right side. Andrew suspected he had a knife hidden under the rags that covered him.

Simon nodded to the dark-eyed man, who retreated into the hall. Louis took a few steps to the back of the room and stood in a half shadow with his hand on his sword.

Andrew moved nearer to the cot. "What happened to you?" he said.

"Have you seen him?" Simon asked, his voice a strained rasp.

"Who?"

"The assassin," he said as if it should have been obvious. "The Ravager. Vincent."

Andrew was alarmed. "He is here?"

"'Twas he who did this," Simon said, then threw the left side of the ragged cover aside.

Andrew saw a blood-soaked bandage draped over Simon's hip.

CHAPTER TWENTY-SEVEN

"He followed the Maiden to the vineyard," the old man continued. "I saw him and stopped him from his evil intent. He escaped with a wound equal to my own." Simon pulled the cover back over his chest. "If there is justice in God's world, he will die slowly and painfully from that wound."

"He went there to kill Jeanne?" asked Andrew, his mouth going dry.

A single nod from Simon, his eyes closing.

"What can I do about it?" Andrew asked as fear laid a cold hand on his heart.

"You are her angel. You must be vigilant," Simon said, his voice fading. "He is looking for ..." The words disappeared.

"What is he looking for?" Andrew asked.

Simon's eyes opened slightly. "Hope Springs."

Andrew felt a jolt as if an electric current had gone through him. "What did you say? He is looking for Hope Springs? Is that what you said?"

Simon's eyes were fully closed. The old man's chest rose and fell with labored breaths.

Andrew turned to Louis. "Did you hear that?"

Louis nodded. "I heard him say 'hope springs.' Does he mean the hope that springs within us?"

The dark-eyed man came to the doorway. "You must leave now."

"Is he going to die?" Andrew asked.

The man snorted. "Him? I do not believe anything can kill him. But this will add another scar to his collection."

Andrew and Louis ventured back to the Boucher mansion. Andrew walked silently, confounded by what Simon had said. Had Andrew ever said those two words to him? Was it a coincidence?

As he walked, he realized that he was looking at every face in the crowd, wondering if the Ravager would suddenly appear. He gripped the hilt of his sword so tightly that it hurt his fingers to let go when he finally reached the safety of the mansion.

"Perhaps Eve will know why he said 'hope springs,'" Louis said.

"Do not tell her," Andrew said.

"Why not?"

"There is no reason for both of us to worry," Andrew replied.

Jeanne could not sit still. She announced Sunday night that she would leave first thing in the morning to speak with the Dauphin. "We have kept faith and freed Orléans. Now we must see the Dauphin properly crowned in Reims."

Dunois begged her to wait. "You must rest."

As he sat against the wall in the meeting room, Andrew felt drained. Eve looked at him. She looked exhausted. Waiting and resting sounded like the perfect plan.

CHAPTER TWENTY-SEVEN

"How am I to rest when the mission is not yet completed?" Jeanne asked. "We have already lost too much time."

Andrew and Eve shared a glance. Wherever Jeanne went, they went.

"I will accompany you to the Dauphin," Dunois promised. "Once we find out where he is."

It was rumored that the Dauphin was in Chinon. They knew that much because he had written letters from there to announce the wonderful news about Orléans. Then they heard he had moved to Blois, and then Tours.

"Will someone *please* find him!" Jeanne begged, clearly exasperated. "I do not understand why he has not sent for me already."

"The Dauphin is surrounded by people who do not like Jeanne," Eve said to Andrew later. "La Trémoille is one. The Archbishop of Reims is another. You watch. They will do anything to stall her."

Knowing they were going *somewhere*, Jeanne's company packed the next morning. When the city officials heard that she was going to depart, they came to the mansion to express their thanks for all she had done. They offered her gifts as a reward.

"I am here for God and whatever reward He may give me later," she said. "I cannot accept your gifts."

A messenger arrived in the early afternoon and reported that the Dauphin was at his castle in the small town of Loches. He agreed to receive Jeanne if she wanted to come.

Andrew noticed that the Dauphin still had not actually summoned her.

Jeanne hardly took time to say goodbye to her many friends. Andrew learned that Bertrand de Poulengy and Jean de Metz were returning to Vaucouleurs to take on other duties. Louis had been ordered back to Chinon to serve Guillaume Bellier once again. Jeanne's brother Jean had said he would return home to Domrémy, though Pierre was resolved to continue on with Jeanne.

The squire Jean d'Aulon remained as part of Jeanne's company, along with Brother Pasquerel. Dunois, of course, had his own business to attend to.

As Jeanne and her company departed, the people of Orléans crowded the streets. They wept with joy and shouted their praise to her. She waved and thanked them until the travelers were well beyond the Burgundy Gate and out of earshot.

From a distance, Loches looked small compared to the other towns Andrew had seen. It sat at the foot of a rocky mount, with a castle perched on top and a monastery nearby. The town itself was not walled in but spread

CHAPTER TWENTY-SEVEN

around the castle like moss around a tree. The spires of various churches sprung up like pointed arrows. Like so many other towns and cities in France, it sat near a river.

Jeanne pushed them to move faster as they came closer to the town. "We must not keep the Dauphin waiting," she called out, making sure to hold her banner high.

Andrew and Eve shared a horse that d'Aulon had found for them. Riding at a gallop, Andrew was sure one of them would bounce off. Dunois kept pace with Jeanne, probably fearful of what the Maiden might do when she greeted the Dauphin.

Just outside the city was a large company of men on horseback. The Dauphin had come out to greet her. He sat regally on a black stallion, wearing a brightly colored tunic. Seeing Jeanne, he broke the line and rode across the field, meeting her halfway.

Jeanne brought her horse to a halt and quickly dismounted. She took off her cap and bowed as far as she could.

The Dauphin climbed off his horse and, with a great smile, reached down and gently encouraged her to stand. She obeyed. Still smiling, he suddenly wrapped his arms around her.

Andrew reined in his horse only a couple of yards away.

"Did he *kiss* her?" Eve asked, craning to see.

"It is too hard to tell from here," Andrew said.

Soon they were surrounded by members of the Dauphin's court: a scowling Archbishop of Reims and a disdainful La Trémoille. Their sour expressions told Andrew that they did not like the Dauphin's open show of affection for Jeanne.

The Dauphin invited Jeanne and her companions to his royal lodge in Loches so he could hear her account of the battle at Tourelles. Andrew was glad that the Dauphin gave Jeanne so much attention and respect. Even the members of the royal court seemed to appreciate her. Sadly the feeling was short lived.

Over the next several days, the Dauphin's counselors squeezed Jeanne out of his schedule. She reminded them that they must now march to Reims to crown him as the one true king. In response they insisted that the subject needed further discussion. The Dauphin himself was indecisive.

"See?" Eve said to Andrew. "They are stalling everything."

Theologians and scholars wrote long and involved essays about Jeanne and sent them to the Dauphin for consideration. They concluded that the Dauphin should "do what the Maiden commands and prudence directs. For everything else, give yourself to works of piety and prayers of devotion."

Meanwhile, the military captains fumed again about taking commands from a girl like Jeanne. La Trémoille

CHAPTER TWENTY-SEVEN

and the Archbishop of Reims did all they could to thwart Jeanne's influence on the Dauphin.

A servant in the royal court told Andrew and Eve that La Trémoille had advised the Dauphin "to allow the *average* people and soldiers" to draw inspiration from her. "*You* are above that," he told the Dauphin.

When Jeanne wasn't waiting for the Dauphin, she was answering yet more questions from the council. Privately she met with Brother Pasquerel to pray and study. He began to teach her to read and write. She also went into the fields to hone her sword-fighting skills and learn to use a battle-ax. The exercise helped restore the strength in her chest and shoulder. Andrew discovered that her greatest pleasure was riding her horse alone in the nearby forests. Otherwise, she regularly made her confession and attended Mass with Brother Pasquerel. Andrew often saw her weeping.

He learned from Jean d'Aulon that the council's latest argument centered around the expense of an ongoing war. They claimed the royal treasury could not afford it. Yet they also understood that the victory at Orléans would be lost if they did not continue the fight to drive out the English. But how were they to be driven out? Every positive statement was met with a dozen negative responses.

Eve reported that Jeanne often paced in her room like a lion.

"I may live a year, barely longer," she said. "Why does the Dauphin destroy my time with delays?"

One day Andrew overheard Jeanne tell Brother Pasquerel that she had been given four things to do: Deliver Orléans—which she had done; see the Dauphin crowned and anointed at Reims; drive the English out of France; and rescue the Duke of Orléans from the hands of the English.

"How am I to do any of those things waiting here?" she asked.

"Had God not given her this mission, she would have been the holiest of women in a convent somewhere," Brother Pasquerel later said to Andrew and Eve.

Meanwhile, the Duke of Alençon was promoted to the rank of lieutenant general of the Dauphin's armies. He and Dunois went off with the troops to fight. First, they marched to the besieged town of Jargeau to get rid of the English there. They believed they would be victorious, just as they were at Orléans. They weren't. The high waters of the river Loire flooded the trenches, blocking their access to the fortress. The French forces unhappily returned to Loches.

"They would have won if they had taken Jeanne," Eve said.

Jeanne was deeply distressed. Unable to wait any longer, she stormed to the Dauphin's chambers. Andrew and Eve followed closely, afraid of what was about to happen.

Bursting through the doors, Jeanne found the Dauphin meeting with a few of his council members. The councilmen leapt to their feet, appalled at the interruption.

CHAPTER TWENTY-SEVEN

Jeanne dropped to her knees and begged, "Gentle Dauphin, do not continue with your tedious councils, but come with me to Reims to claim the crown that is yours!"

The Dauphin politely said, "Do not be impatient. You know better than most that the will of God will be accomplished in His good time."

"I know that," Jeanne countered, then gestured to the council. "But do they?"

Christophe d'Harcourt, an arrogant nobleman whose lips always seemed to purse into a frown, asked, "Is interrupting the Dauphin in his chambers your idea or the idea of your council of angels and saints?"

"My heavenly council has urged me forward," Jeanne replied.

"Show us," d'Harcourt said. "Here, in the presence of your king, show us how your council speaks to you."

Andrew was surprised to see Jeanne blush.

The Dauphin held up his hand. "Jeanne, does it please you to answer this request here, publicly?"

Jeanne glanced at the Dauphin, then fixed her gaze on d'Harcourt. "I know what you want and would provide it willingly, if I could. However, I am at the beck and call of my Voices. They are not at mine."

"A good answer," said the Dauphin.

She turned to him again. "Gentle Dauphin, I am sad that you and your council do not believe me. Yet the Voices of *my* council comfort me and say, 'Daughter of God, go, and we will be your help.' These Voices fill me with so great a joy that I would stay in that condition forever, if I could."

Andrew sensed that something had changed in the room. It was as if the light of the sun had somehow penetrated the thick walls and bathed Jeanne in a beautiful radiance. Her eyes were filled with tears, but her expression had a look of peace that Andrew would never forget. Then, almost as quickly as the change had appeared, it faded again.

Wide eyed, Andrew turned to Eve. Her expression told him that she had felt it too. He glanced at the faces of the council. They all looked astonished.

D'Harcourt put a hand on his heart and said, "Good Maiden, I apologize for any doubt I have had in you."

The other council members looked unsettled. Even a heavenly light was not going to stop them from their meeting.

"Your Highness, I beg you to allow us to resume," one of them said.

"Yes, yes," the Dauphin stammered.

The moment was gone.

Jeanne knew it. Without another word, she bowed to the prince and left the room.

Eve and Andrew followed close behind, eyeing each other with the same question: *What just happened?*

CHAPTER TWENTY-SEVEN

Whatever had happened in the room impacted the council. Soon after, they gave their approval for a great army to be gathered at the city of Selles-en-Berry, south of Blois. Jeanne would be reunited with the Duke of Alençon and her fellow Orléans commanders, including Jean de Dunois, La Hire, and Gilles de Rais. From Selles-en-Berry, they would march again on the English-held towns along the river Loire, learning the lessons from their failure at Jargeau.

The challenge from the royal council was simple: *If* Jeanne and the French army conquered the English strongholds and cleared the passage to Reims, the Dauphin would go there to be crowned.

Jeanne looked delighted. It was what she had hoped to do all along.

"Why did it take them almost a month to decide?" Eve seethed.

Jeanne and her company journeyed to Selles-en-Berry. It was another small town, hardly able to sustain the many soldiers who had come to fight. The military camp spread out from the city limits along the river Cher.

The troops were well assembled by the time Jeanne arrived. She greeted the men she already knew and was introduced to a few new captains who had come to join the fight. One was an old friend of La Hire named Jean Poton de Xaintrailles. He was a stern-looking man with jet-black hair, a matching moustache, and dark, penetrating eyes. He gave her a swift salute.

Two of the new men were young brothers, Guy and André de Laval. Both were noblemen. Yet Andrew noticed that Guy actually blushed when he met Jeanne, and he stammered like a fan meeting a famous rock star. Andrew thought it was funny. Eve said she thought it was "sweet."

Jeanne reminded the commanders of their duties: the soldiers must make a regular confession and go to Mass, no women were allowed in the camp, and there was to be no swearing. Considering the victory at Orléans, the men readily agreed.

Wanting to waste no more time, Jeanne marched the army to Orléans, the starting point for their campaigns along the river.

It's almost like coming home, Andrew thought as they passed the wreck of Tourelles and crossed the great bridge to the gate into Orléans. The people cheered, more bells rang, and the cannons thundered to welcome them.

The Bouchers greeted Jeanne as one of the family. They even put her back in the room she had shared with Madame Boucher and her young daughter, Charlotte.

In no time at all, the commanders were in a heated argument about where to attack first. Jargeau was the obvious choice, if only to finish what Dunois had started. But rumors had reached them that the English had recently brought in a great number of reinforcements.

"We must be cautious," one of the captains said.

Jeanne had heard enough. "Friends! Do not be afraid. No matter the numbers against us or the difficulties

CHAPTER TWENTY-SEVEN

ahead of us, God leads this work. If I were not sure of it, I would be home tending sheep rather than enduring this. We must go on *now*!"

The next day they marched to the English fortress at Jargeau. The rumors about reinforcements turned out to be false. But the English commander, the Duke of Suffolk, had used the time following Dunois's attack to prepare for an invasion.

On the first day, Andrew and Eve were told to stay near the supply wagons. They watched as the townspeople from Orléans unwisely rushed ahead of the army to attack the fortress on their own. As had happened before, many lost their lives for their reckless bravery. A company of French soldiers, young and inexperienced, also attacked in a disorganized frenzy. Many were wounded and driven back.

It took Jeanne to bring order to the chaos. Riding in with her banner, she led a renewed attack. The Duke of Suffolk took the hint and sent a message to the French commanders.

"Give us fifteen days to surrender," Suffolk offered. "If reinforcements come in that time, then we will fight. If not, we will surrender."

The commanders considered the idea. It was part of their military tradition to allow such an offer.

Jeanne was furious. "No!" she said. "Tell them to leave *now*, with the clothes on their backs, if they want to live. Otherwise, we will continue our attack."

Suffolk refused Jeanne's demands. The next day, the battle began again. Both sides stood strong, no closer to victory. Once again Jeanne rode from one end of the field to another, urging the French soldiers on.

The story was told later that she had found the Duke of Alençon with his men trying to establish a new position near the city wall. Jeanne told him to move or he would surely be killed. He was surprised enough to obey her advice. Later, another captain took the same position and was struck down by cannon fire.

At the end of the day, the English waved a white flag for another round of negotiations. They demanded the same terms as before. Jeanne refused. The fight would continue.

Andrew watched as she personally directed the placements of the French cannons and catapults. With a renewed bombardment, she sped to a wall with a company of men carrying a ladder. As she began to climb, a stone was thrown down, knocking her to the ground. Her banner flew from her hand. From where Andrew stood with the supply wagons, it seemed as if everyone froze where they were in the fight.

Jeanne leapt to her feet and raised the banner again. She shouted for the French troops to move ahead. The English recoiled as the French forces thundered their way toward Jargeau. La Hire used the time to position a catapult even closer to the fortress. He let fly three huge stones, each one slamming into the tower and turning

CHAPTER TWENTY-SEVEN

it into a jagged ruin. The French forces now entered the city.

The English abandoned the wall and fell back among the houses and shops. Many hurried to the river. The French chased them wherever they went. Finally, the Duke of Suffolk was captured and the battle ended.

The army returned to a jubilant Orléans. Jeanne expressed thanks to God for the victory and urged everyone to attend Mass.

That evening, Dunois came to Jeanne with servants carrying a trunk.

"A present for you from my father, the Duke of Orléans," he said. "Though he remains a hostage in England, he arranged to send this to you."

Jeanne opened the trunk with the happy look of a young girl at Christmas. She took out a beautiful red cloak and a green tunic fringed with white silk.

"The colors of our house," Dunois explained.

Jeanne was clearly touched by the gesture and promised to wear those colors proudly when the time was right.

"But for now," she said, returning to business, "we must move on to the next English stronghold."

"The men must rest," Dunois said.

"I will give them two days," she conceded.

28

The campaigns to defeat the English strongholds on the way to Reims became a fuzzy memory to Andrew. Each one was a variation of floods of soldiers in glistening armor and colorful banners, stone walls and ladders, flying arrows and cannon fire, swords and lances, shouts and screams, blood and death.

"We're only twelve years old," he complained to Eve one night. "How are we supposed to cope?"

Eve, looking pale, nodded. "In our time, generals push buttons and fire long-range missiles. We hear about the numbers of casualties on a list or see on a map what cities were captured. If we had to fight this way all the time, maybe we wouldn't fight so often."

Andrew shook his head. "The commanders here see how terrible it is, and they still fight all the time. It isn't the way we fight; it's the way we are."

Outside of a town called Meung-sur-Loire, the French army captured a bridge that would allow the troops and their supplies to move freely between the north and south.

They moved on to the ancient town of Beaugency, passing through lush vineyards, colorful gardens, and stretches of cornfields before reaching a few outlying homes.

The English were ready for them. Guards had been posted among the houses, waiting to attack. It worked. The French began to retreat. Once again, Jeanne rallied them to push forward.

The English quickly withdrew into the town and its castle. Rather than fight any further, the English commander presented terms for their immediate surrender. Jeanne agreed that they could leave the next day, taking their horses and personal property with them, if they promised not to fight again for ten days.

Jeanne's commanders were surprised. Why would she allow the English to leave?

Andrew knew the answer: Jeanne had a soft spot for any who would surrender.

That same day, Andrew heard about a different problem.

"Another French army has shown up," Eve explained to him, after hearing Jeanne talking with her captains.

"Another French army is good, right?" he asked.

"But this army belongs to Arthur de Richemont. He is the constable of France. Though, he had a falling-out with the Dauphin, and no one is sure if he is here to join us or fight us. Jeanne said we should attack him before he attacks us."

"What do the commanders say?"

CHAPTER TWENTY-EIGHT

"They told Jeanne that if she attacks the count, their soldiers will not fight with her."

Andrew found that hard to believe. "What is Jeanne going to do?"

"Ride out to meet him," Eve said. "The Duke of Alençon will go with her. So will Dunois and a couple of others. The duke wants us to go too."

"Us? Why us?"

"Because we are her angels. He thinks she will be less hotheaded if we are with her."

"It has not worked so far," Andrew said.

Eve smiled. Andrew had not seen her do that in a long time.

Andrew could feel the tension as Jeanne and her company rode out from their camp to meet Arthur de Richemont. The adults had their own horses. Andrew and Eve shared one.

The constable of France sat on horseback at the head of a vast army. He had at least as many men as Jeanne had on her side. If it came to a fight, it would be a terrible one.

De Richemont was dressed in royal colors and wore a dark cape along with a broad hat that had a long feather sticking out of it. He carried a sword at his side. Andrew noticed that he did not bother to wear any protective armor.

The constable spurred his horse and trotted away from his army to greet Jeanne. As they drew closer together in the middle of the field, Andrew saw de Richemont's face. He had sad eyes and a long nose that seemed to pull his face down, setting his mouth in a permanent frown.

When they were only a few yards apart, de Richemont reined in his horse and dismounted. Jeanne did the same. Andrew saw Dunois's hand slip over to the hilt of his sword.

De Richemont took a few steps and looked surprised when Jeanne came close and then knelt down in front of him.

He made the Sign of the Cross and urged her to stand. She slowly got to her feet.

He said, "Jeanne, I have been told that you want to fight me. I do not know whether you come from God or not. If you come from God, I do not fear you in any way, for God knows my good intentions. If you come from the devil, then I fear you even less."

"Then let us talk, my lord," she said.

The two of them strolled away. De Richemont clasped his hands behind his back and lowered his head to listen to Jeanne. They stopped at a distance where no one else could hear them. He nodded as Jeanne spoke. Then Jeanne listened to him and she, too, nodded.

They returned a few minutes later. The constable mounted his horse and rode back to his army.

Jeanne watched him, then turned and announced to all, "We have peace."

CHAPTER TWENTY-EIGHT

There was a collective sigh of relief.

She mounted her horse and said with a smile, "He has offered the best of his men to fight with us."

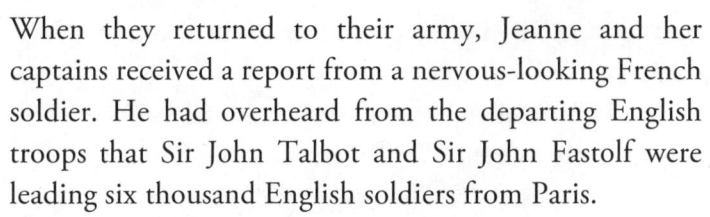

When they returned to their army, Jeanne and her captains received a report from a nervous-looking French soldier. He had overheard from the departing English troops that Sir John Talbot and Sir John Fastolf were leading six thousand English soldiers from Paris.

Andrew knew that the French already feared Talbot, but the mention of Fastolf struck absolute terror in their hearts. They would never forget that Fastolf and his army had brutally defeated them in what had become known as the Battle of the Herrings.

"Even now the English troops are headquartered at Meung," the soldier said.

Andrew listened as the French commanders argued again for caution. Jeanne should wait, they said. Better yet, she should retreat to a safer position. Anything would be better than to face Fastolf and his army.

Andrew couldn't imagine that they had been fighting alongside the warrior Maiden all this time and still didn't know her. The pattern always seemed to be the same: news would come, they would react, and she would act.

"I do not care what numbers they bring," Jeanne said. "God has sent us as His rod of iron to discipline them."

To Arthur de Richemont, she sent a message: "I was not responsible for your coming, but since you have come, you are welcome." The arrival of de Richemont's army would bolster their mission, she told her commanders. Retreat was not an option.

"We will not wait for the English army to attack us," Jeanne insisted. "Let us go and drive them out at sword point."

The commanders reluctantly accepted her order. The French army marched on to Janville.

As they passed fertile fields and great thick forests, Andrew heard Dunois warn the others, "There are many places for the English to hide. Watch for a surprise attack."

Jeanne agreed. "By God, if they were hanging from the clouds, we would have them by now." But she quickly added, "Still, my council has assured me that they will be ours."

Along the way, news came that the English forces had already been marching in *their* direction and had established positions on the vast Beauce plains a few miles ahead.

Jeanne was unafraid.

The French reached a broad hill that gave them a clear view for miles around. In the distance, they could see the town of Patay. They also saw evidence of the English army's presence. Just ahead of a narrow pass between two woods, a long line of pikes had been staked into the ground. The points were sloped toward the enemy.

CHAPTER TWENTY-EIGHT

It was the same kind of barricade the English had used at the Battle of Agincourt. The pikes prevented a charge on horseback.

Dunois frowned. "The English are hiding in the woods behind those pikes. Their longbowmen will slaughter us."

Two English messengers appeared behind the pikes. They passed through the blockade, crossed the field, and eventually ascended the hill. Bowing to the French commanders, they issued a challenge from Talbot. "If you have the courage, come down and fight us."

Jeanne smiled at this obvious lure into their trap. "God and Our Lady willing, we will see you face-to-face at noon tomorrow."

The messenger nodded, then returned the way he came.

"Noon?" asked La Hire.

Jeanne shrugged. "Would you prefer we engaged them sooner?"

"Not when I do not know where they are," La Hire replied. He nodded. "Noon it is."

The French spent the rest of the day preparing for battle.

"There is much we cannot see" became a common refrain among the commanders. "The English could be hiding their archers anywhere in the hedges and forest."

Andrew kept hearing the name *Agincourt* whispered among the troops.

The French captains met to assess the situation. "How do we fight what we cannot see?" was the question they asked.

"We must draw them out," said La Hire.

"How?" asked Dunois.

"God will show us," Jeanne said, her eyes alight.

Andrew could see that her words were not comforting the captains.

She stepped away, stating that she wanted to spend time thinking and praying. She signaled for Eve and Andrew to walk with her.

They strolled back along the road to Beaugency, passing soldiers who now rested on the roadside or in the neighboring fields.

A disturbance caught their attention. Across a field, a group of soldiers had circled around a stag that had unwisely ventured from the forest. With swords and spears ready, the soldiers were about to kill the poor beast.

"We shall eat it when we are victorious," one of the soldiers said proudly to Jeanne as she approached with Andrew and Eve.

Andrew was amused. "I am sure you could lure the English out with one of those."

Jeanne turned to Andrew with a look of wonder. She then shouted, "Wait! Do not kill it!"

The soldiers groaned from disappointment.

"What do you want us to do?" one of the soldiers asked.

"Set it free," she said.

Once again, the soldiers groaned. "Why?" another asked.

Jeanne smiled. "By God's grace, it will be a gift to the English. *Then* we will have our victory."

The soldiers looked at her, perplexed. Then they slowly spread out. The stag stood tall and proud. Andrew noticed a jagged scar along its flank.

Another narrow escape, he thought.

The stag bounded away in the direction of the English army.

"I hope the English enjoy their feast," said the soldier.

"I doubt it," Jeanne said.

Andrew turned to Eve. She gave him a look that said "I don't know what she's thinking."

That night, Jeanne told her commanders that she wanted an advance guard to march across the plain for the town of Patay early the next morning.

"Stay in tight formation as you go," Jeanne said.

"To what purpose?" asked the Duke of Alençon. "Do you want the advance guard to attack early? Is that why you told the English messengers we would see them at noon?"

"How can they attack what they cannot see? I want the English to show themselves," she said firmly. "Once we know where they are hidden, the remainder of the army will follow, ready for battle."

The duke was not assured. "Are you suggesting that an advance guard will serve as bait to draw out the English?"

Jeanne looked at him calmly. "It is another kind of bait that will show us where the English are. My angel has said so." Her gaze went to Andrew.

Andrew suddenly realized that all of the commanders were looking at him.

His cheeks burned from the embarrassment. Especially since he didn't know what Jeanne was talking about.

"If this is your angel's plan, then he should travel with the advance guard," said La Hire, giving Andrew a coy look.

"Yes, he should see his handiwork," said Jeanne.

Andrew swallowed hard. *What handiwork?* he wondered. *What is she doing?*

"I will lead the advance guard," La Hire announced.

"As will I," said Captain de Xaintrailles. "I know this region."

Guy de Laval stepped forward with his brother. "André and I will take a company of men with them."

As the meeting broke up, Jeanne gave a final instruction to her commanders. "Wear your spurs, good men. You will need them to pursue the English as they run away."

The night passed at a painfully slow pace. Andrew couldn't sleep. His mind raced. He didn't fear traveling with the advance guard, but he couldn't figure out what

CHAPTER TWENTY-EIGHT

Jeanne had been talking about. What idea had he given her?

Before the light of dawn touched the sky, La Hire, Captain de Xaintrailles, and the two Laval brothers assembled the men who would form the advance. La Hire instructed them to stay in tight formation. "We do not know where the English are hiding, but our Maiden is certain we will find them."

Eve showed up while Andrew was putting on a few sections of armor.

"Will you be all right?" she asked as she helped him fasten his breastplate.

"How am I supposed to know?" he countered. "Did Jeanne tell you anything?"

"No," Eve said. "But I think it has something to do with that stag she set free."

Andrew shook his head. "I thought about it all night. I don't get it."

"Neither do I," Eve said. "But Jeanne does, and that's all that matters."

Andrew sighed as he slid his sword into its sheath. "I hope so."

La Hire and the other captains led the advance guard down the hill toward the plain. Andrew marched between La Hire and Captain de Xaintrailles. La Hire had insisted on it. "You should be one of the first to see whatever you put in the Maiden's mind," he said.

Andrew didn't reply.

The morning dew soaked their boots and helped to muffle the sound of their footfalls. The air was still. Not even a bird greeted them with a call.

Andrew thought the English barricade seemed farther away than it had looked from the top of the hill.

"The Battle of the Herrings was near the town of Patay only four months ago," La Hire said softly. "Fastolf was the victor there."

"Will this be payback?" Andrew asked him.

"Payback?" La Hire repeated, as if he had never heard the word before.

Andrew realized he probably hadn't. "Never mind," he said.

"Brace yourselves," whispered Captain de Xaintrailles. "Shields up."

Andrew heard the sounds of the soldiers' shields being gently raised. The barricade was closer. If the English archers were hiding nearby and prepared, then the arrows would come buzzing at them at any moment.

But the arrows did not come as they reached the barricade. It looked half finished. Andrew thought that with a single hard push, it might even collapse.

"The English are not prepared," La Hire whispered as they moved past it.

"Or it could be a trick," de Xaintrailles said.

CHAPTER TWENTY-EIGHT

The tension felt like electricity in the air all around them. They entered the path that cut through some woods. Birds sang to the left and the right. There was no hint of anyone hiding anywhere.

"This is unbearable," said de Xaintrailles. "Send a scout ahead."

La Hire nodded. He began to turn and signal one of the soldiers when Andrew made a quick decision.

"I will go," he said.

"I do not think the Maiden intended that," said La Hire.

Andrew began to unbuckle his armor. "I am a fast runner and smaller than any of your soldiers. I will go." He tossed his armor into the bushes nearby. He felt twenty pounds lighter.

"Brave lad," de Xaintrailles said. He clapped the boy on the shoulder.

"I want to end the suspense," Andrew said, half smiling.

A moment later, he was jogging up the path. He picked up speed, glancing back to see La Hire and the advance guard grow more distant. He hadn't thought about what might happen if he came upon the English. Would they shoot him? Take him prisoner? *Better not to think about it*, he decided.

The woods on both sides of the path seemed to thin out. It looked as if he was coming to another open field. He thought he could see the outline of a village far ahead. Was that Patay? He squinted at the shapes dotting a field ahead. There were hedges and what looked like carts of hay. Had something moved off to the left?

Still there was no sign of the English. Slowing down, he moved off the path into the protection of the trees. He watched for a moment.

The call of a bird caused him to turn. He saw a shaft of sunlight cutting through the trees several yards to his right. A stag stood in the middle of the golden rays. It reminded him of when he and Eve had first arrived. He had seen a deer standing in light just like that. And he felt then that maybe God wanted him in this time for some good purpose.

The stag took a few steps. Andrew saw a jagged scar on its flank.

He realized it was the stag that Jeanne had set free. *What are the chances of that?* he thought.

The stag looked at him. Then, with a nod, it leapt away and darted through the trees into the open field.

Andrew was surprised to hear a man shout. He was even more surprised to see several men with longbows suddenly appear from behind the hedges and carts. They were struggling to get their arrows in place to shoot at the stag. One or two arrows flew but missed the mark. The stag zigzagged and bounded onward, drawing more men out of hiding. Their English accents were unmistakable.

Andrew sprinted to the path. Then he ran with all of his might back to La Hire and the advance guard.

CHAPTER TWENTY-EIGHT

Seeing them up ahead, he put on the afterburners like a marathon racer sprinting to the finish line. He threw himself at Captain de Xaintrailles, who caught him and lowered him to the ground.

The world was spinning as Andrew choked out the word "Found!"

"Get your breath, boy," said the captain.

Andrew sat up and tried to breathe. "The ... English ... are ... just ahead. In ... a clearing."

"Have they set up a blockade? What are they doing?" asked La Hire.

"Hunting ... a ... stag."

La Hire gave orders to one of the soldiers to run back to the other commanders. "Tell them to hurry," he said.

De Xaintrailles pulled out his sword. "Shall we?"

La Hire gave a sharp nod. "*Attack.*"

The Battle of Patay, as it was later called, was won within two hours.

The English archers were completely surprised when the French advance guard came at them. They had expected a slow-marching army later in the day, not a smaller group of fast-running soldiers first thing in the morning. Worse, they had not completed their own preparations for the battle. They were still establishing their positions when the stag drew them out.

Jeanne and her commanders had fooled them in another way. Rather than come as one army straight toward Patay, they had sent companies of soldiers around to the left and the right in a flanking maneuver.

The fierce and feared Captain Fastolf had bounded upon his horse and fled. Captain Talbot was not so fortunate. He was captured and brought before the French commanders.

"You did not think this would happen," the Duke of Alençon said to him.

The captain shrugged. "It is the fortunes of war."

Those fortunes had changed very suddenly for the English in France. Upon hearing that no one was coming to protect them, the English commanders at other fortresses set fire to their strongholds and retreated.

Andrew heard La Hire say it was the French revenge for the Battle of Agincourt.

That evening Andrew was reunited with Eve and Jeanne. He asked the Maiden directly, "Did you know the stag would show me where the English were? Is that why you set it free?"

She gave him a slight smile and said, "How could I know such a thing?"

Andrew never heard what became of the stag.

29

The Dauphin sat on a thick-cushioned chair in front of Jeanne. She was on her knees before him. He had a bored expression on his narrow face.

Eve finally realized what it was about him that bothered her so much. He reminded her of a kid she once knew at school who became whatever the kids around him were. If he was hanging out with nice kids, he was nice. If he hung around the bullies, he acted like a bully. Right now, the Dauphin was hanging around the snobs.

Jeanne traveled with her company and the Duke of Alençon to the home of Georges de La Trémoille. His castle was only twenty-five miles east of Orléans at Sully-sur-Loire. She had gone from the wonderful victory celebrations in Orléans to the stifling indifference of the men who bent the Dauphin's mind whichever way it suited them.

Jeanne pleaded with anyone who would listen: "Talbot is captured. Fastolf is fleeing. The English army is scattered. We must march to Paris *now* and reclaim it for France."

In response, Jeanne was given various excuses.

"Wait. The time is not right."

"We do not have the funds."

"Our soldiers must rest."

"It is too risky."

"Speak first with the Dauphin."

"Do *not* speak with the Dauphin."

"You said he must be crowned in Reims next."

Other commanders, like the duke, sided with Jeanne. "Let us march to Paris!" he affirmed.

But they needed the Dauphin's blessing to do anything.

Now the Dauphin sat in his chair, with his bored expression, and said to Jeanne in a sympathetic tone, "I pity you because of the suffering you have had to endure. Rest now."

Eve felt like screaming.

Jeanne's eyes glistened. She did not work for the Dauphin's praise, but she was clearly upset by his response.

"Gentle Dauphin," she said, "you will receive the whole of your kingdom. You will be crowned."

Eve saw the briefest exchange of looks between the Dauphin and La Trémoille, who stood nearby.

Jeanne waited for a response. When the Dauphin said no more, she asked, "Gentle Dauphin, will you recognize the valiant work done by Arthur de Richemont at the Battle of Patay?"

The Dauphin flinched.

CHAPTER TWENTY-NINE

"Whatever has divided you in the past should be forgiven," Jeanne continued. "If nothing else, it would help to reunite the kingdom under you as king."

Eve saw the blood rush to La Trémoille's face. He pressed his lips together so tightly that they became thin white stripes.

"Yes, of course," the Dauphin said. "De Richemont is forgiven. But he will *never* again serve as a member of my court. I will find another way to reward him."

La Trémoille's lips twisted into a smirk.

This was his influence at work, Eve knew. She had come to learn that he disliked anyone and anything that would lessen his hold on the Dauphin. This mere maiden from Domrémy was no match for him. He would get rid of Jeanne if he could. That much was an open secret. But he would not dare. Not now. He would use her for as long as he could, then dispose of her when he was finished.

Eve had seen the royal announcements about the French army's successes. The Dauphin gave credit to Jeanne and the commanders of royal blood. But he did not mention Jean de Dunois, La Hire, Captain de Xaintrailles, or any of the other great men who had fought alongside Jeanne.

It's none of my business, Eve reminded herself, then fumed, *But it is my business*.

It had become her business after spending so much time with Jeanne. There was something about the Maiden that made Eve want to help her, no matter what.

When Eve first arrived in this time, her greatest desire had been to go home again. Now she did not want to leave Jeanne's side. Was it loyalty? Survival? No. It was more than any of those things. Eve had come to love Jeanne, which was a big surprise. It was a struggle for Eve to love anyone. To love meant to trust—and trust was something that her life's experience had taught her not to do.

Eve knew that Jeanne was in greater trouble now than she had ever been on any battlefield. Jeanne was now famous all over the known world. People in other countries were arguing over whether she had been sent by God or the devil. She was compared to David fighting against Goliath, and even the donkey's jaw that Samson had used to wipe out the Philistines. Jeanne's exploits were on the lips of every traveling merchant, monk, sailor, and soldier. Word had spread to the largest cities and the smallest villages. Men like La Trémoille hated her for it.

It made sense to attack Paris while the French army was strong. Paris was the heart of the nation. To reclaim it would be the final victory. But if Jeanne was not allowed to do that, then surely she should be allowed to accompany the Dauphin to Reims to officially crown him as king.

Eve admitted to Andrew that she didn't understand the importance of Reims, since the Dauphin had already declared himself the king after his father had died seven years before.

It was Brother Pasquerel who gave her the answer.

CHAPTER TWENTY-NINE

"Reims is where our kings have been crowned for hundreds of years," he said. "The sacred anointing with holy oil is the seal of the king's true position. And the cathedral is glorious, a place of majesty. It is the only place truly worthy of a king."

Eve heard stories that the English wanted to have a coronation of their own in Paris. Not the Dauphin's coronation, of course. The English Duke of Bedford planned to crown Henry the Sixth there. Henry was a mere boy, but that didn't matter. Bedford wanted a dramatic show to rally the people of Paris against the Dauphin. The event would also remind everyone of the role the Dauphin had played in the murder of the Duke of Burgundy's father.

"The Dauphin denies killing the father of the Duke of Burgundy," Eve told Andrew one evening.

"It's like a Shakespeare play," Andrew observed.

"I think it *was* a Shakespeare play," Eve said.

The one person who seemed thrilled by Jeanne's determination was the wily Archbishop of Reims. Eve did not like the Archbishop. There was something about his eyes that bugged her. They darted back and forth too quickly, like an animal looking for prey.

Jeanne once admitted that she thought the Archbishop was "very clever and sharp-minded but loves money a little too much."

Brother Pasquerel added that the Archbishop was a shrewd man who knew how to play every situation to his advantage. He was allied with La Trémoille and manipulated the Dauphin behind the scenes. On the other hand, he had put up a lot of his own money to defend Orléans. Though some said he did this not because he believed in Jeanne's mission but because he knew it would help his standing with the Dauphin.

After Jeanne's indecisive audience with the Dauphin, she went off to pray. She dismissed Eve to go off somewhere to walk, think, and play.

Eve considered taking a walk but dreaded going outside. The castle sat like an island in the middle of a large moat. The only way in or out was a single bridge that led to the town. It was too much effort.

She had to admit that the castles and manor houses all began to look the same to her. They were impressive from the outside. But inside, the hallways and rooms were variations of the same kinds of walls and floors.

After considering climbing one of the towers, she decided to look for Andrew. She stood in a large corridor and tried to remember in which direction his room was. Suddenly he ran around the corner and nearly fell when he saw her.

"We're leaving," he puffed breathlessly.

"What? Why?" she asked.

"The Dauphin has finally agreed to be crowned in Reims."

CHAPTER TWENTY-NINE

In a day, everyone was on the move—not only Jeanne and her company but the Dauphin and his court. Carriages, wagons, and horses were loaded. They departed Sully-sur-Loire in a long procession destined for the town of Gien, more than seventy miles southeast.

"Why Gien?" Eve asked Andrew. "Isn't that the wrong direction from Reims?"

"The Dauphin has a castle there. And that's where the army is being assembled," he explained.

The castle at Gien was a relatively modest one and was soon overrun by tailors, seamstresses, and various craftsmen tasked with making sure everything was prepared for the coronation. Even Jeanne wanted her banner cleaned for the occasion.

Queen Yolande arrived, explaining that her daughter Marie was the Dauphin's wife and had to be properly dressed. Eve was glad to see the queen again, though it now meant running errands for her and other ladies of the royal court. She had no idea that people could spend so much time discussing the lengths of a robe or the shoulder width of a cloak or the choice of satin versus silk. It became dizzying trying to understand whether this red would match that gold or this yellow would go with that purple.

"There is one thing you can do for me," Queen Yolande said to her one afternoon while they were comparing fabrics. "The royal jeweler is here, working on a broach for the Dauphin's cape. Please ask him when he expects to have it finished."

Eve wandered the castle until she found someone to direct her to the royal jeweler's residence. It was in an unfamiliar wing. She entered a large room where men and women were busy cutting and sewing fabrics at long tables. In a small room in a back corner, she found an old man hunched over a desk with his back to the door. As Eve came around to his side, she saw his fingers working carefully with a thin silver tool. He used the tool to press a purple gem into a gold case.

"Pardon me," Eve said.

The man grunted at her.

"Queen Yolande wants to know about the broach for the Dauphin's cape," she said.

"This afternoon," he said in a low growl.

Eve had been watching the delicate way the man worked with the gem. Then her gaze went up to his face. She staggered back.

It was Simon Le Fantôme.

"Oh," she said, startled.

The old man's hair had been cut and his beard trimmed. And he now looked distinguished in a deep-blue robe. But even from the side, Eve thought his narrow face seemed aged and sickly pale.

He did not even glance up at her. His eyes were fixed on his work. "You are still here," he said.

She wasn't sure what he meant. "Where else would I be?" she asked.

He grunted again. "Did your 'servant' warn you about the assassin?" he asked.

CHAPTER TWENTY-NINE

"You are the only assassin I am worried about," Eve said, then rushed out of the room.

In the hallway, she leaned against a wall and tried to calm herself. Seeing Simon was the last thing she had expected. She had hoped he'd gone away for good.

She took a few deep breaths, then pushed away from the wall. She had almost forgotten why she was there. She shook her head sharply and ran off to deliver the message to Queen Yolande.

And then she was going to have a talk with Andrew.

Eve eventually found Andrew in the small closet that served as his bedroom. She told him about her unhappy surprise.

He looked sheepishly at her.

She realized what the look meant. "You *knew* he was here?" she asked. "Why didn't you tell me?"

"I didn't want you to worry."

"I would rather be worried than surprised," she said, frowning.

Andrew looked at her. She could tell he was thinking about something else.

"What?" she asked.

"There's something else I haven't told you."

"What?"

"I saw Simon in Orléans after the battle. He was wounded."

"A lot of people were," Eve said.

"He said something to me that I haven't been able to figure out."

"He says a lot of things that no one can figure out."

"Will you stop throwing my words back at me?" Andrew snapped. "This is why I didn't tell you about Simon."

"Say something that makes sense!" Eve complained.

Andrew gazed at her, then rushed to get the words out. "Simon was delirious. He said he had been wounded trying to stop the Ravager from killing Jeanne. And then he said the words *Hope Springs*."

Eve flinched. "Why?"

"I wish I knew."

"You must have mentioned it to him," she offered.

Andrew shook his head. "I've thought it over. I never did."

"Then ...?"

Andrew groaned. "I think he said 'Hope Springs' because ... he knows."

"Knows what?"

"That it's where we came from."

Eve was doubtful. "How can he know that?"

Andrew shrugged. "That's the hard part. I think ... he's from the future. Maybe he's from Hope Springs."

"No," she said. "That isn't possible."

"Just like it isn't possible that we're from a town called Hope Springs in the future? Or that we're now living in medieval France?"

CHAPTER TWENTY-NINE

Eve shook her head.

"He saw us arrive," Andrew reminded her.

"Okay," Eve said, trying to sound reasonable. "If he is from Hope Springs, then why not say so?"

"He's been here for *years*," Andrew said. He held up a finger like a teacher presenting a theory. "Maybe that's why he's crazy. He's been here too long. Alfred Virtue said it might happen, right?"

"He didn't say it *would* happen."

"But it *could* happen."

"And what? He's forgotten all about his life in the future? How could anyone forget something like that?"

Andrew frowned. "It was only a guess."

Eve felt drained talking about Simon. "Next time, *warn* me when you know he's around," she said. "No more secrets."

"No more secrets," Andrew said.

The Dauphin was committed to going to Reims. But he wanted assurances that there would be no English assassination attempts or uprisings by those still allied to the English. He would be traveling through two hundred miles of territory that had been loyal to England, after all. It could be dangerous.

Jeanne didn't share his worry. She assured him that God would give the French the power to push back the English and their supporters. To ease his mind, she sent letters to officials and nobility alike, appealing to them to give their hearts to God and their loyalty to the Dauphin. She invited them to the coronation in Reims to personally witness God's blessing on their sovereign.

She also wrote, by her own hand, a letter to the dreaded Duke of Burgundy. The duke was England's greatest ally in France and hated the Dauphin. In the letter, Jeanne begged him to embrace the will of the King of Heaven. "Come to the coronation of France's *true* king," she wrote.

Guyenne and Ambleville, the Maiden's heralds, were kept very busy.

The Dauphin also sent letters. He assured the town governors along the way to Reims that he would forget any past betrayals if they gave him their obedience now. If not, they should expect trouble.

For all of their efforts, Jeanne still felt as if the Dauphin was stalling. She became exasperated and left the castle, choosing to sleep in the fields alone.

"Should I not go with her?" Eve asked Brother Pasquerel.

"Why?" he said. "She'll come back when the Dauphin finally gets on his horse to ride to Reims."

It happened two days later.

Eve would never forget the sight of the Dauphin sitting on his royal steed at the head of his vast army. Following

CHAPTER TWENTY-NINE

Jeanne's victory at Patay, men came from all over France to join the coming fight.

"Where are we supposed to be in the procession?" Eve asked Andrew as she looked at the long line of people.

"Somewhere back here," he said.

Together they walked past the Dauphin, with Jeanne next to him. The Duke of Alençon was on her other side. Eve saw the Archbishop of Reims, then Dunois, La Hire, and Captain de Xaintrailles. La Trémoille was there but had been relegated to a spot even farther back and didn't look happy about it.

Finally they came to a collection of wagons carrying provisions for the commanders and nobility. Jean d'Aulon sat at the head of one and offered them both a hand up so they could join him. Eve turned to look at the spectacle behind them. The column of soldiers stretched on and on, out of sight.

It was more than a day's march to the first city: Auxerre. The people there had taken the Dauphin's earlier letter very seriously and responded quickly with money and supplies to keep the peace. Against Jeanne's wishes, the Dauphin's army stayed there for three days before moving on.

The people of Troyes, on the other hand, were not happy to open their gates to the Dauphin. The city had sworn allegiance to the Duke of Burgundy and the English. It also had a garrison of several hundred soldiers ready to fight for that allegiance.

The Dauphin's commanders had to admit that attacking the city would be difficult, and a siege would be fruitless. The city was self-sufficient.

"They could stubbornly resist us for months," La Hire said.

"What are we to do?" asked the Dauphin.

They were considering their options when the officials of Troyes sent a new message. Before they would discuss terms, the officials had asked a friar named Richard to meet with Jeanne. They wanted assurances from the friar that Jeanne was not actually a witch who had put a spell on the Dauphin.

Eve heard rumors that Friar Richard had been a preacher in Paris and had cried out against Jeanne. He had called her the "Antichrist" who would come to destroy the people's souls. Now it looked as if he was going to find out if she really was.

The city gate opened, and Friar Richard walked out. He was a large man with a long beard. As he trekked across the field, he kept crossing himself and sprinkling holy water as if he were about to encounter a demon.

"This is ridiculous," Eve said.

"Do not be offended," Jeanne said. "I have heard good things about him. He preaches good works to prepare for the return of our Lord Jesus. They say the people of Paris were so moved by him that they gave up their sinful practices and turned to holiness."

CHAPTER TWENTY-NINE

Friar Richard came nearer.

"You see?" Jeanne called out to him. "I will not fly away. Approach boldly."

He took her hands and looked into her eyes. A smile slowly worked its way onto his grim, bearded face. "This is a time of marvels," he said. "I see in you great hope. The Lord Himself will establish His kingdom in France. And you, dear child, must lead His people to deliver the Holy Sepulchre in Jerusalem. Then we shall see the consummation of the ages."

"As God wills it," Jeanne said.

She invited Friar Richard to her tent. There, she dictated a letter to the officials in Troyes. "As a servant of the King of Heaven, I urge the people in Troyes to give obedience to the Dauphin." She turned to Friar Richard. "One way or the other, the Dauphin, as king, will enter all the cities and towns of France to bring peace."

Friar Richard took the letter back to Troyes. The city's council did not reply. Worse, they would not admit the Dauphin's own messengers through the gates.

"What are they up to?" La Hire demanded.

Dunois said, "The garrison in the town supports the English. The council is afraid of what the soldiers will do if they allow the Dauphin in."

The Duke of Alençon added, "Or they may be awaiting reinforcements from the Burgundians. Either way, they are stalling."

The Dauphin looked unhappy. "We cannot allow such a strong fortress to stand against us," he said. "They will cut off our return."

"We should attack them right away," La Hire said.

Dunois disagreed. "The city is too well defended."

Jeanne finally proclaimed, "Enough of this. We must not delay on a course that God has set. By love, by force, or by courage, I will lead the Dauphin through the gates of Troyes."

She climbed onto her horse and rode to the town gate. The soldiers followed. Jeanne gave the command to prepare for battle. The people of Troyes gathered on the walls to watch as archers were put into position. Brushwood was placed against the walls, and guns were mounted and aimed. Under blazing torches, Jeanne worked the men tirelessly through the night, giving the townspeople a clear view of what would come if they didn't surrender.

By dawn, Jeanne was adorned in her white armor. She was helped onto her horse and handed her banner. She lifted it up and turned slowly, giving every appearance that she was about to give orders to attack.

With loud shouts from the wall, the gates of Troyes were opened. Out came the town officials—and Friar Richard.

Much later, the story was told that Friar Richard had urged the city officials to surrender. He explained that Jeanne was a holy maiden, a true saint, who could bring

CHAPTER TWENTY-NINE

all of the king's soldiers flying over the walls if it pleased her to do so. The officials were convinced to yield.

As promised, Jeanne led the Dauphin through the gates.

The soldiers of the garrison slipped away through another gate.

The bells rang for Sunday Mass, and Jeanne marched straight to the church.

News of the surrender of Troyes helped cleared the way to Reims. Town after town declared its loyalty to the Dauphin.

Twelve miles from Reims, the entire procession stopped at the fortress at Sept-Saulx. It had been built by ancestors of the Archbishop of Reims. The Archbishop invited them to rest there while he rode ahead to reclaim his place at the Reims cathedral, something he hadn't been able to do for more than a dozen years. It was his role to welcome the new king, even though they had been traveling together. Meanwhile, dignitaries from Reims came and went from the fortress, all assuring the Dauphin of their loyalty.

Eve went with Jeanne to a chapel in Sept-Saulx, and they prayed together. Afterward, Jeanne lingered, sitting quietly. Eve assumed she wanted to be alone, but Jeanne asked her to stay.

Eve sat down next to her on a wooden bench. The altar was lit by two candles in red holders. The crucifix had an amber glow.

Jeanne suddenly said, "I have come so far in such a short time. A peasant girl who has become …" She couldn't seem to think of the word to describe herself. "Still, there are those who believe I am simple-minded. Perhaps that is what will undo me. My simple trust. Only those who trust can be betrayed."

"I understand," Eve said.

Jeanne continued. "Now that we are so close to the fulfillment of what was promised, I fear that the simplicity of my mission will change. The affairs of state and the intrigues of politics will become a loud scream to me, drowning out my Voices. Then what will become of me?"

"God knows," Eve whispered.

Jeanne nodded. "Yes, my angel. God knows. I am safe with you nearby." She patted Eve's leg and added, "Watch over Andrew."

Eve was surprised. "Why?"

"Combat can be intoxicating for young men," said Jeanne. "They drink it in. It becomes part of them. It can impair their judgment."

"Has it done that to you?" Eve asked.

Jeanne was silent for a moment. "The taste of that drink does not appeal to me. If I could have completed this mission by methods of peace, I would have been happier. For soldiers of either side to die in their sins grieves me."

CHAPTER TWENTY-NINE

Jeanne stood up, genuflected, then walked to the door. "I must find Brother Pasquerel," she said. "I must give my confession."

Eve watched her go with a deep sadness. Once the Dauphin was crowned, they would be even closer to the end.

30

The Dauphin, with Jeanne at his side, led the long procession to Reims. Eve sat behind Andrew on a slow-moving nag of a horse. It smelled of dirt and manure and constantly flicked flies with its tail.

Peasants had trod the road for them along great fields of poppies and lilies. As the procession passed by, the people cheered and waved white handkerchiefs. Fathers and mothers lifted children up to be blessed—not by the Dauphin, but by Jeanne.

The procession came to the high road along the bank of the Vesle River. It was evening, and the view of the city was breathtaking. People lined the ramparts waving flags. Bells rang and cannons boomed. The drawbridge at the southern gate lowered, and the iron gates lifted up to greet them.

Inside, the crowds lined the streets with blazing torches. Townspeople waved hats and handkerchiefs. Trumpets and drums sounded in great fanfare. "Noel! Noel! Peace to our king!" the people shouted, but Eve noticed that their eyes were on Jeanne.

When the procession reached the cathedral steps, the Archbishop and the city's dignitaries formally received the Dauphin. The moon bathed the majestic building in pale white light. Eve looked in awe at its size. Twin towers stood like giant sentries. Three high arches crowned the front doors. Magnificent pillars and spires reached heavenward. A large stained-glass window, rounded and webbed like a giant flower, glowed with red and blue and purple from the burning lights within. After many speeches were made, the Dauphin was taken inside for private prayer.

The Dauphin and Jeanne were invited to stay at the Archbishop's luxurious palace. As Eve left to accompany Jeanne to her room, she gave Andrew an apologetic look. He was going to stay with Jean d'Aulon and the other squires in the servants' quarters.

According to tradition, the coronation had to take place on a Sunday. That was the next day. While the dignitaries slept, the cathedral workers spent the night making preparations. Eve had thought she might sleep a few hours, but the pounding of hammers woke her up.

As it turned out, no one around Jeanne slept anyway. Her armor and sword had to be polished. Tunics and tights were stitched and cleaned. Jeanne's banner was given another fresh scrubbing. Formal dresses were delivered, but Jeanne insisted on wearing her armor. Brother

CHAPTER THIRTY

Pasquerel and Friar Richard, who had accompanied them from Troyes, were ready to hear Jeanne's confession or offer her spiritual counsel at any time.

Louis de Coutes arrived from Chinon that night. Guillaume Bellier had given Louis formal permission to remain with Jeanne for as long as she needed him.

An even greater surprise came when Jeanne's father, Jacques, arrived at the palace door. He had traveled from Domrémy for the coronation. They had not seen each other since Jeanne set off for Vaucouleurs seven months ago. Eve thought Jacques had the hard look of a man who had spent his life working the fields. She could not imagine him being soft and emotional. Yet he embraced his daughter with great tenderness and a few tears.

Jeanne returned his embrace not as a young peasant girl but with the confidence of an adult. They moved off to talk in private. Eve later heard that Jacques had spoken to Jeanne about petitioning the newly crowned king to ease the tax burden on the people of Domrémy.

Jeanne offered to pay for her father's lodging in Reims. But she discovered that the people of Reims had covered the cost in her honor. They had also given Jacques a beautiful horse to take home.

Eve didn't know at what hour she was finally able to lie down. All she knew was that her eyes were open when the light of dawn shone through the small windows of her room.

Soon, a new commotion of activity began. Mass was celebrated and then a light meal was served. There was also a final check to make sure everything was ready for the coronation that would start at nine o'clock. Eve was given a dress of heavy red velvet to wear.

Jeanne wore her white armor, which had been polished to a radiant sheen. Over the armor was draped a cape of blue and red, woven through with gold thread. Jeanne's cropped hair had been combed back but still fell forward in places, as if invisible fingers moved it around.

"You look beautiful," Eve said.

Jeanne tearfully waved her away. "Go. Find Andrew. Seek out a place to watch the ceremony."

"Why are you crying?" Eve asked.

"Because my gentle Dauphin will finally be crowned king today," she replied.

Venturing into the city square, Eve was shocked to find the crowds already waving flags and pennants. She guessed they had been gathering all night. She squeezed into the cathedral, which was overflowing with nobility, officials, soldiers, and toward the rear, peasants.

The cathedral itself was more than Eve could take it. It must have been three or four hundred feet long with pillars lining each side. Vast arches rose up to smaller pillars and a vaulted ceiling of stone ribs. At the far end of the cathedral was an arrangement of stained-glass windows, dominated

CHAPTER THIRTY

by one that looked like a kaleidoscope. Beneath that were more arches and stained-glassed images framed by two walls with countless statues of the saints. An ornate altar stood in the center beneath all the arches and windows. Banners hung to greet the nobles. The smell of hundreds and hundreds of flowers filled the air.

"Eve!"

The voice was a distant call amid the noise and echoes. She looked around.

"Eve!"

Her gaze followed the sound up to a gallery above her on the right. Andrew was there waving.

She held her arms up in a "What are you doing up there?" gesture.

Pointing with exaggerated effort, Andrew shouted. "Go under to the door! On the other side of the pillars. I'll meet you!"

Eve pushed her way through the crowd and came to a long aisle on the back side of the pillars. She had to maneuver through another crush of people as she searched for a door. There were a lot of doors. Then Andrew appeared at one and beckoned her over.

"This is crazy," she said, breathless.

He pulled her through the doorway and closed it quickly. They stood in a small passage, with dim light from somewhere above.

"You look good," he said, gesturing to her dress.

She curtsied as a thank you.

She saw that Andrew was wearing a bright-green tunic with gold stitching around the neck, and a belt of gold ringlets. The leggings were a dark-blue wool.

"These leggings itch," he said. "Come on."

They followed a narrow passage to yet more passages.

"This reminds me of the secret corridors at Chinon," Eve said.

"It was Friar Richard's idea to come here," Andrew explained. "There are upper galleries that'll give us a great view of the ceremony."

They eventually came to a staircase that ascended higher and higher, until they reached another door that led to an upper aisle. Guards were posted there. One of them recognized Andrew. With a nod, he signaled them to go through.

Friar Richard was right. The gallery overlooked the main part of the cathedral and the altar where the ceremony would take place.

It was hard for Eve to keep up with all the traditions of the day. She learned from Andrew that Gilles de Rais and three other knights from a nearby abbey had retrieved an ancient flask of holy oil at six o'clock that morning. The sacred oil of Clovis, named after the first French king, would be used to anoint the Dauphin as the true king of France. In a separate ceremony, the four knights escorted a bare-footed abbot to the cathedral and handed the oil over to the Archbishop.

Andrew learned about this firsthand because he was dragged out of bed to help with it all.

CHAPTER THIRTY

Following the delivery of the oil, the constable of France brought the royal sword to the altar. A specially chosen sword bearer held up the sword for the rest of the coronation.

Andrew nudged Eve. "Look." He pointed down at the crowd.

Eve looked, unsure of what she was supposed to see. Then she spotted Simon Le Fantôme standing in the midst of the crowd. Instead of watching the ceremony, he was staring up at them. Eve shivered.

Trumpets sounded, echoing loudly throughout the cathedral. The Dauphin had arrived, along with his generals, clergy, officials, and delegates. They walked slowly toward the altar as a choir sang. The Dauphin was wearing a dark robe, open at his chest and shoulders to reveal a dull-colored shirt. He had a sad expression on his face. Eve thought he looked scrawny compared to the nobles around him.

Jeanne also entered the cathedral carrying her standard. She reached the sanctuary, bowed to the altar, then stood a few feet away from the Dauphin. Her face was alight with joy.

The Archbishop offered prayers, and then the Dauphin took his place in front of the altar and swore an oath to serve Christ and the nation. A pair of royal shoes was then placed on his feet, and he knelt down.

The Duke of Alençon was given the royal sword. With it, he knighted the Dauphin. Golden spurs were added to the royal shoes.

The Archbishop then led a solemn High Mass with prayers and psalms. Afterward, he anointed the Dauphin's head, chest, shoulders, and arms with the sacred oil and loudly consecrated the Dauphin to God.

The people shouted in response, "Noel! Noel!"

The Dauphin was then dressed in royal robes and given a ring and scepter. Then the crown was placed on his head.

Again, the people shouted, "Noel! Noel!"

Even now, Eve thought the Dauphin looked small and miserable as he sat down on an ornately carved throne. From this moment on, he was no longer the Dauphin. He was Charles the Seventh, the true king of France.

Eve saw Jeanne kneel at the king's feet. She said something to him, then began to weep.

The ceremony continued with various lords and peers of France pledging their loyalty to their sovereign. Then, to Eve's surprise, a group of them lifted the throne high on their shoulders so that everyone could see their newly crowned king. Deafening shouts and cheers went up, along with chants of "Long live the king!"

The trumpets sounded again. The king and the nobles marched out of the cathedral in a grand procession. Five hours after the coronation ceremony had started, it came to a rousing end.

Eve turned to Andrew. He was leaning forward on the rail of the gallery, looking intently at the crowd below.

"Is Simon still there?" Eve asked.

"I'm not looking at him. I'm looking at ..." Andrew gasped, then stepped back from the rail. "It's him. I'm sure it's him."

"Who?" asked Eve.

"The assassin!" Andrew whispered. He moved forward again and pointed at a man wearing a dark cloak and hood at the edge of the crowd. "It's Vincent the Ravager."

From where she stood, it was hard for Eve to get a clear look at the man's face. He was making his way through the jostling crowd. Suddenly the hood slipped back. Eve saw a strap circling a shaved head. The man turned slightly. The strap was attached to an eye patch. A chill went down her spine.

"He can't be the only man in France with an eye patch," she said, hoping it wasn't him.

"He is the only man in the cathedral who was watching *Simon* instead of the coronation," Andrew said.

Eve looked again. As the man with the eye patch moved with the crowd, he was staring at Simon. Simon didn't seem to notice. His head was turned to the altar. He was watching Jeanne.

Eve kept her eyes on the Ravager. "Why is he here? Who did he come to kill?"

"I have to go down and warn Simon," Andrew said and sprinted away.

"Be careful!" Eve said.

But Andrew was already beyond hearing her.

Eve looked over the railing. Both Simon and the one-eyed man were out of her sight. She couldn't see Andrew at all. She wasn't even sure where he had gone. Now all she could think to do was warn Jeanne. With the crush of the coronation crowds, it wouldn't be an easy task.

Though the coronation ceremony had finished, the celebrations were just beginning. The king rode through the streets to hear the praises of the townspeople. Then he presented gifts to the Archbishop and the various officials of Reims for their services. He honored a few men with new positions. Gilles de Rais was made the marshal of France. La Trémoille was given the title of count. The Laval brothers were also made counts. La Hire was given as much land in the county of Longueville as he could reclaim from the English. Jeanne remained with the king at every moment.

With great difficulty, Eve drifted through the crowd, watching for Andrew or Simon or even the one-eyed assassin.

Later, the Archbishop hosted a lavish meal in an ancient banquet hall at his palace. Tradition demanded that the royal table stretch into the street to encourage feasting throughout the town. A bronze stag was placed in one of the courtyards and filled with wine so the people could drink from it.

CHAPTER THIRTY

Eve prayed that Andrew would suddenly appear and all would be well. But he didn't.

What could she do? There was no police station where she could file a missing-person's report. What could anyone do to help?

She kept her eye on Jeanne, who stayed near the king throughout the day. Once or twice she tried to get close enough to warn Jeanne, but the king's guards blocked her way. Even explaining that she was Jeanne's "angel" didn't make a difference. And screaming didn't seem like an option, since there was no imminent danger. For all Eve knew, the assassin was nothing more than a story a madman had made up and Andrew had believed.

It was late afternoon now. Eve watched as Jeanne slipped away from the king's table and disappeared behind a decorative screen. Maybe this was her chance.

She circled around to a doorway, but one of the Archbishop's guards stopped her. She explained that she was the Archbishop's guest and Jeanne's servant. The guard recognized her and allowed her through. It took a few minutes, but she eventually found her way back to Jeanne's bedroom.

Jeanne was sitting in a chair next to her bed. She had taken off her armor and dropped it on the floor at her feet. She now rubbed her face wearily.

"Jeanne—," Eve began to say, but Jeanne spoke instead.

"The Duke of Burgundy sent a delegation to the coronation today. They claim the duke wants to negotiate a peace. The king desires to meet with all of his advisers first thing tomorrow." Jeanne sighed a deep and weary sigh. "I fear it is a ploy. I am weary of ploys. I fear that hidden within all these ploys, there is treason."

She tilted her head back and closed her eyes.

Eve opened her mouth, but suddenly she didn't have the heart to bring up Andrew or Simon. What would be the point? What could Jeanne do? Even telling her about the assassin would not help. Jeanne had thrown herself into far more dangerous situations. And as it was, Eve knew that Jeanne would not die by an assassin's hand.

She realized it would be better for her to talk to Jean d'Aulon. Or Louis.

She nodded to herself. *That's what I'll do.*

Jeanne was looking at her. "Are you all right, my angel?"

"Are you going out again to the celebrations?" Eve asked.

"No. I want to stay here," she said. "I need to pray."

"Good."

"Why?" asked Jeanne.

"It may not be safe . . . out there," Eve said.

Jeanne gave a small giggle. "It is never safe for me out there. And yet I am safe. God is my shield."

"Please pray that God will shield the rest of us," Eve said.

"Dear Evangeline, have you not seen that He already does?"

CHAPTER THIRTY

Throughout the evening and into the night, Eve exhausted herself searching for Andrew. It seemed impossible, with the city lights reduced to torches and bonfires. She was a stranger to Reims and knew nothing about its many streets or what might await her down the dark alleyways.

She approached random people to ask if they'd seen a boy in a bright-green tunic. They looked at her as if she was insane. How could they possibly spot a twelve-year-old boy in such a crowd? She then asked passersby about a man with a patch over his eye. No one had seen him.

She eventually found Louis outside the Archbishop's palace. He was alarmed to hear what had happened and promised to search for Andrew himself. He would also tell Jean d'Aulon if their paths crossed.

The revelries showed no sign of ending. Eve began to despair. There was no explaining Andrew's disappearance except to think that something bad had happened.

Finally Eve decided to go back to the cathedral to pray. Maybe stopping for a few moments would clear her wearied brain.

As she approached the steps to the great cathedral doors, she saw a dark figure in a long robe. The figure was pacing slowly back and forth in the half light of a torch. It could have been a monk, but her instincts told her it wasn't. The figure turned as she reached the top step. It was Simon.

She froze, just out of arm's reach.

"Where is Andrew?" she demanded.

"Your friend is a fool," said the old man.

"Where is he?" she asked again.

Simon looked annoyed. "By what manner of ignorance did he think he could approach a known assassin?"

Eve felt her heart lurch. "He went to find *you*. To warn you."

"The only warning I received was a message from Vincent," he said.

Eve swallowed hard. "What message?"

"He has taken Andrew hostage."

31

Eve slumped down on the cathedral step. "He kidnapped Andrew?"

Simon stood over her. "Vincent has been watching me. He has seen Andrew in my company. He assumed Andrew is worth a ransom to me."

Eve put her face in her hands. She couldn't believe this was happening. "What kind of ransom?"

"He wants something from me."

Eve looked up. "What does he want?"

"Something of mine that he has sought for years."

A realization came to her. "So he was here for you? He did not come to kill Jeanne?"

"He came for her. But he also came for me."

"You have to save Andrew. Give him what he wants," Eve said.

Simon snorted. "What is the boy to me?"

"He was trying to save you!"

Simon seemed unimpressed. "He failed."

"What if the Ravager kills him?"

Simon gave a slight shrug. "A man like Vincent can do far worse things than that. Terrible things."

"What are you talking about? What does he want?" Eve could not imagine it was worth more than Andrew's life.

"It is not for you or anyone else to know," he replied.

Eve was stunned. "You will let Andrew die?"

Simon walked down a few steps until he was eye level with Eve. "I do not believe he will kill Andrew."

"Why should I believe you?" Eve asked, avoiding his gaze.

"What other choice do you have?" the old man said.

"Then what is going to happen if you will not give the Ravager what he wants?" she asked.

"I will rescue your friend."

"How? Do you know where he is?"

"They are well on their way to Paris by now," said Simon. "It is there the assassin will want me to hand over my treasure."

Eve stood up. Knowing *where* Andrew was gave her hope. "Paris? How far is that?"

"Two or three days' journey."

"Can we run after them? If we catch up, then—"

Simon interrupted her. "Vincent is half a day ahead of us by now. He will not travel a normal route. He will take the boy somewhere secret."

"And then what?" she asked.

"I will send a message that I will pay a ransom."

CHAPTER THIRTY-ONE

"Where will you send the message?"

"There is an inn that we both know," Simon replied.

Eve clenched her fists. "Then we have to go there."

Simon shook his head. "Not *we*, child. *Me*."

"I am going with you."

"Oh? You will leave your Maiden?" His question was like a taunt. "What will become of her without her angel?" Simon asked.

"Do not tease me," Eve said.

"It is a serious question," Simon said. "Will she live without you? Will she live at all?"

Eve looked at him. Suddenly she had the feeling that he already knew the answer. "Do you know?"

He gazed at her without expression. "An imbecile can venture a guess," he said.

"Not a guess. Do you *know*?" She wondered if Andrew had been right about Simon.

He blinked, then shook his head as if he was trying to rid himself of an unwanted thought.

Eve's temper flared. "What if I say to you *Hope Springs*?"

Simon looked as if she had struck him.

"What does Hope Springs mean to you?" she persisted. "You said those words to Andrew. Why? Does it have something to do with the Ravager?"

Simon staggered back, his heel catching on a step. He stumbled and caught himself. "You are an enchantress!" he shouted. "You are sowing evil seeds in my mind!"

A man and a woman passing on the street stopped to look at him, then her. He glared at them.

Eve came closer to him than she had ever dared. "Help Andrew, and we will help you. We will figure out why words like *Hope Springs* mean something to you."

"I do not know what you are talking about!" Simon protested in a harsh voice. Then he turned and rushed away, fading into the shadows of the cathedral.

Eve's legs felt as if they were about to give out. She sat down on the step again.

"Are you all right?"

Eve turned to the sound of the voice. Louis was ascending the cathedral steps. His hand was on his sword.

"Andrew was taken hostage by the Ravager," she said.

Louis groaned.

Eve lowered her head. "And I just chased away the one person who can help him."

Louis convinced Eve that the only thing she could do now was get some rest.

He escorted her back to the Archbishop's palace. Music and laughter echoed down the many passages. She thanked Louis and went back to Jeanne's bedroom. Jeanne was sound asleep.

Stepping back into the hallway, she gently closed the door again.

CHAPTER THIRTY-ONE

There's nothing I can do, she thought. She slumped wearily to the floor. Cradling her arms on her knees, she put her head down. She was too drained to think.

A hand touched her shoulder.

She looked up into the face of Brother Pasquerel. "Are you well?" he asked.

Eve burst into tears.

Brother Pasquerel sat down next to her on the floor. He listened as she explained about Andrew.

"What could Simon Le Fantôme possibly have that the Ravager would kidnap Andrew to get?" he asked after she had finished.

"I wish I knew," Eve said.

"I will pray for wisdom," said Brother Pasquerel. "Given the right moment, we should also tell Jeanne. But I am afraid there is little any of us can do at the moment."

Eve felt tears coming again.

"It is difficult for me to say, but I am afraid you will have to trust Simon."

Eve looked at him. "Trust him?"

"The Ravager is part of Simon's world. He knows that world better than anyone. Simon may be the only hope you have of getting Andrew back."

Eve suddenly sat up in bed. She had fallen asleep, but for how long?

Throwing aside the bed covers, she went to the door and peeked into the adjoining room. Jeanne was not in her bed. The light streaming through the window suggested it was well into the morning.

She changed quickly from her nightdress into the plain red dress Jeanne had given her. She laced up her boots and ventured out to find the dining room where she'd had breakfast the day before. It was empty. The table was cleared of dishes, except a single bowl of fruit in the center.

Eve was about to leave when a door opened on the opposite side of the room.

Louis walked in. He saw her and smiled. "You are awake."

"Where is everyone?"

"I am here," he said, as if that should be enough.

"Where is Jeanne?"

Louis plucked an apple from the bowl on the table. "She is in a meeting with the king and his council. The Duke of Burgundy wants to negotiate a truce with King Charles." Louis took a bite of the apple. "The king wants to meet with the duke's emissaries. Some of us think it is a trick. The Duke of Burgundy and the Duke of Bedford are stalling for time while they build up their reinforcements in Paris."

"Paris?" Eve asked. "Are we going to Paris?"

"Not while the king meets with the duke's men." Louis looked at the apple, then took another bite. "Jeanne and La Hire have protested. The king will not listen."

CHAPTER THIRTY-ONE

"I will go to Paris on my own," she said.

Louis asked, "Do you know how to get there? Do you have money or food for the journey? How will you survive?"

Eve could not answer.

"Even if you reached Paris, how do you think you would find Andrew?"

Eve pouted. "I thought you were going to help me."

Louis put the half-eaten apple on the table and came to her. "I am. I know where Simon is. He has not left the city yet. I must say, he does not behave like a man who intends to go anywhere anytime soon."

"What am I to do in the meantime?"

"Be patient and wait," he said.

Eve felt as if she was going mad. Waiting was torture for her.

The king delayed his decision about Paris.

Louis reported to Eve that Simon was going about his usual business at the garrison as if nothing had happened.

Jeanne filled her time riding through the streets of Reims to meet the citizens. Though, privately she told Eve that she was becoming irritated by the king's indecision. She also felt as if the king and his counselors no longer cared what she thought. Now that Charles was officially the king of France, they assumed her mission was over.

Eve was with Jeanne one afternoon when she caught the Archbishop coming from a meeting with the king. The king had not changed his mind, he told her.

Jeanne said, "Then by God's grace, I wish the king would allow me to put aside this fighting and return to my father and mother. I would prefer the peace of keeping sheep with my sister and brothers. *They* will rejoice to see me."

The Archbishop merely smiled and walked on.

Three days later, the king announced that he and the Duke of Burgundy had agreed upon a truce of fifteen days. After this time, they would resume negotiations in the city of Arras.

"*Fifteen days!*" roared La Hire. "It is enough time for the English and the Burgundians to join forces in Paris."

King Charles was determined to give every chance for peace. Meanwhile, he would honor an age-old tradition for newly crowned kings: he would travel with his entire court to the Abbey of Saint-Marcoul de Corbeny. The abbey was founded by Saint Marcoul, who, according to tradition, could cure the evil disease of scrofula by the power of his touch. It was believed that the kings of France were given this same miraculous ability if they went to the abbey after being crowned.

"Sick people are waiting for me to come cure them," the king said.

Jeanne asked to accompany him. He agreed.

CHAPTER THIRTY-ONE

Eve did not want to leave Reims. She worried about all of the things that might happen to Andrew. Finally she told Louis that she wanted to talk to Simon again.

Louis led the way through Reims to the garrison near the castle. Many of the king's soldiers were quartered there. Simon was brushing a horse as they approached. He glanced over and saw Louis first.

"This is not the time for our fencing lesson, is it?" Simon asked.

Eve now understood how Louis had been able to keep an eye on him.

Louis nodded to Eve.

Simon looked at her and said, "What does she want?" He went back to brushing the horse.

"Is this all you plan to do?" Eve asked.

"I have not heard from the Ravager," he said. "What else am I to do until then? March to Paris? Search every house, room, and hovel until I find him?"

"You said something about an inn," Eve reminded him.

The old man turned to her. "I know what you are thinking. It will not work. If I go there before I am summoned, the Ravager will know it. Do you want him to kill your friend?" He spun back to the horse. "There is nothing to do but wait."

That night, Eve did not eat. She could not stomach any food while she thought about Andrew. Where was the Ravager keeping him? Was he tied up? Beaten? Was he fed?

Jeanne pushed her own plate away. A servant quickly appeared and took the plate from the table. Her glass of wine was refilled. Jeanne ignored it.

"Brother Pasquerel told me about Andrew," Jeanne said to Eve. "I have been praying for him."

"There must be something else we can do," Eve said.

"I would go to Paris myself to rescue him, but the king forbids me from venturing near that city. So I will go with him to the Abbey of Saint-Marcoul de Corbeny. I bid you come with me. To lose one of my angels is grievous. To lose both would break my heart."

Eve struggled with Jeanne's invitation to go to the abbey. Louis insisted that she go. He assured her he would stay at Reims and watch Simon. If anything happened, he would send a messenger immediately.

Eve unhappily agreed and traveled the next day to the abbey with Jeanne and the king's court. There, the king worshiped and presented offerings at the shrine of Saint Marcoul. Then he touched those afflicted with scrofula. Jeanne offered prayers and blessings for the many who asked. Eve got the impression that the king was not pleased to be upstaged by the Maiden.

News reached them that many of the nearby towns were pledging their loyalty to the king of France. King

CHAPTER THIRTY-ONE

Charles decided to visit each town to pay his respects. Eve found herself taken farther and farther away from Paris—and Andrew.

She wondered why she couldn't ask the king to help. Couldn't he send his soldiers to Paris to find Andrew?

She put the question to Jeanne, who answered that the king was as helpless as anyone. "Paris is in the hands of the Duke of Burgundy. Until the king decides to trust me rather than him, there is nothing we can do."

32

One night, Eve found Jeanne praying in the chapel of yet another manor house where they had been staying. Eve could not even remember which town they were in. Was it Soissons or Château-Thierry?

Eve knelt next to the Maiden and prayed for Andrew. Then she sat back and wished God would do *something*. Andrew believed that God had brought them to this time for a purpose. Was that it? Being held hostage by an assassin? Was this her purpose: sitting and waiting yet again for an indecisive king?

"The Voices are not clear," Jeanne said.

The statement yanked Eve away from her own thoughts. "What did you say?"

Jeanne sat on the bench next to Eve. "All along I have felt as if my Voices have been holding my hand, guiding me as a child. But now they have let go. They want me to decide for myself."

"Decide what?" Eve asked.

"What my place is now that the Dauphin has become the king," she replied. "You see? He has been my mission. Now I must think differently about why I am here. My Voices have gone silent, so I will think on my own."

Eve wondered if this had something to do with what she was just thinking about. "What if there is no purpose?" she asked.

Jeanne took Eve's hand in hers. "There is always a purpose with God. It is against His very nature not to have a purpose."

Eve thought about that for a moment. "What do you think your purpose is now?" she asked.

"To attack Paris."

Eve knew there was little hope of a lasting truce between King Charles and the Dukes of Burgundy and Bedford. She was now hearing that Bedford had been sending insulting messages to the king. He also made scathing comments about that "deranged woman who dresses like a man."

In recent days, there were a couple of close calls when the French and English armies came very near each other but backed off from actual combat.

Though more towns around Paris pledged their allegiance to King Charles, the city itself remained in the clutches of Bedford. The English duke did exactly what

CHAPTER THIRTY-TWO

the French king's commanders had said: he reinforced his army in Paris.

One morning, yet another inflammatory letter arrived from Bedford. The king was finally offended enough to act. He ordered his commanders to claim the village of Montépilloy, just north of Paris. Jeanne joined them, but only as an adviser to the king.

When the French army arrived at Montépilloy, they discovered that the English had fortified their positions with their usual rows of sharpened stakes.

Jeanne urged the commanders to attack, but they were ordered to wait for permission from the king. The French and English forces sat stewing in the sweltering August heat.

King Charles arrived with La Trémoille. Together they rode around the battlefield and then left again that evening.

Reinforcements had arrived that afternoon from Reims. They brought with them complaints from the citizens of that city that the English would invade now that the king had left. Jeanne sent a letter promising that she would never abandon them, no matter what truces were made.

Louis and Simon were among the reinforcements. Eve was pleased to see Louis again, and asked if any word had come from Vincent the Ravager. The answer was no.

Eve insisted that Louis take her to Simon. They found him on the far edge of the camp.

"Why have you not heard from the Ravager?" Eve asked the old man.

"It is a war of nerves," Simon told her. "Much as you see with these two armies. Though we know who are the true masters."

"Who?" asked Louis.

"The Duke of Bedford has made the Duke of Burgundy the official governor of Paris," Simon replied, then mocked, "The king giveth, and the dukes taketh away."

The next morning, Jeanne took to her horse and rode along the front lines, waving her banner and daring the English to attack.

They did not take the bait.

She dictated a letter to the English commander, warning him to prepare for battle. She did not receive a response.

Then, without warning, the English gave up Montépilloy and marched back to Paris. The entire confrontation was a waste of time.

"They are gathering their forces to strengthen the city," said the Duke of Alençon. "Paris will be harder to invade."

Jeanne was unconcerned. "Let them go to Paris. I would rather fight there than sit idly here for days on end."

CHAPTER THIRTY-TWO

Eve watched the English army march away. "I wonder if I could sneak into Paris with them," she said to Louis.

"Do not think about it," he warned.

She went to see Simon again. "We are so close," she said. "Why not go to Paris now to save Andrew?"

"Why are you bothering me?" Simon grumbled. "I have told you that *we* will not save Andrew. You are a wicked child. You must be patient. There are forces at work that you know nothing about. We will get closer to Paris before you expect it."

Furiously she asked, "But what happens to Andrew while we wait?"

"He also waits," said Simon.

"In what condition?" she asked. "What is happening to him?"

33

What is happening to me? Andrew wondered. He knelt on the cold stone floor and winced. There was little left of his leggings to protect his knees. Both the cloth and his skin were worn away. The open sores burned.

He grabbed a cloth, and a terrible stinging came back to his palms and fingers. Some of the blisters that had formed now broke open again.

"Work!" a raspy voice commanded. It was an innkeeper by the name of Henri, though Vincent the Ravager always called him Scab. The name suited him. Hardly a skeleton of a man, Henri had red scars on his forehead and cheeks that made his face look like a wound that would never heal.

Andrew grabbed the rag again and, ignoring the pain, scrubbed at the floor. He knew what would happen if he didn't. Scab owned a fat walking stick and liked to use it. If Andrew had a question, the answer was a blow with the stick. If he did a job poorly, a blow with the stick. If he did a job well, a blow with the stick. If he did nothing at all, a blow with the stick.

Scrubbing was Andrew's morning job. Later he would pick up cups and plates from drunken townspeople. Often he would have to mop up after soldiers who had gotten sick on the floor.

A large, dog-faced woman with dark whiskers on her upper lip forced Andrew to help her in the crude kitchen. He helped her make stew in a large pot, boil water in the kettle, cut vegetables, and make the bread. He never heard the woman's name. She never offered it.

The August heat outside and the infernal heat in the kitchen made Andrew thirsty. He was allowed one cup of stagnant water a day.

At night he was chained to an iron ring in the wall in a back room. The woman threw him some moldy bread to eat. There all alone, he often wanted to cry. But he refused. He didn't want to give Scab or anyone else the satisfaction of knowing he had done it.

One day as Vincent the Ravager watched Andrew work, he said, "You still have hope. That's good. Always have hope. Hope is what keeps people alive right up until I kill them. I enjoy the look on my victims' faces when hope drains away with their lives."

Andrew blamed himself for his situation. He had gone to warn Simon about Vincent, but then he saw the assassin leave the cathedral in the massive crowd. He stupidly decided to follow the man and find out where

CHAPTER THIRTY-THREE

he was staying. He thought, unwisely, that he could report back to Simon.

Vincent had disappeared around a corner, and Andrew dashed after him. Vincent was waiting.

A hard knock on the head left Andrew stunned enough that he could be dragged off. He was taken to a storehouse, maybe. Somewhere with barrels and boxes. He was tied and gagged and put in a crate.

"Kick and scream all you want," Vincent had said in a voice like broken glass. "No one will hear you. But if you do make a commotion, you will suffer."

Andrew wasn't sure how many hours he was stuffed in the crate. Nor could he figure out where the crate was being moved to after it was loaded on a wagon. Vincent let him out from time to time, when they were away from anyone who might ask why a boy was tied up and locked in a crate.

They eventually came to a noisy city. Andrew was unpacked and put in the care of Scab until Vincent returned. Scab didn't ask where Vincent was going. Vincent never said. Andrew got the impression they had done this sort of thing before.

He overheard enough conversations to learn that he was in Paris. He also learned that he was being kept at an inn called the Captain's Cat. He was never allowed to venture beyond the door to look outside. He didn't know in what part of the city the inn was located.

Andrew looked for ways to escape, but Scab watched him constantly by day and chained him up at night. Scab warned him, "Do not let me catch you trying to escape. Do not let me catch you *looking* like you want to escape. Otherwise, you will not live long enough to know what the consequences will be."

Andrew believed him.

Scab only ever called Andrew "boy" or "the hostage." He often talked about how things would change once Andrew was ransomed. Andrew tried to explain that it was a waste of time. No one would ransom him.

Scab hit him on the back with the stick and said, "Why would you say such a thing? Do you want to die now? The ransom is the only thing that is keeping you alive."

Andrew kept his mouth shut after that. He said so little that most of the customers thought he was a mute. Instead, he listened.

It was from the soldiers that he heard rumors about the "pretender to the throne." They meant King Charles. They also talked about the "French peasant girl." Andrew figured they were talking about Jeanne. He heard them say how the Duke of Bedford and the Duke of Burgundy were making fools of them with all of their talk of a peace treaty.

Andrew overheard some of the peasants say that the French were marching near Paris. Then came rumors that they weren't.

The Duke of Bedford kept reminding the people of Paris that Charles was not really the son of the king. Worse

CHAPTER THIRTY-THREE

than that, he had murdered the Duke of Burgundy's father. *Killed him in cold blood!* the duke cried.

All of this talk seemed to make Vincent the Ravager angrier. He and Scab had been convinced that Jeanne would march the French army straight into Paris after the coronation. Simon would come with them and hand over his treasure in exchange for Andrew. It was as simple as that. But the French army did not attack. Maybe it never would. Vincent would have to contact Simon and arrange another way to meet up for the exchange.

Andrew wished he knew his history better. Had Jeanne ever marched into Paris? Was this where they burned her at the stake? He didn't know.

Then the night before, Andrew had heard one soldier say that Jeanne and the Duke of Alençon had captured the town of Saint-Denis. It was only four miles outside Paris. The same soldier suggested that more French captains were on the march to Paris with hundreds, if not thousands, of soldiers. King Charles himself might even show up.

Vincent sat at a table, drank watered-down ale, and told Scab to beware. "Simon is bound to show up now, with or without the stone."

Andrew had heard the words *ransom* and even *treasure* before, but nothing about a stone. *What stone?*

Scab argued that Simon would not hand over something so precious. Not for Andrew, not for anybody. "Why should he care what happens to this boy?" He hooked a thumb at Andrew, who was scraping something disgusting from the leg of a chair.

"There is something special about the boy," Vincent said. "I do not know what, but it is enough for me to believe that Simon will come."

"If he does not?" asked Scab.

Vincent sneered. "Then we will sell him as a slave."

Chained again to the wall, Andrew spent the night thinking about all he had heard.

La Hire had told Andrew that Simon was married to Vincent's sister. They fought over a treasure. The sister was killed. Simon stabbed Vincent in the eye. For what? A treasure they called a stone. Was it a jewel?

What if it was a stone like the Radiant Stone? What if Simon had used it to travel back in time from the future? Maybe even from Hope Springs?

In the middle of the night, it all seemed possible. In the light of day, it all seemed stupid.

The next day, Andrew became aware of a lot of noise outside. It sounded like the whole city of Paris was in an uproar. There were shouts that the peasant Maiden was leading an attack *today*—a *holy* day—the Feast of the Nativity of the Blessed Virgin! Who but a witch would attack a city on such a day?

Even Scab took offense, and he was as profane as a man could be.

The cannon fire started around noon. Scab went to the door of the inn. "Look at them scamper," he said, laughing.

CHAPTER THIRTY-THREE

Andrew picked up a few cups near the front window. People were rushing into the streets. Soldiers ran in every direction.

Later came screams and shouts. "They have broken through the gate! All is lost!"

When he heard the thunderous sounds of more cannons, Andrew stopped scrubbing the floor and looked up.

Scab swung the stick at him. "Do your work!"

Andrew ducked.

Scab grabbed Andrew by the nape of the neck and dragged him to the small back room.

"I know what you are thinking," Scab growled. He fastened a manacle around Andrew's ankle and chained it to the ring on the wall.

"It does not matter who comes. You will not escape," he said. He walked out, pulling the wooden door closed behind him.

Andrew waited. It sounded as if Scab had gone to the front door again. Maybe he had left the inn to see the fighting for himself.

Looking down at the manacle, Andrew thought, *One way or another, I'm going to get out of here.*

He twisted his foot around, trying to squeeze it through the iron. The rough edge of the manacle scraped at his skin. He tried to grease his foot with some lard he'd been given to eat the day before. Slowly, painfully the foot was slipping through.

There was a loud crash. It was so loud that Andrew thought a cannon ball had hit the inn. He hadn't thought that he might die in a barrage. He heard voices and shouts from somewhere. He worked harder to get his foot free. He scraped at the skin, hoping the blood would make his foot more slippery.

Then the door burst open. Scab stumbled into the room with a look of utter disgust on his face. He hit the ground as dead weight.

A man in monk's robes stepped through the doorway and kicked the fallen villain. In the man's right hand was a bloody knife. He pushed back his hood.

"Simon," Andrew said, relieved.

"Where is Vincent?" Simon asked.

"Not here."

Simon looked at him, clearly annoyed. "I hope this was not a waste of my time."

34

This is nothing like the Battle of Orléans, Eve thought as she watched the campaign for Paris from a supply wagon on the hill.

The trumpets had sounded at noon. At the western gate of Saint-Honoré, Jeanne had raised her banner to lead the soldiers. Her courage was endless. Stones and debris were thrown down at them from the ramparts. Arrows and bolts buzzed. Artillery fire went back and forth.

Then the gate opened, and both English and Burgundian soldiers streamed out to protect the city. Savage hand-to-hand combat followed, with the terrifying noise of crashing armor and pain-filled cries. Neither side made any progress in one direction or another. Then the trumpets sounded for the enemy soldiers to retreat into the city.

Jeanne met with the commanders. "You must cross the moats now. Go forward, my friends! Do not give up the assault until Paris is taken!"

As they had done at Orléans, the soldiers now needed to fill the moat with wood. As many bundles as they could find. The soldiers dashed down to the moat, throwing more and more wood into the water below. But the water flowed from the river Seine and carried the wood away.

The English and Burgundian soldiers on the walls released more arrows and bolts. Jeanne urged her soldiers on. "Victory is yours if you persevere!" she shouted.

She also shouted to her enemies on the wall. "Surrender and be saved, or suffer death without mercy when we enter the city!"

Hour after hour this went on. Jeanne finally dismounted and raced for the wall to cheer on the flagging French soldiers. Her page Raymond stayed by her side, carrying her banner.

Eve watched, clutching her hands to her stomach, trying to calm her anxiety. Her eyes went to the top of the wall. She watched with horror as one of the English archers aimed his crossbow at Jeanne. He was clearly following her as she moved. Then she stopped to say something to Raymond. The archer released his bolt.

Eve screamed as Jeanne clutched her leg and dropped to the ground.

Another bolt flew, and Raymond fell. Eve was sure he was dead. But then the poor young man suddenly sat up. He tore off his helmet and clawed at the bolt sticking

CHAPTER THIRTY-FOUR

out of his foot. He had just caught hold of the bolt with both hands when another arrow buzzed from the wall. It struck him between the eyes. He slammed lifeless to the ground.

Captain de Gaucourt and another captain named Guichard Bournel scrambled to Jeanne. De Gaucort shouted, "Sound the retreat! Retreat!"

Eve took a few steps. Then before she realized what she was doing, she found herself running as fast as she could to Jeanne.

Meanwhile, another soldier picked up Jeanne's banner to rally the scattered men. It was too late. The trumpets sounded the signal to retreat.

De Gaucourt and Bournel put Jeanne's arms around their shoulders and lifted her up. The end of the bolt stuck out of her thigh. They began to move her off the battlefield.

She fought against them. "No! We must take the city! More wood into the moat! We can make a bridge!"

"The *king* commands you to retreat," Bournel begged. "The Duke of Alençon pleads with you to come away."

Eve was now running with them.

"Help me!" Captain de Gaucourt gasped to Eve. "Speak to her!"

Eve pleaded, "You must retreat, Jeanne!"

Jeanne pulled her arms from the shoulders of the two men. She limped a few steps for the city gate. "In God's name, the city can be taken!"

Bournel's face turned crimson with rage. "Stubborn girl! You risk all our lives!" He grabbed Jeanne's arm and yanked her back.

Jeanne fought him, but he was too strong. He pinned her arms with his. De Gaucourt reached down and grabbed her kicking legs.

"Please, do not hurt her!" Eve cried out.

With Jeanne firmly in their grip, the two men carried her away from the gate and joined the retreating troops.

Jeanne screamed the entire way, her cheeks covered with hot, angry tears.

Eve wept to see her so upset. And she wept because she had lost all hope of rescuing Andrew.

At the camp, Eve watched as a physician dressed Jeanne's wound. The crossbow bolt had split the piece of armor meant to protect her leg and had sunk into her thigh.

Jeanne was heartbroken. "We would have won the city if only we had kept fighting."

Eve stayed with her throughout the night, pressing a cool wet rag to her forehead. Jeanne thrashed in her sleep, crying out words that made no sense.

The next morning, Jeanne was on her feet again, wincing as she struggled to get into her armor. "Victory will be ours today," she told Eve. "Where is my duke?"

CHAPTER THIRTY-FOUR

Eve helped Jeanne to the tent of the Duke of Alençon. The commanders were all there to plan the next attack. They were divided as usual, with some arguing to delay a renewed attack. An hour passed. Then another.

Jeanne sat in a chair off to the side, excluded from the debate. Eve saw her fidget. Finally she hit the palms of her hands against the arms of the chair. "I beg you to stop arguing! Claim the victory that awaits you!"

A messenger arrived with news that a party of nobles was approaching the camp. One was the Baron de Montmorency. He was well known for switching his allegiance from the English and Burgundians to King Charles. With him were the Duke of Bar and the Duke of Clermont.

"This is good news!" Jeanne said. "Surely they have brought reinforcements to take Paris."

The three noblemen entered the tent, dressed as if they were going to a formal ball.

The captains gave them a respectful bow.

"What goes on here?" the baron asked.

"We are discussing our attack," the Duke of Alençon explained.

"Attack? There will be no attack today or any other day," declared the Duke of Clermont. "Have you not heard? King Charles has commanded that you retreat!"

The commanders were incensed. Jeanne tried to rise from her chair but fell back again.

"If you will not obey," the duke continued, "the king has commanded us to stop you by force. All of you must return to his court at Saint-Denis immediately."

Jeanne groaned as she sunk farther into the chair. "It cannot be."

The Duke of Alençon glared at the three nobles.

"See to it!" the baron said. Then the three turned and walked out.

The Duke of Alençon knelt next to Jeanne. "Ride with me to Saint-Denis."

She gave him a painful nod.

The Maiden tried to hide her agony as she and the captains rode the two miles on horseback to King Charles at the Abbey of Saint-Denis. Eve sat behind Jeanne and tried not to add to her pain by holding on to her too tightly.

When they arrived, King Charles was sitting at a table in a small room. La Trémoille stood nearby. Both men watched silently as the commanders entered and bowed. Jeanne held on to Eve and managed to lower herself into an awkward kneeling position.

The king rose to his feet. In a sudden outburst, he shouted, "*Fifteen hundred men* were killed! Fifteen hundred!"

His gaze went to Jeanne. For only a second, it softened. Then it hardened again.

Jeanne remained kneeling, her face twisted in pain. "Gentle Dauphin," she started to say, but the king held up his hand.

CHAPTER THIRTY-FOUR

"Why do you call me Dauphin? Am I not your king?" he asked.

"You are," she replied. "Forgive me. I forgot myself."

"You forget much, my valiant warrior," he said. He scanned the faces of his commanders. "We are *ceasing* our campaign."

La Trémoille smirked at them.

"Paris is included in our new truce with the Duke of Burgundy," the king announced. "It is not our city to take."

"A new truce, my king?" the Duke of Alençon asked.

"It awaits my signature," he replied. "There is no need for further battle."

Jeanne fell forward and crawled to the king. She wrapped her arms around his knees. "I beg you, gentle king! If this is so, then please allow me to remove this armor and go home."

The king patted her head. "Alas, no, Jeanne. We have need of you yet."

Eve couldn't bear to hear anymore. She wanted to scream at the king, "I know how this will end! You will blame her for *your* mistakes. You will betray her and make her suffer for daring to speak for God!"

Instead, Eve waited silently. She could not leave Jeanne to struggle out of that room.

Eve helped Jeanne to a bedroom the king had provided for her. Jeanne did not speak as she limped through the abbey. She did not look at Eve as she eased onto the bed.

Eve slipped out of the room. She wanted to find a chapel where she could pray for Jeanne and Andrew. She wanted to ask God to ease her anger.

She followed one passage, then another. It was an abbey. How hard could it be to find a chapel?

Rounding a corner, she ran straight into Simon Le Fantôme. She did a double take. He was wearing something that looked like a monk's robe.

"What are you doing?" she snapped. "Why are you dressed like that?"

"You are a rude little girl," Simon said. He grabbed her arm and began to drag her down the hallway.

She struggled against him. "Let go or I'll scream."

"Scream. I do not care." He pushed open a door with his free hand and shoved her through.

She stumbled and was about to turn on him when she saw something out of the corner of her eye.

It was Andrew. He was sitting on a small bed, holding a bowl with bandaged hands. Brother Pasquerel sat in a chair next to him, putting ointment on his bloodied knees and feet.

Eve let out a little squeak, then put her hands to her mouth.

Andrew smiled at her. "Hi." His voice was weak.

CHAPTER THIRTY-FOUR

She ran over to him and hugged him so hard that the soup in his bowl splashed onto his chest.

"Careful!" he said.

Eve knelt next to the bed. "What happened? How did you get away?"

Andrew nodded toward the door. "Simon went to kill Vincent and found me instead."

They turned to the doorway, but Simon was gone.

"Simon sneaked into Paris in disguise," Andrew explained to Eve. "He was supposed to join up with an underground movement of Carmelite monks. Their plan was to wait until a French attack started. Then they would run around the city claiming that the French army had broken through. They spread rumors that the French would kill them all if they didn't surrender. They had rebels ready to fight inside the gates."

Eve was astonished. She wondered if Jeanne knew.

"It was working," Andrew said. "The officials were discussing their surrender. But then our army retreated."

"I think I know who sounded the retreat," Eve said. "La Trémoille. Except he hid behind some noblemen."

"That was too bad. They were very close to capturing the city," said Andrew.

"If Paris fell, the English would have lost France," Brother Pasquerel said as he dabbed at Andrew's wounds.

"La Trémoille is no friend to the king," Eve said bitterly.

Andrew nodded. "Simon told me that La Trémoille is on the side of the English. Or the Burgundians. Or maybe himself. He convinces the king to do things that undermine putting France back into his hands."

Eve saw how pale Andrew's face was. His cheekbones stuck out more, probably from lack of food. His eyes had dark circles under them.

"I have to tell you something about Simon's *treasure*," he said, trying to wink at Eve.

"Not now," said Brother Pasquerel. With a grunt, he got to his feet. "You need food and rest."

Eve stood up. "He is right. We can talk about treasure later."

Andrew frowned. "But it is important."

"So is your health," Brother Pasquerel said. He nodded for Eve to leave as he took the bowl and sat it on a bedside table. He gently pushed Andrew to get him to lie down and then tucked him in.

As she closed the door behind her, Eve heard Andrew yawn loudly and say, "But I am not tired."

Eve later found Jeanne in a small chapel in a remote part of the abbey.

Eve entered as quietly as she could. Jeanne was on her knees at the altar. Her hands were clasped in prayer. Eve

CHAPTER THIRTY-FOUR

glanced at the altar, surprised by what she saw there. She knelt next to Jeanne and said a few prayers of her own. Then the two sat on a rough wooden pew together.

In a soft whisper, Eve told Jeanne about Andrew and what she'd heard about La Trémoille.

Jeanne looked at her. With a forced smile she said, "I did not lose Paris because of La Trémoille. I lost it because I did not have both of my angels with me."

"Jeanne, please. You have to be careful with La Trémoille," Eve said.

"I must be careful with everyone," Jeanne said quietly. She was silent for a moment, looking at her calloused hands in her lap. She sighed deeply. "Sweet Evangeline, my Voices have gone silent. I hear only the clamor of the king and his council. What am I to do? I have nothing to offer their world of politics."

Eve's heart ached. "I will not leave you again."

Jeanne nodded to the altar and said bravely, "I have made an offering to Our Lady Mary. I have vowed to follow my king and do as he commands."

Eve suspected that Jeanne was trying to sound positive, but the fire had gone out of her voice. Jeanne stood up slowly, gave a slight bow, and limped out of the chapel.

Eve rose and followed, glancing back at the altar.

Jeanne had placed all of her armor there.

35

The retreat from Paris had wrecked the morale of everyone who had fought so hard for King Charles. Everyone, that is, except Charles himself and La Trémoille.

Few now doubted that La Trémoille was manipulating the king to his own ends. Many wondered why. There were whispers that La Trémoille had been bribed by either the Duke of Burgundy or the Duke of Bedford—or both.

The king announced that he and his court would be on the move again. He included Jeanne, Eve, and Andrew in his plans. He led his vast court around Paris to the east and then south.

"We are going home to the Loire valley," he said happily.

Eve wondered which home in the valley the king meant. He had a lot of them.

The Duke of Alençon assembled an army of his own to strike into the territories that once belonged to his family. He asked the king to allow Jeanne to go with him. The king and his council refused.

"For you to attack on your own is your right as a duke," said La Trémoille. "For the Maiden to accompany you will be seen as royal approval of your efforts. We must not upset our diplomatic efforts. The king has signed the truce, you know."

Jeanne and the duke offered heartfelt goodbyes to each other. She also bade farewell to the other commanders, who were going their separate ways. Eve suspected Jeanne knew she would never see them again.

Jeanne's brother Pierre, who had been fighting for Jeanne since Orléans, now admitted defeat. "I cannot stay here and watch the king treat you so poorly. I am going back to Domrémy."

Thanking him with a long hug, Jeanne blessed him for his help and sent her love with him to their family.

King Charles commanded Jeanne to rest and fully recover from her various wounds. She unhappily obeyed. Privately she said to Eve that she now feared their drive to reclaim France had been lost.

Over the next several days, the royal court visited the towns of Provins, Courtenay, and Montargis. They even returned to Gien. It was all a blur to Eve.

They finally settled in Bourges, where the king stayed at his residence. Jeanne, Eve, and Andrew lodged at the home of Madame Marguerite La Touroulde, a friend

CHAPTER THIRTY-FIVE

of Queen Marie's. Eve found out that Madame La Touroulde's husband had something to do with managing the king's money.

Madame La Touroulde was an energetic woman in her forties. She was attentive to Jeanne and often riddled her with questions about her life. Jeanne answered politely but vaguely. Eve could tell that she was wary of the woman's motives.

Jeanne was right to feel that way. Eve learned later that Madame La Touroulde would repeat and embellish Jeanne's answers to her socialite friends. She liked to give the impression that she was a *very* close personal friend of Jeanne's.

Eventually Eve realized that Madame La Touroulde was putting Jeanne on display. Guests came to the house to see her, just to say they had done it. A few brought their rosaries for Jeanne to touch and bless. She refused. Their own touches would be as effective as hers, she said.

Madame La Touroulde was also nosy about Eve and Andrew. She quizzed them about where they were from, who their parents were, and how they had become Jeanne's "angels." They tried to answer her questions without really answering at all.

For a while, life was nothing more than a flurry of social encounters and mundane living. After so many adventures, Eve and Andrew both began to feel restless and bored.

Jeanne's wounds, old and new, slowly healed. But Eve noticed that she did not go out into the field to practice with a sword, or even to ride her horse. Instead, she studied Scriptures with Brother Pasquerel and prayed, often for hours.

To Madame La Touroulde's dismay, Jeanne still insisted on wearing a squire's clothes.

After all the battles, Eve thought they had found peace in their lives. She wondered if she would ever return to Hope Springs. The thought made her think of Simon. She remembered her encounter with him on the cathedral steps. She still couldn't believe that he had come from Hope Springs. The odds seemed impossible to her.

She asked Andrew one afternoon what had become of Simon.

"He's disappeared," Andrew replied. "I think he's gone to find Vincent the Ravager."

While Andrew and Eve were in Bourges, a new young man became an ever-present part of their lives. His name was Sir Charles d'Albret. Eve thought he looked familiar, then later realized that he was the one who had held the royal sword at the king's coronation. D'Albret was related to La Trémoille somehow—a half-brother or a nephew or something like that. That made Eve suspicious of him. She wondered if he had been sent to spy on Jeanne or even

CHAPTER THIRTY-FIVE

sabotage her efforts. D'Albret was only in his twenties, but the king put him in charge of the now-shrunken royal army.

"You have work to do," the king told him, then gestured to Jeanne. "You will need her help."

It was October now, and the king wanted d'Albret and Jeanne to reclaim the small town of Saint-Pierre-le-Moûtier. It sounded like busywork to Eve, but Jeanne was excited about the chance to get away from Madame La Touroulde and do something constructive.

Eve had vowed to stay by Jeanne's side. However, Jeanne insisted that she remain behind. Only her squire, Jean d'Aulon, was allowed to accompany her on this new venture.

"You do not need your angels?" Eve asked her.

"This task comes from the king, not my Voices," Jeanne replied.

"You need protection either way," Eve said.

Jeanne laughed. "Jean d'Aulon will give me that."

Off they marched with a modest-sized army. Eve and Andrew waved them on at the town gate. Eve assumed it would be a quick skirmish, and then they'd return. But a week went by, and very little word came back. Then word trickled down to Eve that a messenger had informed the king that the town would not fall easily.

A few days later, a report came that Saint-Pierre-le-Moûtier was taken, thanks to Jeanne's courageous efforts.

Jean d'Aulon returned to Bourges with a wounded foot. He told Eve and Andrew that at one stage of the battle, the army had fully retreated. Jeanne had refused and remained at the moat, trying to build a makeshift bridge to cross it. D'Aulon had raced up to her and asked why she was still there with only a handful of men. She had laughed and said she had *fifty thousand* men at her side. D'Aulon scratched his head. "I counted only five men."

Eve smiled at him. Sometimes the squire didn't understand Jeanne at all.

"What happened then?" Andrew asked.

"She shouted for everyone to 'Lay down wood! Build a bridge! I will not leave this spot until we take the town!' So we did as she said. And we took the town as if we had fifty thousand men with us."

Eve knew it was a repeat of what had happened in Paris. But unlike that campaign, the soldiers obeyed and secured their victory.

When Jeanne eventually returned to Bourges, La Trémoille publicly praised her for adding Saint-Pierre-le-Moûtier to the list of the king's victories. Jeanne replied that she was grateful to have served him.

However, Eve learned that La Trémoille's motives were not pure.

CHAPTER THIRTY-FIVE

"La Trémoille wanted revenge," Andrew told her as they walked in a field outside of Bourges.

"Revenge for what?" Eve asked. She knew that Andrew was now getting information from servants of the council members he'd befriended.

"The town was run by a mercenary named Perrinet Gressart."

The name meant nothing to Eve.

"Gressart works for whoever pays him the most," Andrew explained. "Right now he's on the side of the English and Burgundians. A couple of years ago, he kidnapped La Trémoille and held him prisoner until a big ransom was paid. La Trémoille has never forgiven him. Now Gressart has his own little kingdom, including Saint-Pierre-le-Moûtier. That's why La Trémoille sent Jeanne there."

"It does not seem like much of a revenge," Eve said.

Andrew frowned. "That's just the beginning. He will send Jeanne off to another town in Gressart's area, where the battle will be bigger and harder."

"Is he trying to get her killed?" Eve asked.

"Killed—or captured," Andrew replied, giving her a worried look.

Eve made it a point to stay close to Jeanne in Bourges. If she couldn't protect her in battle, maybe she could protect her there. Eve bristled every time the king or his council summoned Jeanne. The Maiden often returned looking worn out. Eve felt that more and more, the king and his advisers were trying to beat her down. Or worse, she was nothing more than a pet or mascot.

Eve didn't know her history well enough to remember when or how Jeanne was captured.

"I don't remember either," Andrew said. "What difference does it make if we know?"

"We can warn her," Eve told him.

"*Warn* her?" Andrew exclaimed. "We can't mess with history."

Eve stiffened. "I don't care."

Andrew looked stunned. "What? But you're the one who told me that we can't change history, or it will backfire on us—or something like that."

Eve shrugged. "That's what Alfred Virtue said. What if he was wrong?"

"What if he was *right*?" Andrew shook his head. "You once told me that trying to change history is a big mistake. Time fights back. Remember? Alfred Virtue said so!"

"Since when did you become such a rule follower?" she asked, sulking.

Eve knew he was right but couldn't bring herself to admit it. The thought of standing by while Jeanne was captured—and burned at the stake—was too much for her to endure.

CHAPTER THIRTY-FIVE

That afternoon she saw Brother Pasquerel. He was still teaching Jeanne to read and write. Eve asked if he would hear her confession after their class. He happily agreed.

Sitting down with him in the empty chapel, she began trying to remember her sins since her last confession. After he offered her absolution, she lingered.

"Is there something else?" he asked.

"I was wondering ..." She didn't know how to put it into words. "If a person knows that something bad is going to happen to another person and might be able to stop it, should she?"

Brother Pasquerel looked thoughtful, then said, "We are duty bound to save others from trouble if it is within our power."

Eve smiled.

The priest added, "If I can help you with this person, let me know."

"If I can, I will," she said.

Eve learned quickly that castles were cold in November. The rooms were cold, the chairs were cold, the beds were cold, everything was cold. Fires gave warmth only to those standing next to them.

No matter how many layers of clothes she put on, Eve felt like she was shivering constantly as a damp chill soaked into her bones. At night she slept on her cot under a stack of blankets and furs.

She grumbled that at least Andrew could do things to warm up. He was often racing through the woods, hunting for food, chopping wood, and practicing his skills with swords and staff.

Madame La Touroulde took a dim view of girls doing such things. She insisted that Eve become better at needlework and overseeing a proper household. Otherwise, she was invited to recite Scripture and poetry or play parlor games. Some of the games had boards like tic-tac-toe and nine-men's morris and draughts, which was kind of like checkers and chess. Eve learned various card games, too. But being housebound made everyone a little cabin crazy. Jeanne became the most restless.

Friar Richard had become a mainstay at the house. Jeanne had drawn him close as a spiritual adviser, but lately she began to distance herself from him. Not only did he try to position himself as a spiritual authority to the king, but he had assembled a group of women who claimed to see God in human form, wearing a white gown under a red tunic.

"Like Santa Claus," Eve joked to Andrew.

One of the women, named Catherine, claimed that a woman wearing white with a gold mantle came to her in visions. Catherine had left her husband and children to travel through all the towns in France and raise money

CHAPTER THIRTY-FIVE

for the king's army. She demanded that people give her the money, or the woman in white would expose them to shame. It worked. Donations were up. Even the Archbishop of Reims seemed impressed with her.

Catherine was loud and arrogant and insisted that the king should make peace with the Duke of Burgundy.

Jeanne was furious and said to Catherine, "Our king has done more than enough to make peace. The duke is a traitor and should be met with the point of a lance."

Friar Richard slowly turned his loyalty from Jeanne to Catherine.

One night Jeanne confided to Eve that her Voices had told her that Catherine and her "white woman" were frauds. To prove it, she invited Catherine to stay in her room so she might see the white woman for herself.

The test was a failure. The woman did not appear. Catherine made excuses.

Jeanne lost patience with the fake prophetess. "Go home to your husband and children. I will personally tell the king that you are not what you claim to be."

Catherine turned red with anger. "You will *lose* your next battle," she proclaimed.

Later, Friar Richard railed at Jeanne for her accusation, then stopped speaking to her completely.

Jeanne kept her promise and warned the king about both of them.

It did not matter. The king had lost interest. He announced he would be moving yet again to another palace in the west of France. He did not invite Jeanne to join him.

Now that she was no longer near the king, Jeanne relaxed. She was still fiercely devoted to him, but his court and council had worn her down. It helped that Friar Richard and his flock of followers left too.

In a side room that served as a kind of library, Andrew admitted to Eve that he'd been thinking about Hope Springs a lot more lately. It was now late November. He assumed everyone would be celebrating Thanksgiving.

"But they're not," Eve reminded him. "It's still the same time there as when we left. Maybe a few minutes later. I don't know what the formula is."

Andrew sighed. "Technically, Thanksgiving hasn't been invented yet. The Pilgrims won't go to America for another two hundred years."

Eve chuckled. "Here's something else to think about..." She tugged at her hair. "We've been here for months, and my hair has hardly grown. The same with yours. Normally I would need a haircut by now. Why is that?"

"This whole time-travel thing is enough to drive me nuts." He paused, his face alight with a thought. "Hey, what if Simon is nuts because he came from the future but stayed here too long?"

CHAPTER THIRTY-FIVE

"Why would he stay here on purpose?"

"How should I know? Maybe he lost the stone or ..."

"He fell in love and got married," Eve said.

"Or that." Andrew nodded.

"Or maybe he is just crazy, and the stone is just a jewel that Vincent wants to steal," Eve said. She still thought it was too far-fetched that there was another time traveler nearby.

Andrew looked as if he was on the verge of a pout. "It gives me hope."

"I feel a lot better without hope," Eve said, joking.

But it wasn't really a joke. Eve had been so focused on Jeanne that she had given up on ever going back to Hope Springs. She thought about the message she had left for Alfred Virtue at Chinon but dismissed it as a wild fantasy.

The next day, there was a sudden flurry of activity in the house. Jeanne had been summoned to a battle for the town of La Charité. This time she seemed agitated, even worried, about going.

"We are low on gunpowder, arrows, good crossbows, and supplies. We need to take this town," Jeanne explained as Jean d'Aulon helped put on her new suit of armor. "The king has written from Mehun-sur-Yèvre that he cannot send money to help."

"If the attack turns into a siege?" he asked her.

"Then we must pray for help from the nearby towns that are loyal to the king."

Eve began to pack her own things for the journey.

"No, my angel. You must stay here," Jeanne said.

"Why?"

"I will not have you suffer the bitter cold."

"I want to be wherever you are," Eve replied. "How can I protect you if I do not go?"

"By being my eyes and ears here," Jeanne said.

The king was gone, so Eve did not know what she could see or hear that would help Jeanne. But arguing with Jeanne was not an option. So Jeanne marched off to another battle with the Marshal of Sainte-Sévère and Sir Charles d'Albret.

Eve felt sick while Jeanne was gone. Would the Maiden be captured by the English at this battle?

The days turned into a week. And then another week. Then news came that La Charité was under a miserable siege. The townspeople were comfortable enough, but Jeanne's soldiers were dealing with hunger and the numbing cold.

Eve fumed. "Jeanne took Orléans in only four days. How much time did the king give her to take Paris? *One.* Now she is stuck for weeks at some outpost, all because La Trémoille wants revenge."

Meanwhile, Madame La Touroulde decorated the house for *Noël*, as Christmas was called. Holly and ivy were placed in the windows and around the doors. Rushes and herbs were thrown onto the stone floors. Eve

CHAPTER THIRTY-FIVE

wondered when they would set up the Christmas tree, only to remember that the idea hadn't migrated from Germany yet.

The siege at La Charité dragged on until a few days before Christ's Mass. Word came that Jeanne had launched a decisive attack, though it was decisive only in its failure to capture the town. Sainte-Sévère and d'Albret gave up.

So Catherine was right, Eve thought.

Guests arrived at Bourges. Eve was not introduced properly to many of them. She didn't mind. Together she and Andrew joined them to eat, play games, and watch plays that retold the story of the first Christmas or recounted local myths and legends. On Christmas Eve, a large piece of wood—called the Yule log—was brought in and placed in the largest fireplace. It was set ablaze and left to burn while the household went off to three Masses that night.

On Christmas Day, Andrew and Eve went to Mass again. Afterward, they enjoyed a lavish meal that included goose, duck, partridge, rabbit, pheasant, and fish. Goblets of wine, ale, and punch were served.

Later, Andrew was invited outside to play a game called *soule*, which was like a mixture of soccer, rugby, and hockey. It was a violent game that left Andrew with a swollen lip and a few bruises.

The only Christmas present for Eve was the arrival of Jean d'Aulon. Delighted as Eve was to see him, she was disappointed to learn that Jeanne was first going to

Jargeau and then back to Orléans to attend to some kind of business. He also informed both Andrew and Eve that the king was summoning them to Mehun-sur-Yèvre.

"Us?" Andrew asked.

"Do we have to go?" Eve was not happy. Staying near the king without Jeanne was the last thing she wanted to do. Madame La Touroulde's house had become a comfortable home.

"If you refuse, you will miss the honors," d'Aulon said.

"What honors?" asked Andrew.

"The king is going to present Jeanne with an official act of ennoblement."

The act of ennoblement was the king's way of rewarding Jeanne and her entire family with a special rank in the kingdom, as if they had been born with noble blood. They were given a royal crest to use and were relieved of paying taxes.

Eve was happy for Jeanne and said so often when Jeanne arrived from Orléans. Jeanne admitted that she was pleased for her family but did not care about the honor herself.

"Any honor for me comes from serving God," Jeanne said, then smiled. "Besides, I have my banner."

They stayed a couple of months at the king's residence in Mehun-sur-Yèvre. Spring arrived and lifted their spirits. The truce with the Duke of Burgundy had been

CHAPTER THIRTY-FIVE

extended a couple of times. It was now set to end at Easter. Tensions were still evident, but there was nothing to be done. Jeanne wrote letters to friends and supporters who had asked for her help.

Eve caught herself pacing, distracted by the feeling that Jeanne's capture was coming closer and closer.

Andrew refused to give in to despair. Instead, he tried to fill the time with new games. He actually taught the servants how to play baseball.

"Aren't you afraid of changing history?" Eve teased him.

He smiled. "It won't catch on. It isn't violent enough for them."

Another move approached, and they traveled with the king and his court to La Trémoille's castle in the town of Sully-sur-Loire. The castle had become an important stronghold between central France and the northern areas held by the Duke of Burgundy.

Those around Jeanne were miserable. Living under La Trémoille's watchful eye in his own home was an unpleasant idea. Eve imagined there were secret corridors and spies behind every portrait and door.

"That would be so cool!" Andrew exclaimed. And from then on, he checked every panel and large painting for evidence that Eve was right.

They hadn't settled in very long before letters came to Jeanne from Reims. The people were afraid the English were going to invade. Rumors abounded that the Duke of Bedford, who had crowned the very young Henry in

England last November, wanted to do the same at the cathedral in Reims.

Jeanne wrote back to reassure the people that there was nothing to fear if they shut their gates and refused him entrance. "I will deal with the English before they ever reach Reims.

"Compiègne," d'Aulon said after the letter had been sent.

"What about it?" asked Eve.

"The Duke of Bedford has told the Duke of Burgundy that he may have the entire region around Compiègne if he can conquer it."

"Wouldn't that break the truce?" Andrew asked.

"The truce ends at Easter," d'Aulon said. "They have been gathering their army for the moment it does."

The spring brought more sun and rain. It was also as if France was slowly awakening to the idea of fighting again. Those loyal to King Charles had started an uprising in Paris, but it was squashed. Other towns followed, trying to shake the English stranglehold. Most of the attempts failed.

"This is how it will happen," Eve said to Andrew. "The battles will start again, and Jeanne will be taken."

Jeanne paced around Sully. All of her most trusted military friends were off living or fighting in other regions. How was she to assemble another army?

CHAPTER THIRTY-FIVE

Her brother Pierre returned from Domrémy.

"I thought you would need me," he said to Jeanne as they embraced.

Eve felt comforted that Pierre had come back. She hoped he would lift Jeanne's spirits. She needed the help.

King Charles was of no help whatsoever. Either he would not meet with Jeanne, or he would not give her any advice or consent when he did. "Do what you must" was all he would say. He alone seemed to believe that there was a peaceful solution with the Duke of Burgundy and the English.

La Trémoille met with Jeanne quietly, encouraging her to take up the cause of France again. But Eve noticed that he always spoke in a way that would allow him to deny it later. She was convinced that La Trémoille didn't want Jeanne to win anything. He wanted her captured or killed.

One day, Eve found Jeanne was in a state of excitement. "My new army is at Lagny, west of Paris," she said. "One hundred horsemen and over fifty archers and bowmen. All commanded by Captain Bartolomeo Baretta of Lombard. He has gathered Italian soldiers ready to take on the fight."

"Why would the Italians fight for the French?" Eve whispered to Andrew.

"I think Lombard was once part of France," Andrew guessed. "Or maybe they just hate the English."

Jeanne commanded Jean d'Aulon to prepare to depart immediately.

Eve pleaded with her again, "Andrew and I must come with you."

Once again Jeanne said no.

"If you will not let us come to the battle, then *please* take us away from here," Eve begged. "I do not trust La Trémoille."

Jeanne thought it over. "If I can find somewhere safe, I will move you," she said.

In the following days, Eve *really* missed having cell phones and the internet. News about Jeanne came to her slowly. One report confirmed that Jeanne had gone to Lagny to meet her new army. Her commanders were Captain Baretta, a Scot named Hugh Kennedy, and Captain Ambrose de Loré, who had fought with Jeanne at Orléans.

The next report stated that there was an intense battle against the Burgundians outside Lagny. Jeanne and the French forces were victorious.

Another report said there was a problem. The story was that Jeanne had captured a Burgundian captain named d'Arras. He had been held for ransom as part of a prisoner exchange. The exchange went wrong, and d'Arras was given to the people to stand trial. He confessed to his various crimes as a captain and, to the shock of the Burgundians, was immediately beheaded.

The Burgundians were enraged that their esteemed captain was dishonorably executed instead of ransomed. They blamed Jeanne and said it was further proof that she

CHAPTER THIRTY-FIVE

was acting not for God but for the devil. Jeanne denied any wrongdoing.

Another story emerged that in a fit of anger, Jeanne had broken the Sword of Saint Catherine. According to one version, Jeanne had broken the sword across her knee after finding unholy women sneaking into her army's camp. Another version stated that Jeanne had broken the sword over an unholy woman's *head*. Either way, Eve had a hard time believing it.

Meanwhile, the king surprised everyone by sending out a royal letter admitting his own failure to find a peaceful resolution with the Dukes of Bedford and Burgundy. He had done all he could, he said, but the dukes had used his good intentions to deceive him. They had taken advantage of the truce to build up their armies for renewed attacks on the king's territories.

Too little too late, Eve thought.

Jeanne and her army continued on through France. They captured a town called Melun, just south of Paris. Then they circled around Paris to the north and took Senlis. Then Jeanne took a break from the fighting and went on a pilgrimage to the Church of Élincourt, paying homage to Saint Margaret, one of her Voices. After this, there were a few other skirmishes at other towns. Eve needed a map to keep track of them all.

Every day she hoped that Jeanne would send for her and Andrew. She didn't.

One morning Eve felt especially exasperated and went off to find Andrew. Various servants pointed her in different directions. She finally found him near the garrison where the soldiers tasked with protecting the area lived. Andrew was walking across a courtyard when she called out to him. He turned, looking as if she had startled him.

"What are you doing?" she asked.

"Nothing," he said. But he looked uneasy, as if he'd been caught doing something wrong. "Why are you down here?"

"I am worried," Eve said. "We have to find Jeanne."

"*What?*"

"I am so tired of sitting around here waiting."

"Do you know where she is?" he asked.

"No. But we can find out."

He gave her an awkward smile. "I have a *better* idea. We should go back to Chinon."

"Chinon!" Eve exclaimed. "Why?"

Andrew took her arm and drew her off to the side, away from the soldiers. He said softly, "That's where Simon has hidden the stone."

Eve pulled her arm away. "You are kidding me."

Andrew caught hold of her arm again and said, "Come on." He gently tugged at her.

She groaned and walked with him over to a large door. They passed through to the garrison's dining area. Only one soldier sat at a table near the back: Simon Le Fantôme.

CHAPTER THIRTY-FIVE

"No," Eve said and tried to pull back.

"*Please*," Andrew begged, still holding her arm.

Simon looked up at them. He saw Eve, and his face went rigid. Then a wry smile formed on his lips.

"I really don't like him," she said under her breath.

They sat down across from him, and Andrew said, "She will not go to Chinon. She wants to find Jeanne."

"The Maiden is in the thick of battle now. It is pure folly." His eyes went to Andrew. "Vincent will be where there is a battle, looking for me. Perhaps he is looking for you as well. What he wants must be put into safe hands. Do you understand the trust I am placing in you?"

"What does the assassin want?" Eve asked.

"Tell her about your treasure," Andrew urged him.

Simon said, "It will help you."

"Help us *how*?" Eve asked, thinking they might need money in the days to come.

His eyes narrowed and his voice took on a hard edge. "Why do you ask so many questions?" he asked through clenched teeth.

Eve got ready to run out. This was how the old man looked before he acted crazy.

"Is it not enough that I said I have a treasure that will help you?" he demanded.

"Why do you want to help us?" she asked.

"You are ..." He pressed his hands onto the table as if to keep them from turning into fists. "You must repair what I have broken."

"What does that mean?" she asked.

He glared at her. His lips moved as if he did not know how to form the words. Finally, with great effort, he said, "It is impossible to explain until you have done it."

Eve turned to Andrew. "He does not make sense." She stood up and walked out.

Andrew chased after her, catching her in the middle of the courtyard. "Will you stop for a minute?"

"Why do you believe anything he says?" she asked.

"Why do you want to go back to Jeanne when you know what will happen?" Andrew countered.

Eve looked around and gestured for him to lower his voice. She said in a harsh whisper, "How can you ask me such a stupid question? I don't want her to feel abandoned."

Andrew held up his hands. "Okay. I get it."

She frowned at him, ready to walk away.

"Eve," he said gently. "You know you cannot save her. Your name is not in the history books. We are not supposed to be here."

"I have to be there for her," she said, "even if there is nothing I can do."

Andrew eyed her. "But you think there is. You think you can change what happens."

Eve didn't respond.

"Listen to me. We have a chance to go *home*. But we have to go to Chinon. That is where Simon has hidden the stone."

"*A* stone," she said. "What if that is all it is? I mean, if it is like the Radiant Stone, then why doesn't he come out and say so? The words are easy: 'I have a stone that will let you travel in time.'"

"Because he has been here too long," Andrew replied. "He cannot bring together what his memory knows is true but his brain cannot accept. He remembers what the stone does, but his brain cannot make sense of it. It is like his life here has pushed everything he knew out of his mind and locked it away."

"You just made that up," she said.

"This is *all* I have been thinking about!" Andrew cried out. "That is why he is going crazy. He knows there are things he should remember but cannot. What he does remember does not make sense. Our showing up makes it worse. Throw Vincent into the mix, and it is enough to send him over the edge."

"You think Vincent knows what the stone does?" Eve asked.

Andrew shrugged. "I hope not. I hope he wants the stone because he thinks it is valuable. But Simon is right: if someone like Vincent got the stone and traveled through time, he might do some terrible things."

Suddenly Eve felt as if they were being watched. Andrew must have sensed it too. They both slowly turned toward the dining hall.

Simon stood in the doorway. "Let us make a deal," he said. He walked toward them, a look of serenity on his face. "I will take you to Jeanne. If we survive, then we will go to Chinon together."

"*If* we survive?" Eve said.

He sneered at her. "The Maiden is at Compiègne. It is being surrounded by four thousand Burgundians. I am certain Vincent the Ravager will be among them. So we may live, or we may not. If we do, then we will make the journey to Chinon."

"Deal," Eve said.

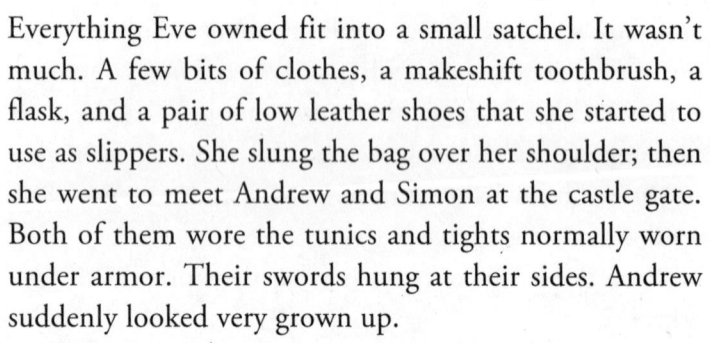

Everything Eve owned fit into a small satchel. It wasn't much. A few bits of clothes, a makeshift toothbrush, a flask, and a pair of low leather shoes that she started to use as slippers. She slung the bag over her shoulder; then she went to meet Andrew and Simon at the castle gate. Both of them wore the tunics and tights normally worn under armor. Their swords hung at their sides. Andrew suddenly looked very grown up.

"We are walking," Simon told them. "My horse was killed by the Ravager the last time I saw him."

"Can we borrow one?" Eve asked.

"One cannot simply borrow a horse," said Simon. "Nor does one steal a horse. Not without a fear of being executed."

They departed from Sully. Eve had no idea that it would take almost three days to walk to Compiègne. Nor could she know what dangers awaited them there.

36

Along the way, Simon explained that Compiègne was one of the largest and strongest cities in France. It was north of Paris, a vital position for whoever had its loyalty. For now, its loyalty belonged to King Charles, even though the king and his council had given the city up to the Duke of Burgundy as part of the truce.

Guillaume de Flavy, the captain of the city's garrison, refused the king's order to yield the city to the duke. De Flavy replied that the city would remain loyal to the true king of France, truce or no truce. With more than four hundred men in the garrison, no one wanted to force the issue in combat.

La Trémoille, on the other hand, tried other means. He offered a huge bribe to de Flavy. The captain refused it.

Now that the truce was officially broken, Captain de Flavy was considered a hero for holding his ground.

The Duke of Burgundy sent four thousand men to take Compiègne, along with artillery that could fire stone balls larger than any army had used before. He also brought in mortars and a great catapult. His archers and crossbowmen were exceptionally skilled, hitting whatever they aimed at with barbed arrows. In addition, the duke brought in men who specialized in laying powder mines around the town, along with an ancient type of flamethrower to make them explode.

That is what Eve, Andrew, and Simon were about to experience as they approached the city from the southeast. Standing at the edge of a forest, they saw the river. On the north bank, the Burgundian camp spread out on a distant hill and adjoining fields.

"Where will we find Jeanne?" Eve asked. Her heart filled with alarm as she gazed at the city's stone towers that now looked like broken teeth.

Just then, a tradesman and his family came toward them from the city. Eve assumed they were trying to get out of harm's way. Simon hailed them to stop, assuring them that he was not a robber but a soldier seeking information.

As his young children played among the trees, the tradesman explained that the Burgundians now had control over most of the towns surrounding Compiègne. Jeanne, he had heard, was with the Archbishop of Reims and the Count of Vendôme and his army in Soissons to the east. However, the people of Soissons feared any Burgundian reprisals and would not open the gate to the Maiden.

CHAPTER THIRTY-SIX

"It has been said that she may be in Crépy-en-Valois to gather more troops," the tradesman offered.

Simon tossed the man a coin by way of thanks. Then he announced to Eve and Andrew that they would stay where they were and wait.

"Wait!" Eve said.

"Crépy-en-Valois is to the south. If she has gone for troops and supplies there, she must pass us here on the way back to Compiègne."

Since the three travelers were not strangers to staying in the woods, they quickly found a comfortable spot near the main road to rest and watch. Andrew caught a rabbit, which Simon prepared and cooked over a modest fire. Night came to them on a cold breeze. A mere sliver of a moon hung overhead. Eve curled up in a ball and fell asleep beneath a tree.

She was awakened by Andrew. "Someone is coming," he whispered to her.

She sat up and listened. The sound of horses' hooves and the marching of many feet was unmistakable. Worried that it might be the Burgundians, they hid behind a grove of trees near the road.

Jeanne, on horseback, came into view. She lifted her hand to bring the column to a halt. Then she dismounted to consult with her officers under torchlight. Jean d'Aulon was there. And a captain with dark hair and eyes whom Eve remembered from earlier battles. The name quickly came to her: Captain Poton de Xaintrailles, a friend of

La Hire's. There were also a few other men Eve had never seen before.

Eve heard Jeanne saying softly that she would enter Compiègne first to apprise Captain de Flavy of their whereabouts. The troops should remain hidden in the forest until dawn.

Eve was about to step out, when Simon moved first and called Jeanne's name. There was a loud rattle as the commanders and nearby soldiers grabbed their weapons. Simon held up his hands and identified himself. He waved for Eve and Andrew to come out.

Jeanne gasped at the sight of Eve, her hands going to her face like a little girl. She embraced Eve, then Andrew, then both of them together. "My angels, my angels! What are you doing here?"

"I was tired of waiting for you," Eve replied.

"Come, then," Jeanne said after thanking Simon for bringing them to her safely.

Jeanne and the three travelers made their way to the city, along with Captain de Xaintrailles and Jean d'Aulon. They entered by a small gateway Jeanne said she had used before. Guards stopped them just inside and then, seeing who it was, welcomed them in. They walked down the darkened streets to a large house. A bewildered servant girl answered the door. Jeanne demanded to see the master of the house, Captain de Flavy.

They were taken to a large study. Jeanne paced while Simon stood with his back to the feeble flames of a hastily

CHAPTER THIRTY-SIX

made fire. Eve sat down with Andrew on a small sofa. D'Aulon gazed at Jeanne. Captain de Xaintrailles leaned against the wall and watched them all with an expression of disapproval.

Wearing a long robe and looking as if he'd been dragged from his bed, Captain de Flavy entered the room, a sullen look on his face. It was clear that he was not happy about his unwelcome visitors. "You have come back," he said.

"I promised you I would," Jeanne said. "Tomorrow I will fight the English and the traitors of France."

Captain de Flavy groaned. "Not so fast, Maiden. They have tightened their grip around the city. Wait until we can assess their numbers."

Clearly, Captain de Flavy did not know how Jeanne reacted to the word *wait*.

"What will their numbers tell us? We will fight tomorrow," she said again.

He looked at Captain de Xaintrailles for help. "Do you agree?"

"Of course," he said.

De Flavy grunted. "As you wish," he said, snarling, then walked out of the room. The servant girl pulled the door closed.

"Do you trust him?" Simon asked Jeanne. "He is known to be ruthlessly corrupt."

"He has remained strong for our king," said Jeanne.

Captain de Xaintrailles nodded, though Eve wasn't sure what he was nodding to.

"We must rest now for what is to come," he said. "We have only a few hours to sleep."

The captain pulled the door open. The servant girl was standing there, red-faced. She had been listening to their conversation.

"I will show you to your rooms," she stammered.

Captain de Xaintrailles and Simon followed her out.

"Leave us for a moment," Jeanne told d'Aulon. He bowed, then strode out.

Jeanne sat on the couch between Eve and Andrew. "Why are you here?" she asked, her expression serious.

"Like I said—," Eve began to say.

"You should not be here," Jeanne interjected. "It is not safe."

"If it is not safe, then you need your angels nearby," Eve reminded her.

"Perhaps it is best for me not to have my angels at all." Jeanne's eyes glistened in the firelight.

Eve shot a look at Andrew, then took Jeanne's hands. "Jeanne, you are going to be captured. If not tomorrow, then soon."

Andrew screwed up his face and said, "No."

Eve ignored him. "They will capture you and ... and ..." She couldn't bring herself to say any more.

Jeanne smiled at her. "Evangeline, you are saying what I already know."

"What?" from Andrew.

"How do you know?" from Eve.

"My Voices," Jeanne told her. "Saint Catherine and Saint Margaret proclaimed that I would be taken before Saint John's Day."

"When is that?" asked Andrew.

"A month from now," she replied. "So all that I have done, I have done knowing that it might be the last."

With a trembling voice, Eve asked, "Did the Voices tell you anything else?"

"No," she said. "Though I asked to die immediately, without suffering long."

"What did they say about that?" Andrew asked.

"They said only that I must be taken, and so it should be. But I am not to be troubled. I must yield, knowing that God will help me." Jeanne looked at Eve, resolved. "I would rather they had told me something else, but that is what they said. So I accept it, knowing that God is always with me."

Burning tears fell on Eve's cheeks.

"Come what may," Jeanne said, "you have inspired me in all I have done."

"Inspired you? How?" asked Eve.

"By being here."

Eve did not sleep that night. She sat across the room, looking at Jeanne on the bed. D'Aulon was sprawled on a cot, snoring softly. Andrew had stretched out on the floor.

Eve prayed, fighting her feeling of helplessness. The words "Thy will be done" kept coming to her. It was what Jesus said. It was what all of the saints eventually said. And without a doubt, Jeanne was a saint.

As the gray dawn filled the room, Jeanne sat up. Stretching, she said to Eve, "I have something for you." She slipped out of bed and went to a bag she normally kept tied to her saddle. It contained the few personal items she carried with her. She took out a leather purse and handed it to Eve. "Take this," she said.

It jingled in Eve's hand.

"If anything happens to me."

Eve tried to hand it back. "No, please."

Jeanne pushed her hand away. "Keep it. You may need it."

Eve looked at the purse, the urge to cry coming upon her again.

Brightly, Jeanne said, "Let us go to Mass."

"Should I wake the others?" Eve asked.

"Let the Holy Spirit awaken them," she said, giggling.

The Church of Saint-Jacques was only a few streets away. Pierre, Jeanne's brother, joined them. He had been staying in the city as a point of contact between Captain de Flavy and Jeanne. After Mass, they returned to Captain de Flavy's house, where Andrew stood, scratching his head.

"You should have gotten me up," he said to Eve.

Captain de Xaintrailles, Jean d'Aulon, and Captain de Flavy were eating breakfast with the newly arrived

CHAPTER THIRTY-SIX

Captain Bartolomeo Baretta. Eve thought Baretta had the look of a pirate, with olive skin, a pudgy face, a scraggly beard, and a mop of unkempt hair.

Simon sat off to the side, nibbling on a piece of cheese and watching the officers.

A map had been placed in the middle of the table. Captain de Xaintrailles, who had finished his modest meal, stood and said, "The Burgundians are on the north side of the river Oise. A single bridge from the city, here, crosses to the meadowlands, which go some three-quarters of a mile and rise beyond the slope of Picardy. The meadow is low and often flooded. We remember well what low, wet meadows have done to our armies in the past."

There were grunts of assent. The English frequently won against the French in wet meadows.

"The road to Margny goes off to the west," the captain continued. "It follows the steep slope of the hill. The enemy is there, commanded by Baudot de Noyelles. And north in Clairoix is the commander Jean de Luxembourg and his Picards. In Venette, to the south, we have Lord Montgomery from England. The Duke of Burgundy himself is now only two miles north in Coudun."

Captain de Flavy nodded. "It is good military strategy for them to spread their troops out, forcing their enemies to do the same. It diminishes concentrated strength."

Captain Baretta reached over and stabbed a finger at the mark representing Margny. "Let us attack there. The enemy has had no time to build strongholds. It is small and easily captured. We will make that our outpost."

From his seat, Simon asked, "What if the enemy swings around from the north and cuts you off from the bridge?"

Baretta looked offended. Simon was an uninvited participant and had no right to speak.

"They will not move their forces quickly enough to cut us off," Baretta said.

Captain de Flavy cleared his throat. "I will post archers on my walls to repel any who attempt to block the bridge. There will also be covered boats on the river. Your soldiers may use them to retreat."

Baretta snorted. "We will not retreat."

Simon did not seem impressed.

"You will march out this morning?" Captain de Flavy asked.

"This afternoon," said Captain de Xaintrailles. "They will expect us in the morning. Taking Margny this afternoon will allow us time to fortify it as our outpost before they attempt to take it back in the morning."

Jeanne was silent for the entire meeting. No one asked for her advice or input. Did she trust these men completely, or had she been relegated to the role of a mascot again?

As the day progressed, Jeanne's army made its way from the forest into Compiègne. The troops were told to prepare for an afternoon fight. With the words "Bring me my banner" from Jeanne, they came alive.

Jeanne wore a new set of armor. It was still her traditional white, but was now covered with a vest of rich gold.

"What is that sword?" Eve asked.

Jeanne held it up for her to see. "It is Burgundian. I captured it at Lagny," Jeanne explained. She mounted a gray horse. A young man Eve did not know served as her standard bearer.

Jean d'Aulon climbed onto a brown steed next to her.

"Watch from the city tower," Jeanne said to Eve. "Pray for me as I go—and always, if you do not see me again."

"This reminds me of Orléans," Andrew said as he climbed the stairs of the tower.

Eve couldn't speak. She felt nauseous from her anxiety about Jeanne.

They reached the top, moving to the turrets where Captain de Flavy's archers stood ready. Below, the trumpets sounded, and Jeanne rode out onto the bridge, with Jean d'Aulon, Captain Baretta and Captain de Xaintrailles alongside her. Then came the other horseback riders and four hundred foot soldiers with lances and spears pointed to the heavens. They marched quickly, as if getting a running start for the slope of the hill ahead of them.

Even from the tower, with its view of the meadow and Margny, Eve found it hard to follow the battle as it quickly unfolded. Only when she had time to think later did it become clearer.

The French army crested the hill to Margny and, from all appearances, caught the Burgundians off guard. Victory seemed assured.

Then a strange thing happened. A group of men without armor rode down from the north, accompanied by only a dozen soldiers. It looked as if they were noblemen who had gone off for an evening ride. Eve learned later that they were, in fact, two commanders from Clairoix, including the commander Jean de Luxembourg. It was possible that Luxembourg had come to explore the state of the city. At the sight of the assault on Margny, their horses reared back. Luxembourg shouted, and two of the soldiers galloped away.

"This is really bad," Andrew said. "They are going for help."

A couple of longbowmen released their arrows at the men, but they were too far away.

"They should have taken Margny by now," Andrew said as a column of smoke rose above the town. "Why are they not returning?"

"It is their right to plunder the village," an archer standing nearby said.

Andrew turned to him. "Can you signal them? They have to be warned about the reinforcements."

"I see no reinforcements," the archer said simply.

An agonizing hour went by. The sounds from Margny suggested combat, but nothing like the cacophony of a full battle.

CHAPTER THIRTY-SIX

Eve wrung her hands. "Come back. *Please* come back."

Movement to the north caught her eye. Then, with growing fear, she saw the Burgundian army racing for Margny. The Duke of Burgundy was leading them, his banner held high. Suddenly, half of the army split off and rode toward Compiègne.

Only then could Eve see the French soldiers casually emerge from the village. Many carried sacks of plunder. They did not know what was coming at them.

Eve moved back and forth along the turret, searching for Jeanne.

"She will come last," Andrew said. "She would never leave the field while her soldiers are still there."

The Burgundians came within sight of the French soldiers. With frightening shouts, the French dropped their sacks and ran for the bridge into Compiègne. Some angled away, hoping to reach the boats on the river. In their panic, a few stumbled and fell into the water, thrashing before their armor dragged them under.

"Do something!" Andrew shouted at the archers. "Give them cover!"

"We have no orders," one archer said.

"You must help them! Use your arrows! Your cannons!" Eve cried.

"We will strike our own soldiers," the archer snarled at her.

It was true, Eve realized. The Burgundians were now too close to the French soldiers.

A shout came from the wall. "Raise the bridge!" It was Captain de Flavy. He was leaning over the edge and waving.

Eve heard a loud grating sound as the bridge was slowly drawn up. "But our soldiers are still coming!"

"So are the Burgundians," Andrew said, his voice filled with despair. "If they breach that gate, then the city could be taken."

Jeanne now appeared in the meadow and beckoned the French soldiers to turn and attack the Burgundians. They ignored her as the sight of the rising bridge caused greater panic. More soldiers scrambled to catch the lip of the bridge. Failing that, they threw themselves at the boats.

Jeanne spurred her horse toward the enemy. "Go forward! They are ours!" was her rallying cry. But there were fewer soldiers to rally now.

The Burgundians came at her, circled around and behind her like water around a large rock. More Burgundian riders came from the east. It seemed endless. Eve saw that they had completely cut Jeanne off from Compiègne.

"Oh no," Andrew whispered.

Fighting back her tears, Eve asked, "How will she get back?" She grabbed the arm of the nearest archer. "*Do something!*"

Jeanne turned her horse in one direction, then another. Burgundian foot soldiers closed in. One reached up and caught hold of her vest. She pulled away. He grabbed it with both hands and yanked hard. Jeanne came off her horse and disappeared into the mob of men.

"No!" Eve sobbed. She threw herself against Andrew's chest. "It is too hard to watch."

Andrew wrapped his arms around her. "Wait ... Look! Jeanne is on her feet."

Eve spun around. The Burgundian soldiers had spread out. Jeanne now stood in the center, saying something to them.

A single soldier stepped forward and held out his hand. Jeanne turned her sword around and offered it to him, grip first. He took it, then held it up and shouted a single word that eventually echoed throughout all of France.

"Surrender!"

37

Jeanne was captured.

There were no French soldiers left to fight for her. The Burgundians put her back on her horse and led her away.

Eve swayed. Andrew thought she might faint. He put an arm around her. "It is over," he said and guided her off the tower.

They made their way slowly through the city, looking like they had just come from a funeral. They headed for the house of Captain de Flavy. It was the only place Andrew could think to go.

The servant at the door claimed she did not know them. It was the same girl who had answered the door the night before. She would not let them in without Captain de Flavy's permission.

They went to the Church of Saint-Jacques. Andrew told Eve to go inside. "Pray for Jeanne while I try to figure out what to do."

She looked at him with a dazed expression, as if she didn't know what he was saying. Then she turned and walked to the doors.

Andrew wasn't unprepared. He had thought a lot about what they should do when Jeanne was captured. One way or the other, they would get to Chinon. But for now, they were in a strange town with no money and no friends.

He made his way to the city's garrison, hoping to find Jean d'Aulon, Captain de Xaintrailles, or Simon. Many of Jeanne's soldiers were there, tending to their wounds. The place had a tomb-like silence.

Then Andrew heard one man whisper, "They have taken the Maiden. What will become of France?"

After a bit of searching, Andrew found Simon sitting on a patch of straw with his back against a hitching post. His head was hanging down, and for a moment, Andrew feared he was dead.

"Simon?"

Simon lifted his head, only a little.

"They have taken her prisoner," Andrew told him.

Simon nodded, only a little.

"What about everyone else?"

"Jean d'Aulon was also captured," Simon said. "And Jeanne's brother Pierre. I am not sure of the others."

Andrew crouched in front of him. "Are you wounded?"

Simon's head came up, more than a little this time. Blood trickled down the right side of his face from a gash under his hair.

CHAPTER THIRTY-SEVEN

Andrew winced. "You need a doctor."

"I need to rest," he said.

Andrew hurried into the garrison. A man was attending to the soldiers on stretchers. Andrew recoiled from the gaping wounds and half-severed limbs. The ground was soaked with blood. The screams made him want to put his hands over his ears.

"I need help," Andrew cried out. "There's a man with a gash outside."

"Is he conscious? Able to speak?" the man asked.

"Yes."

The man shook his head. "Look around you. I am too busy to deal with a mere head wound. Take a few rags. Bandage it yourself."

Andrew grabbed a few strips of cloth from a pile on a table. He found Simon where he'd left him. He began to dress the wound, but he bungled the effort. The rag kept falling into Simon's face.

Simon snatched the cloth away from him. "You do not know what you are doing," he snapped, then tied the rag tightly around his head.

Andrew stepped back. "What will happen to Jeanne?" he asked.

The old man snorted. "She will be taken as a trophy to the Duke of Burgundy, probably at his castle. It is in Luxembourg, a dozen miles north of here."

"Will she be ransomed?"

"Not her," he said. "She is not nobility, or even a soldier. They will treat her as something else. A witch perhaps."

"Someone will rescue her," Andrew said hopefully.

"Someone may try, but she is too valuable for the Burgundians—and the English—to lose. They will fight harder to keep her than they have fought for any city."

"But the king—"

"Listen, boy," Simon said. "The only thing the king or La Trémoille or the Archbishop will do is forget that Jeanne ever served them. They will say she brought it on herself somehow. She was too arrogant and willful, they will say. She did not listen to her superiors. And some will say she was never sent from God at all, but from the devil to deceive them. You know as well as I do what the end will be."

"What the end will be?" Andrew asked, waiting to hear a response that would confirm what he suspected.

Simon gazed up at him. "She will be declared a heretic and burned at the stake."

"You *know* that," Andrew said. "You are not guessing."

"I know my history," he said and looked away.

Andrew wanted to drag Simon back to the church. He wanted Simon to repeat to Eve what he had just said. Simon refused to go anywhere. He was tired. He wanted to rest.

"Prepare to leave for Chinon in the morning" were his parting words.

CHAPTER THIRTY-SEVEN

Andrew made his way through the crowded streets, feeling as if he was swimming upstream no matter which way he turned.

The people looked stunned. Women and children cried openly. The Maiden had been captured. How was that possible? France was doomed. So they went into the streets to talk, or to the inns to drink, or to the cathedral to pray—anything to cope with the horrible news.

Eve was still at the church, kneeling in a back pew. Andrew touched her shoulder. She nodded and came outside. Her eyes were red and swollen.

"We have to stay somewhere tonight," Andrew said.

"I saw an inn around the corner."

"We don't have any money," Andrew reminded her.

"Jeanne gave me a purse," Eve said. "I hid it in my room back at Captain de Flavy's house."

"I hope it's still there."

This time they didn't give the servant a chance to close the door on them.

"Our belongings are here," Andrew stated, then pushed past her. She looked startled but didn't try to stop them.

He grabbed a lit lamp from a side table. Then he marched up the stairs to the room where they had stayed the night before. He saw that it had been tidied up. Obviously someone had already gone through the few things Jeanne had left there.

"Please, God," Eve whispered, then went to the canopied bed.

Andrew assumed she had put the purse under the mattress. He braced himself. Whoever had searched the room would have looked there first.

Eve reached up to one of the slats holding the canopy and felt along the ledge. "Ah," she said, smiling. She pulled down a leather purse.

The servant girl watched them from the hallway, a look of disappointment on her face.

"You did not think to search there, did you?" Andrew teased her.

Eve grabbed her satchel. Andrew picked up a shoulder bag in the corner. It was Jean d'Aulon's. He upended it. A few items of clothing fell out.

"The bag may come in handy," Andrew said. "Jean will not need it."

The servant girl followed them to the door. Andrew handed her the lamp on the way out.

The lodging house reminded Andrew of every other lodging house he'd slept in: rough, crude, and uncomfortable. But it was a roof over their heads. They shared a large room with a half-dozen other people. Eve slept on a straw mat on one side of the room, and Andrew slept on the floor under the window. He decided to wait until morning to talk about Simon and Chinon. He told himself it was a good call. He was sure he heard Eve crying in the night.

CHAPTER THIRTY-SEVEN

In the morning, he was awakened to a clamor of street noise. Compiègne was overrun with soldiers from Jeanne's army and refugees from nearby villages who had come to escape the Burgundians.

"We have to leave," Andrew said to Eve, shaking her gently. She got up without speaking. They gathered their things. He noticed she was wearing the red peasant dress Jeanne had given her.

"Wait," Eve suddenly said.

"What is wrong?"

"What if they rescue Jeanne? We have to be here when she comes back." She pulled a dark cape over her shoulders and tied it at the neck.

Andrew said as kindly as he could, "She is not coming back, Eve. You know that."

"I do *not* know that."

He said firmly, "They will put her on trial as a heretic and burn her at the stake. It will all happen miles away from us. You will not see her. You cannot help her."

"I can try." She gave him a grim look.

"You will die trying," he said. "And what is the point of that?"

"We made a deal," Simon reminded Eve outside the garrison. The bandage was gone from his head, but there was a large scrape of dried blood near his hairline.

Eve was still objecting to leaving Jeanne.

Simon was impatient. "Child, *if* you found out where they were keeping her, and *if* you were able to go there, what do you think would happen? They would catch you and burn you at the stake as a witch. It is what *I* wanted to do when I first saw you."

Eve glowered at him.

"It is the color of your eyes," Andrew added, wiggling two fingers at them. "They freak everyone out."

"I will not argue with you," Eve said, sulking.

"As it is, we must go," said Simon. "Captain de Xaintrailles and the other officers are leaving Compiègne. Only Captain Baretta has promised to stay behind with his company. He will assist Captain de Flavy should the Burgundians attack."

Simon stepped back and looked at Andrew and Eve.

"Is something wrong?" Eve asked.

"Weapons?" he asked.

Andrew pushed back his coat to show the sword in the sheath.

"You?"

Eve turned slightly, drawing aside her cape. A knife was tucked into her belt.

They headed for the small gate Jeanne had used a couple of nights before. Emerging into the bright light of day, they stopped to look out at the fields and forest. Andrew wondered how the day could look so beautiful when they felt so bad.

"How long will it take to reach Chinon?" Eve asked.

CHAPTER THIRTY-SEVEN

"If the weather spares us and we walk briskly and avoid trouble, six or seven days," Simon told them.

"I did not think it was so far away," Andrew said.

"It is only as far as it has ever been," said Simon.

Andrew thought about all the moving around they had done since they'd first arrived in France. One day he hoped to sit down with a map to see where all the towns were.

With Compiègne behind them, they entered the forest where they had met Jeanne and her army two nights ago. They walked in silence. Eve sniffled a few times and rubbed her eyes.

Andrew tried to block out the shock of Jeanne's capture—and the cruelty of what would happen to her.

The clip-clop of horses' hooves and the rattle of wooden wheels caused them to turn. It looked like a potter's wagon, with large clay pots in the back and smaller jugs hanging from rope on the side. The potter drove at a leisurely pace, as if he didn't have anywhere special to be.

"Maybe we can get a ride," Andrew said.

Simon's hand went to the hilt of his sword. "Move from the path." He swept them back with his outstretched arm.

"What is wrong?" Eve asked.

The potter's head was lowered, a hood covering his face. He slouched at an odd angle.

The wagon slowed as it came alongside them, the reins pulling back.

Andrew now saw that the reins were not in the driver's hands but around both his sides, stretching to the back of the wagon.

A second later, the potter fell lifeless off the seat. Vincent the Ravager sprang up from the back of the wagon, his sword drawn.

Simon stepped in front of Andrew and Eve, knocking them out of the way. Andrew kept his footing, but Eve tumbled backward.

Simon's sword was in his hand, but he stumbled while trying to avoid the falling dead man. He attempted a first strike at Vincent and missed.

Vincent leapt from the wagon and was now on the path. He thrust at Simon, stabbing the old man in the right shoulder.

Simon swore at the pain but regained his stance.

Andrew glanced at Eve, who was rubbing her head. He reached for his sword, fumbling to get it out of his sheath.

Simon lunged back at Vincent.

Andrew stepped forward with his sword drawn.

"Stay back!" Simon shouted.

Vincent jeered. "Yes, boy, I will deal with you after I have killed him."

The two men exchanged fierce blows, the ring of steel echoing all around. Simon drove Vincent back, and he stumbled into the horse. It snorted at him, moving forward and backward uneasily. The cart moved with

CHAPTER THIRTY-SEVEN

it. Vincent sidestepped the animal and blocked Simon's blade with the flat of his sword.

The men fought with equal force. Vincent was younger and more agile. Simon had great strength and years of experience.

Eve came alongside Andrew. She had a long straight branch in her hands. She cut at the twigs with her knife, keeping her eyes on the battle.

Andrew thought, as he often did, that fights in real life were not like they appeared in the movies. All of the smooth routines in action films were replaced by stumbles, grunts, and falling into each other like wrestlers. In no time, both men were on their knees, their hands on each other's wrists as each one tried to get the other to drop his sword.

Eve tucked her knife away. "I have had enough of this," she said, then rushed forward with her newly made staff. Using both hands, she stabbed it at Vincent, hitting him on the side of the head. He shouted and fell sideways.

Simon gave her a grateful nod and got to his feet. He flicked his sword at Vincent's sword arm, catching enough of the wrist to make Vincent drop his weapon.

"Now," he started to say to Vincent, but Vincent wasn't ready to give up. He suddenly rolled toward the horse and spider-crawled under the wagon, kicking up a lot of dust as he went.

"Yield," Simon shouted. He kicked Vincent's sword off the path.

Andrew heard the sound of feet and knees scraping on the dirt path. Simon moved in front of the horse, watching one side of the wagon, then the other.

"What is he doing?" Andrew asked, moving away in case Vincent tried to grab his leg.

"Perhaps the snake has found a hole in the ground," Simon said.

Vincent suddenly popped up at the back of the wagon, a crossbow in his hands. He released a bolt, striking Simon in the chest. Simon staggered back and looked down with an outraged expression. Then he dropped his sword, reeling off balance.

Andrew reached out to catch him. They both crashed onto the dirt road. Andrew rolled to his knees and bent over the old man. The bolt jutted from the left side of Simon's chest.

Panicked, Andrew whispered, "What do I do?"

Simon turned his head. He coughed. A line of blood slid from between his lips. He grabbed Andrew's tunic and pulled him close. "Secret. Pass. Box. Under. Nails." His words were a gurgling whisper. He coughed again. Then more clearly, he said, "A mistake ... Man should stay ... own time."

Those last words were English, spoken with an American accent.

Simon exhaled a long breath, his eyes fixed on something beyond the top of Andrew's head. They stayed there.

Andrew fell back, dazed.

CHAPTER THIRTY-SEVEN

Eve cried out. Andrew spun around.

Vincent had Eve by the hair, a knife pointed at her throat.

"What did he say?" Vincent asked. "He said something to you in English. What was it?"

"I could not understand him," Andrew said.

"Get up!" Vincent shouted, a wild look in his eyes.

Andrew stood. His sword was a few feet in one direction, and Simon's sword was a few feet in the other. Andrew raised his hands.

"Where is the stone?" Vincent said. "Tell me or I will kill her."

"I do not know anything about the stone." Andrew's eyes went to Eve. He wondered if she had a plan to do something to escape.

She merely rolled her eyes.

Vincent jerked her head sharply, as if to get their attention.

"Ouch," she said. "That hurts."

"You know where the stone is hidden! Take me to it!" Vincent shouted.

"It is somewhere in Chinon," Andrew confessed. "Simon was taking us there. That is all we know. You killed him before he could tell me anything else."

"Chinon," Vincent repeated. He yanked at Eve to step back toward the wagon. "You," he snapped at Andrew. "There is rope in the back. Tie her. Then I will tie you. Together we will go to Chinon."

"It is better than walking," Andrew said.

Once Eve and Andrew were securely tied, Vincent lifted them onto the wagon seat. He put another bolt in the crossbow, then set the weapon on the ground. "At least one of you will die if you try to escape," he said. He dragged Simon's body into the woods, then the potter's.

"He has weapons and supplies in the back," Andrew whispered to Eve. "Maybe we'll find a way to escape."

"Escape to where? We have to go to Chinon either way," she whispered back.

Andrew shrugged. "Good point."

Vincent gathered the fallen weapons and tossed them into the back of the wagon, covering them with a tarp. He climbed onto the seat next to Andrew. "Is this not cozy?"

"No, it is not," said Andrew.

Vincent snapped the reins, and the horse lurched forward with a jolt.

38

Vincent did not allow Andrew and Eve to talk unless he first asked a question. He had a lot of questions. How did they know Simon? Did they know about his past? Did they know why Vincent had been after him?

Andrew answered honestly. He even repeated what he had heard about Vincent killing Simon's wife and Simon stabbing him in the eye.

Vincent sniffed. "Is that how they say it? Simon's *wife*? She was my sister before she was Simon's wife," he told them.

Andrew decided not to quibble. He looked over at Eve. Her eyes were on the road ahead.

"So why did you kill your sister?" he asked.

"It was *his* fault," Vincent said. "Had he given me the stone, we would not have fought. If we had not fought, my sister would not have placed herself between us. She should have known better, but there you are. My knife was aiming for him, and she got in the way."

"Is a stone worth that much?" Andrew asked.

"Do you know that stone? Have you seen it?"

"No."

"When you see it, when you understand its power, then you will not ask such stupid questions," Vincent said.

So he knows the stone isn't a normal jewel, Andrew thought. *But does he know what it really does?*

The forest was hot and muggy, but at least they had shade. The open road now put the summer sun heavily on their backs. Vincent kept the horse moving at a fast pace, stopping only occasionally for water.

He drove around the west side of Paris, since it was country held by the English. Then he continued south. Andrew did not recognize the names of the towns they passed. They trotted along colorful meadows and wild woodlands. They happened upon other travelers on the road, men of trade, beggars, soldiers marching to their assignments. Most saw the one-eyed man and averted their gaze.

Late in the afternoon, they reached an inn, where they watered the horse. A tinkerer nearby questioned Vincent about the two bound children. He gave the man a cold look and said, "They are thieves. I am taking them to justice."

The tinkerer looked doubtful, but Vincent put a hand on the knife in his belt. The tinkerer walked off.

That night, they slept in the middle of a field. To prevent Eve and Andrew from trying to escape, Vincent bound them to the wagon wheel. By morning their hands and feet were so numb, they could hardly use them. It took almost a half hour before they could stand up on their own.

"Stop complaining," Vincent said.

On the second night, Vincent roasted a rabbit he had caught. As he crouched by the fire, there was a loud snap from somewhere in the woods. Andrew and Eve both turned, sure that someone was coming.

Vincent grabbed his sword and shouted, "Come out!"

No one answered or appeared.

Andrew was sure that whoever it was remained nearby. Vincent suddenly spun to the left, his sword pointing in that direction. At the same time, Eve turned to the right.

"What did you see?" she asked Vincent.

"What did *you* see?" Vincent countered. He shouted again, "Whoever you are, *come out*!"

Andrew did not know whether he should be glad or worried that a mysterious stranger was nearby. Maybe it was one of Jeanne's allies. He thought of Louis, or other people they had come to know. Or maybe someone saw what had happened with Simon on the road and was following to help.

Or it might be an outlaw waiting for the chance to rob and murder them.

"Is it Simon? Is it possible he survived?" Eve whispered to Andrew that night.

"No," Andrew said. He would never forget that last look on Simon's face. The life had truly left him.

"Stop whispering!" Vincent said. He was using the wagon as cover. He looked in all directions, his crossbow ready to shoot.

The next day Vincent kept both his sword and his crossbow close at hand, his eyes darting in the direction of every sound.

"Do not be hopeful," he said. "If it is a friend of yours, he will die."

That evening they found another inn to refresh the horse.

Andrew thought he saw the flickering silhouette of a man in a long coat under a torch near the door. The man was watching them.

Vincent followed Andrew's line of sight and spun around. "What were you looking at? What did you see?"

"A man was standing under that torch," Andrew said.

Vincent stared for a moment. "He is not there now." He held the point of a knife close to the kids' faces. "Do not try to scare me. I get reckless when I get scared."

"I did not think a man like you was ever scared," Eve said.

Vincent grunted at her and put the knife away. "This is true."

Andrew noticed that Vincent whipped the horse to a faster pace and looked over his shoulder more often.

CHAPTER THIRTY-EIGHT

The next day, they entered territory held by King Charles. Vincent showed the kids his knife and sword again, just to remind them of what would happen if they tried to get help. His threat was real but lacked confidence. The mystery man was clearly unnerving him.

They were riding to Chinon from a direction Andrew did not know. He searched for anything that might look familiar. The idea of returning to the town was a relief. He realized it was like going home.

"What will happen when we get there?" Eve asked.

"We will find the stone," Vincent said.

"How?" she asked in a bored tone.

"The boy will tell us what Simon told him, and we will search."

"I told you, I did not understand what Simon said to me," Andrew said.

"Speak the words to me now," Vincent demanded.

Andrew groaned. "He muttered something about a pass and a secret and nails and a box. I do not know what it means."

"Why would he speak words to you unless he knew you would understand?"

"He was *dying*. You put a bolt in his chest, remember?" Andrew said. As he spoke, he realized he felt grieved about Simon. Andrew had come to like him in spite of his craziness.

"Think!" Vincent said, pounding his fist against the side of the wagon. "Where would Simon hide the stone?"

"In the castle somewhere," Andrew replied. "He lived in an officer's room. He guarded a box there."

Eve gave him a "Why are you telling him everything?" look.

Andrew tried to give her an "I know what I'm doing" look.

It didn't work. She looked confused.

It wasn't until the afternoon of the next day that the towers of Chinon came into view. Vincent brought the wagon to a halt and took out his knife. Andrew flinched. Vincent cut the ropes that bound their hands.

Andrew and Eve gently rubbed the chafing on their wrists and hands. They compared who had it worse.

"You win," Andrew said to Eve.

Vincent leaned in close. "Say anything I do not like, or do anything to escape, and one of you will die," he warned them. "Both, if I have my way."

Andrew made a face. Vincent's breath smelled of old onions and cabbage.

"How do we know you will not kill us if we find the stone?" Eve asked.

"You do not know," Vincent replied.

He drove the wagon around to the road that wound up to the main gate. Andrew felt comforted by the familiarity of the people and houses and the rushing sound of the river.

Eve sniffled next to him and wiped her nose with her sleeve. "Only a year," she said.

Andrew knew what she meant.

CHAPTER THIRTY-EIGHT

"What is it you are saying?" asked Vincent. "Why are you crying?"

She said, "This is where we met Jeanne. We were with her when she met the Dauphin for the first time."

"Ah," said Vincent. "You are friends of the king."

"Not friends," Andrew corrected him.

"It is enough to serve our purposes," he said. "I had hoped to get into the castle by using the name of Simon Le Fantôme, but the names of the Maiden and the king are better."

"What are you going to do?" Andrew asked.

Vincent stood on the footboard. "Move aside." He dropped down between Andrew and Eve.

They were crossing the bridge to the castle gate when Vincent suddenly swung his fist around, slamming it against the side of Eve's head.

"Hey!" Andrew cried out.

Then Vincent threw his elbow hard into Andrew's stomach. It knocked the wind out of him. Andrew doubled over. Black spots danced in front of his eyes.

Amid the ringing in his ears, Andrew heard Vincent shout out to the guards at the gate. "Help! The king has sent me! I have come from Compiègne with these two children! They were with Jeanne the Maiden! They are hurt! Let us enter!"

The words, the names, and the urgency were enough for the guards to let the wagon pass. Vincent pulled the horse and wagon around to an isolated spot in the courtyard. He put his arms around Eve and Andrew and rubbed their shoulders. In a creepy voice he must have thought was soothing, Vincent said, "There, there. No harm done. Breathe slowly, boy."

To Eve, he said, "Your senses will come back to you. And once you have recovered, we will solve the mystery of Simon's last words."

39

Vincent climbed down from the wagon and walked around to assess the area.

It took a while before the pain in Andrew's stomach had eased enough for him to think clearly.

Eve sat next to him, gently touching the side of her head. "I'm going to have a headache for a week," she said.

Andrew practiced breathing. He slowly drew air in and let it out again.

"I hope you have a plan," she said to him. The side of her face was red from the blow.

"I had an idea," Andrew replied. He *had* planned to expose Vincent to the guards at the gate. But now it was undone. They could scream for help, he thought, but Vincent was close enough to make quick work of them with his knife.

Vincent sidled up to the wagon. "If you are well enough to talk, you are well enough to take me to Simon's room."

They walked from the wagon to the courtyard where Simon had taught Andrew to sword-fight. Andrew looked at the many faces around them but did not see any he recognized. He wondered how many soldiers from a year ago had gone away to fight in battles.

"There." Andrew pointed to the door. "Another soldier may be living there now."

Vincent did not seem to care. He pushed the door open, then pulled Andrew and Eve inside. He closed the door behind them.

The room was filled with someone's clothes and belongings, but not Simon's. The new owner was not there.

Vincent grabbed Eve by the arm. In a flash, the knife was at her throat.

"Not again," Eve moaned.

"Find the stone," he said to Andrew.

"But I do not—," Andrew started to protest.

"You know what Simon was telling you," Vincent insisted.

"He does not!" Eve said.

Vincent grunted and edged the knife closer to Eve's skin. "How much pain will you allow before you tell the truth?" he asked.

Andrew gave in. "None," he admitted. "I *think* I know where Simon hid the stone."

"What?" Eve said.

"But do not blame me if I am wrong," he added quickly.

Vincent's mouth twisted into a smile. "Tell me."

CHAPTER THIRTY-NINE

"He said 'secret' and 'pass,' which must be the secret passage." Andrew went to the wall, found the hidden latch, and sprung the panel door open to reveal the corridor behind the wall.

"Be careful, boy," Vincent warned. "Disappear and she will suffer for it."

"You have made that clear." Andrew stepped into the secret corridor. It was exactly as he remembered it. The old oil lamp was there, with the flint. The shelves were still covered with dust and cobwebs. He saw the bottles and jugs, the ragged leather pouches, and the boxes with the old tools and ironworks. A knife had been there, but it was gone now. Andrew was disappointed about that. He had hoped to have a weapon. He looked at the rest of the junk, trying to think of a way to escape.

Simon's box was still in its place on a shelf. As he reached for it, his foot touched something on the ground that made a scraping noise. He looked down. The knife was there. He knelt and saw that the latch and lock on a crate had been broken.

"Hurry," came Vincent's voice from the room.

Andrew tucked the knife into his belt, just under his cloak. He grabbed the box.

"This is it," Andrew announced as he entered the room again.

Vincent pushed Eve onto the bed. "Come away from that passage," he said to Andrew.

Andrew did as he was told, taking a few more steps into the room.

"Put it on the bed. Empty it out," Vincent told him.

Eve moved out of the way, dropping her legs on the side of the bed facing the secret passage. Andrew opened the lid and upended the box onto the bed. There was not much to be seen. Some parchments bound with ribbons ... and a small pouch.

Vincent grabbed the pouch.

"Do not touch the stone with your bare hands," Andrew warned him.

Vincent sneered as he lifted the pouch and shook it. Something gold fell onto the bed. It was a wedding ring, embedded with small jewels.

"That is my sister's wedding ring," Vincent told them. He squeezed the empty pouch and threw it down. "Where is the stone?"

"It is supposed to be there!" Andrew said.

Vincent pointed the knife at Andrew. "Where is it?"

Andrew gave him a helpless expression. "I do not know. Maybe it is hidden in the passage." He suddenly had the idea of getting Vincent into the secret corridor and closing the door on him. They could escape while he tried to get out.

Vincent's face turned red. "You are lying!"

Andrew gestured to the passage. "There are shelves in there, with crates," he said.

Vincent looked as if he might fall for it.

CHAPTER THIRTY-NINE

Just then, the door opened. A bearded mountain of a soldier walked in. He looked at the three intruders and bellowed, "This is my room! What goes on here?"

Vincent swung his knife around to slash at the soldier.

The soldier was quick and caught hold of Vincent's wrist. "I see. You want violence?" With his free hand, he punched Vincent in the side of the face.

Vincent let out an animal-like noise and threw himself into the soldier.

The two men began to struggle.

Andrew pulled Eve with him into the secret passage.

Vincent saw them and reached out to catch hold of Andrew. But the soldier caught Vincent by the neck and pulled him back into the room.

Andrew grabbed the ring on the inside of the panel and pulled the door closed. He heard the click of the latch. There were bumps and crashes on the other side of the wall as the men fought.

With the light from the room gone, the passage was almost pitch-black.

"Was this your plan?" Eve asked.

Andrew felt around the shelves, bumping the bottles and jars. His fingers came to the oil lamp and the flint. He grabbed the lamp and put it on the ground. Feeling for the wick, he slipped the small ring of the starter around his fingers and struck it against the flint. There was a spark. He tried it again. Another spark. And again.

"What are you doing? We have to run!" Eve said.

"How are we supposed to see where we're going?" he asked. More strikes, more sparks, and then a flame caught onto the wick. They had light.

Andrew stayed on his knees. By the small glow of the lamp, he looked at the crate with the broken latch. "Simon opened this."

"*Let's go!*" Eve begged. The noise in the room had changed. The struggle was coming to an end.

Andrew dragged the crate out and lifted the lid. Inside were old iron spikes.

"Nails," he said. He lifted them out, tossing them aside.

Things were now very quiet on the other side of the door.

"Andrew?" Eve said.

Beneath the first layer of spikes was a small wooden box. Andrew lifted it up. He flipped open the lid. Inside was a large gemstone with facets that seemed to glow, even in the darkness.

Eve gasped. "That looks like the Radiant Stone."

Someone was clawing at the other side of the wall, trying to find the latch to open the door.

"Come on, Andrew!" Eve pleaded.

"Take the lamp," he said. Once she had it, he upended the crate of spikes onto the floor. He hoped they would slow down whoever was about to come through the panel.

He picked up the small wooden box and pointed down the dark corridor. "That way."

They ran.

40

Following the passageway, they eventually came to the drinking room Andrew had found before. A drunk soldier was leaning against a stack of barrels as they came out. He looked at them with thick-lidded eyes, puzzling over their sudden appearance. As Andrew closed the secret door, he said to the man, "If anyone comes through that door, hit him with a chair."

The man slurred a "Yes, Cap'n."

"To the tower or the gate?" Eve asked as they raced back into the courtyard.

"Not the tower," Andrew replied. "We have to get out of the castle. Vincent could raise an alarm and accuse us of being thieves. Then we'll have a lot of questions to answer."

Eve said, "Down to the bridge. If this stone can get us home, we'll want our clothes."

Andrew nodded. They ran for the gate. There was a terrible crash behind them. They turned to see Vincent stagger out of Simon's old room. His clothes were torn, and his face was swollen, bruised, and scratched. He clutched his side.

Vincent saw them just as they were seeing him. "Stop!" he yelled and limped toward them.

Andrew and Eve ran away as fast as they could. Andrew held tightly to the wooden box.

At the gate leading to the town, he grabbed the guard and pointed back at Vincent. "That is Vincent the Ravager! He just murdered one of your soldiers!"

Startled, the guard turned to look. The two kids raced across the bridge for the road to town. Andrew heard violent shouts back at the castle.

They quickly reached the streets of Chinon itself. Lamps were being lit for the approaching evening. They followed the road that cut through the town to the bridge, passing the familiar shops and buildings.

Rounding a final gentle curve to the bridge, they came to the south gate. Andrew said to the guard there what he had said to the castle guard, just in case Vincent was still following them. They came to the bridge and collapsed against the rail, gasping for breath. The river Vienne gurgled and splashed below.

"We can't stop," Eve said, then launched herself to the right.

They soon reached the path down to the riverbank.

"It's poetic," Eve said, dropping to her knees on the wet bank.

"I remember throwing up on this very spot." Andrew laughed. He looked at the water swirling around the

CHAPTER FORTY

pillars. "The river has risen since we were here last. Getting our clothes could be harder."

"I noticed," Eve said. "It's getting dark, too."

Andrew went to the waterline. He dreaded the thought of getting wet while trying to reach the place where Eve had hidden their bundle of clothes. More importantly, he worried that the current might carry them off.

"Any ideas?" he asked.

Eve didn't answer.

He turned and saw why. Vincent was there. He had grabbed hold of her again, his knife held in the usual place.

"You are more trouble than you are worth," Vincent said. "Give me the stone."

Andrew looked down at the box in his hand. There was no point denying he had it.

"All right." He slowly put the box on the ground. As he did, he stretched the fingers of his right hand to claw a single pebble from the damp earth. He stood up again, the pebble in his palm.

"Move away," Vincent said.

Andrew stepped back.

Vincent shoved Eve toward Andrew. Keeping his eyes on the two of them, he crouched to pick up the box. He opened the lid and saw the gem. "Yes," he hissed.

Eve moved closer to Andrew. Her eyes were filled with despair.

"What will you do with it?" Andrew asked Vincent.

The Ravager lowered his hand to the stone, his fingers poised to grab it.

"Don't touch it!" Andrew shouted.

Vincent jerked his hand back. "Why not?"

"Do you know what will happen if you do?" Andrew asked.

"It will take me to other times and places," Vincent said. "My sister told me."

"Do you know which facets to touch?" Eve asked. "Each one will take you to different times."

"How do you know?" Vincent asked. He grabbed the box, then stood up. He had that wild-eyed look again. "Who are you? Where are you from?"

"The future," Andrew told him.

Vincent looked as if he did not believe Andrew. Then he looked as if he did. "If that is true, you can guide me. You can take me to those places, just as I wanted Simon to."

"We cannot," Eve said.

"You *will*," Vincent threatened.

"We do not know about *that* stone," Andrew explained. "It would be dangerous for us to take you until we know what it does."

Vincent's lips curled. "Then you are of no use to me." He put the box down, then lifted his knife again. He positioned himself to block their escape to the path.

I have a single stone, Andrew thought. *I use that, or I pull Eve with me into the river.*

The stone was his best option. He wasn't going to allow Vincent to leave with that box. But the shadow of the bridge was now merging with the darkness of the night. Vincent was becoming a dim figure to him.

"I know what you are thinking," Vincent said, nudging the box with his foot. "Are you fast enough to grab the box without feeling this blade?"

Eve gasped.

Andrew glanced at her. She was looking past Vincent. He followed her gaze. He saw a shadow move at the entrance of the path.

Vincent must have seen the change in their eyes. He began turning his head to look, then stopped. "You are trying to trick me."

"I wish I had thought of it," Andrew said. He moved his fingers around the stone, getting ready to throw. He had no idea what the shadow was, but the distraction was a good opportunity to act.

The shadow moved forward and took the form of a man in an overcoat and hat. "That would be quite a trick," the man said.

Vincent whirled around with his knife. "This is not your business," he said defiantly as he carefully stepped over the box and reached out for Andrew.

Andrew tried to move, but Vincent caught his tunic and pulled him close.

Andrew wondered if punching Vincent with a stone-filled hand would do any good.

"I will cut his throat," said Vincent.

"Is that your only threat?" the man asked.

"See for yourself, if you dare take another step." Vincent replied.

"I do not need another step," the man said. His hand came up, holding a revolver. He leveled it at Vincent.

Eve whispered, "What?"

Andrew was wide-eyed.

"What is that, pray tell?" Vincent asked. He sounded as if he was not taking it seriously. Why should he?

Andrew did not wait to find out. With a kick, he threw himself away from Vincent, catching Eve in his arms as he flew. They both fell onto the grassy bank.

Vincent's instincts betrayed him. Catlike, he twisted to slash his blade at whatever piece of Andrew he might catch.

A deafening explosion echoed up to the castle walls and under the bridge.

Vincent jerked as if an invisible string had suddenly yanked the left side of his body in the wrong direction. He looked bewildered and furious. His legs buckled, and his free hand clawed at the air. He fell lifeless into the river. The current quickly carried him away.

Still on the wet ground, Andrew scrambled to get between the mysterious stranger and Eve. The man had saved them, but for what purpose?

Only then did Andrew realize that the man was wearing a *modern* overcoat and a *modern* hat to match.

The man pushed the hat back on his head. "Well," he said.

CHAPTER FORTY

Eve put her hands over her mouth.

"It can't be!" Andrew exclaimed.

They were looking at a face they'd only ever seen in a large portrait at the Old Bank Building and in black-and-white photos in a dusty office.

The man smiled and said, "I am Alfred Virtue."

41

Alfred Virtue tucked the gun into the pocket of his overcoat. "We have to go. The sound of the gunshot will draw a crowd."

They took the path up to the bridge. They turned away from the town and crossed over to an open field. Walking quickly, they headed for a forest beyond.

The rustling of Alfred's overcoat and even the sound of the soles of his shoes on the ground were different from anything Andrew had heard in a year. He found himself looking at the man from the corner of his eye.

"I'm guessing you are from the future," Alfred Virtue said, "but not my future."

"That's right," answered Andrew.

"Which century?" he asked.

"The twenty-first," Eve replied.

He stopped and looked at them with an expression of pure wonder. "Well, how about that," he said, then started walking again.

They reached the forest and made their way to an isolated spot in a thicket.

"How are you at making a fire?" Alfred Virtue asked.

"Pretty good now," Andrew said. He gathered kindling and wood, then cleared a space. "It might take a few minutes while I get it lit."

Alfred pulled a silver lighter from his pocket. "This will speed things up."

By the light of the fire, they sat on logs in a small circle.

"Now, I would like to know your names." He pointed to Andrew. "You must be a Perry. The resemblance to Ted is uncanny."

"I'm Andrew Perry, his great-great-whatever grandson." He turned to Eve.

"I'm *your* relative," Eve said. "Evangeline. *Eve.* Virtue."

He smiled. "I'll resist asking about your relatives. It's better I don't know. But you have to tell me what you're doing here."

Andrew nodded for Eve to go first. She explained about finding the Radiant Stone in his office and her few time-travel experiences and how Andrew had joined her to meet Robin Hood.

"And here?" he asked.

"This was an accident," she said. "We've been trapped here without the Radiant Stone."

"That's very interesting," Alfred Virtue said. "I've wondered what I would do if that happened."

CHAPTER FORTY-ONE

"We learned that panicking doesn't help," Andrew offered.

Alfred looked down at the wooden box. "Mind if I look?"

"It belongs to you," Andrew said.

He opened the lid. The stone was there, though it had been jostled by all the running around.

"Do you know it?" Eve asked.

"I do indeed." With a gloved hand, Alfred lifted the stone. "This is the Valiant Stone. I acquired it here in France."

He turned the stone slowly so the facets glittered in the firelight. "It was discovered during renovations on the bridge in the late 1800s. A worker unearthed it and took it home. He thought it was cursed because it made him nauseous and gave him terrible dreams. He boxed it up and got rid of it. After changing a few hands and locations, it wound up with an archaeologist I happened to meet during one of my expeditions here. He knew I collected these particular gems, so he sold it to me."

"Did the archaeologist use it to go back in time?" Andrew asked.

"That's the funny thing about the stones. They don't work for everyone," he said. "Not everyone who touches them goes off to other times. Only certain people. I don't know why." He nodded to them. "It works for you two, obviously."

Something caught his eye, and he looked more closely at the box. "What's this?" He reached in and pulled out folded sheets of paper. He handed them around.

Andrew saw that they were handwritten pages of a journal. "Simon's diary?"

"Ah," Eve said and held up a familiar-looking page.

"That came from my notebook," Alfred said.

"You wrote 'Beware' at the top of it. I guess Simon tore it out," said Eve. "If I ever get home, I'll put it back."

"You have my journals?"

"Some of them. I think you hid the rest somewhere before you—"

"No," he said sharply. "Don't say it. I don't want to know."

Andrew fidgeted. "Okay. But there is a lot *we* want to know. Like how are you connected to Simon?"

"And how did you find us?" Eve threw in.

"The first question is easy," Alfred Virtue said. "Simon was a geologist I consulted about the stones."

"The Radiant Stone and the Valiant Stone? Or are there more?" Eve asked.

"A few more," he said. "The more I acquired, the more I realized I needed to consult with an expert. Simon was one of the best in the area. He lived in Denver but often came to Hope Springs to dig around in the caves. I trusted his expertise. But he seemed to change when he found out what the stones could do. He demanded that I take him back to England during the time of Henry the

CHAPTER FORTY-ONE

Fifth. He wanted to witness the Battle of Agincourt, of all things."

"Why there?" asked Eve.

'He loved that period of history. He had to see the event for himself."

"He *demanded* that you take him?" Andrew asked.

Alfred nodded. "He threatened me, actually. He said he would tell everyone about the stones if I didn't do what he wanted. I couldn't have that. I foolishly agreed. I hadn't figured out the Valiant Stone yet, but I knew the Radiant Stone would get us to England during the time he wanted. So we went back to London. Simon actually saw King Henry. But it was *before* the Battle of Agincourt. I kept telling him I couldn't get him to that exact place and time, but he didn't care. He said he wanted to stay long enough to witness the battle. I said no."

"What did he do?" Andrew asked.

"He knew the Valiant Stone had come from France, so he kept asking me to let him test the facets. He believed that one of them was bound to take him to Agincourt. I refused."

"Why?"

"Because he was becoming obsessed. He was irrational and angry. He threatened me again. I called his bluff and told him to go public if he wanted. He marched out of the bank, and I assumed it was over. I wasn't very smart. I'm sure he broke into my office and stole the Valiant Stone. He disappeared from my time without a trace."

"Wasn't his family upset?" asked Andrew.

"He was a widower. But yes, his grown children were worried. I couldn't tell them what I really believed he'd done." Alfred pointed to the pages from the box. "The details of what happened after that may be in his documents. You should read them to see what you'll learn."

"You don't want to read them yourself?" Eve asked.

Alfred shook his head. "Time travel has made me wary of knowing more than I should in the natural course of events. Otherwise, I would go mad trying to alter the future to my advantage. The future is and always shall be God's domain."

"So why did you come back?" Andrew asked.

"Did you find my message?" Eve interjected.

"What message?" he asked.

"I put it with our clothes under the bridge," she explained. "I wrote your name and asked you to come help us."

Alfred laughed. "That was you?"

"You got it?" Andrew asked, amazed.

"I did, but not the way you intended," Alfred said. "The archaeologist who had the Valiant Stone also had what was left of a parchment he discovered. It was over five hundred years old. Most of the message was too faded to read. He contacted me because he saw *my* name written clearly at the top. He wanted to know how that could happen, since the paper was five hundred years

CHAPTER FORTY-ONE

old. Obviously I didn't know. Until now." He laughed again.

"What about our clothes?" Andrew asked.

"Sorry. There were no clothes that I know of."

"So you didn't come back to rescue us?" Eve asked.

"Not directly," Alfred said. "I didn't know you were here."

"Then ... why?" asked Eve.

"I have come back from time to time to check on Simon. When he disappeared from my time, I was sure he was here somewhere. I traveled back to England and found enough evidence to tell me that Simon had come to France. He took the name Simon Le Fantôme and gained the reputation of a talented jeweler turned man of war. That made it easier for me to track him. I had found obscure writings about him in this time period. I also knew his life overlapped with Joan of Arc, so I decided to retrace her various battles, suspecting that Simon might fight in one of them."

"More than one," Andrew added.

"Finally I saw him from afar at the Battle of Orléans."

"We were there!" Eve said.

"I may have seen you," he said. "But I couldn't have known it."

"So you went to Compiègne to find him?" asked Eve.

Alfred nodded. "I got there just in time to see him die by the hand of the Ravager. I also saw the two of you. Andrew, you looked so much like Ted Perry that I knew it wasn't a coincidence. I decided to follow you to see what was going on."

"What did you plan to do if you met Simon face-to-face?" Eve asked. "Drag him home?"

Alfred's brow furrowed. "I couldn't force him to go back. And how would I explain the way he had changed after disappearing?"

Andrew asked, "Then why were you searching for him?"

Alfred looked a little embarrassed. "To be honest, I wanted to see the impact time was having on him here."

"He went crazy," Eve said.

"So it would seem," Alfred said sadly.

Andrew gestured toward Alfred's coat pocket. "Do you always carry a gun when you time-travel?"

"Not always. This is the first time I've had to use it."

"I'm glad you did. You saved our lives," Andrew said. "Thank you."

"My pleasure." Alfred shook his head. "I don't think anyone will miss the Ravager."

"Aren't you worried that you've changed history?" Eve asked.

Alfred shrugged. "In my experience with time travel, if the gun was going to change history somehow, it wouldn't have gone off. Time won't let us change some things."

"So I keep hearing," Andrew said, rolling his eyes.

Alfred looked at him with a curious expression.

CHAPTER FORTY-ONE

"*Please* tell us about the Radiant Stone," Eve said. "We know it was from England, but we can't figure out why it brought us here."

Alfred gave it some thought, then said, "Its history goes back to Ireland during the time of Saint Patrick. Then I *think* it traveled to England with Saint Brigid to the Beckery Monastery near Glastonbury. It's possible a monk or nun carried it here to Chinon or one of the many abbeys in France. Or it might have been a thief. I know it wound up in England again later. Some things I don't know for sure."

"Somebody should lock these stones up," Andrew teased. "They're dangerous."

"I'm thinking of building a special vault, for safekeeping," Alfred said.

Andrew and Eve exchanged looks.

Alfred noticed. "Don't tell me."

They laughed.

"It's dangerous for me to be with you," he admitted. "I had better leave."

"You're leaving us? Aren't we going with you?" Eve asked.

"I'm not sure what the Radiant Stone will do with people from two different times. It might take you to my time, not yours. Or worse, it could take us back to *your* time. That could be a problem. I don't belong in the future. It might kill me instantly, or I might die quickly of old age. I would rather not take that chance, if it's all the same to you."

"But won't the Valiant Stone take us back to the moment Simon stole it from you in your time?" asked Andrew.

Eve brightened up. "If it does, then we can use the Radiant Stone to go back to our time," she suggested.

Alfred chuckled. "Like changing trains at a station?"

"Why not?" she asked.

"I'm not sure it works that way. If you take the Radiant Stone from my time to your time, then I won't be able to finish my research."

"Oh," Eve said thoughtfully. "If you don't finish your research, then I won't know how the stone works."

"That could change both our histories in ways we can't anticipate," Alfred said.

"But you said we can't change history," Eve reminded him. "You're very clear about it in your journals."

"Really? Oh." He laughed. "Clearly you know more of what I know than I do at this point."

"What should we do?" Andrew asked.

"Any hope you have of getting back to your time is with the Valiant Stone," he said. "Unlike the Radiant Stone, it hasn't been part of your history. Until now."

Eve looked worried. "Are you sure it will take us home?"

Alfred rubbed his chin. "I'm making an uneducated guess about that. I believe it will take you back to your

CHAPTER FORTY-ONE

time because that is where you belong. The stones have an uncanny sense of order and place. The individual facets go backward, but if you clasp the stone with your entire hand, the stone defers to the one clasping it, as if it *must* return you to your true place."

Andrew struggled to understand what Alfred Virtue was saying. "Why?"

"I believe it's because God has so ordered it. The stones are part of the wonder of His creation. He places us in our times and places to serve Him there and then. The stones aren't meant to change that."

"We served Him here," Eve said. "We helped Jeanne."

Alfred nodded. "That may be so, but you were not born to be here. To stay here would eventually drive you insane, like it did Simon. The answer may be in his papers." He stood up.

"What if the Valiant Stone doesn't work?" Eve asked.

"I will come back to check on you." He tipped his hat to them. "With that, I will say goodbye." He gestured to the box and papers. "And I'll say a sad farewell to poor Simon Howard."

"Simon *Howard*?" Eve said.

"Yes. Why?"

"That's the name of a professor my aunt knows."

"A descendant?"

Andrew remembered that Dr. Howard had said his ancestor knew Alfred Virtue and Theodore Perry. "It has to be," said Andrew.

Alfred reached into his pocket and pulled out a small pouch. He carefully removed the Radiant Stone. "It's clumsy trying to carry it without touching it," he said.

"You should design a case for that," Andrew suggested. "Like a pocket watch."

Alfred chuckled. "Theodore Perry said the same thing." He took the glove off his right hand.

"Thank you for saving us," Eve said.

Alfred Virtue smiled at her. "It was a providential accident."

Alfred clasped the Radiant Stone.

"Wait!" Andrew called out. "Theodore Perry *knew* about the time travel?"

It was too late. Alfred Virtue had disappeared.

42

As much as Andrew and Eve wanted to go back to Hope Springs right away, they wanted to return in their modern clothes just as much.

"It's too dark to get them now," Eve said.

They agreed to retrieve their clothes in the morning.

Too excited to sleep, they took out Simon's parchments. Andrew was right: they were his personal journals. Passing them back and forth, they put together his story.

Simon Howard was determined to witness the Battle of Agincourt for himself, and he refused to take Alfred Virtue's *no* as an answer. He stole the Valiant Stone, believing he would go, watch the battle, and then return to his time. The problem was that the Valiant Stone had never been to Agincourt. Instead, the stone took him to Paris the year *before* Agincourt, so he had to bide his time until the battle happened.

He wasn't idle. He used his knowledge of gems, science, warfare, and even his high-school French, to good advantage. He made a decent living in Paris that year and then—*oops*—he met a peasant woman named Catherine and fell in love. Though he knew it was wrong, he married her. To make matters worse, he told her about the Valiant Stone.

At this point in his journal, Simon admitted that he had tried to bring Catherine to the Hope Springs of his time, but the minute she arrived, she began to feel extremely sick. She also began to age very quickly. "She didn't belong there," Simon wrote. So they returned to Paris.

The time for Agincourt grew closer. He was about to journey to that part of the country, when Catherine's brother, Vincent, showed up. According to Simon, the man was "as foul and unworthy a creature as ever allowed by God to exist." Vincent wanted money to buy a commission in the army so he could fight the English invaders. Simon was willing to lend him some, but it wasn't enough.

Unfortunately, Catherine had told Vincent about the Valiant Stone. He believed they could all enjoy a wealthy life if only Simon would use it. Vincent imagined the benefits of investing money in areas they knew would succeed.

Ironically, Simon had refused to help Vincent in much the same way that Alfred Virtue had refused to help Simon. Undaunted, Vincent demanded the stone from Simon. Knives were drawn, and the two men fought. Catherine tried to intercede, and Vincent stabbed her by accident. Simon attacked Vincent, wounding him in

CHAPTER FORTY-TWO

the eye. Vincent escaped. But Catherine died a slow and painful death.

Simon wrote, "All of my modern knowledge could not save her."

In his despair and grief, he sought revenge against Vincent. Certain that the fiend would be at Agincourt, Simon went there to kill him. The men came upon each other the night before the battle. They fought again. This time, Vincent cried for help. French soldiers rushed in. Vincent claimed that Simon was an assassin from the English side. The French tried to take Simon prisoner, but he escaped.

Knowing that Agincourt would end in a decisive victory for the English, Simon joined their forces. After the slaughter, he departed from France, knowing the poverty the long war would bring. He returned to England with Henry's troops and was welcomed as a hero. Again Simon used his modern knowledge to good advantage and became a royal jeweler, armorer, and soldier. He fought in battle like a man who didn't care whether he lived or died. He knew he would encounter Vincent again and eventually fulfill his obsession for revenge.

Simon also began to realize that being a man out of time had affected something else. He was aging more slowly than everyone else. He speculated he could live for another hundred years. But would he want to?

After this, the journal entries became more random. Andrew and Eve concluded that Simon was losing his mind. He wrote again and again about forgetting things he should remember, and the nagging sense that he belonged somewhere else. In his growing madness, his knowledge of history became little more than instinct. He could sense what was going to happen without remembering that he once *knew* what would happen. He chronicled how he reread the earlier parts of his journal and decided he was insane for believing what he wrote.

Meanwhile, he fought for the English against the French, until he saw firsthand what English rule was doing to the French people. He could not justify England's claim to the throne or the country. He placed his allegiance with the Dauphin and journeyed to Chinon. He'd heard about *la Pucelle*, and the memories began to torment him. He *knew* about Joan of Arc but couldn't explain why. Then in his last scribbled note, he admitted that he saw two children arrive. He was sure they were of the devil. It filled him with an unexplainable rage.

"He forgot to mention how he attacked our sneakers," Eve said.

At first light, Andrew and Eve went back to get their clothes. They made their way down to the riverbank. The water had receded enough for Andrew to climb the pillars and supports and pull the sack from the space where Eve had stashed it.

CHAPTER FORTY-TWO

Hidden by the bridge, they changed into their modern clothes. Then Eve decided to put the sack and her note back in their hiding place.

"That archaeologist will find my note years from now and contact Alfred Virtue," Eve said. "He won't know what it means, but it'll be a fun mystery."

"This stuff gives me a headache," Andrew complained.

They looked at each other's clothes and the way Simon had mangled the stitching.

"Are you ready?" Eve asked.

Andrew held open the wooden box. *Please let this work*, he prayed.

Eve took Andrew's hand, then wrapped her fingers around the Valiant Stone.

"I hope—"

But Eve didn't get to finish her sentence in fifteenth-century France.

———

"—it takes us back to our own time," Eve was saying when they arrived.

Andrew was looking down at Simon's box. It was still in his hands. Then he looked around.

"Oh no," Eve said.

They weren't in Alfred Virtue's office in the Old Bank Building. They were standing in what looked like the living room of someone's apartment. The style of the furniture and decorations were old-fashioned, maybe from the early twentieth century.

"Did it take us back to Simon's time?" Eve asked.

The sound of a horn outside sent them both rushing to the window. They were on the second floor of an apartment building across the street from the Old Bank Building. The sign declared that it was the home of the Virtue Curiosity Shoppe.

"And the cars are modern," Andrew said.

Eve gave a sigh of relief. "Thank God."

"But whose apartment is this?" Andrew asked.

Looking around, they spied a picture on the wall. It was Dr. Vince Howard at a ceremony. Next to the picture was his framed master's degree from a university in Denver.

"This is Dr. Howard's place?" Andrew was beginning to feel nauseous.

"His name is Vincent," Eve noted. "I knew there was a good reason not to like him," she added.

"But why did the stone bring us here?" Andrew asked.

Eve pointed to another framed photo of a young-looking Simon Howard sitting on a side table.

"Maybe it was Simon's apartment then, and Vincent stays here now when he visits Hope Springs," Andrew suggested. "So the Valiant Stone brought us here because ... Are you feeling sick? I'm feeling sick." Andrew felt as if he was turning green.

"I am too. But we can't throw up in here. It isn't ours."

CHAPTER FORTY-TWO

They suddenly looked at each other and realized that, at the moment, they were guilty of breaking and entering.

"We have to get out of here," Andrew said.

They tiptoed as fast as they could out the door and down the stairs to the front door of the complex.

Eve carefully put the Valiant Stone in her pocket. "Remind me not to touch that," she said.

Not wanting to be seen from across the street, they found a rear door leading to a parking lot. They navigated around the apartment building and across the street to the Old Bank Building, then slipped through a side door by the stairwell.

Eve's Aunt Catherine and Dr. Howard were still talking in the main area of the shop. Eve and Andrew crept down the stairwell that led to the vaults and Alfred Virtue's private office.

Once inside again, Andrew dropped the box on the desk and collapsed into Alfred Virtue's old chair. He felt better now. The radonite was doing its job.

"Home again," Eve said happily.

Andrew looked at the Radiant Stone. It was sitting where it had been a few seconds ago. Then he remembered that more than a year had gone by almost six hundred years ago. He groaned.

"This stuff gives me a headache," he said again.

Eve looked up at the wall. A framed photo of Alfred Virtue looked back at her. "We met him," she said proudly.

"And Joan of Arc," Andrew added.

Eve held up her hand. "I don't want to think about that right now. It breaks my heart."

"All right," Andrew agreed. "But you have to admit, these stones are making our lives really weird."

Eve found a cleaning cloth and used it to take the Valiant Stone out of her pocket. She looked around. "Where should I put it?"

"In Simon's box," Andrew suggested. "Then hide it in one of those file drawers."

Eve put the Valiant Stone into the box and set the box on the desk.

Andrew could hear Mrs. Drake and Dr. Howard coming down the hall, talking. Mrs. Drake peeked into the office. "I was just showing Dr. Howard the vaults." She stepped aside so Dr. Howard could look in.

"This was Alfred Virtue's office," she told him.

Now that he knew Dr. Howard was related to Simon, Andrew could see a resemblance in the eyes and mouth.

"Fascinating," Dr. Howard said. He looked down at the desk. "What is this box? May I see it?"

Eve put her hand on the top. "No."

"Don't be rude." Aunt Catherine spoke politely but with a "Let him look if he wants" edge.

"I have some personal things in it," Eve said quickly. "It's embarrassing."

Dr. Howard was undaunted. "The wood, the hinges. It looks medieval. That's quite a thing to put personal items in. Where did you get it?"

CHAPTER FORTY-TWO

Eve shuffled nervously. "It was mixed in with Alfred Virtue's stuff."

"He collected all sorts of things," Aunt Catherine said. She touched Eve's shoulder, her fingers tugging at the crude stitching on Eve's pullover. She looked at Eve with an unspoken question.

Dr. Howard scanned the desk. His eyes landed on the Radiant Stone. It was still sitting in its open case. "What is that?" he asked as he reached for it.

"Don't touch it!" Andrew and Eve cried out together.

His head jerked toward them even as the tip of his finger touched the stone.

He disappeared.

Aunt Catherine shrieked.

"Oh no." Andrew stood up. The stone was still on the desk. He looked at Eve.

"He went without the stone." Eve's face went pale.

"What have you done with him?" Aunt Catherine cried.

"I haven't done anything with him," Eve said. "He touched the stone. He went somewhere in time."

"Well, *do something*!" Aunt Catherine sputtered.

Andrew looked at the stone. In a worried tone, he said, "He didn't take it with him."

"What does that mean?" asked Aunt Catherine.

Andrew swallowed hard. "He can't get back."

Aunt Catherine put a hand on her hip and wagged a finger at Eve. "Then you will have to go get him!"

"Which facet did he touch?" Eve asked Andrew.

Andrew took a closer look. "I think it was *that* one. Or maybe it was that other one. I don't know. We'd have to dust for fingerprints to find out."

"Magnifying glass," Eve muttered and searched through the desk drawers and shelves. She found one, wiped the dust off on her pant leg, and checked the stone.

"Well?" Aunt Catherine stood with her arms folded, her foot tapping.

"Was he eating any candy?" Eve asked.

"He had one of my homemade strawberry pastries."

"Powdered sugar?"

"Yes!" she said, obviously annoyed. "Please stop playing Sherlock Holmes and go find the poor man!"

Eve looked at Andrew. "It's this one. But I don't know where it goes."

"Touch it and we'll find out," Andrew said.

Eve picked up the case holding the Radiant Stone. She draped the chain over her head and around her neck. "Here we go again."

"Where were you before?" Aunt Catherine asked.

"I'll explain when we get back." She held out her hand for Andrew.

He grabbed it.

She carefully touched the facet with Dr. Howard's sugary fingerprint on it.

The office—and the world as they knew it—disappeared.

Hope Springs™

THE VIRTUE CHRONICLES

THE SAINTLY OUTLAW

Hope Springs
The Virtue Chronicles

The Saintly Outlaw
The Warrior Maiden
Hidden Heroes

Hope Springs™

THE VIRTUE CHRONICLES

THE SAINTLY OUTLAW

By Paul McCusker

AUGUSTINE INSTITUTE
Greenwood Village, CO

Augustine Institute
6160 S. Syracuse Way, Suite 310
Greenwood Village, CO 80111
Tel: (866) 767-3155
www.augustineinstitute.org

Cover Design: Christina Gray

© 2019 Paul McCusker
All rights reserved

ISBN 978-1-7338598-7-5
Library of Congress Control Number 2019941585

Printed in Canada

Adapted with gratitude from the works of Henry Gilbert and through the generosity of the Palmer Family.

THE SAINTLY OUTLAW

PROLOGUE	1
CHAPTER 1	11
CHAPTER 2	19
CHAPTER 3	33
CHAPTER 4	41
CHAPTER 5	49
CHAPTER 6	63
CHAPTER 7	81
CHAPTER 8	101
CHAPTER 9	107
CHAPTER 10	115
CHAPTER 11	127
CHAPTER 12	143
CHAPTER 13	159
CHAPTER 14	177
CHAPTER 15	193
CHAPTER 16	201
CHAPTER 17	213

PROLOGUE

It all started just before Christmas when Andrew Perry's family went Christmas shopping in downtown Hope Springs. They weren't there as part of the crowds of tourists who came from Denver and the other bigger towns to find some bargains or reasonably priced antiques. The Perrys lived in Hope Springs.

Andrew had gone off on his own to look for presents. His first priority was to go to the Pen & Paint Art Store to find some pens, pencils, and art supplies for his sister Lizzy.

He was walking along, looking in the shop windows, when he passed the Old Bank Building. That's what all the locals called it: "The Old Bank Building," even though it had stopped being a bank building sometime back in the 1970s when the state and national banks opened branches in other parts of town. The bank—the Hope Springs Bank & Trust—closed down and the building was abandoned. Small businesses used it from time to time, and even the City Hall was housed there when work was being done on the real City Hall. After a while, a family with a personal interest in the place bought the whole building and restored it as a giant antique shop.

Andrew had been past the Old Bank Building a lot of times, but he'd hardly paid attention to it. But this time something caught his eye and he stopped.

He realized the front of the building was the exact same image that had been painted on the front of his family's Advent calendar.

The Perry family's Advent calendar had been in the family for almost a hundred years. It was made of wood and stood about three feet tall and was half-a-foot thick. The front was painted to look like a red brick building and had large windows on the bottom and a big door and smaller windows going up for three stories. The windows were made with little hinges that opened up to small compartments to reveal the Advent surprises.

Theodore Perry, Andrew's grandfather (well, he had a couple of "greats" in front of "grandfather," but Andrew could never remember how many) had built the Advent calendar for his kids back in the 1920s. It was handed down from generation to generation and wound up with Andrew's dad.

Andrew always felt a small surge of pride when his family set up the Advent calendar for the season. People who visited often commented on how amazing it was. It was unique.

But Andrew now saw that it wasn't unique at all. There, right in front of him, was the real thing: the Old Bank

Building was the model for the Perry Advent Calendar. And there, in the picture window of the Old Bank Building, was an Advent calendar just like the one Andrew had at home.

Andrew couldn't believe it. There it was, on display standing on fake snow, dwarfed by a huge Christmas tree made of silver pine needles, with a multicolored spinning wheel that slowly turned in front of a bright bulb to change the color of the tree. The entire spectacle was lined with old-fashioned Christmas garlands and lights with gigantic bulbs.

What is this place doing with our Advent calendar? he wondered.

He stepped back and looked up at the sign above the door. Bold black cursive letters announced: *The Virtue Curiosity Shoppe.* (The word "shop" really had an extra "p" and "e" at the end. Andrew assumed that whoever did the sign took the spelling from a Charles Dickens story.)

Andrew thought, *It's a curiosity shop and now I'm curious,* so he went through the double doors.

"Sensory overload" was the phrase that came to his mind as he entered. The vast room that greeted him must have been the lobby to the old bank, but now the entire area looked like a department store for antiques. Racks and stands held old-fashioned dresses, suits, and all kinds of hats: hats with feathers, stove-pipe hats, and hats shaped like plates. Old furniture had been arranged as dining rooms, kitchens, bedrooms, and living rooms. There were glass cabinets and lamps and vases and old dial telephones and wooden toys. Dark wooden cases were gathered in clusters, their shelves cluttered with leather books and knickknacks and lots of things Andrew didn't recognize. He heard a tinkling sound and looked up. A giant chandelier hung from the ceiling, reaching down at least two stories with a gold chain.

Closed doors lined some of the other walls. Open doors led to more rooms with smaller displays of antiques. One was filled with Christmas decorations. He noticed a long counter in the back that sat on marble pedestals and had small iron windows. He was pretty sure the bank tellers had worked there.

Andrew hadn't moved from the front door. He'd been standing there, his mouth hanging open, slowly taking in all he could see. Suddenly, something clicked next to him. He turned to see an upright piano. "Silent Night" started to play all by itself. The keys moved without fingers touching them.

"That's our player piano," a woman's voice said.

Andrew spun around to see a woman standing behind a broad counter to the side of the front door. It was the kind of counter he'd seen in a fancy old western hotel, with panels of gold and red velvet on the front and a polished wood top. There was even a large silver bell on the counter to summon a clerk.

"Have you ever seen one?" The woman had a friendly smile and round silver glasses framing her big brown eyes. Her brown hair was piled in a loose bun on top of her head. She came around the counter to the piano and pointed to two panels on the front above the keyboard.

She slid them aside to reveal a wide scroll that was rolling down. The scroll had holes all over it. She explained, "There is a mechanism inside that moves the scroll. The holes in the scroll trigger the levers inside that move the keys and play the music."

"Like an old computer," Andrew said, looking closer at the scroll.

The woman pulled her glasses down the bridge of her nose and looked at Andrew. "You are one of the Perry kids," she said.

Andrew nodded.

She smiled and said, "I knew it!" She put out her hand for Andrew to shake. "I'm sure you don't remember me. I'm Catherine Drake. I went to school with your father. You were a lot younger the last time you came into my store. I saw you from time to time when your family came for summer visits."

Andrew could never forget his summer visits to Hope Springs. His father had grown up in the town but went off to college in Denver and later founded a successful computer programming business. The family had lived in Denver until the previous summer, when Andrew's parents decided it was time to move to Hope Springs for good.

Mrs. Drake put a finger to her chin and tapped lightly. "It's you and your younger sister and ... the twins," she said.

"Yes, ma'am," Andrew said. "Lizzy, Nick, and Sam."

She looked at Andrew's face and slowly shook her head. "You look just like him, you know."

"Like who?" Andrew asked, thinking she was likely talking about his dad.

She turned and pointed. Dominating a section of a far wall was a massive painting in a gold frame. In the painting stood two men dressed in old-fashioned suits, the kind with long jackets and big collars and vests and ties. Both men had their hands on an oversized globe of the world.

"Take a closer look," Mrs. Drake said and gestured for Andrew to walk over. "The man with the moustache and gold wire-framed glasses there on the left is Alfred Virtue. He founded the bank."

Andrew had heard of the man, maybe in school. Or maybe his parents had mentioned him. His eyes went to the man on the right.

"That's Theodore Perry," she said.

Andrew let out a small gasp. Theodore Perry looked like an older version of Andrew. Or maybe Andrew looked like a younger version of Theodore Perry. He wasn't sure which way to think about it.

"Alfred Virtue was my great-great-grandfather. I always get confused about how many 'greats' he was," Mrs. Drake said.

"Me too," Andrew said.

"Alfred Virtue and Theodore Perry were best friends and business partners."

Andrew gazed at the painting and suddenly felt as if all the antiques and clothes and displays had been cleared away and there was Theodore Perry, live and in-person, standing in the bank with customers, all dressed in clothes of that time. The bank tellers stood in their stations behind the iron grates on the long counter, with customers passing slips of paper or receiving money. Their voices echoed inside, and from outside came the sounds of horses clip-clopping along the street. Through the big front window, Andrew saw the carriages and wagons and even a black Model T car, whose driver was scowling as he tried to navigate around the slow traffic. A police officer in a blue uniform, twirling a big nightstick, walked toward him.

It was so vivid that Andrew had to blink a few times to check himself. Then, in an instant, the scene was gone and he was standing back in the Curiosity Shoppe with "Silent Night" playing from the piano and the normal traffic moving outside.

"Are you all right?" Mrs. Drake asked, looking at him with a puzzled expression.

Andrew would later try to think about how that moment triggered something inside of him. He had a powerful desire to go *into* that painting, into the moment when the two men posed for the painter. He wanted to stand in that room as it once was. He wanted to pick up the antiques all around the room, not just to hold them, but to experience them as they were when they weren't considered antiques. He wanted to feel what it was like to live in the past.

"I could stay here all day," Andrew heard himself say to her.

She smiled at him and said, "I know what you mean."

Just then, other customers came in. Mrs. Drake said, "Excuse me," and went off to talk to them.

Andrew wasn't sure where to begin with such a huge shop. He slowly turned in a circle to take it all in. That's when he saw something move behind the old bank counter. A girl appeared in one of the teller's slots. She had a round face and round glasses and short dark hair. He figured she was his age.

She saw him looking back at her and ducked down.

Weird, he thought. He wondered if she was related to Mrs. Drake. Or maybe she worked there. Or, worse, she might be sneaking around. *Should I say something to Mrs. Drake, just in case?* he thought.

Just then Andrew's little sister Sam was at his side. "Hi, Andrew!" she called out.

The rest of his family had come in when Andrew wasn't paying attention.

"Hi," he said to her and followed her back to the front door. Andrew's dad and Mrs. Drake talked like old friends and even discussed the painting and how much Andrew looked like Theodore Perry. The burst of chat and interest in the shop took Andrew away, though he kept seeing the mystery girl out of the corner of his eye. She kept peering from behind the clothes racks and bookcases. He wondered why she was watching them. Then he realized that she was watching *him*.

His dad said it was time to go and everyone was walking out when Mrs. Drake leaned down and said to Andrew quietly, "Come back any time you want."

He nodded.

She added in a whisper, "Alfred and Ted were up to some really interesting things. You should see what's in the basement some time."

Andrew would think much later, *That was the start of the adventure.*

1

It was April in Hope Springs, which didn't mean it was springtime yet, since the Rocky Mountains were known for quick changes in the weather. One day it might be 60 degrees with buds appearing on the trees, the next day it could be 34 degrees with a foot of snow on the ground. On this particular day, Andrew was wearing a heavier coat because, though the sun was bright, there was an arctic wind blowing through the town.

Andrew didn't mind. He enjoyed the unpredictability of the weather.

He opened the door to the Virtue Curiosity Shoppe and stepped in. The Christmas displays in the window were of course gone. Catherine Drake had replaced them with antique shelves lined with first editions of classic works of literature, all in leather bindings and a few opened up to show off the colorful artwork inside.

Andrew had been to the shop a few times since Christmas. He liked to look around at all the antiques and wander through the rooms. He was especially interested in the collection of local history books, many that told stories of the town's legends. His ancestors were mentioned a few times.

The girl he'd seen at Christmas was sometimes there. But she did what she'd done before: watch him from behind the displays and the furniture in a game of hide-and-seek.

Finally, he had asked Catherine Drake who the girl was.

She gave him a knowing smile. "That's my niece," she had said. "Evangeline, but we call her Eve." She cupped her hands around her mouth and called out, "*Eeeee-v.*"

Eve didn't answer. A door slammed somewhere in the back of the shop.

"*Eve Virtue!*" Catherine Drake had called out again. She gave Andrew an apologetic look. "I don't know why she's being so shy."

On this particular Saturday morning, Catherine Drake said hello as Andrew walked in and she directed him to a section in the far-right corner with some new history books she'd recently picked up from a family estate. "It's near the old teller counter," she said.

Andrew made his way past the tables and displays and found the collection of books. He had just picked up one about Native American tribes in the area when he saw a face looking at him through the bars of one of the teller stations.

He sighed. It was Eve Virtue playing her game again.

He looked directly at her, but she didn't hide this time. She held steady and gazed at him.

CHAPTER ONE

Her face wasn't as round as he remembered, and she wasn't wearing the round glasses, but her hair was still short in a pixie style and he now realized it was almost jet-black. But it was her eyes that caught his attention. They were like a color he had never seen: pale blue and green, maybe, but not exactly. They shone bright, even though the corner was in a shadow.

"Aren't we a little too old for hide-and-seek?" he said to her.

Eve smiled and dropped down behind the counter. Andrew put down the book and took a few steps to see where she'd gone. He saw her crouched down, moving along the back wall like a cat past the doors to the different rooms. Then she ducked inside one, leaving the door open.

Andrew slowly followed her, not sure if he was supposed to or even if he wanted to. Then he heard a clock chime from inside the room. Then another. And another.

He peeked around the door. The girl was standing in the middle of the room. He saw only now that she wore a dark blue sweater, light-colored blue jeans, and gray sneakers. She was waiting for him, that smile still in place. She lifted her right hand to the base of her neck. She clasped something in her fist that was attached to a thin silver chain.

The chimes increased, singing in high and low notes, and Andrew realized the room was filled with clocks. All kinds of clocks: large and small, of different shapes and colors, sitting on tables and shelves and hanging on the walls without any clear order. Grandfather clocks stood proudly like soldiers along one wall. The biggest of them was in the far corner, as tall as the ceiling. It had a giant face that glowed yellow and a door as big as one you'd find on a closet.

The clocks were chiming eleven o'clock. But Andrew noticed the giant clock was showing one o'clock. He waited for the chimes to stop, then asked the girl, "Why do you keep playing hide-and-seek?"

"I had to be sure," she said. "I wanted to know if you are serious."

"Serious about what?"

"The past."

"What past?"

"The past."

"What are you talking about?"

"Are you serious, Andrew Perry?" It was the first time she'd said his name.

"Serious about *what*, Eve Virtue?" he mimicked her.

"An amazing mystery."

"I like mysteries," he said, thinking about stolen money and murders and weird creatures from outer space.

She said, "Decide now."

"Decide *what?*"

"If you're coming or not," she said. She turned and went to the giant clock with the huge door. The door had a key in the lock. She pulled it out and held it up for him to see. It was an old-fashioned skeleton key. "It took me a long time to figure out what this key went to," she said. "Alfred Virtue has a lot of keys hidden around."

She put the key into the lock again and gave it a hard turn. The latch clicked loudly. She pulled the door open.

Andrew stepped forward to get a better view. He saw the pendulum inside swinging back and forth in slow, wide movements. Behind the pendulum was dark space. He squinted but couldn't see the back of the clock.

"Coming?" she asked.

The pendulum swung far to the right. To Andrew's surprise, Eve jumped past it and into the darkness.

It can't be that big, he thought. He peered into the clock cabinet. A black nothing peered back at him. *Is there an opening in the back of the clock to a secret room or a tunnel?*

Eve laughed from somewhere inside.

"Don't be afraid," she said. Her voice echoed like she was in a big room.

"I'm *not*," he called back to her, annoyed at the suggestion.

She said impatiently, "Then *let's go!*"

Andrew waited until the pendulum swung past and jumped through.

He took a few steps and then stopped. Pitch-black. He looked back and could see the swinging pendulum and the light from the room of clocks. But he couldn't see anything ahead of or around him.

"Hello?" he called out. His voice echoed, as if he stood in a vast space. "If you jump out to scare me, I'm leaving," he said.

"Come on," she said. Her voice was somewhere ahead—*far* ahead.

"This is creepy," he said to the vast darkness. "How big is this place?"

He imagined he was in a big warehouse, maybe a stock room where Catherine Drake stored a lot of the antiques.

"Walk straight," Eve called out. She sounded even farther away.

He held his hands in front of him and began to walk slowly. He feared bumping into something hard. "Where's the light?" he asked, but she didn't answer. The room went on and on. He turned to look behind him again. The pendulum and light from the room were like a distant window.

He hadn't taken *that* many steps.

"Come on," Eve said, startling him. She sounded like she was only a foot away, though he still couldn't see her. She took hold of his hand.

Suddenly, bright colored lights shot past them to the left and right, over their heads and below their feet, like they were surging forward—except they were not moving. The *lights* were. He saw Eve in silhouette against the speeding lights. She was looking ahead. Then she let go of his hand and the lights went out.

It was dark again. *But not the same kind of dark*, Andrew thought. *More like a gray.*

CHAPTER ONE

He was aware of the sound of birds. He also felt as if the air had become heavy, like it did on really humid days. And there was a smell that reminded him of grass after it had been cut. *It smells green*, he thought.

He saw a vertical line of light flickering just ahead. It reminded him of the sun shining through the middle of closed curtains.

Was it a stage curtain? he wondered. *Did Catherine Drake set up some kind of historical presentation? Am I about to walk into a show?*

He shoved his hands into the vertical line of light and pushed the curtains aside. Only, they weren't cloth curtains. They were wooden and bristly, scratching the backs of his hands and rustling with the sounds of leaves and branches.

He emerged into a new light and had to blink a few times to adjust his eyes.

He froze where he was. He couldn't believe what he was seeing.

2

Spread out in front of Andrew was a forest, a *large* forest with countless trees and a golden haze of sunlight mixing with the greens and browns.

He thought hard and couldn't connect what he was seeing with what he knew to be reality. There was a parking lot behind Virtue's Curiosity Shoppe, not a forest. And, as he looked, it occurred to him that this wasn't the kind of forest he knew in Colorado, with slender pine trees and stick-like branches and needles on the ground and the kind of crisp air that came with being high above sea level. These trees were fat and had knotholes and branches reaching out like muscular arms. The air was thick with the smell of damp leaves and moss.

He thought hard about it some more. *It's a virtual display*, he decided, *like they have in museums and amusement parks. I'm looking at a 3-D screen in front of me and they have machines doing tricks with the light and making the air feel like it does.*

To prove he was right, he took a few steps forward. He came to a tree and touched the bark. It was rough. An ant marched near his finger.

He looked up. The tree reached high. Through the branches he could see blue sky and white clouds. A bird darted past.

Turning around, he looked at the curtain he'd passed through. It was actually heavy vines covering the mouth of a cave.

He thought, *This is amazing technology!*

He considered going back, just to see if the cave was a warehouse, but the shout of a man stopped him. He turned to look. Off to the right, someone or something was racing through the trees. Whatever it was ran in his direction.

He heard shouts and then dogs barking and, coming closer, the sound of a low snarling and snorting, like a really angry pig.

Then he saw it. A big black hairy beast with a long face and tusks on each side of its snout. And it was running straight for him.

He didn't know what to do. If it was a virtual machine, the beast would run through him. But his instincts said to get out of the way—*and fast.*

Andrew staggered backward a few steps, looking around. He half-ran several more steps.

"Up here."

He stopped and looked up. Eve was stretched out on a thick tree branch.

CHAPTER TWO

"You better hurry," she said. "That boar will trample you."

He ran over to the tree and jumped for the lowest branch. Catching hold, he pulled himself up and scrambled higher until he was on a branch near her.

"They'll be chasing it," she said. "Keep quiet. We mustn't let them know we're here."

"*Who?*" Andrew asked.

She put a finger to her lips and pointed down.

The boar was underneath them now, moving in a small circle, unsure of where to run. Dogs came from different directions and quickly had it surrounded. They snarled and barked at the beast, their hair high on their backs. The boar squealed and snorted, darting back and forth between the dogs. It charged at one with its tusks. With a yelp, the dog stumbled back, then fell to its side, whining as blood poured out of a gash.

Andrew heard a sharp buzzing sound. The boar shrieked as an arrow hit it in the neck. It shrieked furiously and circled in a frenzy. A spear struck its right side. Then another arrow flew from yet another direction, joining the spear. Then a spear caught the left side of its body. The boar dropped, its legs kicking. It made a loud and horrible noise as it lay dying.

None of this makes sense, Andrew thought. *It can't be virtual reality.*

Four men appeared below and kicked at the dogs to move them aside, then stepped up to the squirming animal.

Though they were below him, Andrew was at enough of an angle to make out their features. One man was older, with silver hair and a matching beard. He wore a dark blue robe with gold trim laced with patterns Andrew couldn't see very well. A gold belt of chains hung loose around his waist. Black shoes peeked out from under his robe.

Two of the other men were younger, each with dark curly hair. One had a short beard and the other was clean-shaven. They wore tunics, one red and the other purple, that also had gold trim with the same kinds of patterns that the older man wore. Their legs were covered with dark leggings, though one wore brown leather boots that folded down at the top. The other wore dark shoes that looked like slippers.

There was a fourth man in a plain brown tunic that went down to his knees. A belt that looked like a rope was tied in the middle of his waist. He wore leggings like the other men, though his were dirty and torn. His brown shoes had leather straps that held them together.

The whole scene reminded Andrew of a medieval fair his parents had taken him to one summer.

The squirming boar made another terrible squeal.

Animatronics, Andrew hoped. *Some kind of robot.* But the blood looked very real.

He glanced at Eve. She was still watching the men.

The silver-haired man came nearest to the boar. He raised a sword high and brought it point-down into the chest of the beast. The boar stopped squirming.

The two young men laughed as the older man handed his sword to the fourth man, clearly a servant. "Clean that," he said. He gestured to the dead boar. "Get this back to the house. Put it on the spit for dinner."

"Yes, my lord," the fourth man said.

The whining dog caught the older man's attention. "Stop that," he said.

The clean-shaven, curly-haired man drew a knife from his belt and, with one swift stroke, silenced the dog.

The servant put his fingers to his mouth and let off a loud shrill whistle. Andrew heard voices and footfalls crashing through the forest. Through the branches of his hiding place, he saw a dozen men, dressed like the servant, rushing toward them.

The three men walked away, but the dogs moved in to smell the dead boar. The older man gave a shout and the dogs broke away to follow. Soon, the servants arrived with a carrier made of wooden slats. With grunts and gasps, they began the work of loading the boar and carting it away.

The forest fell into a peaceful silence. Eve beckoned Andrew to follow her. She scampered like a squirrel along the branch, then up to another that stretched across to an adjacent tree. She paused there and waved for him to hurry.

Carefully, he did what she had done. The branches were thick enough not to shake very much. He gained his footing and grew more confident as he went.

Eve led the way, crawling from one branch to another, finding ones that bridged to another tree and then another.

Andrew struggled to keep up. *Now I feel like I'm in a Tarzan movie*, he thought.

Everything his senses experienced—the humid air, the rough bark of the trees, the effort to keep balanced—told him that it was all real, but his brain couldn't make sense of it. How could a 3-D image or virtual reality program or a stage show be this *real*?

"This way," Eve whispered and climbed down to the ground.

Andrew did the same and, once he was sure they were alone, said, "What is this place? Am I dreaming?"

"If you're dreaming, then I'm dreaming, too," she said.

"Not unless you're just saying that in my dream," he countered.

"We need to get dressed," she said.

"Get dressed? For what?"

"You don't want anyone to see you like that." She took a few steps and Andrew realized they were back at the ivy curtain and the cave. Reaching behind some bushes nearby, Eve pulled out a sack. "I hope these fit. I grabbed them along the way."

"Along the way?" he asked.

She pulled clothes out of the sack and handed them to him. "Put those on."

Before he could say anything, she disappeared behind another thick bush.

"Are we part of the show?" he asked as he looked at the clothes she'd given him. They were made of a rough fabric.

CHAPTER TWO

"Hurry, before someone sees you," she called out. "The clothes will feel itchy at first."

Andrew had to make a decision. Was he playing along or putting an end to this craziness? What if he refused? What would happen if he dashed back into the cave to go home? Would he see the clock pendulum and the light from the room of clocks?

He pushed the ivy aside. A wall of stone faced him. The cave was gone.

"You can't get back like that," Eve said from behind the bush. "Now, get dressed."

Andrew changed into the clothes Eve had given him. He pulled on a green shirt that felt like it was made of leather. It came down to the middle of his thighs. It was rough and uncomfortable. Next came thick brown leggings, probably wool and definitely itchy. They fit his legs like a tight pair of jeans, but hung loose around his waist. A belt fixed that. It was made of interwoven strips of leather. There was no buckle, so Andrew had to tie it in the front. He sat on the ground to yank on a pair of dark brown leather boots. They covered his feet with room to spare and went up to his knees.

Eve emerged from behind the bush. She wore a brown tunic, probably wool, that reached down to her knees. A thin strap cinched it around her waist. A vest of leather hung over the tunic. Green leggings covered her legs. Leather shoes reached just above her ankles.

She nodded to him, then gathered up their clothes and shoved them into the sack. She hid it behind the bush again.

"Come on," she said. She picked up a satchel and slung it over her shoulder. She strode into the forest.

"To where?" Andrew asked, following her yet again. He stumbled over fallen branches. He groaned. "Don't they have hiking trails here?"

"Just watch where you're going," Eve said. "You'll get used to it."

"Used to what?" he demanded. "Where are we? Where are we going?"

"*There*," Eve said and pointed.

Through the trees, Andrew saw a mansion with big gray stones, tall windows, and chimneys sticking out here and there. It was like something out of an old movie.

He picked up his pace, now running through the woods toward the mansion, stumbling more.

They reached the edge of the forest. A field stretched out between them and the mansion.

The field is real, he thought. *The mansion is real.* He didn't know what to do with all the things his eyes and ears and sense of touch were telling him was true. He felt a growing sense of panic. His mind kept saying, *This can't be happening. It's impossible.*

Eve touched his arm.

He jerked away from her. "Have I gone crazy?" he asked. "Did I take the wrong allergy medicine this morning?"

She gave him a coy smile and those funny-colored eyes of hers seemed to sparkle. "I asked if you were serious."

"But you didn't say anything about *this*," he said.

"It'll make sense as you go along," Eve said. "Just stay close to me."

"You've done this before?" he asked.

She nodded and said firmly, "Do what I say and you'll be okay." She looked around and signaled for him to follow her as she picked up her speed for the mansion. She ran like a graceful animal, leaping over the pits and potholes that threatened to trip Andrew.

They reached a high stone wall that led to a wooden gate. They went through to a stony courtyard. A ramshackle stable made of rocks and wood sat on the opposite side.

The servants Andrew had seen in the forest were now in the middle of the courtyard, their eyes focused on their task to skin the boar. Andrew paused to look at the mess of fur and muscle and bone until Eve tugged at his sleeve.

They crept along the wall to an arched opening. A passage led between two walls to an open gate. Eve stopped.

The silver-haired man and the two younger ones from the forest were sitting at a table in the center of another courtyard. Servants moved around them with plates and pitchers.

Andrew's mind raced with questions. *A lot* of questions. Apart from anything to do with where they were, he wanted to know who these people were and why they had followed them here. *Surely this is trespassing*, he thought.

He put his hand on Eve's shoulder and was about to ask, but someone shouted, "My Lord, the Lady Anne is here to see you!"

"This is what I came to see," Eve said over her shoulder, as if she knew Andrew's question.

With the announcement about Lady Anne, the three men at the table looked at each other. The clean-shaven younger man smirked. The bearded one sneered.

The older man waved at the servant and said, "Bid her enter."

The servant disappeared through a door and returned seconds later with a woman wearing a long dark dress—or it might have been a coat; Andrew wasn't sure. Her long brown hair was adorned with a purple headdress, held in place by a gold ringlet. She looked young and walked confidently to the table.

The men stood up. The older man gave a terse bow. "You are a vision of loveliness," he said.

Lady Anne curtsied to him, "You are too kind, Sir Reynauld." She gave an obligatory curtsy to the two young men. "My lord Maurice," she said to the one with the beard. "My lord Everard," she said to the one without.

The two young men bowed to her.

"Sit, my lady," Sir Reynauld said. "Refresh yourself with us."

Lady Anne shook her head. "Forgive me, my lord, but I shall not. I come bearing news."

The men remained standing. Everard shifted uncomfortably.

"I have paid the ransom for my husband Bennett's release," Lady Anne announced.

"Have you?" Sir Reynauld asked with undisguised surprise.

"The treasure has been delivered to the castle of Cormac at Loch Earn. My husband will be returning."

"I am overjoyed to hear it," Sir Reynauld said, not sounding overjoyed at all.

"When do you expect your husband's arrival?" asked the young man called Maurice.

"Within a fortnight, my lord," she said. "I believe that will give you sufficient time to depart from our home."

Sir Reynauld and the two young men gave each other sideways glances.

"*Depart*, dear woman? Why would we do that?" Sir Reynauld asked.

Lady Anne looked stunned. "My lord, the estates of Havelond rightfully belong to my husband and his family. Our lord, the abbot, gave you possession of them merely as service to maintain the lands in my husband's absence."

"So we have," said Sir Reynauld. "We have worked diligently, sparing nothing."

"You have done well by my husband's misfortune and benefited from the abundance of our lands," she said quickly. "More so than ever you did at your home in Prestbury."

"I will not deny it, my lady," Sir Reynauld said, his voice silky smooth. "Your husband has been gone for *two years*. Such a long time! We might be forgiven to think of Havelond as our home."

"'Tis home, but not yours for the taking," Lady Anne said.

Sir Reynauld held up his hand. "By law, we are permitted—"

Lady Anne cut him off. "You will remember, Sir Reynauld, that my husband departed to fight for the king against the Scottish plunderers. He was taken captive in that effort."

Sir Reynauld nodded. "A noble effort with a tragic turn. And we have honored him by maintaining the lands in good faith, however—"

Lady Anne's tone sharpened. "In *good* faith? My lord, you drove me from my home and forced me to a cottage on the outskirts of our estate."

"Have you not been comfortable, my lady?" he asked. "How was I to know unless you told me?"

"Are you saying you received none of my messages?" Lady Anne asked.

Sir Reynauld looked insulted. "I have *not*, my lady. Be assured I shall have the servants beaten for their incompetence."

The servant by the door looked worried.

"Sir Reynauld," Lady Anne said, "upon my husband's return, he will reclaim what is rightfully his."

Sir Reynauld gave her a snake-like smile. "We shall discuss the matter when he does."

"So we shall. Good day, sir." Lady Anne gave him a stiff curtsy, turned on her heels, and strode across the courtyard.

"My lady!" Sir Reynauld called out. "Allow me to have my sons accompany you!"

CHAPTER TWO

"I would rather walk alone," she called back to him as she went through the door. The servant hustled after her.

Andrew had been watching the scene and was suddenly confused in a whole new way. Their English was not his English, he realized. And not just their accents. He'd seen enough movies and had even gone to a production of *Hamlet* in Denver. He knew how the British sounded. But the *words* he heard were different. They were from an older kind of English. They reminded him of a book a teacher had read to his class in sixth grade. Something *Tales* by Somebody Chaucer. He had struggled to keep up with that old English. What confused him now was that he *understood* what Lady Anne and Sir Reynauld and the others had been saying, as if they'd been speaking in a kind of English he recognized. *How?* He would have to add that question to all of the others.

Maurice said, "Surely we will not give up Havelond, Father."

Sir Reynauld sat down, and the other two did the same. He picked up a chalice. "In truth, the law sides with the Lady Anne and her husband Bennett. Upon his return, the lands belong with him. However . . ." His voice trailed off and he upended the silver chalice into his mouth.

Everard said, "*However?*"

"If something befell him on the road from Scotland . . . then our circumstances would most-assuredly change." Sir Reynauld slowly shook his head. "How sad it is that, in these times, a man may not be safe from robbers and unscrupulous men."

Maurice suddenly stood up. "Come along, brother."

Everard looked puzzled. "Are we going somewhere?"

"Let us hope to find our lord Bennett along the road from Scotland, to give him protection," Maurice said. He grinned.

Everard smiled as he also stood. "Yes. I see."

Maurice and Everard bowed to their father and marched to the door. A moment later, servants brought Sir Reynauld plates covered with food. Andrew thought he saw vegetables and various small animals.

He turned to Eve, but she was backing away, gesturing for him to retreat down the passage. He began to turn, when he bumped into something big and solid. A heavy hand fell on his shoulder. Another grabbed Eve.

"Now you are in for it," said a low growl.

3

A gigantic man with the face of a potato and a thick black beard dragged Andrew and Eve back to the stable courtyard.

"I have warned you beggars to keep out," he said. He tossed them to the ground.

The other servants lifted their heads, turning their attention from the boar.

"A beating will teach you," the man said and snatched a horse whip from a hook just inside the stable.

"Please, sir," Eve said. "We did not come to beg."

"You shouldn't be here at all." He raised the whip.

Andrew crawled between Eve and the bearded man, ready to take the blow.

Another voice shouted, "Stay your hand!"

The bearded man scowled.

A man emerged from the stable. It was the head servant from the forest. "Are you mad?" he cried out. "Why are you dealing with beggars when you must light the fire for the pit? The master is waiting! Their beating will be nothing compared to *your* beating if we're delayed."

The bearded man snarled, then kicked at Andrew. "Out," he said.

Andrew scrambled to his feet, pulling at Eve's arm.

The man waved the whip at them as Andrew half-pulled Eve through the gate and back to the field beyond.

"Will you *please* tell me what is going on," Andrew said.

"There's no time," Eve said and darted off, running along the wall.

Andrew chased after her. "Where are we going?" he asked. "The woods are *that* way!"

"We have to follow the Lady Anne," Eve called back to him.

"*Why?*" Andrew asked.

"She needs our help," she said and sprinted away from him.

It was all Andrew could do to keep up. They followed the wall to the front gate of the mansion and a road that cut through the forest ahead of them.

Eve slowed to a fast walk. "There she is," Eve said.

Lady Anne walked with her head down and shoulders slumped. As they approached from behind, she suddenly whirled around, as if she thought she was about to be attacked. She then relaxed when she saw the two kids.

"I beg your forgiveness, children," she said. Her eyes were red, as if she'd been crying. "I have no purse, nor money to give."

"We are not beggars, my lady," Eve said. "Master Robin has sent me to you."

Lady Anne's eyes widened. "My dear cousin Robin?" She glanced back at the mansion nervously, then said, "Come. We must not speak in the open."

They followed the road until it came to a narrow path. The path took them a short distance to a cottage made of dark stone and a roof made of branches, twigs, and leaves. The front entrance was arched, with a door made of one piece of solid wood.

Lady Anne lifted the latch and pushed open the door. She stepped in, looking around to make sure no one was there. She waved them in and closed the door.

The inside of the cottage was all one room. A fireplace took up one wall, with black pots and pans and long utensils hanging from its mantelpiece. Fat wooden beams held up the roof. A small bird flitted in the rafters. The floor was made of uneven slabs of stone.

A round polished table and four chairs sat in the center of the room, a vase and flowers placed on top. Nearby stood a hutch with two shelves of plates and cups as its upper half, and a cabinet with drawers comprising its lower half. A smaller chest with drawers sat next to it.

In one corner of the cottage was a bed with a carved headboard and matching frame and footboard. A thick homemade quilt covered a thin mattress. A small stand holding a bowl and pitcher sat to the side. On the floor at the foot of the bed lay a small cot. In another corner stood a spinning wheel and a wooden box of raw wool.

It was a warm day and the cottage was hot and stuffy. The smell of wood and dampness was oppressive. There were only two windows, and square holes with wooden shutters closed over them.

"I dare not leave the shutters open when I am away," Lady Anne said and quickly unlatched them. She pushed them open and a hint of fresh air wafted in. She bade them to sit down at the table while she took plates from the shelf of the hutch. "I have a servant," she said, "but she is at the market now."

She opened the doors of the cabinet and brought out plates of bread and cheese. Then came small wooden cups that she filled with water.

Lady Anne sat down at the table. Andrew noticed that she didn't have a plate. Still, she did the Sign of the Cross and said softly, "For these gifts and your many abundant blessings, we give thanks, O Lord."

Andrew and Eve made the Sign of the Cross.

"Please, eat," Lady Anne said.

The bread was hard and broke apart as Andrew picked it up. He put some in his mouth. It was dry and crumbly. He drank from the cup, just to wash it down. He nearly spat everything out as he coughed and gasped. "This is not water," he choked.

"'Tis ale," Lady Anne said. "Is it not to your liking?"

Andrew didn't want to be rude and said, "I was surprised."

Eve laughed at him. "Ale is often better for you than the water."

CHAPTER THREE

Andrew looked at Eve and all the questions he wanted to ask her came back to mind.

"What are your names?" Lady Eve asked.

"I am Evangelline," Eve said. "Though I am most often called Eve."

"I am Andrew."

"How long have you been in the service of my cousin Robin?" Lady Anne asked.

"A short time," said Eve.

"Since he became an outlaw?" Lady Anne asked.

"Aye," Eve said.

Lady Anne looked at them with eyes of sympathy. "I am saddened to think of what circumstances took you to him."

"I was lost and he found me," Eve said.

"And you?" Lady Anne asked Andrew.

"I am . . . new here," Andrew said.

"Please, then: tell me of my dear cousin," Lady Anne said to Eve.

"He sent me to see if you are well and in need of anything. He heard that your husband is finally returning home," Eve said.

Lady Anne's eyes filled with tears. "Robin is so kind," she said. She pulled a handkerchief from her sleeve and dabbed at her eyes.

"You are having trouble with the men in the mansion," Eve said.

Lady Anne gave a deep sigh. "'Tis a sorrowful business," she said. "My husband Bennett fought for King Henry against usurpers in Scotland. He was captured and has been held for ransom these past two years. The abbot, who owns these lands, allowed Sir Reynauld and his sons to care for the house and fields in my husband's absence. I believed it was an act of mercy. Then their carousing and decadent living caused me great fear. I left my house and came to our gamekeeper's cottage. Here I have been while I raised the money for my husband's ransom. By the grace of God, it has been paid and he will return."

"Do you believe Sir Reynauld will depart?" Eve said.

Lady Anne shook her head.

"I will tell Master Robin of your plight," Eve said firmly. "He will come to your aid."

Lady Anne put her face in her hands and sobbed. "I know he will. Yet I fear for him. Sir Reynauld is befriended by evil and corrupt men."

Eve stood up and said to Andrew, "We must go now, if we're to reach him before dark."

Andrew choked down a piece of bread and rose to his feet.

Lady Anne rose. "You must take the bread and cheese for your journey." She took two large rags from the hutch and wrapped up the food.

Eve put the food inside her satchel and bowed. "Thank you, my lady."

"May God give you strength and speed," she said.

Andrew bowed too and said, "Be of good cheer," because he'd heard it in a school play once and it seemed like the right thing to say.

CHAPTER THREE

Out in the sunshine again, Lady Anne stood in the doorway, weeping and waving to them until the path took them out of sight. They came onto the main road. Eve quickened her step.

This time, Andrew moved faster, getting a few steps in front of her. Then he turned and stopped. Eve nearly ran into him.

"What is wrong?" she asked.

"*What is wrong?*" Andrew asked. "I don't know where we are or how we got here or what we're doing here or if any of this is even real, and you ask, '*What is wrong?*'"

She frowned and pushed past him. "Keep up and I will try to explain. We have to get this news to Master Robin."

"Let's start there," Andrew said, staying by her side. "Who is Master Robin?"

"Robert of Locksley," she said.

"I've heard that name," Andrew said, but he couldn't remember from where.

"You know him as Robin Hood," Eve said.

Andrew stopped again. "Robin Hood? *The* Robin Hood? The steals-from-the-rich-to-give-to-the-poor Robin Hood?"

"That's all wrong," Eve said, walking backward to coax him along. "He doesn't steal from the rich. Some of his best friends are rich. He takes from those who have harmed others by cheating or stealing or . . . worse."

She turned and walked on.

Andrew was stunned. "But Robin Hood isn't real," he said, catching up again.

"You should say that to him when you meet him," she said, giving him a wry look.

"How do you know him?" Andrew asked.

"Like I said to Lady Anne, I was lost and he found me."

"You were lost? *Here?*"

"It was my first trip back," she said.

"Your first? How many trips have you taken?" Andrew asked, not even sure what he meant by the word "trip."

"A few," she said. "And I was like you. Completely confused."

"Confused is hardly the word for it," Andrew said, then pleaded, "*Please* tell me all the things you aren't telling me!"

A sideways glance and a small smile came to Eve's face. "It's going to be hard for you to believe."

"It can't be harder than this," he said, spreading his arms. "I'm walking on a dirt road that you say is in the time of Robin Hood. How hard can the rest of it be?"

She looked at him, the unusual color of her eyes alight. "You'll find out."

"Explain it to me," he insisted.

And she did.

4

This is what Eve told him.

Once upon a time, back in the early part of the twentieth century, there was a respectable and successful businessman named Alfred Virtue. Everyone in Hope Springs knew him. He was likable when it came to people and shrewd when it came to money. He served on the city council and established a profitable bank and invested in all kinds of businesses like railroads, mines, and property.

More than making money, Alfred Virtue loved adventure and exploration. He often ventured off to places like Europe and Africa. He journeyed to the northern reaches of Canada and the southern-most parts of South America. Some said he had sailed to both the North and South Poles.

"It was the time of the great explorers," Eve explained. "Writers marveled at the vast unknown parts of the earth. Jules Verne, H. G. Wells, Arthur Conan Doyle, and Edgar Rice Burroughs told stories of lost worlds and ancient civilizations. People were discovering the world in a whole new way."

During his many travels, Alfred Virtue had heard about the "Radiant Stone." Some said the stone was like a black diamond; others described it as being red or green, with the facets of a diamond or some other precious gem. The Radiant Stone was called by different names in different parts of the world, and historical accounts and archaeological findings put the stone in different times. The myths claimed the stone had magical, even fearsome, powers. Stories told of people who touched the stone and disappeared forever. Others touched it, disappeared, but came back babbling like the insane about the impossible things they'd seen.

At first, Alfred Virtue thought they were merely legends, like the lost city of Atlantis, the Fountain of Youth, or the Loch Ness monster. But the more he heard the stories about the stone, the more he began to believe that there was an element of truth to them.

Eventually, Alfred Virtue concluded there wasn't just one Radiant Stone, but many of them scattered all over the world. They were found in caves and forests, on mountainsides and in riverbeds.

Alfred Virtue slowly collected the legends and the stories, and dared to hope he might find one of the stones on one of his many expeditions. Then, during a trip to Ireland, he met an old man at a pub who professed an intimate knowledge of the Radiant Stone. The old man told how the ancient Druids had found one and thought its power and magic came from the goddess Arianrhod, the "Keeper of the Circling Wheel of Silver" in the sky. She had the power of time and reincarnation and "sky-weaving enchantments." The Druids put the stone in an idol dedicated to her and worshiped it for years.

The arrival of Saint Patrick and Christianity to Ireland changed everything. The old gods were chased out as the people committed themselves to Jesus Christ. The idols were put aside or destroyed. A Druid priest hid the idol with the Radiant Stone in a labyrinth of caves. But a Christian named Aeric, nicknamed the "God Hunter" because he dedicated himself to hunting the idols, found where the Druids had hidden the Radiant Stone. A battle ensued. Aeric was killed, but a young Christian named Brendon escaped with the stone and delivered it to Saint Brigid. Brigid later carried the stone to the Beckery Chapel in Glastonbury, England. Glastonbury was famous for its stories about King Arthur, and that's where Alfred Virtue eventually recovered it.

Alfred Virtue brought the stone back to Hope Springs for examination. It was then he discovered what the stone *really* did.

"And what was that?" Andrew asked.

They were now deep in the middle of a forest somewhere. Birds called out far away. The buzzing of the many bugs had faded off. It seemed like his voice was the only sound for miles around, the thick gathering of leaves overhead and bed of detritus underfoot muting the world.

Andrew asked, "Well? What did Alfred Virtue discover?"

"Time travel," Eve said. She reached up to her neck and pulled at the silver chain. She lifted it over her head and revealed something that looked like a large medallion.

She held it out and Andrew thought it actually looked more like an oversized pocket watch, with a silver cover and a stem on the top. "That's the Radiant Stone?" Andrew asked.

"That's the case," she said. "It needs one to keep anyone from touching the stone by accident." She held the case in her palm with her fingers around one side and her thumb on the stem at the top. She pressed down on the stem. The silver cover sprung open on a little hinge.

"This is the Radiant Stone," she said with a hint of pride.

Andrew expected to see the face of a clock. Instead, the inside was filled with a shiny jewel. It was covered with a lot of facets that caught the light in different ways, sometimes looking green or red or blue, even black.

"What happens if I touch it?" Andrew asked, lifting his finger as if he might.

Eve pulled her hand back to make sure he didn't. "You'll go to another time." She presented it again. "All those facets are different points in time. If you touch one with the tip of your finger, you'll go there."

Andrew put his hands behind his back and looked closely. Some of the facets were bigger than others. "Which one did you touch to get here?"

She carefully pointed to a green facet near the lower left-hand side of the stone. "That one."

CHAPTER FOUR

"Why that one?"

She shrugged. "I don't know. All I know is that Alfred Virtue drew a diagram of the whole stone. It shows every facet and where it takes you if you touch it. He tested them all."

"He went back to all those different times?" Andrew asked, amazed. "There are dozens of facets."

"Even more on the back," she said.

Andrew tried to imagine Alfred Virtue touching a facet, going back in time, then returning to the present to make notes. "It must have taken him ages to figure them all out."

"It didn't take any time at all," Eve said. "While we're here, no time is passing for us back home. And when we're back home, no time is passing here."

"Time *stops*?" Andrew asked.

She shook her head. "It's hard to explain. Time is moving, but the stone lets us step *out* of it. And then, if we go back, we enter the same point we left. Like a book mark, I guess. The story doesn't really stop because you put it aside. There are a lot of pages left. It only seems to stop because you came away from it."

Andrew rubbed his forehead. This felt like figuring out a really hard math problem. "So, right now your aunt is in the shop and she has no idea we've been gone for hours? And when we walk out of that room of clocks again, it'll be like we had just walked into it?"

Eve nodded again. "I left here over a week ago, according to our time. I went to see Lady Anne, like Master Robin told me, but I had to leave. It was a week for me, but no time here."

"Why did you have to leave?"

"Homework," Eve said.

Andrew laughed.

She snapped the cover closed.

"Is it heavy?" Andrew asked.

She handed him the case. It wasn't heavy at all. In fact, he was surprised by how light it was.

He handed the case back to her. She slipped the silver chain over her head and dropped the case under her tunic.

As they walked on in silence, Andrew's mind was spinning. If she had told him all of this back at the shop, he wouldn't have believed her. But there was nothing left to doubt. They were *here*, not in the shop. That thought led Andrew to another important question. He asked, "How do we get back to our time?"

"It's simple," she said. "You just press your hand on the entire stone and it takes you back to where you belong. I guess touching all of the facets at the same time is like a reset button."

"Wait a minute," he said. "I never touched the stone. How did I get here?"

"I held your hand," she said. "It worked through me to you."

They climbed over a fallen tree, worked their way around a thick section of bushes, and emerged from the dense woods onto a narrow path. It was getting late in

CHAPTER FOUR

the afternoon. Andrew realized his legs were aching. He had no idea how long they'd been walking, or if they were anywhere near where they were supposed to be.

Eve suddenly put a hand up to stop.

"What's wrong?" he asked.

"Hide," she said and pushed him back into the bushes.

They crouched down. Andrew peered through the tangle of branches, beyond the path to the woods on the other side. A young girl came into view—he guessed she was seven or eight, the age of his little sister Sam. She had dark unkempt hair and wore a long coat with a hood. Hanging from her hand was a small sack. She walked as if she was searching for something. She came to the path, paused to look around, then crossed in their direction.

The girl stopped at their hiding place and began to pluck berries, putting them into the sack. Andrew saw tears falling down her face, making dull white lines through her dirty cheeks, but she made no sound. Her face was thin, her lips were drawn in, and her eyes looked big against the dark circles underneath them. She reminded him of pictures he'd seen of starving kids in foreign countries. She used her free hand to rub at her runny nose. He noticed her hands were scratched, the skin on her fingers split. Her coat was torn in places.

She was only a couple of feet away. Her gaze was fixed on the berries in front of her, but Andrew could imagine her alarm if she suddenly saw them. *Do we stay hidden or let her know we're here?* he hoped his expression asked Eve.

Eve answered by standing up. "Greetings!" she said.

The girl jumped and stumbled back.

"Do not be afraid," Eve said as calmly as she could. She slowly stepped out onto the path.

The girl jerked her head to the left and right. She was checking her options to run.

"We will not harm you," Eve said, raising her hands. She gestured for Andrew to stand up.

When he did, the girl let out a little screech and dashed across the path to the woods.

They both watched the girl run away. She tripped, clambered to her feet, and raced onward, looking back to make sure they weren't following her.

"Do you think she's lost?" Andrew asked. "Maybe she needs help."

"We don't have time to find out," Eve said.

"What if she's in trouble?"

"We have to deliver our message to Master Robin," she said. "Someone else will find her." She turned and started down the path.

"Who?" he asked impatiently. "There's no one else out here. We can't abandon a young girl."

"She'll be found," Eve said firmly.

He was about to argue with her when they heard a terrified scream.

5

Andrew and Eve rushed through the woods toward the sound of the scream. It was the girl, Andrew had no doubt, but he couldn't imagine why she was screaming. *Do they have bears here?* he wondered.

Up ahead he saw a man with his back to them. He was dressed in the rough clothes Andrew had seen on the servants at the mansion: a brown tunic with a belt made of rope and pants made of the same material as the tunic, but with patches sewn to it. A large knife was tucked in a sheath in his belt on the right side. A pouch hung from the belt on the left. He had hold of one of the girl's wrists.

She struggled to free herself.

The man said something to her, but she squirmed all the more and screeched at him.

Eve darted behind a tree and pulled at Andrew's arm to follow.

Andrew pulled away. He wasn't going to stand by while the girl was being hurt. He said so to Eve in the form of a grunt and grabbed the first stick he could find. *I'll sneak up on him*, he thought and tried to tiptoe in their direction.

As he drew closer, the girl saw him. Her expression betrayed that he was coming.

Still clutching the girl's arm, the man spun around. He had a rugged face with deep lines around his eyes and on his forehead. His chin was covered with stubble. "What is this?" he asked.

"Leave her alone!" Andrew shouted and raised his weapon.

The man looked at the stick. "What are you going to do with that, tickle me?"

"It is all right," Eve called out from behind Andrew. "God be with you, Master Will Scarlet!"

Will Scarlet? Andrew thought, remembering the name from the Robin Hood stories.

The man's eyes went from Andrew to Eve. He smiled and held up his free hand. "Hail, Waif of the Woods!"

Waif of the Woods?

Eve strode passed Andrew, whispering out of the corner of her mouth, "Get rid of the stick."

He threw down the stick and followed her.

"Please tell this child I will not harm her," Will Scarlet said to Eve.

The girl was pulling at her arm and attempted a few kicks at him.

"She might believe it if you will let go of her wrist," Eve suggested.

CHAPTER FIVE

Will Scarlet frowned. "If I let her go, she will run. You know Master Robin will not suffer to have children alone in the forest."

Eve stepped close to the girl, who was wild-eyed from fear. "Listen to me," Eve said softly. "We can help you, if you will tell us who you are and why you are here."

The girl kept her eyes on Eve and slowly stopped struggling.

"What is your name?" Eve asked her.

"Ruth," the girl said.

"Do you promise not to run if he releases you?" Eve asked.

The girl looked unsure, looking at Eve, then Will Scarlet. She nodded.

Eve nodded to Will Scarlet. He reluctantly released his grip.

The girl didn't run. She looked at him unhappily and rubbed her wrist.

"Where are your parents?" Eve asked. "Are they hurt somewhere? Hungry? You were picking berries..."

"Hear me, little lass," Will Scarlet said. He knelt down next to the girl. She backed away. "There is not a village nor house anywhere nearby. From the tears in your cloak and the wear of your boots, you are either lost or you are running from someone or perhaps both. Is that so?"

The girl nodded.

"You are in good company," Will Scarlet said. "Have you heard of the outlaw Robin Hood?"

The girl's face brightened. "We are searching for him," she said.

We, Andrew thought.

Will Scarlet smiled. "You are closer to finding him than you know. Take us to your kin and, together, we will go to Master Robin. We have better food than berries and enough for all."

Her face betrayed her uncertainty. Andrew imagined her parents had told her not to reveal wherever they were hiding.

Her eyes locked on Andrew's.

He gave her an encouraging smile and a nod.

She let out a deep breath. "This way," she said.

Ruth led them through the forest and, eventually, to almost impassable growth of bushes. She easily slid beneath and through them. Eve, Will Scarlet, and Andrew pushed through, coming to a cliff at the edge of a ravine. A stream trickled at least twenty feet below. Ruth gave every appearance of stepping over the edge.

"Ruth?" Will Scarlet called out. The three of them rushed to the precipice and only then saw a path, hidden by the angle and sloping down to a ledge. Ruth stood waiting for them and then disappeared again.

One at a time, the three carefully walked down the slim path and came to a cave, obscured by the thicket. The girl was already inside. Andrew could hear her speaking in soft tones.

CHAPTER FIVE

The three of them entered the cavity. The daylight, filtered by the thicket, cast a gray shadow. Andrew's eyes slowly adjusted, and he saw Ruth kneeling next to an old man lying on a makeshift bed of leaves. He was bundled in a coat that might have once been worn by a wealthy man but was now ragged and filthy. A large satchel sat nearby. Andrew noticed the blackened remains of a fire in a small circle of rocks nearby.

Ruth trembled as she glanced from the three to her father and back again. Even now, she looked afraid they might hurt them.

The old man slowly sat up, looking at them with watchful eyes. "Who is this? Ruth, are we betrayed?"

"Have no fear, master," said Will, bending down on one knee. "Your daughter has brought you aid." He drew the pouch from his belt and presented some slices of bread and meat to the old man. He gave some to Ruth.

The girl drew a small knife from the satchel and began to cut up the portions.

"There is enough for both of you," Will assured her.

The old man cried as he nibbled on the bread. "We have not eaten for three days," he said.

"Then you must eat slowly," Will Scarlet said.

"I thank you, good woodman," the old man said in a low quivering voice. The tears continued to fall. "It is not for myself that I am afraid, but in my present state, I am sure I have not long to live. I suffer anguish to think of my daughter left desolate."

"She will not be left desolate, nor shall I allow you to die," Will said. He grabbed a leather flask from another part of his belt. "Ale," he said.

The old man and his daughter drank, and a new light came into their eyes. Color returned to their cheeks.

With the help of his daughter, the old man crawled onto his knees. "Pray with me," he said and, without waiting, said, "O God of power and might, I give thanks to you for having delivered us from our misery..." He began to cry again. Ruth drew close and cried with him.

Eve and Andrew looked at each other. Andrew wondered what had happened to these poor people.

Will cleared his throat loudly and said in a gruff voice, "Are you able to travel?"

"I fear I am too weak from my illness. But I beg you to take my daughter to safety," the old man replied.

"You will both have safety," Will said. "Leave it to me."

The old man reached out and took Will's hand. "Hear me, good fellow. I am Reuben of Stamford, a Jew of York, and I pledge that if you will get me to my kinsmen in Nottingham, you will have the gratitude of me and my people forever, and our aid wherever you desire it."

"You offer more than I would ever ask," said Will. "What aid I may give you is not for your gratitude or your gold, but because it is always in my heart to help those in trouble."

The old man's eyes filled with new tears.

CHAPTER FIVE

"Bide here until we return," Will said and gestured for Eve and Andrew to come out of the cave with him. They made their way up to the top of the cliff.

"I shall have a few words to say to Dodd about this," Will Scarlet grumbled when they were out of earshot. "'Tis his job to keep watch over this part of the forest. How does he not know about this man and girl?"

Eve gave a wry smile. "Dodd is known for his good heart, not his brains," she said.

Will chuckled. He gave Andrew a close look. "Who are you?"

"Andrew."

"Well, Andrew," he said. "Are you good with a staff, a bow, or a blade?"

Andrew stammered, "I am good with a bat and ball."

Will frowned and said, "Nevertheless, I have a task for you and our good waif Evangeline. Fly you both with all speed to Master Robin. Tell him of our need here. He will give his command about what to do."

For the next hour they ran. Eve bounded like a deer, but Andrew stumbled and tripped and could think of little else than the stitch in his side and how tired he felt.

They came to a part of the forest that looked as it probably had when prehistoric cave people walked through. *If they or anyone had ever walked through it*, Andrew thought.

"Are you sure we're going the right way?" he gasped.

Eve said, "Aye," and darted through a cluster of trees. Andrew was only a few steps behind her. They entered a clearing and Andrew stopped. Men, dressed much like Will Scarlet, sat on the grass or leaned against the trunks of trees; a few were at roughly made tables and benches, eating from wooden plates and bowls, or drinking from wooden cups.

"The Men of the Greenwood," Eve said to Andrew.

The men glanced at them with a cursory grunt or nod. A couple of them greeted her—again calling her "the waif." They came to a magnificent oak tree. More men sat in a circle under its broad branches. They looked as if they were in a serious business meeting, talking in low and earnest voices. One of the assembly saw Eve and signaled to a fellow sitting next to him, who stood up and turned to them. This man had a tanned, handsome, and honest face with lively, sharp eyes and a broad, open smile. Dark brown curls adorned his head. He was dressed in a tunic made of a rough green cloth. Around his waist was a broad leather belt with a sheath holding a dagger. He wore short breeches of leather and leggings of green wool that reached down to his ankles. His shoes were also made of a dark brown leather.

"Master Robin," Eve said with a gentle bow.

"Evangeline! Our dear Waif of the Woods!" he shouted happily. "I have been awaiting your return from Havelond. How is my dear cousin Anne? Were you forced to endure her bread-making skills?" He laughed and turned his gaze to Andrew. "What is this, pray tell? You have found a boy?" he asked.

"His name is Andrew," Eve said.

"You are most welcome, Andrew," Robin said with a courteous bow and wave of his hand.

Robin Hood, Andrew thought, his mind seizing up. *I am meeting Robin Hood—live and in person!*

"Th—tha—thank you, good sir," Andrew stammered and blushed.

"Master, we have two urgent matters," Eve said. She told him about the Lady Anne and her problems with Sir Reynauld, then continued with their encounter with Reuben of Stamford and his daughter Ruth.

Robin swung around to the men in the circle. "Good fellows! On your feet!"

The men were up in an instant. One, a giant of a man, rose above the rest and asked, "What is it, Master Robin?"

"Little John," Robin said to the giant, "take a few men with you and spread out to the main roads leading to Scotland. Search them for my cousin's husband, Bennett of Havelond. See that he is conducted safely to me."

Little John! Andrew thought.

Eve nudged him and whispered, "You're not going to faint, are you?"

"That is Little John," Andrew whispered back.

Robin added, "Oh—and send Hob o' the Hill to my cousin's cottage to make sure she is protected. I do not trust Sir Reynauld nor his sons to leave her undisturbed."

"Aye, Master," said Little John and he strode off with big lumbering steps.

"Someone find Dodd for me," Robin called out.

Andrew could hear voices calling Dodd's name echoing throughout the camp.

A few minutes later, a very round man came bustling up, pulling at his breeches as if they might fall down. "You summoned me, Master Robin?"

"That is Dodd, son of Alstan," Eve whispered to Andrew.

Robin gave him a stern look. "Dodd, why have I received a message from Will Scarlet about an old man and his daughter living in a cave in Barrow Down? 'Tis your area to watch, is it not?"

Dodd turned red-faced and said, "An old man and his daughter? In Barrow Down?"

"They have been there for a few days." Robin's face lost its amiability.

Dodd stammered, but said nothing helpful.

Robin frowned. "Take Nigel and anyone else you need, along with two horses. Carry the old man and his daughter to the Huntsman's Lodge. You know where it is? You will not lose your way?"

"Aye, Master Robin," Dodd said. "I mean, *no*, Master Robin."

CHAPTER FIVE

"See to it, Dodd. I will not countenance any excuses," he added.

"No, Master Robin. That is to say, yes, Master Robin. I mean—"

"*Go!*" Robin commanded.

Dodd rushed off, still pulling at his breeches.

Andrew turned to Robin again. The outlaw was looking at him with a curious expression.

"From what village do you hail?" he asked.

"Hope Springs," Andrew replied.

He looked puzzled. "I know it not."

"'Tis far from here," Eve said.

Robin kept his eyes on Andrew. "I feel as though I have met someone who looks very much like you, though older. Your father, perhaps?"

"My father has never been here," Andrew said.

"Another relative perhaps," Robin said, dismissing the subject.

"Perhaps," Andrew repeated, unsure of who Robin was thinking of.

Robin put one hand on Andrew's shoulder and the other on Eve's. "Eat now. Rest well this night. By God's grace, we will go to the Huntsman's Lodge tomorrow to see about our mysterious cave dwellers."

"Thank you, Master Robin," Eve said.

As the two walked away, Eve whispered to Andrew, "Theodore Perry."

"What about him?" Andrew asked.

"He was best friends with Alfred Virtue," she said. "You look like him."

"So?"

"I think he's been here. That is why Robin thinks you look familiar."

Andrew was stunned. "My great-great-*whatever* traveled through time? He met Robin Hood?"

Eve was amused. "Why are you so surprised? Alfred Virtue trusted Theodore Perry more than anyone. Why not let him take a trip to the past?"

Andrew shook his head. *What else am I going to learn about the Radiant Stone and my family?* he wondered.

Eve led him to a campfire where a short, elf-like man named Arthur a Bland ladled stew from a large black cauldron. He was happy to see "the Waif."

The stew had big chunks of meat and potatoes and a green vegetable that might have been cabbage. Andrew wasn't sure.

"The meat is venison," Eve said. "If we came earlier, we would have had venison pies, some fish, roast duck, and partridges."

Andrew was given a big portion of bread that was easier to chew than the Lady Anne's version. Dunking it in the stew made it even better. The meat was chewy and had a tangy taste.

Darkness fell and Eve showed Andrew to a tree under which someone had made a bed of leaves. "This is where Dodd usually sleeps. He won't be back tonight. It's yours."

"Where will you be?" Andrew asked.

She pointed to another tree a couple of yards away.

"Do they have wild animals here?" Andrew asked. "I won't be attacked by a boar, will I?"

She smiled. "There aren't a lot of boars in England now. The boar you saw this morning was probably brought in from France by Sir Reynauld. The rich can afford them, to hunt for sport."

"No wonder the boar was so unhappy." Andrew stretched out on the bed. It felt the way he expected a mattress of leaves to feel. "I won't be able to sleep," he said, thinking how his day had started with a normal breakfast at home and ended with him in the camp of Robin Hood.

Eve said good night and went to her tree.

Andrew tossed and turned, tossed and turned again, found a comfortable position, and kept thinking, *What a strange day*, when he fell into a deep sleep.

6

Something was nudging Andrew's foot. Then he felt a tug at the tip of his boot.

"Stop it," he said, thinking his brother Nick was messing around.

More nudging and tugging.

He groaned and rolled over to see a deer trying to eat his foot.

He shouted, pulling his legs away as he sat up. The deer gave him a dull look.

Andrew hugged his knees as it all came back to him: The woods. Robin Hood. *Time travel.*

Eve was sitting up in her makeshift bed. "Don't mind him. That's Rodric. He wandered in one day as if no one would even *think* to eat him for dinner. Everyone says he's got sawdust for brains."

Andrew shook his head. "Maybe he does if he thinks my foot is food."

Seeing that the foot would not be returned, Rodric wandered off.

"How did you sleep?" Eve asked.

Andrew moved his head back and forth and up and down. His neck ached. He realized he'd used a fat tree root as a pillow.

Robin's men were up and moving this way and that as if they had important things to do.

"Let's go down to the pond and wash," Eve said.

They traversed the camp, passing some men practicing with swords, others with long staffs. Andrew heard rustling in the trees overhead and saw a few men leaping from branch to branch. One misjudged the distance and fell to the ground with a painful thud. A short distance away, archers shot arrows from longbows at something Andrew couldn't see.

"Robin makes them practice a lot," Eve said.

They walked down a grassy hill to a large pond. Arthur a Bland and a young man were filling pitchers with water.

Eve and Andrew knelt on the bank. She splashed water on her head, face, and neck. Andrew leaned forward to do the same and saw a fish darting away under the surface.

There was a big splash on the far side of the pond. Andrew looked up to see a man swimming. He hoped the man was dressed.

After trying to scrub himself with the cool water, Andrew lay back on the soft grass to let the morning sun dry his face. "I dreamt about traveling through time," he said to Eve. "But the dream was a jumble of Lady Anne's cottage and the long walk through the woods and the little girl picking berries. And I think I saw a man standing somewhere in the forest who might have been Theodore Perry. He was watching me."

"Alfred Virtue wrote about the effect time travel has on our minds," Eve said softly, looking around to make sure no one was listening. "He wondered if it might drive a person crazy."

Andrew said, "Right now, I'm going crazy wondering how a stone can let us travel through time. How does it work?"

"That is the mystery," Eve said. "Alfred Virtue had a theory that the Radiant Stone somehow absorbs time and makes time part of itself. Then it becomes a gateway back to the time it has absorbed."

Andrew considered the idea. "You mean, it'd be like a computer camera capturing images and putting them on a hard drive and then letting you enter into the images?"

Eve shrugged.

"But how can a *stone* record time?" Andrew asked.

"How does anything in nature do what it does? I'm not a scientist. I really don't know. Alfred Virtue didn't know either. He had all kinds of theories, but none he thought was the answer."

"Can the stone send us *anywhere* in time?" Andrew asked.

"Do you mean, to any time or any location in time?"

"Both."

"Alfred Virtue said a Radiant Stone picks up history in the area where it is located." She put a hand to her tunic and Andrew knew she was touching the case underneath.

"*This* stone can take us to points of history in Ireland and England or wherever it's been. Even Hope Springs, I guess, because Alfred Virtue took it there. Other stones can take us to whatever places and points in history they picked up around them."

"So, a Radiant Stone in Rome would take us back to Roman history. One in Moscow would take us to Russian history…"

"That's the idea."

"Did Alfred ever figure out where the stones originally came from?"

Eve nudged at a pebble with her foot and said, "Maybe they came from a meteorite that hit the earth in prehistoric times."

"That wouldn't explain the stones being all over the world," Andrew said. "Unless it *rained* meteorites."

"Maybe they're the same meteorites that killed the dinosaurs," Eve suggested. "But Alfred also wondered if the Radiant Stones came from deep inside the earth itself."

"They worked themselves up through the crust?" Andrew asked.

Eve nodded.

"Then why aren't they lying all over the place?" Andrew countered. "Why doesn't everyone know about them?"

"They're not like diamonds or the kinds of gems people are looking for."

"Okay, but shouldn't there be more stories about people disappearing or showing up back in time, like us?"

Eve tucked her arms behind her head and lay back on the grass. She closed her eyes. "The stone doesn't work for everyone," she said.

"What do you mean?"

"I mean, there are some people who could pick one up and nothing would happen to them. Other people touch one and—*zoom*—they're gone."

"Why would it work for some and not for others?" Andrew asked.

"I don't know," Eve admitted. "Maybe it's like people who are allergic to some things and others aren't. Maybe it's a special combination of whatever the stone is made of and something about the person holding it. I really don't understand it. But it worked for me, and I knew it would work for you."

Andrew turned to her. "How did you know that?"

She pushed up onto her elbow and looked at him, her pale eyes shimmering. "Remember the first time you came into the store, before Christmas? I saw how you reacted to the place."

"It was an interesting store," Andrew said. "I like history. And I was surprised that it was connected to my family. It was a shock to find out that I look like Theodore Perry."

"It was more than all that," she said, coaxing him.

"Well, yeah. I guess I felt like—it's weird to say—but it was like the past came alive, just for a minute."

"That's what I saw in you," Eve said. "Your face looked like the way I felt the first time I came into the shop."

"Is that why you were watching me?" he asked. "Is that what the whole hide-and-seek thing was about?"

She smiled at him. "I see people come in and out of the shop all the time, and you are the only one who reacted like I did. Even Aunt Catherine doesn't get it."

Andrew thought about that. "Are you saying there is something inside of me that's connected to the stone, or something in the stone that's connected to me? Like a magnet?"

Eve sat up. "It's not just the stone. There is something about the Old Bank Building. Alfred Virtue built some strange things into it. You should see the basement when we get back."

He remembered that Catherine Drake had said something about the basement.

"Are you sure it's not some kind of magic?" Andrew asked. "Maybe we're messing around with . . . something evil."

Eve grimaced. "It isn't supernatural. I'm sure an expert could explain it all with wormholes or dark matter or things like that. Besides, Alfred Virtue wouldn't have messed with anything supernatural. He was a good Catholic. So was Theodore Perry."

Maybe we should show the stone to an expert," Andrew said.

"And have them take it away from me for tests? No way," she countered. "Somebody will want to turn it into a new kind of weapon. They always do in the movies."

A horn blew back at camp.

"We're late," Eve said and leapt to her feet.

Andrew stood up and, feeling his face go red, asked, "What do we do about . . . you know . . . going to the bathroom?"

Eve giggled. "Try behind that big tree to the left. Use the shovel."

Robin Hood assembled everyone for morning prayers. In the name of God the Father, Jesus the Son, and the Holy Spirit, he asked for guidance for steps throughout the day. He also appealed to the Holy Mother to keep them vigilant and true. After that, he gave orders to different men about the things he wanted done while he was tending to the old man and the girl at the Huntsman's Lodge.

When the meeting was dismissed, Andrew found Eve putting food and a flask in her satchel.

"I didn't expect Robin and his merry men to be Catholic," Andrew said.

"I thought you knew your history. It's in all the legends," she said. She handed him a knife in a leather sheath. "Tuck this in your belt."

"Will I need it?" he asked, worried.

"Everyone who walks in the forest should have one," she said. "You never know who or what you will meet along the way."

She stood up and Andrew saw that she had a knife too.

"Have you ever had to use yours?" he asked.

"Not on anything human," she replied and walked away.

He wondered what she meant as he fixed the knife to his belt. "Is the lodge far?" he asked, following her.

"A few miles," she said. "Why? Are you sore from yesterday?"

"A little."

She slung the satchel over her shoulder. "So was I, the first time."

The two of them trailed behind Robin and an older man named Warren the Bowman. Warren was short, with wild gray hair and a bushy beard. At first, Andrew wondered how such an old man would keep up, then realized he would have a hard time keeping up with the old man.

"Robin will ask you how you came to the forest," Eve whispered to him.

Andrew gulped hard. He hadn't thought about anyone asking him questions. "What am I supposed to tell him?"

"The truth," she said. "You have no family here, which you don't. You are an orphan like I am, which you are. We met and I brought you with me to Robin, which I did."

CHAPTER SIX

That is *the truth*, Andrew thought. And that's what he told Robin when the outlaw asked him a few miles later.

"I am vexed about *Hope Springs*," Robin admitted. "I have traveled the length and breadth of England and do not recall such a place. What is the nearest town or city?"

Andrew wasn't sure how to answer.

"Denver," said Eve.

Andrew gaped at Eve.

Robin's eyebrows lifted. "Denver? In Norfolk? Then, surely, I should know it."

"It is easy to miss," Eve said. "A blink and you have passed it."

Robin gave them both a skeptical look, which ended the conversation.

Andrew didn't know how many miles they walked. He was surprised that his muscles, which felt stiff at first, limbered up along the way.

From time to time, Robin made sounds like a bird call or a whistle. The same sound came back to him, as if the birds themselves were responding.

"We have men hiding all over the forest," Eve explained. "They watch for those with bad intentions, or those we know who have taken advantage of the poor."

"What do you do with them?"

"If they're really bad, we tie them up and drop them off at the nearest jail. If they are corrupt noblemen or clergy, we make them pay a toll from whatever they have."

"And then what?"

"Robin shares whatever we get with anyone in need," Eve said. "The scouts are also supposed to watch out for anyone who is lost or suffering. That's why Robin was so unhappy with Dodd."

Robin, who was several yards ahead, suddenly turned. "Wait there while Warren and I go ahead."

"Aye, Master Robin," Eve said.

"Signal if you encounter trouble," Robin said.

Eve put her fingers to her lips and gave a long shrill whistle.

"The very one," Robin said, smiling at her. He and Warren strode away.

Eve found a sturdy log just off the path and sat down. Andrew sat next to her and dug a stone out of his boot. "What's up ahead? Why did he want us to wait here?"

"He is probably going to meet up with Ket the Troll." Eve took a small waterskin from her belt and drank.

"Troll?" Andrew asked, staring at her. He imagined a very short creature that lived in rocks and mounds, like Tolkien's hobbits. "Is that just a name or is he a real troll?"

"He is a real troll." She offered the waterskin to him.

Andrew took it, but eyed her doubtfully. "You've seen him?"

She nodded. "He is very private and likes to meet with Master Robin alone."

"I thought trolls didn't like humans," Andrew said.

"They are usually shy of humans," she said. "But Robin saved the lives of Ket and his brother Hob o' the Hill. They are firm friends."

"Trolls," Andrew said thoughtfully as he took a gulp of water.

Eve knew what he was thinking. "There are a lot of things in this forest you have never seen—the kinds of things we heard about in fairy tales. They still exist in this time."

"Trolls? Giants? Pixies?"

Eve smiled at him but didn't answer.

He handed the waterskin back as a loud bird call came from somewhere ahead on the path. Eve lifted her head. "That is Robin. Come on."

She dashed off and Andrew scrambled to follow her.

Robin Hood stood in the middle of the path with a boy at his side. "It is safe to go on to the lodge," he said.

As Andrew drew closer, he realized the person next to Robin wasn't a boy, but a small man, a little shorter than Andrew, with a broad chest, and long, hairy arms and legs covered with muscle like rock. The hair on his exposed head was black, thick, and curly. He wore a cropped leather jacket, which laced in the front, and breeches that reached to his knees. He had no shoes on his big feet. His face was weather-worn and friendly.

"It is the troll," Eve whispered to Andrew.

"Meet Ket," Robin said.

"Welcome to the forest," Ket said in a low and gloomy voice. He gave Andrew a stiff bow.

"My pleasure," said Andrew, bowing in return. *He really does look like a hobbit,* he thought.

Ket gave a nod to Robin and dashed into the woods, disappearing quickly among the bushes and trees.

Andrew gave Eve a wide-eyed look. She grinned at him.

"This way," Robin said.

It was another mile before Andrew saw the lodge tucked back into a grove away from the path. The lodge was actually a shack that looked as if it had been built from whatever could be found in the woods: logs, branches, stone, mud, and leaves. Dodd was standing with Warren the Bowman, guarding the door. Dodd gave Robin an apologetic look and pushed the door open for them.

Inside, Will Scarlet sat on a stool, sharpening a knife with a stone. He stood up for Robin, who waved for him to sit again.

Reuben of Stamford lay in a crudely made bed. His daughter Ruth sat in a chair next to him. Andrew thought they already looked better and healthier than they had in the cave.

At the sight of Robin, Reuben tried to sit up.

"Save your strength," Robin said. He reached out to shake Reuben's hand, but the old man grabbed Robin's hand and kissed it instead.

"God bless you for your mercy to us," said Reuben.

Robin gently pulled his hand away. "Tell me, good man, if you have the strength: how have you fallen into such a wretched state?"

"You have heard, I am certain, of Sir Guy of Gisborne," Reuben said.

Robin snorted. "An evil-hearted fiend if ever there was one," he said.

"Then perhaps you have also heard of Alberic de Wisgar," said Reuben.

"A knight of York," Robin said. "I know of him for his hard-hearted indifference to his fellow man."

"Over time, he has borrowed a great sum of money from me," Reuben said. "As the time for repayment came, he devised a plan to destroy my ledgers and any evidence of the loans."

Robin folded his arms. "I see it all too clearly. He reasoned, in his vile mind, that destroying the ledgers would relieve him of honoring the debt. What, pray tell, did he do?"

The old man glanced at his daughter. "I wish that my dearest Ruth did not have to relive the terror of those days."

"I am not afraid, Father," Ruth said bravely.

Reuben patted his daughter's hand and said to Robin, "Alberic de Wisgar sent a mob against those of my race living in York. My daughter and I escaped, but they ransacked my home and mercilessly attacked my neighbors, wounding and killing anyone who might hand us over."

"Were they able to find your ledgers?"

"No," Reuben said. "Had Sir Alberic been thinking at all, he would have known I did not keep any records or ledgers in my home. They were kept securely with Father Barnabas, a good priest at the cathedral. It was to him that we ran for sanctuary, never believing the mob would follow us or dare to attack such a sacred place."

"Men such as Alberic de Wisgar have no regard for the sacred or the beautiful," Robin said. "What, pray tell, befell you at the cathedral?"

"One of my neighbors, beaten almost to death, revealed the hiding place of my ledgers and, thereby, gave us away. The mob stormed the cathedral, but the valiant Father Barnabas rebuked them, invoking the authority of the Church. He went so far as to threaten them with excommunication if they did not hasten to depart. The frightened mob were cowed, and they retreated. But Father Barnabas feared Sir Alberic would later enter the cathedral by stealth to murder us and steal the ledgers. The good priest believed all would be safer away from York. We sneaked away that night."

"How were you able to escape?" Will Scarlet asked.

Reuben's eyes glistened with new tears. "Thanks be to God, a man-at-arms found soldiers' cloaks to disguise us. That very night he led us out of the town by a privy gate, placing us on the road to Nottingham."

"Why then are you here rather than Nottingham?" Robin asked.

"Sir Alberic, upon discovering our escape, was enraged. He summoned the aid of Sir Guy of Gisborne and the wicked brood at Wrangby Castle to search for us. Fearing anew for our lives, we left the highway and made our way into the deepest part of the forest. Our hope was to find you before the evil assassins found us. I do not know how many days we have wandered. I know only that what little food we carried from York was gone. I fell gravely ill with a fever. Ruth discovered the cave and there we hid until your good man found us."

Robin gave an appreciative look to Will, then Eve and Andrew. "Who or what awaits you in Nottingham?" he asked. "The sheriff there is as corrupt as Sir Guy of Gisborne and Alberic de Wisgar."

Reuben clasped his hands together and pressed them to his heart. "My oldest son lives in Nottingham. Even now I fear he grieves for us as dead."

Robin put a hand on the old man's shoulder. "Take heart. One of my men shall go to his house and make it known you are safe with us. When you are strong enough, you will be united with him."

"Bless you, master, bless you!" Reuben cried out.

Will Scarlet stood and sheathed his knife. "Gladly will I go, Master Robin," he said. He looked at the old man. "You need only give me your message and tell me where I may find your kinsfolk. I shall set out posthaste."

"You will not go alone," Robin said to Will. His eyes fell on Andrew and Eve. "A meal first, before the journey."

Andrew didn't realize how hungry he had become until they sat together at a small table and devoured portions of bread, cheese, and cured meat.

Suddenly they heard shouts outside. Robin and Will were on their feet in an instant, hands on the knives in their belts.

"They have found us!" Reuben said with a pitiful cry and pulled his daughter close.

The door burst open and Little John raced in, with Warren the Bowman on his heels. "Master Robin! We found your cousin's husband, Bennett of Havelond, on the road from Scotland. He was beaten to the brink of death."

"God have mercy!" the outlaw exclaimed.

"We have taken him to the inn at Ravenswood," Little John said. "I left him in the care of the good innkeeper and well-guarded by Much the Miller's Son and Reeve the Baker."

"Did Bennett say who committed the foul deed?" Robin asked.

"No, Master. He fell into a delirium and was unable to speak." Little John's face twisted with a dark anger. "'Twas no robbery nor mere beating, Robin. The wicked assailants intended to leave him for dead. We know who is behind it, and why."

"'Tis so," Robin said. "Hasten now, Little John, to the village of Angston. Seek out Dedric, a wise physician with great skill. Bear my name and he will accompany you to the Ravenswood Inn to give what help he can to Bennett."

"Aye, Robin," Little John said.

Robin turned to Warren the Bowman. "Fly to Lady Anne at the cottage on the north side of Havelond Manor. Hob o' the Hill is already there. Under cover of darkness, bring the Lady Anne safely to me."

"'T'will be done, good master," said Warren, and he departed with Little John.

Robin spun around to Will Scarlet. "Now, Will. To this other business in Nottingham. You must have a disguise. A pilgrim's robe."

"What about us?" Eve asked.

"Beggar children are abundant there. You'll need no change of clothes," he said. "Go swiftly or you will not reach the gates before they close for the night."

Will, Eve, and Andrew were given fresh provisions and set off.

If Andrew felt confident he had the energy to travel another great distance that day, he soon repented of it.

7

Few people standing near Nottingham's Bridlesmith Gate would have noticed the pilgrim in the long dark robe, with his feet in ragged shoes and a staff in his hand, or the two beggar children who followed him. It was less than an hour before sunset and the three of them pressed through the crowd of people trying to get into the town, or out of it, before the gate closed for the night.

More than one person noticed the beggar boy who kept gasping and pointing at the great stone castle on the rock overlooking the town. He said words they didn't understand like "wow!" and "cool!" until he was firmly *shushed* by the beggar girl with him.

"Keep your eyes down," Eve said to Andrew. "Do not draw attention to yourself."

"But it's a *real* castle!" Andrew said back to her.

"I know, I know," Eve said, exasperated.

Will Scarlet, wearing the hood of his pilgrim's robes, stopped to look for landmarks to find the house of Silas ben Reuben. "We seek the street of the Jews," he said softly to the kids.

"A street for Jews?" Andrew said. "Why do they have their own street?" he asked, and his mind went to the Nazi regime and the Jewish ghettos it had created.

"'Tis their way, I suppose. They are secretive," Will said, but his tone betrayed that he didn't really know.

Secretive or protecting themselves or ostracized? Andrew wondered. *Which is it?* He exchanged a look with Eve. She shook her head in a better-not-to-ask way.

Will rounded a corner and stopped at the end of a narrow street. He said "aha!" and slowly counted the number of doors from the corner. Though there were people walking nearby, Andrew noticed that Will didn't ask for directions.

Andrew saw that several of the house doors were open, giving him glimpses of women at work with their laundry and sewing, and children playing nearby. Other houses were shut up, with doors and shutters closed.

Will stopped at the ninth house and waved for Andrew and Eve to come close. He tapped on the wooden door. Andrew heard a heavy click and the door slid open only a few inches. A man's dark eyes peered out at them.

"What is it you want?" the man asked.

"Silas ben Reuben," replied Will. "I have a message for him."

"How am I to know you are not a traitor who would do to me and mine as has been done to others of my people?" the man asked.

"Trust me by these words," Will said and leaned in close to the door to whisper the words he had been given by Reuben. Andrew assumed, from his classes at St. Clare's, that they were Hebrew.

Instantly bolts were slid aside and the door swung wide open. "I am Silas. Come in, friend," said a short, sturdily built man. He looked surprised to see the two children, but gestured for them to enter, then quickly checked the street before barring the door again.

He led the three of them into a small, sparsely furnished room.

"What is your message?" he asked.

Will pushed the hood of his robe back and said, "Your father, Reuben of Stamford, and your sister Ruth are safe and well."

Silas clasped his hands, bowed his head, and murmured a prayer in the same language as Will's message. "Now, thanks be to God!" he exclaimed. "Tell me of my father and sister, and how soon may I see them?"

Will told Silas the story of Reuben and Ruth. When he had finished, Silas thanked him for his kindness to his father and sister and, with a gesture for them to wait, disappeared into a back room. He returned a moment later carrying a belt of green leather, with a pattern of pearls and other precious stones.

"Your kindness is beyond recompense," Silas said. "I would have you accept this from me as a proof of my thanks to you."

"I am grateful," said Will, "but 'tis too rich a gift for me. It suits my master more."

Silas said, "Please, present it to him on my behalf. But, please, you must tell me what I may give you for your kind service." Then his eyes suddenly lit up and he said happily, "Wait!"

He dashed out of the room again and returned, unfolding a cloth. "This is a Spanish knife. They are known throughout Christendom to be of the best craftsmanship."

Will held up the knife. The blade shone a bright silver, was about six or eight inches long, and ended in a razor-sharp point. The wooden handle was ornately carved. Will examined the knife and said, with a tone of awe, "'Tis indeed of the finest make."

"Now," Silas said with hushed urgency, "we must make arrangements as to how and when I may send horses and men to meet my father and sister." He bade them to sit at a small table. "I am sorry I cannot offer you a meal, but I have sent my wife and children away to safety until I know the attack against my father will not be repeated here."

Andrew found himself sitting, then standing to stretch his stiff legs, and then pacing to keep from falling asleep.

Night had fallen by the time all things were settled.

"You must stay here until the morning," Silas said.

"Thank you," said Will, "but it would be better for us to find an inn near the gate, so we may slip away quickly when it is opened at dawn."

CHAPTER SEVEN

Silas reluctantly agreed and, with another blessing, sent the three of them on their way.

As they carefully navigated the narrow streets toward the gate, they passed a man walking the other way. Andrew noticed that the man gave Will a second glance.

Andrew looked up and saw that Will had forgotten to put the hood over his head.

They turned to one street, then another. Andrew glanced back. The man strode several yards behind them.

"He is following us," Eve whispered.

Will nodded and picked up his pace, his hand falling onto the handle of the knife under his robe.

Suddenly, another man with a long beard staggered out of an alley and tumbled into them. He grabbed onto Will's robe, as if for support, but whispered, "Friend of Silas ben Reuben, make haste. Come with me."

Will pushed the man away and said loudly, "Leave us, drunken fool!"

The man fell back into the alley, clutching at Will's robe to drag him down with him. To an outsider, it looked as if they were fighting. Andrew and Eve blocked the entrance to the alley, as if watching.

The man who'd had been following them stopped behind Eve, craning to look. Eve turned on him and held out her hand. "Can you spare a few florins, sir?"

The man pushed her aside.

"Ale!" the bearded man cried out. He still had hold of Will's robes, pleading with him.

"You have had enough for one night," Will said to him. "Let go of me."

Eve said loudly to Andrew, "Summon a guard."

Andrew wasn't sure if she was serious or not.

With the word "guard," the man in the street looked alarmed and moved quickly away.

When he was out of sight, Eve said, "He is gone."

The bearded man let go of Will, who helped him to his feet. They clasped hands in friendship. "Come this way."

He led them down the alley to another passage. At the end of that was a door, which he opened noiselessly. Will, Andrew, and Eve followed him into a dark and low-ceilinged hall. They then came to an open courtyard. Andrew felt a night breeze blowing upon his face. He looked up and saw stars twinkling as brightly as he'd ever seen in his life.

"Go through the door on the left," said the bearded man. "'T'will lead you to the Fletcher Gate."

"I thank you, friend," said Will.

The bearded man retreated into a different passage.

They went through the doorway on the left and, in only a few steps, came to a street. They followed it to the Fletcher Gate. Nearby, an inn leaned precariously toward the city wall, as if it were trying to peek over the top.

CHAPTER SEVEN

The landlord asked Will no questions, nor did he speak to the two children. Will's money seemed to be the only thing he cared about.

There was a common room with a few rough-hewn tables. Three men sat at one near a small window and talked loudly, laughing and hitting their fists against the table top.

Will went to a table in a back corner and took the seat facing the room and the entrance. The kids sat with their backs to the door. A moment later the innkeeper approached and took orders for their supper and drinks. The supper turned out to be a stew that Andrew couldn't identify.

Two more men arrived and sat at a nearby table. Andrew saw them out of the corner of his eye. They were big fellows, dressed in well-made tunics and leggings. He assumed they were the servants of a nobleman. They bent across the table to speak in low voices, which made Andrew want to listen even more closely.

With his eyes on Will, who looked wearily at the three men by the window, Andrew heard the names "Alberic" and "Reuben." He noticed that Will tipped his head ever so slightly, glancing at Andrew to indicate he'd also heard them.

Andrew turned toward the two men, bending as if to adjust his boot. One man had dark shaggy hair hanging over a craggy face. The second man was bald, with a broad face and an angry scar circling his right eye.

The door to the inn opened and a man strode in with a loud stomping of his boots on the wooden floor. Andrew sat up again, turning quickly to glance at the newcomer. It was the young man with the beard Andrew had seen at Havelond.

Eve nudged Andrew. "Maurice, the son of Sir Reynauld," she whispered.

Andrew gave a sharp nod.

"There you are," Maurice said and marched over to the two men.

"Greetings, my lord," the craggy-faced man said.

Maurice sat down at the table. "Fools!" he said. "One small task and you failed!"

"My lord!" protested the scar-faced man.

Maurice's voice dropped low. Andrew strained to listen and heard him say in a sneering tone, "Bennett of Havelond is alive."

"Impossible," the craggy-faced man said. "No man could have survived that beating."

Maurice growled. "Even now he is being cared for at the Ravenswood Inn. You must go without delay and finish the job for which you were hired."

The scar-face man stammered, "My lord, with respect, we have been given new orders from Sir Alberic."

"What is that to me?" asked Maurice.

"We are his servants and duty-bound to him," the craggy-faced man said. "You will remember, I am sure, that he lent us to your father's service out of respect."

"What will Sir Alberic say when he learns you did not perform that service?" asked Maurice.

Andrew could hear the men shuffle nervously.

"I shall see to Bennett at Ravenswood," the craggy-faced man offered, then said to the scar-faced man, "You remain here in Nottingham to keep watch over the house of Silas. Reuben will undoubtedly send a message to his son."

The scar-faced man nodded.

"What is this? Tell me of what you speak," Maurice insisted.

The two men took turns explaining about Sir Alberic's hunt for Reuben and the discovery of an eldest son in Nottingham.

"Why seek the son?" asked Maurice. "Where is the old Jew?"

The craggy-faced man said, "The outlaw Robin Hood harbors Reuben somewhere in the forest. There is no finding him without battling the outlaw and his men."

Maurice was silent for a moment, then said, "I shall go with you to Ravenswood, to ensure that you do not fail again. Bennett of Havelond must not leave that inn alive."

"We shall go nowhere tonight," the scar-faced man said. "The gates are closed."

"As we are here, let us eat and drink and be friends," the craggy-faced man said.

"We shall eat and drink together," said Maurice sourly. "But we are not friends."

Andrew saw out of the corner of his eye that Maurice now turned in his chair to observe the room. His gaze fell on Will Scarlet for a moment, then he turned back to his own table. The innkeeper came to take their order.

Will signaled the kids and they rose. Down a short hall, they climbed a flight of rickety stairs to an upper floor with several rooms. The three of them went into the one closest to the stairs. A single lamp on a small table offered more shadow than light to the dingy chamber. There were no beds, only mats of straw scattered on the floor.

"We are supposed to sleep in here?" Andrew asked, aware of a foul odor coming from somewhere, or everywhere.

Will pointed to two piles of straw nearest a long wall. "The finest accommodations," he said to them. "I shall return in due time." He slipped out of the door again.

Andrew sat down on the bed of straw. It pricked him in the backside. He tried to adjust the lumps. Nothing helped. So, he pushed at the mat to serve as a makeshift pillow and stretched out on the floor. *A hot shower*, he thought wistfully. *Modern mattresses, air conditioning, pillows, clean floors, lighting...* His gaze went to a small round pot in the corner. He shuddered to think what it was used for. He groaned.

"You will get used to it," Eve whispered. She sat on her mat and placed her satchel at the top end as a pillow.

Andrew kicked off one boot, then the other, and rubbed his feet, aware of the callouses forming on the heels and balls of his feet. He lay back. Black wooden beams crisscrossed the ceiling. He remembered seeing similar beams in a restaurant in Denver. The owner said the beams were once part of an ancient pub in England. Andrew wondered if the ancient pub had been located in Nottingham. *How strange would it be if I am now looking at the same beams that wound up in Denver hundreds of years later?*

"How does time work?" he asked Eve.

She groaned. "You want to talk about that *now*?"

"Why not?" Andrew said. The dim flicker of the lamplight made the grooves in the wood shift and change. "What did Alfred Virtue say about time? He must have come up with a few ideas, since he was jumping all over it."

Eve sighed, then said, "Alfred Virtue wrote in his journal that time may be like the surface of a lake."

Andrew thought of the pond he had sat next to that morning.

"He said that time is there, smooth and peaceful," Eve continued. "But then something drops into the water and the surface ripples out in little waves."

"Ripples and waves," Andrew repeated.

She said, "Small grains of sand will make tiny ripples that spread out a little bit. And big rocks make bigger ripples that spread further out. The grains of sand or the bigger rocks are like the different kinds of events that happen in time."

Andrew cradled his arms behind his head. "So, an event like World War II would be like dropping a giant rock in the water," he said.

"That's right. It makes *huge* ripples that affect everything around it," Eve said.

"What about a normal life?" Andrew asked. "Is that a tiny grain of sand?"

"What is normal?" she asked. "If you grow up to be an Albert Einstein or a Saint Francis or a guy who sets off a nuclear explosion, then you have made a big ripple. But I guess that most of our lives are like tiny grains of sand, affecting only what is close by."

Andrew studied the ridges in the cracks of the wooden ceiling. "The top of a lake is almost never smooth," he said.

"What?"

"The water is almost never smooth," Andrew repeated. He turned and propped himself up on his elbow to face her. "Time is always rippling because stuff is always being dropped into it, like rain."

Eve was sitting against the wall. She folded her arms and frowned at him. "The idea is still the same, though. Small ripples, big ripples, a lot of ripples. Go to sleep." She lay down on the mat.

Andrew rolled onto his back again and tried to find a comfortable position. He couldn't.

The door opened again, and Will Scarlet walked softly in. He gestured for both Andrew and Eve not to speak and extinguished the lamp. Pale moonlight came through a single small window on the far wall. Andrew saw the shadow of Will Scarlet slide down to the floor beneath the window.

CHAPTER SEVEN

Andrew squinted against the darkness.

Will whispered, "The men below are the very scoundrels Robin wants to meet. Alas, we are unable to send word to him, or capture them. We must bide our time until the morrow." He folded his arms across his chest.

Andrew squirmed and thought the bed of leaves and a pillow made of a tree root was more comfortable than this.

A harsh whisper of "Andrew!" in his ear brought him awake. Suddenly hands were on his arm, shaking him until he turned over.

He opened his eyes to see Eve crouching over him. "What's wrong?" he asked.

Another voice—a man's—demanded, "Who are you?"

Startled, Andrew sat up. The man who had followed them the night before was standing in front of Will Scarlet.

Will was on his knees, cowering. "I am but a poor pilgrim who journeys to the holy shrine at Walsingham." He sounded afraid, but Andrew noticed that his hand was on his hip, the hilt of the Spanish knife within easy reach.

A gray light came through the small window on the wall.

"A pilgrim?" shouted the man from the street. He laughed derisively. "A pilgrim's robe covering a rogue's body."

"I was not always a pilgrim," Will said. "Our Lord works in the stoniest of hearts."

"And to whom do these children belong?" the man asked.

"They are beggars. I have allowed them to travel with me, out of Christian charity."

Andrew noticed Mr. Craggy Face and Mr. Scar Face, the two servants of Sir Alberic, standing in the doorway. They peered in with sleepy eyes.

The man snorted. "Why were you on the street of the Jews?"

To this, the men at the door straightened up. "Say that again?" the craggy-faced one said.

"This is none of your affair," the man from the street said to him.

"How, sir, is it your affair?" Will asked the man from the street.

"'Tis my affair because I am Cobb the Brewer and I know you are not a pilgrim, but one of the band of cutthroats that serves the outlaw Robin Hood! You were at his side in the forest, where I was stopped and relieved of half of my purse."

"You are mistaken, sir," Will said. "Though, if the outlaw took any of your purse, it was because you gave him cause."

Cobb sneered at him. "As I would expect one of his rogues to say! Come downstairs. The captain of the guard will determine whether I am mistaken or not."

Will tipped his head to Andrew and Eve to come along and crossed the room.

CHAPTER SEVEN

The two men at the door stepped aside as the three followed Cobb into the hall and down the stairs. Andrew noticed that Eve grabbed her satchel, returning it to her shoulder.

The servants of Sir Alberic stayed closely on their heels. All of them entered the common room, where two men sat at a table.

"Captain!" Cobb the Brewer called out.

The two men rose from the table. Long swords hung at both their sides. One man was thin with a twisted nose and small bird-like eyes. He wore a blue and gold robe that made him look like an official. Andrew assumed he was the captain. The second man wore a silver hauberk and drew his sword.

"Who have you there?" the captain asked.

Cobb said, "He declares himself a pilgrim, Captain, but I know him to be an outlaw in league with Robin Hood."

"Show me your hands," the captain said to Will. "Then I will know if you are a pilgrim or something else."

Will hesitated.

The captain stepped forward and grabbed Will's hands. He yanked them into view, inspecting the left and then the right. "Callouses and corns. You are no stranger to archery."

At that moment the door burst open and the innkeeper, with a bucket in hand, bustled in.

The open door was enough for Will to shout to Andrew and Eve, "Run!"

Andrew sprang forward but bumped into the captain and fell. Eve darted straight through the men to the door, pausing for a second to turn to check on Andrew. Andrew half-crawled toward her.

The innkeeper, startled by the commotion, dropped the bucket and fell back against the door, closing it again. Andrew reached Eve, but they were stuck as the innkeeper stumbled one way, then another. Andrew glanced back and saw that Will was now in the clutches of Sir Alberic's servants. They pulled at his arms, but he slammed a heel onto the foot of one and gave a sharp elbow to the other. They reeled back and he threw himself at the door.

The innkeeper shrieked and tried to step out of the way.

The five men came after Will, but he seized the dropped bucket by the handle and swung it around, striking Cobb on the side of the head. Knocked senseless, Cobb fell back into the captain and the guard, then onto the floor, effectively blocking the way for Sir Alberic's servants.

Eve and Andrew struggled with the rusty latch on the door as Will swung the bucket again, driving the five men back.

Andrew managed to lift the latch and began to pull the door open just as the captain pushed the craggy-faced servant hard at Will. Both men slammed against the door, closing it again. Now Will, Andrew, Eve, the craggy-faced man, and the innkeeper were heaped up there. Andrew dropped to the floor and crawled to one side. Eve did the same, crawling to the other.

CHAPTER SEVEN

Will struggled against the weight of the craggy-faced man, who was trying to regain his balance. The innkeeper, who was stronger than he looked, let out a grunt and pushed both Will and Mr. Craggy Face back toward the room. The captain and the guard caught hold of Will's robe and, tripping over the still-fallen Cobb, crashed to the floor. Andrew saw the Spanish knife fly from Will's belt. It hit the floor and slid under a table. Andrew scurried after it, unseen by anyone in the fight.

The captain and the guard pinned Will's shoulders to the floor. The scar-faced servant pounced, landing on Will's kicking legs.

"Ropes! Bring me ropes!" the captain shouted at the innkeeper.

The innkeeper looked startled. "Rope? Do I have rope? Where do I keep it?" he muttered and ran back and forth.

"The sheriff will hear of your thick wits!" the captain yelled at the innkeeper. The craggy-faced man was now on his feet, ready to attack if Will tried anything.

"Have mercy, good captain!" cried the innkeeper as he fumbled loudly behind a counter.

Cobb dragged himself to a wall and propped himself up, rubbing the side of his head.

The innkeeper banged around, finding nothing helpful. Finally, Mr. Craggy Face pushed him aside and went to a back room. He returned seconds later with a coil of rope and scowled at the innkeeper as he threw it to the captain.

Andrew crouched near a table and looked at Eve for help. Should they attack the men to help Will? Should they run?

Eve, standing near the closed door, lifted her hand ever so slightly as a signal for Andrew to wait.

Will's arms were roughly bound, the knots pulled tight. The captain and the guard yanked him to his feet.

Just then Maurice, son of Sir Reynauld, came down the stairs, adjusting his tunic as if he'd just awakened. "This is a riotous place," he complained.

"Open the door," the captain commanded the innkeeper.

The innkeeper obliged, jerking the door open wide. A small crowd had gathered outside but quickly scattered as the captain and guard pushed Will Scarlet out. Cobb, still rubbing his head, followed.

The two servants raced over to Maurice and whispered, with grand gestures, what had just happened.

Maurice's eyes lit up. "That outlaw may solve both of our problems," Maurice said. "Get out of my way." He pushed past them and marched through the doorway.

Eve signaled for Andrew to follow, but the innkeeper stepped in front of them and closed the door. "Wait," he said. "I am a friend to Robin and the Men of the Greenwood."

Andrew and Eve looked at one another, surprised.

The innkeeper dropped into a chair and fanned his face with his apron. "Be a good lass and bring me a cup of ale."

Eve went behind the counter and soon had the drink in the innkeeper's hand. He gulped it down. "If you know how to find the outlaw, then be quick. Tell him about his friend," he said.

"What will they do to Will?" Andrew asked.

"He will be hanged if no one comes to his aid."

Eve turned to Andrew, "You stay here. I will go to Robin."

Andrew felt the blood drain from his face. "Stay here? Alone?"

"I am the faster runner and know the way," Eve said. "You need to keep an eye on Will—and Maurice."

"But . . ." Andrew glanced at the innkeeper, whose head was tilted back and his eyes closed. "The *stone*. If you go and something happens, how will I get home?"

She brought out the chain from her neck. "You hold onto it."

This idea scared him even more. "What if I lose it?"

"You cannot have it both ways," Eve said. "Take it or leave it."

"You keep it," Andrew said, swallowing hard. "Go. I will stay here. Alone."

With his eyes still closed, the innkeeper said, "You won't be alone, lad."

8

It wasn't hard for Andrew to catch up to Will Scarlet. The parade of the captain, Cobb, Maurice, and the two servants drew a lot of attention as they made their way through the streets. Guards had now joined their captain in the march. Andrew overheard the captain asking the names of their party, to serve as witnesses. The craggy-faced servant was Jenkins of Dove's Field. The bald, scar-faced man was Walter of Larimore. Maurice gave his own name with a tone of great significance, but the captain didn't seem to notice.

The captain stopped to turn and announce, "I am Captain Butcher, second in command to the Lord Sheriff of Nottingham. As the Lord Sheriff is in London for a fortnight, I am in command and will administer justice."

Will snorted at the word "justice."

It was a short walk to the gray stone building that served as the town's prison. Will was dragged inside by the captain and the guard, with Cobb following. The captain told the rest to wait. He pushed the door closed, but Maurice held it fast with his hand.

"I have an interest in your prisoner," Maurice said.

Captain Butcher looked him over as if seeing him for the first time. "I shall be the judge of that." A handful of guards assembled in front of the doorway, pushing back Maurice and the crowd.

"Keep order here," the captain said and slammed the door in their faces. The crowd milled for a few moments until, seeing there would be no further drama, they slowly went their separate ways.

Andrew moved off to the side, as close to the door as he could get. He crouched down next to the wall, mud and filth threatening to cover his boot tops. He thought he smelled rotten vegetables.

There were occasional shouts from inside. Maurice, Jenkins, and Walter moved a few yards down the street and conferred among themselves.

A half hour went by, then an hour. The door eventually opened again and the captain stepped out. The guards—five of them—snapped to attention. "The prisoner is defiant," he said to anyone who was listening. "He has told us to do our worst to him, and so we shall."

"What are your orders?" one of the guards asked.

Captain Butcher gave a sinister smile. "Prepare the gallows for him! He shall swing at dawn."

The guards saluted and marched away.

Andrew sprang to his feet. "You are going to hang him? Without a trial?"

The captain glanced at him like a man surprised that a monkey could speak.

"Go before I have you arrested as well," he said.

Andrew took a few steps, as if to obey, but looked past the captain. He saw Will inside, being punched and dragged to an inner door. Will kept a proud look as they manhandled him into a passage, and then he was gone.

The captain glared at Andrew. Andrew backed away into the shadow of an empty animal pen that had partially collapsed against a wall. He tried to disappear behind the last standing post.

"Captain Butcher!" Maurice shouted, striding forward. "By what authority do you hang this man? It is for the sheriff alone to render such a judgment."

"I am the sheriff when the sheriff is away," Captain Butcher said simply.

"I beseech you to allow me inside so I might have a word with you," Maurice said.

"If you must speak, then do so here," the captain said brusquely.

Maurice glanced around. He gave a stern look at Andrew, who ducked behind the post. "I have a way for you to capture Robin Hood himself," he said.

The captain's eyebrows shot up. "Speak," he said. "'Tis a fair reward to have that rogue imprisoned or, better still, slain."

"It is this," said Maurice, and his villainous face took on a crafty look. "Do not hang this man here, but in Ravenswood."

"Ravenswood? What does Ravenswood have to do with this business?"

"A man dear to the outlaw's heart lies there, ill to the point of death. The outlaw will surely go there to aid him. Yet, it is a surer thing if his fellow outlaw is taken there to be hanged. The outlaw will come and, when he does, you and your men will capture him. Think of it, captain. *Two* hangings rather than one."

The captain was thoughtful for a moment, then asked, "Who did you say you are?"

"I am Maurice, son of Sir Reynauld of Prestbury and ally to Sir Alberic de Wisgar. You know them as men of nobility, men who show lavish gratitude to those who assist their cause."

The captain straightened up. "Is that so?"

"The man who lies ill is a hindrance to my father's interests."

"And Sir Alberic?"

"The outlaw harbors a fugitive, a Jew who runs from Sir Alberic de Wisgar's demand for justice."

"What fugitive?"

"Reuben of Stamford."

"The father of Silas?" Captain Butcher suddenly looked to the left and the right, as if he feared who might be listening. "Come inside," he said to Maurice.

The two men went inside and closed the door. Jenkins and Walter came near, pressing close to the door to hear what was being said inside. A few moments later, the door opened again and Maurice stepped onto the dirty street. He had a smug look on his face.

"My lord?" Jenkins asked.

"The man is a dolt. A sheep's head," Maurice said under his breath.

"What are we to do?" Walter asked. "My master will be angry if I do not find the home of Silas ben Reuben."

"Put Silas ben Reuben out of your mind," Maurice snapped. "The captain has agreed to take the outlaw's man to Ravenswood."

"My lord, I fear you have not considered the violent skill of the outlaw's men," said Jenkins. "They may ambush us in Ravenswood."

"The captain assures me that he will take more than enough men to do battle and capture the scoundrel," Maurice said. "They will not all march with us, but many will take to the surrounding forest. He believes his guards are as crafty as the Men of the Greenwood. If he is true to his word, all will come to a satisfactory end."

Andrew slid down behind the pole. His mind raced as he drew his knees up and embraced them with his folded arms. What was he to do? How could he get a message to Robin Hood about this scheme?

He heard the scuff of footfall on the dirt next to him. He looked up. Maurice stood in front of him.

"Spare something from your purse for a poor beggar boy?" Andrew asked, holding up his hand.

"Your clothes are not that of a beggar, nor is your manner of speech," Maurice said. "You are a spy for the outlaw."

Andrew was about to protest, but Maurice reached down and caught Andrew's collar in a firm grip. He jerked the boy up and leaned in close. "You will journey with us to Ravenswood."

9

Eve ran as fast as she could from Nottingham, racing north to the forest she was growing to know and love so well. She had become used to running long distances but now felt as if her legs were turning to rubber and a rib had turned inward to stab at her side. More than any fatigue from running, she felt the weight of leaving Andrew behind. Guilt pressed on her for tricking him into traveling back in time.

It wasn't clear to her—even Alfred Virtue wasn't entirely sure—what happened if a time traveler was hurt.

A mile into the woods, she heard a birdcall, a familiar signal. She whistled the call of a whip-poor-will in response, a tricky effort.

Nidd of Whitby leapt down from a nearby tree, clumsily landing on a thick root and stumbling. "Greetings to you, Waif of the Woods," he said, quickly recovering.

"Greetings, Nidd," she said, breathless. "I have urgent news for Robin from Nottingham."

"By God's grace, he is not far," Nidd said. "He is now in Hares Hollow, meeting with his cousin Anne. Come."

Nidd dashed away. Eve groaned as she clutched her side and chased after him.

Hares Hollow was the name of a thicket that, to the untrained eye, wasn't noticeable from any nearby path. Its landmark was an ancient willow that stood in the center, its thin branches lazily spread out in a broad canopy that reached to the ground. Over a dozen people could sit inside that canopy without being seen.

Eve approached and Nidd, who had arrived first, pushed an arm into the cascading leaves and spread them apart for Eve to enter.

Robin and his cousin Lady Anne sat inside on crude stumps that had been brought in to serve as chairs. Lady Anne's back was to Eve, but Robin saw her clearly and gestured for her to wait.

Lady Anne was saying, "Good cousin, why have you brought me here when my husband is in Ravenswood?" She sounded anxious.

Robin said in a soothing tone, "To be assured you were not followed by any of Sir Reynauld's allies. To lead them to your husband through you, my lady, would endanger both your lives."

"Murder?" Anne shook her head. "Evil as he may be, I cannot believe Sir Reynauld is capable of that."

"My dearest lady," Robin said, "Sir Reynauld had your husband savagely beaten and left for dead. You must not be naïve about his capabilities."

"Why?" she cried out. "For Havelond? Is a house and land worth condemning his immortal soul?"

"I fear he is not a man who cares about his soul," Robin said sadly. "Havelond is superior in every way to his own house and lands in Prestbury. He is determined to keep his hold on it."

"What can I do?" she asked, her voice choking with tears.

"Dearest cousin, you must trust me. I will give Sir Reynauld good cause to return to Prestbury. He will also pay the price for inflicting such pain on you and your husband."

"When may I see my husband?" she asked.

"We shall go under the cloak of darkness. Rest now, refresh yourself," Robin said. He turned his attention to Eve. "Come forward, Waif of the Woods. Tell me all. Where is Will Scarlet and your friend?"

Eve knelt at his feet. "Sad news, Master Robin," she said, and told him everything about meeting Reuben's son and Will being taken to the prison.

Robin leapt up. "This is grave news indeed."

"There is more," Eve said, and added what she knew about Maurice and the two servants from Sir Alberic. "Master Robin, Maurice knows Bennett is recovering at Ravenswood."

Robin looked at her, wide-eyed, then shot like an arrow through the curtain of branches. Eve and Anne looked at one another, surprised. Eve helped Anne to her feet, and they followed him.

In the open again, Eve heard Robin summoning the men to his side.

"What, pray tell, does this mean?" Lady Anne asked her cousin. "What has Sir Reynauld to do with Sir Alberic? I do not know the man."

Eve gave a sympathetic look to Anne. "Sir Alberic's servants beat your husband, my lady."

Anne gasped, clasping her hands together. "Why? Why would two of his servants carry out that evil task?"

"It was a favor," Eve said.

"Evil men readily aid one another in their foul conspiracies," Robin said. "This is a troublesome alliance. If Sir Alberic's men are in league with Sir Reynauld, then Sir Alberic must have something to gain."

Over a dozen men had now gathered. Robin raised his hand to bid them to silence and said, "Lads, good honest Will Scarlet has been seized in Nottingham. What say you?"

"He must be rescued!" came the fierce cry. "If we have to pull down every stone of Nottingham town, we will save him!" The hard looks on the faces of the outlaws showed their resolution.

"We may also suffer hardship in Ravenswood if we are not diligent," Robin said. Then he gave assignments to the various men, sending some men to Ravenswood to protect Bennett and others to devise a means to rescue Will from Nottingham. Once that was done, he proclaimed, "With our Lord's help, Will shall be rescued and brought safely back amongst us!"

"Or many a mother's son of Nottingham shall be slain," a voice in the crowd called out.

"Pray it does not come to that," Robin said.

Anne came alongside Robin and put a hand on his arm. "I implore you, cousin. Spare the innocent from a deed that was none of their doing. Allow me, for my part, to seek justice according to the law."

Robin turned to her, a skeptical look on his face. "How will you accomplish such a miracle, my lady?"

"I shall go forthwith to the Abbey of Saint Mary's and appeal to the abbot himself," she replied.

A few men laughed. Robin gave a harsh look to silence them. He said to her, "You will not receive justice from the abbot, good lady. He is corrupt to the very core of his being."

"I must try," she said.

Robin relented. "You will not reach the abbot tonight, but with good speed, you may arrive in the morning."

"And if the sheriff hangs Will Scarlet while she makes a vain appeal?" Nidd called out.

"The sheriff is not there. He has gone to London," a man named Brawby said. "Captain Butcher is in command, a man worthy of his name. He will do anything to advance his position in the eyes of his superiors. If hanging Will Scarlet will gain him status, he will do it."

"We must go! We must attack!" the men cried out.

Robin waved his hands for calm. "To attack Nottingham would be an act of war. If we are to go to war, then we must do so based on a just cause. Remember, *we* are the outlaws in this fight."

More shouts erupted from the gathering. "Are we to do nothing?" was the prevailing cry.

Robin spoke over them: "While my cousin seeks out the abbot, I will send Geoffrey the Palmer, our fastest runner, to scout out Nottingham. Only then may we discern a course of action."

Geoffrey the Palmer, a tall man with the longest legs Eve had ever seen on a human, pushed through the assembly. He said, "Master Robin, give me leave to depart now or I shall not arrive before the gates close for the night."

"Go," Robin said. "Enter by way of the Fletcher Gate. Seek out Harold, the innkeeper there. He will know what has become of Will. He also knows how to aid your escape, though the gate be closed. Report to me in Ravenswood."

"Aye, Master Robin." Geoffrey turned, making his way back through the men and onward into the woods.

"My dear lady," Robin said to Anne. "To meet the abbot, you must go to York. If you hope to be there on the morrow, you must forgo seeing your husband in Ravenswood tonight."

She looked at him gravely. "I know, cousin. If it will save further bloodshed, then I must yield my own heart's desire."

He took her hands in his. "You, good lady, are a saint."

She clasped his hands in return, her eyes filled with tears of sorrow. "I am not as yet. God willing, I will become one."

Robin said, "Summon your servant. You must depart."

"My servant fled in fear when she heard of my husband's beating," Anne said.

Robin turned to Eve. "Evangeline, you will ride with Anne as her servant."

"Me?" she asked. "But what about Andrew? He remains in Nottingham."

"You are of no help to him even if you returned to Nottingham. Geoffrey will bring us news," Robin said. "Go with Lady Anne."

"Yes, Master Robin," she said, though her heart sank at the thought of Andrew making his way in such a strange world.

Robin smiled at her, then turned and called out, "On your knees, men and women of good faith. Let us ask for our Lady's protection and help in what we must do, believing our cause to be just."

They knelt, performing the Sign of the Cross as Robin began to pray. It was a very short appeal to Mary and all the saints for their aid. Eve was a Catholic and sometimes prayed in this way, but only now did she feel it as a burning in her heart.

They finished and Robin quickly stood up. "Look lively, good friends! We do not know what time we have, nor what we face in the day to come! But by the grace of God, we shall face all things well."

10

Eve lost track of the time as they journeyed to York. The afternoon light drained away to the night and she found it harder and harder to stay awake. She nodded off more than once as her horse trudged along, and only occasionally did she see the shadows of small villages and a house or two in the distant darkness. Robin had sent Nidd to accompany them. Eve marveled at his attentiveness to every movement and sound around them, his hand ready on his sword, or reaching for his longbow.

They eventually came to the Barstone Inn, not far from York. Nidd knew the owners well and believed it was best for the Lady Anne to have rest, if only for a couple of hours, before meeting the abbot. Eve felt like she sleepwalked from the front door of the inn to a spacious room in the back. Lady Anne collapsed onto a framed bed. Eve fell onto a mattress stuffed with feathers on the floor.

She dreamt of her own bed at home and, in her dream, wondered why she had ever come to a place without paved roads and cars and comfortable hotels and electricity and running water.

The dream ended when Nidd shook her shoulder. "Up, good waif. Attend to your lady."

Eve stood up, swaying where she stood, feeling as if she hadn't slept at all. She drew the curtains on two large windows, allowing a dim gray light into the room.

The Lady Anne was sitting on the side of her bed.

"What may I do for you, my lady?" Eve asked, holding back a yawn.

"Fetch water for the pitcher and bowls," she said.

Eve looked around and saw that the room had not only the expected bed and stand, but also a small table and chairs, a bench near yet another window, a wardrobe, and a small room for storage at the back. Eve was about to go to the door when the door suddenly flew open.

A thin woman bustled in with a pitcher and bowl. "Good morrow," she said. "I am Margaret, wife of the proprietor. Water for your washing. I shall bring food anon."

Margaret left and, several minutes later, returned with plates of bread, cold meat, and cups of ale. She placed them on the small table and said, "Ring the bell when you have finished," and pointed to a bell hanging by the door. Eve and the Lady Anne ate in a sleepy silence.

Nidd came to the door and reported, "The gates of York are opened. We must hurry to the Abbey of Saint Mary's or the crowds will reach the abbot ahead of us."

CHAPTER TEN

Eve and Lady Anne hurriedly ate and were soon on the road again.

York was an ancient city, with Roman walls and gates, narrow roads, and a shamble of shacks that served as houses and shops. Eve had to dodge the occasional sheep or sidestep a tradesman pulling a cart. Nidd led the way, with a new man, Hal the Smith, following several steps behind them. Nidd explained that Hal was an old friend and often served as Robin's eyes and ears in York. Hal was short and elderly, with dozy eyes and sagging cheeks. But when he helped Eve onto her horse, she detected a great strength in his unassuming body. He did not speak the entire journey.

The Abbey of Saint Mary's sat along a river. Walls with arches and gates enclosed the grounds. Eve expected it to be a quiet place of prayer and meditation, but it was bustling with servants, tradesmen, workers, and laypeople who had come for reasons of their own.

As they crossed a vast courtyard, the Lady Anne explained that the abbey had dozens of Benedictine monks, scholars, and a school for boys. "It is a rich abbey," she said, lowering her voice. "Some say it is too rich, tempting the abbot to lavish self-indulgences."

"Aye, my lady," Nidd said. "A gathering of holy men rebelled, demanding a change to a simpler life. They were cast out and formed their own haven, the Fountains Abbey, to the north and east of here."

"Nidd?" a voice called out.

Nidd turned. A young man wearing a black robe crossed the courtyard. He smiled and stretched out his hand to shake.

"Father Simon," Nidd said and clasped the young man's hand.

The priest pulled him close, his smile held frozen while he said, "Why have you come to this lion's den?" His whisper was harsh. "What if you are recognized?"

"Who would recognize a poor peasant like myself?" Nidd asked in the same whisper. "I accompany the Lady Anne, at my master's bidding. She is his cousin and in need of help."

Father Simon stepped back. He bowed to Lady Anne. "My lady, welcome."

Lady Anne curtsied in return.

"Father Simon has been our spiritual guide in the Greenwood," Nidd explained, never raising his voice. "He hears our many confessions and offers the Mass. He is a great comfort to us."

Father Simon saw Eve and cried out, "Our dear Waif of the Woods!"

Eve smiled and curtsied.

Father Simon turned to Nidd again and asked, "Pray tell, why are you here?"

Nidd stepped closer to the priest and quickly told him why they'd come to the abbey.

Father Simon nodded. "The abbot conducts his business in the chapter house. I shall take you there,"

CHAPTER TEN

he said. "There is already a vast assembly of men and women at the door, waiting to pay their rents with money or goods. Others come to appear in answer to some charge or demand made by the abbot, or by one of the knights who manage his lands. Most come with complaints about the abbot's bailiffs or the stewards who have oppressed them."

"How is it that an abbey, dedicated as it is to the love of Christ, would employ oppressive bailiffs?" Lady Anne asked.

Father Simon lowered his head. "'Tis a question often asked, but never answered."

They passed from the courtyard through a doorway and into a broad hall. It was just as Father Simon had said: a crowd of men and women, mostly in peasants' clothing, were there.

"Follow me," Father Simon said and pushed through the crowd.

Some of the people assumed he was a man of importance and began to ask him for help. Others thrust parchments at him, asking if he'd give them to the abbot. He held up his hands, apologizing again and again as they pressed on. "Allow the *lady* through, if you please!" he said.

"Are we cheating by going to the front?" Eve asked Nidd.

Nidd looked puzzled by her question. "Knights and ladies are always to be heard first."

Soon they reached a set of double doors. Two taller guards stood straight with even taller spears held upright.

They suddenly crossed the spears to block the door. "No further," one said.

"The Lady Anne of Havelond is here to see the abbot," Father Simon said.

The guards lifted the spears and stepped aside. "Tell the prior," the one said.

Father Simon slipped in, closing the door behind him. A moment later he returned and gave an encouraging nod. "We are to wait here."

They moved to the side.

Eve was crowded close to Father Simon. She looked at the young, clean-shaven face, the kind eyes that scanned the crowd in the hall, and the thin lips that moved ever so slightly. His hands were clasped in front of his chest.

Father Simon met her gaze. He smiled.

Eve asked, "Are you praying?"

"They are in most need of it," he replied.

An hour went by as the door opened and a short bald man wearing a white robe summoned various people to enter. Most entered with expressions of hope but came out with looks of sadness or anger.

Finally, the bald man called out for "Lady Anne of Havelond."

"This is where I bid you *adieu*," Father Simon said. "My presence will only hurt your case. The abbot and I often disagree."

CHAPTER TEN

Lady Anne thanked him, and the priest began his journey through the crowd again, waving away more parchments and appeals.

"I shall await you in the courtyard," Nidd said.

Lady Anne, with Eve close behind, was led into the large meeting room. The Abbot Robert sat behind a table covered with parchments. He was a plump man with curved lips that moved readily from a pout to a sneer. His red face was like a cascade, his forehead rolling down to pig-like eyes, thick jowls rolling to a double chin that then rolled over the collar of his robe. He looked fierce and unhappy. Next to him was the prior, his second in command, whose slender face and sad eyes contrasted sharply with the abbot's appearance.

To the right of the abbot sat the sheriff of York, along with two severe-looking knights.

"A pack of grumbling rascals," the abbot complained loudly and threw a parchment aside. "What am I to do with them?"

"My lord abbot," the prior responded in a calm and steady voice, "when wrongs are charged against the stewards of the abbey, we must reflect up on the honor and grace of the Holy Virgin, after whom our house is named. If our servants are shown to have acted without mercy, they should be punished."

"Save your breath, prior, for I would rather leave my bailiffs to do as they think needful than meddle in matters of which I know little." The abbot turned a squinty eye to the prior. "If things were left to you, we should all go naked and give these rascals all that they craved. Say no more. I am abbot and, while I am chief of this house, I will do as it seems fit."

The abbot looked up at the Lady Anne and was about to speak when the doors crashed open and a tall man strode in. He was dressed in a hauberk, with a sword slung from his belt. On his head of rough black hair was a hat of velvet, which he lifted as he entered. Behind him came his squire, bearing his helmet and a heavy mace.

The abbot half-rose in his seat. "Sir Guy," he said with a gurgling cough of a laugh, "you have come at last."

"There are one or two cases I wish to hear," Sir Guy said with a very sudden and sharp glance at Lady Anne. He dropped into a vacant chair at the table. "One involves that villainous robber and murderer Robin Hood."

"My lord sheriff," the abbot said, turning to the sheriff of York, "we look to you to take stronger measures than you have. You must root out the band of vipers in Barnsdale."

"Barnsdale or Sherwood?" the sheriff replied with a disdainful sniff. "He seems to be in both forests at the same time."

"He must be found, wherever he has nested," Sir Guy said. "His deeds are an offense to all men of nobility."

The prior coughed gently and said, "Yet, if I am bold, Sir Guy, his deeds are no worse than deeds done by barons and lords to the poor of our county this past year.

None of them ever received punishment from you, my lord sheriff."

Sir Guy glowered at the prior and muttered curses under his breath.

The sheriff turned away angrily, but said nothing.

"You are a quarrelsome man," the abbot said to the prior, his heavy face shaking with anger. He pounded his fist on the table. "I want to eat. Where is my cellarer?"

"My lord abbot," the prior said and gestured to Lady Anne. "You have yet to hear this good woman, who has been waiting patiently. The Lady Anne of Havelond."

"Of Havelond?" Sir Guy said with a low snort. "I think not."

The abbot looked up as if he hadn't already seen Anne. "What do you want?"

Lady Anne stepped forward and curtsied. "God save you, my lord abbot. I have come to seek justice."

"What is your complaint?" the abbot asked.

Lady Anne explained about her husband's service in Scotland to King Henry, how he was taken captive and held for ransom, and how, now that the ransom had been paid, Sir Reynauld of Prestbury would not relinquish their lands. "Where is your husband?" the abbot asked, looking around the room. "I cannot address this case unless your husband comes to me in person."

"He would have come, my lord abbot, but he was severely beaten on his journey from Scotland." She looked down at her clasped hands and said, "There is evidence enough to believe Sir Reynauld was responsible for the attack."

Sir Guy rose to his feet. "This is a spurious accusation! What evidence?"

"I shall present it at the proper time," Lady Anne replied. "As it is, my lord abbot, it may be weeks before my husband is able to walk again."

"Then there is nothing to be done until he comes here himself," the abbot said.

Lady Anne took another step forward. "What am I to do, my lord? I fear for my life and the life of my husband. Sir Reynauld is prepared to commit any vile act to fix his hold upon my house and lands. I demand justice, my lord abbot."

The abbot gave a loud snort.

"Is there none to be found here?" Lady Anne asked.

Sir Guy hit the table with his hand. "You Saxons did not know the meaning of the word until we Normans taught it to you."

Lady Anne said calmly, "Sir Guy, the only thing the Normans taught us is that justice serves only the Normans."

The abbot jabbed a finger at the table. "Bennett must appear before me. *Here.* Until then, Sir Reynauld remains my steward at Havelond."

"My lord abbot, you force me to pursue justice by other means," Lady Anne proclaimed.

"Pray tell, what means are those?" Sir Guy asked. "You are cousin to the outlaw Robin Hood, are you not? Do you seek his aid? Do you know where he is even now? Perhaps the lord sheriff should arrest you as an accomplice."

"That would serve you and Sir Reynauld well," Lady Anne said. "'Tis a grievous feat to turn your victims into criminals." She held out her arms, pressing her wrists together. "Arrest me, then. Bind me. Then shall I present the evidence I have against Sir Reynauld, and the king's own justice will be forced to take action."

A nervous look came over the sheriff's face. "We must be calm," said the sheriff.

The abbot waved his hand to dismiss Lady Anne. "I am fatigued by this prattle. Bring your husband to me. In the meantime, you must pray that the Lord will provide," the abbot said wearily.

Lady Anne stepped to the very edge of the table. The abbot's narrow eyes opened ever so slightly. "I shall *pray*, my lord abbot, that our Lord will deal truly with wicked men who desire land that is not theirs, ever yearning to add acre to acre, grinding down the souls and bodies of the poor tenants who slave for them. For what? More wealth and more power to ruin and oppress those who cannot fight against their evil power! May the Lord provide an end to them, by whatever hand it may come."

The abbot fell back in his chair, his red face deepening to a dark purple. He sputtered, "Out, before I have you thrown out!"

Lady Anne gathered her skirt, turned, and marched out the door. Eve glanced back at the abbot, sure he was having a heart attack.

The prior seemed unconcerned and asked calmly, "Shall we hear the next case?"

Eve struggled to keep up with Lady Anne. The crowd in the hall, sensing her anger, parted like the Red Sea to allow her through.

"You were bold, my lady," Eve said as she came alongside her. "What evidence would you have given against Sir Reynauld?"

"I have none," Lady Anne said. "But they did not know that."

Nidd approached them in the courtyard, but Lady Anne did not break her stride to greet him.

"My Lady?" he asked, walking briskly to keep up with her.

"Robin spoke the truth," Lady Anne said to him. "There is no justice to be found here."

11

Andrew had been held captive overnight by Maurice and the two servants of Sir Alberic. They kept him at their sides at the inn for yet another night on stiff straw and hard wood. Now, as they stood outside of the prison waiting for Will Scarlet to be brought out by Captain Butcher, he was sandwiched between them. Walter of Larimore kept a heavy hand on his shoulder.

Voices could be heard from the other side of the stout iron-plated and rivet-studded gates. With creaking and jarring the great double doors swung open and twelve of the captain's guards marched out. Each had a steel cap on his head and wore a shirt of heavy mail. They held their swords high. In their midst was Will Scarlet, his hands held in front, bound with stout cords. His look was bold and his head held high as he walked. His expression changed only when he saw Andrew standing with his three adversaries.

Captain Butcher followed, barking commands for horses to be brought out.

"Why is the boy here?" the captain asked.

Maurice explained his conviction that Andrew was a spy for the outlaw's band.

Captain Butcher gave Andrew a malevolent look. "Put him on the horse with our other prisoner."

"I never learned how to ride a horse," Andrew said.

"You will learn," Maurice said. "Or die in the attempt."

The horses were trotted out. One was a scrawny nag. The guards heaved Will onto the nag, then Jenkins and Walter tossed Andrew in front of him. They gave Andrew the reins.

The captain insisted on a slow procession through town. Andrew assumed he was showing off his victory. The people gathered to watch as they passed, with eyes on Will Scarlet and Andrew and words whispered behind raised hands.

Andrew turned, speaking as softly as he could over his shoulder, "I have the Spanish knife under my tunic. I can cut you free."

"Not now, lad," Will said. "I will use it when the time is right."

They passed through the gate and set out on the open road. Maurice urged them to pick up their speed, swatting the rear of the old nag with his whip. The horse lurched forward, but only enough for Andrew to bounce uncomfortably.

As they rode, Andrew looked around at the countryside anxiously. He had hoped to see the outlaws rushing from the dark woods, but there was no sign of help anywhere. Peasants worked their lands, travelers walked with packs on their backs, and the occasional tradesman pulled a cart or urged a donkey along.

The warmth of the morning sun turned into an oppressive afternoon heat.

"Not far now," Will said.

As if on cue, the captain's guards spurred their horses and rode more quickly ahead, soon disappearing into a cloud of dust.

"Where are they going?" Andrew asked Will.

"Taking their positions," Will said. "Dare we hope that Master Robin is there to receive them?"

"What if he has gone to Nottingham to save you?" Andrew asked, remembering that Eve carried a message to Robin to do that very thing.

"Then we must make good use of that Spanish knife," Will said. "Pass it back. I will tuck it under the folds of my shirt."

Andrew waited until the eyes of their captors were elsewhere and then carefully slipped the knife into Will's hands.

They rode on, stopping only once for a few gulps of water and to stretch their legs. Andrew saw that three guards had stayed behind with them, hands on swords and eyes on the fields and woods around them.

Sometime late in the afternoon, Ravenswood came into view. It was little more than an inn with a handful of houses and shacks, fences for animals, and a few plowed fields. The inn sat at a crossroads, with a large empty field along side it. In the distance, Andrew saw the square tower of a church. The captain shouted to come off of the road and onto the barren field. They crossed to a lone oak tree standing in its center, the branches thick with green leaves. The guards dismounted.

The captain circled the nag and then pulled Andrew to the ground. His grip on the boy's arm was vice-like. "Try to run and an arrow will drop you before you take but a dozen steps," he said.

Will Scarlet was left on the nag.

Maurice sneered up at him. "No false moves by word of warning or deed, knave, or you will know suffering as never before."

Will Scarlet grunted.

Maurice summoned Jenkins to his side. "Go to the inn. Find Bennett."

"What if it is a trap?" Jenkins asked, worried.

"You will be the first to know," Maurice said with a low laugh. "Do you have a knife?"

"Aye," said Jenkins, touching his belt.

He gave Andrew a hard push toward the servant. "Take him with you," Maurice said. "Use him to protect yourself."

Jenkins grabbed Andrew by the scruff of the neck and pulled him across the uneven field, walking at first, then picking up the pace to a jog. "Pray, lad, that the outlaw is up to no tricks," Jenkins warned him.

CHAPTER ELEVEN

They reached the front of the inn. Jenkins opened the door and stepped back, as if he expected an attack. Nothing happened. They stepped inside a large room with tables and chairs and a long counter, but no people.

A burly man came from a back room, wiping his hands on an apron. "Good day," he said.

Jenkins took Andrew's arm and led him to the counter. He leaned on the top of it and scowled at the innkeeper. "Where are the outlaws?" he demanded.

The innkeeper looked puzzled. "Outlaws?"

Jenkins pulled the knife from his belt and held it up. "Outlaws."

The innkeeper flinched and took a step back. "I serve all sorts in here," he stammered.

"Tell me, or you will feel this blade in your fat carcass." Jenkins's voice shook as he spoke, and Andrew realized he was afraid.

The innkeeper's eyes stayed on the knife. "The outlaw was here with some of his men, but received word that one of his own was to be hanged in Nottingham. They hastened away."

Andrew felt his heart sink. He had hoped that, somehow, Robin would know where Will Scarlet really was.

"Who is here now?" Jenkins asked.

"Myself," the innkeeper said. "Also a sick man lies upstairs in bed. He was terribly beaten and is near death."

"Is he alone? Who is with him?" Jenkins asked.

"The outlaw left an old woman to care for the man." Beads of sweat had formed across the innkeeper's brow. He wiped at them with a rag from his apron pocket.

"Take me to him," Jenkins said and tucked the knife back into his belt.

The innkeeper waved for them to follow and led them down a hall to a set of stairs near a back door. Jenkins held Andrew in front of him, his grip hard on Andrew's shoulders. They went up the stairs, each step creaking loudly as they did. At the top, the innkeeper took them down another hall, past an open door on the right, and then stopped at the second.

"He is here," the innkeeper said softly.

"Open the door," Jenkins said.

The innkeeper obeyed, pushing the door open and stepping back into the hall. The windowless room was dark, apart from a lit candle on a bedside table. Andrew saw a man lying in a bed. Sitting on a stool next to the bed was a small figure in a hooded robe, leaning on the edge of the mattress as if praying.

Jenkins took a step past Andrew into the room. His hand drew the knife from his belt.

The innkeeper reached out and gently pulled Andrew back. The floorboard groaned under their feet. Jenkins turned in time to see them move and his sour expression suddenly changed as he realized, too late, what he should have known.

CHAPTER ELEVEN

In a quick move, the figure on the stool was on his feet, a knife held ready. It was a man Andrew didn't recognize. Then the quilt was thrown aside and the sick man—Robin Hood himself—came off of the bed with a laugh.

Jenkins lifted his knife, but the innkeeper now had a knife of his own and held it against Jenkins's neck. Robin caught hold of Jenkins's wrist and twisted until Jenkins fell to his knees and dropped the knife. "Mercy! Have mercy!" Jenkins said through clenched teeth.

Robin picked up the knife and handed it to the innkeeper. "With gratitude," he said.

The innkeeper nodded, then quickly retreated down the hall to the stairs.

"How many of you are there?" Robin asked Jenkins.

"Only three," Jenkins said. "Captain Butcher, Master Maurice, and myself."

"He is lying," Andrew said. "The Captain brought a dozen guards with him, maybe more."

Robin gave a disappointed look at Jenkins. "What is your name?"

"Jenkins."

"I am the one they call Robin Hood, and this is Much the Miller's Son," Robin said cordially. Much nodded.

Jenkins looked puzzled by the introduction.

"Today you will be sorry you chose to serve the wrong master." He gave Jenkins a stunning blow on the side of the head with the hilt of his knife.

Jenkins fell, dazed, to one side, but Much's hands were on him, dragging him onto the bed. Rope seemed to come from nowhere as Much bound Jenkins's hands and feet.

Robin turned to Andrew. "What about you, lad? Are you hurt?"

"Saddle sore," he said.

Robin chuckled. "And Will Scarlet? Unharmed?"

"They have knocked him around, but he is tough," Andrew said. "How did you know we weren't in Nottingham?"

"Thanks be to God for men with fast legs," Robin said. "Where are they keeping Will now?"

"Under the tree in the middle of the field."

"So, they will see us coming, should we attack. Though we are positioned better than they know," Robin said. He bowed down to face Andrew. "I would not have you in harm's way again, lad, but I have need of your help."

"I will do whatever you want," Andrew said.

Andrew crossed the field alone. He could see Maurice and the captain pacing under the tall oak. They were watching him, the guards standing ready behind them. Will Scarlet was still on the horse but, as Andrew came closer, he saw that they'd put a noose around his neck and stretched it over a branch of the tree.

The captain drew his sword as Andrew approached. "Where is Jenkins?" he demanded.

Andrew swallowed hard, trying not to sound nervous. "At the inn. He wants you to come to see Bennett."

Maurice asked, "The outlaw left the man unguarded?"

"There was a guard," Andrew explained, "but Jenkins took care of him."

"What of the outlaw?" the captain asked. "Has he been here?"

"The innkeeper said Robin Hood and his men went to Nottingham to save Will Scarlet," Andrew replied. He looked at Will Scarlett, who gazed back at him with a blank expression.

Maurice gave a proud smile. "This is good news. I shall have Bennett and you will capture the outlaw when he rushes back from Nottingham."

"It is a trap," Captain Butcher said. In a quick move, he grabbed Andrew, drawing him close. "Is it a trap? Is the outlaw at the inn?"

Andrew acted surprised, which wasn't hard to do. He stammered, "Yes. Robin Hood is inside."

The captain snorted at Maurice, who turned red.

Andrew continued, "Robin wants you to know that you are surrounded by his men, though you cannot see them. He will strike a bargain with you: Jenkins for Will Scarlet."

"Let him kill Jenkins," Maurice said. "It was his incompetence that brought us to this trouble."

The captain sheathed his sword. "Does the scoundrel expect us to bring Will Scarlet to him?"

"He will meet you in front of the inn to make the exchange," Andrew said.

The captain shook his head. "He will have the advantage there. The rogue and his men must be drawn out."

"How? Invite them to make the exchange in the middle of the field?" Maurice asked.

The captain scowled at Maurice. "There will be no exchange, you fool. We must prepare for battle."

Maurice looked stunned. "A battle?"

"I did not come this far to trade men with an outlaw I mean to capture," the captain snarled. "We will draw him and his hidden bandits out into the clear."

"By what means?"

The captain pointed to Will on the horse. "By hanging this brigand."

Will turned to the captain but said nothing.

Andrew cried out, "No!"

The captain gave a look to one of his guards, who took hold of Andrew and dragged him over to the side of the nag. "Move and I have orders to kill you," the guard snarled.

Andrew looked up at Will. The noose was fixed tight around his neck, the rope disappearing into the foliage of the tree, then dropping down again. His eye went to Will's hands. He hoped Will had secretly used the Spanish knife to cut the cords, but they were still there.

The captain gave orders to another guard. "Ride to the inn. Tell the outlaw to surrender or I will hang his friend. If he doubts me, then let him but watch from his hiding place."

The guard mounted his horse and sped across the field. He dismounted at the front door of the inn. Andrew saw Robin come out to greet the guard. They spoke for a moment and the guard climbed upon the horse and rode back.

"What does the robber say?" the captain called out.

"He sends this message: 'Release Will Scarlet and the boy or you and all with you will suffer grievous harm, even to the pain of death,'" the guard said.

"So be it," the captain said and, taking out his sword, strode over to the nag. He lifted the sword and turned the flat side to strike the flank of the horse.

Andrew and Will exchanged glances. With a voice of stone, Will said, "A battle with great bloodshed is needless. If I must die, grant me this much: give me a sword and let me be unbound to fight with you and your men until I lie dead on the ground."

Captain Butcher looked at him scornfully. "A thieving varlet does not deserve to die so honorably. You will hang, as will the rest of your cutthroat comrades."

Maurice's face bunched up with worry, and he called out, "Give them a moment to change their minds."

The captain snorted. "I shall not." He brought the flat of the sword down with a loud slap onto the back end of the horse.

The horse bolted forward, and Will Scarlet slid off the back. Andrew was prepared to rush forward to grab Will's legs, with a vain hope of holding him up so he wouldn't hang. The guard gripped him tighter.

"Stop!" Andrew cried out.

Will hung for only a few seconds, then suddenly jerked his hands apart, the cords flying aside. With both hands, he grabbed the rope above his head to alleviate its strangling hold. Then, like magic, Will seemed to fly up into the tree and disappear into its thick leaves.

"By the devil!" Captain Butcher shouted, lifting his sword and moving under the tree to look.

There was a buzz like the sound of a bee as a small black arrow flew down from somewhere in the tree, striking the captain on the top of his shoulder. He staggered back with a loud cry. The guards raced to him, pulling him from danger.

The guard holding Andrew pushed him away and left to see to his captain. Andrew fell at the thick base of the tree. Looking up, he saw Will on a high branch, cutting the noose from his neck. Next to him was Ket the Troll, with his small bow held up in his left hand and his right hand stringing one arrow after another and letting them fly.

Maurice and the guards scattered from under the tree, exposing themselves in the surrounding field. Arrows now flew from different directions, from both the inn and the distant woods. Andrew saw Robin Hood and

CHAPTER ELEVEN

Much the Miller's Son running in their direction. The captain's guards turned this way and that, seeking cover but not sure which direction to go. "Haste, haste," cried one guard. "Away! Away!"

There was a *thud* next to Andrew as Will Scarlet dropped from the tree. He grasped the boy with both hands and tossed him up to Ket the Troll. "For safekeeping," he said and sprinted toward Captain Butcher with his Spanish knife drawn.

"Hello, lad," Ket said in his usual low, mournful voice.

Andrew positioned himself on a thick branch and strained to see what was happening below. A guard and Will Scarlet, both with knives at the ready, circled one another.

More guards, with swords held high, erupted from their hiding places in the forest, on horseback and on foot.

Andrew saw it all, feeling as if he'd slipped into a nightmare. Swords and knives were brandished, clashing loudly as they struck one another. Spears were thrown, arrows buzzed, men struggled in hand-to-hand combat. Fear surged through Andrew's body. *This is nothing like the movies*, he thought. Then came a wave of adrenaline that sharpened his focus and heightened his sense of everyone's movements, almost as if in slow motion.

Robin Hood was closer to the tree now, clashing swords with a guard. Captain Butcher emerged from somewhere out of Andrew's view, clutching his sword. He circled behind Robin, whose attention was on the guard. Andrew knew that, unless someone did something, the captain would strike Robin down. Andrew shouted, but his voice disappeared in the noise below.

Andrew turned to Ket the Troll, who had moved to another branch to release his black arrows in another direction.

Andrew half-scrambled, half-fell, from branch to branch to the ground below. The captain was coming up behind Robin, his sword ready for a terrible thrust. Andrew knew he had to do something and, looking around, saw a stone the size of his fist on the ground. He whispered, "God help me," and, in one swift move, snatched up the stone and threw it as hard as he could at the captain.

The stone curved in the air—better than any curveball Andrew had ever thrown—and hit Captain Butcher hard on the left temple. The man spun as his legs went limp. He fell in a heap behind the outlaw.

The sudden distraction of the fallen captain allowed Robin to dispense with the guard in front of him. He swung around to the fallen captain, looked puzzled, then saw Andrew standing by the tree. A quick nod of thanks and Robin dashed into the battle again.

Andrew pressed against the tree, worried he might be struck by an arrow or a swinging sword. The fight continued with a terrible ferocity on the field. Then, a single man broke away, running from the combat for the forest. It was Maurice.

CHAPTER ELEVEN

"He is getting away!" Andrew shouted to no one in particular. Getting no response, Andrew ran after him.

Only after he had made it across the road and into the woods did Andrew wonder what he would do if he caught up to the man.

The sound of a horse's snort turned his attention to the right. Through the trees, Walter, Sir Alberic's other servant, was climbing onto a horse. A second horse came into view and Andrew knew how they would escape.

A twig snapped and Andrew turned in time to see Maurice reaching for him. He tried to dodge, but Maurice caught hold of his tunic and threw him to the ground. The man followed it with a hard kick to his side, knocking the wind out of him. Andrew doubled up, wheezing, trying to breathe as black spots formed in front of his eyes.

Maurice's hands were on him again, dragging him across the ground by his arm. A moment later, he was thrown onto a horse. Maurice climbed on behind him, whipping at the horse to move.

Andrew heard a sharp hiss, followed by a loud cry from Walter. The servant fell to the ground, a black arrow sticking from his chest.

Maurice spurred his horse into a gallop, then a full run through the trees.

Still straining to get air into his lungs, Andrew struggled to stay conscious and wondered if he'd ever get out of this world alive.

12

Havelond.

Andrew, who had recovered enough to watch where they were going and hope for a chance to escape, now saw the familiar grounds. It was near evening and the manor house was taking on an ominous darkness.

Maurice guided the horse along a side path to the courtyard and stable. He dismounted and barked commands for the "beggar boy" to be brought inside. The large man who'd grabbed Andrew when he'd first arrived now seized him again and hooked an arm around his waist. Andrew cried out as a sharp pain shot through his side where Maurice had kicked him. The thug was unconcerned and carried him into the manor.

Andrew was brought to a large dining hall. A massive rectangular table framed by a dozen chairs dominated the center. A wall-sized stone fireplace stood at the far end. Tall narrow windows lining another wall were propped open and fresh air wafted in.

Maurice was leaning over a side table, splashing water from a bowl onto his face.

The thug dropped Andrew onto a chair near the side table and lumbered out again. Andrew gingerly touched his side. He knew it was bruised but worried that Maurice's kick had damaged a rib.

Maurice lifted a pitcher and poured a drink into a tall silver cup. "You want some, I am sure," Maurice said.

"Yes please," Andrew said, realizing how thirsty he was.

With a cruel smile, Maurice drained the cup, then slammed it down with a contented "ah!" He didn't offer any water to Andrew.

A set of double doors at the head of the room opened. Sir Reynauld walked in with his son Everard and a man with a pointed face and narrow eyes that reminded Andrew of a rat. Maurice greeted them and only then did Andrew discover that the man was Sir Alberic.

Sir Alberic was taller than the other men, though his slumped shoulders curved his lean body slightly forward. He clasped his hands loosely in front of his chest, the thin fingers threaded into each other. He wore a long black robe that contrasted the pale skin on his rodent-like features.

"I am surprised you would greet me so cheerfully," Sir Alberic said to Maurice in a voice that matched his look, "since you have suffered to fail so miserably."

"Failed, Sir Alberic?"

"Where are my servants? Why have they not returned to me with news of Bennett?"

CHAPTER TWELVE

"Your servant Walter is dead," Maurice reported. "I know not what has become of Jenkins. It was their failure you should consider, not mine." He gave Sir Alberic a sharp look. "I would have thought a man of your stature would have had more competent servants to do his bidding."

Sir Alberic's lips pulled back into a smile that also served as a sneer.

"Mind your tongue," Sir Reynauld said to his son. "Where, then, is Bennett?"

"He is missing," Maurice replied.

"Perhaps you should tell us all that happened after your arrival in Nottingham," Sir Alberic said.

Andrew listened as Maurice told his tale, which mixed a little fact with a lot of fiction. He claimed it was Captain Butcher who came up with the foolish scheme to travel to Ravenswood to capture Robin Hood, kill Bennett to please Sir Reynauld, and find Reuben to gain favor with Sir Alberic. "I was a reluctant participant," Maurice concluded and explained how the scheme had gone wrong after they were ambushed by the outlaws.

Sir Alberic paced calmly as he listened, his hands rubbing together.

Sir Reynauld's face contorted with rage. "Fools to a man! And you, my son, were the biggest of them all."

Maurice reeled back, as if struck. He glared at his father, but did not speak.

Everard gave an apologetic look to his brother. He turned to his father and asked, "What are we to do now?"

"The abbot and Sir Guy of Gisborne have given us additional time by rebuffing the Lady Anne," Sir Reynauld said. "She may not make a claim against us unless Bennett himself appears before the abbot in York. We may yet find him before that happens."

"Their aid allows you more time in Havelond, but it does not help me with Reuben of Stamford," Sir Alberic said with a loud sniff. "Reuben may yet still demand the money he expects from me. The Jew must be found."

"No doubt the outlaw is hiding the two of them," said Sir Reynauld.

"Now you see why I have brought the boy," Maurice said.

With that, all eyes in the room turned to Andrew.

Sir Alberic stepped to the chair and leaned over Andrew, his hands still clasped in front of him. "Speak, young beggar. What reward would satisfy you if you would tell us how to find Reuben of Stamford and Bennett?" Sir Alberic's beady eyes locked onto Andrew's.

At that moment, Andrew realized that Sir Alberic reminded him more of a praying mantis than a rat. "Sir, I do not know where they are," he said. "I am not from these parts. Free me now to walk the forest and I would be completely lost within mere minutes."

The men looked at one another.

"I will beat it out of him," Sir Reynauld said.

CHAPTER TWELVE

He had taken only two steps when, suddenly, Andrew heard a familiar buzz and a black arrow slammed into the top of the dining table, narrowly missing the man.

The men were startled, throwing themselves to one side and the other while craning to see from where the arrow had come.

"Are we under attack?" Everard cried out from behind a chair.

"I know that black arrow," Maurice said, half-hidden under the table. "'Tis one of Robin Hood's men."

Sir Alberic had pressed himself against the wall next to Andrew. He glanced at the window, then grabbed at the arrow. It was firmly embedded in the wooden tabletop. He knelt and peered close. "A parchment is tied to the shaft."

Sir Reynauld snatched up a long pole that had been leaning against the wall between the windows. Positioning himself out of harm's way, he used the pole to close the thick wooden shutters. He dropped the pole and walked with renewed confidence to the arrow. The others also relaxed. Sir Reynauld undid the thin string that held the roll of parchment in place.

"*Sir Reynauld of Prestbury and Sir Alberic de Wisgar,*" he read aloud, "*your debts are now due. Depart Havelond by daybreak with all that is yours. Heed this warning or suffer the pain of your treachery.*"

Everard went pale. "The outlaws know you are here, Sir Alberic."

Sir Reynauld slammed a fist against the table. "Who is that lawless wretch to dictate to us?"

"What shall we do?" asked Everard.

His father looked at him with contempt. "You mew like a coward," he said. "Call the men-at-arms. Command them to guard every corner of this manor."

"You would have them lay siege to us?" Maurice asked.

"I do not believe the outlaw has enough men to entrap us here," he said. "However, I would have you and Everard depart with great speed to Prestbury to summon our allies."

"Now?" Everard asked. "To travel by night will lay us open to ambush by the outlaw's cutthroats."

"Only if you tarry."

Everard came closer to his father. "We cannot make the journey there and return before dawn," he said. "Father, you do not know the strength of the outlaw. If you are not seen departing by the morning, he will attack."

"I do not fear the scoundrel as you do," Sir Reynauld said firmly. "Do as I say!"

Everard bowed and left the room. Maurice lingered, looking as if he wanted to say something, but changed his mind. He glanced at Andrew. "What about the boy?"

"Leave him to us," said Sir Reynauld.

Maurice turned on his heels and walked out.

Sir Reynauld went to the door and pulled at a long cord. "Sir Alberic, 'tis safer for you to stay here than to attempt to journey home. Let us see to supper."

CHAPTER TWELVE

Sir Alberic gave a bow of gratitude. "It would seem we must now fight the outlaw together."

The two men turned their attention to Andrew again.

"Pray tell, what shall we do with you?" Sir Alberic asked.

"Give me a drink of water and set me free?" Andrew suggested.

Sir Alberic leered at him. "You have the saucy tongue of your master," he said.

Andrew shrugged.

"We shall cure you of that," Sir Alberic said.

Andrew was locked in a closet with no food nor drink nor light, save a thin gray line that shone from under the door. Once his eyes adjusted, he saw shelves lining one wall. He felt plates and pitchers on one. He didn't find any food or water. His fingers touched rough blankets on another shelf. He grabbed them and spread them on the floor as a bed. With nothing better to do, he lay down with his head close to the crack under the door, hoping for a clue about what was happening. He prayed for someone to rescue him.

His bruised side ached no matter which position he took. Eventually, from the sheer exhaustion caused by the long day, he fell asleep. How long he slept, he didn't know, but he woke up to the same foreboding darkness. His mouth was dry. He had trouble swallowing. His head began to hurt. A wave of nausea hit his stomach.

I'm dehydrated, he thought.

Performing the Sign of the Cross, he prayed, "Dear God, please provide me with water."

Lying down again, he closed his eyes and fell into a fitful half-asleep/half-awake state, like a fever-dream. He came out of it when a sound—he didn't know what it was—caused him to sit up. He listened. A low rumbling of thunder came, followed quickly by a torrent of rain that fell heavy against the house.

If only there was a window, he thought. *I could reach out for a handful of water.*

He lay back down, praying again for God to help him. He hadn't finished the prayer when a drop of water hit him on the forehead. Then another. And another.

A leak in the roof!

He pushed himself up a few inches and opened his mouth. A drop of water hit his tongue. He held his position as more drops fell, giving him relief.

Thank you, God, he thought, as more drops came.

He had an idea and placed a pitcher from the shelf where his head had been. The drops splashed inside, spraying him and the blankets.

"You can stop now," he said to God after he'd filled that pitcher and started another.

He curled up in a ball away from the leak and fell asleep feeling better than he had for hours.

A gentle scratching sound woke him up the next time.

Rats, he thought. Then he realized the sound was coming from the lock on the door. He crawled over and listened. Someone was turning a key in the lock. There was a gentle click and the door slowly opened.

"Andrew?" a low and mournful voice said.

"Ket?" whispered Andrew. "Ket the Troll?"

"Aye," he said. "We must move quickly. The wicked knights intend to deliver your dead body to Master Robin to prove they do not fear him."

Andrew's mouth went dry. His hand bumped against the pitcher of rainwater. He drank some of it but felt a new wave of nausea.

"They are coming for you now. Follow me," Ket said.

Andrew stood up, his legs cramping, and entered the dark hallway with Ket. The troll closed the closet door and locked it again.

Heavy footsteps sounded from somewhere down the hall. Ket tugged at Andrew's sleeve and together they went down a hall in the opposite direction of the noise. They reached the double doors of the dining hall and slipped in.

"How will we get out?" Andrew asked.

"By going up," Ket said. He went to a tall hutch in the far corner of the room and climbed the shelves to the very top. He reached a hand down to Andrew. Andrew caught it and climbed as Ket pulled with greater strength than Andrew imagined.

"Further on," Ket said, and now leapt up, grabbing a crossbeam on the ceiling. He swung up and, as before, reached down for Andrew, who took his hand again. And so it went until Ket and Andrew were high in the rafters, crawling along the beams to the far end.

"You did not shoot the black arrow through the window, did you? You shot it from up here," Andrew said.

"Near enough to the open window so they would think it came from outside."

"How will we get out?" Andrew asked, thinking of the narrow windows.

"'Tis the only way," the troll replied. "You must squeeze through as I did."

As the two crept along the crossbeam, the doors below were thrown open. Ket signaled for Andrew to stop.

The large servant that had manhandled Andrew earlier entered with a lamp.

"What do you mean, 'the closet was empty'?" Sir Reynauld shouted, coming in behind the servant. "Dullard! Did you forget to lock the door?"

"No, my lord," the servant said. "He was there most of the night. He used blankets as a bed and collected rainwater to drink. Someone from outside must have taken the key from the hook and set him free."

"Raise the alarm," Sir Reynauld thundered. "Search the house. Find that boy!"

The servant started through the door.

"Leave the lamp!" Sir Reynauld barked.

The servant put the lamp on the table and hurried out.

Sir Reynauld put both hands on the table and leaned forward, groaning loudly.

"Is it time for breakfast?" Sir Alberic asked casually as he walked in. He was fully dressed.

"Someone freed the boy."

"Pity," he said, his hands coming up and clasping in their familiar position. "How did the boy escape?"

"The clumsiness of my servant, no doubt," Sir Reynauld said. "He shall pay dearly for his mistake."

A maidservant came in, still wearing a dressing gown and looking terrified. "My lord?" she asked.

"Food," Sir Reynauld commanded.

The maidservant bowed and rushed out.

The two knights lit candles around the room, though a gray light was creeping across the windows. They sat at the table in silence.

Sir Alberic looked up at the window. "The outlaw demanded that we leave Havelond by sunrise."

"Let the outlaw demand what he will. I am not afraid of him." Sir Reynauld gazed at Sir Alberic. "Are you? Do you intend to repay the Jew?"

Sir Alberic gave a light laugh. "Let him come to collect."

A flurry of servants arrived with trays covered with plates of food and goblets. Without a word, Sir Reynauld began to eat. Sir Alberic waited until the servants left again, then delicately nibbled at his food.

Andrew's mouth watered. He couldn't remember the last time he'd eaten. He looked at Ket, who sat perfectly still with his eyes on the scene below. He lifted his head and turned it slightly as if listening to something. Andrew listened but couldn't hear anything, apart from the sounds of the men eating below.

Suddenly, shouts erupted from somewhere in the house, then came the sound of feet pounding hard in the hall. Everard appeared in the doorway.

"Father!" he cried out. "Thank God you are not dead."

He was soaked from head to foot. His hair was matted against his skull and his face was streaked with mud.

Sir Reynauld stood up. "Dead! Whatever are you talking about? What has happened?"

Everard dropped into a chair, slouching wearily. "Prestbury House has been burned to the ground." He covered his face with his hands and sobbed.

Andrew looked at Ket. Ket gave a slight nod, then turned his attention to the scene below.

Sir Reynauld snapped his fingers at a servant standing in the corner. "Bring him a cup of ale."

The servant did as he was told.

Everard drank quickly and said, "The outlaws caught us as we reached the grounds of Prestbury. We fought them. Maurice most valiantly of all."

Sir Reynauld clutched a fist to his chest. "Where is Maurice now?"

CHAPTER TWELVE

"Captured, my lord. The outlaws have stolen him away into the forest." Everard pounded the cup on the table. The servant fumbled to pour him another drink.

"How is it that you are unscathed?" Sir Alberic asked.

"The outlaws spared me so I would deliver a message to you." The young man drained the cup again.

"What message?"

"We must depart Havelond *now*, taking only what we can carry, knowing we will never return."

Sir Reynauld snorted. "If they have destroyed our home, where do they expect us to go?"

"To Thornbridge," his son said. "They have demanded that we come to Thornbridge, with Sir Alberic. They said to obey and we may see Maurice yet alive."

"I am to go to Thornbridge?" Sir Alberic asked. "For what purpose?"

"To face your accusers," said Everard.

"What accusers?" asked Sir Alberic.

"Reuben of Stamford will be there."

"The brazenness! The effrontery!" Sir Reynauld roared. "I will not suffer the threats of that swine!"

Everard reached out and caught his father's hand. "My lord father, we must do as they say. I fear for the life of Maurice. I fear for all of our lives. Let us do as they say: depart with what we have, the flesh on our bones if nothing else. I beg you. Had you seen the devastation that was once our home, you would not doubt them."

Sir Reynauld pulled his hand away. "You are like the daughter I never had," he said. "Let them come here. See if they have the will or men to drive us out."

"We have not the men! Maurice and I never reached our allies!" Everard cried. "Be wise, Father. This manor house was not built to withstand a siege."

"'Tis true," Sir Alberic said with a sigh. He dabbed at his mouth with a napkin and threw it onto the plate. "We must go to Thornbridge."

"What?" Sir Reynauld shouted.

"I will remind you again, Father, that the life of your oldest son depends upon our going," Everard said.

"Hear me," Sir Alberic said. "I shall send a servant to York to rally the sheriff and all of the forces he can muster. They will surround the outlaws at Thornbridge. Not only will you keep Havelond, but I shall be rid of Reuben."

"If you are resolute to fight, then I beg you to send a message to Wrangby Castle for Sir Guy and the knights there to give us aid!" Everard said.

"Coward!" Sir Reynaud suddenly struck his son with the palm of his hand. The slap was so hard, and the sound so sharp, that Andrew recoiled and his hand stirred dust from the top of the beam. Ket grabbed his shoulder to steady him. Alarmed, Andrew watched specks of dust float downward toward Sir Alberic, who was still seated at the table.

"You are an embarrassment to me," Sir Reynauld snarled. "We shall show Sir Guy of Gisborne and all the knights of the realm our true power. All will know our mettle when we deliver the outlaw's head by our own strength."

Everard stood, glowered at his father, and stormed out of the room.

Sir Reynauld gave a contemptuous look to Sir Alberic, who turned just as the dust settled on the table near his plate.

"We must depart," Sir Reynauld said and marched out.

A moment later, Sir Alberic stood up and finished the last of his drink. He grimaced and smacked his lips as if he'd tasted something he didn't like. He put the cup down and sauntered out.

Ket moved toward the far wall. Andrew crawled behind him, still wishing he could grab a few of the leftovers from the plates below. Ket stopped again and looked down.

A maidservant entered the room and stacked the plates onto a tray. Then she turned and went to the window. Using the long pole, she unlatched and pushed open the heavy shutters. A cool morning breeze blew in and the yellow glow of sunrise touched the small panes of glass.

The maidservant stopped where she was and tilted her head up. She looked directly at Ket and Andrew. "God be with you," she said and took the tray from the room.

"We must hurry," Ket said and hurried forward.

13

The world seemed to glisten in the morning light as Andrew and Ket sprinted along the outer wall to the closest edge of the forest. Andrew braced himself for the sudden shouts from guards standing watch, but all was silent.

They moved into the trees and seemed to circle Havelond. Andrew had the sense that they were near the cave he'd first come through and wondered what he'd find if he went there now.

Ket stopped and said, "I shall intercept the servant bearing the message to Sir Alberic's men in York."

"What about me?"

"The way to Thornbridge is lined with forest," Ket said. "You must follow Sir Reynauld and Sir Alberic, lest they change their plans."

"What good will that do?" Andrew asked, thinking that he had no way to signal anyone if anything changed.

"Master Robin's men will be watching in the woods. Should you sense any danger, signal them with this whistle."

Ket cupped his hands around his mouth and whistled one long note, followed by two short ones. To Andrew's ear, it sounded like another bird call. "Now you."

Andrew tried the same signal, though it didn't sound as good as Ket's.

"That will do," Ket said and patted Andrew on the back. He was off, sprinting through the trees until he seemed to blend in to the forest itself.

Drops of water fell from the leaves above Andrew's head. He tilted his head back and let the drops fall into his mouth. Then he made his way toward the clearing that separated the forest from Havelond Manor.

A movement just ahead made him stop. He peered through the trees and saw Everard walking along the edge of the trees. Andrew crept closer to see what he was up to.

The young man hung his head, his hands clasped behind his back. He seemed lost in his thoughts as he strolled along the field, parallel to the house.

Andrew climbed the nearest tree, crawling along the branches, as he'd done before with Eve, leaping quietly from tree to tree, the leaves shivering only slightly as he did. *I'm getting pretty good at this*, he thought. He kept Everard in sight, allowing him to walk several yards ahead.

Everard reached a point where, to continue on, he would have gone around to the front of the house. Instead, he stopped. Andrew couldn't see why and carefully crawled along a branch to find a better vantage point. At the end

CHAPTER THIRTEEN

of that branch, he reached for another and slipped. He lost balance and, with a lot of unhelpful grabbing and clawing, fell to a branch below, then bounced to one side into open air and soon found himself with his back flat against the ground.

If the kick to his side from Maurice hadn't fractured a rib, then his fall might have done the trick. With great effort, he rolled onto his hands and knees.

Everard was sitting on a tree stump, his elbows on his knees, his head still hung low. He looked over at Andrew with a forlorn expression. "Why are you here? Why have you not run to freedom?"

"That is a good question," Andrew said, groaning. He climbed to his feet and brushed himself off. His bruised side throbbed with a dull ache.

Everard sighed. "This is folly," he said. His eyes were red and the side of his face swollen where his father had struck him.

Across the field, servants led horses out from the stable. Soon, a cart followed. Then another. Everything was being moved to the front of the manor.

Everard turned to Andrew again. "Do you have a brother?"

"Yes," he replied.

"Would you not do all in your power to save him if his life were in danger?"

"Not when he uses my stuff without asking," Andrew said, adding a chuckle to show he was joking.

Everard didn't notice. "I must find the outlaw and plead for my brother's life."

Andrew was surprised.

"Will you lead me to the outlaw?" Everard asked.

"You will find Robin at Thornbridge," Andrew said.

"I must speak with him *before* the meeting with my father. Otherwise, I fear there will be no time for sensible talk," Everard said. He stood up and faced Andrew. "Will you lead me to him?"

Andrew shook his head. "I do not know where he is."

"Surely, if we walk in the direction of Thornbridge, you have the means to signal the outlaw or one of his men. I hear they are everywhere."

Andrew thought of the whistle Ket had taught him. "Yes, but . . . how do I know you are not part of a trap?"

Everard spread his arms wide. "I go with no more than what you see here, without the benefit of a sword or my father or any other aid. You, beggar boy, are the only aid I have in the world."

Andrew gazed at him. What was he supposed to do? Ket's orders were to follow Sir Reynauld, not guide one of his sons to Robin Hood. *But*, he reasoned, *if Everard is able to talk to Robin Hood and stop a battle, then it has to be worth it.*

"My family is doomed unless I intercede," Everard said.

Andrew made up his mind. "If you know the way to Thornbridge, I will try to send a message to Robin Hood."

CHAPTER THIRTEEN

"God bless you, boy," Everard said, relieved, and turned away from the manor. Together they went into the woods.

Everard followed the same path through the woods that Eve and Andrew had taken when they followed Lady Anne. This time, Everard didn't join the road, but veered off in a different direction that took them around the other side of Lady Anne's cottage. "She deserved better," he said as they passed and picked up his pace.

Andrew asked, "Why did you make her move there?"

"My father and I fell in love with Havelond. My brother fell in love with Lady Anne," Everard said. "Alas, she did not feel the same for him."

"She was married," Andrew reminded him.

Everard frowned. "He did not care. He wanted her. That was enough."

"Your family takes whatever it wants," Andrew said.

Everard eyed him, then nodded. "Aye. 'Tis a great fault that infects us, a deep pride that drives us to possess what we covet."

They walked on in silence. Andrew stayed watchful, staying at least an arm's length away from the young man, never losing his worry that Everard was using him to set a trap for Robin. His instincts seemed sharp, sharper than he'd ever known before. He saw things he normally wouldn't notice: a bird with speckled brown wings perched upon a branch; a hare moving cautiously through the brush; the deep earthy smell of the forest; the hint of smoke from a distant fire. Even the trees that had all looked the same before now took on distinctive characteristics. He was aware of their different shapes and sizes, the way the branches reached out, the shapes of their leaves. The world seemed more alive to him, and he was more alive within it.

With that feeling came another: they were being watched. Andrew was sure he saw a figure just behind a tree in one direction, and another figure crouching on a branch in a tree the other.

"The Thorn Bridge is but a mile ahead," Everard said.

"Is it an actual bridge?" asked Andrew.

"What else would it be?" Everard put to him.

"I thought it was just a name," Andrew said, thinking of his own time and how often streets and neighborhoods were named things that had nothing to do with what or where they were. "Is it made of thorns?"

"'Tis a bridge that sits on the Thorn River," Everard said.

"Makes sense," Andrew said and, without explaining, cupped his hands around his mouth and whistled loudly one long note and two short ones.

Everard stopped and looked at him, startled.

CHAPTER THIRTEEN

The voice of a boy came from only a few feet away to their left. "We have been wondering if you would signal, Friend of the Waif," he said, as he came out from behind an oak tree.

"Greetings," Andrew said, surprised to be looking at a boy younger than himself, dressed in the clothes of an outlaw, complete with a long knife on his belt. He held a bow in one hand and reached back to a quiver of short arrows slung on his back.

Everard looked him over and said, "Is the outlaw's band made up entirely of boys?"

"I am Gilbert of the White Hand," the boy said, notching an arrow into the bow string. "I am the nephew of Will Scarlet, the man your brother attempted to hang."

Everard held up his hands in surrender.

"He has come to beg Robin Hood for his brother's life," Andrew said.

"Alone?" another voice said from behind them.

Everard and Andrew turned. A tall man Andrew hadn't met stood with a spear ready to be thrown.

"We are alone," said Andrew.

"Follow me," Gilbert said.

They walked deeper into the woods, with Gilbert occasionally glancing back at them. The tall man with the spear stayed several yards behind them.

"The Thorn Bridge is that way," Everard said, pointing to the right.

"We are not going to the Thorn Bridge," Gilbert said, and walked to the left.

They arrived at a meadow. In the center, standing with his hands on his hips as if he'd been waiting for them, was Robin Hood. He took off his hat and gave them a low bow. "Hail, Everard, son of Sir Reynauld of Prestbury."

"Greetings to you, Robin of Barnsdale and the Outwoods, Robert of Locksley, and all other names and lands you claim as your own," Everard said, also bowing.

"The Greenwood is the only land I call home," Robin said. He came alongside Andrew and placed a firm hand on his shoulder. "You have done well, lad."

Andrew felt a blush of pride creep into his cheeks.

"Where is my brother?" Everard insisted.

"Are you demanding to know?" Robin said, glaring at the man. "Hardly the tone of one who has come to beg."

Everard bristled. "*Beg*, outlaw?"

Andrew looked at him with surprise. What had happened to the red-eyed man he saw sitting on a tree stump? Where was the man who was ready to plead for his brother's life?

Robin suddenly laughed. "You truly are the son of your father. The walk from Havelond has rekindled your pride and stiffened your neck."

"It was not the walk," Everard said, speaking through gritted teeth. "It is standing face to face with a man I know to be a thief and a murderer."

CHAPTER THIRTEEN

Robin stepped back from Everard, giving him a steely look. "If I am a thief or a murderer, then you may thank men like yourself for having made me so, as I take only to give back to others in need, or kill only to spare the lives of those who cannot defend themselves. You, son of Sir Reynauld, rob and kill for your own good pleasure."

Andrew saw Everard's fists clench.

Robin saw it as well and cried, "By the rood! I have consented to meet you in good faith, believing you to be of a character apart from your kin. Before Our Lady, the Mother of Our Lord, I vowed to hear you as an act of peace. Was I mistaken?" He raised a hand and several men emerged from different parts of the forest surrounding them.

Everard turned, his hand going to his belt to find a knife that was not there. "Scoundrel, wicked and foul—"

"I am done with you, Everard. You will be led away to join your father's caravan, come what may," Robin said.

Andrew felt anger burn like coals through his body. He couldn't stand it anymore. "Stop!" he suddenly shouted.

Surprised, both Robin and Everard looked at him.

"You are worse than kids on a playground," he said, his voice full of scorn. He stepped up to Everard. "What are you doing? You came here to save your brother's life! You said you wanted to stop this battle!"

Everard stood, stunned.

Andrew continued, "Remember what you said about pride? Are you going to let it kill your brother today? Are you really like your father after all?"

Everard reached up and gently touched the place on his face where he'd been slapped by his father. His expression, which had grown hard while talking to Robin, now softened. "Aye," he said to Andrew. "'Tis a family curse that comes upon me like a fever."

"'Tis the curse of Adam and it may bring us all to a sorrowful end," Robin said, his tone also softening. "You have spoken wisely, lad. Young Everard, let us begin anew."

Everard unexpectedly knelt down on one knee in front of the outlaw. "The boy is right, noble outlaw. I have come to beg for my brother's life and to secure peace so that others will not die from an act of pure vanity."

Robin took the young man's arms and guided him to his feet. "Rise, Everard. You are worthy to be heard. Let us pray you will prevail upon your father to subdue his pride this day. Come! I shall take you to your brother, who is recovering from his wounds."

"Wounds?"

"Mere scratches, of little concern. 'Tis his broken leg that troubled us."

"How, pray tell, was his leg broken?" Everard asked.

"A foolish attempt to escape in a part of the forest he did not know. He spurred the horse to hurdle a fallen tree and was thrown off. Our physician assures us of his recovery, thanks be to God. See for yourself."

"With gratitude," Everard said.

The two men walked off across the meadow, with the tall man following, spear in hand.

CHAPTER THIRTEEN

Andrew turned, unsure of where to go, and saw Gilbert waiting nearby. "Gilbert, where is Eve?"

Gilbert looked unsure. "Eve?"

"Evangeline, the Waif of the Woods," Andrew corrected himself.

Gilbert's face lit up. "This way."

The young boy led Andrew back into the forest. A path took them to a cabin partially obscured by dense trees. A guard, whom Gilbert called Thomas of Helmsdale, stood watch. He gave the door a sharp knock and moved aside. The door opened. Eve was coming out with a silver pitcher in her hand.

"Andrew!" she shrieked and, before Andrew could react, dropped the pitcher and gave him a hug. Then, just as suddenly, she pushed back, her face red.

Gilbert and Thomas turned away, but Andrew saw that they were laughing.

Eve stammered, "I am sorry. I have been worried about you."

"Me too," he said, his cheeks burning.

They looked at each other, neither one knowing what to say next.

Eve bent down and picked up the silver pitcher. "Water," she said. "I am getting water for Reuben and Ruth. You can help."

They used the short walk to a stream to tell briefly what had happened since they parted ways in Nottingham, leading to this final meeting in Thornbridge.

"Reuben and Ruth are afraid," Eve admitted. "They believe Sir Alberic is going to trick Robin and attack them. They say he is a son of the devil."

Andrew nodded. "He is creepy. He does this thing with his hands that makes him look like a praying mantis."

The stream cut through the woods between wall-like ridges of trees and brush. They found their footing down a gentle slope that put them on a bank where a small waterfall, created by a natural formation of rocks, formed a pool. Eve knelt down and filled the pitcher.

Andrew stooped to splash water onto his face, head, and neck. It was so refreshing that he decided it wasn't enough and fell into the pool.

Eve screamed with laughter.

The pool was only a few feet deep. Andrew splashed, went under, and emerged again closer to the waterfall.

"Silly boy," Eve called to him.

The sound of the splashing water roared nearby.

Eve shouted and gestured, "Your belt! Your knife will get rusty."

Andrew hadn't thought of that. A small clump of bushes sat within arm's reach by the waterfall. He undid his belt and tucked it, with the knife, underneath. He dropped into the pool again and rolled to let the water clean off the day's dust and dirt.

The ripples in the water reminded him of the conversation he'd had with Eve earlier about Alfred Virtue and time travel, and the questions rushed back to his mind. He half-swam to the bank and said to her, "I was wondering: Everard was able to find Robin Hood because I was there to guide him. If I had not been in Havelond, he would have traveled with his father and never talked to Robin."

"So?"

"*So*," Andrew said, "history is changed because I came from our time. It is like that thing you said about ripples on the lake. I came from our part of the lake to *this* part and I am making *new* ripples by being here."

Eve gazed at him and said with true affection, "You are such a *Perry*."

"What does that mean?"

"Your brain works in such a weird way," she said. "The Virtue family has the same problem."

"Am I right? Have I changed history?" he asked.

Eve sat down on a large rock and embraced the silver pitcher on her lap. "All I can tell you is what I read in Alfred Virtue's journal. There was a page where he underlined the phrase, '<u>Always Remember: You Don't Belong</u>.'"

"Don't belong?"

"In the past," she said. "We don't belong here, and Time knows it."

"Time *knows*? How does Time know anything?"

"The same way your body knows that something doesn't belong in it," Eve said. "Your body fights to get rid of the foreign invader. If you get a splinter in your thumb, your body isn't going to change much. If you get cancer, your body does *big* things to fight it from changing your body. Alfred Virtue said the same thing is true with Time. We're like splinters in this Time and can get away with little things. But if we try to do something *big*—if we tried to kill the king or burn down London—then that's more like cancer, and Time will counterattack to stop us."

Andrew pushed back into the pool. "That doesn't make sense. How can Time fight to stop anything at all?"

"Maybe that's the wrong way of putting it," she said when he came close again. "The point is, Time *can't* allow us to change the past, just like gravity can't let us fly. It is the way it works, the nature of it. The rules."

Andrew laughed. "Ripples, splinters, gravity, rules..."

Eve smiled. "Or maybe it's like wet cement."

Andrew laughed again. "Wet cement?"

Eve said, "Alfred Virtue noted that if you carve your initials into wet cement, the initials slowly dry and get harder and harder to change."

"Unless you have a jackhammer," Andrew said.

"Try to go back in time to change what has already happened and you can't," Eve explained. "You think Everard came to find Robin because you were around to lead him. But it is also possible that he would have come by himself and found Robin on his own."

"Maybe," Andrew said, not convinced. "What if I want to go back in time to stop Adolph Hitler?"

"You won't be able to," she said. "One way or another, Hitler will do what he did. Those initials in the wet cement are dry."

"Yeah, but what if I keep trying?" Andrew challenged her. "What if I am like a jackhammer to Time and . . . and came up with a plan to—?"

Eve cut him off. "The plan would fail and he would go on to do whatever he did the first time. You can't change anything that big."

"How do you know that for sure?" Andrew asked.

"Because Alfred Virtue *tried* and couldn't do it."

Andrew was shocked. He stood up in the pool. "Whoa, wait a minute. Alfred tried to change history?"

"Over and over," she said. "No matter what he did, Time stopped him. And there were a couple of situations when he thought Time was trying to throw him out."

"Throw him out!" Andrew exclaimed. "How did it do that?"

"Alfred wrote how he tried to change the past and suddenly fell sick for no reason. When he persisted, he noticed that bad things happened to him. A large planter fell out of a window and nearly hit him on a street, a horse almost ran him over, a wooden staircase collapsed under him. He realized that Time was trying to get rid of him, just like your body tries to get rid of a virus in your bloodstream. Time fought to keep him from infecting the past. *That's* why he wrote: '<u>Always Remember: You Don't Belong</u>.'"

"The whole thing sounds crazy," Andrew said.

Eve laughed. "It *is* crazy. But we're here."

Andrew swam around in a small circle, thinking about it all. He asked, "What about God?"

"God can change whatever he wants," Eve said simply. "Alfred Virtue didn't question that part. I'm sure he didn't want to be at odds with Time *and* God."

Andrew ducked beneath the water again, swimming for the waterfall. He came up and found himself in a small cave behind the waterfall. Reaching up, he grabbed a ledge and pulled himself up.

This would be a great hideout, he thought.

He looked around, wondering if other people in history had found this place. Maybe he'd find a tool or a trinket from some other time.

He saw a small dark something at the far end of the cave, almost hidden in the shadows. Andrew scooted over for a closer look. It was a satchel made of some sort of cloth or leather, with a long strap and a flap over the top. He picked it up. Something inside rattled. Lifting the flap, he found a balled-up tunic, a wooden bowl, an empty water flask, and a leather pouch with three coins. He shoved everything back into the satchel so he could show Eve.

Slipping back into the water, he moved along the ledge to the rock wall. He pushed through the wet curtain of the waterfall. Bushes hid him from the view on the bank and he crouched down into the pool with the idea of lunging out to surprise Eve. Maybe he'd throw the pouch of coins in her direction.

CHAPTER THIRTEEN

He inched around the bush and saw the rock where she'd been sitting. Next to it, the pitcher lay on its side, the water spilling out.

He looked around, thinking she might be about to do something to scare him instead, but she was nowhere to be seen.

Eve was gone.

14

Andrew was about to call for Eve, but his instinct told him to wait. He stayed hidden where he was, looking this way and that. Then his eye caught a glint of light near a tree at the crest of the ridge. The light had caught a man's helmet. The wearer was standing and had chain mail on his chest and a long spear in his hands. Even from this distance, Andrew recognized that he was one of Captain Butcher's guards from Nottingham. The man gave a quick look around the stream and disappeared beyond the ridge.

Andrew's mind raced with the possibilities. Was it one guard or a whole army of them? He couldn't imagine just one would venture into the woods, so there had to be more. They must have grabbed Eve. But why were they there? Had they come to rescue Captain Butcher? Were they part of a plan concocted by Sir Reynauld or Sir Alberic to ambush Robin at Thornbridge?

After waiting to be sure the guards had left, Andrew came out of the pool. He retrieved his belt and knife next to the bush and stood soaking wet on the bank, his clothes hanging heavily on his body.

What was he supposed to do?

He had to warn Robin about the guards. But how? They were between him and the outlaws. He wrapped the belt around his waist and touched the hilt of the knife. He couldn't launch an attack on the guards by himself. There must be something else.

An idea came to him and he emptied the satchel he'd found, shoving the contents under the bush. He searched the bank for smooth stones and threw as many as he could into the bag. Slinging it over his shoulder, he crept up the ridge and made his way into the woods.

He saw a dozen guards fanned out ahead, moving slowly forward, with Eve captured in the middle. From the back, he saw a strip of cloth around her head—they'd gagged her—and from the position of her shoulders and arms he assumed they'd bound her hands.

Andrew climbed the nearest tree and, as he'd done with Everard, followed the guards from above. It was hard work to move noiselessly, with his wet clothes, the heavy satchel, and the ache in his side, but somehow his limbs and the limbs of the trees didn't betray him.

He saw the cabin in the thicket off to the right and wondered if anyone there might see the invaders. The guards moved to the left and came to a stop. Three of them conferred, their heads turning together to something he couldn't see. Andrew used the moment to climb as high as he dared.

Through an opening in the branches, he saw what the guards had pointed at: a bridge. Robin and some of the men were on one end of the bridge, looking across to a road beyond. Andrew's gaze followed the road as it snaked in and out of view in the forest. Something glinted in the light and Andrew saw a caravan made up of men on horseback, carts, and people on foot. He had no doubt that it belonged to Sir Reynauld.

Andrew climbed down a few branches and crossed from tree to tree until he was above the gathered guards. They now had their swords drawn and the bowmen readied their bows and arrows. He saw Eve struggling to free her hands. A guard also saw her and backhanded her. She stumbled but stayed on her feet.

Andrew decided to raise the alarm somehow. A shout wouldn't be enough, he knew. He needed to cause a commotion. Reaching into the satchel, he brought out a stone. He moved into position and flicked the stone at Eve, grazing her shoulder. She looked down at the stone, then up at Andrew. Her eyes widened, but she quickly looked away again, so as not to attract the attention of the guards.

Andrew crept from branch to branch, establishing places from which he'd have clear shots and the freedom to move quickly away.

The guards below spread apart. They were about to move again. Andrew took out a stone, aimed carefully and threw hard. The stone hit the helmet of one. Startled, the man spun around to see what had struck him. By then, Andrew had jumped to another branch, throwing another stone and hitting another guard on the shoulder. Soon he had the guards around Eve spinning and turning, trying to figure out what was hitting them, and from where.

From a different branch, Andrew found an angle that allowed the stone to strike a guard next to Eve on the jaw. The throw hurt the guard more than Andrew expected and the man almost lost balance, dropping to his knees. Eve seized the moment to leap onto his back, throwing her bound hands over his helmet and around his neck. This caused even more chaos as the guards now had to deal with the wild waif even as stones rained down on them, seeming from all directions.

Andrew leapt like a squirrel, changing positions again and again. As he reached for the last stone in the satchel, he looked down just as a guard looked up directly at him. An arrow was already notched into his bow. He shouted and let it fly. Andrew leapt away just in time, the arrow striking the branch where his leg had been. He flew with his arms outstretched and caught hold of a branch on the next tree over. But the guards now knew where he was and began to release one arrow after another, splintering the wood and leaves around him.

CHAPTER FOURTEEN

Just as he prayed that Robin and his men would hear the chaos, a collective roar came from the direction of the bridge, followed by shouts and the buzz of distant arrows. Soon, Andrew heard the heavy clanging of swords.

The guards below were no longer interested in the boy with the stones, so Andrew scampered back to where he'd last seen Eve. He hoped that she'd somehow escaped and was now hiding up in a tree.

He let out a startled gasp. Eve was lying between a bush and a tree, as if she'd been carelessly thrown there. A helmet sat next to her.

Andrew dropped down next to her. He shrugged off the satchel and used his knife to cut the bonds from her hands. As he pulled the gag away from her mouth, she slowly opened her eyes.

"Ouch," she groaned. "He hit me on the side of the head. What kind of man hits a girl?"

"Maybe the kind that has a girl on his back with her hands around his neck," Andrew said. "Can you stand up?"

She nodded. He helped her to her feet.

There was a crunch of leaves behind Andrew. He heard a low "aha" and saw Eve's eyes widen.

Instinctively, Andrew grabbed the helmet and spun around as fast and hard as he could. The heavy piece of metal served as a solid weapon against the guard who was coming at him with his hands outstretched. The helmet caught him on the side of his bare head. He fell, hitting the other side of his head against a tree. Dazed, he slid to his hands and knees.

"We have to go," Eve said and took Andrew's hand. They stumbled at first, found their footing, and sprinted away from the guard and the fighting nearby.

"You were pretty good with those rocks," Eve said when they reached a safe space behind a tall line of bushes.

"I'll bet he wished he had kept his helmet on," Andrew said.

"I pulled that off when he was trying to throw me off of his back," Eve explained.

The two of them paused to catch their breath. It was only a few minutes, but they both realized at the same time how quiet the woods had become. They slowly stood up to see what had become of the battle, but the battle was finished. Robin's men were leading the Nottingham guards back to the bridge.

"We won," Andrew said.

"All thanks to you," said Eve. She touched his arm. "We can go home now, if you want." Her hand went to the chain around her neck.

"And miss the ending? I don't think so."

They scrambled to catch up to the outlaws and their captives.

CHAPTER FOURTEEN

"How dare you miscreants attack the sheriff's guards! I defy you. I swear by all the saints that your heads will rot on pikes!" Andrew recognized the voice as Captain Butcher's. Robin had brought him from wherever he'd been kept and now placed him with his captured guards in a line near the bridge.

Robin stepped over to him, a smile on his face. "Why do you complain, good captain? Your men are alive. And we have fed you and kept you in greater comfort than even the sheriff himself afforded you." The outlaw put a gag over the captain's mouth. "Be watchful now. Bear witness in silence."

Andrew and Eve moved under a tree, waiting to see what Robin would do next.

Robin saw them and saluted. "Is it true that I am to thank you for this?" He waved a hand at the captured guards.

Eve hooked a thumb at Andrew. "He saved the day."

Robin strode over and took Andrew's hand, giving it a hardy shake. "Lad, I am indebted to you yet again."

Andrew nodded. "You are welcome," was all he could think to say.

"Why were they here?" Eve asked the outlaw.

"I was careless," said Robin. "A tradesman from Nottingham recognized the captain when we carted him from Ravenswood, and he followed us. I was sure the tradesman was a friend and paid him no mind. The tradesman, thinking he would receive a reward, returned to Nottingham and told the guards. They came to rescue their beloved captain." Robin shot a look at Captain Butcher, who continued to glare at him. "It would have served them better to think through their plan of attack. Poor training on the part of their captain, I think."

The captain snorted at him and turned away.

Robin said to Eve, "I bid you, my waif, to return to Reuben and his daughter in the cabin. Two men guard on the outside, but I would have you inside, since they find great comfort from you."

Eve cast a disappointed look at the bridge but said, "Aye, Master Robin." She gave a quick nod to Andrew and walked away.

"Now to business," Robin said to Andrew and went to the bridge, calling out final orders to his gathered men.

Sir Reynauld's caravan was now in view, slowly making its way forward. A single rider on horseback at the head carried a red banner adorned with the image of a white tower and, above it, a bird descending with its talons outstretched. Behind the bearer rode Sir Reynauld and Sir Alberic, side by side, both in chain mail and tunics. Sir Reynauld's tunic was decorated with a coat of arms identical to the banner. Sir Alberic's tunic was a simple white with a red sash cutting across at an angle. Behind them trailed another half-dozen men on horses, several horse-drawn carts with servants and crates, and, finally, the servants on foot.

Andrew wondered where Robin was keeping Everard and Maurice, and why he hadn't brought them to the bridge yet.

CHAPTER FOURTEEN

Sir Reynauld held up his hand and the caravan came to a halt on the far side of the bridge. He dismounted, as did Sir Alberic, and the two men crossed with heavy steps to the midway point.

Robin spoke to Little John and Warren the Bowman, who were positioned at the foot of the bridge on the outlaw side. Someone in a hooded cloak stepped from behind a tree and walked with Robin to meet the two knights. As they drew close to the center of the bridge, the hooded man pushed back his head cover. It was Everard.

Sir Reynauld gave his son a scornful look. "Am I betrayed by my own flesh and blood?"

"Nay, Father," said Everard. "I am here in good faith to avoid bloodshed."

Sir Reynauld looked at Robin Hood as he asked Everard, "Has the scoundrel bewitched you? Are you now another rogue among his outlaws in the Greenwood?"

"I am not, though there are worse things I could become," Everard countered.

Sir Reynauld grunted. "Why are you here, then?"

Everard cleared his throat and said in a formal tone, "My lord Father, promise to yield Havelond and we shall depart safely with Maurice. I have the word of Robin Hood."

"The word of this man is of no value to me," said Sir Reynauld. "However, *my* word is that I will skin his carcass for the birds."

Robin calmly asked, "You are unrepentant for your evil deeds, Sir Reynauld?"

"I will not repent for you, outlaw."

Robin turned to Sir Alberic. "What say you, Sir Alberic?"

"What would you have me say?" Sir Alberic responded.

Robin laughed. "I see you glancing back at the road as if you expect someone. Might it be the sheriff's guards from Nottingham, who you will see bound on the other side of the bridge, should you crane your neck to look?"

Sir Alberic looked at Captain Butcher and the guards. He gazed at Robin with an expression of indifference. "They are nothing to do with me."

"No?" Robin asked, a tone of amusement in his voice. "Perhaps you are looking for your allies from York?"

Sir Alberic's face twitched.

Robin continued, "Alas, your messenger, good man that he is, never reached York to deliver your message. However, he has been treated kindly and given a hearty meal for his troubles."

"You are without honor, every one of you!" Sir Reynauld shouted, his face matching the red in his coat of arms. "Give me but a chance and I shall show you—" Faster than anyone would have thought possible, Reynauld's hand went to the knife in his belt and, quick as lightning, had it drawn and thrusting toward Robin.

Everard shouted, "Father!" and stepped between his father and the outlaw.

CHAPTER FOURTEEN

The knife plunged deep into the young man's chest. He fell into Robin and sunk to his knees. Sir Reynauld reared back, the bloody knife in his hand. His face filled with the horror of what he'd done. He dropped the knife and it fell off of the bridge into the river.

Little John rushed to Robin's side. Warren the Bowman had his arrow notched and ready to shoot.

"Vile!" Sir Reynauld cried out and knelt next to his son. His face was twisted in anguish and anger. "I shall be avenged of this before my eyes close in death."

Robin looked at the man, astonished. "Avenged, Sir Reynauld? 'Twas your knife that has done this evil deed. Turn it on yourself if you seek to avenge him."

Sir Reynauld spat at the outlaw.

Robin ignored the insolence and said, "Save the life of your remaining son. Promise now and forever to yield Havelond and leave its true owners in peace."

Sir Reynauld stood up. "Hear me, knave. I shall see you and your men hanged for this." He took a few steps back and only then did Andrew realize that Sir Alberic had already retreated to the far end of the bridge. Sir Reynauld pulled the sword from its sheath and lifted it.

Too late did Warren the Bowman realize that the sword wasn't for Robin but was a signal of some sort. He let fly an arrow that struck Sir Reynauld in the arm. The sword flew from Sir Reynauld's hands, hitting the rail of the bridge and joining the knife in the water below.

"Attack!" Sir Reynauld yelled, clutching the arrow in his arm and rushing back across the bridge.

A horn sounded from somewhere in the caravan. The servants in the carts, sitting passively until now, leapt to their feet. They cast aside their rough robes and tunics to reveal chain mail. Swords, spears, and bows seemed to come from nowhere. The servants at the back of the caravan drew knives and lifted up spears. Over two dozen men now rushed to the bridge.

"Back!" Robin shouted to Little John as he grabbed Everard and, with surprising strength, lifted the dead man onto his shoulder and carried him to the outlaw's side of the bridge. He crossed to Andrew and put Everard down at the base of the tree. "See to him," Robin said, dashing back to the bridge to meet the oncoming assault.

Andrew was puzzled, wondering why Robin wanted him to watch over a dead body. Then he saw Everard's eyes twitch and open wide, ablaze with fright and pain. He took a deep, wheezing breath and thrashed his arms as if defending himself.

"Calm down!" Andrew said and suddenly thought of all the movies he'd ever seen where someone had been wounded. "I need to stop the bleeding," Andrew said.

"Allow me to help." A figure came near and knelt on the other side of Everard. It was a young man with curly hair. "I am Father Simon," he said. He pushed the sleeves up on his black robe. Grabbing the knife from Andrew's belt, he deftly cut at Everard's clothes. He soon

CHAPTER FOURTEEN

had Everard's bare chest exposed, revealing a severe gash on the right side of his rib cage.

The priest cut the sleeve from Everard's robe and pressed the cloth against the wound. Everard cried out.

An arrow suddenly buzzed between Andrew and the priest, slamming into the tree behind them. If Everard had been sitting up, he'd have been struck and killed.

"Lift his feet," Father Simon said, grabbing under Everard's arms. The two of them carried Everard behind the tree and lay him down again. Father Simon worked again on the wound.

Andrew peeked around the tree to see the Battle of Thornbridge in all of its savagery.

Robin had allowed many of Sir Reynauld's men to cross the bridge so the band of outlaws would have the full advantage of their positions in and around the trees. Arrows flew like a swarm of angry wasps, swords rang against one another, spears and staffs parlayed, shouts and cries punctuated successes and failures.

Sir Reynauld was in the thick of it, the arrow broken in his right arm. He swung another sword with his left, raging at Robin's men like a wild animal.

Sir Alberic was back on the bridge, not fighting at all, but making his way slowly through those who were.

"What is he doing?" Andrew asked no one.

"Hold this," Father Simon called out behind him.

Andrew turned. The priest gestured to the cloth on Everard's chest. Andrew knelt and pressed the cloth on the wound while Father Simon shoved his hands under his robes. He brought out a small pouch, undid the string that held it closed, and retrieved a vial. He yanked out the stopper and poured oil on his fingers. He marked the Sign of the Cross on Everard's forehead.

He leaned close to Everard's face and, in Latin, whispered, "*In nomine Patris, et Filii, et Spiritus Sancti...* Everard, son of Sir Reynauld of Prestbury..." Everard nodded once or twice, and said, "Aye." Then, in English, Father Simon said, "By God's grace, we will carry you to a place where I may properly treat you."

Father Simon looked at Andrew with sorrowful eyes and put the stopper in the vial, tucking it away again. "We need help carrying him," he said, and he rushed off to find it.

Everard's hand suddenly took hold of Andrew's. "I beg you, take me to my brother ere I die. He must be told..." His voice trailed off.

"Told what?" Andrew asked.

"Told ... there is no glory in our pride, only eternal pain...beg him to yield..." His hand relaxed in Andrew's. He closed his eyes, his chest rising as he drew in a harsh breath of air. Then he slowly exhaled.

Andrew heard a terrible rattling sound coming from somewhere inside of the young man. He waited for him to breathe in again, but he didn't and never would.

Andrew lowered his head. Tears formed in his eyes and spilled hot down his cheeks.

CHAPTER FOURTEEN

The battle subsided as Sir Reynauld's men were slowly defeated. Robin's men rounded them up to join Captain Butcher and his guards. Sir Reynauld himself had collapsed due to the loss of blood from his wound and now had a second arrow in his side. Father Simon bent over him to administer first aid, but the obstinate man pushed him away.

A question slowly worked its way through the Men of the Greenwood: where is Sir Alberic?

The prevailing answer was that the coward had run for York.

Andrew wasn't so sure. He remembered his last glimpse of Sir Alberic, slipping past the fighters on the bridge. Maybe he was hiding behind a tree, waiting for a chance to attack Robin. The thought made Andrew nervous enough to make his way past the prisoners and the bridge to the part of the woods Sir Alberic had fled. Walking along the road, he searched to the left and the right, hoping for any clues about the praying mantis's whereabouts.

He heard a groan and stopped. Through the trees, a lone figure was crouching low to the ground. Andrew raced toward it, pulling his knife from his belt. Coming closer, he saw that it was Ket the Troll crouching down next to one of Robin's men.

"Ket?" Andrew asked.

"He is still alive," Ket said, his hand on the man's head. "He's been stripped of most of his clothes. Why, pray tell, would someone take a man's clothes in the heat of battle?"

"It was Sir Alberic," Andrew said.

"He disguised himself to escape?" Ket asked.

Andrew had an alarming thought. "Not to escape, but to do what he came to do. I know where he is!"

15

Together, Eve, Reuben, and Ruth had been praying. The battle was a distant commotion, but that did no less to calm the fears of the old man and his daughter. They worried all the more when Dodd, son of Alstan, told them that he and the other guards were leaving to join the conflict.

Eve had bolted the door and shuttered the two windows.

Less than an hour had gone by when they noticed the clamor had ceased.

"It is finished," Ruth said, relieved.

"Who won?" asked Reuben, worried.

From the door came a gentle knock.

Eve called out, "Who is there?"

"Thomas the Tanner," the voice said. "The battle is won. Robin bids you to come, with all your belongings."

Reuben said, "Thanks be to God."

Ruth clasped her hands and closed her eyes, whispering the same.

"Open up," Thomas the Tanner said. "Master Robin is waiting."

Eve hesitated. She was suspicious. She had never heard of Thomas the Tanner.

"Please, dear girl, do not keep him waiting," Reuben said to Eve, gesturing to the door.

She undid the bolt.

Thomas the Tanner slouched into the cabin. He was draped in a long cloak that hung as if it was too large for his body. His face was obscured by a hood. "My thanks, dear child," he said.

"I have never seen you before," Eve said.

"You are unlikely to have ever seen me," the tanner said. "My face is horribly disfigured, owing to the treachery of Sir Alberic and his evil hordes. I keep to myself, even among the Men of the Greenwood."

The explanation sounded reasonable. Eve relaxed.

"Gather all your things," Thomas the Tanner said. "Today we shall have justice."

Reuben's face filled with gratitude and he knelt next to a small trunk. He opened the lid and began to rearrange what few belongings they had inside. "Bring me the candlesticks," he said to his daughter.

Ruth picked up two silver candlesticks from a side table and handed them to him.

"Take only what you most cherish," the tanner said, with a hint of impatience. "Religious items, as you will. Any legal documents . . ."

The tanner's emphasis on "legal documents" caught Eve's attention.

CHAPTER FIFTEEN

Reuben shuffled the clothing and keepsakes, then brought out several bound parchments. Some bore wax seals.

"Ah," said the tanner as the old man placed the parchments on the floor next to him. The tanner's hands slowly rose to his chest. He rubbed them together, the left inside the right, then the right inside the left, and the thin fingers intertwining and coming loose again.

At that moment, Eve thought of a praying mantis, and she remembered what Andrew had said about Sir Alberic.

Reuben looked up and must have realized the same, for he cleared his throat nervously and put a protective hand over the ledgers, pulling them protectively back to himself.

"Now sir," the tanner said, his voice oozing with assurance, "those are the very documents you must give to me for safekeeping."

"Thank you, kind man. I shall hold these close," said Reuben, standing with the ledgers clutched tightly.

Ruth heard the change in her father's tone and now stood erect, a puzzled look on her face.

The man's shoulders stiffened. "I insist," he said, and shoved his hood back with one hand, while the other emerged from inside his cloak with a long knife. All doubt was gone. Sir Alberic himself stood before them.

Ruth shrieked and Reuben stepped back, pushing his daughter behind him.

Eve used the distraction to seize a quarterstaff that one of the outlaws left leaning against the wall. Her practice with Robin's men paid off as she used both hands to bring the staff level, then thrust it at Sir Alberic, hitting him solidly with the blunt end on the side of the head. He howled as he reeled back but recovered quickly and lunged forward with the knife pointed her way. Cat-like, she jumped aside, swinging the staff around, hitting him in the shoulder.

"Run!" Eve shouted at Reuben and Ruth. But the old man and his daughter were too slow getting around Sir Alberic to the door.

The evil knight leapt between them and their escape, brandishing the knife again. "The deeds!" he commanded. "Place them in my hand now and you may live."

"I do not believe you," Eve said, gripping the staff for a renewed attack.

As she thrust forward, Sir Alberic swung his free arm and knocked the staff off its course. Eve lost her balance and tumbled forward. Sir Alberic brought his knife-wielding hand around to stab at her as she fell, but Reuben threw himself forward, using the ledgers to swat Alberic's arm.

The knife flew from Alberic's hand as Eve hit the ground on her side, losing her grip on the staff. Alberic kicked at her, his foot catching the side of her head. A burst of light flashed, followed by a sharp pain.

Alberic, with surprising dexterity, swung his elbow back, hitting Reuben in the chest. The old man staggered backward, knocking Ruth to the side and landing hard against the opposite wall.

CHAPTER FIFTEEN

Eve saw Alberic's knife only a few feet away and rolled to grab it. He kicked at her again, catching her arm. Grabbing her by the scruff of her neck, he jerked her to her knees. "I shall have those deeds, whether you are dead or alive. Beginning with you," he said to Eve. He grabbed the knife from the floor and held it near her throat.

"Mercy!" Ruth cried out.

Eve braced herself. She had wondered if it was possible to die in the past and feared she would now find out. A prayer went through her mind, interrupted by a thin whistling sound that was quickly followed by a dull thud. She felt Sir Alberic's hold on her release as he let out a fierce cry and stumbled a few steps. Eve dove away from him, crab-crawling across the floor to Reuben and Ruth. A small stone skittered nearby and she knew immediately what had happened.

Sir Alberic's hand pressed against his forehead, a trickle of blood sliding through his fingers. He had a dazed expression and muttered, "By the saints." He looked at his bloody hand.

Another stone whistled through the open window and slammed into the wall to his left. He jerked his head toward the sound, holding up the knife as if it would protect him somehow.

Another stone rocketed in, striking him hard on his right shoulder. Realizing the assault was coming through the open window, he dropped to his knees to take cover.

Only a few feet away, the ledgers lay where Reuben had dropped them. Sir Alberic now reached for them, his face a picture of greed.

Eve made as if to jump at Alberic, but Reuben caught her arm.

He gave Eve a grim look and shook his head.

Sir Alberic reached up for the latch. Another stone hit just above his head. He flinched but was undaunted in his escape. Yanking the door open, he climbed to his feet. Eve heard a sharp buzzing sound and Alberic screamed, falling onto his side, the ledgers tumbling away. He clutched his leg. A small black arrow jutted out from above his knee.

Ket the Troll stepped into view, a fresh arrow in his bow pointed at Sir Alberic.

"God be praised," Reuben said.

"Amen," Eve whispered and picked up the fallen ledgers, handing them to Reuben.

Sir Alberic snarled at Ket, "I am in agony."

"'Tis only the start," Ket warned.

Andrew appeared in the doorway, next to Ket. His eyes darted around the room until they caught Eve. "Are you all right?"

"You missed with two of your throws," she said.

He looked indignant. "I did that on purpose!" he said.

Voices outside told her that more of Robin's men had come. She took a deep breath, hoping to calm her pounding heart.

Reuben and Ruth, huddling together, prayed, "O give thanks unto God for he is good and his mercy endures forever . . ."

16

Two of Robin's men carried Sir Alberic to the bridge. Father Simon made efforts to treat the man's wounded knee. The Men of the Greenwood came from their different positions in the forest, bringing more captives.

Sir Reynauld lay among his captured men, a long arrow rising from his side. His face was a sickly pale color and his eyes were closed. Maurice, Sir Reynauld's remaining son, sat propped up on a makeshift carrier nearby. His right leg was bandaged and pressed between two wooden planks that served as splints. Will Scarlet stood close by, a hand on the hilt of the Spanish knife in his belt.

The members of Sir Reynauld's household who had not fought now sat in a nearby thicket. Robin had ordered food and drink for them. Captain Butcher and his guards were still bound and sat in a dusty patch under the sun. The captain was gagged, though there was no hiding his frown beneath the cloth.

The dead—of which there were two among Robin's men and seven among Sir Reynauld's—were taken to another part of the forest where prayers would be offered and burials undertaken.

Andrew and Eve found a place to sit under a broad tree at the edge of the crowd.

"What will Robin do?" Andrew asked.

"Put an end to it," Eve replied.

Robin Hood, his clothes dirty and stained from the battle, strode to the center of the gathering. "We thank God for his mercy today," he said. "Now we pray for his wisdom and justice."

Sir Reynauld opened his eyes, a look of raw malice filling them. The hatred there said more than any words Sir Reynauld could have expressed. He sullenly glanced from face to face, landing on his son's, who returned a similar look.

Robin looked down upon Sir Reynauld and said, "You are dying, Sir Reynauld. Your wound cannot be mended by anyone here. For the sake of your soul, speak to our good priest. Repent of your sins."

Sir Reynauld glared at the outlaw. "I will appeal for no mercy from you, vermin! Outlaw! Wolf's head! Runaway rogue!" The words were mere sputterings that ended in a sharp gasp from a sudden spasm of pain. His back arched and he slumped to one side, his eyes now staring, drained of his hate-filled life.

"This is justice," Robin said and performed the Sign of the Cross.

Maurice grabbed both sides of the carrier, shaking it as he let out a piercing cry of anguish. "As God is my witness, you will pay for this," he railed at Robin. "How it will be accomplished, I do not know. But I shall have revenge against you."

Robin gazed at Maurice. "Against me?" he asked and crouched next to the dead man. He pointed to the arrow in Sir Reynauld's side. "The colors on this arrow are not mine, nor of any man in my service."

Maurice looked at him doubtfully.

"Do you not recognize it?" Robin asked him. "This arrow belongs to the house of Havelond."

"By the black rood," Maurice shouted, "how is that possible? Has Bennett come to the battle?"

"Nay, he still remains bedridden from the beating your men gave him," Robin said, his tone of accusation clear.

"To what rogue does that arrow belong?" Maurice demanded.

Robin's men shuffled, stepping aside as Lady Anne passed through them. "It belongs to me," she said. "I am the rogue."

Maurice was astonished. "You?"

She stood in front of him, her hands clasped tightly in front of her. "Your father, dishonorable man that he was, stood ready to slay Warren the Bowman while his back was turned. I let fly the arrow to stop him. Glad I am to see the end of the accursed man."

Maurice's face contorted with rage. "Then, with all of my might, I shall seek my revenge against you, my lady."

"By all the saints!" Robin cried out and stormed over to Maurice. "Have you not lost enough?"

Maurice recoiled, though his look remained defiant.

Robin leaned in until his face was only inches away from the man's. "By God's grace, you have been given many warnings this day. Your family begat this tragedy when you sought to steal Havelond from this good lady and her noble husband. To worsen your sin, you set cruel men to kill Bennett for no reason other than to possess what was not yours. Has the death of your brother, who sought to right your wrongs, not taught you anything? Has the death of your father, prideful and unrepentant, not shown you the folly of your days if you do not change your heart? I spared your life at Prestbury for this very purpose: to allow you to repent."

Maurice flinched at Robin's words but said nothing.

Robin raised a hand as a signal. Little John and Dodd carried out the body of Everard and laid it next to Sir Reynauld.

Maurice groaned and turned away. There was a loud hitch in his breath of a stifled sob.

"See the end of your days!" Robin said to him. "Will you repent or not? If not, I shall give Will Scarlet leave to satisfy his own vengeance upon you for the wrongs you committed against him in Nottingham and Ravenswood."

Will drew his knife.

Andrew suddenly raised his hand, as if he were at school, and walked forward. "Master Robin!"

Robin turned, surprised by the boy's interruption. "Speak, young Andrew."

"I have a message for Maurice."

Maurice looked affronted. "What message could a *beggar* have for me?"

"Everard's own words, spoken to me as he died."

All eyes were on him now. He could feel his face turning red. He hated giving oral reports at school. He felt his mouth go dry now. "He wanted you to know that there is no glory in your pride, only eternal pain. He said to beg you to yield.'"

Maurice's face fell. "What is this trickery?"

"They were his last words," Andrew said. "I swear."

"The boy would not lie," Robin said. "Indeed, your brother's heart speaks the truth that, had you and your father embraced, we would have been saved from today's suffering."

Maurice's body slumped as if the thing that held it so rigid had been suddenly taken away. He put his hands over his face and muttered something.

"Speak again," Robin said.

Maurice's hands came away from his face, the dust of the day now smeared by his tears. "For the love of my brother, I yield," he said.

Robin looked relieved. He pointed at Captain Butcher. "Bear witness, Captain, to what you have heard!"

The captain tried to speak through his gag, but it only came out as muffled complaints.

"For the sake of justice," Robin announced, "all of Sir Reynauld's belongings in Havelond, and those of any value in the carts, shall be given as compensation for the trouble he has given to Lady Anne and her husband Bennett of Havelond."

Lady Anne, still standing nearby, said, "Nay, dear cousin, I want none of his belongings, nor anything that will remind me of these dark days."

Robin nodded. "I understand, my lady," he said. "However, you *will* keep the box of treasure we discovered in Sir Reynauld's possessions." It was not a request.

Lady Anne bowed and curtsied to him.

"I, then, have nothing," Maurice said.

"You have your life," Robin countered. "You have the generous offer of your father's property from Lady Anne."

"Where shall I put it? I have nowhere to live," he said, now sulking.

"You have the gamekeeper's cottage on the grounds of Prestbury," Robin said. "We saved it from the burning."

"A cottage?" Maurice said.

"'Tis not the grandeur you believe you deserve," Robin said with strained patience. "Remember how this good lady lived in a much smaller cottage while you feasted in her home. Be grateful!"

Maurice folded his arms and said no more.

Done with him, Robin now turned and called out, "Where is the vile and oppressive knight who gave generously to our grief on this day? Sir Alberic de Wisgar!"

Sir Alberic was propped up on the rail of the bridge, one of Robin's men on each side. His leg was bandaged and soiled with blood. With an overdramatic show, he pushed the men away. "I shall stand on my own," he said. They let him go and moved aside. Sir Alberic swayed, then fell to the ground with a cry of pain.

The crowd laughed.

"Just as well," Robin said to him. He nodded to Dodd, who had been standing at the edge of the crowd. Dodd retreated and, a moment later, brought forward Reuben and his daughter, accompanied by Ket the Troll and four other outlaws.

Ruth cast a shy glance around the assembly and suddenly caught sight of the face of Alberic. She retreated, backing into her father, holding him with both hands.

"Reuben of Stamford," Robin called out, "is this the man you know to have incited the mob and attacked your people at York?"

"Aye," replied the old man. "By his command, men, women, and even little children were grievously injured so he might be released from his great debt to me."

Robin gazed down at Sir Alberic. "You attacked the cathedral, as well. For that, evil knight, you will suffer more punishment than I may impose upon you here."

Sir Alberic looked up at Robin with cold eyes.

"What are we to do with him?" Robin asked the crowd.

Cries came out to hang the man; others wanted him whipped; still others called for him to be drawn and quartered.

"I am a knight of the realm!" Sir Alberic snarled. "I will not be judged by peasants. The law demands that I—"

"Do not speak to me of the law, Sir Alberic!" Robin shouted. "You bend the laws with a breathtaking impunity. Do you invoke them now to escape punishment? Coward! My purpose here is one of *justice*, not adherence to your unjust laws!"

Captain Butcher squirmed and tried to shout through his gag.

Robin held up his hand. "Hear me! There are two matters to which we attend. The first is the debt owed by Sir Alberic to Reuben of Stamford. Are you prepared to repay the money, Sir Alberic?"

"Are you mad?" Sir Alberic said. "I would not carry such a treasure with me."

"Where is it stored?"

Sir Alberic hesitated to answer.

"Do not test me," Robin warned.

"'Tis safely kept at my estate," Sir Alberic said. "Send me to fetch it."

Robin laughed. "Deceitful creature that you are, I am sure that if I were to allow you to leave this forest, you would renew your efforts to slay the one to whom your debt is owed. Reuben and his family will not be safe as long as you owe him the money." Robin paused, giving the man a stern look. "For that reason, I have transferred your debt from Reuben of Stamford to *me*."

Sir Alberic blinked as if he did not understand what Robin had said. "To you?"

"I have paid Reuben from my own treasure," Robin said. "You must now repay *me* the debt you once owed to him."

"Why?" Sir Alberic asked.

"You will not bully nor hound me as you have this poor man. I shall collect it from you forthwith."

Sir Alberic suddenly laughed. "You have been declared an outlaw! I am under no obligation to pay you."

"According to your law," Robin said.

"According to *the* law," Sir Alberic repeated.

"I have stated my views upon your law," Robin reminded him. "Look now upon the body of Sir Reynauld. Think also of his estate at Prestbury, burned to the ground. Do you doubt that I shall collect the debt from you?"

Sir Alberic slowly shook his head.

"This very day, we will send messengers to your family to return henceforth with the money you owe," Robin announced. "Or know, wicked man, that you will not leave this forest alive."

Sir Alberic went pale. "You would not dare."

Robin gave him a cruel smile. "Will you wager your life to find out?"

Again, Sir Alberic shook his head.

"Once we have settled the first matter, we will attend to the second matter," Robin said.

"What second matter?" Sir Alberic demanded.

"The crimes you committed against the people of York—the wanton destruction, the invasion of the cathedral," Robin said.

"You cannot judge me for those!" Sir Alberic shouted.

"I can, but I will not," Robin said. "I have not met him as yet, but I believe Sir Lawrence of Raby, the marshal of the king's justice, is a stern but honest man. Unlike the sheriff of York, he does not take bribes nor partake in the corruption of Sir Guy of Gisborne, the knights of Wrangby castle, nor even of you, Sir Alberic, though you have made every attempt. To him you will be delivered. By *his* judgment, as the appointed marshal of our good king, justice shall be rendered. A hanging, I suspect."

Sir Alberic's face went from a pale white to a sickly green.

Just like a praying mantis, Andrew thought.

Robin gestured to Little John. "Take him away for safekeeping."

"Aye, Master Robin," Little John said. He grabbed Sir Alberic by the arm and pulled him up. The last Andrew saw of the praying mantis man, he was being half-carried, half-dragged, into the woods.

Before the end of the day, riders from Nottingham arrived at Thornbridge. Leading them was Silas, son of Reuben, along with armed men ready to escort Reuben and Ruth to greater safety. Andrew heard them mention the town of Godmanchester as a haven for their people. Their reunion was sweet and full of grateful tears.

At their goodbye, Reuben clasped Andrew's hand and said, "God's blessings be upon you, brave boy." He embraced Eve and gave her a silver ring. "'Tis only a small token of my gratitude," he said.

Over the next two days, it was joked among Robin's men that the children of Sir Alberic hotly debated whether or not to pay their father's debt. Apparently, greed ran deep in the family and they were willing to let him die to keep their treasure. Sir Alberic sent a renewed appeal, with threats and promises and a reminder that Robin would collect from them with or without their cooperation. It was enough to persuade them, and the amount was delivered to Robin by the end of the third day.

Sir Alberic was taken by a party of Robin's men to the king's marshal, Sir Lawrence of Raby. Jenkins, who had been held prisoner in Ravenswood since his capture, was also handed over. It was later reported that Sir Lawrence, well aware of the knight's terrible deeds in York, was more than ready to dispense the king's justice.

Later, Andrew heard it said that the Battle of Thornbridge, as some called it, was told as a legend throughout the countryside. The legends included stories of a boy who, like the shepherd David in the Bible, wielded stones to bring down evil men, and a girl with magical eyes who saved an old Jew and his daughter from great harm.

Word returned that men and women breathed freely again to know that men as evil as Sir Alberic de Wisgar and Sir Reynauld of Prestbury had met true justice. Robin's reputation for brave and good deeds spread far and wide.

Andrew and Eve agreed they were ready to go home and found the perfect way to go when Robin asked them to help with one more task.

17

Robin organized a party of men, led by Robin himself, to escort Lady Anne and her husband Bennett back to Havelond. Andrew and Eve were asked by Robin to join the caravan. "You are good for her spirits," he said to them quietly.

Lady Anne thanked her cousin profusely for all he had done. "I beg you, dear Robin," she said, "permit me to return the favor, any favor of any kind, to show my gratitude."

Robin bowed to her, "With pleasure, good lady. I shall remember, should the time ever come."

The journey was long, since Bennett had to be carried in a covered cart, traveling slowly to ease his discomfort. Andrew saw the man only once, when they placed him into the cart on a bed made of a goose down mattress. Bennett wore bandages on his head and across the side of his swollen face.

Andrew heard that Bennett had awakened just once since his beating. He held his wife's hand. "My darling," he had whispered before falling to sleep again. Lady Anne believed that, by the help of the Blessed Mother and all the saints, Bennett would recover, though it would take months, perhaps years. Andrew wanted to believe it too.

The manor at Havelond looked different now that Sir Reynauld was gone. Maybe it was Andrew's imagination, but he thought it seemed brighter, the stones themselves aglow with sunlight.

It became clear that Sir Reynauld did not really believe he'd have to vacate the place. The carts he had used in the caravan were filled with his mercenary soldiers, the treasure to pay them, and crates stuffed with mostly junk. The house still contained his more valued possessions, which Lady Anne promised to send away immediately.

Lady Anne stood in the dining hall and wept with joy to be home again. "There is much I must do to free this house from the sinful hold Sir Reynauld had upon it," she said. "I will have endless days of joyful work."

"While you are at it," Andrew said to her, "you have a leak in one of your closets."

Andrew and Eve were about to leave, making it as far as the courtyard by the stable, when Robin caught up to them.

"Where are you going?" he asked.

"Into the woods," Eve replied. "We may practice stone-throwing, to improve Andrew's aim."

"Hey!" Andrew protested.

"A worthy endeavor," Robin said. He suddenly gave them both affectionate embraces, as if he knew he may not see them again. "Thank you for saving my life and the lives of my men, which I am reminded you did on more than one occasion."

Andrew blushed and Eve smiled.

The outlaw stood at the gate and watched them as they crossed the field to the woods.

Andrew's mind went back to the day he'd first arrived and how unreal it felt then. Even now, he wasn't sure whether or not this was all just a dream.

As they came closer to the cave, Andrew asked, "What happened to him? Alfred Virtue, I mean."

"He disappeared," Eve said.

"That's it? He just disappeared?"

"He went on an expedition and disappeared," she said.

"Maybe he's still alive," Andrew said. "It's like that rule in all the stories: if there is no body, then the character is probably not dead."

Eve laughed. "He would be a hundred and fifty years old by now."

"Maybe he figured out how to slow down time for his body," Andrew suggested. "He might be a hundred and fifty in our time but, in another time, he might be only forty, or twenty."

Eve shook her head. "I think we age in the same way, no matter what time we're in."

"Are you sure? What if we don't go back to our time for twenty years?" Andrew asked, thinking of the children in *The Chronicles of Narnia*. "Will we show up right after we left, but look twenty years older? How does that work?"

Eve groaned. "I don't know. It gives me a headache to think about."

Andrew had more questions, but he didn't ask them. He hoped to read Alfred Virtue's writings once they returned. He had a lot to learn.

They retrieved their clothes from behind the bushes and got dressed in their modern outfits. Andrew thought his jeans and shirt felt strange: a little too loose and too soft, not rugged enough. His sneakers didn't fit as comfortably as they had before. Maybe his callouses had made his feet bigger. He wondered how he would explain it all to his parents.

"Ready?" Eve said and pulled out the necklace.

"Ready," Andrew said, but he held up his hand. "Wait."

"What's wrong?" she asked.

Andrew was looking at a tree nearby. He called out, "I see you, Ket the Troll! Come down!"

The troll dropped from the tree. "Your eyes are sharper than they were, Master Andrew," he said.

Eve looked at Andrew nervously, then asked Ket, "What are you doing here?"

He gazed at her for a moment. "We trolls know greater mysteries of the world than ever we tell. I have believed, from the first moment I saw you, good waif, and you, lad, that you were not of this world. I wonder how it is so."

Eve presented the case to him, showing him the stone and explaining what she knew about it. Andrew noticed that she didn't mention exactly where the stone was about to take them, only that they would go away to another land. He assumed any explanation about time travel would be too long and involved.

Eve finished and Ket nodded his shaggy head. "The stone is well known in our legends," he said.

"You know about it?" Andrew asked.

"Aye. I know the whereabouts of others like it."

Surprised, Andrew and Eve looked at each other.

"We'd love to see them," Eve said.

"Perhaps, as God wills," Ket said. "Until then, your secret is safe with me." The troll gave them a low and respectful bow. He turned and walked away, disappearing quickly into the trees as he always seemed to do.

Eve took Andrew's hand and they stepped behind the ivy curtain. A rock wall faced them until Eve touched the Radiant Stone, and a new opening appeared. They stepped through.

For the complete story of Robin Hood and his adventures, listen to *The Legends of Robin Hood*, a six-hour audio drama from the Augustine Institute featuring over 60 acclaimed British actors, full production of sound, and original music.

Go to airtheatre.org to find out more.

Hope Springs™

THE VIRTUE CHRONICLES

The Hidden Heroes

Hope Springs
The Virtue Chronicles

The Saintly Outlaw
The Warrior Maiden
Hidden Heroes

Hope Springs™

THE VIRTUE CHRONICLES

The Hidden Heroes

By Paul McCusker

AUGUSTINE INSTITUTE
Greenwood Village, CO

Augustine Institute
6160 S. Syracuse Way, Suite 310
Greenwood Village, CO 80111
Tel: (866) 767-3155
www.augustineinstitute.org

Cover design: Ben Dybas

Editor: Jennifer Lonas

© 2021 Paul McCusker
All rights reserved.

ISBN 978-1-950939-82-4

Printed in Canada

*To the many men and women
who have served the Church courageously
throughout history.
And, as always, to Elizabeth, Thomas, and Eleanor.*

The Hidden Heroes

CHAPTER 1	1
CHAPTER 2	9
CHAPTER 3	23
CHAPTER 4	39
CHAPTER 5	53
CHAPTER 6	65
CHAPTER 7	81
CHAPTER 8	91
CHAPTER 9	101
CHAPTER 10	123
CHAPTER 11	139
CHAPTER 12	145
CHAPTER 13	163
CHAPTER 14	179
CHAPTER 15	187
CHAPTER 16	199
CHAPTER 17	213
CHAPTER 18	227

CHAPTER 19	239
CHAPTER 20	251
CHAPTER 21	257
CHAPTER 22	271
CHAPTER 23	283
CHAPTER 24	295
CHAPTER 25	305
CHAPTER 26	313
CHAPTER 27	321
CHAPTER 28	331
CHAPTER 29	341
CHAPTER 30	353
CHAPTER 31	359
CHAPTER 32	367
CHAPTER 33	375
CHAPTER 34	379
CHAPTER 35	383
CHAPTER 36	395
CHAPTER 37	411
CHAPTER 38	417
CHAPTER 39	435
CHAPTER 40	449
CHAPTER 41	465

This was a mistake, Andrew Perry thought as he shivered in the cold darkness. He was on his knees. One knee was in a small puddle; the other was on misshapen rocks that stabbed through his jeans. He tried to stand, lost his balance, and grabbed at the air. His hand fell against rough stone. It was solid enough but damp. He steadied himself. He felt as if he might throw up.

Something moved near him, and he heard soft breathing.

"Eve?" he whispered.

"I'm here," Eve Virtue said. She groaned. "We left too fast."

Andrew started to agree but had to put a hand over his mouth to keep from hurling. He closed his eyes and took a deep breath. The wave of nausea passed, but his head hurt.

"We should have checked Alfred Virtue's diagrams of the Radiant Stone to see where we were going," Eve whispered. "And we didn't bring the radonite."

"We didn't have time to grab any," Andrew said, scrubbing his face with his hands. Radonite was a mineral discovered by Alfred Virtue that helped ease the impact of time travel on their bodies. "And I'm sure we're wearing the wrong clothes for wherever we are." He felt another wave of nausea and threw up with sudden violence.

"That's disgusting!" Eve cried out. Then he heard her wretch and cough quietly. That was her version of throwing up.

Andrew took another deep breath. The damp air was chilled. He could hear Eve's soft breathing and the rain tapping on the roof overhead. Drops of water splashed on the stones all around him. The echoes told him he was in a large, empty building of some sort.

He screwed his eyes up against the darkness and tried to make out the shadows.

Eve's hand found his arm and squeezed. "Something moved over there," she said.

He had no idea where "over there" was. He looked harder. The shadows blended with more shadows. Then he saw one of the shadows move.

There was a flash of lightning, and the shadow took the form of a man. He was a few yards away, facing them. Andrew blinked as the darkness returned. He couldn't see anything at all for a few seconds.

Eve gasped and squeezed his arm harder.

Another flash of lightning showed the man again. He was now in front of them.

Surprised, Andrew stumbled, his foot slipping into a rut in the stone floor. His back pressed against the wet stone wall.

A different kind of light suddenly pierced the darkness as the man raised a lantern. His face was half hidden under a wide-brimmed hat. His eyes seemed to glow beneath the brim. His clothes looked like layers of rags. He leaned forward and said, "Kneel. Use the penitent crawl to escape through the hatch." His breath smelled of old vegetables.

"What?" Andrew whispered.

The man put a hand on Andrew's shoulder and pushed down. "*Kneel*, I say, or thou shalt surely be taken." He turned and moved away with a gentle shuffling sound. The light disappeared with him.

Eve slid down. "What should we do?" she asked.

"What other choice do we have?" Andrew asked. He lowered himself into the rut, his knees touching stone and water again. "What's a penitent crawl? What hatch?"

A loud wrenching sound drew his eyes to the left. A set of doors at the far end of the building were thrown open. Half a dozen men stood framed in the large doorway, the rain hanging like a gray curtain against the night behind them. They held torches with flames that jumped wildly under the drops. In the flickering light, Andrew saw dripping hats, scraggly beards, and long overcoats.

It looks like a scene from a Frankenstein movie, he thought.

Eve pulled at Andrew's shirt. "This way," she said and began to back away.

Andrew followed. In only a few feet, they came to what looked like benches that had been thrown carelessly into a pile. There was a space between the benches and the wall. Like a mouse, Eve crept into the makeshift tunnel.

Andrew scooted in but kept his eyes on the mob of men. They stepped slowly through the doors, as if they were afraid. By the light of their torches, Andrew now saw stone walls and arched windows. *We're in a church*, he thought.

The mob walked forward. Then the raggedy man stepped in their path. As one, the men lurched back, startled.

"Who goes there?" the man at the front of the mob shouted, his voice breaking with fear.

The raggedy man laughed. "Who wouldst thou expect to find here?"

The mob boss lifted his torch and squinted. "Ambrosius."

"Tell me, John Buxton, why dost thou and thy fellow ghouls haunt this house of God on such a night?" asked Ambrosius.

The one called John Buxton snorted. "We search for traitors in this pagan ruin."

"Thou wilt find neither traitors nor pagans here."

"Dost thou deny that thou art a Papist?" Buxton asked.

"I deny that I am a traitor," said Ambrosius.

Buxton sneered. "Give thanks to her gracious majesty that my warrant is not for thee. Otherwise, I would see thy body stretched upon the rack, with all good strength."

Ambrosius chuckled. "Strength, perhaps, but there is little good about it."

"Worm's breath! Thou art a thorn in my flesh," Buxton cried out. "Had the Privy Council given me leave, I would have long ago torn down this house of idolatry."

Ambrosius waved a hand. "I see no idols here," he said.

"It stinks of old incense," Buxton said, then strode farther into the church.

The men lifted their torches to follow. Andrew shrunk back.

"Where hast thou hidden the seditious priests?" Buxton demanded.

"There are no priests here," Ambrosius said, then gestured to the men. "Come, good gentlemen, to the house for a cup of hot cider."

The men made noises as if they were happy to take up the offer.

Buxton shouted, "Fools! He would lure you away whilst the priests make a swift escape." He turned to one of the men. "Hold fast those doors."

The doors were pulled closed with loud bangs. The men then spread out into the church. They kicked at the few remaining pieces of furniture against the opposite wall. Each one toppled with a loud clatter.

Eve wiggled deeper under the pile of benches.

Andrew stayed near the mouth of their little den. By the torchlight, he caught glimpses of the damaged chapel. Tapestries that had been violently torn were hanging askew along the walls. Some had blackened edges, as if they'd been set on fire.

He watched the men vandalize what remained and felt anger rising in his heart. *Why are they hunting priests and wrecking churches?* he wondered.

Ambrosius positioned himself with his back to Andrew and Eve. His hands were clasped behind him, half hidden by the sleeves of the odd coat he wore. Then his right hand slipped into view. He pointed to Andrew's left.

"He wants us to run for it," Andrew whispered to Eve.

She came close and pointed to the rut. It stretched along the church wall and ended in a small square wooden flap. "Penitent crawl and hatch," she whispered.

Andrew and Eve prepared to creep toward the hatch, but Buxton suddenly returned. Andrew withdrew, squeezing next to Eve. They watched the mob boss through the tangled legs and seats of the benches. Buxton lifted his torch and peered into the pile. Andrew and Eve froze.

Buxton stepped back. "Happily would I throw my torch onto this heap and let the blaze bring down thy offensive abode."

"Would the queen applaud such waste?" Ambrosius asked Buxton. "Is it not her custom to turn these chapels into houses of worship for her faith?"

Buxton sniffed. "This place of idols is not worthy of our true faith." He held his torch high as if he might actually throw it onto the pile. Andrew braced himself.

Suddenly, one of the other men called out from somewhere beyond Andrew's view. "My lord! Come see. 'Tis one of their books of witchery, hidden under their altar."

Andrew saw Buxton's head snap around. He shouted, "Hound's teeth! Why doth the altar remain? Why hath it not been burned?"

"Perhaps because it is made of *marble*?" Ambrosius queried.

Buxton scowled at him, then marched away.

Ambrosius spun toward Andrew and pointed again to the left. "Crawl," he whispered. Then he turned back to the mob.

The light drained away as the men carried their torches to what was once the front of the church. Andrew signaled Eve to follow him. They crawled on all fours along the rut to a small square hatch. The top of the door hung on hinges.

It's like a cat flap for humans, Andrew thought.

He turned to make sure the men were looking away. For the moment, they were busy tearing pages out of the book they'd found. One of the men used his torch to start a small fire. Three of the other men now tried to upend the altar. They grunted and gasped but couldn't move it.

"Do not strain yourselves," Ambrosius taunted the men.

Andrew pushed on the hatch, but it held fast.

"How do we get out of here?" Eve whispered.

Andrew felt around the edges of the door. His fingers touched a wooden latch. He moved it to one side, and the door swung free.

"Get ready to go," he said softly to Eve.

She moved past him and positioned herself in the hatchway.

Andrew watched the men rocking the altar back and forth. The large marble table tipped to fall. He tapped Eve on the shoulder, and she pushed through the small door.

The men cheered as the table crashed to the ground. Andrew threw himself through the hatchway and landed in a deep puddle of cold mud.

2

Eve helped Andrew out of the mud. The rain fell heavily on both of them, streaking their hair and faces. Andrew rubbed his eyes to clear away the mud.

"Where should we go?" he asked.

Eve pointed. "There."

Through the veil of rain, Andrew saw a light in the window of a cottage. "Do you think it belongs to Ambrosius?"

"Let's hope so," Eve said. She ran forward.

Andrew slipped and fell again. He clawed at the outside wall of the church to get to his feet.

They reached a wooden door at the front of the cottage. Andrew lifted the latch and pushed. The door didn't budge. "Let's try around back," he said. "We have to get out of sight."

Rounding the corner, they came to a waist-high fence enclosing a small yard. Beyond the fence was the back door to the cottage and, next to that, a small window. Andrew noticed a candle flickering in the window. The flame was tiny, yet it glowed brightly.

The rain fell harder. Andrew couldn't figure out if the fence had a gate.

"Climb over the fence," he said.

Eve hoisted herself up and over, then lost her footing and fell on her backside. Andrew laughed as he followed her, but the rickety wooden slats gave way and tossed him into a puddle.

From a small shack nearby, chickens clucked at them. Then, from another direction, Andrew heard a loud snort. An enormous pig lumbered out of a small barn and charged at them.

Eve pressed against the cottage wall.

Andrew scrambled to his feet. He reached out to the beast. "Good piggy. Nice piggy."

The pig head-butted Andrew and knocked him down again. Then it shoved its snout into his face.

"Ew," said Eve.

"Get off!" Andrew shouted and gave the pig a hard shove.

The pig snorted indignantly.

Farther along the cottage wall, beyond the flickering light, a door suddenly opened. Ambrosius leaned out. "Come anon," he beckoned them. "The men have gone but may yet return."

The kids plodded through the mud to the door. The raggedy man stepped aside to let them in. He pointed to a barrel just inside. "Wash yourselves," he said. "A fire awaits you beyond that next door."

CHAPTER TWO

Eve went to the barrel. Andrew was about to follow but glanced back to the small window. There was no candle or flickering flame.

"The water is warm," Eve said as she splashed her face and arms.

Andrew took a turn. He wondered how the water had been heated.

When they finished, they continued through to a spacious room. Andrew would have sworn that the various candles placed around them lit up more brightly as they entered. The room had a few sticks of furniture—tables of various sizes, shelves on the walls, and simple wooden chairs. Two chairs were positioned in front of a fireplace that dominated one wall. A stack of wood blazed on an iron grill. The flames licked at a black cauldron hanging on a hook just above.

Ambrosius waved at them. "Warm yourselves by the fire. Dry off your wet clothes."

The kids obeyed, turning slowly in front of the fireplace.

Andrew watched Ambrosius move to the far end of the cottage. He now saw that the man's coat was a wild assembly of rags, animal fur, and long bird feathers. The raggedy man tossed his hat onto a hook on the wall and went to a table. A candle suddenly flickered to life there, just as Ambrosius approached it.

Andrew turned to Eve. Her gaze was on an oversized candle sitting alone on a stand next to a window. The flame at the top was small, but its light illuminated the room.

Eve looked at Andrew with a puzzled expression. "How does the flame burn so bright?" she whispered to him.

Andrew shrugged.

Ambrosius brought them two tin cups. "Water from the saint's well. You will feel restored in the drinking."

Andrew drank and felt his nausea ease away. He didn't feel as cold or wet either.

Standing in front of them, the raggedy man didn't seem much taller than the kids. He had looked quite a bit taller in the church. His hair was silver and cut short. It reminded Andrew of drawings of Julius Caesar. Ambrosius had a narrow face with stubble over his lips and chin. His eyes were pale brown and large, like an owl's. They held an expression that made him look as if he was thinking of a joke. Andrew thought he seemed young and old at the same time, if that was possible.

"Who were those men?" Eve asked after she drained her cup.

"The queen's priest hunters," Ambrosius replied. "They came in the vain hope of finding priests hidden here."

"Why would priests have to hide?" asked Andrew.

Ambrosius smiled and nodded to their clothes. "From what time have you come that you do not know the answer to that question?"

Andrew and Eve exchanged looks.

CHAPTER TWO

"Our time?" Eve asked.

"The time from whence you came." The raggedy man took their cups and gestured for them to sit in the two chairs facing the fireplace.

As Andrew sat, he realized his clothes were completely dry. And then he remembered that both he and Eve were still wearing their modern clothes. Eve was in a pullover and jeans, and he was wearing a shirt and jeans. The stitching on their clothes had been sewn and resewn. Their sneakers had been scarred by a knife. All at the hands of a madman they had met in the time of Joan of Arc.

Ambrosius pulled over a third chair and sat down opposite them. "Fear not. I am here to help you."

"Help us do what?" Eve asked. "We have not told you anything."

The man's gaze went back and forth between them, pausing on Eve's unusually colored eyes. Andrew expected it. Everyone seemed to notice them. Sometimes they appeared to be a pale blue, or perhaps azure or opal, sometimes a kind of green or hazel, and sometimes a stormy color, depending on the light or Eve's mood. People often commented on her eyes, and some feared her. But Ambrosius didn't react. Instead, his own eyes twinkled.

"I saw you arrive." He lifted his hands and exploded his fingers outward. "*Poof.* Out of nowhere. I never tire of it."

Andrew turned to Eve, his eyes wide. Then he shifted his gaze to the man and asked, "You have seen it happen before?"

Ambrosius said, "It would be courteous to tell me your names."

"I am Andrew Perry."

"And I am Evangeline Virtue."

The raggedy man bowed his head in greeting, then paused when Eve said "Virtue." He glanced at her with a knowing look. "I am Ambrosius, the Keeper of the Flame and Guardian of the Stone."

"What stone?" Eve asked.

"Perhaps the same one thou hast hidden in that locket around thy neck," Ambrosius said.

Eve's hand went to the case enclosing the Radiant Stone. "How do you know about that?"

He chuckled. "Dost thou not know where thou art?"

"Nay," Eve said.

Nay? Andrew glanced at her. Then he remembered that the Radiant Stone somehow changed their words to match the language people spoke in the time they were visiting. Sometimes it happened without Andrew and Eve realizing it.

Ambrosius continued. "Thou art in Beckery. Though some have called it *Little Ireland*, since it is something of an island, if one can call a patch of dry land in the middle of a marsh an island." He suddenly laughed and said, "Bees Wax!"

CHAPTER TWO

"Bees Wax?" asked Andrew.

"Yet another name for the island," Ambrosius explained. "Since I am the only one here, I reckon 'tis mine to call Beckery."

"But *where* are we?" Andrew asked.

"To answer broadly, you are in England. To be exact, you are in a cottage once owned by the good priests who lived here. 'Twas they who once celebrated Mass in the chapel more than forty years ago. Left to ruin, it was, by the command of King Henry the Eighth," Ambrosius said sadly. "For centuries, pilgrims trekked here to pray, to receive absolution, to drink of the water, to see the flame of Saint Brigid."

Andrew shook his head. "They came to see a flame?"

The raggedy man eyed him. "Saint Brigid of Ireland herself visited Beckery many centuries ago. 'Tis her well from which the water comes. She brought relics with her, including the stone you possess. It hath been called by many names. You call it the Radiant Stone."

Eve asked again, "How do you know that?"

"You are not the first to travel back to this time," said Ambrosius. "The one called Alfred the Virtuous hath been here as well."

"*Alfred Virtue?*" the two kids said together.

"Aye. He is a relative of yours?" Ambrosius asked.

Eve nodded. "Mine," she said.

"'Twas rude of him not to warn me that he would be sending *children*," he said.

"He could not have known," Andrew said. "Or maybe he did. It depends on ... on ..." Andrew wasn't sure what it depended on. Alfred Virtue had lived one hundred years *before* Andrew and Eve, but he met up with them in the time of Joan of Arc. Andrew groaned. "The whole Radiant-Stone-time-travel thing is still confusing to me."

Ambrosius laughed. "'Tis so indeed!" He leaned forward. "Now, I pray, speak freely. Why have you come?"

Eve began by explaining how she was a descendant of Alfred Virtue and lived with her aunt Catherine in a town called Hope Springs. "My aunt owns an antique shop that used to be a bank. Alfred Virtue founded the bank in the early part of the twentieth century."

Ambrosius nodded. "Pray, continue."

"I knew that Alfred Virtue was an explorer, so I started poking around," she said. "I found the Radiant Stone in his old office, along with a few of his journals that describe what it does. I tried it out and went back in time to the age of Robin Hood."

"Ah, dear Robin," Ambrosius said warmly as if he knew him.

Eve continued. "I met Andrew and—"

Andrew cut in and said, "She tricked me into going back to Robin's time."

"'Twas no trick!" she snapped, glaring at him. "It was thy choice to come along."

Andrew looked at Ambrosius and shook his head. "She tricked me."

CHAPTER TWO

"Doth it matter now?" Ambrosius asked.

Andrew realized that it didn't.

"We had an adventure with Robin Hood and then went back to our time," Eve explained. "Right after we got back, we had an *accident*." Her eyes darted over to Andrew. "There is no point arguing about *how* the accident happened. But we went to the time of Joan of Arc. We did not have the Radiant Stone, so we could not get home again."

"A fearful plight," said Ambrosius.

"Alfred Virtue used the Radiant Stone to come back and save us," Andrew said.

Ambrosius lifted an eyebrow. "How then did you journey home, since he was from one time and you another?"

"We used the Valiant Stone," Eve said.

Ambrosius looked surprised. "The Valiant Stone? 'Twas in fifteenth-century France?"

"Aye," said Eve.

Ambrosius looked thoughtful. "You used it to return to your time and country far into the future?"

Andrew tried to explain. "A man stole it from Alfred Virtue in the twentieth century and took it back to France in the fifteenth century." He decided to leave out the part about the thief being an ancestor of Dr. Howard's.

The man's bushy eyebrows lifted up. "Indeed! Pray, then, how did you know the Valiant Stone would take you home?"

"We did not know," Andrew replied.

"'Twas a bold venture," Ambrosius said.

There was something about the man's expression that made Andrew think they had taken a bigger risk than they knew.

Eve continued the story. "When we got home, my aunt was giving a tour to her friend—"

"*Boyfriend*," said Andrew.

"Her *friend*," Eve said sharply. "He saw the Radiant Stone on the desk and touched it before we could stop him. He disappeared, so we used the stone to follow him here. Now all we have to do is find him and take him back to Hope Springs."

"Ah, that will not be so easily done," Ambrosius said.

"Why not?" Eve asked.

Andrew sat up. "Have you seen Dr. Howard?"

"Aye," Ambrosius said. "He arrived here in the same fashion as you, though he was wild eyed and overwrought. 'Twas clear he did not know what had come upon him. He ranted and wailed. I feared a blow to the head was my only means to calm him down."

"You hit him?" Eve asked.

"Nay. I persuaded him to drink the water." Ambrosius gazed at the two kids. "He was here a fortnight. When no one came to rescue him, he lost patience. He determined to venture forth."

"He is gone?" asked Andrew.

CHAPTER TWO

"Aye. Two months hence."

"*Two months?*" Eve cried out.

Ambrosius nodded as if to confirm the timing. " 'Twas July. I am certain of it. 'Tis September now."

"We were only a couple of minutes behind him," said Andrew. Then he remembered that the past and the present seemed to move at different speeds.

"Where is Dr. Howard now?" Eve asked.

"He set his mind upon London."

"Why London?" asked Eve.

Ambrosius sighed. "He was of a mind that his kinfolk would be found there. I beseeched him then to journey south, to the Howards in Arundel Castle. He would find them also in North Yorkshire. But I begged the man not to go to London."

"What is wrong with London?" Andrew asked.

" 'Tis a perilous age in all of England, but 'tis worst of all in London. Strangers are beheld with suspicion." Ambrosius stood and went to a wooden trunk in a corner of the room. Kneeling, he undid the leather straps and opened the top. "These are his." He held up a tan shirt, a pair of jeans, a brown waistcoat, and a pair of socks.

"Dr. Howard was wearing those when he left Hope Springs," Eve said.

"Where are his cowboy boots?" Andrew asked.

Ambrosius pulled his cloak aside. He was wearing the boots. "We traded," he said. "In exchange for these, I allowed him the use of my best clothes."

There was a loud bang from somewhere behind the cottage. Andrew and Eve stood up.

"Are the men back?" Eve asked.

Ambrosius slowly stood up. "Nay. 'Tis Gwendolyn, my mare. She kicks at her stall when I neglect to feed her. Come. The rain has stopped."

As they followed him out the back door, Andrew glanced at the solitary candle on the table. The flame still burned steadily, but the candlewax itself wasn't dripping or shrinking in size.

Ambrosius led them past the pigpen and chicken coop to a stable. Inside was a single stall holding a tall gray horse. It stomped as Ambrosius came forward.

"I know," he said to the horse in a soothing tone. "I am a poor master."

The horse turned its attention to the two children. Eve rubbed the bridge of the mare's nose. "Hello, Gwendolyn."

Andrew patted the horse's neck.

The raggedy man reached somewhere in his cloak and brought out an apple. He handed it to Eve. "Feed her this," he said.

While Eve gave Gwendolyn the apple, Ambrosius went to a corner of the stable and lifted a large bale of hay. Andrew was astonished. The size of it was more than one man could carry. But Ambrosius not only carried it; he balanced it on one shoulder as he opened the gate to the stall and stepped in with the horse.

CHAPTER TWO

"Your Dr. Howard seemed to understand the danger of these times," Ambrosius said.

"Why is there so much danger?" Eve asked.

"Our sovereign Queen Bess—"

"Queen Bess?" interrupted Andrew.

"*Elizabeth*," Ambrosius clarified. "She dreads a revival of the old religion."

"The old religion? You mean the Catholic religion?" asked Andrew.

"Aye," said the raggedy man. "Sadly, the queen hath been given cause to believe its followers wish her dead."

"What year is this?" Eve asked.

"One thousand five hundred and eighty."

Fifteen eighty! Andrew did the math in his head. Fifteen eighty was more than four hundred years *before* the twenty-first century. More than three hundred years *after* Robin Hood. And one hundred and fifty years *after* Joan of Arc. He suddenly felt very far from home.

"'Tis against the law to be a Catholic now." Ambrosius came out of the stall and closed the gate. "To be Catholic is to risk imprisonment, or worse. By law, Catholics may be stretched on the rack, or their heads may be thrust on a pike." Then he called out, "Is it not true, good fathers?"

As if in response, there was movement all around the stable. Wooden slats in the walls were slid aside. A gentle shuffling and creaking could be heard in the hayloft over their heads. In a matter of minutes, four men assembled around them. All were young, probably in their twenties.

They smiled at Andrew and Eve as they dusted off their clothes.

Ambrosius said, "Here are the priests the mob could not find."

3

Back in the cottage, Ambrosius explained that the priests had come to England secretly from France. Their mission was to encourage Catholics by offering them the Sacraments, sermons, and teachings about living a faith-filled life in difficult times.

Andrew wondered how being Catholic could be illegal.

Ambrosius offered the priests a meal, but they all refused. They said they were fasting. Instead, they asked for a place to pray. He showed them to a room through a door to the right of the fireplace. He entered the room with them and closed the door.

Andrew drifted to the large candle by the window. "It's not melting or burning down," Andrew said.

"I noticed," Eve said, coming alongside him. She reached out her hand to the flame, but she drew it back at the sound of Ambrosius's return.

Ambrosius gestured to Andrew and Eve. "Now to your needs," he said. "Clothes I have not. However, I know where they may be found. We must hasten to Glastonbury."

"Where is Glastonbury?" Eve asked.

"Across the marsh. We shall take the boat," replied Ambrosius.

"Will the priests be safe here?" asked Andrew.

"As safe as they shall be anywhere. They know where to hide should anyone come in search of them." Ambrosius grabbed his hat from the hook on the wall.

Andrew pointed to the candle. "It burns, but it doth not burn down."

" 'Tis the flame of Saint Brigid. It hath burned day and night since she brought it here," Ambrosius explained.

"It *never* goes out?" Eve asked.

"Many of ill intent have attempted to extinguish it, but I would not allow it," he said. "After all, I am the Keeper of the Flame."

"You have been here for centuries?" Andrew asked. It was meant to be a joke, but Ambrosius merely grinned at him.

The raggedy man pressed the hat on his head and ruffled his cloak as if it didn't fit properly. Suddenly, he reached into a pocket and took out a small brown mouse. "Nay," he said. "Thou mayst not come along." He set the mouse on the floor.

The mouse sniffed at them, then scampered to the fireplace. It disappeared into a crack in the stonework of the hearth.

Eve lifted her hand as if she were in school. "You said that Saint Brigid brought the Radiant Stone when she visited Beckery. Do you have it here?"

"Aye. 'Tis well hidden."

"But I have it *here*," Eve said, touching the silver case around her neck.

" 'Tis true," Ambrosius acknowledged. "The stone in the locket is indeed from *thy* present time. And the stone in my keeping is from *this* present time," he said.

"They are *two* stones but the *same* stone?" Eve asked.

"Aye," said Ambrosius.

Andrew had to give that some thought. "If you have the Radiant Stone, why did you not let Dr. Howard use it to return to our time? Just like we used the Valiant Stone to do it," Andrew asked.

Ambrosius offered Andrew a patient look. "Time is being etched into the stones as it passes. 'Tis a perilous thing to leap ahead of the stone's true time, as you did with the Valiant Stone. God alone knows what may come of such an action."

Andrew shook his head. What the raggedy man said made as much sense to him as anything else he'd learned about the stones and time travel. There were rules for them, but the rules weren't easy to follow.

"Now we must make haste before the night draws to a close," Ambrosius said.

The rain had moved on, but clouds like fists covered the moon. Andrew found it hard to know where the sky ended and the land began.

Ambrosius had hooked a small lantern to a rod at the back of a rowboat. He now sat beneath the lantern working the oars—down, back, up and over, then down again. With each stroke, the boat seemed to glide faster and farther than the man's efforts should have allowed.

Andrew listened to the gentle rhythm of the oars and water. He felt an occasional bump as the boat's hull nudged against a rock or scraped the shallow bottom of the marsh. Thick reeds brushed against the boat on every side.

Eve asked Ambrosius, "Where are we going?"

"To Glastonbury," he answered. "You will have need of clothes and provisions if you hope to find Dr. Howard in London."

"How will we travel to London? We have no money and no way to get there," Andrew said.

"The methods and the means await us," Ambrosius proclaimed without any further explanation.

The front of the rowboat slid onto the shore and jolted to a halt. Ambrosius leapt out and pulled the boat farther aground. Andrew and Eve climbed out, their feet sinking and slurping in and out of the mud. With the lantern in hand, Ambrosius led the way across an open field.

Andrew gazed up. The thinning clouds now looked like bony fingers clawing at the light of the full moon. The three travelers walked from the boat and soon came to cottages and huts. A dirt road led to large stone buildings. They rounded a corner and came upon a vast ruin that looked like a yawning mouth filled with broken teeth.

"Glastonbury Abbey," Ambrosius said sadly. "King Henry the Eighth sent his minions to ransack it. They murdered the abbot, stole all that was valuable, and dispersed the monks. It hath been broken apart a little at a time ever since."

They continued on in silence as Andrew glanced back at the ruin. He tried to imagine what the abbey must have looked like in its days of glory.

They made their way down a mere sliver of a street and stopped in front of a tavern. A sign above the door said "The Thorn Tree" and had a crude painting of a long thorn emerging from a wild-looking bush. The tip of the thorn dripped red.

Ambrosius suddenly spun to Andrew and Eve. "Are you faithful to the one, holy, Catholic, and Apostolic Church?"

The question so surprised Andrew that he stammered, "Aye."

"I am," Eve said.

"Good," said Ambrosius. "Do not confess it again unless you speak to one you trust with your very lives. Trust few."

Ambrosius continued walking toward the tavern. Rather than approach the door, he stepped into a passageway on the left. It was so narrow that the raggedy man had to turn sideways to fit. He shuffled along. Eve gave Andrew a nervous look and then followed. Andrew squeezed in and went after them.

The passage stretched the length of the tavern and the building next to it, then opened to a courtyard behind them both. A carriage was there. Andrew's immediate impression was that it looked like a circus wagon or a gypsy caravan, with steps up to a door in the back of a tall wooden covering.

The back door opened. A tall man stepped out, lowering his head to keep from banging it on the wood frame. He had a round and cheerful face, thick black hair, and a full beard. He wore a waist-length burgundy jacket that stuck out like a pod for peas. Andrew remembered that the jacket was called a *doublet*. The man's arms were covered with white sleeves that were tight at the top, then puffed out down to his wrists. Below his doublet were breeches that looked like baggy shorts that stopped at the knees. Black leather boots covered the rest of his legs.

Stopping on the top step, the man put his hands on his hips as if he had just taken the stage to make a speech. "Ah, my dear wizard," the man said to Ambrosius in a deep, warm voice.

"Dear William," Ambrosius said.

William stepped to the ground and clasped both of the raggedy man's arms. Then his gaze went to Andrew and Eve. "Pray, what are these?"

"Two helpers for thy journey," Ambrosius replied. "Andrew and Evangeline. They have need to go to

CHAPTER THREE

London. As thou art going, I hoped thou couldst deliver them safely."

"Oh?" William asked. He gave Andrew and Eve a once-over, his gaze pausing on Eve's face—and her eyes.

Ambrosius added softly, "They are Children of the Stone."

He nodded. "That would explain their costumes." He gave them a low bow. "William Brookes at your service."

Andrew and Eve both bowed in return.

The raggedy man dug his hands into his cloak and fished around as if he had forgotten something. Then he brought out a small leather bag. "This will ease the expense of new costumes, and their safe passage." He handed the bag to William. It made a clinking sound.

William tucked the bag somewhere under his doublet.

Ambrosius nodded his head toward the tavern. "Where is Matthew?"

"He hath gone to meet members of the audience," said William. "We performed Saxo Grammaticus's *Amleth* this past afternoon. The onlookers were effusive in their praise. A few members sought a private meeting."

"William and Matthew are actors," Ambrosius explained to Andrew and Eve. "They journey the length and breadth of the country, performing wheresoever they may. Where two or more are gathered, they perform."

"Comedies, tragedies, and romances, presented in story, song, and sonnet," William said. He beckoned them into the caravan. "Sit ye down whilst I consider your attire."

The inside of the caravan was a mess of clothes and props, all hanging on the walls, tossed over crates, sticking out of trunks, and scattered on the floor. Andrew saw swords, shields, and helmets from different ages. There were long cloaks and robes, wigs, and masks. The entire wagon smelled of musty, old drapes. The kids squeezed to the sides as William moved back and forth. The caravan rocked like a ship on unsteady waters. Once or twice William hit his head on the lantern swinging from a hook in the ceiling. Its light danced fiercely.

Ambrosius watched from the door with an amused expression on his face.

Soon enough, William had unearthed clothes for Andrew and Eve. "These belonged to the children of a patron," he explained. "Anne and Henry, they were. They traveled with us through Yorkshire when we performed the Roman plays. Henry was a remarkable Cleopatra."

"But Cleopatra is a woman. A boy played her?" Andrew said, suddenly worried about what kinds of shows these actors performed.

"Girls and women are forbidden to take the stage," Ambrosius explained. "Boys play women's roles."

William turned to Andrew. "So *thou* couldst perform—"

"*Nay*," Andrew said quickly. "But I thank you all the same."

With a look of disappointment, William said, "Then thou shalt be the master of the props, and Evangeline shall be the mistress of the costumes."

Eve disappeared behind a blanket, hung up as a curtain, to change her clothes. Andrew changed his as well. A few minutes later, Eve emerged wearing a blue peasant's dress. Andrew was dressed like a smaller version of William. He sported a light-blue doublet, breeches of dull gold, and long woolen stockings of pale blue. He was given a cape of fine blue velvet but thought he would look silly wearing it and set it aside. His brown leather boots came up midthigh.

William gathered up their modern clothes and tossed them into the bottom of a trunk. He paused only to inspect their shoes, turning them over and around. Andrew wondered what he thought of the rubber soles, modern stitching, and laces.

With a grunt, William tossed the shoes into the trunk and covered everything up with assorted costumes. He gave Andrew a curious look as he stepped out of the cabin.

The kids gave each other a once-over.

"You look like Puss in Boots," Eve said with a giggle.

Andrew blushed.

Eve tugged at her dress. "The fashions are a lot different from Joan's time."

"Everything is so puffy." Andrew wiggled his feet. "These boots are a little too big."

"Shove a rag in front of your toes," Eve suggested. She lifted the hem of her dress slightly to reveal brown leather shoes on her feet. The tips of the shoes bulged out.

Andrew took her suggestion and found a couple of small rags. "I hope I don't get blisters."

A moment later, Ambrosius came to the door. "It is all arranged. William and Matthew will see that you reach London safely."

"How will we find Dr. Howard in a city as big as London?" Andrew asked.

"He will find you," came the reply.

"How?" Eve asked. "He doth not know we are here."

"The stone draws travelers together," Ambrosius said. "Circumstance leads them one to another. I have seen it happen again and again."

Andrew thought about the first time he met Eve at her aunt's shop. She had been watching him while he looked around. He thought she was being weird, playing a kind of hide-and-seek. She later told him she knew somehow that he would understand about time travel. So she led him through the Clock Room ... and back to the time of Robin Hood. Then in the time of Joan of Arc, she and Andrew encountered Simon Howard. He turned out to be the great-grandfather of Dr. Howard, a friend of Eve's aunt Catherine. From what Ambrosius had said, Andrew realized this was no coincidence.

"You have come here for Vincent Howard, but there may be a greater purpose at work," Ambrosius added.

"Nonetheless, I am certain the man will cross your paths. Though I cannot be certain what his state of mind will be."

William climbed into the caravan. "'Tis late," he announced. "We must sleep." He pushed costumes and props off a bench set in the front wall. "Thou mayst use that," he said to Eve. To Andrew, he said, "There is room for thee underneath."

Andrew looked at the cramped space under the bench and wondered how he would be able to sleep there.

William pulled a latch on the left side of the wagon. Part of the woodwork came down like a hideaway bed. "Matthew sleeps here."

"Where do you sleep?" Eve asked him.

"Thou art reclining upon my bed," William said, pointing to the long, narrow bench they had been sitting on.

Ambrosius lifted a hand to them. "I shall bid you farewell."

At that moment, running footsteps outside drew their attention to the door. A man appeared, breathless and red-faced. "William!" he gasped. "The hunters come this way!"

"To action," William said, clapping his hands. "We must lock up and put out the light."

"If John Buxton and his brutes are on the prowl, then I must hasten my return to Beckery," Ambrosius said. He squeezed past William and the kids and put a hand on Matthew's shoulder. "Courage, friend."

"Godspeed," said Matthew.

As Ambrosius stepped out of the wagon, Eve called after him. "Will we see you again?"

He nodded. "As long as you possess that stone, I am never far away."

"Thank you," Eve said.

"May the wings of angels fly you speedily to London," he said and was gone.

Matthew scrambled into the wagon, pulling the door shut behind him. "The hunters stopped me outside the Poole cottage. They accused me of priestly behavior. Imagine that! I walked on, but one of them followed me back to town. I hoped to lose him by dodging this way and that, but I am not confident." He fixed his eyes on Andrew and Eve. "Pray tell," he said, "to whom do these creatures belong?"

"They are journeying to London with us," William explained, adding in a half whisper, "Andrew and Evangeline are Children of the Stone."

Matthew looked impressed. He pushed a hand through his light-brown hair, as if to make himself more presentable. He bowed. "I am Matthew Whyte." He smiled, and dimples appeared under his thin beard.

"To bed," William announced. "If we are to be still, then let us sleep while we do it."

William and Matthew made a quick effort of tidying the wagon. Costumes went onto hooks and hangers. Props were thrown into trunks, which were then pushed aside.

"Why do *we* have to hide from the priest hunters?" Andrew asked.

"They are an ill-tempered lot. They are known to imprison strangers merely for the pleasure of having done so," Matthew said.

"They are also in the practice of taking what is not theirs," William added. "They seek to compensate themselves for the trouble of having bothered us. If you have anything of value, give it to me now so I may hide it."

He reached up to the arched ceiling of the wagon. Andrew noticed that it had been crudely painted with a design of light-blue tile squares outlined in dark red. William pushed on one of the tiles, and it lifted up. He took the pouch of money Ambrosius had given him and tucked it into a space in the roof. Matthew took off a gold necklace and a pouch from his belt. He handed them to William.

"Do you have anything?" William asked Andrew and Eve.

Andrew looked at Eve.

She reached up to her neck and grasped the silver locket that contained the Radiant Stone. She slipped the chain over her head and gave the necklace to William.

William held up the necklace and gazed at the locket. It looked like an oversized pocket watch, though Andrew doubted that William knew what a pocket watch was.

"I am curious but will not ask," William said, then grabbed a small cloth from nearby. He wrapped the locket in it, then tucked it up in the hiding place. He lowered the tile again. "Places, everyone," he said, as if directing a scene.

Andrew crawled under the bench. A feathered quilt served as a mattress. It was more spacious and comfortable than he had expected. He heard Eve get settled above him. Matthew lay down on his cot. William extinguished the lamp and stretched out on the long bench.

"Is this your home?" Andrew whispered.

"'Tis," said William. "When money allows, we indulge in proper lodgings."

They fell silent.

Andrew didn't know what time his body thought it was. Was it morning when they left fifteenth-century France? Was it afternoon in Hope Springs? He thought about people who had jet lag when they travel to different time zones. Perhaps he suffered from time lag.

He must have fallen asleep, because a loud banging at the door jolted him awake. He sat up—and hit his head on the underside of the bench. Groaning, he lay down again. Then he remembered where he was.

"I heard something inside," said a man outside. Someone pulled at the door handle.

Andrew stayed still.

"Shall I break the door in?" asked another man. "'Tis bolted from the inside. Someone must be in there."

"Fool! There is also a lock for a key," said a third man.

Andrew was sure the third voice belonged to John Buxton, the leader of the mob at Beckery.

"Take an axe to it," said the first man.

"Whose wagon is it? The queen's warrant doth not allow the destruction of property without cause," Buxton said.

"What are we to do?" the second man asked.

"Wouldst that thou had not allowed the stranger to escape with such ease," Buxton grumbled. "It could have been the traitor Edmund Campion."

"He was not priestly," the second man protested. "Nor did he have the look or bearing of Campion. On the contrary, this man was lowborn."

"'Twas an *actor*," the first man said. "The Pooles may be notorious Papists, but the law doth not prohibit the entertaining of guests, even actors."

Andrew heard Matthew let out a soft snort.

There was silence for a moment, then Buxton said, "Let us make haste to the island. That foul wizard will not expect us. We may yet find ourselves a priest or two this night."

Andrew knew it would take more than these men to outfox Ambrosius.

The priest hunters moved off.

Andrew thought about the name *Edmund Campion*. It sounded familiar to him. He wondered if he had learned about the man in history class at school. He was about to ask William and Matthew who Campion was, but suddenly he saw a shadow move beyond the thin crack between the door and the jamb.

Someone was waiting outside the caravan, hoping to catch them.

A minute went by. Then another. Rain began to drum at the roof. Finally, with a disgusted *harrumph*, the shadow at the door moved off.

Andrew let out a small puff of air. Only then did he realize that he had been holding his breath.

4

The wagon suddenly gave a violent jerk backward and then forward. Andrew sat up and once again bumped his head on the underside of the bench. "Ouch," he said. He had been sound asleep.

Crawling out from his little nest, he saw that the caravan door was open. He caught a glimpse of Eve outside. He heard William and Matthew calling to each other.

He slowly walked down the caravan steps to the damp ground.

Eve was standing at the corner of the wagon. "I thought the jolt might awaken thee," she said. "They are hitching up the horse."

Andrew frowned at the half light of the dull-gray dawn.

Eve nodded to a barrel in the corner of the courtyard. "That will help," she said.

Andrew went to the barrel. Cupping the cold water in his hands, he splashed his face, head, and neck. It did the job. He felt more awake.

"Do not stand idly by, lad. Fill those up," Matthew said, pointing to a half-dozen jugs sitting next to the barrel. "Place them inside the wagon."

Andrew pulled out the stoppers and filled each jug. He now noticed that the courtyard was three sides of a square between a collection of buildings. A door to his right opened up. A heavy-set woman came out carrying a wicker basket.

She winked at him. "A little something for your journey," she said and handed the basket to Eve.

"I thank you for your kindness," Eve said.

William came around the corner. "Molly! Thou art a treasure!" he cried out, then kissed her on the cheek.

She giggled. "Safe journey," she said. With another wink at Andrew, she bustled back through the doorway. He heard her secure the latch inside.

It wasn't long before everything was set for them to leave. William announced he would drive. Matthew was tasked with preparing the costumes and props for the next performance. Eve volunteered to help him. Andrew was to be another set of eyes for William at the front of the wagon.

"For what should I watch?" Andrew asked, puzzled over why he had asked the question that way.

"Watch for highwaymen, priest hunters, and markets or fairs where we may ply our trade," William replied.

Matthew made the Sign of the Cross. "In the name of the Father, Son, and Holy Ghost," he said softly. "Teach us, good Lord, to serve Thee as Thou deservest, to give and not to count the cost; to fight and not to heed the wounds; to toil and not to seek for rest; to labor and not to ask for any reward, save that of knowing that we do Thy will."

"Amen," William said, then laughed. "Apart from the bit about not asking for any reward."

William drove the wagon out of Glastonbury. Andrew sat next to him on the front bench. Merchants and tradesmen moved the opposite direction into town. Some pulled two-wheeled carts. Many carried large loads on their backs, and a few had horse-drawn wagons filled with goods.

"Market day," William said sadly. "Ah, to think of the audience."

"Why do you not stay?" asked Andrew.

"We have business elsewhere," William answered, with no further explanation.

Andrew's eyes went to a giant cone-like hill off to the left. A stone tower sat on top. "What is *that*?" he asked.

William turned to look. "That is the Tor. Hast thou not seen it before?"

"Nay," Andrew said. The strangeness of the hill astonished him. It stood tall and separate from the landscape all around it.

Behind him, he heard a sound like a window opening. He twisted around to see a panel slide to one side. Eve's face appeared in the rectangular hole. "Did you see the Tor?" she asked. "Matthew was just telling me about it."

"I can tell you many legends about the Glastonbury Tor," William said. He seemed happy to have an audience.

As they bumped along the uneven dirt road through the countryside, William wove together tales about the hollow underworld of Annwn beneath the Tor. Fairies, led by King Gwyn ap Nudd, played cruel practical jokes on humans, unless they were given presents.

He told other legends of King Arthur freeing Queen Guinevere from the top of the tower. Later, Arthur was taken there to heal from his battle wounds. Some believed he was buried there, while others said that the Holy Grail was placed near the Chalice Well closer to the town. Older tales spoke of Joseph of Arimathea coming to preach the gospel in that area not long after Jesus ascended to heaven.

"Then there are tragic accounts," William said, his tone becoming somber. "Abbot Richard Whiting and two other monks were taken to the top of the hill and executed for treason. What treason did they commit? They refused to recognize Henry the Eighth as the head of the Church. 'Twas not enough for the king to dissolve the abbey. He determined to stain its memory with blood."

CHAPTER FOUR

Andrew wondered how the country had become a place of such violence.

The horse labored as the wagon lurched along drunkenly, tipping this way and that on the uneven pathways. Andrew jostled in his seat as they traveled over broad-shouldered hills and along a patchwork of green and brown fields tucked between. There were few houses, only huts that looked like housing for animals and their keepers. Flocks of sheep gathered between hedgerows. Some fields looked as if the harvest season had passed; other fields showed signs of life. Most of the fields were open and untilled. More than once, William slowed the wagon to allow sheep to cross in front of them, or to follow behind a few meandering cows. He often had to coax the mare to the left of the path and then to the right to avoid getting stuck in the mud.

The trees clung to summer's green foliage, while the yellow and amber colors of late September began to invade. Andrew was surprised to see entire sections where trees had been cut down. When he asked about it later, Matthew explained that the demand for wood was taking its toll. It was used for fuel or to build new houses, furniture, and even warships.

Parish church towers stood like weather-beaten lighthouses in the distance.

It reminded Andrew of England in Robin Hood's time. But he noticed that the terrain in the south of the country had a different character from the north.

Every couple of hours, they stopped briefly at small villages to water their horse and give it a rest. Andrew switched places with Eve so she could enjoy some fresh air. William and Matthew also swapped duties, with Matthew driving while William stitched torn costumes and repaired damaged props.

"Matthew hit me in the head with this," William told Andrew, holding up a wooden sword. The top half was broken off. "A swordfight in a pirate play. My blood spilled everywhere. And the audience gave *him* a standing ovation."

William opened the back door of the caravan so Andrew could watch the road behind. As far as he could tell, few people took notice of them.

The wagon rattled over a bridge that crossed a large river. Then it slowly circled a deep forest. Greater hills appeared, and a field with a dull-green blanket of grass that stretched out for miles. After a while, William switched places with Matthew, and Andrew joined William on the bench. Eve remained, sitting on the bench between William and Andrew.

"Salisbury Plain," William said. "Keep watch like a hawk. The plain is the abode of many a beggar, ruffler, mort, palliard, rogue, or highwayman and his doxy."

"I would," Andrew said, "if I knew what those things were."

William laughed. "They are the names of various types of lawbreakers who prowl the land. I shall point them out should we encounter any of them."

They came within view of a mound of earth with a cluster of tall, gray stones standing on top. Andrew thought it looked familiar.

"Is that Stonehenge?" Eve asked, just as the name came to Andrew's mind.

"Aye," said William. "Hast thou been here before?"

"I have seen it only in pic"—Eve stopped and corrected herself—"in *drawings*."

As they rode closer to the mound, Andrew saw that the stones varied in width and height. It looked as if someone had placed them in a circle that had later been broken. The circle now had a kind of horseshoe shape. The tallest stones were rectangular and stood upright. He guessed they might be twenty feet high. Other stones lay like crossbeams along the tops. Long shadows stretched out from the setting sun.

"The local folk say that the Druids placed the stones here as part of a temple. You can see what might have been the altar." William gestured toward a grouping of smaller stones set up like a table. "Or this structure may have been a monument on the site of a bloody battle between foreign invaders and the Cangi—the great giants of Somerset. 'Twas said the stones danced in celebration. Many a night they still do."

Andrew shot him a look. He was smiling.

William guided the horse and wagon along a ditch that circled the base of the mound. "Perhaps it was the work of Merlin in the days of King Arthur," he said.

Andrew saw more clearly that the stones inside the broken circle seemed to have the same shape, like arms reaching around to invite people in. A few stones looked as if they had fallen or been chipped away. Off to the side was a fat slab leaning to one side.

They look like gravestones to me, Andrew thought.

They came to an earthen bridge. William pulled the reins and the horse slowed. They crossed to the mound and rode to the edge of the stones.

Andrew wasn't superstitious, but he felt a strange uneasiness about the place.

"Why are we stopping here?" asked Eve.

"We dare not journey on in the dark," William replied. "Rocks, ditches, and thieves will curse us along every mile."

"Will they not rob us here as well?" Andrew asked.

"They may try," said William. "But darkness blinds them just as it blinds us. And some of the robbers fear the stones at night more than any weapon made by man."

William pulled a bundle of wood from a holder under the wagon and built a fire. He then set an iron rack over the top, with a small black pot and a kettle. He sat down on a stool next to the fire and began to pull vegetables from a small bag. He cut them up and tossed them into the pot.

"What skills do you have?" he asked Andrew and Eve.

"Skills?" asked Andrew.

"Dost thou cook?" he asked Eve.

"I can cook a little," she said. "If you tell me what to do."

"Weapons? Art thou handy with any weapons?" William looked at Andrew.

"I am handy with a staff," Eve said.

William looked surprised. "There is one just inside the wagon door. Show me," he said to her.

While Eve went to fetch the staff, he asked Andrew, "And thou?"

"I am best with rocks," said Andrew.

"Rocks?" William gestured for Andrew to show him.

Andrew knelt down and picked up a couple of pebbles. He pointed to one of the standing stones a few yards away. "The middle one?"

William nodded.

Andrew took a step back, wound up his arm, and launched the pebble. It hit the tall stone dead center.

William grunted. "That will do."

Eve returned, tossing a long staff from hand to hand as if checking its balance. Suddenly, with a shout, Matthew lunged at her from the side of the wagon. Eve spun quickly, swinging the staff around. She caught Matthew on the side of the head. He cried out and fell to his knees.

Andrew gasped. William let loose a hearty laugh.

Eve shrieked and ran to Matthew's side. "I am so sorry!" she said, kneeling next to him.

Matthew rubbed his head. "We are in safe hands," he said, groaning.

William was now rocking on his heels, tears in his eyes. "We are safer with thee than thou art with us!" he roared.

Matthew got to his feet and said, "Let us assign positions for the night." He gestured to Andrew. "The stone thrower shall be on top of the wagon. The maiden shall hide inside. William, stay by the fire. I will be hidden behind the standing stones."

"I shall take the first watch," William offered.

"And I the second," said Matthew.

Andrew raised his hand. "And I the third?"

"Two watches are enough," said William. "We will signal if thou art needed."

"What is the signal?" Eve asked.

"A loud shout will usually do the trick," William said, laughing again.

That evening, the four of them sat around a small fire and ate vegetable stew. Matthew then led them in nightly prayers. Afterward, Andrew followed Eve into the wagon.

CHAPTER FOUR

He hoped this would be a good chance to talk. Eve must have thought of the same thing, because she leaned the staff against the wall and sat down on her makeshift bed.

She hugged her knees in her arms and said, "Well, here we are again. I have no idea what we're doing."

"That seems to happen everywhere we travel." Andrew sat down on William's cot and nodded toward the door. "What do you think of them?"

"I trust them because Ambrosius trusts them," she said. "And I trust Ambrosius."

"How does Ambrosius know so much about the stone?" Andrew asked.

"I don't know, but he does," Eve said. "That's good enough for me."

Andrew said, "I wish I knew more about this time in history. Henry the Eighth, Queen Elizabeth, closing down abbeys, and hunting priests ..."

Eve shook her head. "I heard the hunters mention Edmund Campion. He is a saint. I *think* he died in England because he was a Catholic." She frowned. "I don't like the idea of hanging around another saint who gets killed. Joan of Arc was enough for me."

"I wish we could go back to a time that wasn't so *historical*," Andrew added, knowing it was a silly thing to say.

Eve didn't laugh. She looked worried. "I hope Ambrosius is right about the Radiant Stone. The part about drawing people together. Otherwise, we'll never find Dr. Howard."

"What does 'Children of the Stone' mean?" Andrew asked. "Are we part of a club? Does it make us special?"

"I don't know," Eve said, shaking her head again. "We'll figure it out as we go."

Andrew sighed. "How am I supposed to sleep when thieves might sneak up on us?"

"Think of our days with Robin Hood," she said. "We always slept in the woods with one eye open."

Andrew remembered the feeling. In Robin Hood's time, he was aware of every sound in the forest. He could even tell which sounds were friendly and which weren't. He hoped the same sense would come back to him now.

"It'll come back to us," Eve said, as if she knew what he was thinking.

With nothing else to say, Andrew picked up a blanket and stepped out of the wagon. He circled to the front. After tossing the blanket onto the driver's bench, he went in search of pebbles that were good for throwing. He found enough to fill a pouch and tucked that into his belt. Then he climbed onto the wagon bench. Reaching up, he caught hold of a metal rail that edged around all four sides of the wagon's roof, like a luggage rack. The rail seemed solid enough. He used it to pull himself up; then he crawled to the center of the roof. Only then did he notice that the roof had a slight arch. He hoped the rail would catch him if he rolled to one side or the other in his sleep.

Andrew spread out the blanket on the side of the wagon facing Stonehenge. He put the pouch of pebbles nearby, then lay down so his head was at the top of the slanted roof. He eased onto his back and tucked his left arm behind his head. The night air was crisp and the sky was clear. A soft breeze blew, whispering among the standing stones. He sat up and listened. He was sure he could hear a low hum, as if someone had plucked a bass string, and it now vibrated all around them.

The starlight danced in wild rhythms. Andrew wondered how different those stars would look if he were in this exact spot, at this same moment, in his own time. They didn't seem so different from the stars he saw in the times of Robin Hood and Joan of Arc. Maybe some new ones had shown up or some old ones had disappeared.

A Bible verse came to mind. It said something like, *The heavens tell of God's glory.* He thought, *Whether it's five thousand years ago, or two thousand, or five hundred, or even five minutes, God is always God.*

A soft whistle yanked him from his musings. He grabbed the pouch of pebbles, then slid onto his stomach. He crawled to the railing and carefully peeked over.

Stonehenge was bathed in a pale-blue light. Matthew was nowhere to be seen. William stood by the dying fire with a sword in his hand. Andrew wondered if it was real or a prop.

Off to the right, a large black stallion carrying a hooded figure slowly entered the ring of stones. The rider came alongside William. William sheathed his sword. The hooded figure handed him a small bundle. Just then, Matthew emerged from behind a standing stone and joined the two men. Soft words were spoken. William passed the bundle to Matthew, who retreated into the shadows. William gestured to the wagon. The hooded rider turned and lifted a hand in a wave to Andrew. Andrew waved back. The rider made the shape of the Cross in the air as a blessing. Then, jerking the reins, he spurred his horse to a gallop and rode off into the darkness. William stood where he was for a moment. He jabbed at the logs on the fire, then lay down again.

Back on his blanket, Andrew mused about why William and Matthew would be receiving a bundle from a hooded rider in the middle of the night.

5

" 'Tis a new play," William said, winking at Andrew.

It was dawn. The four campers were sitting by the smoldering fire, nibbling on some bread, pieces of salted fish, and some pickled herring. There was a time when Andrew would have thought it was an unusual meal first thing in the morning, but jumping around in time had changed all that.

"Someone brought you a new play in the middle of the night?" Eve asked.

"The wisest course is for each of us to know little about the other's business," Matthew said gently.

Eve looked at him suspiciously.

William picked at something in his teeth and said, "Child, if the priest hunters capture any of us, we might say more than we intend to say."

"I would not," Andrew said.

"If thou felt the pain of hot pokers put to thy skin—" Matthew began to say.

"They would not do that, would they?" Eve interrupted, her eyes wide.

"Indeed they might—and worse," said Matthew.

"Surely not to children," Eve insisted.

Matthew gave her a look that suggested *Aye, they would*.

"Hath England lost its mind?" Andrew asked.

"She hath lost her soul," said William.

They finished breakfast in a brooding silence. Then they readied the wagon and trekked across the plain in a northeasterly direction. Matthew was tasked to drive. Eve sat next to him, with Andrew next to her. William opened the small sliding door behind them. He occasionally appeared there, when he wasn't banging around in the wagon.

"Where to now?" Andrew asked Matthew.

"Winchester," he replied.

"The famous cathedral?" asked Andrew.

"Aye."

Eve frowned. "Would it not be a ruin now?"

"The cathedral was spared by King Henry's villains," Matthew said. "Instead, they plundered the priories. The lands were sold. The stones of those sacred dwellings were placed in the city wall."

The caravan bounced along a path that led to a wider road. Fields, distant cottages and shacks, and grazing livestock were the recurring sights of the day. Farmers stopped their work to watch the travelers pass. The hills seemed to multiply and become the landscape of a different country.

CHAPTER FIVE

"We are diverting ever so slightly to the south," Matthew explained. "Soon we shall arrive in the village of Nether Wallop."

"Funny name," Andrew said.

"A *wallop* is a mix of two ancient words—*waella* and *hop*," Matthew said. "It means a 'spring of water.'"

There wasn't much to the village, or even a spring of water, as far as Andrew could see. They rode along a narrow road and passed a few cottages with thatched roofs hanging over white walls and dark beams. Matthew pulled up to a tavern. William leapt out of the wagon, stretched, then strode inside. A moment later, he returned with a tall, spidery-looking man. Andrew had never seen such long arms and legs on such a small trunk.

"Mr. Stokes is the owner of this fine establishment," William announced. "He will see to the care of the horse and provide a modest meal for our journey."

Mr. Stokes gave them a low bow. Andrew thought the man's limbs might get tangled up in the process.

Eve perched on the wagon steps. Andrew watched as Matthew drifted back to the main road. He stopped and glanced one way, then the other. He looked left, straightening his back as if gathering his strength, and walked off.

"Whither is he going?" Andrew asked.

William slid over to Andrew and said softly, "Matthew's family lived not many miles hence. He often came to this village as a boy. The family did worship at the ancient church yonder."

"May we see it?" Eve asked, jumping down from the step.

"If it pleases you," William said.

The three of them followed Matthew along the road to the base of a hill. A path led to the church at the top. Its square stone tower stood like a guard over the entire village.

"The Parish Church of St. Andrew," William announced. "'Twas built during the time of the Saxons."

"How long ago was that?" Andrew asked.

"More than five hundred years," William replied.

Cresting the hill, Andrew saw the tower standing at one end of a long stone nave. Tall stained-glass windows lined the walls. William led them to a worn oak door on the side of the church. The door stood open.

Andrew was about to go in, but William put a hand on his shoulder.

"Wait," William said.

A moment later, Matthew came out. He was shaking his head and rubbing tears from his eyes.

"What is wrong?" Eve asked.

Matthew looked at her, shook his head again, then walked away.

"Should we go in?" Andrew asked.

"With all good speed," said William, and they stepped through the doorway.

CHAPTER FIVE

Pillars lined the aisle that led to the altar and a huge stained-glass window behind it. The wooden pews were simple and unadorned. The walls were painted white. A man stood at the far end of the chancel. He looked busy wiping an oversized wooden chair with a cloth, but Andrew noticed his eyes were on them.

Eve began to make the Sign of the Cross, but William reached over and held her arm.

"We have seen enough," he whispered sharply and waved them out.

They walked quickly across the lawn and back down the hill. Matthew stood waiting for them by the road.

"What happened?" Andrew asked as they returned to the tavern.

Matthew looked at him with a miserable expression. "I attended Mass there when I was a small boy. Then the church was faithful to the Church of Christ. Now it is faithful to the Church of *England*, the one founded by the eighth Henry and Queen Elizabeth. I had forgotten ..." He put a hand over his eyes for a moment, then continued. "The walls ..." Again, he stopped to compose himself.

Andrew didn't understand what was wrong with the walls.

Matthew cleared his throat. "There were paintings on the walls," he said. "One showed Saint George killing the dragon. Another presented Saint Nicholas. Yet another showed work tools being used to wound Jesus' legs—as a lesson to all who would work on the Sabbath. But the most glorious was a painting of our Lord Jesus Himself, in majesty, surrounded by angels."

"What happened to the paintings?" asked Eve.

Matthew took a deep breath as if to gain strength, then said, "By royal decree, Henry the Eighth commanded that any images reminding the people of our Catholic faith be removed. The walls of the church were whitewashed. The precious sacramental articles were declared idolatrous and were stolen or destroyed."

Andrew felt a burning in his cheeks. He knew how he would feel if someone ransacked St. Clare's in Hope Springs. Yet he couldn't imagine it ever happening.

When they returned to the tavern, Eve climbed the steps to the back of the wagon. She sat on the top step with her elbows on her knees and cradled her chin in her hands. She looked sad.

Andrew paced back and forth in front of her. He felt as though he should say something. He watched as William went inside the tavern to see about the food. William returned with a stooped white-haired man following behind. He whispered to the old man and then to Matthew, who was checking the hubs of the wagon wheels. The white-haired man hobbled to Matthew. They spoke together quietly. Then the two walked off, disappearing around the side of the tavern.

Curious, Andrew went to the corner of the old stone building. He saw Matthew and the old man on a footpath, crossing a field to a knot of houses on the other side.

CHAPTER FIVE

Andrew returned to the wagon. Eve gave him a questioning look. She leapt down from the step, and the two of them went to William. He was now brushing the horse with long, broad strokes.

Eve looked around to make sure they were alone. Then she asked the question that had also been on Andrew's mind. "Is Matthew a priest?"

William stopped brushing but kept his eyes on the horse. Then he sighed deeply and said, "Aye. He is."

Andrew and Eve looked at each other.

William began brushing the horse again and added, "As am I."

Andrew and Eve learned from William that Matthew had gone to hear the confessions of a few Catholics nearby. "They live in fear. They have no access to the Sacraments. He gives them words of encouragement."

They were now sitting inside the wagon. They didn't want anyone to hear them.

"You are not truly actors?" Andrew asked.

William laughed. "True actors would say we are not. However, we perform so we may travel freely. The queen's hunters do not expect priests to be actors. Some of our fellow priests think it a scandal."

"Are there still a lot of priests in England?" Eve asked.

William grew serious. "I will speak no more about it. As we have told you, there are those who would inflict terrible pain upon you to discover what you know."

Matthew returned an hour later. He looked happier than before, smiling and whistling as they prepared to leave the village.

Andrew was inside the wagon, putting newly filled water jugs away, when he heard voices outside. He went to the door. A handful of men had surrounded Matthew and William. One was the man Andrew had seen at the church earlier.

"You are *Papists*!" the man was shouting. He jabbed a finger at William's chest.

"How now? Why wouldst thou accuse us of such a thing?" William demanded.

"I saw thee and thine in the church," the man replied.

"Is it a Catholic church now? Are all who visit thy church accused of holding the Catholic faith?" William asked. "The queen would be very interested to know thou thinkest so."

The man grabbed Eve, who was standing nearby. He pushed her to the middle of the circle. "I saw this child make the Sign of the Cross!"

William laughed. "Didst thou? Art thou so sure of thine eyes? Might she not have been waving away a bug?" To make his point, William waved his hand as if swatting at a fly and made what looked like the Sign of the Cross.

A few of the men laughed. The man from the church scowled.

"Thou art misinformed," William continued. "*If* we were Catholics, why would we go into a heretical church?"

"Why would *actors* go into a church at all?" Matthew added with a light chuckle.

"'Tis enough, Benjamin," an older man in the mob said.

Benjamin rounded on the mob. "I am not so readily fooled. By the authority of the Crown, I *demand* that the wagon be searched. See what Papist rubbish is hidden within!"

The man pushed Andrew aside and stomped into the wagon. There was a lot of crashing and banging. Boxes were thrown through the doorway, smashing to the ground. Costumes and props followed.

The men in the mob gave one another nervous looks.

Benjamin appeared at the door again and shouted, "See to it!"

With a lot of grumbling, the men shuffled over to the boxes and began searching through each one.

Eve caught Andrew's eye and touched her neck. She wiggled a thumb at the wagon. Andrew realized she meant that the necklace with the Radiant Stone was still inside. He understood that she was worried about what would happen if the men found the secret compartment where it was hidden.

William stepped forward. "What authority of the Crown do you invoke? Show me your warrant!"

No one in the mob responded.

A crowd from the village gathered, watching the commotion.

"Well, then!" William called out. He stepped onto one of the boxes as if it were a podium. "Why waste our time as these men are doing? Allow us to present a selection of dramatic scenes in which we tell the tragic tale of Julius Caesar and his betrayal at the hands of his beloved friend Brutus. Matthew!"

With a flourish, Matthew snatched a couple of robes from a pile of costumes on the ground. He gave one to William and quickly threw the other around his own shoulders.

William and Matthew began to deliver long speeches as Julius and Brutus. The words reminded Andrew of something William Shakespeare might have written. Then Andrew wondered if William Shakespeare was alive in that time. The two actors spoke loudly, with dramatic hand gestures. Soon, the villagers—and the mob—were watching and applauding them. Benjamin stepped out of the cabin. He glared at his comrades, then marched away.

The inside of the cabin was a wreck. Andrew checked the secret compartment. It was safely closed up.

"Let's clean up this mess," Eve said to Andrew. The two began to put the contents back inside.

CHAPTER FIVE

Andrew found their modern clothes in a corner. "I wonder what he thought of these." He held up their sneakers.

"At least he didn't take a knife to them," Eve said.

William and Matthew finished their performance, with Matthew, as Brutus, stabbing Caesar with a prop knife. William fell to the ground but still had enough energy to give another speech for five minutes. Then he collapsed. Brutus then gave a tearful speech over the fallen Caesar, with a sobbing finish. The crowd applauded as the two actors took their bows. Some coins were pressed into their palms as the villagers left.

The older man from the mob patted William on the shoulder. "Sorry about all this," he said. "Our Benjamin Beard is strung a little too tight. He sees Catholics *everywhere*."

"I understand," said William. "One can never be too careful these days."

The tavern owner came over with a large container of soup and a loaf of bread. "For your troubles," he said.

Alone again, the four of them ate. Then they put the wagon back into traveling condition.

Once they were on the road again, Andrew was sure he saw the man from the church hiding behind a tree, watching them depart.

6

Night fell, and a heavy rain slowed their progress. Again and again, a wagon wheel slid into a deep rut or hole, and the four of them were soaked trying to coax it out.

"Thankfully the thieves do not care for the rain," Matthew said.

The roads curved in and out of steeper hills. The horse snorted loudly, shaking its mane, and the wagon seemed to move mere inches at a time. Finally, William suggested they find cover in a thicket. "Let us await the morn," he said.

It was too wet to make a fire, so they went to their sleeping places in the back of the wagon. The constant drumming of rain on the roof helped Andrew fall asleep.

The morning sun was well hidden behind iron-gray clouds. The rain became a fine spray as they continued on. Late in the morning, they saw through a thin mist Winchester Cathedral rising high over the trees and rooftops of the city. They entered through the west gate and slowly navigated the main street to the market. The cathedral loomed large to their right. The rain had stopped by the time they reached a tall, open-sided monument with arches and pinnacles and statues of various saints.

"'Tis a goodly place," exclaimed William as he leapt from the driver's seat.

"No wagons or horses here," said a man with a body shaped like a building block. "Move through there." He pointed to a narrow road. "For a short time, thou mayst use the field in front of the cathedral."

William obeyed. They passed between rows of shops that opened up to a wide patch of land. The cathedral stood in the middle.

Andrew gasped at the majestic structure. "It must be over a hundred feet high," he whispered to Eve.

A square tower of gray stone formed the central part of its cross-like shape. Thin spires lined the longest of the four wings, each one topped with a cross. The walls were lined with windows, some adorned with pointed arches, others with more rounded tops.

Andrew came around to the main entrance. Dozens of stained-glass windows gazed down at them beneath a giant arch of stone. High above the arch was a section shaped like a triangle, with a spire on top and two on the sides. At the base of it all, three sets of doors sat under arched porches.

"This is what all cathedrals should look like," he said to Eve, his eyes following the detailed lines and angles intricately carved into the many pillars.

CHAPTER SIX

She stared for a moment, then said, "I think it is more beautiful than the cathedral at Reims."

Andrew thought of the many cathedrals he and Eve had seen in France during the time of Joan of Arc. But something about this cathedral impressed him more.

"Thou hast seen the cathedral in Reims?" Matthew asked. He had been standing close by and now looked at Eve with raised eyebrows.

Eve stammered, "I ... I should have said, it *must* be more beautiful than the cathedral at Reims."

"Have *you* been to Reims?" Andrew asked Matthew.

Matthew glanced around, then gave him a sharp nod. "I believe I have spent more of my adult years in France than I have in my home country."

At midday, William and Matthew returned to the monument in the center of the main road. They were dressed in armor and carried painted wooden swords. They summoned all within hearing distance. Andrew and Eve walked up and down the street, inviting everyone they saw to a "grand performance by two highly skilled actors." Soon, a modest crowd had formed.

Andrew climbed the steps to the monument and searched the crowd. He had a sudden impossible hope that Dr. Howard might be there. Instead, he felt his heart lurch when he saw Benjamin Beard, the troublemaker from the church in Nether Wallop. Andrew turned to tell William and Matthew, but they were already waving for the crowd's attention.

William proudly declared that they would now begin a drama about "Winchester's favorite son—King Alfred the Great—in which Alfred must repel the notorious Danish hoards led by Guthrum, king of the Danes!"

The show began with William and Matthew alternating the narration, fighting with their swords, narrating some more, then fighting with their swords again.

"Methinks it is an excuse to do fight scenes," Eve whispered to Andrew.

"Methinks?" Andrew asked.

"Is that what I said?" Eve looked surprised. "Those words keep slipping in."

Andrew chuckled.

As William and Matthew performed, Andrew thought that a lot of the speeches sounded like the ones the two actors had used for their Julius Caesar scenes. Only the names were changed. And rather than William being stabbed as Julius Caesar, it was Matthew as Guthrum, king of the Danes, who was run through—under the armpit.

There were shouts and applause at the end. Coins were thrown at the actors' feet.

As Andrew and Eve picked up the money, Matthew said, "It will go to the Hospital of St. Cross outside the city."

The crowd dispersed. Andrew searched the faces for Benjamin, but he wasn't there. An older woman approached Matthew and laid a hand on his arm. She came close and whispered something to him. He gave a slow nod as she spoke. Then, eyes brimming with tears, she slowly walked away.

Andrew saw Matthew give William a knowing look. The two men quickly gathered up the show props and walked briskly back to the wagon. Andrew and Eve followed them. At the wagon, Andrew told the other three about seeing Benjamin in the crowd.

William and Matthew looked concerned. William said to Matthew, "Be cautious."

Matthew nodded.

After changing back into his peasant clothes, Matthew left them. He said nothing, not even goodbye. Andrew watched him walk up the lane alongside the cathedral.

"We shall find an inn and have a proper meal," William said cheerfully. He patted the neck of the horse. "But first, we must find a stable."

William learned from a passerby that he could stable the horse and secure the wagon just a couple of streets away.

"Wait here," he said, then drove off.

"What about Benjamin Beard?" Eve asked.

Andrew shrugged. "There's nothing we can do about him. Let's look inside the cathedral!"

They crossed the soggy grounds to the huge doors. They hadn't gone far when Andrew noticed crude wooden crosses and blocks of stones marking rough rectangular patches in the earth.

"We're walking on a graveyard," Eve said.

Andrew shivered. He was about to make the Sign of the Cross but stopped himself. He looked around quickly to make sure no one was watching.

They reached the largest of the doors at the front of the cathedral. It was fastened with fat chains. The other doors were also chained or locked. They followed footpaths that presented views of the cathedral from different sides. Then they went back to the corner of the grounds to wait for William.

William did not come.

Andrew and Eve paced for a while, then split up to watch for him from different directions. Andrew was aware of suspicious looks from passersby. Some were in peasant clothes; others wore the robes of officials or clerics.

He rejoined Eve. "Do you think Benjamin had William arrested?" he asked.

Eve looked as worried as Andrew felt. "Should we walk in the same direction William went with the wagon?"

Andrew agreed that it was a good idea, so they walked back to the main street and the monument. People were going about their business. There was no sign of William.

"Did he go left or right?" Andrew asked.

"I'm pretty sure he went right," Eve said. They headed that way.

A handful of women had gathered outside a poultry shop. They were haggling with a butcher over this goose or that particular duck or the small size of the chickens.

Andrew's gaze went from there to the shop next door. Benjamin Beard from Nether Wallop was leaning against a pillar outside the shop.

Andrew tugged at Eve's arm.

"Run," she whispered. She backed away.

Andrew hesitated. He was afraid that running might make them look guilty. He simply stared at the man.

"For whom do you search?" Benjamin asked, walking toward them.

Eve tapped Andrew's back. "Behind us," she said.

Andrew glanced over his shoulder. Two men were walking up the street in their direction. One of them was William. He looked grim. The other was a short man wearing official robes.

"That is Sir Edward Goddard, the *High Sheriff*," Benjamin explained with a note of triumph in his voice.

William gazed at Andrew and Eve, then his eyes went to Benjamin. Andrew thought a look of understanding crossed his face.

"Where is the other one?" Benjamin asked the High Sheriff.

"He is yet to be found," said Sir Edward in a surprisingly high voice. He stroked his long dark beard. "'Tis likely he will go to Lady West's house. The Wests are known recusants."

"Good sir, you confound me. Why do you claim we are Papists?" William demanded. "By what evidence do you accuse us? Is it the nature of this city to trouble humble men in this way?" He pointed a finger at Benjamin. "This varlet searched our belongings at Nether Wallop. Now he hath followed us here. Is he part hound? Are we foxes for his vain hunt?"

"I have a nose for traitors," Benjamin said, sneering.

"*Traitors!* Scurvy knave! I am so vexed that every part of me quivers!" William shouted.

The High Sheriff held up his hand. "The truth shall come forth," he said. "Pray, attend me."

"Where will you have us attend you?" William asked.

"The jail. We shall speak there." The High Sheriff gestured for Andrew and Eve to follow as well.

William stood his ground. "Take me, if you must. These two are mere children and should not set foot in such a place."

"Our jail is homely enough. 'Twill do them no harm," said the High Sheriff. "Dispute me, and thou wilt be hard put upon."

William shook his head but then urged Andrew and Eve forward. They marched up the main street in the same direction they had entered the city. Just before they reached the west gate, they veered right and soon came to a squat building made of brick and stone. Sir Edward pushed open the door, and they crowded into an entry hall. A desk sat to the right. Parchments were neatly placed on top, with a quill pen and inkwell next to them.

A door opened in the back wall. A tired-looking man with shaggy hair and a beard came through. He wore a faded robe that might have been official looking once but was now worn and tattered.

"Pray, what creatures are these?" the man asked the High Sheriff.

"Catholics!" Benjamin shouted.

The High Sheriff reeled around to Benjamin. "Begone! Thou wilt be summoned when I have need of thee."

Benjamin glared at the sheriff, then turned sharply away. He slammed the door behind him as he left.

The High Sheriff signaled to the tired-looking man. "Take him to thy custody." The *him* was William.

The man grunted and moved aside so William could walk through the rear doorway.

William gave the man a friendly smile. "I am William Brookes, an actor."

The tired-looking man said in a low, miserable voice, "I am Anthony Dovedale, a jailer."

The jailer followed William through and gave the door a tug that didn't quite close it. Andrew felt nervous. Without William, he suddenly felt unprotected. All the talk about being tortured came back to his mind.

The High Sheriff pointed to two chairs against a wall near the desk. "Sit down," he said.

Andrew and Eve sat down, clasping their hands on their laps like two naughty children in front of a principal.

The High Sheriff said, "Answer my questions honestly, and you will soon be on your way once more."

Andrew heard a soft sigh come from Eve.

The High Sheriff peppered them with questions. How did they know William? Were they relatives? Why were they traveling with him now? Did they know men named Edmund Campion and Robert Persons? Had they met any other men or women professing the *evil* Catholic religion?

Andrew thought he and Eve answered the questions well. He remembered how they answered similar questions in the times of Robin Hood and Joan of Arc. They were learning the art of answering without saying too much or lying. In this case, they said they were not relatives of either actor. They were serving as apprentices until they met up with their guardian, a man named Vincent Howard, in London. They said they didn't know either of the men the High Sheriff mentioned, nor anyone professing the evil Catholic religion.

The High Sheriff gazed at them for a moment. He then went to the door leading back to the cells. "Come hither," he said.

"You are locking us up?" Eve asked. She had gone pale.

"You will wait there whilst I speak with the actor," the High Sheriff explained.

Andrew stayed in his chair. "Will you torture us?" he asked.

The High Sheriff chuckled. "Tools of that kind are not to be found here."

Eve gave a sigh of relief and stood up.

The man's answer didn't reassure Andrew. If they *did* have tools of torture, would they use them on kids?

The jailer bustled through the door. "What is your pleasure?" he asked.

"Detain them," the High Sheriff said.

The rear door to the cells led to a corridor lined with other wooden doors. Each door had a single window in the middle, with iron bars. The jailer stopped at a door on the right and pulled it open. He waved the children inside the cell. They obliged him, turning to watch as he closed the door. He gave it a final pull to make certain it was secure. Keys rattled, and the lock made a loud, dismal sound.

Andrew stood on the tips of his toes to look out the barred window.

"Oh!" said Eve, sounding surprised.

Andrew turned. Eve was facing a corner of the cell. In a dull shadow, a young boy and an even younger girl were huddled on a patch of straw. Their faces were dirty. Their clothes were little more than tattered rags.

"Greetings," Eve said.

Two sets of eyes peered up at her, then darted to Andrew when he asked, "Why are you here?"

"Mother and father invited a priest to the house," the boy answered slowly. "He heard our confessions. He said the Mass. Someone told on us."

Eve knelt down beside them. "Why would someone betray your trust?"

"For the reward," said the little girl.

"Where are your mother and father now?" Eve asked her.

The girl shook her head.

The boy said, "Father was taken to the Queen's Privy Council in London. We do not know where our mother is."

"How long have you endured this jail?" Andrew asked the boy.

"Days and days," the boy replied.

"Perhaps our company will cheer you," Eve said hopefully.

The boy and girl huddled closer together.

Andrew and Eve tried to make themselves comfortable. It was hard to do. The boy and girl had taken most of the straw. Andrew didn't have the heart to ask them to share.

The boy's name was Peter. The girl's name was Marjorie. They had lived outside of Winchester their entire young lives. When they learned that Eve and Andrew had come from far away, they each took turns asking questions. The children treated them as if they were worldly-wise, older siblings. Andrew felt as if they were being interrogated all over again. Peter eventually asked about Andrew's and Eve's faith. Did they believe in the new religion or the old one? Andrew and Eve shared a look. It was a dangerous question.

They were spared answering when the jailer arrived with stale bread and water. That was all they would get from him. "Do not ask me any questions, because I have no answers to give," he said sourly.

Andrew nibbled on the bread, then lay down on the cold stone floor. He wondered what had become of William and Matthew. He wondered what time it was. He wondered if they would ever get out of the jail or if they would be stuck there for "days and days." He fell asleep thinking of questions he couldn't answer.

Deep in the night, Andrew felt a sharp kick strike his leg.

"Wake up," Eve said.

Andrew sat up. A dim light from the corridor showed Eve standing in the middle of the cell. Marjorie was cowering in the corner. Peter rubbed his eyes, looking as if he had just awakened.

"Speak! What wast thou doing?" Eve demanded.

The little girl gave a tiny whimper.

"What happened?" Andrew asked, standing up.

"She tried to steal my necklace," Eve said, clasping the locket that held the Radiant Stone.

"Nay!" the girl cried. "It came out from under your clothes. I hoped it was a crucifix. I desired only to touch the holy item and pray."

Eve frowned. "Thou should have asked."

"I am heartily sorry," Marjorie said. She tucked in close to her brother. He put a protective arm around her and glared at Eve.

Eve sat down and slipped the locket under her dress collar.

"Do you have a crucifix?" the girl asked.

Andrew touched Eve's arm to stop her from answering. The question sounded to him like a trick. If either of them had a crucifix, it would prove they were Catholics. If not, they might be considered Protestants.

"If thou wouldst pray, then say the 'Our Father,'" Andrew suggested.

"Aye, sir," Marjorie said. But she didn't pray at that moment.

Turning his back to the two children, Andrew drew close to Eve and whispered, "Why do you have *that*?" He gestured to the locket.

"I was afraid the wagon might be searched again," she whispered back.

What if you're searched? he wanted to ask but realized it was a gamble no matter where they hid the stone. He gave her a quick nod.

Eve lay down again, pulling her dress tightly around her. Andrew turned to the children. They had closed their eyes. He settled on the floor again and dozed off.

Noises at the door jarred Andrew awake. A dull-gray morning light now filled the little cell. The door was yanked open. The jailer stood in the passage.

"Out with you," he said.

"You are letting us go?" Eve asked as she got to her feet.

CHAPTER SIX

"Wouldst thou rather stay?" the jailer asked gruffly.

Andrew stood up. His back and knees hurt. "All of us? Them as well?" He hooked a thumb at the two children.

"They can go whenever they want," the jailer said. "I cannot get rid of them."

Andrew looked at him, puzzled. What did that mean?

Peter suddenly pointed at Eve. "She is a Catholic," he said. "She possesses a Catholic necklace. Marjorie saw it in the night."

Eve put a hand to her neck. "'Tis not a Catholic necklace!"

"They are Catholics!" Marjorie shrieked.

"Show me thy necklace," the jailer said. He held out a hand to Eve.

"Give us our reward," Marjorie said, dancing from one foot to the other.

The jailer pushed her away. "Begone! Await me at my desk," he said.

Peter and Marjorie scampered out of the cell. Marjorie gave Eve a final look of victory before she disappeared around the corner.

The jailer pushed his fat palm closer to Eve. "Pray, give it me or suffer a lash."

"'Tis only a family keepsake of little worth," Eve said. She slowly lifted the chain over her head. Rather than hand him the locket, she held it up for him to see.

"Wicked child," the jailer said and snatched it from her.

Andrew slowly drifted between the jailer and the door. He worried the jailer might steal the stone.

The man held up the locket by the chain. He watched it twirl in the dim light. "What is inside? How dost thou open the case?"

"'Tis a stone, coated with poison," Andrew said. "The case protects the one who carries it."

"Why wouldst thou carry a poisoned stone?" the jailer asked Eve. He thrust the locket toward her but held on to the chain. "Open it."

Eve touched the small nob at the top of the locket. The front sprung open. Even in the dim morning light, the Radiant Stone seemed to sparkle and glow.

The jailer eyed it with obvious greed. "What manner of gem is that?" He jerked on the chain, pulling the locket away from her.

"Stop!" Eve said, reaching to take the locket back.

The jailer knocked her hand away. "'Tis a curious thing," he said as his forefinger touched the stone.

In an instant, the jailer disappeared.

7

Eve put a hand over her mouth. Andrew stepped forward as if he might grab the man somehow. But the jailer was gone.

"No, no, no, no!" Eve said. She felt dizzy. "He took the stone with him," she said to Andrew.

Andrew looked dumbfounded. He pointed to the open door. "Should we run?"

"And do *what* without the stone?" Eve snapped. She placed her hand against the wall to steady herself. Her heart pounded frantically in her chest. *What are we supposed to do?* she thought.

The sound of footfalls came from the passage. The High Sheriff appeared in the open doorway. William stood behind him. Then, to Eve's surprise, Matthew also came into view.

"Why are you here? Master Dovedale was told to release you," the High Sheriff asked the kids.

Andrew began by stammering, "We ... uh ... we were ... uh ..." but made it no further than that.

"Where is Dovedale?" the High Sheriff asked impatiently.

Suddenly a loud cry came from the front of the jail. The screams of the two children quickly followed.

"How now?" the High Sheriff asked as he sprinted away. Matthew followed him.

William lingered, looking bewildered. "What have you done?" he asked Andrew and Eve. Another shout caught his attention and he dashed away.

Eve was hot on his heels, with Andrew pressing in behind her. They came to the small office in the front. It was chaos there.

Peter and Marjorie were behind the desk, screaming and pointing.

Anthony Dovedale was lying on the floor, curled up in a ball and shaking violently. He was dressed in rags. Patches of his pale face shone through streaks of black soot.

"By the rood!" the High Sheriff shouted.

Wild eyed, the jailer scrambled to his feet and let loose a torrent of words. "Caves and ... and ... pagans ... and ... the stone! The *stone*!" He held up the Radiant Stone by the chain, his eyes the size of dinner plates.

"Make sense, man!" the High Sheriff shouted. He moved toward the jailer. "Thou art spouting gibberish!"

"A wizard!" the jailer screamed. He saw Eve and threw the locket at her as if he couldn't bear to touch it any longer. It hit her arm and fell to the floor. Eve quickly snatched it up.

Peter pointed at the jailer again and said, "He came from nowhere!" Both children began screaming again.

"*Be still!*" the High Sheriff yelled at the children.

Peter and Marjorie drew back, cowering.

The jailer was quivering, his ragged head jerking in one direction and then another. He mumbled random words again.

Eve knew what had happened. Anthony Dovedale had traveled somewhere back in time. Perhaps he had landed in a cave. Perhaps he had come across people he thought were pagans or wizards. There was no knowing for sure. She had no intention of asking him.

"Hast thou been drinking again?" the High Sheriff yelled at the jailer.

Anthony Dovedale shook his head and muttered softly.

"Must we remain for this spectacle?" William asked.

The High Sheriff turned, an impatient look on his face. "Go! A pox upon me! The man is a babbling idiot."

William waved his hand for Eve and Andrew to go. Matthew followed.

The High Sheriff jabbed a finger at the two smaller children. "Irksome creatures, begone!" he snapped.

Given the chance to escape, Peter and Marjorie dashed past them all through the doorway.

William was the last one to leave. He closed the door behind him and gave Eve a curious look.

From the street, they could hear the jailer's voice rising to a shrill pitch. But nothing he said made any sense.

The wagon and horse were stabled at the far end of the main street. William and Matthew quickly hitched up the horse. The four travelers crowded onto the driver's bench, with William at the reins. They passed through a towered gate and onto a bridge. Once they reached the other side, a road took them left, along the outside of the city wall.

None of them spoke. The clip-clopping of the horse and the irregular scraping sound of the wheels on the uneven dirt road were as much noise as anyone seemed to want. Eve waited and wondered when one of the two men might ask about the jailer and the stone.

William spoke first, with a question for the kids. "Were you asked about Edmund Campion?"

"Aye," said Andrew.

"'Tis as we feared," Matthew said. "We must delay our journey to London."

"Why?" Eve asked.

William frowned. "Too many eyes are upon the roads. The scene at the jail may draw hunters to us. We shall travel forth to Reading. By God's grace, guidance will be given there."

Matthew turned to Eve and Andrew. "Ambrosius warned us of the power of the stones," he said. "For my part, I would rather know nothing more than what I have seen this day. Some mysteries are best left as mysteries."

"I am sorry," Eve said. "I should not have been carrying the stone. As soon as we stop, I shall hide it in the secret compartment again."

"We departed without a meal," William complained. "Robbed of supper, robbed of breakfast, robbed of any of the delicious food from a Winchester inn. Alas!"

"Thou fillest me with guilt," said Matthew. "I had a delightful meal at the home of Lady West."

"Do not speak of it," William said with a groan.

"How did you find us at the jail?" Andrew asked Matthew.

"'Twas Benjamin Beard who found me and took me there," Matthew replied. "I was given little choice in the matter."

"I pray we see no more of that vile man," said William. "His zeal strains my patience."

Outside a village called Alresford, William drove the wagon off the path. They bounced onto a narrow patch of land between the road and the edge of a forest. He reined the horse to a stop. The four climbed down to inspect their stores of food. Eve used the opportunity to put the Radiant Stone back in its hiding place in the wagon.

William brought out a loaf of brown bread with butter and currants, some salted fish, and pickled herring. He spread them out on a blanket like a king's feast. He also passed around a jug of watered-down wine.

The sky threatened rain the entire time they ate, but none came. The clouds hung heavy like a warning.

As they finished their meal, Eve heard a low rumbling. She looked up, assuming it was thunder. Then she realized the noise was coming from the south. All four of them turned to look. A dozen men on horseback were racing down the road at full speed.

"Pray they are not for us," Matthew said.

They were.

The lead rider was Benjamin Beard from Nether Wallop. Like a herd on the run, the riders left the road and rode toward the travelers, soon circling their campsite.

"Hail, fellows!" William called out. "Are you here to search our wagon again?"

Benjamin leapt from his horse and strode to the priest. "Nay, foul spawn of Satan. We come to do justice, in the name of the queen."

"Justice of what sort?" William asked. "The queen's justice takes many forms."

"Were it within my power, I would hang each of thee by the neck from the branches of yonder oaks!" Benjamin snarled.

William looked offended. "Pray tell, good man, what offense have we caused to warrant thy wrath? Surely our performance yesterday was not so dire. Or dost thou accuse us once more of popery?"

"I accuse thee of witchcraft!" Benjamin shouted.

"Witchcraft!" William cried out. The cheerful expression on his face turned to something far more serious. Eve thought that if William hadn't been a priest, he might have punched Benjamin.

"Aye," said Benjamin. "The *girl*! The unnatural color of her eyes surely tells of her companionship with the dark angel."

"Oh, brother," Eve said. She had hoped that the color of her eyes wouldn't cause any problems here, as it often had in other times and places.

"Show me the stone that made the city jailer stark-raving mad," Benjamin demanded.

"We have no such stone," Matthew said. "If the city jailer is stark-raving mad, then that is his business and hath nothing to do with us."

"It hath *everything* to do with you!" Benjamin fumed.

The men with Benjamin had quietly dismounted. Eve thought they looked enraged, ready to attack if they were given an excuse. Two of the men had their backs to her. They were doing something, but she couldn't see what.

"If thou canst find a stone with the powers of which thou speakest, then search and lay claim to it," Matthew challenged him.

"I will not waste my time attempting to find your hiding places." Benjamin signaled the two men who had been facing away from them. They swung around, two torches in each hand. They gave one torch to Benjamin and another to a burly man nearby. The four men then moved toward the wagon.

Matthew put himself in Benjamin's path. "Pray, what dost thou intend?" he asked.

Without a word, Benjamin slammed a fist against the side of Matthew's face. Matthew tumbled aside and dropped to his knees.

William came forward with his fists clenched. One of the other men swung a club and struck him on the head from behind. William fell like a dead weight to the ground.

Hands seemed to come from nowhere and grab Eve. She struggled but was held firm. Another of the thugs caught Andrew. He fought back but was also restrained.

Eve heard a shout from the front of the wagon. A man was shooing the horse away. It trotted a few yards toward the road, then looked back, as if watching to see what would happen next.

The four men took the flaming torches to the wagon, spreading out to different corners.

"Purge it with fire!" Benjamin shouted.

The torches were held against the wagon. Parts of the wood caught fire quickly; other parts smoldered. One of the men came from the forest with an armload of branches. He tossed them through the back doorway of the caravan. Benjamin set them alight.

CHAPTER SEVEN

Matthew tried to stand but was knocked down again. William slowly came to and sat up with a great effort. Eve thought she saw blood in his thick head of hair.

She strained against the hands that held her. Panic surged like boiling water through her veins. She could feel tears burning in her eyes.

"There is nothing we can do," Andrew said next to her. The man holding him relaxed, his eyes on the fire.

Eve turned to Andrew. "*Radiant*" was all she said.

Andrew looked at her face, then his eyes went to her neck. They widened and shot over to the wagon. Then Eve saw his expression change to one of sharp determination.

Andrew broke free from his captor and bolted to the wagon.

One of the men nearby reached for him, but Andrew sidestepped his grasp. Benjamin spun around from where he stood and also dove for the boy. But Andrew leapt over him like a deer over a fallen log. Then, with a bound, he threw himself into the back of the wagon and disappeared in a cloud of smoke.

Eve heard screaming and realized it was her own voice.

The back of the wagon was engulfed in flames. Part of the roof collapsed.

Matthew and William now fought against the men guarding them. Fists flew in all directions. The hands clasping Eve tightened. She thought they would have to wrap around her throat to stop her from screaming.

All eyes were on the wagon now. Was there any way Andrew could escape?

Then came a terrifying explosion, and a great wave of fire devoured the wagon.

Eve's scream stopped. She couldn't breathe now. Darkness overtook her.

8

Eve opened her eyes.

She was propped up against a tree. Matthew was leaning over her, pressing a damp cloth against her forehead. His eyes were red-rimmed. She looked past him to the wagon. It was a ball of fire. Smoke rose like a pillar into the slate-gray sky. William was on his knees several yards from the burning wreck. Eve couldn't tell whether he was praying or weeping.

The men from the mob stood farther away. A couple of them had climbed back onto their horses. Each of them wore stunned expressions, except one. Benjamin paced back and forth. Eve couldn't make out what he was saying, but his gestures made her think that he was berating his men. He kept pointing to William.

Eve felt as though her brain had gone numb. There was a high-pitched ringing in her ears. She looked at the wagon again and squeezed her eyes shut. *Andrew*, she thought and wanted to scream again. She rubbed her eyes and tried to think. That was hard too.

Matthew straightened, and she watched him cross the distance between her and Benjamin in long strides. He was shouting at Benjamin. The rest of the men mounted their horses and spurred them to move. Soon, Benjamin stood alone, facing a red-faced Matthew.

Eve thought she heard him shout the word *murderer*.

William was on his feet now and went to Matthew. His hands were raised. He stepped between Matthew and Benjamin. With one hand, he held Matthew back. With the other, he gestured at Benjamin.

"In the name of God, depart!" William cried out.

Eve's gaze slowly returned to the wagon. She hoped that Andrew had escaped somehow. But he'd only just leapt into the wagon when the roof caved in. The explosion came only a few seconds after that.

She began to cry again, even as she told herself that he couldn't be dead. *It's not possible. He can't die outside his real time.*

She was hardly aware of the sound of a horse galloping away. A quick glance, and she saw Benjamin racing down the road. She shook her head and sobbed.

"What has happened?" Andrew asked her.

She turned toward his voice. He was sitting next to her. His face was smudged with soot. Patches of red appeared in streaks across his cheeks. His hair stuck up at wild angles.

I'm dreaming, she thought. *I passed out again, and now I'm dreaming.*

"Why are you crying?" Andrew asked.

She was willing to play along with the dream. "Because you *died*, you idiot! Why did you go into the wagon? It was on fire!"

He looked hurt. "You left the Radiant Stone inside. I went to get it. And I did," he said and held out his hand. The locket with the stone was there. "I got the purses of money, too," he said proudly. Then he frowned. "Except ... I don't know how it happened. It's really fuzzy."

She gazed at him. He gazed back at her.

"What?" he asked.

She reached out to his face. Her fingers brushed real skin. "Andrew?" she whispered.

"What?" he asked again.

She shrieked and threw herself at him, wrapping her arms around his neck. He lost his balance, and they both tumbled into a patch of leaves.

"Cut it out!" Andrew shouted, pushing her away.

Then William grabbed them and shouted, "God be praised!"

Matthew came over and caught Andrew with both hands, lifting him to his feet and embracing him. Breathlessly, Matthew said, "Thou shouldst be dead! How art thou living?"

Andrew suddenly looked unsure of himself. "I know not," he said.

Eve saw his expression and knew that he *did* know something.

The blackened remains of the wagon now smoldered. Thin lines of smoke drifted up like black ink scribbling in the air. One wheel remained, tilting the wagon to one side. Half of the front wall and the driver's bench were still intact. Matthew said he was grateful for that much. He then went to the driver's bench and reached underneath. After fiddling with something for a moment, he said, "Thanks be to God!" and brought out a rectangular metal box. Inside he had hidden a prayer book, a crucifix, and a few other priestly items.

William poked at the charred wreckage with a long stick. He occasionally pulled out a small box or a piece of clothing, as if in the hope it would be useful, only to throw it back again. Their costumes were ashes.

"The explosion must have been our jars of makeup," Matthew said.

Eve kept an eye on Andrew. He hadn't moved from his spot next to the tree. She thought he looked tired, perhaps even stunned. He stared at nothing and seemed slow to answer questions. She wanted to ask him what had really happened inside the wagon but decided to wait.

With a happy shout, William yanked at something in the pile. With both hands, he pulled out a trunk. He made noises as if the wood was still hot, flapping his hands and then trying to get a better grip. Finally he had the trunk on the ground. The clasps were warped, so it took both men to wrench the lid open.

Inside the trunk were various scorched scripts, along with items of clothing and shoes. William called out to

Eve and Andrew. He held up the clothes they had worn from the twenty-first century. Eve had forgotten all about them. She was glad to see they hadn't burned up. She nudged Andrew. He nodded to acknowledge the find but said nothing. Then he leaned back against the tree and closed his eyes.

The horse hadn't ventured far from where it had stood in the field earlier. William tied what was left of their possessions into bundles or placed them in a couple of small sacks he'd recovered. Then he secured them onto the beast's back. "We shall have to walk," he said. He looked up at the sky. " 'Tis late, but I fear Benjamin will yet return for us with another violent crowd. Let us put a greater distance between us and them."

"How is Benjamin allowed to do this to us?" Eve asked.

Matthew said, "To be accused of the Catholic faith is to forfeit our rights. There is no justice for what they have done here."

"Certainly not for a pair of actors or their servants," William added.

Eve retrieved Andrew from his place under the tree, and the four of them gathered around the horse. William said a soft prayer, thanking God for their safety and asking for strength and courage on the journey ahead.

They marched slowly and silently for half a dozen hours, stopping only to find water and rest for a few minutes at a time. Eve was aware that every unidentified noise from the woods or the fields made her jump. She expected a mob of men or thieves to come at them from every possible direction.

"Basingstoke is ahead," William announced. "A lovely market town. There is an inn called the White Hart. We will stay there, thanks to Andrew saving our purses."

The town was dark and still by the time they arrived later that night. It took a lot of pounding on the door to rouse the innkeeper at the White Hart. When he opened the door and saw William, he smiled and warmly invited them all in. With sharp shouts, the innkeeper roused his sleepy-eyed servants. A boy took the horse down a passage alongside the inn. Two other servants took bundles from the horse and disappeared through a doorway to a hall.

The innkeeper offered the travelers some leftover sausages and vegetables and some pints of ale while he prepared their chambers.

The "chambers" were two small rooms in the back of the inn. There was hardly enough space for William and Matthew in one room, so Andrew and Eve went to the other. A four-poster bed with curtains around it dominated the space. The mattress was made of feathers and rested on a straw mat that was slung to the bed frame by ropes underneath. A gentle fragrance came from a tin plate filled with dried flowers on a nearby table.

Andrew insisted that Eve sleep on the bed. He made himself comfortable on a makeshift cot—something the innkeeper called a *truckle bed*. It was there for any servants traveling with their masters.

With the single candle blown out, Eve lay in the darkness and thought about the burning wagon. In her mind she replayed Andrew rushing to the rear door and leaping inside the wagon. She saw the roof collapse and even winced at the memory of the explosion. She sat up.

"Andrew," she whispered.

"Hmm?" he responded.

"What really happened in the wagon?" she asked.

She heard him shuffle. The floorboards creaked.

"I think I was hit on the head," he finally said. "What happened doesn't make any sense."

"Tell me anyway."

He hesitated, then cleared his throat and began. "When I jumped into the wagon, I knew I'd made a big mistake. The fire was all around. I wasn't even sure I could get to the secret compartment. So I was about to jump out again when …"

Andrew was quiet.

Eve prodded him. "When what?"

"When a *hand* grabbed my arm and pulled me in," he said.

"A hand?" Eve asked. "Whose hand? No one else was in there."

"I *know*," Andrew said. "Let me finish. A hand pulled me in. And it was a good thing, too, because the roof would have fallen on me if I'd tried to get out that way. The hand pulled me inside, and I turned and—*I'm not making this up*—Ambrosius was there."

Eve gasped. "Ambrosius!"

"He was just standing there in those weird clothes of his. He had the locket and the purses in his hand. He gave them to me and said, 'Hold fast.' Then he grabbed my shoulder and ... and ... we *disappeared.*"

"You disappeared like we disappear when we travel in time?" Eve asked.

He shook his head. "We didn't travel in time. The next thing I knew, we were standing in the forest—away from everyone. I could see the burning wagon through the trees. I could hear the voices. Ambrosius looked at me and said, 'Foolish boy. Why wouldst thou rush headlong into a burning wagon?' I told him I went in to save the stone. He said, 'The stone hath not lasted all these years to be destroyed by ignorant men and their fire.' Before I could say anything, he was gone."

"He walked away?"

"No. He disappeared again," Andrew explained. "I stood there and thought, *I can't go out in front of everybody*. So I waited. And the longer I waited, the fuzzier the whole thing became. It was like I had dreamed it. By the time I found you by the tree, I was confused about what happened."

Eve thought about it. "Ambrosius is the Guardian of the Stone. He has one of his own," she reminded him.

CHAPTER EIGHT

"But he used it to go to the wagon at that *exact* time," Andrew said. "How could he know to be there right then?"

Eve gave a slight shrug. For everything she thought she knew about the stones, she realized she still didn't know much at all.

"Maybe I'm wrong," Andrew said. "Maybe I breathed in too much smoke or hit my head on something."

"But you have the Radiant Stone and the money," Eve said. "You couldn't have rescued them from the secret compartment in the few seconds you were inside the wagon. And you *escaped*."

He slowly exhaled. "It's so confusing," he said.

"I believe Ambrosius was there," Eve said firmly. "I don't know how he did it, but he was there."

9

Eve awakened the next morning feeling anxious. They were in a new town, and that meant a new chance to be stopped or interrogated or even arrested for being Catholic. She had never felt so unsafe before. Not even when she was running all over the woods with Robin Hood and his men, or fighting in battles with Joan of Arc. In both places, she knew who and where her enemies were. Now there was no way to know until they were right in front of her.

She said as much to Andrew when they walked out to the main hall of the inn.

"I feel the same way," he admitted. "I keep looking over my shoulder, scared that someone is going to grab me."

The hall was a large room, open to the rafters. A broad stone hearth made up a far wall. Black pots of various sizes hung on iron frames.

There were a handful of people sitting at long bench-like tables. Andrew lowered his voice. "Any one of these people might be out to get us," he said.

"Don't say that," Eve scolded him, looking around nervously.

The innkeeper who had opened the door for them during the night was busy at a massive oak cupboard. Eve could see that the door to the left of the cupboard led through to a kitchen, where cooks were preparing food on a vast table. The innkeeper turned and carried two plates of food to customers at the end of a table.

The man saw Eve and Andrew. "You will find your actors outside," he said and poked a finger at a side door.

The door led them to a cobblestone courtyard. The horse was already hitched up to a simple open-topped wagon—nothing as fun as the one that had been burned.

"I am sure I paid more than I should have," Matthew explained. He pushed at one of the wooden sides. It rattled loudly. One of the slats looked as if it might come loose.

"We are in no position to haggle," said William.

"Do we have cause to linger here?" Matthew asked the two kids.

Andrew shook his head.

"No performance today?" Eve asked.

"No costumes," William said. He leaned closer and said, " 'Tis best for us to find a safe haven. I fear for our lives after the events of yesterday." He patted Andrew on the shoulder as if to acknowledge how close the boy had come to death itself.

CHAPTER NINE

Eve and Andrew climbed into the back of the wagon, while William and Matthew took the driver's bench. Eve was grateful they weren't walking all the way to Reading. Her legs ached.

Basingstoke sat at a crossroads that had made it a popular stopping point all the way back to Roman days. There was a square in the center for the weekly market. Eve saw only four main streets. One led to a church, and another led to a town hall. The main road connected Winchester to London. Small shops for bakers, butchers, tailors, and blacksmiths sat on each side of the street.

The wagon seemed to catch every rut, hole, and ridge on the road. Andrew and Eve bounced up and down and were thrown from side to side. Trying to have a conversation was impossible, so the two silently held on to the sides of the wagon.

They reached the town of Reading by midafternoon. They entered on a road lined with houses, just like Winchester. A bridge took them over a broad river into the town center. Crowded with merchants and customers, the town seemed larger than any of the others Eve had seen.

They came to a square where a town crier declared the latest news to the dozens of people who had gathered to listen. Eve heard him say the name *Edmund Campion*, with a warning to be watchful for him or any other "Catholic traitors" in their midst.

"Beware of strangers!" the crier shouted.

Eve felt sure that the eyes of those in the crowd suddenly fixed on her.

She averted her gaze, and it landed on the lonely ruins of an abbey off to the right. It reminded her of the ruin at Glastonbury. She crawled over to the driver's seat and, rising onto her knees, asked, "What happened there?"

Matthew said over his shoulder, "Reading Abbey was dissolved by King Henry more than forty years ago. The abbot, Hugh Faringdon, was convicted of treason and executed. The land was sold off."

"It must have been beautiful in its time," Eve said.

"I am told that it was," Matthew said sadly.

Andrew came alongside Eve and asked, "Are *all* of the Catholic buildings wrecked in England?"

"Alas, they are," said Matthew.

They followed the street as it curved around to the west, then turned north again. They were soon out of the town. Eve felt relieved. After a mile or so, William drove the horse from the road onto a narrow track along a barren field.

"This land belongs to the Josephs family," Matthew said. "They are faithful Catholics. Arthur Josephs is a merchant, a seller of many things, mostly wool. Margaret, his wife, is a virtuous woman. The lady spends her time in prayer and needlework, and oft she sews vestments for the priests who have visited her hither. Their children are grown and live nearer to Oxford. The servants are Catholic, though we must not take that for granted.

Any one of those folk could be bribed to betray the family."

They came to a house made of sand-colored stone. It was an enormous rectangle, with chimneys at each end. Rather than bring the wagon up to the large front door, William continued around to the back of the house. They stopped at a courtyard cluttered with barrels, crates, and baskets. Chickens wandered aimlessly around the courtyard. Somewhere, sheep were bleating. A goat stood under the eaves of a low-ceilinged stable.

A servant carrying a tub emerged from a back door. She saw the wagon and gave the travelers a startled look. She tossed the tub aside and ran back through the doorway.

"Are we sure we are welcome?" Matthew asked William.

"We will find out in a moment," William replied, then leapt from the wagon.

A woman wearing a gold-and-red dress stepped outside. She had a lean face and a long nose, with wide eyes set atop high cheekbones. She wore a white hat that looked like a bonnet. It was held in place on her silver hair with lace that tied under her narrow chin. At first she looked at them anxiously. Then her eyes caught William's face, then Matthew's, and her whole expression lit up.

"God save you, Lady Josephs," William said, bowing to her.

Matthew slid off the driver's bench and went to her. She clasped his hands in hers and said warmly, "My dear Father Matthew!"

"We apologize for not warning you of our coming," Matthew explained. "We had unexpected trouble."

"You gave Agnes quite a fright. The girl feared you were priest hunters. I bid you, friends, to enter," she said. Then she noticed Andrew and Eve in the back of the wagon. She beckoned for them to join the others.

"The children have journeyed with us from Glastonbury," William explained as Eve and Andrew presented themselves. "We are delivering them to London on behalf of Ambrosius."

The woman's eyebrows lifted. "He is alive and well?"

"Indeed, my lady. Very much so," said Matthew.

Lady Josephs moved to Andrew and Eve, then put her hands on their heads like a kind of blessing. "God save you, dear children."

The party went inside, passing through a sizable kitchen. The servant named Agnes now stood against one of the walls, her hands clasped in front of her and her head lowered. Eve wondered if she knew that William and Matthew were priests. Perhaps this was her way of showing respect.

Eve caught glimpses of several smaller rooms off to the side of the kitchen. One had fat barrels. Another was filled with giant wheels of cheese. Another had different-sized pans, buckets, and oversized iron utensils hanging from the ceiling.

They went through a doorway and into a passage with flagstone flooring. The passage stretched alongside a staircase. They then came to a foyer and a wide front door made of oak. To the right was an archway that led to a Great Hall. A gigantic wooden table dominated the room. A dozen chairs lined each side. Ornate candleholders were spread down the center of the table. There was a wide hutch on one wall and a narrow serving table on another. An enormous hearth took up most of the far wall. The ceiling went up to the very rafters of the house.

Eve was staring at this gigantic room when she heard a "pssst" from Andrew. She spun and saw that the rest of the group had moved left. She stepped quickly to catch up and passed through another archway into a parlor. Unlike the Great Hall, this room was cozier, with a low ceiling and dark paneling on the lower half of the walls. Above the paneling hung neat rows of framed paintings of stern-looking faces and the English countryside. Two broad windows gave a golden light to the room. A carpet bearing a deep-red-and-black design covered most of the floor. There were cushioned chairs of various sizes, a long couch, and small tables. A modest-sized fireplace was centered on the far wall, with a chimney that disappeared into the ceiling.

Lady Josephs asked them to sit down. No sooner had they obeyed than three servants arrived from adjoining rooms. They moved the small tables to positions in front of the guests.

"You must be famished from your long journey," Lady Josephs said.

The servants exited as quickly as they had entered.

Lady Josephs watched them, as if making sure they were out of earshot. Then she said softly, "We are cautious. The search for Edmund Campion is a feverish frenzy. Watchers are everywhere."

"Hath Campion been here?" Matthew asked in a hushed tone.

"The gentleman hath not graced us with his presence. 'Tis said he hath visited the Yate family at Lyford. Those are but rumors. 'Tis all we hear."

"Where is your good husband?" asked William.

"My lord is at our London home, conducting business. I do not expect him for another week," she said at a greater volume, as if for the benefit of any eavesdropping servants. Then she lowered her voice again. "If you are bound for London, you must go to him. Until that time, make this your home so that we may be assured of your safety."

The servants returned with trays of food—bread, cheese, sliced vegetables, and meats. Silver cups contained something that tasted to Eve like weak wine.

The conversation returned to Edmund Campion, but Eve noticed that they spoke as if they were merely interested in him as a news topic. It seemed like the way they might talk about a new law or the economy.

Finally Andrew said, "I keep hearing his name, but I know not why Edmund Campion is so important."

The grown-ups looked at him in surprise.

"Why should a mere child know the man?" Lady Josephs asked. "Why should anyone?"

"Let us explain," said Matthew.

The three adults took turns telling Andrew about Edmund Campion. He had once been a popular young man as a student at Oxford University. The nobility, even Queen Elizabeth, were taken by his charm and intelligence. He would do great things, they thought. But then he shocked everyone by embracing the Catholic faith.

It was a scandalous decision, made at the worst time possible. Queen Elizabeth viewed Catholics as a threat, especially after many in the north had united to rebel against her. Her armies defeated them. But later, Pope Pius the Fifth excommunicated her, thus releasing her Catholic subjects from any obligation to obey her. The queen and her Privy Council assumed that Catholics all over the country would rise up against her. Laws were put in place to force Catholics to join the Church of England. When that failed, the laws forbade Catholics from practicing their faith at all. The Queen's Privy Council made allegiance to the Pope illegal. To be a faithful Catholic meant accusations of high treason and a sentence of death.

Edmund Campion fled England for France. He studied and became a priest with the Society of Jesus, an order that Saint Ignatius of Loyola established only a few decades before. Campion taught at colleges throughout Europe. Then, in Rome, Pope Gregory the Thirteenth blessed Campion to engage in a secret mission to England. His purpose was to find and encourage Catholics through preaching and delivering the Sacraments. Political activism and rebellion against the queen were forbidden.

Father Campion, Father Robert Persons, and a handful of other priests sailed to England in June. Using an underground network, Campion traveled throughout the northern part of the country. His work was so effective that the Queen's Privy Council officially banished all Jesuit priests from the country. It became a crime to welcome them, help them, or worship with them. Campion became England's most wanted man. Yet very few people knew where he was.

Lady Josephs now laughed. "Rumors have placed him in Middlesex, Berkshire, Oxfordshire, and Northamptonshire—all at the same time!"

"We know Father Campion is meant to return to London soon," Matthew said. Then, in a whisper, he added, "William and I desire to join his effort."

Lady Josephs shot a glance at the door, then said abruptly, "For now, you must refresh yourselves! My good servants will show you to your rooms."

Eve's room was furnished with a four-poster bed, a cushioned chair, end tables, and a wardrobe. Agnes was Eve's attendant and stood by, waiting for Eve to get rid of her dusty clothes. Eve began to undress but felt awkward with Agnes watching her with a puzzled expression on her face. Then the girl's eyes lit up when Eve took the Radiant Stone locket from around her neck.

"Pardon me, miss, but I ne'er have seen a locket of that size," Agnes said.

"Where may I put it for safekeeping?" Eve asked.

"Everywhere in this house is safe," Agnes said.

Eve hung the locket on one of the bedposts. She looked at the stack of linens. "Why so many? Am I that filthy?"

Agnes seemed even more puzzled now. "One is for thy hair, another for thy feet, another for thy legs, another for thy upper body ... Dost thou not have linens where thou livest?"

"Just one, to dry off after I have bathed," Eve explained.

"Bathed? Art thou often ill?"

"Nay. Must I be ill to enjoy a bath?" Eve asked.

"Aye, mistress," said Agnes, frowning. "However, 'twill take time. Thither is the firewood to be laid, and the water to be heated. I have heard it said that the queen herself bathes but once a month."

"Once a *month*?"

"Why would her highness desire more than that?" Agnes asked. "Rubbed down with clean linens is a far better way to be clean."

Eve decided not to argue. She took one of the linens and rubbed her face. As she did, Agnes knelt down and began to wipe her feet. Eve leapt back. "What dost thou?" Eve cried.

"My duty," Agnes said. "My lady will be angry if I do not serve thee."

Eve rolled her eyes, then nodded. She felt like a two-year-old being scrubbed by her mother. But by the end, she had to admit that she felt as clean as if she'd had a full bath.

"Thy clothes will be laundered before the morn," Agnes said.

"What am I to wear now?"

Agnes went to a tall wardrobe and brought out a pale-blue gown. Gold swirls were embroidered all over, with small pearls stitched in where the swirls met. The skirt of the gown spread out from the waist and looked like a church bell.

Eve took the dress and held it against her body. It looked as if it would fit. "I thank thee," she said, then added, "I can dress myself."

Agnes frowned. "Then thou wilt want thy other garments." She went to the drawers of a large dresser and began to bring out a variety of garments that she laid on the bed.

"What are these?" Eve asked, looking at all the clothes.

Agnes gazed at her as if she couldn't imagine being asked such a question. Then, like talking to a small child, she began a show-and-tell.

She held up a long tunic that she called a *smock* and explained that it was worn closest to the body. She lifted up a pair of silk stockings, then a kind of vest with sleeves

CHAPTER NINE

attached, which would fill out the dress. The sleeves were lined with pearls. Then came a corset and a red petticoat. Agnes then produced a fabric-covered frame called a *farthingale* which would give shape to the skirt of the dress. There was also a *stomacher* that was pressed against the wearer's stomach. It covered the undergarment where the top of the dress was left open (according to the latest style from London). A *kirtle* covered the laces on the garments. After all those, Agnes said, Eve would put on the gown. Then the servant pointed to another vest that she called a *jerkin*. It was to be worn over the top of the gown and buttoned down. The jerkin was designed to spread out at the shoulders, like wings.

Eve was shocked. "Must I wear *all* of these?"

"Aye, miss," Agnes said, then went to the door.

"Wait," Eve called out. "I need thy help after all."

Agnes smiled, then summoned another maidservant to come in. Both women helped Eve.

By the time she was dressed, Eve thought, *No wonder they needed so many servants back then.*

"Miss, thou art a beauty," Agnes proclaimed.

"I cannot breathe," said Eve.

The maidservants giggled.

Agnes led Eve through the parlor to a long corridor that took them past three other rooms, each as large as the parlor. One was filled with shelves and books. Another was an office, with a spacious desk in the middle and maps and charts hanging on the walls. The third looked to Eve like a crafts room. It had a loom, a spinning wheel, tables for sewing, and fabrics and threads draped on racks.

The Garden Room was at the very back of the house. Windows looked out onto a walled-in garden. The late-afternoon sun gave the room a warm glow. A pair of doors opened to a patio. Flowers of orange, purple, yellow, pink, and white filled the carefully planned beds that lined the stone pavement. Ivy covered the brick walls.

Andrew was standing behind a chair at the dining table when Eve entered. He stepped from behind the chair and bowed. Eve saw that he was dressed more formally than before. His waistcoat was a now a rich red, and his doublet had a pattern of blues, reds, and browns. His tan belt was loosely tied around his waist, draping down to the lower part of the doublet. His breeches were a royal green and went down as far as his knees. Dark-brown laces held up his tan stockings. The brown leather shoes he wore looked like slippers.

"Impressive," Eve said.

Andrew blushed. He gestured to her and said, "That dress is very ... ummm ... *girly*."

She was unsure whether he meant it as a compliment. She curtsied anyway.

William and Matthew came into the room with Lady Josephs. She was now wearing a more formal-looking

CHAPTER NINE

gown, like Eve's. William and Matthew wore grown-up versions of Andrew's outfit. Eve thought it was curious that Lady Josephs had clothes ready for unexpected guests of different ages.

Lady Josephs asked Matthew to say grace for the meal. He obliged, daring to end with the Sign of the Cross.

They sat down at the table, with Lady Josephs at the head and William and Matthew on each side. Andrew sat next to William, and Eve sat next to Matthew. The place setting was basic: a large silver plate with a cup, a sharp knife, and a spoon. In front of Lady Josephs sat a silver bowl with something that looked like salt, and another bowl with pepper.

No fork, Eve thought.

Lady Josephs clapped her hands. "The first course," she said, then added, "Eat no more than you can bear. We take no offense by what you leave."

Servants entered with huge trays and distributed a leafy salad with boiled eggs, smoked and pickled herring, salmon with a kind of mustard sauce, and a few fish that Eve couldn't identify. Eve watched how William and Matthew used their knives and spoons to make up for the lack of a fork. They ate silently.

Soon, that part of the meal was finished, and the servants took everything away.

Lady Josephs asked a few questions about their journey from Glastonbury to Reading. She was alarmed to hear about the jail, the mobs, and the destruction of the wagon.

The second course arrived as the servants brought in gigantic trays laden with various meats. Eve recognized the pig roast—that one was easy—but she had to guess at the beef, lamb, venison, chicken, duck, goose, and pigeon. There were also mutton pies and bowls of stew.

Eve glanced over at Andrew. He took only a few bites of each dish. She did the same. She couldn't imagine anyone having the stomach to eat everything that had been offered.

The dessert—if it could be called that—was served in baskets and included a variety of fruit, tarts, and cheese.

After the servants began to clear away the dishes again, Matthew leaned toward Lady Josephs and said, "My lady, for the delicious meal I give you thanks. Now, if you will allow it, I shall retreat to the master's study. I have placed there my vestments and would be honored to serve you and your trustworthy servants the Sacrament of Confession—and, later, a *spiritual* supper. Everything is there and awaits us."

The lady's eyes grew misty with tears. "Dearest Father, the honor is mine."

Eve also grew tearful. The comfort of this home, the meal, the thought of celebrating the Mass—all filled her with a contentment she hadn't felt in a long time.

The moment was short lived. A loud commotion sounded from another part of the house. Matthew and William were on their feet. All eyes went to the door. They heard the loud footfalls of boots beating the floor.

A red-faced servant came in looking flustered. "My lady—"

The servant was interrupted by the entrance of a stern-faced man with a bushy salt-and-pepper-colored goatee. The man elbowed the servant aside.

Taking a few steps toward Lady Josephs, he yanked at his cap, revealing a mop of hair that matched his goatee. He bowed low. "Good lady, I beg your forgiveness."

Lady Josephs pushed her chair back from the table. "My dear Mr. Nedly! Whatever is the matter? Thou hast given us a fright with thy dramatic entrance."

"A thousand pardons," Mr. Nedly said without sounding sorry. He wore a long burgundy cloak of velvet. The left side was pulled open, exposing a sheath holding a long knife. He put his hand on the hilt of the knife.

Lady Josephs gestured toward the agitated man. "Gentlemen, this is Mr. Hugh Nedly."

Before anyone could respond, Mr. Nedly said, "Mrs. Josephs, I have been reliably informed that *hunters* from Reading are coming this way. They suspect you of entertaining priests." He shot a look at William and Matthew.

"'Tis a grave error," said Lady Josephs. "My guests are actors. William Brookes and Matthew Whyte. Surely thou hast heard of them."

"I am embarrassed to say that I have not," Mr. Nedly replied tersely. "All the same, the hunters will insist on searching the house."

"I have nothing to fear," said Lady Josephs. But her gaze went to Matthew and betrayed her concern. The items to celebrate the Mass were tucked away in the study.

"Perhaps you do not," Mr. Nedly countered, "but these strangers will be taken and questioned."

"The hunters would not dare!" said Lady Josephs.

"The Queen's Privy Council would say otherwise." Mr. Nedly took another step forward. His voice was low but filled with urgency. "Dear lady, the news from Ireland hath inflamed the entire town."

"What news?" she asked.

"An expedition of Spaniards and Italians hath landed there to give aid to the Irish Catholic rebels," he said.

"What is that to us?" she asked.

Mr. Nedly looked astonished at the question. "Dear lady, all believe that Edmund Campion prepares to lead a rebellion in this country. The townspeople are in a frenzy. They believe he is nearby, stirring up peace-loving Catholics."

"Father Campion hath said again and again that he is not a rebel," said Lady Josephs.

"Why would anyone believe him?" Mr. Nedly challenged her. "Indeed, I myself was questioned only this morning by the High Sheriff, for no cause other than being a friend of this family."

"I am saddened for thy suffering," said Lady Josephs. She sighed. "What are we to do?"

"I have brought my wife's coach. Allow me to take your guests away," he offered.

CHAPTER NINE

Lady Josephs looked unsure. "Must they depart?" she asked.

"The eyes of the hunters are upon this house, I fear," said Mr. Nedly. "Would you have them captured if the house were suddenly searched?"

Lady Josephs looked at William, then Matthew. "I am appalled by this turn of events," she said unhappily. "Where wouldst thou take them?" she asked Mr. Nedly.

"To London," Mr. Nedly said.

Lady Josephs frowned. "Is that not jumping from the frying pan into the fire? Are they not searching for Mr. Campion with greater diligence there?"

"The Privy Council follows the rumors it hears about Campion," Mr. Nedly explained. "It is watchful of the countryside first and foremost. London, the council believes, is protected by its many spies. The council is wrong, of course. 'Tis easier to disappear in London than anywhere."

Lady Josephs nodded. "I see."

Mr. Nedly turned to William and Matthew. "I have been told that Mr. Campion and the other holy men with whom he travels will assemble in London soon. If that is so, then I have news that may save their lives."

William and Matthew exchanged a look. William said, "You speak of things beyond our knowledge," he said, then added, "since we are but *lowly* actors."

Lady Josephs gazed up at Mr. Nedly. "Thou dost offer a kind service, sir, and I am forever grateful. Pray, give us leave to discuss thy proposition. Thou mayst await word in the garden."

Mr. Nedly looked hurt. "We have little time, good lady," he reminded her. Then he bowed and walked through the double doors to the patio.

The red-faced servant was still in the doorway. "Fetch him a drink," Lady Josephs said. The servant bowed, then disappeared into the hallway.

Lady Josephs pressed her hands on the arms of her chair as if to stand. William pulled the chair back for her. She rose wearily. "Mr. Nedly hath been a good friend to my husband and me. Though we have never spoken openly of our Catholic faith, his coming here suggests that he knows of it."

"Do you trust him?" asked Matthew.

"I have no cause to distrust him," she replied. "However, let us be cautious. First, remove whatever vestments and instruments of worship thou hast placed in the study. I have a hiding place where they will not be found."

"My lady, if we accept his offer of the coach to London, then I must take everything with me," Matthew said.

She frowned. "If you are stopped and anything of the old faith is found, you will be arrested. I assure you, my hiding place is secure. It was built for this very purpose. Priests have hidden there on many occasions. Your sacred items will be safe."

"Should we hide there now rather than travel to London?" asked William.

Lady Josephs shook her head. "If Mr. Nedly truly has news for Edmund Campion, then you must see to it."

William looked worried. "What of you, my lady? If the hunters come—"

"I know the hunters. They will do nothing to me or this house without cause," Lady Josephs said. "In this, I agree with Mr. Nedly: if you are found here, the hunters will claim to have a just cause to do with me as they will."

"Then we must go to London," William said.

"Make haste, Matthew," Lady Josephs urged. "We shall hide any evidence of your presence here. Your non-priestly belongings will be placed in a trunk for transport. William, pray tell Mr. Nedly that we gratefully accept his offer. Bid him take you to my husband at our home in London."

With that, Lady Josephs and Matthew left the room.

Eve watched Mr. Nedly through the double doors. He paced around the patio, stopping to examine the flowers. She wondered if he could hear the discussion they'd just had.

"Mr. Nedly!" William called out.

Mr. Nedly spun on his heel and marched back inside. He glanced around and looked disappointed that Lady Josephs was no longer there.

"We gratefully accept your offer to go to London," William said. "Lady Josephs would have you take us to her husband there."

Mr. Nedly bowed. "With pleasure, sir. 'Twill be late when we arrive, though. We will stay first at my lodgings near to his home. I shall see you delivered safely to Mr. Josephs on the morrow."

"You are a true friend indeed," said William.

"I would be a truer friend to speed you hence," Mr. Nedly said. "At any moment, the wolves may be at the door."

10

The coach was a fancy-looking black box with a solid roof and walls and curtained windows in the doors on each side. The edges were painted in gold, giving the coach a royal look. It reminded Andrew of the coaches he'd often seen in cowboy movies. The two wheels on the driver's end were large, but the rear wheels were even larger, rising alongside the cabin. The coachman sat hunched over on the high bench, his head tucked low in his cloak and his hat pulled down. He held a long whip that stood up like an antenna. Two horses stomped impatiently between the hitches in front of him. Servants strapped the actors' trunk on a shelf at the back.

Within half an hour of Mr. Nedly's arrival, Andrew, Eve, William, and Matthew were squeezed inside the coach. At first, Mr. Nedly suggested that the two children ride up top with the coachman, but William insisted they travel with the adults. Mr. Nedly shouted at the coachman, who snapped his whip to spur the horses forward. The coach moved quickly along the long driveway to the road.

Andrew noticed that the coach didn't bounce as violently as the wagon they'd used. For that he was grateful. They rode in silence at first. Then, as they approached the center of Reading, Mr. Nedly pulled the window curtain aside. There seemed to be a lot of people with torches on the streets.

"'Tis a boisterous town," said Matthew.

"Bands of hunters search the houses," Mr. Nedly said.

Andrew felt Eve's body stiffen next to him.

"Will they stop us?" William asked from the other side of Eve.

"They may," Mr. Nedly replied. He was sharing the bench with Matthew, facing the others. "However, this coach is known to many, as my wife often uses it. Pray the mob believes it is she inside. They are not inclined to harass women."

At one point the coachman slowed down. "Out of the way, fools!" he shouted. Then they gained speed again.

"We leave the town behind us. This is the main road to London," Mr. Nedly explained. "Sleep whilst ye may. 'Tis a few hours to our destination."

Andrew folded his arms and leaned back into the bench cushions. He closed his eyes. Eve leaned in close to him. Her head nudged against his shoulder, then stayed there.

The road was a straight Roman road built by invaders hundreds of years before. Andrew could hear the sounds of the wheels against the dirt and felt only the slightest bumps.

Nice shock absorbers, he thought.

The rocking and rattle of the coach lulled him to sleep.

Andrew was awakened by the sound of soft voices. He blinked at the light of a small lamp that swung in a nook behind the rear seat. Mr. Nedly was turned slightly to Matthew, his face a dark shadow. He was saying something about Edmund Campion's hiding places. He even suggested the areas of London where the fugitive might be found.

Matthew spoke in a grave tone. "Sir, you speak too freely. Pray, what if we are in league with the Queen's Privy Council and the priest hunters?"

Mr. Nedly smiled at him. "Good sir, I venture to say that you are not. You have no cause to fear me. I am also a Catholic. Why else would I place myself in danger to help Lady Josephs—or four strangers?"

"Still, I would ask you to be cautious with what you say. There are spies everywhere," warned Matthew.

"Indeed there are," Mr. Nedly said. "One or two among the priests themselves. That is one of my messages to Father Campion. I know who the spies are."

Matthew said nothing for a moment. Andrew couldn't make out his expression.

"'Tis on my heart to join the priests in their work," Mr. Nedly said.

"That is your business, sir," said Matthew softly. "'Tis none of mine. Nor should it be. Such an admission is treasonous. Think what will become of you should these two children be caught and questioned. They will be forced to speak truthfully about your words."

Mr. Nedly cocked an eyebrow as he looked at Andrew and Eve. He winked at Andrew when he saw that he was awake. "They will not betray me. I am certain of it. In their eyes I see two children who have witnessed more than we suspect. They guard the secrets in their hearts."

"The Royal Hunt, sir!" the coachman shouted. He then made noises at the horses, and the coach slowed.

With a few sudden bumps, the coach came off the road. Eve stirred, then stretched. William sat up.

Mr. Nedly threw open the two doors and said, "Stretch your legs. I will see to our food and drink whilst the coachman changes our horses."

The grown-ups stepped down from the coach. Andrew leaned out and watched Mr. Nedly and William slowly walk along a stone path to an inn a few yards away. Men's feet, horses' hooves, and coach wheels had churned up the grounds surrounding the inn. The inn itself was made of stone and timber. It was lit up with torches placed on stands lining its sides. A few horses were tied to a hitch at the front. A couple of other coaches sat along a far wall.

It's like a truck stop, Andrew thought as he dropped from the coach's steps onto the muddy ground.

CHAPTER TEN

Eve stood in the doorway of the coach. "Ew," she said. "I am going to get mud all over my dress."

They had left the house of Lady Josephs in such a hurry, they hadn't had time to change into traveling clothes.

Matthew came alongside Andrew and Eve. "Be careful what you say to Mr. Nedly."

"Do you not trust him?" asked Eve.

"Nay, I do not. In these troubled times, it is difficult to trust anyone we hardly know." Matthew took a few steps, slipping a little in the mud. He seemed to find his footing, then walked in the direction of a darkness at the far edge of the grounds.

The coachman had climbed down from his seat. He was a stern-looking man with a face that had seen too many years of being sun drenched and wind beaten. He nodded at Andrew, then tipped his hat to Eve. He staggered toward the inn.

Eve looked up at the sky. "I wonder what time it is."

Andrew shrugged. "Night."

"I can see that," she said. "Do you know where we are?"

Andrew shrugged again. "At the Royal Hunt."

Eve frowned at him. "Is there a town or city nearby?"

"London?" Andrew offered.

"You aren't being helpful," Eve said, then retreated into the coach.

Andrew thought about walking to the inn but was afraid of falling into the mud and ruining his clothes.

He pulled himself onto the lowest step of the coach and looked around.

In a shadow near the corner of the inn, something moved. Andrew narrowed his eyes to focus. "Eve," he said softly. "There's a man over by the inn. He's watching Matthew."

Eve came into the doorway. "Is he a priest hunter? What should we do?" she asked.

Matthew emerged from the darkness and walked toward them. He lifted his legs high because of the mud. His head was bowed, and his hands were clasped behind his back. Andrew thought he looked as if he was praying.

When Matthew was closer to the coach, Andrew said, "Matthew, there is a man—"

"I know," Matthew said without raising his head. "Be at peace. He comes our way."

Andrew looked up. The man had left the shadows. He was tall and rotund. In the flickering torchlight, Andrew saw that he wore a wide brown coat that made him look like an umbrella with a head on top.

"Hail!" called the man, lurching in their direction.

Matthew turned and raised a hand. "Greetings, my lord!"

The man was only a few feet away. Andrew could see his chubby face and red cheeks.

"I know thee," the man said to Matthew. "'Twas in Arundel—no, Brighton. Perhaps Eastbourne in the town square..."

CHAPTER TEN

"What was the occasion, my lord?" Matthew asked.

"Thou didst perform in a drama about Prometheus, or it might have been Iphigenia. Unforgettable!" The man clapped Matthew on the back. "Art thou not an actor?"

Matthew bowed, "Matthew Whyte, my lord."

"Lord Broadhurst," the man said, also bowing as much as his frame would allow. "What brings thee here? Wilt thou perform nearby?"

"We journey to London, with hope of finding an audience there," Matthew replied.

"Perhaps the queen herself?" Lord Broadhurst asked, nudging Andrew playfully.

Matthew nodded. "Pray it is so, my lord."

"I fancied the stage in my younger days," Broadhurst said. "My father would not hear of it. He wanted me to become a clergyman!" He gave a loud laugh. "Imagine that! 'No future in it!' I said to him. I studied law instead. I now serve the Queen's Privy Council."

Andrew felt his muscles stiffen. Eve took a step back into the coach.

"A noble work, my lord," said Matthew.

"'Tis, if one enjoys dashing hither and yon, seeking out Catholics like a rat catcher," Broadhurst said sourly. "Even now I ride to Reading. 'Tis said that Edmund Campion is in hiding there."

Matthew gave a light laugh. "I heard he was in Winchester *and* Basingstoke *and* Salisbury *and* Glastonbury."

The lord rolled his eyes. "The man is everywhere and nowhere at all." Then he brightened up and said, "An idea occurs to me. As one who travels widely, thou must see and hear much. The Privy Council should hire *thee* to be its eyes and ears."

"An intriguing notion, my lord," said Matthew.

"Since thou art bound for London, seek an audience with Lord Walsingham. Tell him Lord Broadhurst hath sent thee." He rubbed his fingers together. "It pays well, should thy information lead to the arrest of any Catholics."

"I thank you for your counsel, my lord," Matthew said.

Lord Broadhurst clapped Matthew on the back again. "God speed thy journey," he said, then waddled off toward the inn.

"My lord," Matthew called after him.

Eve put her hands over her face and dropped onto a seat.

Andrew slumped against the door. "I thought we would be arrested," he whispered.

"God be praised that we were not," Matthew said.

Andrew climbed into the coach. He sat next to Eve. She looked frightened.

"This is scaring me more than anything else we've done," she said softly. "At least in Robin's time—and with Joan—we knew who the enemy was."

Matthew stepped up but lingered in the doorway. Andrew watched as Mr. Nedly and William passed Lord

CHAPTER TEN

Broadhurst at the inn. They exchanged greetings for a moment, then continued on.

When he reached Matthew, Mr. Nedly looked anxious and asked, "Pray tell, was that Lord Broadhurst?"

"It was. He offered me a job as a spy for the Queen's Privy Council," Matthew replied calmly. He stomped the mud from his boots on the coach steps.

"*What?*" exclaimed Mr. Nedly.

Matthew moved into the cab and took his seat. Mr. Nedly also kicked at the side of the coach to loosen the mud on his boots. Then he pulled himself up and in.

William did the same, looking amused as he entered. "He offered thee a position, Matthew? Doth it pay well?" he asked. "If so, I pray thou hast accepted the offer."

The two men laughed.

Mr. Nedly looked at the inn, then turned to them, his brows pressed together. "I shall encourage the coachman to make greater speed to London."

They continued east, crossing a bridge over the River Thames near the village of Stanes.

An hour passed in silence. Then the coachman called out to the horses and brought them to a full stop.

Mr. Nedly leaned his head out of the window and shouted to the coachman, "What is it, Jerome? Highwaymen?"

It was the first time Andrew had heard the coachman's name.

"Not highwaymen," Jerome called back. "*Hunters*, sir."

"Not again," Eve said, sitting up.

A group of men surrounded the coach, coming around to the two doors. They wore matching outfits of dull-brown vests and reddish leggings. A couple of the men had swords; the others had spears. *Guards or soldiers*, Andrew assumed.

"Why hast thou stopped us?" Mr. Nedly asked the man closest to him.

The man wore a large gold medallion around his neck. He said, "Orders, sir. I pray you step out."

"Orders by what authority?" Mr. Nedly demanded.

"The Queen's Privy Council," said the man. "We search for Edmund Campion or any of his wicked company."

The doors were yanked open. The five passengers stepped out. Andrew shivered from the chill in the air. Eve came close to him, an expression of fear in her eyes.

"I am Hubert Nedly from Berkshire. These are my esteemed companions, the renowned actors William Brookes and Matthew Whyte, and their apprentices."

"I am Captain Milne. With apologies for the inconvenience, Mr. Nedly. A quick look is all we need," the medallioned man said.

"I will not suffer such an indignity!" Mr. Nedly shouted.

CHAPTER TEN

"You need not suffer long if you will but stand aside," said Captain Milne.

Mr. Nedly folded his arms and stood firm where he was.

Milne signaled two of his men. They came at Mr. Nedly with their swords drawn.

Matthew held up his hands and cried out, "Stop!"

The soldiers looked surprised.

"Kind sir," said Matthew to the captain, "a private word, if you will."

Milne gave a slow nod. Matthew touched his elbow, and they moved out of earshot. Matthew said something, and with a look of surprise, the captain stepped back. He looked at Matthew, then at the coach. He eyed everyone there. Then, with a quick bow, he waved a hand at his company. "Let them pass!" he commanded.

The soldiers looked confused as they began to separate.

Matthew returned and said quietly to the others, "Into the coach."

Mr. Nedly was the last to climb inside, glaring at the men as he did.

Once the coachman had urged the horses forward again, Mr. Nedly asked Matthew, "What didst thou say to him? Why did he yield?"

Matthew smiled. "I explained that we are traveling to London for an important meeting with Lord Walsingham, on behalf of Lord Broadhurst. I warned the captain that any delay shall surely bring the wrath of Lord Walsingham."

Mr. Nedly began to laugh—a mere chuckle at first. Then it grew into a loud, knee-slapping roar.

The coachman stopped at an inn on the outskirts of a town called Brentford. While stretching his legs, Andrew noticed a great river to the south. "What is that?" he asked William.

"The Thames River, of course" came the reply.

"But we took a bridge over that river a long time ago," Andrew said.

"So we did," William acknowledged. "The Thames meanders all over the countryside, flowing north and south, east and west. As we approach the city, thou wilt see it in the distance, and then it shall be closer, back and forth, as we journey through Chiswick and on to the gates of London itself."

When the journey continued, Andrew sat on the right side of the coach. Leaning forward, he looked out of the small window in the door. Buildings of stone sat in the dark like phantom ships on a lonely sea. Between the roofs and walls on narrow streets, he caught glimpses of anchored boats and slow-moving barges making their way to unknown destinations. They traveled north and east, away from the river.

CHAPTER TEN

The grown-ups debated the best way to Mr. Nedly's house. Matthew suggested they enter London near an area called Tyburn, the famed place where criminals and Catholics were executed. He reasoned that it was unlikely anyone would suspect Catholics of going that way.

Mr. Nedly insisted that they enter the city on a more deserted road south of Hyde Park, the queen's hunting grounds. From there, they would follow straight through to Holborn, where his house was located.

William had an entirely different idea that involved following the river.

"Maybe we should pull over and ask at a gas station," Eve said softly to Andrew.

In the end, the coachman made the decision without asking anyone in the cab. He turned south toward the river, then east again, then north to an area where they were surrounded by the Inns of Court—Lincoln's Inn and Gray's Inn. They then traveled east again and south on Schow Lane. The coachman brought the horses to an abrupt stop.

Mr. Nedly muttered something about giving the man a good whipping.

"Are we not here?" Matthew asked.

Mr. Nedly pointed to a house in the middle of a long row of houses. "There," he said. As he spoke, a light flickered in a front window.

"Then we are delivered safely. There is no need to whip the man," said Matthew.

Mr. Nedly grumbled as he climbed out of the coach.

The party was soon inside Mr. Nedly's modest London home. It was a narrow building, with small rooms to the left and right of a main hall. Two servants who had clearly been roused from bed now busied themselves with their master and his guests. Andrew and Eve were given separate chambers in the servants' area on the ground floor. Mr. Nedly's room was above them on the next floor. Matthew and William were given a room on an upper floor.

As Andrew settled onto a straw mattress, he was thankful not to be in the rocking coach. Then he wondered how late it was. Or early. He'd lost all sense of time.

He may have fallen asleep. He wasn't sure. But a voice caught his attention.

"Wake up," it said.

Andrew opened his eyes. The room was dark.

"Up, lad," the voice said.

"Who is it?" Andrew asked. He saw a light flickering near the corner of the room. He gasped.

Ambrosius was there holding a small candle.

Am I dreaming? Andrew sat up.

"Quickly. See to the door," Ambrosius said.

Andrew slipped out of bed and went to the door. It stood slightly ajar. He turned to ask Ambrosius what exactly he was supposed to be seeing, but the raggedy man was gone. Then Andrew heard a hissing sound, like air leaking from a pipe. There was no mistaking what it was: whispering. He adjusted his position for a better view. By the light of a lamp on a side table in the hall, he saw Mr. Nedly facing Jerome the coachman. Both men were dressed. Mr. Nedly was stabbing a finger at Jerome's chest.

I hope he isn't going to beat Jerome, Andrew thought.

But it became clear that Mr. Nedly was giving Jerome urgent instructions. "Be quick, I tell thee. All will be undone by daybreak."

"Where will I find help at this hour?" Jerome complained.

"Use thy wits, if thou hast any," Mr. Nedly snapped.

Jerome shook his head and walked away.

Mr. Nedly glanced around. Andrew pulled back behind the door. Then he heard the man retreat down the hall, followed by footsteps ascending the stairs.

Andrew sat down on the bed. What was the urgent errand Mr. Nedly had sent Jerome on in the middle of the night? Perhaps it was nothing. Perhaps it was something.

Maybe Mr. Nedly sent Jerome to find priest hunters, he thought.

He dismissed the idea. Why would Mr. Nedly save them from priest hunters at the house of Lady Josephs—and from roadblocks—only to betray them in London?

It can't be that, he thought as he stretched out on the bed.

Yes, it can, he told himself, then sat up again.

11

Andrew clamped a hand over Eve's mouth to keep her from screaming.

"*Sssssshhh!* It's me," he whispered. He lifted the lit candle a little closer to his face.

She pulled his hand away. "When is the last time you washed your hands?" she asked in disgust.

"Something is going on," Andrew said. Then he told her what he'd seen in the hall. He decided not to mention Ambrosius, since that part might have been a dream.

Eve sat up. "We have to tell William and Matthew."

Getting to the two priests was harder than they expected. The floorboards in the hall seemed to creak with every step they took. They had the same trouble with each stair leading to an upstairs hallway. There was a single room to the left and another staircase beyond it at the end of the hall. The door to the room was open. A candle burned just inside.

Andrew peeked into the room. Mr. Nedly was sitting at a desk with his back to the door. Andrew could hear the scratching of a pen on paper. He gestured for Eve to wait while he crossed the doorway to the other side. Mr. Nedly's scratching continued. Then Eve followed. She tried to tippy-toe across, but the floor creaked. She half leapt into Andrew's arms. He hugged her to keep her from stumbling. They froze and listened. The scratching sound stopped. Then the chair scraped on the floor.

Should we run for it? he wondered, but he knew the sound would give them away.

Before they had time to do anything, Mr. Nedly came through the doorway. He held a candle up. Without looking in the kids' direction, he went to the top of the stairs. "Jerome?" he called out in a harsh whisper.

Andrew let go of Eve. They slowly inched along the wall away from Mr. Nedly.

Mr. Nedly called for the coachman again. Then, with an angry grunt, he walked down the stairs.

Andrew tugged at Eve's arm, and they quickened their pace. They reached the second staircase and crept upward. At the top was a short hallway with a door at the end. The door was closed. Andrew thought he heard gentle snoring on the other side. He lifted the latch, and the door opened on greased hinges.

The snoring came from a large bed where William was sprawled out. A lamp on the bedside table gave a dull glow, as if it might go out at any second.

A second light flickered on the left side of the room. Next to the wall, Matthew was kneeling in front of a crucifix on a small table.

CHAPTER ELEVEN

Andrew took a step. The floorboard creaked. William sat up in an instant.

"What is wrong?" Matthew asked.

"Methinks Mr. Nedly hath sent for priest hunters," Andrew said.

Matthew looked at William. William crawled out of bed. He was fully dressed, except for his boots.

"Close the door," Matthew whispered.

Eve obeyed.

The two men moved softly and with the precise movements of cats. Clothes were assembled and put into a leather satchel that Andrew hadn't seen before. The crucifix and a few books were shoved into a second satchel.

"Where are thy shoes?" William asked Andrew.

Andrew looked down at his feet. He'd left his boots in his room.

Matthew eyed Eve. "Thou lookest like a servant girl," he said approvingly.

"My dress is hanging in my room," she said. Her toes peeked out from under her skirt. She wiggled them.

"We will find shoes for thee after we escape," Matthew said.

"How will we go?" Andrew asked. "We must walk past Mr. Nedly's room. He will see us."

William pointed to a shuttered window in the corner of the room. "That will take us to the fat branch of a great tree in a garden that borders a field," he said.

"You already know how to escape?" Eve asked.

"We *always* know how to escape," William said. He pointed to Eve. "Thou shalt ride on Matthew's back." And to Andrew he said, "Thou shalt ride on mine."

That was the plan. To Andrew's surprise, it seemed to work perfectly. They reached the tree easily enough from the window. Their experience crawling along branches and running through forests and fields aided Andrew and Eve with the rest. Andrew felt the cool, damp grass and prickly weeds on his uncovered feet, but he wasn't bothered.

I've been doing this for hundreds of years, he thought with a smile.

They crouched in the darkness of the field, watching the house to see if anyone was following them. No one came.

"Where do we go now?" Eve asked.

"The city home of Arthur Josephs," Matthew replied. "Lady Josephs provided me with its location before we departed."

They crossed the field into a labyrinth of gardens behind another long row of houses. They kept to the shadows, aware of every noise coming from the various inns and houses they passed. Dogs barked at them. They found a narrow footpath between two houses that led to Fetter Lane. They veered right and soon Matthew said, "There it is."

He crept over the lane to an iron gate. It was unlocked. The fugitives slipped through and followed the pathway to the front door of house. The lower half was made of brick; the upper half was made of dark timber and white plaster. Small windows seemed to be placed randomly. Andrew couldn't tell whether it was a two- or three-story home.

They came to a dark porch, and William found the rope for the bell. He pulled only once. Andrew heard a loud jingle inside. They waited.

After a couple of minutes, William was about to pull the rope again, but there was a shuffling sound on the other side of the door.

"Who is it at this hour?" came a low voice.

"We come from Lady Josephs to see Master Arthur," Matthew said to the door.

More shuffling and then scraping sounds. Andrew imagined someone lifting the large plank of wood used to bar the door. The latch clicked. The door was pulled open. A robed man faced them. A woman holding a candle peeked out from behind him.

The robed man looked beyond them, as if checking to be sure no one else was there. Then he beckoned them in. "Await me in the front room whilst I awaken the master."

The woman with the candle ushered them into a spacious front room. Dying embers glowed a faint red in the fireplace.

Voices, footfalls, and banging came from another part of the house. Then the servant entered carrying a lamp. Behind him was a tall silver-haired man who fumbled with the belt of his robe. He looked at the two men. Then his eyes widened with recognition.

"Matthew! William!" he said and grabbed the men's hands.

The adults went off to talk. Andrew and Eve were given their own rooms near the back of the house on the next floor. Andrew suspected they were the rooms that the Josephs' children used. Andrew's room was larger, and the bed was more comfortable than the servant's closet he had at Mr. Nedly's. He went to the single window on the back wall and pulled open the shutters. He squinted at the darkness outside. It looked like there was a back garden with a wall. Beyond the wall was a copse of trees and what looked like the back of an inn.

He tested the latch on the window. It was stiff from rust but eventually gave way. He peered out the window and noted a sheer drop to a patio below. It was too dark to see what else was down there. He hoped that he'd figure it out if trouble came.

Something moved outside to his left. Eve was also peeking out of the window to her room. "No tree," she whispered.

"We'll have to fly," Andrew replied.

They ducked their heads back inside. Andrew latched and shuttered the window. As he fell asleep, he prayed that no one would raid the house. Then he thought how sad it was that he even had to pray such a thing.

12

It was late in the morning when Andrew awakened. He had burrowed under a thick quilt and, for a moment, couldn't remember where he was. Then he slowly surfaced to a cool room. He found a basin of water on a side table, along with a stack of linens for washing. He gave himself a quick scrub.

Clothes had been laid out for him on the end of the bed. They were much like the ones he'd been wearing. Boots sat nearby on the floor. He dressed and marveled that everything fit him almost perfectly.

He left the room. Coming down the hall to the stairs, he heard voices below, along with the chink and rattle of plates and cutlery.

"Good morning, young squire," a man said behind him. It was the servant from the night before, now fully dressed.

"Is it still morning?" Andrew asked.

"Somewhat, aye."

The servant led Andrew down the stairs to a lower hall and into a dining room. Arthur Josephs was at the head of a long table, with William and Matthew. Eve sat next to Matthew. She was wearing a functional peasant-type outfit.

Spread on the table were plates and trays of food that reminded Andrew of the feast they'd had in Reading. He felt famished. He sat down and began stuffing his mouth with portions of the meats and vegetables in front of him.

Eve giggled at him.

Andrew blushed, realizing he was making a pig out of himself. He slowed down.

Arthur Josephs was a soft-spoken man with a narrow, pale face and forlorn eyes.

Andrew wanted to ask about Mr. Nedly. Before he had the chance, the bell rang at the front door. William and Matthew stood up and moved to a large wooden hutch along one of the walls. Andrew thought it was an odd thing to do.

"Rebecca!" Arthur Josephs called out.

The maidservant Andrew had seen the night before came through from the kitchen. She crossed the room and stopped at the doorway to the front hall. She peered around the edge of the door, holding up a hand for them to be still. "James is answering the door," Rebecca said in a voice that sounded much younger than she looked.

Andrew assumed that James was the name of the servant who'd brought him down to breakfast.

Then she relaxed and lowered her hand again. She stepped back into the room and said softly, " 'Tis Mr.

Nedly." She came away from the door and went about her business.

A moment later, Mr. Nedly himself entered the room. He bowed to them with a flourish of his hat and said, "Praise be to God! You are all safe!"

As Mr. Nedly stood straight again, Andrew noticed that he had a black eye and bruises on one of his cheeks.

William and Matthew returned to their seats.

Arthur Josephs invited Mr. Nedly to sit down, waving to the chair at the opposite end of the table. "Good sir, I have heard distressing news," Mr. Josephs said once Mr. Nedly was seated. "Priest hunters paid a visit to thy house last night?"

"Aye," said Mr. Nedly, "The ruffians arrived not long after we had settled in for the night. I refused them entrance. *This* was their response." His fingers lightly touched the corner of his black eye. "I feared we were followed as we approached London. So I sent my servant out into the street to keep watch. The poor man was brutalized."

Andrew shot a look at Eve. Had he misunderstood what he had heard Mr. Nedly say to the servant?

Mr. Nedly continued. "At the hour the louts came to the house, I was sure we were all doomed. I was as surprised as the hunters when they reached the upstairs room and found it empty. Pray, did you escape through the window?"

William said, "We did, sir."

"What warning caused you to depart?" Mr. Nedly asked.

William tipped his head to Andrew. "The children heard something that alarmed them. They came directly to us. Rather than take the time to consult with you, or put you at further risk, we slipped out."

Mr. Nedly looked at Andrew. "Didst thou hear the men at the door?"

"In earnest, I am not sure what I heard," Andrew said honestly.

Mr. Nedly folded his hands on the table and nodded. Andrew couldn't tell whether the man was relieved or disappointed.

"Do we have cause to believe the hunters will come here?" Mr. Josephs asked.

"I fear so," said Mr. Nedly.

Mr. Josephs stood up. "We must hide anything that might be construed as evidence," he said. "James!"

The servant entered the room.

"Bring the books from my room. Thou knowest the ones," Mr. Josephs said.

James bowed.

"The satchels from our rooms as well," Matthew added.

James gave another bow before he left the room.

"I cannot believe you have a hiding place that will escape the hunters' notice. They are thorough," Mr. Nedly grumbled.

Mr. Josephs smiled. He held up a finger, as if to say, *Watch and see.* He turned to the hutch at the back of the dining room. It reached from the floor to the ceiling and was at least seven feet wide and a couple of feet deep. The center of the top half had glass doors showcasing decorative plates that were propped up on small stands. Two solid doors covered the lower half. Mr. Josephs opened one of the doors on the right to show that it had shelves inside for linens.

Andrew felt as if he was watching a magician set up a magic trick.

"Matthew?" Mr. Josephs said.

Matthew stood up and slipped behind Mr. Josephs on the right side of the hutch.

Mr. Josephs faced them, spreading his arms. "Watch," he said.

Here comes the magic trick, Andrew thought.

Mr. Josephs reached up to the top of the right corner of the hutch. There was a gentle thumping sound. Then he stepped to one side.

Matthew was gone.

There was a collective gasp. Andrew wanted to applaud.

"By the rood!" Mr. Nedly shouted as he leapt to his feet. "What conjuring is this?"

William laughed. So did Arthur Josephs. "Come and see," the older man said.

Everyone crowded next to the hutch.

Mr. Josephs explained, "There is a hidden latch on top that releases a door." He reached up and pushed the latch again. Andrew now saw that the right side of the hutch opened inward just enough for someone to slip through. Matthew stood in a space in the wall behind. He held a small candle in his hand, a flame flickering on top.

"Pray tell, how is this done?" asked Mr. Nedly, pressing his hand against the wooden door and peeking in.

"A small room, wide enough for a few men to stand, fewer to lie down," Mr. Josephs said. "If thou goest around this wall to the kitchen, thou wilt see a pantry. This room is behind the shelves there, but looks part of it. Unless one measured the wall, one would not know the room is there. 'Tis said the previous owners of this house used it to store illegal goods."

Mr. Nedly tried to push himself through to the secret room but gave up. "I would lose my buttons attempting that," he said.

"May I?" Andrew asked.

Mr. Josephs nodded. Matthew stepped out of the hutch and handed the candle to Andrew.

Andrew easily went through the doorway. The secret room was the length of the hutch and about three feet deep. A tower of short shelves on the far wall held a lamp, a jug, a basin, and a few other necessities. Thin mattresses

CHAPTER TWELVE

hung like blankets on a line of hooks on the back wall. He thought of the secret passageway behind the walls in the castle of Chinon in Joan of Arc's time.

Andrew heard a shuffling behind him. Eve came into the room.

"Amazing," she said.

"'Tis a tight squeeze for a slumber party," Andrew said.

Eve came close and whispered, "If Mr. Nedly is a spy for the hunters, why is Mr. Josephs showing him this hiding place?"

Andrew shrugged. "I could have been wrong. Perhaps Mr. Nedly is innocent." He blew out the candle. They exited the secret room.

Mr. Josephs used a small knob to pull the door closed. The latch clicked.

"If one did not know the door was there, one would never find it," William said.

"What keeps the door from hitting the shelves inside the hutch?" Mr. Nedly asked.

"'Tis something of a trick," Mr. Josephs said. "The shelves on the top are only as deep as the standing plates. The shelves on the bottom lift as the door moves in, pressing the linens to the front."

Mr. Nedly looked impressed.

Everyone sat down to finish breakfast. While they ate, James returned with an armload of books and the priests' satchels. He opened the hidden door again and placed the items in the secret room.

They then discussed what Matthew and William should do next. Arthur Josephs admitted that he had heard news of Edmund Campion. The now-famous priest was due to return to London at any time. But no one seemed to know where to find him.

"Might he come here?" Mr. Nedly asked. Andrew noticed that the man's eyes kept going to the hutch.

"There is no reason he should," Mr. Josephs replied. "I do not know him. Nor would he know me well enough to trust me."

Mr. Nedly scrubbed his chin thoughtfully. "Be very careful in whom you place your trust," he said.

Mr. Nedly departed an hour later. Once he had gone, the adults seemed to relax.

"We must be very careful in whom we trust, indeed!" Mr. Josephs exclaimed.

Andrew looked at them, confused.

Eve shook her head. "I do not understand."

Mr. Josephs said, "I have suspected for some time that Mr. Nedly is not truly a friend to us."

"If he is not a friend, why did you show him the hiding place?" asked Andrew.

"To prove whether he is a friend," said Mr. Josephs. "If the hunters arrive and seek out that room, then I shall know the truth about Mr. Nedly."

"But then you cannot use the room anymore," Eve observed.

"'Tis only one, and the oldest. I have a better one in another part of the house," Mr. Josephs said.

The men rose from the table. William and Matthew announced that they would go their separate ways to visit Catholic homes around London.

After they had gone, Mr. Josephs asked Andrew and Eve, "Have you been to London before?"

"Nay, sir," Andrew said.

"I have," Eve said.

Andrew turned to her. "Thou hast been to London?"

"Once. When I was a small child. I do not remember it at all."

"Thou didst not say."

"Thou didst not ask."

Mr. Josephs interrupted them. "I shall have James take you in the coach," he said.

Andrew thought about the London he had seen in pictures and movies. Big Ben, Buckingham Palace, Westminster Abbey, London Bridge. Had any of those been built yet?

Arthur Josephs retreated to his study while James arranged for the coach. Andrew now noticed a few other servants in the house that he hadn't seen before.

Andrew and Eve were excited about a tour of London. They went to the front door to wait for James. Just then, the bell rang. James seemed to come quickly from nowhere to answer the door. He lifted the latch and was suddenly thrown back as a crowd of men pushed their way in.

Andrew threw an arm up to protect Eve.

"What is this?" James shouted.

A man with thin, oily hair and a ragged beard held up a medallion hanging around his neck. "By order of the Queen's Privy Council," he said in a raspy voice. He hooked a thumb at Andrew and Eve. "See to them."

A heavy-set member of the gang grabbed Andrew with one hand and Eve with the other. He dragged them down the hall and shoved them into the dining room. "Sit," he barked.

The two kids dropped into chairs at the table.

Andrew felt annoyed. Eve looked frightened. The heavy-set man began to look around the room, stationing himself near the hutch with his arms folded. He scowled at the kids as if daring them to try to escape.

From the hallway, Andrew heard the voice of Arthur Josephs. First, he demanded to know who the men were and why they had burst into his home. The official with the medallion was Philip Tebworth. He said he had trustworthy information that Josephs was harboring priests.

"You will find no priests here," Josephs insisted.

Andrew could hear the gang of men stomp their way through other parts of the house.

Suddenly, a different man appeared at the doorway to the kitchen. He must have come in through the back.

CHAPTER TWELVE

Peering into the dining room, he said, "Mr. Hemple! Why dost thou stand idly by? Search this room anon!"

"I have made a goodly search, Mr. Bland," said Mr. Hemple. "There be few places to hide."

"Under the table?" Mr. Bland asked.

"Aye," Mr. Hemple lied.

"Hast thou searched the cabinets for crucifixes, books, or other devilish devices? Hast thou tapped the walls?" Mr. Bland asked.

Hemple frowned.

"Be quick about it," Mr. Bland said with a snort. He withdrew into the kitchen. Soon there were loud bangs and crashes, suggesting that the man was upending everything.

Hemple looked under the table. Then he drifted around the room as if he thought it was a waste of time to look. He went to a side table and pulled at a drawer. He grabbed a handful of linens and tossed them onto the floor. He yanked at another drawer, allowing the cutlery inside to scatter at his feet.

He stepped to the large hutch and stared at it like a man trying to figure out a strange beast. Andrew saw Eve's body stiffen. He caught her gaze and shook his head. She looked back at him helplessly.

Hemple opened the glass doors and then the smaller door. He pulled at the drawers below.

Mr. Tebworth peered in from the hallway. "Mr. Hemple?"

Hemple spread his arms. "Nothing, sir."

"Hast thou asked the children?" Tebworth asked, jerking his head toward Andrew and Eve.

Hemple shook his head. "Ask the children what, sir?"

"If there are Catholics in the house. Perhaps they are true to the faith of our queen and need only be asked to reveal what they know," Tebworth said.

Before Hemple could reply, Tebworth grunted impatiently and sat down across from Andrew and Eve. "You will do our queen and country a goodly service if you speak freely. Lie to me, and I shall know it. The Tower of London awaits those who lie to me."

"Do you put children in places to rot?" Andrew asked.

"Indeed we do. Catholic children are the most dangerous of all," Tebworth said.

Eve exhaled slowly.

Tebworth reeled on her. He opened his mouth to speak but suddenly stopped. He leaned in more closely to look at her eyes. "God save me! What art thou?"

Eve lowered her head. "A girl," she said.

Tebworth hooked a finger under her chin and lifted her face. "Then speak, *girl*. What dost thou know? Tell me, or thy devilish eyes may be rendered blind."

Andrew glared at Tebworth.

Eve flinched. "These eyes have seen Catholics," she said slowly.

Andrew now turned his gaze to Eve. He was afraid of what she might say.

"Where?" Tebworth asked. A crooked smile took shape.

"In Salisbury. On the plain, near the standing stones," Eve answered.

"At the Stonehenge?"

She nodded. "I saw Catholics dancing wildly in the moonlight. One of them sacrificed a small dog. Or it might have been a hedgehog."

Andrew put a hand over his mouth to keep from laughing. Even Mr. Hemple snorted, then coughed to hide his chuckle.

Tebworth looked at Eve, then Andrew. His eyes narrowed. "Dost thou mock me?"

"Nay, sir," Eve said.

Tebworth ran a hand through his greasy hair. "If we find any evidence of popery in this house, it will be hard going for you," he warned them.

"You shall not find anything, sir," Andrew said.

"We shall see," Tebworth said, sneering. He stood up and went to the hutch. "Stand aside," he snapped at Mr. Hemple.

"I searched it," said Hemple as he moved away.

"Didst thou? I doubt it." Mr. Tebworth examined the hutch, moving from one end to the other and making "hmm" noises.

Andrew had the feeling that Tebworth knew exactly what he was looking for but was pretending he didn't. *If Tebworth gets into the secret room, he'll find all of the things that are hidden there*, he thought.

Eve touched Andrew's arm. She tipped her head toward the door, suggesting that they run while they had the chance.

Andrew shook his head.

Tebworth moved to the right side of the hutch. He reached up to the top, his fingers searching. He smiled. Andrew heard the latch click. Tebworth gave the children a knowing look, then pushed the door in. He stepped through the opening and disappeared from view.

"Now," Andrew said. He propelled himself out of the chair. He shot to the door with Eve right behind him. Just then a man stepped into the doorway. Andrew slammed into him, and Eve ran into Andrew. The man gave them both a hard push back into the dining room.

Eve stumbled and fell. Andrew slammed into the side of the table. He slumped into a chair.

The man had a hefty beard and wild eyebrows that seemed to cover most of his face. The skin on his cheeks and forehead was dotted with red patches. He wore a bright purple robe.

Glaring at Mr. Hemple, the man roared, "What goes on here?"

Mr. Hemple looked puzzled. "Who are you?"

"Mr. Chamberlain is my name," he said impatiently. "Who is in charge of this idiocy?"

Mr. Hemple pointed to the hutch. "Mr. Tebworth is inside there. 'Tis a hiding place." Then he added, "*I* found it."

CHAPTER TWELVE

Mr. Chamberlain caught Eve by the wrist. He jerked her hard to the table. "Must I tie thee up, or wilt thou behave?"

"I will behave," Eve said.

He let her go. She sat down, her eyes wide.

Andrew struggled with what to do. If Mr. Tebworth came out of the secret room with anything belonging to the priests or Mr. Josephs, they were in big trouble.

All eyes were on the hutch.

Tebworth returned. His face was knitted into tight wrinkles. "Thou art Mr. Chamberlain?"

"Aye. Have you found anything, sir?" Mr. Chamberlain asked.

"Nothing," Mr. Tebworth said bitterly. "Mr. Hemple, fetch the master of the house. I would have a word with him."

Mr. Hemple ran out of the room.

Mr. Tebworth scowled at Mr. Chamberlain. "See to it that thou makest a better job of searching this room than that fool Hemple." Tebworth marched out of the room.

Andrew watched Mr. Chamberlain make his way to the hutch. The man nodded appreciatively at the latch mechanism. He pushed open the door, disappeared inside the secret room, and returned with a look of admiration. Then he examined the rest of the dining room, tapping the walls and tugging at drawer handles of a buffet table. He lifted a colorful tapestry on the wall. All the while, his eyes were fixed upon the door. Andrew thought he seemed more interested in the hallway than the search. The man drifted to the door and peeked into the doorway. Then he stepped back and quickly closed the door.

He spun around to Andrew and Eve. "Make haste!" he said. "Flee through the kitchen."

"What?" Eve asked.

He winked at them.

"*William?*" Andrew said.

"Aye," said William, his eyes twinkling. "Make haste," he said with hushed urgency. "Master Josephs will be taken for questioning. We must not allow the same fate to befall you."

They scurried to the kitchen. No one was there. The kitchen utensils, pots, and pans had been thrown onto the floor. The back door stood open. They stepped out to the back garden and crossed to a tall stone wall.

"Mr. Nedly told them about the secret room," Eve said.

"So he did," said William. "We suspected the man was a spy. Exposing the room proved our suspicion."

Andrew and Eve followed him to a section of the wall that had collapsed. They climbed over the rubble to the grounds beyond. The maidservant Rebecca was waiting for them. She stood with her arms wrapped tightly around two coats, a distressed look on her face.

William gave her a scrap of paper. "Take this ... and them," he said, nodding to the kids.

She tucked the paper into an apron pocket, then gave the coats to Andrew and Eve. The kids put them on.

CHAPTER TWELVE

"What about you?" she asked William.

"I shall warn Matthew," he said. "Make good your escape before the villains discover you have gone." He dashed away, running along the wall in the opposite direction.

"Where are we going?" Andrew asked Rebecca.

"To safer lodgings on Chauncelor Lane," she said, then added glumly, "*If* we make it that far."

13

Andrew, Eve, and Rebecca followed a pebbled lane between two brick buildings. Andrew saw a sign identifying one of the buildings as the Swan on the Hoop Inn. The name made Andrew laugh. They came to Holborn Street and turned left. It was midday. The street was congested with people walking with great purpose, navigating among men on horseback, women in coaches, and workers in wagons.

Shrubs and trees lined the road, giving natural borders to the many houses and taverns. Andrew saw grander-looking buildings farther away from the road, surrounded by massive park-like gardens. He thought they might be churches and said so, but Rebecca said they were mostly courts of law.

Andrew pointed to the rubble of an old building. "What was that?" Andrew asked.

"The old Templar ruins," Rebecca said. She kept walking without explaining.

Andrew searched his memory. He had heard the word *Templar* before and thought it had to do with Catholic soldiers.

They came to the walls and gate of Lincoln's Inn and continued onto Chauncelor Lane. It was a narrow stretch of road with a red-brick wall on the left and a stone wall on the right. Andrew saw the tops of trees and grand spires behind the stone wall, and more gates and stately buildings along the way.

"'Tis awfully big for an inn," Eve said.

"It is not an *inn* for food and lodgings," Rebecca explained. "'Tis one of the oldest courts of law in England."

Andrew thought how funny it was that Catholics were hiding in the center of London's courts.

The walls ended, opening up a long row of houses. Rebecca stopped at one gate, looked at the house, shook her head, and then continued on. The next gate stood open. "This one," she said.

They followed the path to the front door of a red-brick house. The windows were shuttered, though it was daytime.

Rebecca lifted the heavy iron knocker. She pounded it three times.

A man dressed as a servant opened the door. Rebecca thrust into his hands the paper William had given her. Without another word, she walked away.

Andrew and Eve watched her go.

"We thank thee," Eve called out.

The servant was a round-faced man who reminded Andrew of Father Tuck from their Robin Hood adventures. The man looked at the paper, then cast a wary look at Andrew and Eve. He stepped back and said, "By thy leave, enter."

They walked into the front hall. It was deeply shadowed, with only thin shafts of light coming through the shuttered windows.

Andrew said to the servant, "We do not know where we are or what the message says."

The servant closed the door. "Be quick," he said, then ambled down the hall to a door on the right. He gave it a sharp knock.

"Enter," said a voice from inside the room.

The servant pushed open the door. "I beg your pardon, sir. Arthur Josephs hath sent two children with a message." The servant went in. Andrew heard the sound of the paper rustling. "They await your good pleasure."

"I thank thee, Mr. Dilber," the voice said, then called to Andrew and Eve, "Come in, my friends!"

They walked into a brightly lit study. An unshuttered window faced the back of the house. Sunshine illuminated assorted chairs, tables, and bookshelves that took up most of the room.

A tall young man stood in front of a modest-sized desk in the corner. His light-brown hair was cut short, and there was only the slightest hint of hair on his face. He had broad shoulders atop a torso and arms that suggested solid strength. His legs were stout and slightly bowed as if they struggled to support the upper part of his body. His eyes were a pale blue and held a look of mirth. Andrew guessed the man was in his early twenties.

"Shall I take their coats, sir?" Dilber asked.

"Nay. We shall not be staying. Fetch my coat anon, after thou art assured these fugitives were not followed."

"Aye, sir," Mr. Dilber said. With a bow, he left them.

"Andrew and Evangeline," the young man said, holding up the paper. "You journeyed to London with my dear friends William and Matthew."

"Aye, sir," said Andrew. "Pray, who are you?"

"I am George Gilbert," he said with a smile.

"A pleasure to meet you, sir," Eve said, curtsying.

"'Tis a joy." Gilbert went to a fireplace, almost lost behind the chairs, and tossed the note onto the red embers. The paper flared and curled into a black ball. "There is something you wish to tell me about Mr. Nedly?"

"He is a spy," Andrew said.

"Mr. Josephs tested him by letting him see a secret room," Eve said. She explained all that had happened.

"Mr. Josephs is a wise man," said Gilbert after she had finished. "He hath been arrested. Thankfully, William and Matthew are safe."

Andrew was relieved.

Gilbert frowned. "I am sick at heart to think of Mr. Nedly's betrayals and the arrests to which they have led."

"Do you think there are other spies in your group?" Eve asked.

"I am afraid there are," said Gilbert. "As our priests reach out in the name of Christ, they touch many people's lives. We cannot be certain who among those many people will be the Judas to betray us."

Mr. Dilber returned with Gilbert's coat. "A man is watching the house from the street," he reported.

"So we shall depart another way," Gilbert said. He shrugged on his coat. Then he gestured to the two kids. "This way, please."

Andrew and Eve struggled to keep up as George Gilbert walked quickly down the hallway. He rounded a corner to a staircase. They climbed the stairs to an upper hallway and followed the passage to a small room. It was only slightly larger than a storage closet. At the back wall sat a big wardrobe. Gilbert pulled open the doors. To Andrew's surprise, he climbed inside.

Eve giggled. "Just like Narnia," she said softly.

The children watched as Gilbert opened a back panel in the wardrobe. Beyond that was a dark space. He went through and beckoned them to follow. Eve went first, then Andrew. Gilbert stepped through the back of the one wardrobe into another wardrobe. He pushed open the doors to a large empty room.

"This is the adjoining house to mine," Gilbert explained as he went back into the wardrobes and closed the various doors and panels.

"'Tis empty, as thou canst see. Should hunters come, we may descend to the ground floor and escape through a side door."

They began the trek downward on a long flight of stairs.

"Do you have hiding places in houses all over London?" Andrew asked.

Gilbert said, "By the grace of God, we have them all over England."

Emerging from the side door of the house, they hurried down a passageway to a low stone wall and shrubs bordering a garden. Beyond that was a pasture enclosed by the walls of Lincoln's Inn to the north and another tall wall to the west. They skirted along the row of neighboring houses, moving away from Lincoln's Inn.

Gilbert said, "Should you ever need to pass this way again, there are orchards and gardens on the other sides of those high walls. You mayst find places to hide there. Or travel, as we do now, past the Harflete Inn just ahead to Ballards Lane. It will return you to Chauncelor Lane and south to Flete Street."

Andrew heard what Gilbert was saying but knew he would be completely lost if he ever came this way again.

Gilbert's coach was waiting for them at the end of Ballards Lane. It was a less lavish vehicle than Mr. Nedly's. Andrew thought it looked as if someone had thrown a big wooden box on top of a normal wagon and held it all together with leather straps. He, Eve, and Gilbert sat inside on benches with thin pillows.

Gilbert looked amused. He shouted over the loud rattling of the wheels on the rutty road, "This is a far cry from the coaches my family is accustomed to. My mother hath three of a much finer make. I brought one with me to London, but I lent it to the wife of a member of the Queen's Privy Council."

Andrew was shocked. "You have given your coach to one of the people who are trying to capture you?"

Gilbert smiled and said, "We have also lodged with many a member. Keeping our enemies close makes them less suspicious."

"You are spying on the spies?" Andrew asked.

"I suppose I am," Gilbert said.

Eve said, "I have noticed that everyone talks about the coaches belonging to women. Do the men not own coaches?"

"The men own coaches but do not often ride in them," Gilbert replied. "Unless they are ill or unmanly."

Eve laughed. "*Unmanly?*"

Gilbert looked perplexed. "Aye. Men ride horses. Coaches are for those with weaker constitutions."

Eve glanced at Andrew. "Thou shouldst be riding a horse," she teased.

"I would if thou gavest me one," he said.

"Coaches are acceptable for children," Gilbert said. "They are also of good use to our priests. An enclosed coach enables them to venture forth unseen."

They traveled west, taking roads away from the main towns and the wide fields that surrounded them. Gilbert explained that they were riding to the home of a faithful friend near the market town of Uxbridge. He said no more than that.

Eve was quiet for most of the trip. Andrew thought she had something on her mind, but the noise from the coach made it hard to talk.

It was three hours before the coachman called out, "Southlands!"

Gilbert explained that Southlands was next to Uxbridge. It turned out to be a tiny village with an inn and a few shops. They ventured off the main street and came to a huddle of houses. At the end of a lane, the coachman halted in front of one thatched cottage made of crisscrossed timber and white plaster. As Andrew climbed out of the coach, he noticed that the cottage was only the front part of a much larger brick house behind it.

Calling to the coachman, Gilbert said, "Return to London, Henry. Fetch our friends, and if all is safe, bring them here."

"Aye, sir," the coachman said, then snapped the reins to get the two horses moving again.

Andrew followed Gilbert and Eve down a path of sunbaked mud and grass. As they approached the cottage, a wiry-looking, older man with unruly gray hair and a long curly beard stepped from the front door. He walked quickly to them with outstretched arms. He gave George Gilbert a friendly embrace.

"This is our good master, William Griffith," Gilbert said to Andrew and Eve.

CHAPTER THIRTEEN

Mr. Griffith shook Andrew's hand and bowed to Eve. "Your servant," he said to them. "Come inside. Refresh yourselves."

Griffith guided them through the thatched cottage. In each small room, men of different ages were either sitting and reading or at small desks writing. A hall led from the cottage to the brick house in the back. The rooms there were larger. One contained a small group of men around a table. They seemed to be engaged in a hushed but intense conversation.

Mr. Griffith took his guests to a sizable kitchen area and invited Andrew and Eve to sit at a hefty block table. A short man with a broad face, long brown hair, and a wispy goatee was busy moving between vegetables cut up on a table and a great pot on the fire. For a moment, Andrew thought of the character Gimli from Tolkien's Lord of the Rings trilogy.

Mr. Griffith introduced the man as Brother Ralph Emerson. Then Griffith turned to Gilbert and said, "Father Persons awaits us."

The two men walked out.

Andrew remembered hearing the name *Persons* somewhere along the way.

Brother Emerson smiled at them. A moment later, he placed cups of ale and plates of bread, cheese, vegetables, and nuts in front of them. "Eat, drink," he said, then went back to his work.

"Are all of the men here priests?" Andrew asked as he nibbled the food.

"Not all," replied Brother Emerson. "Some are deacons. Some are newfound converts and supporters of our cause, members of the society of gentlemen formed by our generous sponsor George Gilbert."

"Mr. Gilbert gives you money?" Eve asked.

"In great abundance," Brother Emerson said. "He hath provided sixty pounds in money, two horses and a servant, two suits of apparel for traveling, books, vestments, and all manner of essentials. He and his friends serve as conductors and companions, without whom we could not travel."

Eve said quietly to Andrew, "I do not know how they live like this."

"What dost thou mean?" he asked. "'Tis a nice house."

"I *mean* being afraid all the time, watching for spies, worrying about capture," she explained.

"Afraid? Worried? Nay, dear girl," said Brother Emerson as he chopped up the stalk of a long green vegetable.

Eve looked embarrassed that she'd been heard.

"To die for Christ is the greatest honor," the priest continued. "Many of us have come knowing we shall be caught, tortured, and killed for proclaiming the true faith. Jesus has called us all to this very purpose."

Eve lowered her head. "Well, I would be afraid," she said.

Brother Emerson nodded to her. "'Tis no sin to be afraid, child. In our fear, God gives us the grace to find courage—if we ask Him."

CHAPTER THIRTEEN

"Andrew, Evangeline," George Gilbert called from the doorway. "Father Persons desireth a word with you."

Andrew and Eve looked uneasily at each other. They followed Gilbert down the hallway to another section of the house. He escorted them into a small study.

Father Persons stood to greet them. He had large, tired-looking eyes, a long nose, and a small mouth nearly hidden by his moustache and beard. His short hair was salt-and-pepper colored. The layers of his clothes were all black, making him look more like a priest than any of the other priests Andrew had met.

The priest stood behind the table in a room filled mostly with plain wooden chairs. He gestured for them to sit down. As they did, he pulled a chair around the desk and sat facing them.

In a low, calm voice, Father Persons said, "So you are Children of the Stone. I thank you for the goodly service you have rendered to Father William and Father Matthew coming from Glastonbury."

"You are welcome, good sir," Andrew said.

"I have been told that you are searching for someone," the priest said.

"Dr. Vincent Howard," Eve answered.

"A few members of the Howards are faithful Catholics," Father Persons told her.

"I do not think he is Catholic, sir," Eve said.

"Nevertheless, I shall use our couriers to inquire into his whereabouts. The gent is a relative of yours?" asked Father Persons.

"Nay. He is a friend of my aunt's," Eve said.

"Pray, who is thy aunt?" asked Father Persons.

"Catherine Drake," Eve replied.

"From where doth she hail?" he asked.

"A hamlet called Hope Springs," Eve said, then quickly added, "'Tis far away, in the west."

"I do not know it," Father Persons said. "Thy aunt sent two *children* to search for her friend?"

Eve nodded. "She is not able to travel, sir. There is no one else she can rely upon."

The priest's expression told Andrew that he was unsure about Eve's response. Andrew braced himself for a series of questions that would be hard to answer.

Instead, Father Persons slowly shook his head. "The days are difficult," he said, as if that covered everything that needed to be said. "We welcome your company and continued service."

Andrew and Eve returned to the kitchen. Brother Emerson was now slicing long loaves of bread.

"May I help you?" Eve asked.

He looked grateful for being asked but said, "Nay, child. Walk in the garden and be at peace."

Eve gave Andrew a look that said *That means you, too*.

CHAPTER THIRTEEN

Andrew was happy to oblige.

Together, they stepped into the garden. The late-afternoon sun shone at an angle that gave clear lines to everything. Long shadows stretched from the house and a ramshackle barn that sat at the edge of a wide field. In the distance sat a grove of trees. Beyond that, Andrew saw the jagged rooftops of the town of Uxbridge.

"It's a real garden," Eve said, pointing to patches of furrowed ground just behind the house. Some late-season vegetables were there, waiting to be collected.

Andrew knelt down to pick up a few small stones in the brown dirt. Training his eye on a post near the barn, he wound up his arm and threw one of the stones. He missed the post by a few inches.

"You're already out of practice," Eve said.

He threw a second stone and hit the right side of the post. A third stone hit dead center near the top. He looked around for something to put on top of the post.

"I haven't had a chance to tell you..." Eve began, then paused.

"Tell me what?" Andrew's search led him toward the barn.

"I had a strange dream at Mr. Nedly's," she said, trailing behind him. "Not long before you woke me, I dreamed that Ambrosius was standing in the corner of my room."

Andrew stopped and turned to her. "Was he holding a candle?" he asked.

"Yes," she said. She looked at him with a curious expression. "He woke me up and told me to go to the door. How did you know that?"

"Did you go to the door?" Andrew asked, his heart suddenly beating fast.

"No. I thought it was a dream. I rolled over and went back to sleep." Her eyes narrowed, and she asked again, "*How did you know?*"

"He appeared in my room, too, and told me the same thing," Andrew said. "Then he disappeared when I went to the door. That's how I overheard Mr. Nedly and Jerome."

"Ambrosius went to you because I didn't wake up?" Eve asked. "But how did … how could he …?" She shook her head. "These adventures are getting weirder and weirder."

"Weirder than leaping all over time?" he asked.

"Well, apart from that," she said.

Andrew was glad to see her smile. He was about to throw another stone but stopped. Beyond the barn, a man was strolling across the field in their direction.

Eve came alongside Andrew. Her eyes were also on the stranger. "What should we do? He might be a priest hunter," she said.

"Go inside. Tell the others," Andrew said. "I'll stall him."

"How will you stall him?" she asked.

Andrew tossed the stone up and down in his hand. "I'll think of something."

Eve jogged toward the house.

Andrew strolled over to the side of the barn. He pretended that he was searching for something on the ground but kept his gaze on the approaching stranger.

The man wore a dark suit. Even at that distance, Andrew could tell they were the clothes of a nobleman. On his head was a hat with a long feather sticking out of the side. He rested a hand on the hilt of a long sword in his belt. His brown leather boots came up to his knees. They looked worn and weathered.

"Hail!" the man called out with a wave.

Andrew gave him his full attention. The man might have been thirty years old. He had wide eyes, tanned skin, a thin moustache, and a trimmed beard that came to a point below his chin.

"Hail, my lord," said Andrew.

The man had reached the barn and took off his hat. His hair was long. He pushed it back with his fingers. "Art thou a Griffith?" the man asked in a low voice. He nodded to the house. "Is that thy house?"

"Not mine, sir. I am a guest," Andrew replied.

"Dost thou know Mr. Griffith?" the man asked.

"I do," Andrew said but added nothing more.

The man chuckled. "Clever lad! Give nothing away to a stranger," he said. "Pray, what is thy name?"

"Andrew."

"Tell me, Andrew, if I were to draw my sword and demand answers from thee about that house, what wouldst thou do?"

"First, my lord, you would have to draw," Andrew challenged him.

The man reached for his sword. Before it was free of the hilt, Andrew threw himself to the right. He did a somersault to get clear of the man. In one move, he sprang to his feet again and launched the stone from his palm. The stone knocked the feathered hat from the man's hand.

Astonished, the man stumbled back. "Take me for a fool to ask such a question!" he cried. He slid the sword back into its sheath and snatched up his hat. "Clearly, the secrets of this abode are safe whilst thou dost stand guard. Fear not, Andrew. The assembly inside awaits me. I am Edmund Campion."

As if to prove the man's claim, Father Persons, Mr. Griffith, and a crowd of men poured out through the back door of the house. They shouted happily and were soon shaking hands and embracing Campion.

"So that is the famous Edmund Campion," Eve said as she came next to Andrew.

Andrew watched the newly arrived hero. "And I nearly hit him in the head with a rock."

14

Father Campion disappeared with Father Persons and Brother Emerson for a lengthy private discussion. The three men eventually came out for supper, which was served at a large table in a windowless back room. Andrew had the impression that the room was once used for storage.

Apart from the men Andrew had already met, there were another half dozen who had been studying or praying in various rooms. Most of them looked as if they were in their twenties. They all had the bright-eyed enthusiasm of men on a great mission. Mr. Griffith sat next to a silver-haired woman with a pleasant face. Before the prayer, Father Persons introduced her as "the lady of the house," Anne Griffith. He commended the Griffiths for the use of their home. She blushed and waved away the attention.

The meal was simple, with a few selections of meat and vegetables given out in small portions. Once everyone had eaten, the plates were cleared and Father Persons stood up.

"We welcome our brother Edmund Campion, who shall speak anon," Father Persons said. "First, I must deliver distressing news. Our dear friend Arthur Josephs has been imprisoned for questioning."

The men groaned and shuffled uneasily.

Father Persons continued. "Father William and Father Matthew are safe at secret lodgings in London."

Andrew was relieved to hear the news.

"The Queen's Privy Council hath employed more spies throughout the city. We must be ever more cautious," Father Persons said. He then gave a brief account of his travels throughout England. He talked about the many people who were strengthened in their Catholic faith by the priests' work. He also spoke of those who became Catholic, including many leaders around Stratford-on-Avon, such as John Wheeler and John Shakespeare.

"Shakespeare?" Andrew whispered to Eve.

"Maybe it's a relative of William's," she whispered back.

Once again, Andrew felt that his lack of knowledge about history failed him. He listened to Father Persons and gazed at the dashing figure of Edmund Campion and had no idea what would become of these men.

Bowing to Edmund Campion, Father Persons said, "Treasured friend, we are glad to have thy good company again after so many months away. 'Twas reported that thou wert in different towns and cities, miles and miles apart, seen by many, captured by some, even declared dead by a few, *on the very same day*!"

Those gathered around laughed.

"I pray thee, rise and speak to us!" Father Persons said.

Father Campion laughed as he stood. "'Tis a delight to see you, whether I am alive or dead! I thank our Lord Jesus and our Holy Mother for the many prayers that allow me to stand before you."

Father Campion touched his fingers along the fabric of his suit. "I confess that these clothes make me feel ridiculous. Please, give me the simple frock of a good priest!"

The men hooted, and some applauded.

Father Campion began to move slowly around the room. His expression turned serious as his voice softened. "Dear brothers, the heat of persecution now raging against Catholics throughout the whole realm is most fiery. Gentle and simple men and women are led to prison. Even children are put into irons."

Eve gave Andrew a worried glance.

The priest went on. "The good folk are deprived of their goods, shut out from the light of day, and publicly held up to the contempt of the people as traitors and rebels. They are blamed for the coming of us, the Jesuits, to this realm. More than battles and bloodshed, our queen and her counselors fear the great number of conversions we have made. They sweetly entice the faithful to yield in outward appearance only. Attend their houses of heresy, they say, show obedience there even whilst our hearts hold fast to other truths. What, then, becomes of our very souls?"

Father Campion then told stories of Catholics imprisoned as traitors and horribly tortured. He recounted how priests cheerfully bore their chains, even when they were paraded down the streets and abused by onlookers.

"Though we resist political debates and proclaim our loyalty to our queen," he said, "we are duty bound to preach the gospel of Jesus Christ and the truth of His Church."

With that, Father Campion led the group in prayers for the success of their mission, for the many people who aided them, for the souls of the English people, and for the soul of the queen.

That night, Andrew was given a cot in the corner of a room with three of the young priests. He slept fitfully. With any sudden noise, he jerked awake, afraid that the hunters were about to grab him.

The next morning, the men gathered with Father Persons and Father Campion to pray and discuss their immediate plans.

Father Persons announced that the house would be emptied of the priests in slow shifts throughout the day. They would be given money, clothes, and aliases. Some would be sent into the countryside; others would reside at addresses around London. The locations were kept secret to all but Father Persons and the priests going to various locations.

"We do not want any of us to know more than we must," Father Persons explained.

Andrew knew they were following the old rule: if you're caught and questioned, you can't reveal what you don't know.

Father Persons said, "Be alert. Do nothing to draw attention to yourselves, save living as men of good character."

Father Campion then rose to bless them. "My brothers, I entreat you to be humble. Do not attempt to be clever in your speech. Allow God to give you the tongues of angels and the truth of the Apostles. Your primary care is to faithful Catholics. Virtue, piety, and prudence must be your weapons. Make moderation your watchword. If you are captured, deny firmly any charges and demand to see any evidence against you. Often, your accusers will play the bluff. If you are convicted and led away to be executed, know that you join many saints by sealing your convictions with your blood."

Andrew wondered what he and Eve were expected to do. The answer came quickly as Eve was tasked with helping Mrs. Griffith and two other priests tidy the house. Andrew was told to help pack satchels of provisions for the departing priests.

Father Persons and Father Campion retreated for a day of writing letters to their superiors in Reims and Rome. Andrew learned that the letters would be carried out of the country by priests posing as merchants, or sent through the Spanish ambassador's personal couriers.

"I shall take the letters to the ambassador myself," Father Persons said.

Later that afternoon, Andrew found Eve pulling up weeds in the garden. There was a crisp edge to the air. He knelt down next to her and tugged at a few stubborn roots.

Eve sighed. "What is going to happen to us?"

"Let's hope the contacts of Father Persons will lead us to Dr. Howard," Andrew replied.

"That could take a long time," Eve said.

"What else can we do?" Andrew asked. "If we return to Hope Springs without him, your aunt will think we've been gone only a couple of minutes and didn't try very hard to find him."

Eve nodded. "What has he been doing all this time? You know what happened to Simon Howard in France—and that poor jailer in Winchester."

Andrew thought of Simon. He had almost lost his mind because he'd been in the past too long. And the poor jailer, Anthony Dovedale, was a complete wreck.

"Our Children of the Stone are now Children of the Weeds?" a familiar voice asked.

William came toward them from the back door. Matthew followed close behind.

Andrew and Eve leapt to their feet and rushed to the two men.

"Thank God you are well," Eve said. She hugged William, then Matthew.

CHAPTER FOURTEEN

"Was there any doubt?" asked William.

Matthew patted Andrew on the shoulder. "We have news," he said.

The four of them went back into the house and met with Father Persons, Father Campion, Brother Emerson, George Gilbert, and the Griffiths. They gathered in the kitchen while Mrs. Griffith poured them warm ale.

Matthew said, "The Queen's Privy Council hath determined that Father Campion is in London no longer. They have sent spies throughout every part of the country to find the fugitive priest. They search for Father Persons as well. Everyone known or suspected to be in sympathy with the Catholic Church is more closely watched."

"Will they harm our brothers and sisters?" Brother Emerson asked.

"'Tis claimed that the council's wrath is directed against the Jesuits only," Matthew replied.

"Though we speak no ill against her majesty," said Father Campion.

"The queen's fear is stoked by her Privy Council," William said. "In turn, she goads them to take more extreme actions."

"Pray, then, what shall we do?" asked Brother Emerson.

Father Persons said, "We must strengthen our plan by changing our lodgings every two or three days—perhaps every day if needs must."

George Gilbert said, "I shall agree upon a schedule with the friends of our society."

The men discussed who should go where. Father Campion would be safest in the towns surrounding London. Father William and Father Matthew would once again travel as actors throughout the region.

"As such, we will deliver words of warning to the Catholics we meet, and we may yet keep abreast of the Privy Council's doings," Gilbert said.

"What of our two guests?" Brother Emerson asked, his eyes on Andrew and Eve.

Father Persons gave them a rare smile. "On the morrow, they shall provide me with the best disguise of all."

15

Bernardino de Mendoza, the Spanish ambassador, lived in an enormous palace near one of the homes of George Gilbert in Holborn. The Bishop of Ely—a bishop of the Church of England—owned the palace. He rented it to Mendoza, even though Mendoza was a devout Catholic.

It was well known that spies for the Queen's Privy Council kept a close eye on the palace. Andrew got the impression that it had become a risky game for priests to sneak in to see the ambassador when they knew they were being watched.

Father Persons came up with the idea that Andrew and Eve should accompany him to the palace. "The hunters will not expect a priest to travel with two children," he said.

George Gilbert arranged for a coach to take them from the Griffiths' home to the ambassador's residence at midday. The coach was much nicer than the one that had brought Andrew and Eve out of London. The outside was a burgundy color, with edges painted in gold. The inside was covered in a rich red velvet.

"Compliments of a member of the queen's own court." Gilbert grinned as he helped them into the coach. "You are unlikely to be detained."

Father Persons wore a flamboyant purple suit with oversized, frilly collars. On his head was a wide-brimmed hat adorned with a peacock feather.

"You are a dandy," Father Campion teased him.

"'Tis appropriate for the place I am going," Father Persons said unhappily.

Andrew was dressed in the fine clothes of a gentleman's son. Eve wore a pale-green dress that Mrs. Griffith's had hemmed for her overnight. Eve didn't look comfortable at all. She kept pulling at the dress.

"It doesn't fit," she said privately to Andrew. "It's too tight in the shoulders, and it's too long. My feet are catching on the hem."

"Shall we run to a department store and buy another dress?" Andrew asked.

"If only," Eve said.

Gilbert instructed the coachman to taxi his passengers at a leisurely pace. "Rushing will draw unnecessary attention," he explained.

They approached London from the northwest. Dark clouds, bloated with rain, settled over the city. The many spires looked as if they might punch holes in the clouds' bellies.

Andrew recognized the road and sites leading into Holborn. He knew which turns would take them back to the homes of George Gilbert and Arthur Josephs. The coachman turned north until they came to an arched gateway. Andrew peeked out the window. He gasped. Beyond the gate was not only a palace but a grand cathedral as well.

A guard wearing a red-and-gold uniform opened the gate. The coachman guided the horses up a drive to a wide portico. More guards, all wearing the same red-and-gold uniforms, surrounded the coach and opened the doors.

"Welcome," one said with a thick Spanish accent.

Andrew stepped out and looked back toward the road. He saw a man just outside the gate. He was pacing along the pavement, craning to see who was paying the ambassador a visit. He stopped at the sight of Andrew. His expression changed from one of anticipation to disappointment.

The plan worked, Andrew thought.

Eve nearly fell getting out of the coach. "I hate this dress," she said, yanking the hem away from her shoes.

Father Persons was the last to exit the coach.

The guards led the three of them through a set of heavy doors and inside to a wide, dark-paneled hallway.

A woman with the stiff-backed demeanor of an office clerk rushed forward to meet them. She curtsied. "The ambassador is expecting you," she said to Father Persons.

The priest fumbled as he took off his hat and bowed to her.

The woman shot a look at Andrew and Eve. " 'Tis a *private* audience, I believe. I was not told to prepare the nursery."

Eve snapped, "We do not need a—"

Andrew interrupted her. "With humble thanks to the ambassador, we shall not stay."

The woman looked relieved.

Father Persons gave Andrew and Eve an apologetic look. "Do you remember the way to George Gilbert's home?"

"Aye, my lord," Eve said.

"I thank you for giving me safe passage," the priest said.

Andrew and Eve were ushered back through the door and down to the gate. The coach had already pulled away.

"I guess we're walking," Andrew said.

The two made their way back to Holborn. Eve complained about her dress the entire time. They reached the main road, and Andrew wondered how they would cross over to the other side. The various horseback riders and coaches seemed to dart here and there, with no sense of direction.

"We'll have to run for it," Andrew said. He took Eve's hand to help her.

Eve hitched up her dress with her free hand. "This will be fun," she said, sounding as if it wouldn't be fun at all.

"At least the road is paved," Andrew said.

They followed a stone sidewalk, looking for a break in the traffic.

A coach slowly passed them and caught Andrew's eye. It looked identical to Mr. Nedly's coach. Then the face of Mr. Nedly himself appeared in the window. He turned his head and saw Andrew.

"Uh-oh," Andrew said, quickening his pace.

Eve dragged behind him. "What's wrong?"

He tugged at her hand. "It's Mr. Nedly," he said and used that moment to cross the street.

Eve shrieked as they navigated the traffic, stopping and starting suddenly, then darting this way and that.

They reached the pavement near the old Templar ruins and pressed on.

Andrew heard shouts behind them. He glanced back in time to see that Mr. Nedly had stopped his coach. Coachmen and pedestrians swore about the sudden traffic jam.

Andrew and Eve passed Lincoln's Inn and crossed Chauncelor Lane. Andrew spied open gates and passageways for them to rush into if needed.

"Stop those children! Papists! Traitors!" Mr. Nedly shouted from somewhere behind them.

Andrew and Eve broke into a full run. Eve jerked her dress up to her knees so she wouldn't trip.

More shouts caused Andrew to look back. A handful of other man had joined Mr. Nedly and his servant.

Andrew reached the corner of a long wall and pulled Eve to the right. They were now on a path with the wall to the right and the start of a row of houses on the left. The kids raced to the back of the houses and darted to the left. A wide pasture opened up in front of them. They followed a worn path that cut between the pasture and a long line of stone walls and tall shrubs enclosing the gardens behind each house.

"Do you know where you're going?" Eve gasped.

"I'm trying to remember!" Andrew cried out. "Gilbert's house is along here somewhere."

"We can't lead them to the house," Eve said.

"We'll find the empty house next door and use the secret passage in the wardrobe."

"What if the house is locked?"

"One problem at a time!" he snapped. They came to a gap between the shrubs. "This way," he said.

Andrew pressed through the shrubs first. Eve followed. An uneven stone path led through a garden to the house. Eve took a few steps, then fell. Andrew helped her up.

"It's my dress," Eve said, sounding exasperated.

They dashed to a door on the side of the house. Just as Andrew reached for the latch, the door opened.

Matthew was there. He looked as startled to see the two kids as Andrew was to see him.

"The hunters are coming!" Andrew said, panting.

Matthew's eyes widened. He motioned them to come inside.

It was too late. As they were entering the house, Andrew saw Mr. Nedly and his mob arrive at the garden. Mr. Nedly shouted at Andrew.

"To the wardrobe," Matthew said, then hurried farther into the house.

CHAPTER FIFTEEN

Andrew slammed the door and slid the lock into place. He turned, bumping into Eve, who had stumbled again. Andrew caught her arm and pulled her up.

"Go on," she said, clawing at her dress. "I will be right behind you."

Andrew went through to the hall. Matthew was already running up the stairs. Andrew spun to Eve. She was a few feet behind him, still struggling to run without tripping over her dress.

"Go!" she shouted.

Andrew shot up the stairs to the first floor. Eve was a few steps behind him. Matthew was already ascending the next staircase.

From down below came the sounds of splintering wood and men's shouts.

Andrew climbed the next flight of stairs and raced from the hallway into the room. Matthew already had the wardrobe doors open.

His head spinning, Andrew turned to tell Eve to go ahead of him.

But she wasn't there.

"Eve," he gasped, then ran back to the hall.

She was at the bottom of the stairs on the first floor. "My dress got caught on a nail!" she cried out.

There was a terrible racket as the men clambered up the first flight of stairs.

"Go on! I'll hide!" Eve said.

Before Andrew could respond, she rushed out of sight.

He took a step to go after her, but arms wrapped around his chest from behind.

"Thou cannot help her if thou art caught," Matthew said as he carried Andrew up to the empty room. "The villains will question both of you and force out what you know."

Andrew struggled against him. "But I cannot leave her."

"Upon my word, Evangeline shall be safely returned to thee," Matthew said.

Matthew threw Andrew into the wardrobe, pushing in behind him. Andrew had no choice but to go through.

He stumbled into Gilbert's house and fell on his hands and knees. He could hear Matthew closing the various panels and doors.

Andrew's heart was pounding. The blood throbbed in his head.

He was aware of Matthew standing nearby. Shouts, footfalls, and banging came from the empty room on the other side.

"Where have they gone?" Mr. Nedly roared.

"They must be here somewhere!" came another voice.

The doors of the wardrobe were thrown open on the other side. Then came an awful pounding, as if Nedly's men were testing the wood.

"They cannot have disappeared!" Mr. Nedly shouted.

"The window is bolted," said another man.

Someone shouted from farther away. Andrew crawled to the wall and listened. From the commotion, it was easy to guess that they'd found Eve. He pulled himself up and reached for the wardrobe door.

Matthew grabbed his wrist and whispered, "Nay!"

They both stayed still. Andrew strained to hear what was happening.

"Evangeline hath locked herself in a closet," Matthew whispered.

Now came a chaotic banging. Andrew imagined the men pounding on the closet door. Then there was a crash. Had they broken through?

He now expected to hear Eve scream. Instead, a strange silence followed.

The shouts of the men turned into a kind of low murmuring. Andrew couldn't tell what they were saying.

Suddenly he heard a new voice. A man was yelling at the others. Andrew caught enough words to know that the man had seen fugitives running out the front door.

The news caused another barrage of noise as the men pounded down the stairs and out of the house.

Andrew slumped to the floor. He felt sick. Matthew put a hand against the wardrobe door. There was an eerie stillness. Then they heard footsteps coming up the steps of the other house and into the empty room. Andrew got to his feet.

The wardrobe doors on the other side opened. The first panel on the back of the wardrobe moved. Then came a rhythmic sound of three knocks, then two, then three again.

Matthew gave a deep sigh of relief. "That is our signal." He opened the wardrobe doors and stepped inside. Andrew heard a series of loud clicks; then Matthew stepped back into the room. A few seconds later, the head of an old man peeked out.

"Greetings, lads," said William, wearing another disguise.

"God be praised," said Matthew.

"Imagine my surprise as I strolled up the lane and heard all the commotion issuing forth from this house," William said. "I readily knew what was occurring. I sent those scoundrels on a wild-goose chase."

"Thank God for thy quickness of mind," Matthew said. "Why art thou in costume?"

"To make my way safely across London," he replied.

As soon as William stepped into the room, Andrew leapt into the wardrobe and through to the other house. He took the stairs two and three at a time down to the lower floor.

William shouted from behind him, "What is wrong, lad?"

"Where is Evangeline?" Andrew asked. In the hall, he saw a wrecked door hanging open by a single hinge. The closet was tiny, with just enough room for someone Eve's size. On the floor was a small strip of cloth. He picked it up. The cloth had come from Eve's dress. Other than that, the closet was empty.

"They took her?" Andrew asked as William and Matthew joined him.

CHAPTER FIFTEEN

"Nay," William said. "Evangeline was not with the men."

"The hunters must have found her hiding here," Matthew said.

William gave them a puzzled look. "I shouted when I came upon the scene. The men were roused to give chase. Evangeline was not with them. Nor was she here when I ascended to yonder room."

Andrew pushed at the closet walls. "Is there another hiding place?" he asked.

Matthew said, "Only the one in the wardrobe."

The three of them searched the hall and nearby rooms, even daring to shout out her name. But Andrew knew that Eve wasn't there. She could not have escaped before the men reached her. She had hidden in the closet.

"We must depart, lest we be captured," Matthew said.

They moved toward the stairs.

Andrew held up the scrap of Eve's dress. "Where is she?" he asked.

"'Tis curiously like the jailer in Winchester, is it not?" William said. He leveled a knowing look at Andrew. "By what means could a Child of the Stone escape from a locked closet?"

16

The more Andrew thought about it, the more certain he was that Eve had used the Radiant Stone to escape.

He now sat in the front room of Gilbert's house. He felt hot and fuzzy brained. Father William, Father Matthew, and George Gilbert were deep in conversation nearby. He looked at the three men as if they were far away. Mr. Nedly and his mob had returned to the house next door, they were saying. The hunters might discover the connection between that house and Gilbert's presence in this one.

George Gilbert called out to his servant Mr. Dilber. "'Tis time to move," he said. "Seal the wardrobe passageway. Pack up our belongings."

The men stood. Andrew remained where he was.

He imagined what had happened. Eve was trapped. She panicked. She used the Radiant Stone to escape.

Eve is gone, he told himself.

He considered the possibility that Ambrosius had saved her. But surely he would have put her nearby, right there in Gilbert's house.

No, she used the Radiant Stone, he thought.

Even now, she was back in Alfred Virtue's office. Maybe she stayed there to give herself time to think.

If that was true, he might be stuck in this time for months, maybe years.

Even if she had immediately touched the facet to come back, it was anyone's guess where she wound up. Back in London? The closet in the house next door? The chapel at Beckery? Somewhere else the Radiant Stone had been in its history? It wasn't as if she could program in a specific date and time.

"Andrew," Matthew said.

Andrew looked up. Matthew was standing over him. The others had left the room.

"Thou art not well?" Matthew asked.

Andrew shook his head.

"I know not what it is to be a Child of the Stone," Matthew said. "Some mysteries are best kept with those who must bear their burdens. But I ask: Wherever Evangeline hath gone, dost thou believe she is in danger?"

"Nay," Andrew replied. "She is safe."

"'Tis better, then, that she is not in the clutches of the vile hunters," he said.

Andrew nodded.

Matthew lifted his hand over Andrew's head, like a blessing. "Then be at peace."

CHAPTER SIXTEEN

Be at peace.

Andrew wished he could be at peace. But losing Eve unsettled him to his very core. Even when they were stuck together in the time of Joan of Arc, with no way to get home, he didn't worry. Being together made it bearable. Now he was alone.

Eve will come back, he reminded himself. *One way or the other, she'll come back.*

The days became like a fever dream to him. He functioned well and did what he was told, but everything felt as if it was happening to somebody else. He helped Dilber and a few other servants pack up Gilbert's belongings for the move to another house in London.

One day, he and William left the moving party. They traveled along a road called the Strand to the next big city just west along the River Thames. It was called Westminster. Their coach took them past the gatehouse of an old palace there. Andrew thought it looked more like a collection of palaces that had been thrown together. A modest clock tower stood on the corner.

William explained that King Canute the Dane may have built the original palace five hundred years before. "Fire often destroyed its wooden pillars, beams, and walls. King Edward the Confessor built a bigger palace for his court here and then gave much of his wealth to building St. Peter's Abbey across the field."

William pointed, and Andrew turned to see the great arches and double sentry-like towers of a building he knew in his time as the famous Westminster Abbey.

"'Twas a Benedictine monastery," William said. "Edward insisted that the church be shaped like a cross. He saw it completed but died on Christmas Eve, only a few days ere it was consecrated. Henry the Third added much to the palace and the abbey. All of our kings—and the queen—have been crowned in the cathedral."

Andrew thought of the cathedral in Reims, France, where the Dauphin was crowned thanks to Joan of Arc.

William looked grim. "Alas, the glory hath departed. The abbey was taken by Henry the Eighth and placed into the hands of the heretics. Queen Mary reclaimed it, but alas, 'twas lost again after her downfall."

Taking a few turns off the main road, they came to a cottage on a small patch of wooded land.

"Where are we?" Andrew asked.

"The home of a virtuous widow," William replied. "'Tis better thou knowest not the name."

The widow was a waxen-faced woman dressed all in black. Andrew later learned that she always wore black as a memorial to her dead husband.

Father Persons was with Brother Emerson and Father Matthew in a simply furnished sitting room at the back of the house.

William delivered a few handwritten messages to Father Persons. He held one up that was bound with a blue ribbon and a red seal.

"From our good friend close to the Queen's Privy Council," William said.

Father Persons opened that message first and read it. He leaned back in the chair, his brow showing deep lines. "'Tis a warning," he said. "The council will announce yet another proclamation against the Jesuits. It will remind all good English subjects that the priests are in England for the singular purpose of overthrowing the queen. The council shall begin immediately to search all of the homes of known Catholics."

"What will you do?" William asked.

Father Persons stood up. "I shall move all the more frequently around London to avoid capture. Father Campion must go farther afield." He scrubbed his chin thoughtfully for a moment. "'Tis untimely news. Yet God's will is always timely. This may give Father Campion much-needed time to write."

Andrew listened as Father Persons and William discussed the need to publish more books and pamphlets arguing their cause. He remembered hearing that Father Campion had written a widely read essay in the summer. Nicknamed "Campion's Brag," the essay challenged the queen's theologians to a debate about the Catholic faith. It had caused quite a stir, and a flurry of nasty responses from various scholars and preachers.

"I shall write on a selection of topics," Father Persons said. "Father Campion must write another challenge."

"How will we print the papers?" Brother Emerson asked. "We dismantled the printing press for fear of the Privy Council."

"We must find another location for the press," Father Persons said.

"An idea comes to my mind," said William, "but I must give it further thought before I speak of it."

Father Persons dismissed them but asked Andrew to remain. When they were alone, Father Persons said, "I have received a message about Vincent Howard."

Andrew came to attention. "Sir?"

The priest continued. "Your man was arrested in Southampton nigh on three months ago. The townspeople complained that the gent behaved like a madman. 'Twas surmised that he was a drunkard, though no one had ever seen him drink."

"Is he there still?"

"Nay. Once the High Sheriff rooted out his name, he was delivered to the Howard family in Arundel. Allowing he was a lost member of that good family, they treated him charitably. They were vexed by the many riddles he spoke. A doctor was summoned but was likewise confounded. Your gent was forcibly removed to Bedlam."

"Bedlam, sir? Where is that?"

"Here in London. 'Tis St. Mary of Bethlehem hospital for lunatics," Father Persons said.

They put Dr. Howard in an asylum? Andrew imagined somewhere horrible with wild-eyed, drooling maniacs locked in dark rooms. "Is he there now?"

"He was there when the letter was written a fortnight ago."

"With permission, I must go to him," said Andrew.

"As thou wishest," said the priest.

William volunteered to accompany Andrew to the asylum. George Gilbert's coach took them east through London, then north out of the city at Bishopsgate.

Andrew had never been to an asylum. He felt nervous.

William seemed to sense how Andrew felt and talked at length about the hospital. "St. Mary's was once the priory for an order dedicated to Our Lady of Bethlehem. Monks and pilgrims who had been to Bethlehem often came there. 'Twas later a haven for the poor and those with burdened minds."

"So it is not a hospital?" asked Andrew.

"'Tis named a hospital because it is run by charity," William explained.

"Why is it called *Bedlam*?"

William looked at him as if the answer was obvious. "*Bethlehem* became *Bedlam* in the common tongue."

Andrew nodded. It seemed obvious once William said it.

William continued. "Whilst cleansing London of all manner of Catholic evils, Henry the Eighth decreed that the hospital be delivered to the custody of the Lord Mayor of London. The Lord Mayor, in his good counsel, then delivered the caretaking of the hospital to the governors of Bridewell."

Andrew looked at William, perplexed.

"The governors of Bridewell Prison," William said slowly.

"The hospital is run by a *prison* warden?" Andrew asked.

"'Tis worse," said William. "It now is under the rule of Roland Sleford, a cloth maker who cares only for what wage he may make from the sick and infirm."

The grounds for St. Mary of Bethlehem were beyond a wide gate. The hospital was a cluster of buildings with no consistent design or construction. Some of the buildings looked like mere houses made of wood. Others were larger structures made of fat gray stones, some with turrets at the top, like the towers of a castle.

The coach came to a halt in front of the main door of a long, low building. William and Andrew stepped out of the coach as a fresh rainfall began.

A man rushed from the building and opened the coach door for them. His face was covered with red splotches. He was dressed in a faded uniform with torn sleeves and leggings that looked as if multiple cats had shredded them. Smiling at them with a mouth full of brown and black teeth, he cackled, "Come! Come anon!"

William gave Andrew a quick nod. They followed the man into the building. Andrew was instantly hit with a terrible smell that reminded him of a backed-up sewer, a gym locker, and rotten fish. William handed him a handkerchief to put over his nose. The priest then used a second one for himself.

Drops of water dripped from the ceiling and gathered in small pools along the dark hallway. A wild scream echoed from somewhere. From another direction came a loud groan. A woman shouted, "Have mercy! I beg thee! Mercy!"

Andrew looked up at William, who shook his head sadly.

Another man hurried over to them. His face was round and clean-shaven, almost baby-like. He wore the tidy robes of a clerk of some sort. "Are you picking up, dropping off, or visiting?" he asked.

"By your leave, we have come to see a patient," William said.

"Does it have a name?"

"Vincent Howard," William said.

"*Howard*, my lord?" The man's eyebrows shot up.

"Is Mr. Sleford here?" William asked in a tone that suggested the man should find someone in charge.

"Nay, good sir," the clerk said. "Yet I know the good Dr. Lazars would desire to speak with you about Vincent Howard. Make haste to the Abraham Ward!"

The clerk spun around and walked quickly down a long hallway. William and Andrew followed. The man turned once or twice to urge them along. They passed rooms on each side, where Andrew caught glimpses of chilling sights. Men and women, dressed in rags, were strapped to tables or chairs. In one room, men were gathered around a bed, where legs kicked violently as a patient writhed. Farther along the hall, a solitary man paced with his hands clasped behind his back. He saw Andrew, suddenly lifted his head, and howled like a dog.

The clerk turned down a short passage that dead-ended at a wide doorway. William and Andrew followed him into a room overrun with shelves of vials and tubes, jars and boxes, iron tongs and saws, scissors and knives. In the center of it all was a bench with leather straps. A wooden vise was attached to the top of the bench, with a kind of corkscrew running through the center. Under the bench were puddles of something brown. Andrew shuddered, realizing he was looking at a crude operating table.

"Good master," the clerk called out. "This gentleman and lad would speak with you about Vincent Howard."

Dr. Lazars stood on the other side of a table covered with jars, vases, and beakers. He was bent over, observing a dozen small bowls in front of him. He wore a long red robe that was splattered with streaks of gross-looking colors that Andrew didn't want to think too much about. The doctor snapped his bald head up as soon as he heard *Vincent Howard*.

"Draw near! Who are you? What do you know about the man?" Dr. Lazars demanded.

Andrew and William came closer to the table. Andrew realized that the bowls were filled with wormlike, squirming things. He recoiled from them.

"This boy knows Mr. Howard," William said.

CHAPTER SIXTEEN

Dr. Lazars spun on Andrew. "How now! Art thou his kinsman?"

Andrew said, "I am a friend."

Lazars squinted. "Art thou *Andrew*?"

Andrew was surprised.

William looked surprised too. "How do you know his name?"

"The patient—er, *Mr. Howard*—spoke of Andrew and a girl. 'Eve,' he called her. 'Adam and Eve?' I asked, believing the patient to be confused. But nay. '*Andrew* and Eve,' he insisted. Two children, of whom he knew little. Yet they were the main players in his feverish rants about a *stone*. Knowest thou aught about a stone, boy?" Dr. Lazars looked at him with fiery eyes.

"Aye, sir," Andrew said. He decided to tell the truth no matter how strange it might sound. "'Tis a stone that moves people from one time to another."

"Vincent Howard came from an age that hath not yet happened?" the doctor asked.

"'Tis so, good sir," Andrew said. "He journeyed here in error."

"Pray, what error did he commit?" the doctor asked.

"He touched the stone." Andrew glanced at William, who was looking at him open mouthed and wide eyed.

The doctor pounded the table with excitement, rattling the bowls. "By the rood! I am astounded. Ne'er have I heard of such fanciful tale telling!"

"Do you believe his account?" William asked.

Dr. Lazars laughed. "I believe it as I would any mythology. From whence did the stories come?" he asked Andrew.

Andrew pointed to his head. "Here."

Lazars gazed at Andrew for a moment. Then he said, "Vincent Howard is a man of many humors."

"You think him amusing?" Andrew asked.

"*Humors*, child," the doctor said.

He then launched into a lengthy explanation of the four humors that beset all of mankind—yellow bile, black bile, phlegm, and blood. If the humors were out of balance, a person would fall ill.

Lazars turned to Andrew. "Tell me, then. What is the cause of the man's illness? Unconfessed sin in his heart? A punishment of God? Foul air or stagnant water? Decay? A poor diet?"

"I know not," said Andrew.

" 'Tis a mystery," Lazars said. "No treatment delivered Vincent Howard from the fancies of his demented mind."

"What treatments?" asked Andrew.

Lazars looked impatient. "The patient was bled, to no avail. Then I sought a worthy apothecary for concoctions to ease the poor man's mind. Enemas, laxatives, and mixtures to induce vomiting were all applied. Alas, no improvement. A course of leeches followed. Then sleep potions. Then an elixir made of hemlock, black and white poppies, henbane, and mandragora. The patient would not be cured. I then made preparations for trepanning—"

"*Trepanning?*" William asked, clearly alarmed. "You intend to bore into his skull?"

Andrew shook his head as if he hadn't heard right.

"Trepanning is customary in these extreme cases," Dr. Lazars said.

"Good sir," Andrew said, feeling sick, "where is Vincent Howard now?"

Dr. Lazars suddenly glared at the clerk, standing just behind Andrew. The clerk shuffled uneasily.

"He escaped, in party with another patient," said the doctor.

"When?" asked William.

"Four days ago," the doctor said.

"'Tis five days," said the clerk.

"Five, then," the doctor snapped.

"With what patient did Mr. Howard escape?" asked William.

"'Twas the notorious George Eliot," Dr. Lazars replied. "A varlet, a charlatan, and a trickster. The rogue was brought to me to cure his murderous impulses. He beat an attendant to the point of death."

"Where did they go?" Andrew asked.

The doctor shook his head. "I know not."

There was nothing left to say. Andrew and William thanked the doctor and made their way back to the coach. Dr. Lazars walked with them, chatting as if he was especially interested in Andrew.

I hope he doesn't want to bore into my skull, Andrew thought.

When they reached the coach, Dr. Lazars put a hand on Andrew's arm. "Lad, there is a phrase Mr. Howard oft repeated. Pray tell, what is *Hope Springs*?"

Andrew felt a chill shoot down his spine. He replied, " 'Tis a land far, far away."

Dr. Lazars smiled and nodded. "A mythical place."

"A place of dreams," Andrew said.

He wondered if he would ever see it again.

17

In the coach again, Andrew assumed that he and William would return to London. He was wrong. William told the coachman to drive them several miles east. "Green Street in East Ham," the priest said.

"East Ham?" Andrew asked.

"Thou wilt understand shortly," William said.

Along the way, Andrew thought about the visit to Bedlam. The news about Vincent Howard seemed both good and bad. The good news was that Andrew now knew that Dr. Howard was in the area. The bad news was that he still didn't know exactly where Dr. Howard was. And even if they met up, he would have to tell the poor man that there was no way to get back to their own time.

Andrew looked up and noticed that William was watching him from the seat opposite.

"Pray, what is wrong?" Andrew asked.

William's normally jovial eyes were now serious. " 'Tis difficult for the small minds of man to grasp the great mysteries of God. The strange ways of Ambrosius and the sudden disappearance of Evangeline confound me. As do thy words about Dr. Howard. Are those mysteries of God? Or is another force at work?"

Andrew thought of the times when he and Eve had been accused of doing the devil's work. "I am a faithful Catholic," he said.

"Dost thou renounce the works of Satan and all his evil deeds?" William asked.

"I do."

"Then may God reward thee for the burden thou bearest."

"Burden?"

"To be part of a great mystery is to bear a great burden," William said. "Few will understand. Many desire to do thee harm."

Andrew remembered that Matthew had also called it a burden. *Sometimes it feels that way*, Andrew thought.

East Ham was well named. It was a hamlet east of London. On a broad road called Green Street, William and Andrew came to an arched gateway along a long brick wall. The coachman, whose name was Mr. Kimble, climbed down from the driver's seat and pushed open the iron gates. He then used the bridle to lead both horses through. After, he closed the gate again and drove the coach onward.

The house was a square, two-story building made of a dull-red brick. A rectangular wing stretched away to one side. Behind it was a stone tower that looked as if it had once been part of a castle.

The door to the main house opened. A man stepped out to greet them. Andrew did a double take. The man looked a lot like William, except he was thinner and had a closely trimmed beard.

"My brother Edward," William said.

William bowed to Edward. "Good day, sir," he said.

"God save thee, lad," said Edward. His voice was almost identical to William's.

They went inside the house, which was large and empty. They strolled from room to room in the main section, then down a passageway to the Great Hall. On one end was a kitchen, with a staircase that Andrew assumed led to the stone tower. He would have liked to go to the top to see the view, but the brothers suddenly turned and went back to the main house again.

"This shall do nicely," William said. "'Tis remote and yet close enough to London to access what we need. Hast thou spoken to father?"

"Aye," Edward replied. "He will want to hear from thee on the matter, but I am certain he shall give us his permission."

"What didst thou tell him?" William asked.

"As we agreed. A young and trustworthy gentleman shall live here." Edward hesitated, cocking an eyebrow.

"Do we know *what* young and trustworthy gentleman shall live here, pray tell?"

William said, "I shall recommend to Father Persons that we install Stephen Brinkley."

"I know the name," said Edward. "A virtuous gentleman with an excellent knowledge of literature."

"Stephen Brinkley is a priest *and* an experienced printer," William added. "He shall secure the printing equipment and manage its functions."

Andrew was completely confused now. "Pray, help me understand your plan."

"Our father owns this property," William explained. "This is where we shall assemble our printing press." To Edward, he added, "Father Maurice hath the means to acquire the paper and fulfill our other needs."

"From whom will the money come?"

"George Gilbert."

A nod from Edward. "Secrecy will be our greatest challenge. Keeping it from father will not be easy."

"Your father doth not know?" Andrew said.

William gave Andrew a forlorn smile. "Our father is a good man, but he is not Catholic. We have been forced to keep many secrets from him."

"Thou being a Jesuit is one," Edward said to his brother. "He would certainly not approve."

CHAPTER SEVENTEEN

Within a week, the "young gentleman"—played by Stephen Brinkley—was living in the house everyone now called Greenstreet. Stephen Brinkley was an energetic young man with blond hair and a goatee. The various parts of the printing press were smuggled in crates hidden alongside the kind of furniture that would suit a man of wealth. Andrew was never sure where the furniture came from. The press was installed in a windowless room at the back of the house. Priests, in disguise as friends or laborers, came and went.

One day while William was away, Andrew was stationed at the front door of the house. Mr. Kimble, the coachman, was positioned at the arched gateway. Two priests were in the middle of unloading a crate of parts for the printing press when Andrew heard a loud whistle. It was a signal from Mr. Kimble.

"Beware," Andrew warned the two priests.

Another priest was standing by the door. "I shall fetch Master Brinkley."

Andrew trained his eyes on the gate. Mr. Kimble was talking to someone on the other side. Then he opened one of the gates, and two men stepped through. One of the men wore a tri-cornered hat, and a dark, fur-lined coat with a white collar draped over the top. The other man was gray haired and dressed as a gentleman of modest means.

"'Tis the parson *and* the churchwarden of St. Martin's Church," one of the priests announced.

"Why have they come?" the other priest asked, his voice shaking.

"They come to greet the new tenant," Stephen Brinkley said calmly as he stepped out of the house.

"What shall we do with this crate?" asked the first priest.

"Carry it inside," Brinkley said.

The two priests strained to lift the crate from the back of the wagon—and nearly dropped it.

"*Carefully!*" said Brinkley.

The parson and the churchwarden were closer now. The parson lifted his hand to Brinkley and called out, "Good morrow, sir!"

"Good morrow," Brinkley called back and walked down the drive to meet them. Andrew lingered nearby.

The men introduced themselves as Parson Benson and Mr. Haig.

Stephen Brinkley introduced himself as Stephen Creed, newly arrived.

Andrew glanced back at the door, just in time to see the two priests disappear inside with the crate. He felt relieved until he saw that the back gate of the wagon hung open. On the wagon's bed lay a long black cylinder sticking out from under a tarp. It had the girth and length of a small log. Clearly, it was part of the printing press. He took in a sharp breath and wondered, *How will Mr. Brinkley explain this?*

CHAPTER SEVENTEEN

The two men asked Stephen Creed from whence he had come, what station in life he held, and why he had chosen this particular home. Mr. Brinkley had clearly worked out his answers to their satisfaction. They then invited him to attend their church, reminding him that it was his duty to do so.

As they spoke, Andrew casually stepped over to the wagon. Keeping an eye on the two men, he pulled at the tarp and tucked it around and under the exposed cylinder.

Andrew heard the parson warn Mr. Brinkley to be watchful of Catholics. "The Jesuits have invaded like rats," he said.

Mr. Brinkley assured them that he would be.

"What, pray tell, is *that*?" the churchwarden suddenly shouted, pointing at the wagon.

Andrew froze where he was. His arm was still draped over the tarp as if he just happened to be standing there idly.

The churchwarden walked to the back of the wagon. Mr. Brinkley and the parson followed him.

"What hath caught thine eye?" Mr. Brinkley asked.

The churchwarden skirted to the left of Andrew and pointed to a chair sitting with an assortment of furniture near the front of the wagon. "By the stars, is that a throne chair?" he asked.

Andrew turned to see a boxy-looking wooden chair with a tall back and wide armrests. The woodwork was ornately carved with a leafy design along the edges and what looked like a large tree carved into the back.

Mr. Brinkley gestured to the chair. "Aye. My father was a cabinetmaker, with an affection for French styles."

"Is it walnut?"

"Every inch." Mr. Brinkley chuckled. "'Tis beautiful to look at but uncomfortable to sit upon."

"'Tis true of all things French," the parson said.

The three men laughed. Mr. Brinkley used the moment to guide them away from the wagon. They chatted and laughed as they strolled back down the lane to the gate.

Andrew slumped onto the tarp, feeling as if he might be sick.

Andrew spent some days helping at Greenstreet and other days assisting Father Persons. Andrew stayed by the priest's side as they moved from one safe house to another in London. Some of their hiding places surprised Andrew. One night, they lodged in the home of a priest hunter who believed Father Persons was a jeweler. Another night, they stayed in one of the queen's palaces.

Father Persons stayed very busy giving counsel to the priests in his charge, arranging help for Catholics in prison, and offering guidance and the Sacraments to the undercover Catholics. Though the priest could be warm and kind, he was very serious and focused on his work.

CHAPTER SEVENTEEN

Andrew once asked William why Father Persons was always so serious.

"When Father Persons returned to England from Rome, he came believing he would be martyred," William explained. "Truly, *all* of the Jesuit priests expect to be caught and killed by the queen's men."

"And they came anyway?" Andrew asked.

"Is it not an honor to die for Christ?" William asked.

In spite of this grim reality, the priests and deacons Andrew met were full of life and energy. Few seemed afraid. On the few occasions when a priest admitted fear, Father Persons advised him to take his fears to the Lord in prayer. "Remember our Lord in the garden of Gethsemane," Father Persons said.

Andrew observed that prayer was a focal point of the priests' lives. Mornings, afternoons, and evenings—at least some part of each day was spent praying alone.

They have to pray a lot to be so brave, Andrew thought. He found himself praying more too.

November was a dark, wet month. The sun and moon rarely broke through the heavy cloud cover, and the air smelled damp from the rain. Smoke poured from the many chimneys in the city. Andrew noticed that the streets were less crowded now. The house and shop windows were often shuttered. Many of the city's day laborers went out into the fields to help with the harvests, or to bring sheep, pigs, and cows to the markets.

On some days, a nagging, drizzly rain fell. The coaches George Gilbert provided were often thin walled and leaky. Andrew was given a heavier coat. It was a little too big but proved to be better than nothing.

The work of the priest hunters did not stop. Word came to Father Persons that the Queen's Privy Council was in a frenzied rage. The council knew the Jesuits were still very busy in and around London, but no one seemed able to catch them. Catholic homes were watched and raided as a daily occurrence. The hunters even intensified the random searches of strangers and coaches, raising an outcry from the nobility.

Father Persons and Andrew had a close call at one of the safe houses. A band of priest hunters suddenly showed up at the door. The family panicked, but Father Persons calmed them and said he would pray that God would hide him from the hunters' eyes. He was so sure of God's protection that he answered the door himself.

Andrew feared the worst.

The hunters didn't even recognize Father Persons. They were searching for someone who looked like Edmund Campion. Father Persons invited them in. While the hunters searched the house, the priest and Andrew quietly slipped away.

A few days later, Andrew traveled with Father Persons to the residence of the Portuguese ambassador. The ambassador kept a private chapel on the grounds. English Catholics in nearby houses often slipped in for

Mass. Father Persons agreed to visit and hear confessions. Andrew remained on the covered porch outside the main door to watch for anyone suspicious.

It was a cold day, but Andrew maintained his post. He was thankful for his heavy overcoat.

As the day wore on, he noticed a man lingering at the gate. The man paced with his head held low. Even when an afternoon storm dropped buckets of rain, the man simply adjusted his hat and kept pacing. Occasionally he stopped to chat with the Portuguese guard posted there.

Andrew was concerned about who the man was and what he wanted.

As evening approached, Matthew arrived at the gate. The man stopped him. They spoke for a moment, and the man handed something to Matthew that Andrew couldn't see. As Matthew entered the gate, the man walked away. The guard waved Matthew through.

As Matthew approached the main door, Andrew pulled it open for him. The two stepped inside the front hall. A servant of the ambassador rushed from a nearby room, saw who it was, and retreated again.

"Who was the man at the gate?" Andrew asked Matthew.

"James Bosgrave," Matthew said, stepping inside the front hall.

The name meant nothing to Andrew.

Matthew sighed. "Alas, the man is a priest."

Andrew was confused. "A *priest*? Why did he not come through the door?"

"He feared he would not be welcome," Matthew replied.

"Why would he fear that?" asked Andrew.

Matthew explained that James Bosgrave was a young Englishman who had lived overseas most of his life. He joined the Jesuits as a novitiate at the age of fifteen and became a priest a few years later in Moravia. He suffered from health issues, so his doctors insisted that he return to England, believing his homeland would serve as a cure.

As soon as Bosgrave set foot on English soil, priest hunters detained him. They sent him to prison, where he was tortured and interrogated by the Bishop of London. According to reports from the Bishop, Bosgrave agreed to attend Church of England services. This was something that both the Pope and the Jesuit leadership forbade. Soon after, Bosgrave was released from prison.

"Henceforth, he hath attempted to meet with us," Matthew said. "We have denied him as we are suspicious of his intentions. Is it his desire to debate us on the matter of attending the queen's heretical churches? Doth he hope to ease his conscience? Is he a pawn for the Bishop of London? A spy?"

"Pray, what did he give you?" Andrew asked.

Matthew held up an envelope sealed with red wax. "A private message for Father Persons, whose presence here I did not confirm or deny."

" 'Tis a sad tale," Andrew admitted.

"I shall entrust this letter to thee for safe delivery to Father Persons." Matthew handed the envelope to Andrew. He dug into his coat and drew out a smaller envelope. "This as well."

Andrew took the second envelope. The word *Pax* was written in large cursive lettering on one side. A modest seal of purple wax was on the other side.

" 'Tis from Father Ralph Sherwin," Matthew explained.

Andrew had heard the name mentioned a few times but had never met him. Father Sherwin had come to England at the same time as Father Persons and Father Campion.

"I must be away," Matthew said. He threw open the door and pushed against a blast of cold wind.

Andrew pulled the door closed after Matthew stepped outside.

The ambassador's servant appeared again. He gave Andrew an impatient look.

"I am sorry," Andrew said.

The servant withdrew.

Andrew looked down at the envelopes in his hands.

Something bad is about to happen, he suddenly thought.

18

After hearing confessions, Father Persons read the two notes. He wrote a response to James Bosgrave right away.

Handing the envelope to Andrew, he said, "Father Bosgrave awaits this message. You shall find him in a coach beyond the gate. Please return with his reply."

It was just as Father Persons said. A coach sat a few yards from the ambassador's gate. The door opened as Andrew approached. James Bosgrave leaned out. He had a thin, pale face and dark circles under his eyes. His hand trembled as he took the note from Andrew. Bosgrave disappeared into the coach. A moment later, the priest leaned out again and said, "Tell the good Father that I agree."

Andrew turned to go back to the house. Bosgrave shouted something to the coachman. With a crack from the coachman's long whip, the coach pulled away.

After Andrew delivered Bosgrave's response, Father Persons nodded, then said, "We journey now to Bridewell."

"The prison?" Andrew asked.

"'Tis also a borough," Father Persons said.

A pale sun dipped to the horizon. Father Persons said farewell to the Portuguese ambassador. A servant announced that a coach had arrived. It was one of George Gilbert's. Father Persons and Andrew climbed in.

"Pray, sir, what are our plans?" Andrew asked as Mr. Kimble steered the coach back toward London.

"We shall meet Father Bosgrave in Bridewell, once we are certain no priest hunters have followed us."

"Will the address you gave Father Bosgrave not give away one of our hiding places?" Andrew asked.

Father Persons shook his head. "The address is not one of our houses."

The address was Bridewell Palace, once a private home and now a prison and a hospital for the poor. It sat along the Flete River, yet another waterway that flowed through London and emptied into the Thames. Gilbert's coach brought them to a street near the wharf adjoining the palace. The driver guided the coach around, ready to dash away if the meeting proved to be a trap. Andrew saw Father Bosgrave's coach waiting near the entrance to the wharf.

Father Persons gave Andrew a few instructions. Andrew climbed out of the coach and walked over to Father Bosgrave's coach. He watched for any sudden movements from the alleyways. He still had an uneasy feeling.

CHAPTER EIGHTEEN

Bosgrave stepped down from his coach. He looked puzzled to see Andrew again.

"Hath Father Persons come?" Bosgrave asked.

"Are you alone, sir?" Andrew said.

"Before God, I promise that I am alone," Bosgrave said.

Andrew said, "Then follow me, sir."

The two walked back to Gilbert's coach. Andrew held the door open for Bosgrave to climb in. Then Andrew climbed up to the coachman's seat and scooted in next to the coachman.

The old man was hunched over. He said with a grunt, "Watch it, lad."

Andrew looked more closely at the coachman.

It was William in disguise.

William drove the coach around London, going in wildly random directions. Andrew checked all around to see if anyone was following them. As far as he could tell, no one was. Finally, Father Persons signaled for William to take them back to Bridewell Palace from another direction. William drove through an area called Black Friars. When they came to the other side of the Flete River, Father Bosgrave stepped from the coach and crossed through a covered bridge.

William then drove the coach to another part of London.

As they entered the small safe house, Father Persons related to William and Andrew what Father Bosgrave had told him. "He hath claimed his days of torture left him weak and confused. The Bishop of London twisted his words. He never agreed to attend the heretical services."

"Do you believe him?" William asked.

Father Persons replied, "I have directed Father Bosgrave to publicly denounce the distortions of his words. Father Bosgrave agreed. We must now watch and see."

After removing his disguise, William led Andrew to a kitchen at the back of the house. A woman, whose name was never offered, served them a light meal of quail, cheese, and bread. While they ate, Andrew heard noises at the front door that sounded as if someone had arrived. He was about to investigate when William put a hand on his arm. " 'Tis Father Ralph Sherwin. He will meet Father Persons in another part of the house.

"I have not met Father Sherwin," Andrew said. He knew only that Father Sherwin was one of the first priests to arrive in England with Father Persons and Father Campion.

"Father Sherwin was one of the original group of Jesuit priests that Pope Gregory the Thirteenth had sent to England," William explained. "Father Sherwin hath not seen Father Persons, nor Father Campion, since arriving in London early this past summer."

CHAPTER EIGHTEEN

Andrew shook his head. He wondered how many priests had sneaked into England over the past few months—and how many had been working alone. He then wondered how many would survive.

William finished his meal and stood up. "Do not wait upon Father Persons," he advised. "The two priests will surely talk through the night."

A small cot in a small room off the small kitchen was Andrew's bed for the night. Cold air sneaked into the room through several cracks in the walls and a single badly framed window. Andrew burrowed under the threadbare blankets. He missed the heating system at home.

He didn't sleep long. A loud bang startled him awake. He sat up and listened. Voices sounded in the hall. He slipped out of bed and crept through the dark kitchen to the hallway that led to the front of the house. Two men stood near a door to a side room. One was Father Persons. The other must have been Father Sherwin. They were talking in hushed and tear-filled voices.

Father Sherwin's voice rose enough for Andrew to hear, "I am not afraid to die. 'Tis my greatest desire, if it be for our Lord."

Andrew froze where he was, afraid that if he retreated, he would draw attention to himself.

Father Sherwin knelt. Father Persons put his hands on the priest's head and whispered a prayer. The two made the Sign of the Cross, and then Father Sherwin rose. Silently they went to the main door. Father Sherwin left.

Andrew shivered as the night air raced at him from the open door.

Father Persons closed the door. He then turned as if he knew Andrew had been there all along. He gave a quick nod, then disappeared through another doorway.

Andrew went back to his small bed and burrowed in again. Falling asleep wasn't easy. He kept thinking about the two priests and wondered if their goodbyes were final. Then he realized that any time the priests parted company, it was possible they would never see one another again.

The parting wasn't a final goodbye. The next morning, Father Persons told Andrew, "Thou shalt attend to Father Sherwin, as he may be in great danger. 'Tis as we already believe: a man traveling with a boy is less suspicious than a man traveling alone."

"Why doth Father Sherwin not leave London?" Andrew asked.

"I have asked him to do so, but there is a certain gentleman coming to London to see him. Father Sherwin will quit London once he hath met with the man."

Father Sherwin arrived midmorning. He was a pudgy-faced man with thick lips framed by an unkempt goatee. A high forehead slid up beneath a mop of thinning brown hair. His eyes were a dark brown and seemed to Andrew as if they'd already seen a lot of sadness.

"Good morrow," he said to Andrew as he passed to meet with Father Persons privately. He was gone only a moment. When he returned, he patted Andrew on the arm. "Shall we?" he said, and they went out to the waiting coach.

The sun made a rare appearance, but the air stayed crisp. Andrew got into the coach, dropping onto the bench across from the priest.

"God bless thee for traveling with me," Father Sherwin said. "We go hence to the home of Nicholas Roscarrock, a dear friend of George Gilbert. He hath sacrificed much for our work."

They journeyed to a part of London Andrew didn't recognize. The neighborhood was filled with modest-sized houses. They stopped in front of one with shingled wood siding and ornate gables. A heavy-set servant met them at the door. He led them to a room crammed with as many men and women as could fit the space.

A dapper man with pale skin, short blond hair, and a long blond beard came forward to greet them. He wore a white silk ruff around his neck and a black velvet robe.

"Good morrow, Nicholas," Father Sherwin said.

Andrew squeezed off to the side of the room, positioning himself next to an unshuttered window. Nicholas Roscarrock and Father Sherwin took their places in front of the gathering.

Father Sherwin led them in prayer and then began to preach. He recited from memory a section of the Gospels about the disciples in a storm at sea.

Andrew listened but kept looking out the window. Along the front of the house was a small yard. A row of bushes lined the street beyond. Andrew watched as a wagon with half a dozen men rode past the house. It was nearly out of view when it suddenly stopped.

Andrew stood up straight.

A coach came slowly to a halt in front of the bushes. Four men climbed out.

Andrew gasped. One of the men was the priest hunter Mr. Tebworth, and the other was the spy Mr. Nedly.

Just then, the men from the wagon joined them.

"Hunters!" Andrew cried out, his voice a loud croak. His mouth had gone dry.

Father Sherwin stopped preaching.

"Hunters are coming!" Andrew cried out again.

Nicholas Roscarrock pushed through the crowd to the door leading to the main hall. He closed the door and locked it.

There was a terrible pounding at the front door. The crowd was on its feet.

"Stay in thy seats!" Roscarrock said.

Andrew was already moving toward Father Sherwin when Roscarrock hissed, "Dear Father, to the back door!"

Andrew saw a narrow passage off the rear of the room.

"Begone!" Roscarrock said and pushed Father Sherwin toward the passage.

They had taken only a couple of steps when bangs and shouts came from the rear of the house as well. The hunters were coming from both directions.

Andrew heard the soft whispers of prayers coming from the men and women still in their chairs. Nicholas Roscarrock pressed his hands against the door to the front hall. It suddenly jerked from the force of someone slamming against it from the other side. Once, twice, and on the third attempt, two men smashed through. Roscarrock stumbled back.

Mr. Tebworth entered, eyeing the crowd. His gaze paused on Andrew, and he sneered. Then his eyes darted to Father Sherwin. "Arrest him!" Tebworth shouted.

The two men who had broken through the door now elbowed their way among the praying men and women.

Father Sherwin raised his hands, as if appealing for calm. The men grabbed him by both arms. The priest did not resist.

Mr. Nedly now stepped through the door. He was red-faced and wild eyed. "At last," he said breathlessly. Then he saw Andrew and pointed. "Take that boy!"

"The priest is enough," said Tebworth.

"The boy will be useful to us," Mr. Nedly said.

Andrew thought about making a run for the back passage, but one of the men from the wagon now blocked the way.

"What of the rest of them?" Tebworth asked.

Mr. Nedly waved a hand at them. "The Privy Council will want to question each of them. Especially my lord Roscarrock."

Andrew was dragged out of the house with Father Sherwin. They were placed in the coach. Andrew sat by himself on one bench. Mr. Tebworth and Mr. Nedly squeezed in on each side of the priest.

"Pray, what charge do you bring against me?" Father Sherwin asked.

"Treason," said Tebworth.

"I am not a traitor," Father Sherwin said.

"Thou art a Catholic," Tebworth said. "Worse, a *Jesuit*. Deny it!"

"*Prove it!*" countered Father Sherwin.

Mr. Nedly smirked. "We shall see."

"Is it by our queen's command that you arrest young boys?" Father Sherwin asked. "In the name of all that is decent, set him free."

Tebworth looked unsure.

Mr. Nedly shook his head. "Nay! This boy aids the priests. By the rood! He shall tell us what he knows."

"Where are you taking us?" Father Sherwin asked.

"Marshalsea Prison," said Tebworth.

Andrew imagined a dungeon with chains on the walls. He felt a burning around his eyes. Afraid that he might cry, he fixed his gaze out of the small window in the door.

The coach followed a major road through the city. To the right, Andrew saw a long bridge stretching across the Thames River. The bridge was covered with what must have been hundreds of tall, narrow buildings. Each seemed to have its own design of brick, wood, and stone. Some of the buildings were several stories high, with slanted roofs and pointed towers. Some hung over the side of the bridge like fat bellies over a tight belt. The very arches under the bridge looked as if they were buckling from the weight of so many buildings.

The coach turned away from London, taking them toward the river and that bridge. The coachman began shouting as they slowed to a crawl. Andrew saw through the window that they were now in the thick of a crush of pedestrians. He could only imagine the congestion of traffic ahead of them.

They crept at a snail's pace along the bridge. The buildings Andrew had seen from afar were now like canyon walls around them. They slipped into and out of shadows as they made their way through tunnels formed where the buildings connected overhead.

Leaning to the left-hand door, Mr. Nedly shouted to the coachman, "Use your whip! Get these wretches out of the way!"

Andrew made eye contact with Father Sherwin. Was it possible to escape while the coach moved so slowly?

The priest tipped his head ever so slightly and darted his eyes to the coach door on Andrew's right. It would be easy for Andrew to escape. But if he leapt out, what would he leap into?

The coach suddenly came to a full stop. Mr. Nedly shouted curses at the coachman while the coachman shouted curses at anyone within earshot.

At that moment, Father Sherwin jerked to Andrew's left as if trying to escape. He slammed against Mr. Nedly, pressing the man against the side of the cabin. The sudden movement startled Mr. Tebworth, who lunged for the priest.

With the three men entangled, Andrew threw himself at the unattended door.

God alone knew where it would take him.

19

Andrew landed catlike on all fours on the cobblestone road.

There were shouts in the coach. Andrew imagined that Father Sherwin was struggling with his two captors.

Andrew launched himself toward London.

He heard Mr. Tebworth shout, "Stop that boy!"

The people on the bridge were deaf to his shouts as they went about their business. Without looking back, Andrew ducked between the stalled coaches and wagons. He dodged peasants carrying baskets and side-stepped servants pulling carts. He raced past shops and booths of merchants selling their wares.

He knew he had to get off the main road. He darted to an alley on the left. Children playing on a tilting wooden staircase shouted at him as he passed by. The alley dead-ended at a railing. The murky brown water of the Thames flowed far below. He spun to the right and ran along a narrow path between the rail and the buildings. He hit another dead end at a stack of barrels. Then he saw a doorway behind the barrels and squeezed through. He raced down a path with a turn to the left and another turn to the right. He slowed, trying to catch his breath.

"What is thy business here?" a woman shouted from a balcony above him.

Andrew sprinted off again. He came to an opening that put him back on the main thoroughfare. The end of the bridge was just ahead, with the ramshackle buildings of London just beyond.

Andrew stopped long enough to look back. He saw the traffic and the people, but no one seemed to be chasing him.

He walked quickly past the riverside wharfs. Men were working on boats of all sizes, adjusting sails, pulling nets or ropes, and hoisting barrels.

Andrew came to the grounds of a parish church that occupied the corner of a busy intersection. He headed east. East, he knew, would eventually take him back to the parts of London he had come to know.

He prayed that the safe house would truly be safe.

Andrew made his way to one of the lodgings the priests had used in Holborn. He hoped the hunters hadn't discovered it. Just to be sure, he watched the house for half an hour before approaching the front door.

CHAPTER NINETEEN

He was relieved when George Gilbert's servant Dilber answered his feeble knock. He was even more relieved when he was taken to a room where Father Persons was meeting with George Gilbert and a handful of priests. Word had already reached them that Father Sherwin had been arrested. Andrew confirmed the news, then added that Mr. Nedly and Mr. Tebworth had taken Father Sherwin to Marshalsea Prison.

The gathering looked stunned.

George Gilbert looked ashen faced. "I know a guard at Marshalsea. He will bring us news of Father Sherwin."

Father Persons then beckoned everyone to kneel. He led them all in prayers for the "first of us to be captured."

Afterward, Father Persons urged the men to make a quick exodus from the house and scatter in different directions.

Father Persons said to Andrew, "Thou wilt return with me to Uxbridge."

Gilbert arranged for another coach, and they departed within the hour.

Father Campion and Brother Emerson were at the Griffiths' when Father Persons and Andrew arrived. The two men had also heard the news about Father Sherwin. They debated how the hunters knew where to find the priest. And they worried anew about having a spy among them.

Father Persons asked, "Hath James Bosgrave betrayed us to the Queen's Privy Council?"

The answer came only a couple of days later. James Bosgrave had indeed gone to the Queen's Privy Council—but not as a spy. Instead, he condemned the Bishop of London for misrepresenting his words and actions. Then he openly challenged the Bishop to a public debate about Catholic teaching. The council arrested him again.

The priests prayed for Father Bosgrave. During their prayers, Andrew sensed that they felt bad for doubting the priest's loyalty.

It seemed that every day thereafter brought more news of Catholic homes being invaded and searched. Nicholas Roscarrock and many other men were locked up for questioning.

Father Persons and Father Campion made two decisions. The first was that Father Campion should travel farther away from London to an area in the north called Lancashire. Brother Emerson would accompany him. Father Persons reminded Father Campion to use the time to write his next essay.

The night before Father Campion and Brother Emerson departed, Father Persons led them in prayers, heard their confessions, and renewed their vows as priests. Goodbyes were said the next morning. Once more, Andrew had the feeling that the priests believed they would never see one another again.

CHAPTER NINETEEN

Andrew watched the two men walk across the field and thought of Eve. She had been standing next to him in the Griffiths' garden when Father Campion first arrived, walking across that same field. Andrew stood alone now and suddenly felt lonelier that he'd ever felt in his life.

Andrew traveled with Father Persons to the Greenstreet house in East Ham. Father Persons wanted to hand-deliver his pamphlet for printing there.

Andrew was glad to see William and Matthew again. They had been busy helping Stephen Brinkley with the printing operations. A Catholic scholar named Thomas Hyde had written a pamphlet for "afflicted Catholics." Another scholar named Richard Bristow had written an essay about heresy. Priests had secretly distributed both pamphlets to Catholic contacts overnight around London and the surrounding countryside. In a mischievous move, the priests also sneaked them into the homes of members of the Queen's Privy Council.

"'Tis against the law to possess our writings," William explained, laughing. "The members of the Privy Council might have to arrest themselves for receiving the pamphlets."

The council was furious.

Andrew wondered how long the printing could go on at Greenstreet. Stephen Brinkley continued to play the role of the gentleman of the house, with the priests dressing up as his servants. But Andrew feared that the wagons coming and going with printing supplies, ink, and paper would look unusual to the people living nearby. His fears seemed to be confirmed one day when he opened the gate to allow a wagonful of paper to enter. The Protestant parson was watching from across the road.

Andrew informed William, who then warned everyone in the house to be ready at a moment's notice in case someone arrived to investigate.

What does it mean to be ready? Andrew thought.

He found out the next day.

Playing guard at the gate again, Andrew was suddenly face-to-face with a tall, broad-shouldered man carrying a long walking stick. His expression seemed fixed in a disapproving frown. He looked like an unhappy version of William.

"I am Thomas Brookes, *the owner of this house*," he announced in a low, sour tone. "My sons William and Edward may be here. I desire to speak with them immediately."

Andrew panicked. Without opening the gate, he ran up the drive to the front door. He found William in the front hall, amid a beehive of activity. From the back, Andrew could hear the low, rhythmic clatter of the printing press.

"Your father is here!" Andrew shouted.

William spun to Andrew. "Where is he?"

"At the gate."

"Didst thou not give him leave to enter?" William asked.

"I forgot to unlock the gate," Andrew said, embarrassed.

Using his commanding stage voice, William called out, "To your places, everyone!"

With those words, the noises in the house changed in a matter of seconds. Andrew heard footsteps running in the halls and up the stairs.

William half ran with Andrew back to the gate. Thomas Brookes was pacing there, red-faced. Andrew fumbled to unlock the gate and pull it open.

"Good day, sir!" William said cheerfully.

Thomas Brookes stepped through. He glared at his son. "Why dost thou have this boy standing guard at the gate?" He lifted his walking stick as if he might hit Andrew with it. "I would have him beaten for leaving me unattended."

"As you wish, sir," William said, and winked at Andrew.

They walked up the drive to the house.

"Why have you come?" William asked.

Thomas Brookes eyed his son. "The parson hath claimed that thou art receiving goods of a suspicious nature. *Paper*, he said."

Andrew nearly groaned out loud.

"Pray, sir, what hath led him to such a claim?" William asked.

"The gentleman happened to be at the paper merchant's when someone from *this* house ordered an overabundance of paper. Yesterday the parson saw the wagon deliver the paper here. Where is the lodger I have allowed to live in my house?" Mr. Brookes asked.

They were at the front door now. Andrew worried about what they would find inside.

As William reached for the handle, the door was suddenly pulled open. One of the priests stood there in the full costume of a servant.

"Ah, good master!" he said. "A thousand pardons!"

Mr. Brookes pushed past the servant into the front hall.

Andrew was surprised by the silence. Another priest, also dressed as a servant, stood at a long table by the wall, wiping it with a cloth.

"I demand to see the master of the house," Thomas Brookes barked. "Tarry not!"

Andrew knew that Stephen Brinkley had been working at the printing press all morning.

"The master of the house hath been riding, good sir," the priest-now-servant said.

William said, "Dear father, had we known you were coming—"

"I desire no explanation from thee," Mr. Brookes said sharply. "Bring me the man!"

CHAPTER NINETEEN

Just then, Andrew heard the clip-clop of horses' hooves on the driveway. Thomas Brookes and William turned at the same time.

Dressed in the full splendor of a wealthy gentleman, Stephen Brinkley arrived on horseback. He trotted to the porch. A servant helped him climb off the steed. "Good day to you, sir," he said to Thomas Brookes with a grand bow.

"Good day, Mr. Creed," Brookes said gruffly.

"My father hath come to inquire about a shipment of paper that was delivered to this very house yesterday," William said. "He is concerned about the use you are making of his house."

"Use, sir?" Brinkley said. "Am I constrained from making use of the house as I see fit? Must I reread our agreement?"

Brookes was undaunted. "Why do you have need of a wagonload of paper?"

"For inspection, sir," Brinkley replied.

"Inspection?"

"My family hath a financial stake in the publishing of high quality books," Brinkley said. "'Tis my task to inspect the paper on behalf of my father. The roll of paper was brought to me here. I was satisfied with its texture. It hath gone to its proper warehouse. Is there anything else you wish to know? I have also taken delivery of various types of cloth for curtains I desire sewn. Should I have presented them for your consideration? Perhaps the next occasion I am delivered clothes from my tailor? Would you require a letter to declare it?"

Andrew saw William make a face, as if Brinkley was pushing his act too far.

Mr. Brookes eyed Brinkley, then said, "Nay, sir, 'tis not necessary."

"I beg you, then. Let us be friends. Come inside for refreshment," Brinkley said.

"I will not, sir. My business here is finished." Brookes turned on his heel and headed back down the drive toward the gate.

William signaled for Brinkley to wait. Then he and Andrew double-stepped to catch up with Mr. Brookes.

"Be not angry, Father," William said.

At the gate, Thomas Brookes rounded on his son. "Mark me, William. I will not tolerate anything of an inappropriate nature taking place on my property. Should rumors concerning this house come to me again, I shall hold thee responsible."

"Aye, Father," William said.

Brookes marched through the gate and out of view down the street.

William put a hand on Andrew's shoulder and breathed a long sigh of relief.

"What are we to do?" Andrew asked.

"Watch to see what comes of my father's visit," William replied.

At the front door, Brinkley stood mopping his brow.

"Well done, good man. A great performance," William said to him. "Pray, how didst thou change so speedily?"

"By God's grace," Brinkley said as he took off his leather riding gloves. "Thy father would have been suspicious had he seen *these*." He held up his hands and wiggled his fingers. They were smudged with ink.

20

The Feast of Saint Andrew the Apostle arrived as it did every year on November 30th. It was also Andrew's birthday. Because of his time travels, he had lost track of how old he was. A year older? Two? And yet he was only a few minutes older according to Hope Springs' time.

The priests encouraged the laypeople around them to commit to novenas in honor of Saint Andrew and to prepare for the usual fasting for Advent.

December arrived with longer spells of wet, cold, sunless weather. The London streets reminded Andrew of black-and-white movies he'd seen about England, with characters like the Artful Dodger and Fagin prowling the alleyways. He reminded himself that Charles Dickens wouldn't write those stories for another one hundred and fifty years. In this time, the only ones prowling the dark alleyways were probably Privy Council spies.

There were some days when Andrew thought, *If I were really smart, I could figure out how to use what I know about the future. Maybe I could make a lot of money.* It was a fantasy that appealed to him. But then he thought, *Someone will accuse me of being from the devil and burn me at the stake.*

Andrew thought often about Eve. He imagined her moving somewhere at a different speed in a different time. While he played out his days and nights in England, she might be standing in Alfred Virtue's office for only a few seconds.

He began to have nightmares. In some of them, he was stuck in this time and place, living out his life as a fugitive for being a Catholic. In other dreams, he was chased by Mr. Nedly, captured, and taken to a prison. Andrew would suddenly awaken in his room at Greenstreet—or sometimes a house in Bridewell—certain he'd heard someone shouting. He realized that he must have been the one who did it.

He felt safest at Greenstreet. But the encounter with Thomas Brookes put everyone on edge. Andrew was sure the local parson was watching the gate. A decision had to be made.

At midnight on a Friday, Stephen Brinkley finished printing the latest pamphlets Father Person had written. By dawn, the printing press had been dismantled and placed on wagons. The priests left Greenstreet at random times during the day. Within a day after that, the house was scrubbed and the disguised priests had departed. Stephen Brinkley, dressed as the gentleman called Stephen Creed, said goodbye to William and Edward. That afternoon,

CHAPTER TWENTY

Edward hugged his brother farewell and rode off for other adventures. Andrew joined William in a coach for the trip to Bridewell.

On the way through London, the coach came to a sudden stop. The coachman named McInerny shouted that a wagon had tipped over on the road ahead.

"Let us walk," William said to Andrew. "Lest any are hurt and in need of help." He stepped out of the coach, with Andrew following.

The scene ahead was pure carnage. A horse lay on its side in the mud. One of its legs was clearly broken. A wagon was also tipped over, with pieces of furniture scattered around. A man sat near the wagon with blood flowing down the side of his face. He looked stunned. Next to him a woman was holding her arm and screaming. William pushed through the crowd and knelt down next to the woman.

That's what I figured, Andrew thought.

Andrew was about to step forward to help, when his gaze landed on the crowd on the other side of the wagon. He froze.

Mr. Nedly was there. His eyes were on William, who was turned away from him, treating the howling woman. Mr. Nedly shifted a few feet, craning his neck as if trying to get a clearer view of William.

Andrew's instinct was to shout at William to run. But that would surely expose the priest. Andrew then decided to distract Mr. Nedly.

Moving to the front of the crowd, he circled around to get into Mr. Nedly's line of sight. Mr. Nedly was still watching William. Andrew moved in the other direction, all the while praying that William would keep his back to Mr. Nedly.

Andrew wasn't watching where he was going. His foot came down on the bandaged limb of an old man with crutches. The man cried out and gave Andrew a hard push. Andrew stumbled and fell. When he got to his feet again, Mr. Nedly was now looking at him.

There was a moment of recognition. Mr. Nedly shouted. Andrew gave a startled shriek and took off, racing away from the scene.

It was then he realized the flaw in his plan. He hadn't thought about *where* he would run. Unlike London Bridge, there wasn't a nearby row of houses for him to hide behind.

It didn't matter. Mr. Nedly was now coming around the wagon at a surprising speed.

Andrew dashed back to the only cover he could find: the bottleneck of coaches and wagons. He glanced up and saw McInerny, the coachman, standing on the driver's bench. McInerny was watching Andrew with an alarmed look.

Andrew grabbed the door handle and pulled himself into the coach. Then he slammed the door shut, crossed the inside of the coach to the other door, and leapt out. He hit the ground and rolled under the coach. Mr. Nedly

CHAPTER TWENTY

arrived. Andrew recognized his boots, though they were now covered with mud. Andrew heard him open the coach door. One foot lifted, as if he was about to climb in. Then he stopped and lowered it to the ground. He was completely still. Andrew imagined that Mr. Nedly had seen the empty coach and was now looking around for him.

Suddenly Mr. Nedly dropped to his knees. He spotted Andrew and shouted, "Aha!"

Andrew rolled away, then got to his feet.

Mr. Nedly called to him.

Andrew weaved in and out of the jammed traffic to get to the other side of the road. When he reached the muddy pavement, he realized that nothing was there but a long, high wall stretching out in two directions. He made as if he was about to go left, then suddenly ran right.

Mr. Nedly was now cutting through the traffic, running at an angle to Andrew.

Andrew knew that Mr. Nedly would intercept him if he didn't find a way of escape. "God help me," he gasped and picked up his speed. The mud was thick and slippery, making it hard to get traction or quickly change direction.

Mr. Nedly found a gap in the traffic and came at Andrew with even greater speed. Just then, Andrew saw a man ahead step out of a doorway in the wall. Andrew quickly calculated how to stop for the door without sliding into Mr. Nedly's clutches.

At that moment, Andrew realized that sliding was exactly what he needed to do.

He turned like a baseball player getting ready to slide into a base. He went down onto his side and hit the mud just as Mr. Nedly dove to grab him.

Mr. Nedly, with outreached arms, flew over Andrew. Nedly's foot slammed Andrew in the side, causing the man to trip. Andrew heard a terrible thud as Mr. Nedly slammed into the wall. Andrew came out of his slide several feet on, stopping just outside the gate in the wall. He leapt to his feet.

The man who had just come through the doorway gave Andrew a puzzled look. He then looked over at Mr. Nedly and said, "Merciful heavens!"

Andrew looked as well. Mr. Nedly was facedown on the ground. A smear of blood had followed his head down the wall. He was deathly still. Then, slowly, his arms moved. His hands clawed at the mud. Then he began to move his legs.

Andrew backed away. He felt a sharp pain in his side where Mr. Nedly's foot had caught him. He took a few more steps, glancing around for any unwelcome attention. Clutching his side, he picked up his pace and rushed away.

21

Andrew half ran and half staggered to the safe house in Bridewell. The pain in his side grew worse with every step.

Matthew met him at the door. He took one look at the boy and said, "Thou art pale, lad. Art thou hurt?"

Andrew nodded.

"Come. Let us see to it."

Matthew helped Andrew down the hall to the study. "My side," Andrew said. He carefully stripped off the layers of clothes above his waist, wincing the entire time. Then he raised his right arm so Matthew could see the damage. The priest gave a low whistle. Andrew peeked down. The right side of his chest was an angry red and purple.

Matthew summoned the servant. It was Mr. Dilber again. The two men conferred and concluded that Andrew must be seen by a surgeon.

"A *surgeon*?" Andrew asked, alarmed. He looked at his bruised side, trying to imagine why he needed that kind of work. "Is he going to cut me?"

Matthew looked baffled. "Cut thee? Why would he do that?"

Andrew tried to answer, but it only made the conversation more confused. He eventually figured out that a surgeon was another word for a doctor. Doctors might also be called *bonesetters* and *barbers*.

The surgeon was a woman named Mrs. Mimms. She was white haired, short, and frail looking. She reminded Andrew of an elderly nun he often saw at his church in Hope Springs.

Matthew explained that she was a devout Catholic who knew much about the workings of the human body. "She hath a gift for healing," he said.

Mrs. Mimms stood before Andrew, closed her eyes, and made the Sign of the Cross. She whispered a prayer and then came around to look at his side. She lightly touched around the bruise, nodding at his pained reactions.

"A broken rib," she said. She turned to Matthew. "Tightly wrap his chest in linens, though not too tight."

"It shall be done," Matthew said.

Mrs. Mimms reached over to a large satchel she had brought. She pulled out a vial filled with a green liquid. Unplugging the stopper, she sniffed. "This will ease thy pain."

She held the vial up to Andrew's nose. The liquid smelled like a minty medicine.

"One drop on the tongue," she said. "That much shall put thee to sleep. Too much, and thou wilt sleep

CHAPTER TWENTY-ONE

permanently." She pushed the stopper back in and handed the vial to him.

Dilber returned with broad strips of linen. Mrs. Mimms carefully wound the strips around Andrew's torso. He felt uncomfortable but not terribly pained.

Matthew thanked Mrs. Mimms and saw her to the door. Andrew slowly put on his undershirt. He tried to ignore the occasional stabbing pain in his side.

"Thou gavest Mr. Nedly quite a run," William said, walking into the room. He was smiling, but Andrew saw worry in his eyes.

Andrew shook his head. "I feel bad. Mr. Nedly hit the wall hard. He was bleeding."

"His wound was not so bad that he could not rage against thee as they helped him to his coach." William paused a moment, then said gratefully, "Thou hast saved my life."

"I am glad you escaped," Andrew said.

Matthew returned. He looked grave. "Lad, I fear thou art easily recognized now. We must move thee from London. To remain would endanger thee—and any priest with whom thou art seen."

"Where can I go?" Andrew asked.

"We shall hasten with good speed to Uxbridge," William said. "Father Persons shall advise us."

The coach ride to the Griffiths' house in Uxbridge seemed bumpier than usual. Every jolt and jerk sent daggers of pain into Andrew's side. He remembered the vial Mrs. Mimms had given him and put a drop on his tongue.

After a while, he said to William, "The medicine is not working."

The next thing he knew, William was carrying him through the doorway of the Griffith's house near Uxbridge.

"What happened?" he asked, feeling very groggy.

William laughed.

The conversation between Father Persons and William was like a scene being played on a stage far away. Another man was there—young and dashing, like George Gilbert. He sat off to the side and listened with his chin resting on his fist. Gervase Pierrepont was his name.

Father Persons was concerned about Andrew and the chase with Mr. Nedly. He said that the Privy Council had issued yet another proclamation. The queen intended to make examples of the Jesuit priests by extreme punishment, to strike terror in the hearts of any who supported them.

The priest agreed that Andrew must now journey to other parts of the country.

"Where will I go?" Andrew asked. His words were slurred, and his voice sounded as if it was coming from someone else.

"North," Father Persons said. "Gervase is going hence to meet with Father Campion and Brother Emerson at the house of his brother Henry in Nottinghamshire."

Andrew perked up. He knew Nottinghamshire. That was where he'd had adventures with Robin Hood. *But that was hundreds of years ago*, he remembered.

"God willing, thou shalt spend Christmas there," Father Persons added.

Christmas! This would be the second Christmas he had spent away from home—even though home hadn't celebrated a single Christmas since he'd been gone. And his last Christmas was more than one hundred and fifty years ago.

The absurdity of it all suddenly caught up to him. He let out a burst of laughter that sent a shiver of pain down his side.

Father Persons and William turned to him.

"Forgive me," Andrew said, groaning but then giggling.

"On the morrow," Father Persons said, as if concluding whatever he'd been saying. "Thou shalt depart with Gervase then."

Andrew nodded with another wave of giggles.

Gervase stood up and gestured to Andrew. "Pray tell, is this boy a fool?"

William chuckled. "He hath partaken of a concoction from Mrs. Mimms."

Father Persons and Gervase both said, "Ah!"

Andrew looked up at them. The men laughed.

Andrew didn't know why.

Dawn illuminated the nearby frosted fields and revealed the first hint of a blue sky in quite a few days. Andrew was grateful. He learned the next morning that they would not be traveling by coach. Gervase Pierrepont had organized for two horses to take them north.

Andrew had a slight headache from the medicine Mrs. Mimms had given him. His rib jabbed at him whenever he moved the wrong way. He looked at the tall black horse Gervase had found for him. How he was supposed to ride it far into northern England without terrible pain every step of the way?

He talked to William about it. William suggested that he talk to Father Persons. The elder priest was sympathetic but maintained that Andrew needed to leave right away. Going with Gervase Pierrepont was the right thing to do. If the pain became unbearable, he should take the medicine.

"But I will fall off the horse," Andrew said.

"Gervase will watch out for thee."

Andrew wasn't comforted. "What if Evangeline returns? She will be sorely vexed if I am not here."

"We shall let her know where thou hast gone. And we shall keep her safe until you are reunited."

"Pray, what if Vincent Howard—"

Father Persons held up his hand. "Lad, this is the best course of action. The Privy Council hath intensified its efforts to find us—to find *thee*. I will not lose thee to one of their prisons. The pain in thy side will be as nothing compared to the pain thou wilt suffer at their hands."

CHAPTER TWENTY-ONE

Andrew fell silent.

Father Persons gave him a kind smile. "Pray that thy sufferings will draw thee into a deeper relationship with God."

As the final preparations were made to depart, sad news came from London. Father Ralph Sherwin had been moved from Marshalsea Prison to the Tower of London, along with a few other captured priests and Nicholas Roscarrock.

"The Tower is often the last stop before execution," Father Persons said. "And yet they entered its chambers with praise and thanksgiving for all they will endure for Christ."

Father Persons offered a blessing, and then William helped Andrew onto his horse. Once he'd seated Andrew, William clasped Andrew's hand for a moment. "Godspeed, lad," he said tenderly.

Andrew adjusted himself in the saddle. He was no stranger to riding a horse, thanks to his time with Robin Hood and Joan of Arc. His side hurt, but he didn't complain. How could he after hearing about Father Sherwin and the others?

Gervase mounted his horse, and they trotted away from the Griffiths' house. They took a road around to the west of Uxbridge, and then north. Andrew had a vague notion that Gervase wasn't happy to be riding with such a young companion, especially one who might be a fool.

Once they were well away from the town, Gervase announced, "We shall journey north through Buckinghamshire. There is a route we might have taken through Hertfordshire, but that county hath become home to many government officials and administrators. They keep their country homes there. William Cecil, the Lord Burghley, maintains two great palaces in that region."

"Who is William Cecil?" Andrew asked. He recalled hearing the name in various conversations.

Gervase looked surprised. "Thou dost not know the villain? When I imagine the snake in the garden of Eden, 'tis William Cecil I see in my mind's eye." He chuckled at the thought, then said, "Lord Cecil is one of the queen's most trusted advisers. He loathes Catholics one and all, but Jesuits in particular. Many of the priest hunters are his men. He would be delighted to see the realm rid of all Catholics."

"Why?" Andrew asked. "Why can Protestants and Catholics not share the country? Why doth one have to drive out the other?"

Gervase paused in thought for a moment, then replied, "Lord Cecil hath said, 'Those who differ in the service of their God will also differ in the service of their country.' He doth not believe the two can share the same space. One must prevail. He is determined that the Protestants shall be the victors. For that reason, we Catholics are outcasts in our own land."

They rode on in silence. Andrew felt more at ease as he moved farther from London. They saw a variety of travelers and sometimes raised a hand to greet them. Andrew slowly lost his fear of being stopped and questioned.

Andrew noticed that the landscape had changed from rolling hills of field and forest to areas that had once been forested but were now cluttered with uprooted trees and stumps.

"Pray, what place is this?" Andrew asked.

"Buckinghamshire," Gervase replied.

"Why, then, the desolation of trees?" Andrew asked, waving a hand at everything around them.

"Ah! The beech trees," Gervase declared. "The abbots who own these lands removed them."

"Why?"

"Thieves," Gervase said, as if that explained everything.

Andrew waited, then asked, "What of the thieves?"

Gervase glanced at him. Andrew felt like a fool again.

Gervase spoke slowly. "Cattle, sheep, and pigs are driven from Wales to the London markets. They stop hereabouts for feed and to graze. The highwaymen and thieves would lurk in the forests and, with boldness, fall upon the poor drovers to steal and plunder. The abbots resolved to thwart the thieves by removing their hiding places."

"That makes sense," Andrew said, unsure that it did.

The day stayed crisp and cold, even when the sun was at its peak. Andrew felt the air bite at his nose and cheeks. His side was now a continual ache, occasionally changing to a sharp pain if the horse suddenly jerked to the left or right. Gervase often stopped to give Andrew a rest. They ate from a supply of food that Mrs. Griffith had given them: salted meat, bread, and cheese. Because it was still a time of fasting for Advent, they ate very little.

Gervase declared that they would soon lodge at the King's Head in Aylesbury. It was a familiar inn where his family often stayed on their many travels to and from London.

"If thou art in great pain, we would be welcome at the home of the Dormer family in Wing," Gervase added. "But to go there would take us a few miles out of our way."

"I am content with an inn, kind sir," Andrew said.

The sun was on its descent when they came to Aylesbury. The town sat on the summit and slopes of a great hill, crowned by the tower of a church.

"'Tis St. Mary the Virgin's church," Gervase said with the same sad tone that Andrew remembered hearing from Matthew at Nether Wallop. "'Tis now in the hands of the enemies of Christ."

Andrew and Gervase rode into the town's market square. They passed an ancient stone cross and then a mix of large halls dominating smaller inns and shops. The shop owners were closing up the shutters and doors. Gervase

CHAPTER TWENTY-ONE

directed his horse off the street into a cobblestoned courtyard. He dismounted, then helped Andrew down.

The King's Head was a unity of three buildings, each made of timber and plaster. The main part of the inn had two stories, with leaded windows jutting out from under a tiled roof. Two smaller wings came off of the main building to the left and right.

A boy, slightly younger than Andrew, suddenly appeared. "Hail, Master Pierrepont," he said. Taking the reins, he led the horses through an archway to the stables.

"I am obliged, Nicholas," Gervase called after the boy.

Andrew followed Gervase through the front doorway and entered a spacious hall. Assorted men, dressed in traveling clothes, sat at tables and chairs spread around the room. A fire crackled in a broad stone hearth. Andrew noticed a scrawny-looking man standing next to the fire. His eyes were on Gervase.

"Master Pierrepont!" cried a stoop-shouldered man shuffling out from a back room. He had a surprisingly wild mop of hair and an equally unruly beard.

"Greetings, Oliver," Gervase said.

"Will you be wanting the Gatehouse Chamber or the Solar Room?" Oliver asked.

Gervase thought about it, then said, "The chamber faces the market square and may be raucous come morning. We shall have the Solar Room."

Oliver escorted his guests up the stairs. The Solar Room was a grand bedroom just above the main entry.

It was spacious, with oak paneling and its own fireplace, already lit. There was a single canopied bed along the back wall, with dark wooden tables and cushioned chairs adorning the rest of the room.

"Good sir, I shall have a cot brought up for your servant," Oliver said.

"The son of a friend," Gervase corrected him. "I am escorting him to Nottingham."

Oliver nodded, then stepped closer and said softly, "There are priest hunters about. A man I know not hath been asking questions about the guests. Be careful, sir."

Gervase thanked him, then asked, "Is the hole intact? I carry papers in need of protection."

Oliver went around the side of the bed and lit a lamp on the stand. He handed the lamp to Gervase, then reached behind the headboard and touched something. One of the panels—the size of a small door—opened near his legs. He pushed the panel in and stepped aside for Gervase to proceed.

Gervase knelt down with the lamp and peered inside. "Excellent," he said.

"May I?" Andrew asked.

Gervase passed the lamp to Andrew.

Andrew knelt down, holding his side to avoid pain. He lifted the lamp just inside the door.

The "hole" was a secret room like the one Andrew had seen at the home of Arthur Josephs. This one was only about three feet wide and extended the length of the bedroom along the wall behind the bed. He gave the lamp back to Gervase and stood up. Oliver closed the panel.

Gervase thanked the innkeeper and gave him a few coins.

Oliver bowed, then said, "Nicholas shall bring your belongings to this room. Mrs. Prescott hath baked a delicious mutton pie. Or, if it is your preference, there is also a tasty pottage."

Gervase and Andrew ate in a private booth in a far corner of the main room. Andrew noticed that Gervase kept his eyes on the room. Andrew was also watchful. He searched for the scrawny man he had seen before, but the man wasn't there. Andrew wondered if he was a priest hunter.

Oliver came to the table to clear up the dishes. Reaching next to Gervase to grab a cup, he said softly, "A man offered a bribe to Nicholas for a look in your saddlebags."

Gervase did not react. "Is the man nearby?"

"Nay. Nor shall he be. I have banned him."

Andrew asked, "Was the man standing earlier by the fireplace?"

"Aye," said Oliver. "A sordid-looking character. If a witch could turn the foulest alley cat into a man, it would look like him."

Gervase laughed. "Did the creature have a name?"

Oliver shook his head. "He did not offer one. Nor did he display any warrants."

"Where are my bags now?" asked Gervase.

"Nicholas put them in the hole in case the man troubled your room."

Gervase placed a hand on the innkeeper's arm. "I am indebted to thee yet again. Name the amount the man offered to Nicholas as a bribe, and I shall give him the same for his loyalty."

Oliver smiled. "We are at your service, as always." He retreated with the dishes.

"I had hoped to sleep in," Gervase said with a sigh. "Alas, we must depart at daybreak."

22

The inn creaked like an old ship. At every sound, Andrew woke up, sure that the Alley Cat Man was sneaking into the room.

Morning came but didn't bring very much light with it. Dark clouds had gathered overnight and remained, threatening to assail them with rain at any moment.

On horseback again, Andrew followed Gervase through Aylesbury. He glanced in the direction of St. Mary the Virgin church. At the edge of the churchyard, standing near a tall monument, the Alley Cat Man was watching them.

Andrew gasped and drew his horse closer to Gervase. "The man is there."

Both riders turned, but the Alley Cat Man was gone.

"He cannot follow us lest we know of it," Gervase said. "Fear not."

They departed the county of Buckinghamshire and entered into Northamptonshire. It was as if they had entered another country. The open roads they had ridden thus far were now narrow, winding paths. There was little room for the two on horseback when cattle and sheep were allowed to roam freely. More than once, Andrew and Gervase were stalled by wagons carrying loads of limestone from the nearby quarries.

Andrew found himself looking back, afraid to see the Alley Cat Man trailing them. There was something about the man that filled him with a sense of dread.

Gervase must have noticed Andrew's worry, because he said, "If the man knows who I am, then he must know whither I go. 'Tis my hope that he abides in Aylesbury and disturbs only travelers there."

Andrew hoped it was true.

The rain arrived midday, lashing at them in violent bursts. Their coats and hoods were soon drenched. They sought shelter in the woods, but the bare-limbed trees offered little comfort.

"We shall not reach Northampton today," Gervase said after they found relief at a small tavern. "We shall stop at Yardley Gobion for the night."

Yardley Gobion was a village with only a few thatched cottages clustered together. Two elms stood prominently in the very center of the town as if they had some significance. Outlying farms bordered the grounds of a manor house called Hall Yard.

Gervase and Andrew arranged for a room at the Pack Horse Inn, a quaint building of stone, timber, and plaster. It was only a little warmer inside than outside.

CHAPTER TWENTY-TWO

"This was once a chapel dedicated to Saint Leonard," Gervase said.

Andrew was sure he knew the rest of the story. King Henry the Eighth had dissolved the chapel. Now it was an inn.

The rain continued to fall throughout the night. There was a leak in the roof of their room that dripped into a puddle in the corner. The noise kept Andrew awake. His shivering from the cold didn't help. He'd hung up his clothes to dry by an unreliable fire in the small fireplace.

Fortunately, the rain stopped by morning, though the sky was still overcast.

As they were about to depart, the innkeeper—a stout woman named Mrs. Marchbank—approached Gervase. She had a worried look as she said, "Sir, a man arrived after you retired. He was asking questions about you."

"Did he look like an alley cat?" Andrew asked.

"Aye. That would be him," the woman admitted. "A vicious alley cat."

"Where is he?" Gervase asked.

Mrs. Marchbank shrugged. "He asked his questions, then hastened away."

Gervase dropped a coin in front of her. "Pray tell, what questions did he ask?"

"Your name and the reason for your travels," she said, slipping the coin into an apron pocket. Then her brow cinched together. "He asked if you are a Catholic. 'How should I know?' I asked the man. 'And what business is it of thine?'"

"Well done," Gervase said and added another coin to the first.

"Much obliged, sir," she said. "I must say, the man asked more about the boy here than he did about you."

Gervase looked at Andrew.

Andrew felt the blood drain from his face.

The woman continued, "As I know no more about him than I do about you, my answers were the same. Then the man skulked out into the rain just as you came in."

Riding on again, Andrew asked Gervase, "Why, pray tell, would the hunter ask about me?"

"Perhaps he seeks a reward," Gervase suggested. "Perhaps he heard about thee in London and desires to claim you for the Queen's Privy Council."

Andrew wasn't comforted by the thought.

Gervase said, "Had he the courage to face me, I would make short work of him. Men of this type do not have courage."

The road north seemed busier with other travelers as the day went on. Andrew found himself looking at each face, expecting to see the Alley Cat Man.

After a few more hours of riding, Gervase told Andrew that they would not be entering Northampton. "Instead, let us circle around to the east. There is an abundance of good friends whom we may visit. I have messages to deliver."

CHAPTER TWENTY-TWO

Andrew suspected the decision to avoid Northampton was due to the Alley Cat Man.

They passed a village called Wellingborough, and just north of it, they came to an estate with acres of gardens and forest. They entered through a massive iron gate and continued to a square manor house made of a light-colored stone. Unusually tall windows caught Andrew's eye.

"Welcome to Great Harrowden Hall," Gervase said.

A servant greeted Gervase and Andrew, then ushered them into a richly supplied library. The walls were covered with bookcases lined with leather-backed books. Andrew glanced at the spines and saw multiple titles on herbs and gardening, cooking, and agriculture. He also saw classics by Pliny and Livy, Virgil, and Plutarch. *Canterbury Tales* was there, along with Aesop's *Fables* and Malory's *Morte d'Arthur*.

Lord William Vaux was the master of the house. He strode into the room with an easy confidence and clasped Gervase's arms. "My dear boy!" he said.

Andrew guessed that Lord Vaux was a dozen years older than Gervase, though his slender build made him look the same age. He had short brown hair and the slightest of beards. A white shirt and ruff contrasted his black-and-gold vest. He gave Andrew an amused look and bowed. "Thy servant, sir," he said.

Andrew bowed in return. "My lord," he said.

Gervase handed over an envelope. Andrew noticed that it was sealed with purple wax. "My Lord, a letter for you from Father Persons."

Lord Vaux took the letter but did not open it. "I am honored, sir. Anon, you will be my guests tonight, or as long as you desire."

"Tonight only, my lord," Gervase said. "We journey to my family estate to collect our mutual friend."

Andrew assumed the "mutual friend" was Edmund Campion.

"I am delighted," said Lord Vaux.

A servant showed Andrew and Gervase to their rooms on the second floor. Andrew's bedroom was the largest he'd been in since his time-travel adventure began. The bed looked big enough for him to roll a dozen times before falling off. Servants delivered a change of clothes, thanks to one of Lord Vaux's sons. A servant took Andrew's travel-worn clothes away to be washed.

After a brief rest, Andrew was summoned to dinner in the Great Hall. There he met the wife of Lord Vaux. Andrew thought she looked older than her husband by a few years. Lady Vaux seemed reserved and spoke very little during their modest meal.

Lord Vaux proudly said, "Edmund Campion tutored our son Henry some ten years ago. Edmund is a member of our family."

After the meal, Lord Vaux invited Gervase and Andrew to yet another large room. A fire burned brightly in the gigantic fireplace. Lord Vaux bid them recline in the thick-cushioned chairs. Andrew was grateful. His rib hurt.

Lord Vaux held up the letter from Father Persons. He read portions of it aloud. "Be courageous. Suffer not a faint heart. Do not be discouraged when thou art persecuted, tempted, and afflicted. With faith, look to our Lord in this hour. The tempest will end. The waves will be stilled."

"'Tis a prayer for us all," said Gervase. He then told their host about Father Sherwin.

With a somber expression, Lord Vaux went to the fireplace. He leaned his hand on the rose-colored mantle and said, "I am of an age when my life should be one of peace. I have often thought, *Let the troubles of these difficult days fall to younger and stronger men to champion.* Our Lord would not have it so."

Reaching down, Lord Vaux picked up an iron poker and jabbed at the burning logs. He continued. "Nay, our Lord hath placed me in such tumultuous times as these. In my life, I have seen a king reject the Church of Christ, a queen attempt to restore it, and another queen reject it again. I have seen the sacred Mass abolished by a charlatan church I do not recognize. I am forced to serve God in secret and worship in hiding. Priests I have loved are exiled or hunted. I have watched my children grow up, surrounded by many who hate the Catholic faith and would have my family imprisoned if they could."

When Lord Vaux turned again to them, Andrew thought he saw tears in his eyes.

"Come, let us pray." Lord Vaux took them to a small chapel in another part of the house. The chapel was simple, with a beautifully carved altar. Lady Vaux was already there, kneeling and praying quietly. The three of them knelt near her. Lord Vaux treated Father Person's letter as a genuine prayer for them all. He ended with an appeal to God that if they should die for the faith, let them die honorably.

Gervase and Andrew traveled on to Rushton Hall the next morning. Larger and more impressive than Great Harrowden, Rushton Hall was a sprawling, palatial manor with dozens of arched windows. Its spire-like roofs thrust upward at different heights, and the walls jutted out with no real consistency. The estate sat on hundreds of well-tended acres near the River Ise.

Gervase seemed entertained by the house. " 'Twas built more than a hundred years ago," he told Andrew. "If we are permitted to tour it, thou shalt see that the design is fixed as a quadrangle. 'Tis of no set style. Thou wilt notice Roman, Gothic, and Italian styles throughout. There is also a triangular lodge built in honor of the Trinity."

Andrew nodded as if he knew what Gervase meant. What he *did* know was that the place spoke of great wealth.

CHAPTER TWENTY-TWO

As they entered through the main gate, Gervase mentioned that the lord of the manor, Sir Thomas Tresham, was related to Lord Vaux by marriage.

A servant welcomed Gervase and Andrew and told them that Sir Thomas was somewhere on the grounds dealing with poachers. Another servant was sent to find him. Other servants made sure the two travelers were given food and ale while they waited for his lordship.

It was an hour before Sir Thomas arrived. He met them in a room set aside for greeting guests. Andrew was struck by the man's overall features. Dark hair came to a point on his forehead, as if drawing attention to his sharp eyes. His beard and moustache highlighted a mouth that seemed shaped in a permanent sneer.

Sir Thomas tossed his coat aside and dropped into a chair. Stretching out his legs, he snapped at a nearby servant to remove his boots. The servant put great effort into the task. While being relieved of his attire, Sir Thomas gave a running discourse about his problems with poachers.

"Most of them are priest hunters, I am sure," he said. "They steal my game even as they look for ways to betray me to the Privy Council. Mark me, I will die by their hands!"

"Let us pray not, my lord," said Gervase.

"I do not will it, but I expect it," Sir Thomas said.

Andrew sensed that the man's bristly manner amused Gervase. Andrew was intimidated. It was a relief that Sir Thomas paid no attention to him at all.

Gervase handed over several letters to Sir Thomas. "They are sent from Father Persons," Gervase explained. "He asks that you see them delivered safely."

Sir Thomas waved for a servant to take the letters away. "What is thy mission?" he asked Gervase.

"To meet and escort Father Campion, my lord," said Gervase.

Sir Thomas gave a quick nod. "Father Campion visited here, perhaps it was a fortnight ago. I do not recall. The man is a saint. We have so few of them these days." He followed the comment with a complaint about Lord Vaux owing him money, which was hardly saintlike, he noted.

Gervase used the moment to announce that he and Andrew must continue on their journey.

Sir Thomas looked disappointed but confessed, "Ah well, 'tis all for the best. I am a terrible host. Perchance 'tis the reason guests stay in other wings of the house. My wife hath often said I am too sour."

Your wife may be right, Andrew thought.

The two travelers continued on to Leicestershire. The landscape there had fewer hedgerows and trees than the other counties they'd been through. The cows and sheep seemed to be spread farther apart as they grazed.

Andrew noticed, too, that the cottages were smaller and made from cruder materials, like clay and straw.

CHAPTER TWENTY-TWO

The peasants they passed looked worn and ragged, often meeting their greetings with looks of anger.

"'Tis a forlorn county," Gervase explained when they stopped near a stream to refresh themselves. "The families that own the land hold their possessions very close. A hefty sum is required of the herders and shepherds to graze the animals. The poor are indeed very poor. There have been riots."

"Are we in danger?" Andrew asked Gervase.

"Nay. The people are bitter against their landlords, not strangers." More softly he added, "If we be in danger, 'tis because of the many Protestants here. To gain a reward for our skins is no small thing."

Andrew wasn't comforted.

He drank from the cold stream, then stretched his aching muscles. Flinching at the jab in his side, he strolled back to the muddy stretch of lane. He looked back the way they'd come. At a turning in the road, he saw a saddled horse standing off to the side. A man came from behind the horse, crouching as if he was inspecting the horse's hoof. The man's face was turned away. Andrew couldn't be sure, but he thought it was the Alley Cat Man.

Andrew slowly backed away, returning to Gervase by the river. "We are as yet still followed," he said.

Gervase was tightening the straps to his saddle. "I saw the man a few miles back."

"What should we do?" asked Andrew.

"'Tis in my mind to make him work for his reward." Gervase gestured to Andrew's horse. "Art thou able to ride at speed?"

Andrew understood. "I shall do my best," he said, checking the saddle.

They mounted, then trotted up to the road. With a loud "Yah!" from Gervase, they spurred their horses on. The horses bolted. The race was on.

23

Andrew did not dare look back. To turn even a little added pain to his side. It was already throbbing from the galloping. He didn't know how many miles they raced. They came to the village of Melton Mowbray rising up from the banks of the Eye River. Melton Mowbray had only four cross streets. Gervase slowed down and then turned right. Andrew followed him to the Horned Cattle Inn. They rounded the old stone building and dismounted in the back.

"Wait here," Gervase said as entered the rear of the inn.

Andrew groaned. His side was in agony. He leaned against the wall and thought of Mrs. Mimms's vial of medicine. He would take a drop before bed.

Gervase returned. He did a double take when he looked at Andrew. "Thou art sickly. Go inside and rest. The innkeeper will bring thee food and drink whilst I see to our room."

"I thank you," Andrew said.

Andrew clutched his side as he walked inside. He came to a hallway crowded with crates and casks. He followed it to a front area that served as an entry and dining room. A huge, barrel-shaped man stood behind a counter. He directed Andrew to a corner table.

Andrew slid into the chair. A sharp pain stabbed at his side. He reached to his belt and found the pouch with the vial. Undoing the leather strap, he retrieved the vial from the pouch and set it on the table.

There were only a few guests in the room. A stack of coal burned bright-orange and red in the hearth.

The barrel-shaped man brought Andrew a cup of cider and a plate of something that looked like a small pie. Slices of cheese were spread around the edges of the plate.

Andrew pulled the stopper out of the vial and intended to put a drop in the cider. His hands were shaking and several drops fell in.

He groaned. *Perhaps the potion will be diluted in such a big cup*, he hoped.

The front door of the inn burst open. The Alley Cat Man stormed in, looking red-faced and winded. He scanned the room and saw Andrew. In a few quick strides, he was at the table. He dropped down into the chair next to Andrew and scooted close.

Andrew shifted to move away but felt the jab of a knife point against his leg.

"Halt," the man snarled, "or I shall have thy guts for garters."

CHAPTER TWENTY-THREE

Andrew froze.

"Thought thou wert clever, eh?" the man said in a raspy growl. "Thought thou couldst outrace me?"

"Who are you? What do you want?" Andrew asked.

The man leaned even closer to Andrew. His hair and beard looked as if they hadn't been washed in weeks. He had a pock-marked face and narrow eyes. His breath was foul, and his teeth were brown.

"Where is thy master?" he demanded.

"He hath gone to our room," Andrew said, then asked again, "What do you want?"

The man's gaze fell to Andrew's plate. He grabbed a piece of cheese and tossed it into his mouth. He spat it out again. "Stilton. I despise Stilton cheese."

Andrew remembered the cup of cider and the medicine he'd poured into it. "Wash it down with this," he said and pushed the cup across the table.

The Alley Cat Man looked suspiciously at the cup. "'Tis what?"

"Ale."

Picking up the cup, the Alley Cat Man took a long drink, paused to burp, then took another. He drained the cup, then slammed it on the table. "An odd taste to it, but I am obliged."

"Why have you been following us?" Andrew asked.

"'Tis for thy master to know," the man replied, wiping his mouth with the back of his hand.

Gervase rounded the corner. His eyes met Andrew's, then shifted to the Alley Cat Man. His face turned stone-cold, and he put a hand on the hilt of the knife in his belt. He slowly stepped forward.

The Alley Cat Man scowled at him. "Draw your knife, sir, and my own blade will carve a piece from this boy."

Gervase looked at Andrew, who nodded. "'Tis true," Andrew said.

Gervase grabbed a chair on the opposite side of the table and sat down. "Well, then. Thou hast caught us. To what purpose?"

"To see you drawn and quartered," the man said. "I know your evil doings. You are Catholics."

"What, pray tell, hath led thee to the idea?"

"I have been following you from the Griffith house in Uxbridge. 'Tis well known that the Griffiths are Papists, as are many others you have seen on your journey north."

"Prove thy claim, sir! Summon the sheriff if thou wilt. I shall then tell how thou hast threatened the life of a mere boy."

"The law permits me to do what I must to capture Catholics," said the Alley Cat Man. "The boy will suffer no harm if he comes with me to the sheriff."

"Is that so?" Gervase replied. "Dost thou truly believe I would allow thee to depart with him?"

"My knife assures me you will," the man said. "If I do not kill the boy, I will assuredly cripple him before you prevail upon me."

Andrew had been watching the man, hoping the potion would take effect. Now he heard the man slur while saying the word *assuredly*.

"I am a man of peace, but I will fight thee," Gervase said.

"I am not a man of peace, but I will not fight you," the man countered.

"Do not brawl," Andrew said, then turned to the Alley Cat Man. "I will come with you."

"Nay!" said Gervase.

The man eyed Andrew. "Thou wilt come?"

"Aye," Andrew said, "*if* you canst but walk from here to the door."

"Walk?" the man asked with a puzzled look.

"I shall go if you canst walk," Andrew repeated.

The man rubbed his hand over his face. "What witchcraft is this?" he asked as he began to sway in his chair.

Andrew smiled and slid away from the Alley Cat Man.

The man was slow to react. He tried to lunge at Andrew, but it was more like a fall. His knife clattered to the ground as he dropped face-first onto Andrew's chair.

Gervase reared back in his chair. He watched in surprise as the Alley Cat Man slid from the chair to the floor under the table.

"What hast thou done?" Gervase asked Andrew.

Andrew held up the vial. "Thank Mrs. Mimms," he said with a grin.

Gervase called to the barrel-shaped innkeeper—a man named Bernard.

Without a word or a question, Bernard pulled the table aside and looked down at the unconscious Alley Cat

Man. He grunted. "I have seen this man before, my lord," Bernard said. "A vile creature that I doubt was born of woman."

"Hath *it* a name?" Gervase asked.

"*It* hath several," the innkeeper said. "John Smith is the latest. Thomas Jones before that. Robert Thompson before that. Hath he caused my lord trouble?"

"He hath indeed," Gervase said. He picked up the fallen knife. "He threatened this good lad who is in my charge."

"My profuse apologies, sir!" Bernard said. "Until such time as the sheriff comes to the village, he shall be locked up."

"Pray, when will the sheriff come?" asked Gervase.

Bernard was giving the question some thought when Gervase handed him a few coins. Then the answer came quickly. "Three days, I should think, my lord," the innkeeper said, pocketing the coins.

The two men smiled. Bernard reached down and grabbed John Smith's legs. With little care, he dragged Smith across the floor and out of the room.

Gervase and Andrew departed Melton Mowbray in the early morning light. They rode through the town under the vacant gaze of yet another church that had been dedicated to Saint Mary. As they continued their journey northward, Gervase insisted they ride at a faster pace than usual. It was an uncomfortable trek. A damp cold seemed to press icy fingers around every bone in Andrew's body.

By early afternoon, they closed in on Nottingham. Andrew felt his heart quicken at the thought of returning to the town. He wondered how much it had changed in almost three centuries since he went there on an errand for Robin Hood. Was the castle still on the hill, or was it now a ruin? Were Bridlesmith Gate or Fletcher Gate still there? What was left of Sherwood Forest to the north—or Thornbridge or Ravenswood? Were the descendants of Ket the Troll still making their way secretly through the deepest and most hidden places in the wood?

Andrew thought of Eve and wished she could be with him to see it all.

"Will we stay in Nottingham?" he asked Gervase.

"Nay," he said. "Holme Pierrepont is to the east. Why dost thou ask?"

"I hoped to see it again."

"Again? When hast thou been to Nottingham?"

Andrew was caught. "A long time ago," he said.

"How long can it have been? Thou art but what? Twelve?" Gervase had a mirthful look in his eyes.

"Twelve only in years," Andrew said.

Gervase shook his head. "I know little of the stone that thou art a child of, but it must have confounding properties."

"You have no idea," Andrew said softly.

They reached the grounds of Holme Pierrepont Hall by midafternoon.

"That is St. Edmund's Church," Gervase explained, pointing to a great tower rising above the tree line. "It hath been our neighbor for over four hundred years."

"Is it still Catholic?" Andrew asked.

Gervase shook his head. "Alas, 'twas ransacked during the pillage of Edward the Sixth. Queen Mary restored the tower, but it fell again into the hands of the heretics. 'Tis said that spies hide in it to watch the comings and goings at Holme Pierrepont Hall." He gave a small shrug. "There is not much for the spies to see. The meadows. The Trent River. The enclosures for grazing."

The Great Hall stood majestically in its place across an open field. It was made of bright-red brick, with oversized windows and turrets lining the roof. By the time they reached the main archway leading to the door, servants appeared from every which way to greet them.

They hailed Gervase and gave greetings to Andrew. It was "Master" this and "Master" that. After helping the two travelers dismount their horses, the servants whisked away their belongings.

The two were led into the front hall. From a terrace above came the shout "Gervase!"

"Henry!" Gervase called back. "Dear brother!"

A man who looked like a slightly older version of Gervase rushed down a broad staircase. The two men embraced.

CHAPTER TWENTY-THREE

"Henry, greet Andrew, the lad Father Persons put into my charge," Gervase said.

Henry nodded to Andrew. "Thou art most welcome."

Andrew bowed.

Henry clapped his brother on the back. "Come!" he said. "Be refreshed!"

They were led to a modest dining room that Andrew guessed was for smaller private parties. Earlier he had seen from the corner of his eye the doorway to a much grander room for feasting. This room was richly paneled with dark wood. Small arched windows allowed light in on one wall, and another wall of brick had a fireplace in the middle. Fat beams of wood crossed the ceiling above them. The servants brought in a meal of pheasant, with vegetables and bread.

Andrew shifted in his chair. His side ached with a steady throbbing.

His host noticed him squirm. "What is it, lad?" asked Henry.

Before Andrew could answer, Gervase explained about Andrew's race from the "wicked betrayer, Mr. Nedly" and the resulting broken rib.

"A boy with courage," Henry said. "'Tis an honor to have thee in my house. But let us see to thy injury. A ride from London with a broken rib is no easy matter."

An older servant named Mr. Hancock was tasked with looking at Andrew's bruised side. Mr. Hancock guided Andrew to a quaint guest room on the second floor. It had a bed framed with oak posts and thin beams to hold curtains on the three open sides. A couple of chairs and tables sat on a woven rug. A fire burned steadily in the small fireplace.

Mr. Hancock ordered two other servants to draw a bath in an adjoining room. Then he helped Andrew remove the layers of clothes above his waist. The servant made a hissing sound when he saw Andrew's side.

"What medicines dost thou have?" Mr. Hancock asked.

Andrew explained about Mrs. Mimms and showed him the concoction.

Mr. Hancock unstopped the vial and held it to his nose. "Aye, the woman knows her craft," he said. "'Tis amazing how she is able to find such rare herbs in London, of all places."

The bathtub was in a closet-like room with a long bench, racks for linens, and a smaller closet in the corner with a toilet.

Once the bath was ready, Hancock brought in a large bottle and poured light brown granules into the water.

"What is that?" Andrew asked.

He gave Andrew a shrewd look. "I have a few tricks of my own."

Mr. Hancock shooed the servants out of the room and closed the door behind him. Andrew slowly took off the rest of his clothes. He climbed into the tub, expecting the water to be cold. It was on the hotter side of warm.

He gently sank into the water. Within minutes, he felt the pain fade from his side.

After his bath, one of the servants brought him a silken nightshirt. He thought he wasn't tired enough to sleep, but he slipped quickly into dreams of racing horses and creepy men with the faces of animals.

24

Andrew awakened to a heavy snowfall. From the window in his bedroom, he watched fat flakes fall on fields already covered in white.

A servant arrived to help him dress. The clothes were the quality of a noble family and fit him well, though he couldn't imagine where they'd come from. He wondered if they were hand-me-downs or had been tailored by a servant while he slept.

Edmund Campion and Brother Emerson were celebrating the Mass in a private chapel. Andrew arrived just in time, sliding into a wooden pew next to Gervase. In front of them were Henry and a woman Andrew hadn't met. A girl of about five turned in the pew to look at Andrew. She had a round, pleasant face and curly red hair. She smiled at him. He smiled back. Then the woman nudged her and she quickly swung around again.

The Mass was done simply. Father Campion spoke about the difficult days that awaited all of them. "But our Lord is with us on the many different paths we shall take," he said.

After Mass, introductions were made. The woman in front of Andrew was Frances, Henry's wife. She had a long face and nose, small eyes, and a mouth that seemed to perch on her chin like a bird about to take wing. She wore large ruffs around her collar that made her head look as if it were floating above a patch of clouds. The little girl was Grace, their daughter.

As the morning went on, Andrew learned that Henry Pierrepont was a politician, often active locally and in London as a member of Parliament. He had also been a justice of the peace and even the High Sheriff for a while.

It wasn't long before Andrew realized that Henry and Gervase argued like brothers often do. They debated the state of the nation and the folly of the queen's handling of her Catholic subjects. Henry seemed to take a moderate stance and called Gervase "radical" and "obstinate."

Andrew saw Father Campion and Brother Emerson for only the time it took to say hello. Then they disappeared for most of the morning. Around noon, Father Campion returned, apple cheeked and bright eyed. He had the look of a man who had been out in the snow. Warming himself by the fire in the smaller dining room, the priest summoned Andrew to the stool at his side.

"Thou hast had adventures since I last saw thee," Father Campion said.

Andrew admitted that it was true.

CHAPTER TWENTY-FOUR

"Evangeline hath not returned?" the priest asked.

"Nay," Andrew said sadly.

Father Campion pressed his hands together under his chin. "I see," he said thoughtfully. "'Tis thee alone to bear the burden."

Andrew was puzzled. "The burden, sir?"

"The burden of preparing me for what is to come," he replied.

Andrew was concerned. "Preparing you, sir? For what am I expected to prepare you?"

"My death," said the priest soberly. Then he suddenly straightened up and said cheerfully, "Meanwhile, as the Lord wills, we shall remain safely here until the Feast of the Epiphany."

Andrew was troubled by Father Campion's words. But he soon put them aside as the Pierrepont family turned its attention to Christmas.

He quickly discovered that Christmas at this time in England's history was different from the Christmas he'd experienced in France. The queen and her Protestant advisers had made many changes to the Catholic traditions the people had known. Even traditions that had not been banned were left unobserved as many families feared being accused of treason. Others kept the traditions in secret.

Henry Pierrepont determined that his family would limit the number of holiday guests and play down the usual festive parties, dances, and activities.

"We must not put Father Campion or Brother Emerson at risk," he said.

Frances Pierrepont was of a different mind. She determined that the Twelve Days of Christmas must not be a morose lamenting of their plight as Catholics. "I shall not have our daughter raised to dread the birth of our Savior as a melancholy occasion. This house shall celebrate in old and new ways!" she announced. She kept the servants busy with daily instructions about their meals, gatherings, and games.

Henry made a lot of harrumphing noises but abided by his wife's wishes.

Greenery went up all over the house. Enormous wreaths were hung above the fireplaces, in the windows, and on the doors. Grace rehearsed a Nativity play with Andrew. She would play Mary, and Andrew was tagged to play Joseph.

Small, oval-shaped pies made of mincemeat—or minced mutton—were prepared. Grace patiently explained to Andrew that the pies represented the manger the baby Jesus slept in. "That is why the pies must never be cut with a knife," she said.

Henry put up his loudest protest when Frances had a tall evergreen tree brought in. "'Tis a pagan symbol that the foul-minded Martin Luther hath made popular!"

CHAPTER TWENTY-FOUR

Frances argued that Martin Luther had not made the tree popular. The couple eventually compromised. The tree would be kept and decorated, but it would be placed in a side room where Henry wouldn't have to look at it.

On Christmas Eve, a Yule log was lit in the fireplace of the largest hall. It was the width of a tree trunk and was expected to burn the entire twelve days.

"Just like they did in France," Andrew muttered to himself. He wished again that Eve were there to share these experiences.

With Christmas morning came the smells of cooking meat and pastries. Father Campion and Brother Emerson celebrated the Mass, and then Henry, Gervase, and a few other gentlemen rode off for early morning foxhunting. Father Campion privately prayed for the poor fox. Another Mass was said at noon.

Presents were exchanged in the afternoon. It would be the first of many occasions for gift giving over the following eleven days. Grace was the center of attention as she opened boxes of new dresses, dolls, and wooden toys. Even Andrew was included. He was given a new pair of boots, tailor-made for him by a craftsman in Nottingham.

The Christmas meal was a foreshadowing of every meal they would have over the season. Pig and wild boar were the dominant meats, but the Pierreponts also served peacock, partridge, goose, beef, and venison, along with bread and cheese. Andrew was introduced to a huge

Christmas pie in an enormous pan of pastry. The pan was filled with a turkey stuffed with a goose that was stuffed with a chicken that was stuffed with a partridge that was stuffed with a pigeon.

Ale, wine, and various types of hot punch were enjoyed, though Andrew thought a lot of the drinks were too bitter for his taste.

That night they performed the Nativity play. Andrew felt awkward as he stood with the five-year-old Grace and placed the baby Jesus in the manger. The joy of the moment turned dark for him as he suddenly imagined hunters breaking down the door and arresting them all.

I will never make it back to Hope Springs, he later brooded. He couldn't shake the fear that he would be stuck in this time, running and hiding from the hunters.

The day after Christmas, Andrew joined the family and the servants to distribute food and drink to the poorest families in the area. It was an all-day activity that took even longer because the priest hunters were out in full force, stopping and questioning the travelers.

Gervase was in a fit of rage. "The varlets harass us because we are Catholics."

Over the rest of the season, small groups randomly appeared at the front door, causing immediate alarm throughout the house. Father Campion and Brother

CHAPTER TWENTY-FOUR

Emerson were whisked away to their hiding places. The groups were nothing more than carol singers, arriving to sing, enjoy a hot punch called *wassail*, and receive a coin or two for their performances.

On the twelfth day of Christmas, Andrew overheard a servant say that Mr. Hancock would ride into Nottingham to visit a cousin. Andrew asked Gervase for permission to go with Mr. Hancock. Gervase agreed.

Mr. Hancock said he was delighted to have the company. "However, the shops will be closed. Few of the merchants work during the Twelve Days. Work doth not begin again until Plow Monday."

Andrew didn't care. He felt restless and impatient. Seeing Nottingham was a good excuse to get away from the house.

He bundled up in a thick fur-lined overcoat and rode the horse he had been given in Uxbridge. Another snowfall made it slow going. They finally crossed a long bridge over the Trent River at midday and entered the town on the south side.

Mr. Hancock was delivering a basket of food and medicine to his cousin and would not be long. Since Andrew intended to wander the town on foot, Mr. Hancock agreed to take Andrew's horse with him.

"Meet me here at the foot of the bridge in an hour's time," the servant said.

They parted company, and Andrew made his way along the rugged street. The large and forbidding castle he knew from Robin Hood's time still overlooked the southwest part of the town. Little had changed about it, he thought.

He walked toward the center of the town. There was no doubt that Nottingham had grown and expanded in the past few hundred years. The buildings were more distinguished than they were before. It was as if the town had become important. The shops were closed, as Mr. Hancock had said, though inns and taverns were open for business.

Andrew wandered until he came to the Bridlesmith Gate on the west side of town. He remembered that it was the gate he, Eve, and Will Scarlet had used when they were searching for Silas ben Reuben. Will had been disguised as a pilgrim. Andrew and Eve had dressed as peasant children. Now, the iron gates were kept open since they were no longer needed to protect the town from invaders. Newer buildings nearly obscured the stone edifice.

Andrew thought about the Fletcher Gate—and the inn where he and Eve had gone to escape from the town. He asked an old woman where he'd find the gate, and she pointed east. A meandering street eventually led him there. A pile of rubble now stood where the inn had once been.

Andrew was disappointed. He gazed at the debris for a moment, remembering how the sheriff's men had overpowered and captured Will Scarlet on that very spot. Eve had to race away to tell Robin. Andrew stayed behind to keep an eye on Will Scarlet, only to be captured himself. He smiled at the memory, but only because he was still alive to remember it.

Lost in his thoughts, he hardly noticed something moving out of the corner of his right eye. Only as he realized that the figure was gaining speed did he turn fully to look.

The Alley Cat Man was rushing at him.

25

Andrew had two conflicting thoughts. The first was how *very* tired he was of people chasing him, and that he should stand his ground this time. The second was that he had better move and move fast.

His good sense told him to go with the second.

Darting to the right, he followed the street down to another and then darted left. He had no idea where he was going. He could hear the pounding of the Alley Cat Man's feet behind him. Once or twice he also heard an animal-like snarl as if the man wanted to shout but couldn't get the words out.

Andrew turned at whatever street came up next. He dodged left and then right. He looked for the castle to give him a sense of direction but found it confusing. One minute the castle was straight ahead, then to his left, then to his right.

Why am I always being chased in this country? he thought as he ran. *It's not fair! I don't even belong here!*

The longer he ran, the angrier he felt. The stabbing pain in his side worsened.

He came back to a road he thought he recognized and stopped to get his bearings. The castle was to his right again. If he ran left, the road would take him back to the bridge where he was supposed to meet Mr. Hancock.

He started off again, gathering speed. He saw the bridge up ahead. Even better, Mr. Hancock was at the foot of the bridge with the two horses.

Andrew put on the afterburners, pouring every bit of energy into his legs.

Suddenly the Alley Cat Man emerged at a full run from a street just ahead, cutting Andrew off from the bridge. "Aha!" he shouted.

The two runners were on a collision course. Both tried to slow down and slipped on the slushy road. They were like bad ice-skaters. Andrew hit the man, glancing off him and tumbling to the ground. The Alley Cat Man spun, nearly fell, then held his balance. He lunged at Andrew. Andrew saw him coming and rolled to the left. The Alley Cat Man slipped again and fell to the right on his hands and knees.

This would probably be funny if I could watch it from a distance, Andrew thought. He rolled onto his stomach to get up.

The Alley Cat Man puffed loudly as he stood up straight. Andrew was hunched over, then pulled himself upright. The Alley Cat Man was only a dozen feet away. He held up his hands, ready for the grab.

CHAPTER TWENTY-FIVE

The two now faced each other, moving back and forth in a slow circle. Andrew held the distance, bracing himself for whatever move the Alley Cat Man might make.

Andrew heard shouts from somewhere behind him. It sounded like a mob was coming his way.

"My men will catch thee," the Alley Cat Man snarled.

Andrew became aware of a new sound: the thundering of horse's hooves coming from behind the Alley Cat Man.

Just beyond the man's shoulder, Andrew saw Mr. Hancock riding hard and fast toward them.

The face of the Alley Cat Man changed from confidence to concern. He clearly heard the thumping hooves coming closer now. The shouts from the men behind Andrew became a warning.

Andrew and the man locked eyes and continued their slow turn. They were now parallel to the mob coming from one direction and the horse coming from the other.

The Alley Cat Man looked panicked, as if he couldn't decide whether to give up the fight or make a move. He then foolishly leapt for Andrew just as Mr. Hancock's horse rode between them.

The front of the horse hit the man in midair. He spun like a propeller and landed in a heap in a pile of slush. The mob roared and ran for the fallen man.

Andrew took off for the bridge. A familiar voice shouted "My hand!" Andrew glanced over his shoulder. Mr. Hancock had brought his horse around and was coming alongside Andrew.

Andrew reached up. Hancock caught him by the wrist and pulled him up. Andrew used his free hand to grab the back of the saddle and then swung his legs onto the back of the horse.

As they reached the bridge, Andrew looked back to see the crowd helping the Alley Cat Man to his feet. Andrew leapt from Mr. Hancock's horse onto his own. The two riders sped away from Nottingham.

Back in his room at Holme Pierrepont Hall, Andrew sat down. The pain in his side screamed at him. He felt dizzy.

"Pulling thyself onto a speeding horse will wrench things apart that are meant to be together," Mr. Hancock said as he looked at Andrew's side and arm.

Word of the chase spread around the house. Gervase, Henry, and Father Campion came to see Andrew. Gervase was astonished that the Alley Cat Man—John Smith, as the innkeeper called him—had followed them to Nottingham.

"'Tis likely he hath been searching those streets since well before Christmas," Father Campion suggested.

"I did not realize we were such prizes," Gervase said.

Henry asked Mr. Hancock, "Did anyone in the town recognize thy face? Might any in the mob know that thou comest from this house?"

Mr. Hancock shook his head. "I was hooded to protect myself from the cold."

CHAPTER TWENTY-FIVE

"We may yet be safe," said Henry.

Still, they all looked worried.

"I thank thee for saving me," Andrew said to Mr. Hancock.

The servant gave a nod, then turned to his master. "My lord, the lad is made of sturdy stuff. I, on the other hand, am not. I have become too old for this kind of sport. May I retire for a short spell?"

Henry laughed and patted Mr. Hancock on the shoulder. "Take thyself to bed. See to no further duties today."

Mr. Hancock bowed, then walked out. Andrew noticed that he was rubbing his arm and shoulder as he left.

"Thou hast been a generous host," Father Campion said to Henry. "However, 'tis necessary for us to depart sooner."

Henry agreed. "I shall make the arrangements," he said, then departed.

Gervase followed his brother out. "I will escort them," he said.

Father Campion sat down in a chair next to Andrew. "I do not know what to make of thee," he said. "Thou hast a special gift for drawing trouble to thyself."

Andrew felt a burning anger rise up within him. "'Tis not my fault!" he cried. "Why can I not go anywhere. I cannot do anything without fearing the hands or shackles of hunters."

"'Tis the plight of all Catholics now," said the priest.

"Why do the Catholics not rise up and rebel against the queen and her wicked men?" Andrew fumed.

He looked into the face of Father Campion and saw something flash in the priest's eyes. Father Campion leaned close and said in a stern voice, "Thou must *never* speak such words again. Not in my presence, *ever*! We are here to comfort the people of the Church and to give witness to the truth. Some of us will die for it. But we are *not* here to overthrow those whom God hath put in authority over us."

Andrew drew back from Father Campion and lowered his head. He felt ashamed.

Father Campion patted his arm. "Rest, lad. 'Tis still Twelfth Night and the eve of Epiphany. We have yet more to celebrate."

The celebrations included singing carols, drinking cups of punch, and cutting into a Twelfth Night cake. The cake tasted to Andrew like french bread with sugar on top. After the festivities, the servants began to dismantle all of the Christmas decorations. Andrew was told that it was considered bad luck to keep them up after Epiphany arrived.

Before bed, Father Campion blessed the house, according to an ancient tradition. He spoke the words of the blessing in a joyful voice, but Andrew noticed that he emphasized safety and protection more than anything else.

CHAPTER TWENTY-FIVE

Father Campion and Brother Emerson celebrated the Feast of the Epiphany with Mass in the morning. Afterward, the Pierrepont family and their servants gathered to eat fresh pastries.

More singers performed at the door throughout the day. The family then met around the charred remains of the Yule log and prayed. This was the end of the holiday season.

Andrew didn't feel festive. He felt angry. He didn't want to be in England anymore. He thought again about Eve. She would understand.

The next morning, the horses and provisions were prepared for the guests to depart.

"Where are we going?" Andrew asked Gervase.

"The bleak and cold north," Gervase replied.

"Will Father Campion be safer there?" Andrew asked.

Gervase frowned. "Alas, I fear that Father Campion is no longer safe anywhere."

26

Andrew now understood how Father Campion had been able to travel the countryside for so many months.

Dressed as a man of moderate means, the priest was accompanied by a gentleman who would vouch for him. For the next part of the journey, that gentleman was Gervase Pierrepont.

The horses they rode were fresh and strong. Their saddles were finely made, and the provisions were well supplied. Brother Emerson would pose as Father Campion's servant. Andrew would be his young ward.

Before leaving Holme Pierrepont Hall, Father Campion blessed the family and the house. He then gathered his fellow travelers together and recited the Itinerarium. It was a Latin prayer for the road ahead that praised God, reminding them of His mercy upon the children of Israel in their travels. It ended with the proclamation, "Let us proceed in peace!"

The four said their thanks and farewells to the Pierrepont family. Andrew was sorry to say goodbye to

Mr. Hancock. He knew he had caused the servant a lot of trouble.

They slowly rode away. When they were only a mile from the manor, Andrew noticed that Father Campion had drifted well ahead of them.

"Should we not catch up?" Andrew asked.

"Nay," said Brother Emerson. "He rides ahead to pray and meditate, read his breviary, and recite the litanies of the saints. He doth so every morning, preferring silence and solitude. When we catch up to him, he will be as pleasant and talkative as ever. Then be warned: as we approach our next destination, he will again separate from us for further meditation on the sermon he shall be asked to preach."

"Doth he always preach?" asked Andrew.

"He preaches, hears confessions, and celebrates the Mass," Brother Emerson replied. "Do not be discouraged."

"Discouraged?" Andrew asked. "Why would I be discouraged?"

"Many of the homes we visit shall seem rather sad. Families are fined burdensome amounts for refusing to attend heretical services. Destitution awaits many of them. Others suffer the imprisonment of family members for their faith. Thou wilt hear much talk of death, fleeing the country, and the ruin of Catholics. Yet there is steadfast courage to be found among them all."

Andrew felt his anger rising again. *It's wrong!* he thought. *No one of any faith should have to suffer like that.*

CHAPTER TWENTY-SIX

By midafternoon, the travelers reached a modest house near a village called West Hallam, just east of the town of Derby. A family of nine greeted them with excitement. Andrew thought the family name was Powdrell or Powtrell, but he didn't ask in case it was better not to know.

Father Campion heard confessions, celebrated the Mass, and preached about the Scriptures and faith in a time of great trial. A light meal was given to the guests, and then everyone went to bed.

Father Campion celebrated the Mass again early the next morning. Afterward, he recited the Itinerarium, and they rode off.

"Will we change houses every night?" Andrew asked Brother Emerson after Father Campion had ridden ahead.

Brother Emerson nodded. "We ride on as often as we must. To stay in one place is dangerous."

Andrew wondered why they had stayed so long at Holme Pierrepont Hall. He put the question to Gervase.

"I insisted upon it," Gervase replied. "'Tis a large house with many hiding places. Should the hunters have invaded to search, they would have exhausted themselves in doing so. 'Twas also in our minds that few of the gentry or workers around Nottingham desire to upset the lord of the manor. Many benefit from his generosity throughout the year."

They did not travel very far that first day. Soon they arrived at the manor of a man who had attended Oxford University with Father Campion. Once again, the priest heard confessions and said the Mass. Rather than preach this time, he sat at a table with his former classmate and discussed the Catholic faith well into the night.

The next day, the travelers rounded the town of Derby and made their way west to the home of the Longfords. This time they stayed for two days to accommodate various family and friends who traveled to see the famous priest.

On the following Saturday, they went to the home of Lady Constance Foljambe in Walton, Derbyshire. The four travelers were pleasantly surprised to find George Gilbert there. He claimed he had ridden from London to visit friends, but Andrew suspected he had really come to check on Father Campion.

Though Gilbert was his usual energetic and good-humored self, he seemed weighted by something. Andrew learned in bits and pieces that the published writings of Father Persons had triggered a new wave of harassments, arrests, and imprisonments of Catholics. Fines that were already crippling were raised even more. The Queen's Privy Council now made it an act of treason to attempt to convert anyone to the Catholic faith.

George Gilbert revealed another reason for traveling to see Father Campion. "Father Persons desires you to know that he awaits your next book."

"'Tis declared a treasonous act, and yet he would have me write it?" Father Campion teased.

"How soon will thy treasonous act be completed?" Gilbert asked.

CHAPTER TWENTY-SIX

"Pray, before Easter," Father Campion said. "Though it may not be the book Father Persons is expecting."

"How so?"

The priest shrugged. "Because I do not yet know what it is about."

Father Campion and his three companions journeyed two days later against an icy wind and snow to Spital, near Chesterfield. It was there that Gervase introduced them to an older silver-haired gentleman with pale skin and a beak-like nose.

"Mr. Henry Tempest of Broughton Hall," Gervase announced. "He shall be your escort north into Yorkshire."

"You are forsaking us?" Andrew asked.

"I leave you in better hands," he said.

Before Gervase departed the next morning, he clasped hands with Andrew and said affectionately, "Farewell, dear fool."

Before Andrew's family had moved to Hope Springs, he often begged his parents to sell everything and travel around the country in a big camper. He thought it would be fun to drive from town to town, see the sights, and then move on.

He was now glad his parents hadn't listened to him. He was tired of traveling. The farther north he went, the worse the bone-shaking cold, dampness, and heavy snow were.

Mr. Tempest had insisted that they stay at inns rather than houses. He said he feared they were being followed. Every stranger who gave them a second glance caught his attention. This went on for a week until Father Campion insisted that his priestly duties were neglected by staying at inns. Mr. Tempest reluctantly agreed to return to the homes of Catholic families.

Father Campion's routine resumed as they toured Yorkshire late into January and February. Everywhere they went, they met people in need. Widows were grieving over their dead husbands. Parents were grieving over the lost faith of their children. Entire families were pressured financially. Husbands and wives, brothers and sisters disagreed about the Church and turned on one another, sometimes violently. There were sicknesses of all sorts. Father Campion offered hope and peace.

The priest hunters were not idle. Often by dumb luck, they happened to show up to search a house, not realizing that Father Campion and Brother Emerson were hiding inside a wall only a few feet away.

On one occasion, the priests were protected by the brute force of a very large man named Sir William Babthorpe. He held the hunters off at sword point while Father Campion and Brother Emerson escaped out of a back window and into a nearby forest.

With every stop, with every heartbreaking story, with every close call, Andrew felt a growing knot in his stomach. He seethed against those who were inflicting

CHAPTER TWENTY-SIX

so much pain. He understood better why Robin Hood fought for justice when the laws themselves were unjust. He appreciated deeply how a peasant girl like Joan of Arc could leave her village to fight against France's oppressors. The thought came to him: *Where are the great leaders from God who would rise up against this persecution?*

Andrew had hoped it would be Edmund Campion. But now, as they ran yet again to escape the clutches of more hunters, he doubted it was this priest. Maybe none of these Jesuit priests were called to lead the Catholics in England to freedom. Maybe their witness would be in sacrificing their lives.

Andrew thought more and more about Father Campion's words to him back at Holme Pierrepont. He was there to prepare Father Campion for his death. *What does that mean?* Andrew asked himself.

Meanwhile, the knot in Andrew's stomach hardened. The freezing northern winter sunk into his bones—and his heart.

27

Mr. Tempest led the travelers to his sister Elizabeth's house near a village called Felixkirk. Elizabeth was married to a gentleman named William Harrington. Their son was also named William. He was a little older than Andrew.

Felixkirk sat on the side of a tall hill, surrounded by rich woodlands. The Harrington house was miles from anywhere the spies and hunters might search for Father Campion. The Harringtons stated that their seclusion was perfect for the fugitives. They invited Father Campion and his companions to stay for the season of Lent.

By this time, they had been riding for more than six weeks. Andrew was relieved to hear Father Campion accept the invitation. For the first time since leaving Holme Pierrepont Hall, Andrew felt secure. He also hoped that young William might become a friend.

Andrew was quickly disappointed. Within a few days, it became clear that William wasn't interested in being friends with anyone but Father Campion. The young man followed the priest everywhere, asking questions about the faith and why Catholics and Protestants were at odds.

Father Campion then had the idea that the book Father Persons wanted him to write should be based on his answers to William's questions. He would write the book as he and William talked.

With little else to do during those cold and wet late-winter days, Andrew sat off to the side of the small study where Father Campion and young William met. The priest explained the reasons why the Roman Catholic faith was the true continuation of the faith of the Apostles. He also discussed why the church of King Henry the Eighth and Queen Elizabeth broke with that faith. Father Campion eventually covered what would become ten essential reasons for being Catholic.

Andrew thought the entire discussion was remarkable. He learned a lot from Father Campion about what he believed.

Father Campion finished his lessons, then said to both young William and Andrew: "Harken unto me, lads. Remember the cause you serve and the time in which you live. Defend the faith with clarity of speech, but know that your adversaries will twist what you say to give it a meaning you never intended. They did so to our Lord Jesus, and they will do the same to you. Rather than respond to my challenge last year, taking it point by point, they attacked me personally. 'Tis because their arguments are weak, though they do not think so. All who speak the truth must expect the same abuse."

CHAPTER TWENTY-SEVEN

Father Campion spent evenings and a few mornings writing his book of reasons in Latin. By the end, young William was convinced he wanted to be a priest like Father Campion.

Andrew, on the other hand, felt a heavy sadness. He had been listening to the words of a great man of God but knew the Privy Council would do all it could to stop those words from being heard by anyone else. The council would kill Father Campion. He had no doubt about it.

He remembered Eve's heart-wrenching despair about Joan of Arc. Eve would have changed history to save Joan's life. Andrew wished he could do the same for Edmund Campion. But he knew he couldn't.

In English, Father Campion's book was called *Ten Reasons*, though the official title was much longer than that. Once the work was finished, the priest sent a message to Father Persons in London. The reply from Father Persons came in the form of a young man named Robinson.

"Father Persons is overjoyed by the news of your work," he said. "A printing press hath been established in a new location. Everyone now awaits the manuscript itself."

The initial plan was for Robinson to take Father Campion's book directly to London. The idea troubled Father Campion. What if hunters followed Robinson, detained him, and destroyed the manuscript?

Brother Emerson suggested that the book be divided into sections and taken to Father Persons by different trusted friends traveling different routes. Father Campion agreed, and they worked out the details of the plan. It reminded Andrew of secret-agent movies he'd seen.

Shortly after Easter, a former student of Father Campion's arrived to conduct them to their next destination. He was a scholarly man named Edward More, the grandson of Sir Thomas More. Andrew had learned about Sir Thomas More. A favorite of Henry the Eighth, More did not side with the king over the split with the Roman Catholic Church. More was executed for treason.

For the journey, Father Campion switched roles with Brother Emerson. Instead of being the master, he became Brother Emerson's servant.

"It may confuse the priest hunters and spies," Brother Emerson said.

Father Campion chuckled and said, "They are so very confused already."

Andrew's head spun over their next round of travels. They moved back and forth like pinballs in a machine from one hall to another. There was Blainscough Hall, Samlesbury Hall, Monk's Hall, Mowbreck Hall, Woodacre Hall, and Park Hall—each one a home to families who had been praying for time with the beloved priest.

While they were at Park Hall, word came that Father Persons wanted Father Campion to read over the *Ten*

Reasons once more and make any necessary changes or corrections. Father Persons would also have one of the priests in London make certain that quotes from the Bible and any other documents were accurate.

The owner of Park Hall was a good man named Richard Horton. (Andrew learned later that the correct spelling of the name was *Hoghton*.) Richard Horton gave Father Campion access to a beautiful library he kept in a tower on the estate. The library provided Father Campion the means to confirm his quotes and facts. Andrew sometimes helped the priest by fetching books and running errands.

One day, a young man appeared at the tower entrance. He was a tutor for the children of Richard Horton and was now seeking a book of ancient plays. Father Campion was busy writing, so Andrew offered to slip into the library to retrieve the book the young man wanted. After a long search, Andrew found the book tucked away on a lower shelf, half hidden in a corner.

"Hearty thanks for thy help," the young man said after Andrew handed over the book.

"I am glad to be of service," Andrew said.

The young man had a round, boyish face, but his eyes gave the appearance of someone much older. He held up the book and asked, "Canst thou read Latin?"

Andrew shook his head. "Why do you read a book of plays in Latin?" he asked.

"I seek inspiration," replied the young man.

"From a book of Latin plays?" Andrew said.

The young man chuckled. "I drink from whatever fount it mayst spring."

"Why do you need inspiration?" Andrew asked. "Is it for your students?"

"Nay. 'Tis for myself," he said. "I desire to write poetry and plays. But alas, my father says there is no living to be made unless I go to London. He would have me dedicate my life to teaching. I defer to his wisdom. To live as an artist in London would be difficult." The young man suddenly thrust out his hand. "Thou art an amiable lad. What is thy name?"

"Andrew." They shook hands. "Andrew Perry."

"William Shakespeare, at thy service."

Andrew froze. "*William Shakespeare?*" he asked.

The young man laughed and pulled his hand away from Andrew's grip. "Aye."

Andrew swallowed hard. "You ... you are ..." Andrew stammered.

William eyed him. "Lad, thou hast gone pale. Art thou unwell?"

Andrew gathered his wits and said, "Go to London, Mr. Shakespeare. Write plays. I believe with all my heart that success will be yours."

"Andrew, I pray thou speakest as a muse." He lifted the book again. "Many thanks for thy kind assistance." He turned and walked away.

Andrew spun to the tower door. Father Campion stood there with a curious look on his face.

"I beg pardon, Father. Did I distract you from your work?" Andrew asked, concerned.

"Nay. I had my eye on that young man. He is from a Catholic family. I had indulged the hope that he would become a goodly priest in our service."

Andrew wanted to say, *He can't become a priest. He's William Shakespeare!*

Before Andrew could speak, Father Campion said, "Methinks he will render a better service in some other vocation." The priest went back into the library.

Andrew held back a laugh and followed him.

Andrew, the two priests, and Mr. More left Park Hall to continue Father Campion's tour. They had traveled a good part of the day when Father Campion realized he'd left some of his personal books back in the Hoghton library.

"'Tis too far to return," Brother Emerson said. "I shall fetch the books when time permits."

Andrew was relieved. He didn't want to backtrack all that way to retrieve some books. He was concerned about being caught by the hunters. A *lot* of people had traveled to see Father Campion at Richard Horton's home. As Andrew watched them come and go, he wondered if there were any spies among them. Crowds flocked to see Father Campion might also draw the hunters' attention.

This was not just a problem at Park Hall. Andrew noticed that at every new house, the gatherings grew larger. It seemed that as soon as people learned that Father Campion was visiting an area, they came from near and far to see him. Stories were told that some had spent entire nights in neighboring barns to be certain they had a place near the priest the next day.

Andrew was worried enough to talk to Brother Emerson about it. "Father Campion is putting himself in danger," Andrew said when the two of them were riding alone.

"Father Campion hath what some have called 'fire,'" Brother Emerson said. "'Tis a certain hidden force that flows only from the Holy Spirit. That fire inspires all who meet him."

"I know," Andrew said. "But his fire may attract those who would trample the flame."

Brother Emerson nodded. "Lad, I prevailed upon him to turn away the crowds. He says only that he cannot be restrained from the work God hath beseeched him to do."

Only a few days later, hunters surprised them all during a return visit to the Worthington family at Blainscough Hall. Isabel Worthington, a widow and dear friend of Father Campion's, had asked the priest to come by again to speak to members of her family. Father Campion agreed.

It later seemed funny to Andrew that the hunters arrived after Father Campion had met with the family

CHAPTER TWENTY-SEVEN

and was now enjoying the grounds of the estate. As soon as the alarm was given, Andrew dashed from the house to warn the priest.

He crossed a rear garden, leapt over a low wall, and saw Father Campion in the distance walking with a maidservant near a large pond. He could have been a gentleman out for a leisurely stroll on any estate in England. The two stopped, and Father Campion faced the pond with his back to the danger behind him.

It was a wide-open space with nowhere for the priest to hide.

Andrew had run only half the distance when hunters came around the house from another direction. They were also making their way to the pond.

He knew he wouldn't reach Father Campion before the hunters and thought that a shout would give the priest away. Andrew slowed down, watching the scene with mounting terror.

The maidservant shifted slightly. It was clear to Andrew that she had seen the hunters. She calmly turned back to the pond and said something to the priest. He gave a slight nod, then faced her. It looked as if they were talking. Then, to Andrew's surprise, the maidservant shouted a very loud "Sir!" Suddenly she slapped Father Campion across the face. He looked stunned. She followed the slap by using the full force of her small body to push him into the pond. As he flailed in the water, the maidservant marched in Andrew's direction.

She huffed angrily as she approached. As she passed Andrew, she gave him a quick smile and a wink.

At the same time, the hunters had stopped in their tracks. They gathered to talk while glancing at the priest climbing out of the pond. Then they spun around and returned to the house.

Andrew raced down to the pond. Father Campion now stood on the bank, dripping wet. He was laughing.

"God bless the girl," he said, wiping a hand through his soaked hair.

"Why did she do that?" Andrew asked.

"The hunters were searching for a priest," he said. "They were not expecting to find a young gentleman who would be slapped and dunked by a maidservant."

28

The priest hunters searched the manor without success, though Brother Emerson—also dressed as a young gentleman—gave them suggestions for places to look.

"Have you tried that closet?" he asked. "Beneath that plank of wood? 'Tis sure to come loose and reveal an entire nest of priests."

The hunters were not amused. They departed empty handed.

That evening, the family and the priests laughed about what had happened at the pond. Isabel Worthington commended her maidservant's quick thinking—and gave the girl a few days off as a reward.

In the middle of the meal, a servant rushed in to report that a stranger was at the door.

"Have the hunters returned?" asked Lady Worthington.

"I do not know, my lady," the servant replied.

Father Campion and Brother Emerson dashed from the room. There were hiding places in the house after all.

The servant took his time returning to the door. Then he invited the visitor to wait in the sitting room. Andrew ducked into an alcove near the main staircase while Lady Worthington went in to greet the stranger.

Suddenly she cried out with an expression of joy. Then Andrew heard a voice he had not heard in a long time.

It was William Brookes.

Everyone gathered around William in the front room. He explained that he had been searching all over the north for Father Campion.

His eyes fixed on the fugitive priest. "Father Persons wants you to return south to finalize corrections on your book and oversee the printing."

"Father Persons wishes me to join him at Southwark house?" asked Father Campion.

William shook his head. "Alas, we were forced to depart Southwark house. An apprentice of Mr. Brinkley's—a man named Roland Jenks—was captured while buying stocks of paper. From fear of torture, he confessed the locations of the houses in Southwark and Bridewell. By the grace of God, we escaped before the Privy Council's men arrived. More than one hundred of the beastly villains tore apart the Bridewell house. They found books, papers, vestments, and rosaries. Father Bryant did not escape in time and is now in the Counters prison."

CHAPTER TWENTY-EIGHT

Father Campion groaned. "Father Bryant will not endure questioning. I fear lest he tell all he knows."

"Pray, what then of the printing press?" Brother Emerson asked.

"'Tis moved to Stonor Park, near to Henley," William said, brightening up. "The park is surrounded by woods, with ready access to the river. I bid you come."

Father Campion agreed, and preparations were made.

Andrew took William aside later and asked, "Hath Evangeline returned?"

William gave Andrew a sympathetic look. "Nay. No one hath seen her."

The next morning, Father Campion, Brother Emerson, William, and Andrew headed south. William insisted that they take back roads. Though it would take more time, they would avoid the priest hunters.

They rode at a quickened pace for long hours. Andrew was grateful that his rib no longer caused him trouble.

Brother Emerson served as their scout. He rode ahead to houses known to be friendly to Catholics and sought lodgings for each night of their journey. But rather than sleep, Father Campion often spent late hours hearing confessions and celebrating the Mass.

It was almost summer now, and the landscapes of the various counties were quite different from how they looked when Andrew traveled north. Scores of peasants worked the fields. Herds of animals grazed within borders of hedgerows or short stone walls. He was more aware of the churches now. Some that the Church of England had taken over stood like memorials in a graveyard. Others were derelict and ruined, their roofs collapsing or the stones in the walls carted away for other purposes.

There was nothing charming or quaint about the view. To Andrew, England now looked scarred. Even in the bright summer sunshine, he felt that a terrible darkness hung over the land. The only hints of light came from the Catholics they met along the way, hiding in their homes or praying and worshiping in their secret spaces.

The travelers arrived in the medieval city of St. Albans, named after the first Christian martyr in England. The city had a clock tower as its claim to fame. There was an impressive cathedral that reminded Andrew of the one at Winchester, though this one needed repairs. The adjoining abbey was abandoned, thanks again to Henry the Eighth.

Though late in the day, there were a number of people on the streets. Many of the shops were still open. Instinctively, Andrew scanned the faces in the crowd, looking for anyone who might be watching them. The knot in his stomach was hard as a rock as they rode through the city.

Andrew saw a figure suddenly retreat from view into an alleyway. Riding past the entrance to the alley, he noticed that no one was there. He dismissed the worry.

They stopped at an inn located at the edge of the city. Simply called the Belfry, it had rooms available and a

CHAPTER TWENTY-EIGHT

substantial dining area. Anyone looking at the travelers would have seen only haggard faces and dusty clothes. They sat at a table in the back of the room. Father Campion sat facing away from the other guests. After they had ordered food from a waiter, the three men settled into an amiable chat.

Andrew only half listened. He sat with a view of the front window and the street beyond. The glass was thick, slightly blurring the shapes of people, horses, and carts moving outside.

He became aware of one lanky figure that hadn't moved since they sat down at the table. Andrew excused himself and walked through to the kitchen at the rear. The waiter was there, along with a cook, setting plates of food on a big tray. The waiter glanced up at him.

"Is there a back door?" Andrew asked.

The waiter tipped his head toward a short hallway lined with shelves of plates and bottles. The door was at the end.

Andrew slipped out the door to a small courtyard. He followed it around to a narrow passageway leading back to the street. At the edge of a wall, he peeked out. His mouth went dry. The Alley Cat Man stood across the street. He was leaning against a post in front of a closed shop, his eyes fixed on the front of the inn. Andrew ducked back, pressing himself against the rough wall. He couldn't believe it. How was it possible that the man had found them again?

He peered out again in time to see another man come alongside the Alley Cat Man. The second man was tall, wiry, and hunched over in the shape of a comma. He had a crooked nose and a long beard. He leaned close to the Alley Cat Man and said something. The Alley Cat Man nodded, then the two walked toward the city.

Andrew noticed that the Alley Cat Man was walking with a limp. Crouching down as if to fix his boot, Andrew raised his eyes in time to see the men rushing away.

Andrew decided that for once, he would do some hunting of his own. He followed the Alley Cat Man and his companion.

The shops were closing, and the crowds began to thin out, making it easy for Andrew to keep the men in sight. They came to an old stone building. A crude sign above the door said "Magistrates Court." The Alley Cat Man pounded on the door. A moment later it opened. Both men stepped inside.

Andrew carefully made his way to the door. It had been left open. He glanced quickly inside. The Alley Cat Man and Mr. Comma stood in front of a tall wooden desk with their backs to the door. A white-haired man sat high up behind the desk. He had a bored expression on his face.

The Alley Cat Man was shouting, "I am Josiah Stowell, empowered by the Queen's Privy Council!"

"Lower thy voice," the white-haired man said.

Stowell lowered his voice, but Andrew still caught a few words: *Jesuit* and *Campion* and *Belfry*.

CHAPTER TWENTY-EIGHT

Andrew raced back to the inn as quickly as he could and burst through the front door. His three companions looked up at him.

The waiter came to the kitchen door, wiping a cup with a rag.

Andrew gave him a quick smile and went to the table. He said softly, "We have been seen. Two men have gone to the magistrate."

The men looked at him but didn't move.

"One is the Alley Cat Man. I heard him say Father Campion's name," Andrew said. "We must flee! *Anon!*"

The three men sprung up. Brother Emerson went to the rear of the inn to talk to the waiter. Father Campion and William dashed to the stairs to retrieve their belongings from the rooms.

Andrew was about to follow them when he heard a shout from outside. He went to the front door and looked out. Josiah Stowell stood in the middle of the street, berating a man on a horse.

"Watch, fool!" Stowell roared as he shook his fist at the rider. He continued across the road toward the Belfry.

As had happened with Mr. Nedly in London, Andrew's instincts told him to lead his pursuer away from the priests.

He stepped outside in full view of Stowell, then shot across the street. Andrew came to a narrow passageway and took it.

He didn't get far. A high wall cut off the road. He spun around. Josiah Stowell and his comma-shaped friend were at the mouth of the passage. Andrew saw an alley to the left and rushed that way. Again he came to a dead end with a high brick wall on two sides and the back of a building on the other side. The building had a single wooden door. The door had no outside latch. Andrew threw himself against the door. It rattled but held firm.

Josiah Stowell and Mr. Comma were now entering the passageway.

Andrew turned to the wall and jumped as high as he could. His fingers grazed the top but not enough to get a grip. He pivoted to face the two men and skidded on rocks and debris at his feet. He fell onto his backside. A few stones jabbed his palms.

"Well, now," Josiah Stowell said, leering.

"'Tis only the boy," Mr. Comma said. "The priests will escape!"

Stowell scowled at him. "Begone! This cur is the one I seek."

Mr. Comma looked confused. With hunched shoulders, he sauntered away.

"*I* am the one you seek?" Andrew asked.

Stowell limped closer. Andrew saw that the side of the man's face was swollen.

"'Tis thy doing," Stowell said, pointing to his face. "'Twas almost a fortnight ere I could walk again."

"*You* were chasing me," Andrew reminded him.

The man spat on the ground. "Where is it?"

"What?"

CHAPTER TWENTY-EIGHT

"The *stone*." Another step closer.

Andrew's blood went cold. "What stone?"

"The magic one. He said thou wouldst have it."

"Who?"

"Vincent Howard," Stowell said. "Met him in Bedlam, I did. He spoke of the stone. I did not believe him then, but I saw thee and the girl. 'Twas I, with Mr. Nedly and his men, who chased you into the house. The girl was in the closet. I saw her enter with mine own eyes. We broke open the door. Gone she was. 'Twas then I knew." White spittle had gathered at the corners of the man's mouth.

Crazy, Andrew thought.

"Give me the stone," Stowell said, holding out his hand. In his other hand, he now held a knife.

"I do not have it," Andrew said.

"Liar!"

"Search me. Search everywhere. I do not have it," Andrew said. He was still on the ground. He considered his options for escape but came up empty handed.

"Where hast thou hidden it?" Stowell asked.

"The girl took it with her when she vanished," Andrew said.

"Where did the girl go?"

"Whither she went is unknown to me." Andrew's fingers wrapped around a large stone.

Stowell took another step toward him. He was only a dozen feet away. He raised the knife. "I will ask thee once more only, and then I shall gut thee like a fish. *Where is the girl?*"

Andrew thought, like a prayer, *Eve, where are you?*

The man rushed at him.

29

Eve was standing in Alfred Virtue's office in Hope Springs. Her heart was still pounding hard from fear. She had been hiding in the safe-house closet as men battered down the door. But she had touched the Radiant Stone just in time.

"Eve?"

She turned to the voice.

Aunt Catherine stood in the office doorway. "What are you doing here? You've been gone for less than a minute. Where are Vince and Andrew?" She came farther into the office. "*What are you wearing?*"

Eve glanced down at her dress. "I can't explain now," she said. She lifted the Radiant Stone and found the facet that would take her back to Elizabethan England.

As she pressed the tip of her finger against the facet, she heard her aunt call out, "Eve!" Then her aunt and the office were gone.

Now Eve was standing in a building she recognized immediately: Beckery Chapel on the island near Glastonbury.

Dim daylight came through the holes that had once held stained-glass windows. The benches that had been thrown along the wall were now a burned pile of sticks and ash. The marble altar was in pieces on the ground. The roof was pitted and in danger of falling in. Eve wondered how much time had passed since she'd first arrived here with Andrew. Unlike that cool and rainy night in September, it was now hot and muggy.

Closing the locket on the Radiant Stone, she draped the chain around her neck. A scuffling noise came from beyond the open double doors. Ambrosius stepped into view, looking exactly as he had the last time she saw him. He smiled and said, "I thought thou wouldst come to the cottage."

Eve began to feel the queasiness that came from time travel. She swayed where she stood.

Ambrosius seemed amused as he moved quickly to her side. He crooked his arm through hers. "Come to the cottage, dear child. Drink a cup of water from the saint's well. Tell me what happened."

They walked to the cottage under a cloudy sky. The path was mere ruts of sun-hardened mud. Insects buzzed in the reeds nearby. Eve breathed in the warm air and the fragrance of nearby blossoms. Her heart sank. She'd been away for months, maybe longer.

Inside the cottage, she was soon settled in the same chair that she had sat in before. The room should have been hotter than it was, but a cool breeze blew from somewhere. She glanced at the table to see if Saint Brigid's flame was still burning there. It was. Yet it didn't flicker in the mysterious breeze.

Ambrosius gave her a cup of water. "This shall clear thy head."

As she drank, her nausea eased.

"Thou didst perform an act of great renown," Ambrosius said, sitting down across from her.

"How do you know?" she asked.

"Stories of that sort come my way."

"We were trying to escape from the priest hunters," Eve explained. "This dress got caught on a nail. I ran into the closet to hide, but they found me. They did not even try the latch. They simply started bashing the door down. I was so afraid. I did not want to be captured. I thought they would make me tell them about the priests. So I took out the locket and grabbed the Radiant Stone."

Ambrosius gave her a kind look and said gently, "Poor child. It must have been terrifying."

Eve nodded. The warmth in his voice made her want to cry. She gathered herself and asked, "How long have I been gone? It was only a few seconds in my time."

"Several months," Ambrosius said.

"But I touched the same facet," Eve said, trying to make sense of it all. "Why did it not bring me back to the same day Andrew and I arrived?"

"The stone is not a machine," Ambrosius said. "'Tis not accurate until one learns to use it properly."

"Is Andrew all right? Do you know where he is?" she asked, panic rising within her.

"He journeyed north with Father Campion, then journeyed south again. He hath been safe. Though I cannot speak of him at the moment."

"Why not?"

"'Tis a fortnight since I have heard about him. All hath been silent."

"What doth that mean?"

"I have sent inquiries. My allies say nothing about him. Curious, as if he disappeared in the same manner as thee."

Eve shook her head. "He doth not have a stone."

Ambrosius lifted his hands as a shrug. "Then it must be something else."

Eve felt tearful again. "I have to find him."

"We shall."

"*How?* You said you do not know where he is."

"'Tis true," Ambrosius admitted. His eyes were filled with mischief. "But I know where he is likely to be."

Using the same old boat he'd used months before, Ambrosius navigated the marshes. Once on land, he and Eve walked into Glastonbury. Eve noticed that some of the people on the street greeted Ambrosius like an old friend. Others stayed clear of him. They returned to the same tavern where Eve had met Matthew and William.

CHAPTER TWENTY-NINE

Ambrosius went inside, leaving Eve to wait in the small courtyard alone. He returned a few minutes later. "Help is on the way," he said.

Within a half hour, a horse-drawn wagon rounded the corner, driven by a young man with dark hair and a pockmarked face. He leapt down from the driver's bench, nodded to Ambrosius, then disappeared through the back door of the tavern.

"'Tis not an actor's wagon," Ambrosius said as he climbed onto the bench. "But 'twill do as well." He took Eve's hand and pulled her up.

The back of the wagon held a couple of barrels and a few crates.

"What are those?" Eve asked.

"Supplies bound for Lyford Grange," he said and snapped the reins to get the horse moving. "'Tis a hamlet near the town of Wantage on the River Ock, at the foot of the Vale of the White Horse."

Eve smiled. The names sounded as if they had come from a Tolkien story. She asked, "Why must we travel to Lyford Grange?"

Ambrosius looked at her from the corner of his eye. "To find something that hath been lost."

Anxious to see Andrew, Eve willed for Ambrosius to go faster as they drove the horse and wagon north. But Ambrosius took his time, pointing out the cathedral in the city of Wells and the Roman baths in a city appropriately called Bath.

To pass the time, Eve asked him to explain all that had happened while she was gone.

"Father Campion hath written a treatise titled *Ten Reasons*," Ambrosius said. "The priest and his allies had the boldness to secretly distribute copies all over Oxford University. 'Twas said that many were so intent upon reading Father Campion's work that the final examinations were disrupted. Some scholars were enraged. Many students were moved by the essay's eloquence, elegance, and good taste. Father Campion challenged the queen's clerics to a debate about each point."

"Did they accept his challenge?" Eve asked.

"They did not." He sighed deeply. "I fear the only platform they shall give Father Campion will be the gallows. His life, not his words, will testify to the truth."

As the day waned, they reached a town called Chippenham. Ambrosius turned off the main road and followed a bumpy path through a thick forest. They ascended a steep hill to a small stone cottage tucked away at the edge of a clearing.

Ambrosius reined the horse at the door and climbed down from the bench. "Enter whilst I take care of poor Methuselah," he said, patting the horse's neck. He unbridled the beast and began the work of unhitching it from the wagon.

The cottage was a single room with a stone fireplace. It had a table with four wooden chairs, a tub with an iron pump, and assorted shelves filled with old pottery. A straw mattress lay in one corner.

Eve went to the pump and worked the handle. It groaned at first, then gurgled, then spat brown water from the spout, soon followed by clear water. She palmed some into her mouth. It was cool and fresh.

Ambrosius came in carrying one of the crates. He dropped it on the table and pulled off the top. "A few provisions," he said and lifted out a small basket.

Eve moved closer. The basket contained some bread, dried meats, and assorted vegetables. He then pulled out a couple of ragged wool blankets. He handed one to Eve.

"That goes on thy bed," he said. "I shall sleep outside. 'Tis a perfect night for it."

"Who owns this cottage?"

"My family hath owned it for years," he said. " 'Twas once a forester's hut."

"No one else lives here? You leave it unattended?" Eve asked.

"Aye. Why dost thou ask?"

"I am surprised it hath not been ransacked," she replied.

"Few would dare do that." Ambrosius took a small lamp out of the crate. He lit the wick. "The folk here believe it is the dwelling place of an ancient family of trolls."

Eve raised an eyebrow. "Is it?" Her memory suddenly shot to Ket the Troll, a friend she had made in the time of Robin Hood. Perhaps Ket's descendants lived there.

"If the trolls were here, they would not make themselves known," Ambrosius said. "Man hath not been kind to them."

Ambrosius laid out their meager meal and put the crate aside. They sat and ate in silence.

Eve had a lot of questions she wanted to ask Ambrosius, but she didn't know where to begin. She took a deep breath. "I want to ask you about time," she said.

"A vast subject," he said. "Immeasurable, and yet we measure it. Seemingly endless and yet finite. Beyond our imaginations, and yet we try to contain it in sundials and clocks and calendars."

"How doth it work?" she asked.

"Work? It doth not *work*. It simply is," stated Ambrosius.

"Like God?"

Ambrosius frowned. "Child, there is nothing *like* God. God is God. Time is God's tool. 'Tis the framework He hath created to prepare us for eternity. Here, we are merely practicing for what is to come. We live and mark minutes and hours and days and years and events and ages and epochs. For what cause? Eternity."

"But how can a *stone* move me back in time?" she asked.

"By what means dost thou move in time at all?" he countered.

Eve puzzled over the question. "I know not."

"Nor do I," he said. "But God hath willed it to be so. We move forward at the same speed, and yet we perceive that time is moving both fast and slow. 'Tis one mystery. Another mystery is moving backward through time by any means at all. God's wonders never cease to amaze."

"Have you traveled in time?"

He simply gazed at her. She couldn't read his expression.

She continued, "How is it that you are the Keeper of the Stone? Did somebody choose you to do it, like signing you up for duty? Or did you decide for yourself?"

"How is it that thou art a Child of the Stone?" he countered. "Was it thy choice?"

"I did not know I was a Child of the Stone until you said so."

"Yet thou became a Child of the Stone the moment thou didst find the Radiant Stone."

"I found it by accident," she said.

"*Accident?*" Ambrosius suddenly burst into laughter. "Dear girl, how canst thou travel through time and still believe in accidents? Thou hast seen many random things come together in unexplainable ways."

"'Tis a coincidence?"

"Accident, coincidence. Let us not quibble over words," Ambrosius said. "Men and women of wisdom know that the great odyssey of life hath no accidents, no coincidences. There are providential activities that, to our limited minds, appear to be accidents and coincidences. But they are merely the woven threads in the great fabric of God's will as it meshes with our will."

Eve paused to think about what he was saying. She remembered first seeing Andrew in her aunt's shop and knowing somehow that he would be her time-travel partner. She thought of their adventures in Robin Hood's time. She recalled how they had met Simon Howard in the time of Joan of Arc and later learned of his connections to Alfred Virtue.

Ambrosius gave her an amused look. "Simon Howard was the ancestor of Vincent Howard. Was it a mere coincidence that thou didst meet in the fifteenth century one man from the twentieth century and his ancestor in the twenty-first century?"

Eve sat back in her chair and wondered how he knew what she was thinking. "Are you a mind reader?" she asked.

"I know minds, which is not the same thing as reading them." He suddenly stood up. "We must depart at daybreak. If we continue talking in this fashion, thy brain will be too overwhelmed to sleep."

"But I want to know—to *understand*," she said.

"These matters cannot be rushed. Thou must understand about time ... in time," he said.

The following day, they journeyed into countryside made up of broad rolling hills. It was early evening when they approached the turn heading north for the town of Wantage.

"Wantage?" asked Eve. "Not Lyford Grange?"

"Someone I lost is in Wantage," Ambrosius replied.

Eve decided not to ask.

As they drew closer to the town, Ambrosius said, "Alfred the Great was born here in 849. 'Twas called *Wanating* then, of the county Berkshire. The mysterious White Horse Hill is not far beyond."

"Why is it mysterious?" Eve asked.

"In ancient times, the image of a running horse was carved into the chalky base of the hill."

"Carving a picture of a horse in a hill doth not sound mysterious to me."

"It would if thou couldst see the pattern from above, like a bird in flight. That is the only way thou canst appreciate the carving." He eyed her. "Pray, how or why would an ancient people create something that can only be seen from high above? For whom was it created?"

Eve admitted, "That *is* mysterious indeed."

Wantage had a large square at its center for a marketplace. A few empty stalls remained from the last market. Buildings with shops and businesses lined the square. Ambrosius brought the wagon to a halt in front of an inn.

"Remain here whilst I make a few inquiries," he said.

Eve obeyed, sitting and watching as a few townspeople strolled around the town square. Some glanced in the shop windows; others seemed to be enjoying the summer evening.

Suddenly, shouts came from a far corner of the square. Eve spun in the seat to see what the commotion was. A man pushed through a small group of people. "I am not insane!" he cried in a way that sounded totally insane. His voice echoed off the buildings.

Eve assumed he was drunk.

The man walked unsteadily to the very center of the square and slowly turned in a circle. "I have seen pagan caves! The rituals of Satan himself! But for a wizard, I would be trapped there still!"

Eve sat up straight, alarmed.

She climbed from the wagon to get a better view of the man.

He suddenly stopped his manic spin and looked in her direction. His face was a hairy and haggard mess. The hair on top of his head was mostly white and looked torn out in patches. His clothes were stained rags. There were no shoes upon his feet. Eve could see cuts and scars on his exposed flesh.

It was the jailer from Winchester.

30

Anthony Dovedale's eyes opened wide at the sight of Eve. He pointed, gasping, as if the shock of her presence had stolen his voice.

Eve stumbled back against the wagon. In a flash, she remembered how the jailer had touched the Radiant Stone and disappeared, only to reappear later in a terrified state of mind. She felt sick to think that this is what had become of him.

He lurched toward her—stumbling, then reclaiming his stride, all the while pointing at her. "Thou art a *she-devil*," the man said in a whispered growl. "See what thou hast done to me!"

"I did not do anything," Eve said.

The man was nearer now. "Enchantress!" he snarled.

"Anthony Dovedale!" Ambrosius shouted as he stepped up behind the man.

Dovedale pivoted and then reeled back. "Wizard!" He dropped to his knees in the dirt and cowered with his hands over his face. He sobbed.

Ambrosius said to Eve, "Help me get him inside." Kneeling down, Ambrosius put a hand on Dovedale's shoulder. He said softly, "Harken unto my voice, poor man. Think not that thou art demented or cursed. Thou hast been given a great gift. God hath allowed thee to see what others never shall see."

Dovedale slowly lifted his head. His dirty face was streaked with tears.

"Come to the inn. Eat and drink, and I shall tell thee a beautiful secret." Ambrosius drew Dovedale to his feet and hooked his hand under the man's left arm. Eve did the same on the right. Then they guided him to the inn.

At a table in a darkened corner, Anthony Dovedale clawed at a plate full of food and guzzled a tankard of weakened ale. Ambrosius explained in very simple terms what had happened back in Winchester. "Thou didst touch a facet on a miraculous stone and wert carried to another age. The pagans and the cave thou sawest were as real as any living being or place thou canst see now. 'Twas I who showed thee how to come home by placing thy hand and fingers thus."

Ambrosius made a fist as if wrapping his hand around the stone.

Dovedale gazed at Ambrosius with red-rimmed eyes. His lip quivered. "By what manner of magic may a stone do such things?"

CHAPTER THIRTY

" 'Tis not magic. 'Tis a mystery of God," Ambrosius said. "There is more thou needest to know. All in good time. I have arranged for the innkeeper to give thee a room, to feed thee, and to bathe thee. Fresh clothes will be given thee. Thou must rest. Allow the fever that hath gripped thy mind all these dark months to ease. I shall return to retrieve thee. Together we will travel to a place where thou shalt learn more."

Anthony Dovedale looked at him gratefully.

On the road out of town, Eve asked Ambrosius, "How did you know the jailer was in Wantage?"

Ambrosius said, "I searched for Anthony Dovedale after the mishap at Winchester. He ran away in a frenzied state of mind. No one seemed to know where he had gone. I discovered that he hath kin in this area. I then heard stories about a madman roaming the streets and speaking of wild and impossible things."

"You look like a wizard," she teased.

"I am *not* a wizard. That would be an offense to God," Ambrosius said sharply. He kept his eyes on the road ahead.

"You were not in Winchester. How did you know that Anthony Dovedale had gone back in time?" she asked.

Ambrosius gave a slight shrug. "I am the Guardian of the Stone. I am tasked to know when things have gone amiss. The man's screams told me."

Eve was astonished. "You heard his screams from the past?"

"In a manner of speaking."

"Do you know every time a stone is used?" she asked.

"In a manner of speaking."

Eve gave it some thought, then asked, "You knew I had touched the Radiant Stone to escape from the hunters?"

"Aye."

"You knew I returned?"

"Aye."

"How do you know these things?"

He glanced at her. "I have been taught by years of experience."

"How many years?" she asked.

He gave her a familiar look that said the conversation was finished.

"A few things thou must know about Lyford Grange," Ambrosius said as they rambled along a dusty road. " 'Tis the home of Francis Yate. Francis hath been locked in a Reading jail for eight years because of his refusal to bend the knee to the queen's religion. His wife, Jane, hath since used the estate to perform a goodly service. In a wing of the house, eight nuns are living in safe solitude. They belong to the order founded by Saint Bridget of Sweden."

"Mrs. Yate is hiding *eight nuns* in the house?" Eve asked.

"Aye, including Francis Yate's mother, who became a nun herself," he said. "During King Henry's reign, the nuns had been placed in the care of hostile families. The queen was petitioned to have them moved to more sympathetic homes. The Yate family took them in. Father Thomas Ford and Father John Collington are there as well, to serve as chaplains."

Eve was amazed. "Why are they allowed to live here? Why are they not in jail?"

"For a time, the queen hath allowed priests and established orders to remain, so long as the members keep to themselves," he explained. "'Tis the Jesuit priests the queen fears."

"Is the house not constantly watched?" she asked.

"What man hath time to watch a house constantly?" he countered. "Thankfully, the hunters cannot be in all places at all times."

The land had flattened out as they reached the drive for the estate. They lurched at half speed along the rutted path, crossing a mound that served as a bridge over a long pond that had once been a moat. They came to a wall and a set of iron gates. A servant stepped out from behind the wall, opened the gates, and waved them through.

The manor was built of stone and timber, with a tall shingled roof. Eve thought it looked more like a hall than a house. But she soon realized the view was deceptive. When they circled around to the side, she saw that multiple wings had been added. They pulled into a courtyard framed by a quadrangle of various outbuildings: barns, stables, grain stores, and pens for livestock.

A burly, bearded man stepped from one of the outbuildings. He wiped his hands on a grimy apron and nodded at Ambrosius.

"Hail, Brutus!" Ambrosius called out. "I have brought gifts!"

There was a bang, and the wagon bounced. Two young servants had lowered the gate to the wagon. A third had jumped onto the back and began pushing the crates to the others.

"Well done, lads," Ambrosius said.

At the rear door, several men and women gathered. They looked with great anticipation at Ambrosius, then Eve, but seemed to look disappointed when they saw no one else.

Ambrosius signaled to the servant on the wagon. "Why the sad faces?"

"They thought thou hadst brought *him*," the man said. "*Father Campion*. We expect him at any time. The master hath arranged it."

"Master Francis hath written to Father Campion from the prison?" asked Ambrosius.

"Aye. With coins placed in the right palms, the jail leaks like a sieve," the servant said.

Eve felt a surge of hope. "Will Andrew be with Father Campion?"

"Let us pray so," said Ambrosius. "If not, then I am confounded as to what hath become of the lad."

31

Andrew and Brother Emerson stood next to their horses, waiting for Father Campion. They had stopped briefly in a town called Wantage, on their way to Stonor Park. Father Campion had gone off to meet with someone. As usual, Andrew didn't know who the person was or the reason for the meeting.

The wide-open market square made Andrew nervous. He felt exposed to the eyes of the townspeople nearby.

Glancing down, he spotted a smooth, round pebble on the ground. He picked it up and tossed it back and forth from one hand to the other. Then he clasped it firmly in his right hand. He wondered if his pitch and aim were still good.

His mind suddenly went back to the alley in St. Albans. Josiah Stowell, the Alley Cat Man, was rushing toward him. Andrew had a single stone in his hand. He launched it at his pursuer.

Stowell reeled back, hitting the ground in a heap. Andrew carefully approached, kneeling just out of arm's reach. Blood trickled from a gash in the man's forehead.

I've killed him! Andrew feared.

He looked at Stowell's chest. It slowly rose and fell. Then Stowell stirred a little, with a soft groan. Andrew picked up the knife that had fallen from Stowell's hand. It was a crude blade with a wooden hilt. He tucked it into his belt.

"What hast thou done to me?" Stowell asked, his eyes still closed.

Andrew scooted farther away. "I hit you with a stone."

"Thy aim is true," Stowell said. He groaned again.

"I have been practicing for hundreds of years," Andrew said. He tugged at the pouch on his belt and pulled out the vial from Mrs. Mimms. He pulled out the stopper and quickly leaned over the man, putting a couple of drops on his lips. "This will help your pain."

Stowell licked at the drops. "'Tis the potion I drank before?"

"Aye." Andrew placed the vial in the palm of Stowell's hand. "You need it more than I."

Stowell struggled to sit up. The man rested on an elbow and used his free hand to touch his wound. He looked at the blood on his fingers. "What kind of accursed creature art thou?" Stowell asked. "I have hunted grown men cleverer and more experienced than thee. Yet thou hast evaded me at every encounter. Methinks God is protecting thee."

"I hope He is," Andrew said.

"Blind me if I think I have chosen the wrong side," Stowell said. His words were slurred. He dropped onto his back again.

CHAPTER THIRTY-ONE

"I must depart forthwith. Mr. Comma will find you here, I hope."

"Mr. Comm—?" Stowell's head fell to one side. Mrs. Mimms's potion did its work again.

Andrew made his way back to the main street. The Belfry was overrun with officials and spectators. Mr. Comma was out front, arguing with both the innkeeper and the white-haired magistrate.

"How now?" Andrew asked a young woman who was watching the event.

"'Twas said that Edmund Campion himself was there."

"Hath he been captured?"

"Nay," she said.

Andrew was relieved.

"Pity, as I had hoped to see him," the young woman said. "'Tis said he is truly handsome."

Andrew wondered what he was supposed to do now.

Go to Stonor Park, he decided. He was sure he would meet up with Father Campion and Brother Emerson there.

Andrew hadn't walked very far from St. Albans when he saw a man sitting under a tree. Two horses stood nearby. As Andrew approached, the man stood up.

It was William. A great smile spread across his face as Andrew approached. "I told Father Campion thou wouldst be along soon enough," he said.

Andrew and William caught up to Father Campion and Brother Emerson a few miles onward. The close call in St. Albans made them even more cautious. They now diverted off the major roads south, seeing out-of-the-way routes and inns. As they drew closer to London, Father Campion sent William ahead to find Father Persons and determine where they should all meet.

That night in their room at a small inn, Andrew had time alone with Father Campion. He confessed how he felt when he threw the stone at Josiah Stowell.

"I wanted to kill the man," Andrew said. He then told Father Campion about the knot he'd had in his stomach throughout his journey in the north.

The priest said in a soothing voice, "The knot is thy fear and hatred. Pray to God that thou wouldst let them go."

"How can I whilst we are hunted? 'Tis unjust."

"Has there ever been a time of true justice?" Father Campion asked. "Hath the example of our Lord not shown us that the wicked will always pursue the innocent unjustly? Lies shall always work to strangle the truth. Our peace is in Christ, not in this world."

"Will you believe it, even at your death?" Andrew asked.

Father Campion was silent for a moment. Then he leaned forward, his face level with Andrew's. "I see now why thou wast brought to me. In thee I see what I might become. A child striving against the world, filled with knots of fear and hatred. As I speak to thee, I speak to myself and say, 'Fear not, for Christ is with us always.'"

"The words are easy to say," Andrew said.

"Easy? Nay, lad. The weight of them is with me each day as I journey closer to my death."

Andrew frowned. "If you know the end, why do you not escape while you can?"

"Take the way of Jonah? Nay, Andrew. To run is to be swallowed up and spat out again. I am here to embrace the cross I have been given. Thou must do the same."

"What is my cross?"

"To bear witness to these things and be a comfort to others."

Andrew pondered what it meant for him to bear witness and comfort others, but the events that followed proved to be distracting.

William returned the next day with a message for Father Campion and his companions to meet Father Persons at a house in Whitefriars, London. Andrew was concerned that they were going into the heart of the city again.

William wryly said, "We may well be safer there than anywhere, since the hunters will not believe we would dare return."

The house in Whitefriars was owned by Lady Mary Babington and her son Anthony. The Babingtons were a well-to-do Catholic family that had been popular with royalty, though they now walked the political tightrope between their faith and the Privy Council. Anthony was one of the many young men who had joined George Gilbert's group to fund and assist the Jesuit priests. Looking at his handsome face, Andrew was sure he'd seen Anthony at one of the other safe houses in the past.

Father Campion and Father Persons embraced, then wasted no time going off in private to discuss all that had happened since they last parted.

Dinner proved to be uncomfortable. Anthony Babington was far more radical than his mother or even Father Campion. He declared that Catholics should rise up against their oppressors, using violence if necessary.

Father Campion remained calm as he countered the young man's argument, reminding everyone that priests were forbidden to take such actions. Father Persons was thoughtful throughout the discussion. At the end, he surprised Andrew by suggesting that the recent proclamations from the Queen's Privy Council might lead to more extreme measures.

The conversation turned to the imprisonment of Father Alexander Bryant. He had been taken to the Tower of London, where the tortures began. Reports leaked out that his captors refused him water and shackled him with the heaviest chains they could find. He was then thrown into an underground cave called the Pit and left in isolation. Upon his release from that terrible hole, he was put on the rack and stretched beyond human endurance. And yet, by his own account, Father Bryant said that God had removed all of the pain. In spite of the torture, Father Bryant refused to reveal anything about the priests' hiding places around London.

Father Campion and Father Persons expressed their admiration for Father Bryant, considering they feared he would prove to be much weaker. They then had a very somber discussion about what they would do if they were arrested and tortured. Each hoped he would also be brave and steadfast.

"I get weak over a leg cramp," Andrew said privately to William after the meal had ended. "I cannot imagine putting up with torture."

William chuckled, then took Andrew aside and said quietly, "Lad, Father Persons hath made a decision about thee."

Andrew suddenly felt as if a principal had summoned him to the school office.

"Your encounter with Josiah Stowell in St. Albans hath reminded him that thou art a draw for unwelcome attention—to thyself and to us. When we move to Stonor Park, thou shalt remain there until Father Persons believes it is safe for thee to venture forth again. We shall not speak of thee in our letters or dispatches. It will be as though thou hast disappeared, much as Evangeline did."

Andrew thought the whole thing sounded dismal, as if he was now a prisoner. "I shall not be permitted to leave at all?" he asked.

"Thou wilt not have the time," William said, giving the boy's shoulder a decisive pat. "Mr. Brinkley will keep thee very busy indeed."

"Busy with what?" Andrew asked.

"We must publish Father Campion's book."

A couple of days later, Andrew left with Father Campion, Father Persons, and Brother Emerson for Stonor Park. They weaved through London, ever watchful for spies and priest hunters. They passed the arch for London's ancient Westgate and came to a barren patch of land with a wooden structure shaped like a triangle. Andrew was chilled to realize that the structure was built to hang criminals.

Father Campion took off his hat and bowed to the wooden posts. He also dared to make the Sign of the Cross.

The priest's act of reverence for the gallows puzzled Andrew. He asked Brother Emerson once they were clear of the city.

"'Tis called the Triple Tree at Tyburn. Alas, more Catholics are hanged there than criminals," Brother Emerson explained. "But only after suffering many great humiliations and tortures."

Andrew felt the blood drain from his face. "Tell me no more. I do not wish to know."

"God willing, thou wilt never have to."

32

Stonor Park was a great estate nestled among the Chiltern Hills, four miles north of a village called Henley-on-Thames.

A widow named Lady Cecily Stonor lived there now. Her son John lived with her. They remained loyal Catholics in spite of multiple fines and arrests for not embracing the queen's religion.

A herd of deer watched the travelers from London as they reached the stone wall and iron gate bordering the grounds. A servant bid them enter a wide courtyard surrounded by a collection of houses. The variety of stone, brick, and timber suggested that different people had built the structures over many years. Andrew got the impression that the Stonor family couldn't stop tinkering with their estate. A medieval chapel to the right was a contrast to the long hall next to it. The main house ahead was rectangular, with smaller wings sprouting off of it.

"Come and see what hath been done," Father Persons said.

Andrew accompanied the priests upstairs to a small room at the rear of the main house. It contained only a few chairs and a table and looked rarely used. They continued through another doorway to a much larger room Father Persons called Mount Pleasant. Andrew assumed it had once been a guest bedroom. Now it was filled with printing equipment.

Stephen Brinkley poked his head out from behind a tall stand of type-setting plates. He saluted them. Then he turned to bark instructions at a handful of assistants busy at various tables and the printing press itself.

Father Campion strolled around the room. He then asked Father Persons, "Pray, how will we escape should the priest hunters come?"

Father Persons wiggled a finger at them. "This way." He took them through a narrow door at the far end of the room. A short hall led to a set of stairs climbing upward. "The attic," Father Persons explained.

The attic was empty, save for a few trunks and some old furniture. Father Persons took them to a rear wall and pulled at a heavy latch. A door opened, exposing a rising hill and forest immediately behind them. He pointed to a ladder on the floor, then to a broad oak tree directly opposite. Attached to the tree was a wooden platform.

"This ladder reaches to yonder tree," said Father Persons. "We shall use it to escape into the forest."

CHAPTER THIRTY-TWO

They returned to the printing room. Father Persons called for silence as he blessed the people, the press, and the outreach of Father Campion's *Ten Reasons*.

Then the work began in earnest.

Within a few days, Andrew became a full-fledged printers' apprentice. He cut large rolls of paper, used "dabbers" to spread ink onto plates of type, checked the printed pages for smudges and smears, and assisted in binding the pages into a book.

Andrew rarely saw anyone but Stephen Brinkley and the other printers. He ate with them in a small room near the press and slept in a slightly larger room furnished with cots.

Lady Stonor appeared on occasion to commend their work. She was elderly but maintained a strength that defied her years. Her son John helped assemble crates of the finished books, bound for Oxford. They were to be smuggled into one of the chapels where the university's official ceremonies would take place.

Andrew heard very little about the world outside Stonor Park. Though William assured him that he would be told immediately if Evangeline returned, Andrew worried that he might somehow miss her. News came that the Queen's Privy Council had issued additional orders allowing for even greater persecution and cruelty against the Catholics.

Several days after the book's release, William arrived. He signaled Andrew to join him outside. "Let us walk," he said.

They strolled across the courtyard and through the front gate. Andrew blinked several times at the summer sun. He couldn't remember the last time he'd been in daylight. It might have been to help unload a wagonful of paper. Now he was aware of the buzzing songs of the insects and the birds soaring over the green lawn.

"The *Ten Reasons* hath been a great success," William told him. "As such, Father Persons is now concerned about the intensity of the hunt for Father Campion. He hath instructed Father Campion and Brother Emerson to ride northeast to Norfolk. Thou shalt join them."

"I must go north again?" Andrew asked, his heart sinking. His mind went back to Eve and Dr. Howard. How would they ever find one another?

"I know thy concerns," William said. "We shall not forget thee. There is yet time before thy departure."

"Pray, time for what?" asked Andrew.

"Father Campion hath asked Father Persons to allow him to retrieve the books he left at Hoghton Tower in the spring."

Andrew nodded. "I shall go as Father Persons wishes." What else could he do? The course of his life seemed beyond his control.

"Come anon," William said. "The servants have prepared a bath for thee for a good scrubbing. Thou shalt travel as the ward of a gentleman and must look the part."

Andrew looked down at his clothes. His apron was stained with ink; his stockings were torn; his shoes were filthy and worn-out. He held up his hands. They were black from his work at the printing press.

"It will have to be a *hard* scrubbing," he said.

The farewells outside the gates of Stonor Park were filled with emotion. Andrew was now dressed in the clothes of a well-to-do ward. He sat on his horse and watched as Father Campion and Father Persons embraced. While Father Campion journeyed north, Father Persons would journey south to Kent.

The men stepped apart. Father Persons shook a finger at Father Campion, like a parent giving final instructions to a child. "Do *not* remain at Hoghton Tower. Avoid the houses of the Catholic gentry on the way. Reside at the inns. Be not detained anywhere. Establish a base in Norfolk and stay there until thou hast heard from me."

"Aye, Father," Campion said.

In an odd gesture, he took off his blue-velvet hat and handed it to Father Persons. "As we once did in Prague," the priest said.

Father Persons laughed. In turn, he gave his green-velvet hat to Father Campion.

The two priests put on their new hats, adjusting them for a better fit.

Satisfied, Father Campion said, "God speed you on your way."

Father Persons mounted his horse. A priest Andrew had not met was on horseback next to him. The two priests waved and started across the field for the main road.

Father Campion mounted his horse. Brother Emerson climbed onto his steed, and the three riders began at a slow trot. Andrew looked back at Stonor Park, already missing the safety he felt there. The knot in his stomach hadn't bothered him for weeks. He could now feel it tightening again.

Just outside the nearest village, a young rider came galloping toward them. He rode like a man on an urgent mission. Andrew expected him to zoom past. Instead, he slowed down and came alongside them.

Andrew braced himself for trouble.

"I have come with a message for you," the young man said to Father Campion. He reached into his vest, pulled out an envelope, and handed it to the priest.

Father Campion tore open the seal and read the letter. He frowned, then handed it to Brother Emerson. "I have refused our friend on too many occasions. Await me here," he said. He suddenly yanked the reins, turning his horse around and galloping away.

"Where is he going?" Andrew asked.

Brother Emerson read the letter, then said, "'Tis from Francis Yate, a Catholic held prisoner in the jail at Reading. He begs Father Campion to visit his family near Wantage. I assume Father Campion hath gone to ask permission from Father Persons to do so."

Brother Emerson was right.

"It took some doing," Father Campion explained to the priest when he returned half an hour later. "Father Persons hath agreed, providing I place myself under your authority. We are to stay one night only."

Brother Emerson gave a deep, long-suffering sigh.

Father Campion smiled and gave the word to the young messenger. "Go hence with all good speed," he said. "Tell them I am coming."

The young man looked overjoyed. With a shout, he rounded his horse and rode away.

"Pray, at what abode doth the Yate family live?" Brother Emerson asked.

" 'Tis called Lyford Grange," Father Campion replied.

The three riders prodded their horses and proceeded west.

33

Andrew pocketed the smooth pebble in his hand. He had been lost in memories of Josiah Stowell in St. Albans and all that had happened in the months since then. He now decided that his time safely hidden away in Stonor Park made him even more nervous in a wide-open market square—like this one in Wantage.

A sharp snap of leather reins echoed like a shot around the square. Andrew looked up. Two men rode in a rickety old wagon across the square. The man at the reins looked uncannily like Ambrosius. A second man looked familiar, but Andrew couldn't think why. He wanted to shout out in the unlikely chance that the first man was Ambrosius. Andrew decided against it, fearing it would draw unwelcome attention.

Brother Emerson came alongside Andrew. A moment later, Father Campion joined them. The three mounted their horses and rode out of town.

Along the way, Brother Emerson explained to Andrew that Lyford Grange had once been the manor house of

Abingdon Abbey. "John Yate of the Buckland Yate family purchased it fifty years ago," he said. "His son Francis later inherited it. Now, his wife, Jane, manages the family's affairs while Francis is imprisoned for the Catholic faith. The house also serves to protect an order of nuns."

They reached Lyford Grange as the sun crested the tops of the nearby trees. They rode past a pond to a gated wall. There, a servant greeted them and allowed them through. They continued past the main door and around to the back of the house. Andrew thought he saw faces framed in the windows as they circled the house. By the time they came to a courtyard, people had gathered there. All eyes were on Father Campion.

Father Campion dismounted as two men came forward. One was tall and dark haired. The other was shorter, with dust-colored hair and a round face. Andrew heard their names: Father John Collington and Father Thomas Ford. They expressed their thanks to God for the safe arrival of Father Campion and Brother Emerson.

Andrew noticed that many of the women were dressed in simple gray-colored dresses and wore scarves in their hair. He assumed they were the nuns. His assumption was confirmed when Father Campion turned to them and they all dropped to their knees in respect.

Father Campion looked startled and commanded them to rise. "'Tis more than I deserve!" he said. "And I am short on time!"

The women rose but blushed as they did.

A gray-haired woman with a youthful face, blue eyes, and a ready smile came to the door. She was introduced as the lady of the house, Jane Yate. Andrew noticed that with her smile were deep worry lines around her eyes.

"Welcome, all!" she called out. "Come in!"

The courtyard quickly emptied. Andrew was left alone.

My weeks of being hidden have made me invisible, he thought as he dismounted. His legs ached. A servant rushed from somewhere and led his horse to a nearby stable.

Andrew dusted himself off. From the corner of his eye, he saw a maidservant lingering at the door.

"Would you care for something to drink, young master?" the maidservant asked.

Andrew's head snapped up at the voice.

Eve stepped out of the doorway.

Andrew gasped.

She smiled at him.

He opened his mouth to speak, but all the words caught in his throat. Conflicting emotions raced through him. He reached out for something to steady him, but nothing was there. "You," he said, then dropped to the ground.

She was laughing at him. "Silly boy," she said. She knelt down next to him. "What are you doing?"

His eyes burned. He knew if he blinked, tears would fall.

Her face was close to his. Tears formed around the bottom edges of her eyes. "I am so glad to see you alive," she said.

Finally, the words that formed in his mind came out. "What took you so long?" he asked.

Eve laughed and threw her arms around him.

"Cut it out," Andrew said. But he didn't push her away.

34

While Father Campion met with the household and conducted confessions in another wing of the house, Andrew and Eve found an empty sitting room to talk privately. They sat down across from each other in fat cushioned chairs.

Andrew told Eve about going to Bedlam to find Dr. Howard and being hunted by the Alley Cat Man—Josiah Stowell. Then he shared the big surprise that Stowell was after him because of the Radiant Stone.

"So Dr. Howard is telling people about it?" Eve asked. "No wonder they think he's insane."

Andrew shrugged. "At least we know he's still around."

Eve explained that Ambrosius had brought her to Lyford Grange because he knew Father Campion would come there. They'd heard nothing about Andrew, but Ambrosius was sure he'd be with the priest.

"How could he know that?" Andrew asked. "We were going to Norfolk. It was a last-minute message from Francis Yate that brought us here."

Eve said, "If Ambrosius was right about you, then he might be right about Dr. Howard coming here."

"What makes you think so?" Andrew asked.

She gestured for Andrew to follow her. They walked down the hallway to a storage room. She went to a crate and lifted the top. Inside were Dr. Howard's clothes. "Why would he bring these if he wasn't sure?"

"He has a lot of tricks up his sleeve," Andrew said.

Eve agreed, then told him about Anthony Dovedale in Wantage.

Andrew thought about the man he'd seen driving the wagon near the market square—and the familiar-looking passenger next to him. "I saw them in Wantage! Now I'm sorry I didn't shout to Ambrosius."

"I think he's taking Anthony Dovedale to Beckery," Eve said as she put the lid back on the crate.

"What about our clothes?" Andrew asked.

"I don't remember where they are. William was keeping them for us, wasn't he?"

Andrew shrugged. "That was a long time ago."

"Does it matter how we'll be dressed when we get back to our time?" Eve asked.

"How will I explain this outfit to my family?" Andrew asked.

"How will you explain *any* of this to your family?" Eve asked.

"I don't know yet," he said.

She giggled softly. "But you've had centuries to figure it out."

CHAPTER THIRTY-FOUR

They came out of the storeroom into the hallway.

Just then Brother Emerson rounded the corner. He had his head down and his hands clasped behind his back. He almost ran into them.

"My apologies," he said, looking startled to see them.

"Are you troubled?" Andrew asked.

"I knew this would be a mistake," Brother Emerson said. "Every nun wants Father Campion to hear a lengthy confession. As do the servants. Mrs. Yate wants to tell her friends to come whilst he is here. He is too gentle to refuse them anything. He will preach and celebrate the Mass in the morning, but I am vexed lest we do not leave as planned."

"Father Persons said he must be obedient to you," Andrew reminded him.

Brother Emerson rolled his eyes.

At that moment, there was a pounding at the main door.

Andrew gasped.

"Fear not. The hunters would never be allowed beyond the gate without Mrs. Yate's permission," Eve assured him.

A servant rushed past to answer the door.

Andrew watched as five people came in. They whispered in excited tones about meeting Father Campion. The servant led them down another hall.

Brother Emerson made some helpless sputtering noises and followed them.

Andrew felt the knot in his stomach again and said to Eve, "This is a problem."

35

Brother Emerson insisted that Father Campion take a break. A modest meal was served in a large dining hall. Andrew thought they now had twice as many people in the house as when he had arrived.

As they ate, Andrew watched Brother Emerson whisper to Father Campion. Father Campion suddenly stood up. "Beloved friends and hostess," he said, bowing to Jane Yate, then to the man at her side. "And Edward, the brother of our absent host, Francis."

The man called Edward nodded.

Father Campion continued. "I am rightly reminded by Brother Emerson that we must make haste at dawn. We have a long journey ahead of us. Pray, forgive me for the speed with which I must do what I have come to do."

After the meal, Mrs. Yate was excited to show the priests the hiding places they'd use if the hunters came.

One priest hole was in a normal-looking side room on the main floor. A fireplace stood near the corner of the room. Next to the chimney was a door leading to a small closet. Inside the closet were small boxes and a short ladder leaning against the wall. A servant named Richard Buckley entered the room and used the ladder to reach a square section of the ceiling. Beyond the square was a vent-like shaft. Slats of wood had been nailed into the wall of the shaft to create a makeshift ladder inside.

"This shaft leads to a hiding place in the attic gables," Mrs. Yate explained.

She then took the small group upstairs to her bedroom. A large window faced the front of the estate. From the outside, the window was up and to the right of a stone archway over the main door.

Richard Buckley moved the curtains aside to reveal a fixed window seat. It was the width of the window and more than a foot deep. To the right of the window and the seat was a wall the same width as the bench. Buckley touched a small lever hidden where the bench met the wall. A panel the width and height of the wall opened. The servant stepped onto the bench, then moved past the open panel. He disappeared into the wall and closed the panel behind him. From all appearances, the servant had never been in the room.

Father Campion was delighted. "Where doth the passage lead?" he asked.

"There is a secret room above the stone archway over the main door," Mrs. Yate replied. "The archway is at least three feet thick, allowing two or three men to hide there."

The panel moved again, and Richard came out, looking proud of his accomplishment.

Father Campion and Brother Emerson tried it. Both men disappeared behind the wall for a minute, then returned.

"Ingenious!" Father Campion proclaimed.

"There are other hiding places, but these are the best," said Mrs. Yate.

After that, Father Campion resumed hearing confessions. Andrew and Eve had nothing to do but wait. It grew late. Finally, Eve admitted she was tired and went off to a cot set up for her in the nuns' area of the house.

Richard Buckley, the servant who had demonstrated the hiding places, showed Andrew to one of the guest rooms.

Tossing his boots aside, Andrew was about to get undressed but decided it would be better to sleep with enough clothes on to make an escape.

In the morning, Andrew learned from Brother Emerson that Father Campion had been up most of the night hearing confessions and leading short spiritual exercises. For that reason, Brother Emerson allowed Father Campion to sleep in longer than usual. Andrew found out later that the priest had not slept in at all. Instead, he had used the time to celebrate a private Mass with the nuns. He then came down in time for lunch.

For a moment, Andrew was alone with Father Campion in the dining hall. Andrew took the chance to say, "I will not be traveling to Norfolk with you."

"Pray, why not?" Father Campion asked.

"I believe that Vincent Howard is in this area—or soon will be. Evangeline and I will wait for him here, if Mrs. Yate will allow it," he said.

"Mrs. Yate will allow it," the woman herself said as she entered the room. Eve followed her and nodded to Andrew.

The men stood. Mrs. Yate acknowledged the gesture but bid them sit. Buckley held a chair for her as she sat down. Her brother-in-law Edward also joined them, as did Father Collington and Father Ford. The nuns ate privately in their own wing of the house.

Those gathered in the dining hall ate and chatted about the state of things in London and the hard conditions Mr. Yate was enduring in the Reading jail. It was close to noon before Father Campion and Brother Emerson were ready to depart. As they said their goodbyes, Father Collington stepped forward with a message he had just received. A group of students from Oxford would be meeting that day at an inn near the university. They were going to debate Campion's *Ten Reasons*. The leader of the group had asked Father Collington to join the discussion. Father Collington thought it would better serve their interests if Father Campion surprised them with a visit.

CHAPTER THIRTY-FIVE

"Oxford is on the way to Norfolk," Father Campion said to Brother Emerson.

"Is the inn safe?" Brother Emerson asked.

"'Tis owned by a Catholic family," said Father Collington. "Ne'er have they had trouble with hunters or spies."

Brother Emerson looked concerned as Father Campion agreed to go.

Father Collington was thrilled and quickly saddled a horse to accompany them.

In the last-minute change to the journey, Father Campion and Brother Emerson said only the briefest of farewells to Andrew. "Be strong" was the last thing Father Campion said to him.

It was a disappointment for Andrew, but he understood that he was only a minor player in this story.

Once the priests had gone, Andrew and Eve took a walk around the grounds. They strolled to a nearby forest. The thick, earthy smells of the woods on a summer day caused Andrew to think of Robin Hood. Then the thought of the saintly outlaw reminded him of another encounter he'd had.

"I met William Shakespeare," he said to Eve.

Eve spun to him. "William Shakespeare? *The* William Shakespeare?"

"Well, he isn't *the* William Shakespeare yet. He's a tutor. But he's interested in going to London to write plays." Andrew added proudly, "I encouraged him to do it."

Eve laughed. "So you've changed the course of history?"

"Maybe," Andrew said. "Who will ever know?"

They were away from the house for only an hour. When they returned, they were surprised to see that a dozen new people had shown up to meet Father Campion. They were displeased about his absence and complained loudly. Less than half an hour later, several more people arrived. They, too, were vocal in expressing their unhappiness.

Mrs. Yate tried to appease them with food and drink.

Someone said, "Please send to Oxford to ask Father Campion to return."

Mrs. Yate explained why she could not do that.

"Why doth she not send them away?" Andrew asked Eve in the kitchen. They were helping the servants put together trays of food for the ever-growing number of guests.

"She is too kindhearted," the cook said from behind the chopping board. His name was Thomas Cooper. He had large, bulging eyes, a small nose, and a wide mouth. He reminded Andrew of a fish.

A moment later, Richard Buckley joined them in the kitchen. He was visibly agitated. "They have sent Father Ford to Oxford," he fumed. "He is tasked with persuading Father Campion to return to Lyford Grange."

"What?" Andrew cried out. "Do they not understand the danger he is in?"

Buckley spread his arms as if to say, *What am I to do about it?*

CHAPTER THIRTY-FIVE

"Thou must ride to Oxford to tell him *not* to come," Andrew said.

Buckley paused. Then his face changed from frustration to agreement. "Aye, lad," he said. "It will serve Mrs. Yate. She is more fragile than she appears and doth not cope well with the pressure of so many demands."

"I shall come with thee," Andrew said. "I will remind Father Campion of the same concerns we faced in the north. He will be sensible."

Buckley dashed for the back door and shouted, "Brutus! Anon! Saddle our two fastest horses."

Mounted and ready to go only a few minutes later, Andrew waved at Eve from his horse.

"Thou hadst better come back," Eve called to him.

"Thou hadst better be here when I do," Andrew called back.

Oxford was only fifteen miles from Lyford Grange. Maintaining a steady gallop, the two riders arrived in under an hour. The King and Lion Inn was tucked away down a side road in a clearing by itself.

Unless you were looking for it, you'd never know it was there, Andrew thought. But the large number of horses and coaches suggested that its location didn't hinder its popularity.

The innkeeper looked up anxiously at them from behind a long counter. When his eyes went to Buckley, he relaxed and tipped his head toward a wooden staircase to his left. Buckley thanked him. Andrew followed the servant up the stairs.

There was a meeting room at the top. As he entered, Andrew could hear that an argument had already started. The scene was almost like a classroom setting. Father Campion sat at a head table. Brother Emerson sat next to the priest. Father Ford stood at one end of the table. Father Collington stood at the other. Almost twenty young men were seated at tables all around the room. The empty plates and cups suggested that they had been there awhile.

"I have been sent to beg you," Father Ford was saying to Father Campion. "How can the appeals of godly men and women who are so desperate to hear your words fall on deaf ears?"

"I am acting under obedience to Father Persons," Father Campion replied.

"He did not envision such an occasion. I cannot believe Father Persons would deny these devoted people your blessing," Father Ford countered.

"I believe he would," Andrew said, stepping forward. His eyes were on Father Campion. "Father, I ask you to remember the danger of the crowds in the northern counties."

CHAPTER THIRTY-FIVE

Father Campion smiled at Andrew. "I have not forgotten."

"Impudent child!" Father Ford said. He reached out his arm and swept Andrew back from view.

Andrew felt his face burn.

The Oxford students moved to the front table and argued that a return to Lyford Grange would rob them of more time with Father Campion.

Father Collington now sided with Father Ford.

Andrew circled behind the students and stood up on one of the chairs. Then on a table. It wobbled but held. He cupped his hands around his mouth and shouted, "*Obedience!*" His voice was lost in the uproar.

Father Campion waved his hands for everyone to calm down. He was teary eyed as he said, "The decision belongs solely to Brother Emerson."

Brother Emerson suddenly went pale.

"Why?" asked one of the students. "He is not one of your superiors!"

"Ah, but he is," Father Campion said. "Father Persons hath made it so."

The dissenting voices now turned on poor Brother Emerson.

The brother slowly shook his head. "I will offer you a compromise," he said quietly. All the voices were stilled. "Father Campion may stay here tonight to continue his discussions with you."

The students cheered.

"On the morrow, he may return to Lyford Grange, where he will stay until I return on Sunday."

"From whence will you return?" a puzzled Father Campion asked.

"Lancashire," Brother Emerson replied. "I shall fetch thy books from the dwelling where they were left."

"Can you make the journey in that time?" Father Campion asked doubtfully.

"Our Lord and the weather permitting, thou wilt see me again on Sunday," Brother Emerson said.

Father Campion patted Brother Emerson on the back. "The wisdom of Solomon," he said.

Andrew didn't consider Brother Emerson's compromise wise at all. Everything in his gut said that Father Campion should leave the area immediately. How could the queen's spies and hunters not hear about this meeting at the inn—or the crowds gathering at Lyford Grange?

But the bargain was struck. Brother Emerson left immediately to ride north to Hoghton Tower. Father Ford and Richard Buckley rode to Lyford Grange to share the joyful news, though Buckley didn't look at all joyful. Father Collington remained in Oxford for a time, then followed them.

CHAPTER THIRTY-FIVE

Father Campion asked Andrew to stay with him and ride back to Lyford Grange the next morning. Andrew agreed but wasn't happy.

Father Campion continued his discussion with the students. The upper room was too stuffy. Frustrated, Andrew went downstairs to get some air.

He passed the innkeeper, who was still behind the counter. The man had the face and body of a baked potato. He stroked his chin and said, "Art thou here with our other guest for the night?'

Andrew nodded.

"Thou wilt be safe," he said, and held up his fists. They looked like huge hams. "I will not allow anyone in."

Andrew thanked him, then stepped outside. The sun was fading, and a warm breeze touched his skin with a motherly gentleness. The inn was made mostly of stone, with a few beams thrown in to hold up the roof. Andrew followed the front wall to the corner of the inn and heard the raised voices of two men. He glanced around to see who or what might be there. His eye caught two men standing next to a coach, just across the clearing. One was dressed in the clothes of a coachman. The other wore the clothes of a gentleman. He held up a cane, gesturing as if he might strike the coachman. Andrew wondered what the coachman had done to make the gentleman so angry.

The gentleman pointed at the inn. Andrew ducked back to keep from being seen. Then he heard the sound of footfalls coming his way. He made his way back to the door and was reaching for the latch when a heavy hand fell hard on his shoulder.

"Out of the way, boy," a voice said.

Andrew turned slightly to look at the man. It was the coachman. His face was narrow, thin, and haggard, with deep wrinkles on the forehead and around the red-rimmed eyes. He had long, shaggy gray hair and an equally shaggy beard. The skeletal face and full beard almost threw Andrew off. But there was no doubt who it was.

"Dr. Howard!" Andrew cried out.

36

The man stepped back. Andrew couldn't tell if Dr. Howard recognized him. So he quickly said, "'Tis me. Andrew. From Hope Springs."

Dr. Howard doubled over as if the words *Hope Springs* hit him like a sucker punch. He put his hand against the wall to steady himself. Then he took a deep breath, drawing his body up again. He grabbed Andrew by the arm and half dragged him to the side of the inn.

"Let go!" Andrew snapped.

Dr. Howard relaxed his grip. "How is this possible? How didst thou find me here?"

"I did not find you. You just found me," said Andrew.

Dr. Howard leaned against the wall. "Where hast thou been?" he asked with a pathetic whimper. "Dost thou know what happened to me?" He reached for Andrew again, then withdrew his hand. "Where is the stone? Let us hasten away from this nightmare!"

"I do not have the Radiant Stone."

Dr. Howard looked appalled. "Pray, where is it?"

"With Eve."

"Is she in Oxford? Let us go with great speed," Dr. Howard said urgently.

"She is fifteen miles away, at Lyford Grange."

"Lyford Grange? Oh, cruel time!" Dr. Howard said pitifully. " 'Tis all atangle. Thou must help me!"

Andrew frowned at him. "As you helped me by sending Josiah Stowell to attack me?"

"Attack thee!" Dr. Howard said. "I hired him to *find* thee. To bring thee to me. Nothing more."

"That is not what he said."

Dr. Howard scowled. "The villain is a liar. I should have known better than to trust anyone in Bedlam."

"Yet you were there."

"A terrible mistake," Dr. Howard said. " 'Twas said I was crazy. I was taken against my will. Thou dost not know what terrible things they conspired to inflict upon me." The man sniffed and rubbed at his nose with the back of his hand.

Andrew was unmoved.

"I beg thee!" Dr. Howard said. "Take me to Lyford Grange now."

Andrew thought of Father Campion and shook his head. "I am duty bound to remain here tonight. We may go back to Lyford Grange on the morrow. Then we may go home."

"What home, pray tell?" came a voice from the corner.

Andrew spun around. It was the gentleman with the cane whom Andrew had seen with Dr. Howard earlier.

CHAPTER THIRTY-SIX

Up close, he looked like anything but a gentleman. He had eyes set in a weasel-like squint, a hooked nose, and lips curled back as if they had been cursed that way. His face was bony and scarred from a few too many bad decisions.

Dr. Howard suddenly stiffened.

"Who is this boy?" the man asked.

"I ... I was questioning him," Dr. Howard answered.

"What could he know?" the man asked.

"Nothing." Dr. Howard gave Andrew a shove. "Begone, urchin."

Andrew moved around the corner but lingered to hear what would happen next.

"Thou art wasting my time. Come anon," the man said.

"But sir, I—" Dr. Howard began.

Then Andrew heard a loud thump. Dr. Howard cried out. He then fled around the corner like a dog escaping a whipping. He saw Andrew, then scrambled away.

The man with the cane stepped into view. He gave Andrew a disdainful look as he passed by.

Andrew went to the door. The innkeeper was standing there watching as the man with the cane climbed into the coach. Dr. Howard scurried up to the coachman's bench.

"Who was that gentleman, sir?" Andrew asked.

"George Eliot," the innkeeper said with a sour face. "He is as wicked a man as ever was born of woman."

Andrew said the name to himself. It sounded familiar. "What doth he do?"

"Things most vile." The innkeeper suddenly chuckled. "He shall be annoyed to learn that Father Campion was here. Missing that bounty will pain him."

Andrew fell asleep at the inn puzzling over Dr. Howard. Why was he working for such an evil man?

In the morning, Andrew looked unsuccessfully for Dr. Howard. He continued looking as he and Father Campion mounted their horses and headed back to Lyford Grange.

The situation at the house was far worse than Andrew expected. More people had arrived to meet Father Campion. He agreed to hear their confessions and, if time allowed, to preach.

Andrew found Eve helping Cooper the cook. Andrew took her aside and told her about Dr. Howard and the man named George Eliot.

"Dr. Howard must be in terrible trouble," she said. "Is he coming here?"

"I hope so," Andrew replied. "But he must escape from George Eliot first. We do not want a man like that coming here."

Richard Buckley rushed through the doorway in a panic. "God spare me from this folly," he said. He went to a cupboard and began taking out cups and plates. "Refreshments," he muttered. "For thirty and four people, not counting our own!"

CHAPTER THIRTY-SIX

"You are like Martha in the story about Jesus," Eve said. "All work and no time to sit down."

Buckley shot her a grim look. "Nay, I am the disciple tasked with feeding the five thousand. May God provide me a boy with a basket of loaves and fishes!"

"We can help," Andrew said. He and Eve went alongside the servant and began to bring out more dishes.

Cooper waved a small ladle at Buckley. "More guests will arrive today, and still more on the morrow. Watch and see."

"Father Campion's net will also draw in spies and hunters," Buckley said in a mournful tone.

Andrew and Eve spent all day helping Buckley and the other servants take care of the guests. By evening, Andrew was sure they now had more than forty people crowding in to see the priest and hear him speak. Father Collington and Father Ford beamed proudly that so many wanted to worship and learn from Father Campion.

Chairs and cushions were placed in the small chapel in the nuns' wing of the house. It was understood that Father Campion would say Mass the following morning and then depart with Brother Emerson, assuming he would return as planned.

Throughout the evening, Andrew heard Buckley muttering words like *reckless* and *irresponsible*.

Andrew felt the knot in his stomach tighten even more.

Just after sunrise, Andrew was awakened by noises outside. Peering from the window, he saw more horses and coaches than could fit in the courtyard. Brutus was serving as a traffic guard, waving people through to a field behind one of the barns.

Andrew saw many of the Oxford students who were in attendance at the King and Lion Inn. "Has the whole university shown up?" he groaned.

Dressing quickly, he dashed downstairs. Buckley and Cooper were already in the kitchen with four other servants and two of the nuns. They were preparing food and drink for after the Mass. Eve soon appeared to help. She gave Andrew a look of despair.

Andrew felt a growing alarm in the lead-up to the Mass. *How can so many people gather and hope to stay unnoticed?* he wondered.

Buckley asked Andrew to attend the gate with Brutus. "Be alert. If anyone suspicious should arrive, raise the alarm."

Andrew spent an hour at the gate, watching as Brutus identified those arriving and questioned those he didn't know. The incoming traffic dwindled enough for Andrew to go back into the house. Angry as he was about the large gathering, he still wanted to attend the Mass.

He was walking across the courtyard when he heard the sound of horse hooves pounding the dirt.

"Boy," Dr. Howard called as he climbed off his horse. "Hurry!" He led the horse by the reins to the barn.

CHAPTER THIRTY-SIX

Andrew followed. "How did you get past the gate?" he asked.

"I said I was here to see thee," Dr. Howard replied. "I slipped away from George Eliot in the night. This is one of his horses." He giggled, his eyes darting this way and that. "I have left him with one less horse and no one to drive his coach. We shall see what he doth about that!"

Andrew watched the man, wondering if he had gone insane.

"Pray tell, where is Eve? Where is the stone?" Dr. Howard asked.

"She is somewhere in the house," Andrew said. "I have not seen her for a while."

Dr. Howard began to pace. "Dost thou know what I have been forced to do? Beg. Work the most menial jobs. Endure a mental asylum. Me! I have a graduate degree. I teach history. This is a period of history I have loved. Now I despise all it is. The people are ignorant. My vast knowledge of history could not penetrate their stupidity. I have spoken at symposiums about Queen Elizabeth as a great monarch. Now I see what she hath truly done, and I detest her."

Andrew glanced around to make sure that no one was listening. "Keep your voice down, sir."

"Why?" Dr. Howard asked. "Begone! Fetch Eve and the stone. We shall depart this accursed place. Go. Hurry. Shoo. Be quick about it."

"Eve is at Mass," Andrew said. "We must wait until she comes out."

"Mass!" Dr. Howard now looked around nervously. "Mass is celebrated here? Now?"

"Aye."

Dr. Howard went pale. " 'Tis Father Campion?"

Andrew didn't answer. Instead, he said, "Follow me, Dr. Howard. I have something for you. *And please stay quiet.*"

Andrew guided Dr. Howard through the house and to the storeroom. He went to the crate that Ambrosius had brought from Beckery. "These are yours," Andrew said as he lifted the lid.

Dr. Howard gasped and put his hands together like a little child at Christmas. He grabbed his clothes and slumped down, pressing them to his face.

Andrew slipped out of the room, not wanting to see the man weep.

Andrew went to the chapel. He saw Eve sitting near the front with the nuns. Everyone was kneeling and praying a litany with Father Campion. Andrew retreated. Dr. Howard would have to wait.

Returning to the storeroom, Andrew opened the door and looked inside. Dr. Howard was gone. Worried, Andrew rushed for the courtyard but came to a sudden stop in the kitchen. Dr. Howard was standing in a corner, watching the cook and the servants. He had a terrified look on his face.

Thomas Cooper gave Andrew a puzzled look.

"Dr. Howard?" Andrew whispered.

The man's eyes flitted to Andrew. He suddenly sprang into action, taking Andrew by the arm and pulling him into a nearby pantry. "He is here," Dr. Howard said in a hushed voice.

"Who?"

"George Eliot."

"The man I saw last night?" Andrew said. And then the name suddenly rang all the right bells in his memory. "George Eliot is the man from the insane asylum that you escaped with."

Dr. Howard nodded. "He saved my life. Dost thou know what the doctors were about to do to me? *Drill into my head!* Mr. Eliot was my protector."

"The doctor at the asylum said that George Eliot is a murderer," Andrew said.

"An accusation never proven." Dr. Howard caught Andrew by the arms.

Andrew pulled back. "Will you stop grabbing me?"

"You must get Eve. We must leave. *Now.*"

"What is George Eliot doing here?" Andrew asked, suddenly fearing the answer. "Is he a spy? Are you a spy?"

"Nay, I am not!" snapped Dr. Howard.

The door to the pantry opened. Thomas Cooper gave them a hard look. "How now?"

"A man hath arrived who may be a spy," Andrew said.

Dr. Howard flinched and seemed to curl into himself.

Cooper's eyebrows shot up. "Name the man."

"George Eliot."

The cook suddenly laughed. "'Tis no spy. George Eliot is a friend. We served the Roper family together. Dost thou know the Ropers? They are related to the great Thomas More."

"He is a Catholic?" Andrew asked.

"Aye."

"Why hath he come here on this day?" Andrew asked.

"He is traveling to Derbyshire and visited family nearby. He recalled that I work here. I have invited him to stay for lunch. Come and see."

Andrew followed the cook back into the kitchen—and then froze.

George Eliot stood there, looking much the same as he had the night before. His hand rested on his cane.

Eliot watched Andrew as he entered but didn't betray any recognition.

Cooper introduced Andrew, then turned to have Andrew introduce the other man. But Dr. Howard wasn't there.

"Dear friend," Eliot said to Cooper, "I left a colleague waiting at the gate. Alas, the gatekeeper would not permit

CHAPTER THIRTY-SIX

him entry. My friend is not a Catholic, but he is well disposed to the faith."

"Bid him enter," Cooper said cheerfully. "I shall tell Brutus to open to him." Then he said in a forced whisper, "We are conducting Mass in the chapel. If thou attendest, thou wilt be delighted. Father *Edmund Campion* is here to preach."

Andrew stifled a groan. A change made its way over Eliot's face, as if the sun had suddenly ducked behind storm clouds.

"Campion himself?" Eliot asked. "I have heard much about him. May I fetch my friend from the gate?"

"Aye," Cooper said.

Andrew watched Eliot slip out the back door. If he was a friend of Cooper's, then maybe he wasn't a spy after all. Andrew went back to the pantry, but Dr. Howard had gone. He tried the storeroom. Dr. Howard was sitting on a small barrel.

He looked up anxiously as Andrew peeked in. "Did Eliot see me?"

"I think not."

He seemed relieved. "Eliot's friend is David Jenkins, an agent of the Queen's Privy Council." He looked at Andrew with a panicked expression. "We must flee."

"Have they come to arrest Father Campion?" Andrew asked.

"They have a *system*," Dr. Howard said. "First, Eliot will attend the Mass to identify Father Campion. David

Jenkins will remain in the kitchen, awaiting a signal from Eliot. If Father Campion is here, they will take action. Excuses will be made for one or both of them to depart. They shall then seek out a nearby sheriff or magistrate who will return with men-at-arms to capture the priest."

"Why are you telling me this?" Andrew asked.

"To assure thee that I have nothing to do with it." Dr. Howard lifted his head a little. His eyes didn't meet Andrew's. "See now why we must hurry?"

Andrew left Dr. Howard in the storeroom again. He arrived in the kitchen just in time to hear David Jenkins decline the offer to attend the Mass.

"I would rather remain in the kitchen to sample this delicious-looking food," the man insisted.

Cooper laughed and pushed a plate of meat in his direction.

George Eliot gave a humorless smile. "The boy here will show me to the Mass," he said.

Cooper nodded to Andrew. "Aye, lad. Lead the way."

Andrew stammered, trying to think of an excuse not to. But Eliot's hand fell on his shoulder and gripped him hard.

"This way," he said to Eliot.

Andrew's mind raced as they walked to the other wing of the house and up the stairs to the chapel. As they entered, Father Ford began the Mass with the Sign of the Cross, then said in Latin, "In the name of the Father, Son, and Holy Ghost."

CHAPTER THIRTY-SIX

Eliot guided Andrew to a chair and forced him to sit down. He whispered, "I mean thee no harm. Be still. All will be well."

Andrew looked around. He guessed there were now at least sixty people gathered. What kind of chaos would he unleash if he suddenly shouted that a priest hunter was present? He wasn't even sure if that was true. Was George Eliot really a priest hunter?

The Mass proceeded. Andrew noticed that Eliot said all of the right things and made the right gestures. *He can't be a spy and do that*, Andrew thought.

Then, as Father Campion stood to give a homily, Eliot fidgeted.

Father Campion preached from the Gospel of St. Luke about the story of Jesus weeping over Jerusalem. It was clear to everyone there that Father Campion was thinking about England when he read from the same account in Matthew: "Jerusalem, Jerusalem, thou that killest the prophets, and stonest them which are sent unto thee."

The homily lasted for an hour, with the congregation weeping over the beauty of Father Campion's words. Andrew felt heartbroken as the priest reminded them that Jesus spoke the words as He went into the city to face His brutal crucifixion. "Our Lord's passion awaits us all. Many of us shall suffer gloriously as He suffered."

Eliot no longer fidgeted but sat with his head down for a moment. Then he abruptly stood and slipped out of the Mass.

Andrew followed him, sure he was up to something. Eliot bumped into Mrs. Yate as he passed her in the hall. He asked her forgiveness and walked on. Mrs. Yate watched him go.

"Who is the man?" she asked Andrew.

"I think he is a spy, though Mr. Cooper speaks for him," Andrew said.

"Watch him most carefully," Mrs. Yate said. "I shall post one of the servants on the roof to keep watch for hunters."

Andrew walked quickly to find Eliot. The kitchen was empty. He went through to the courtyard, stopping just inside the doorway. Eliot and Jenkins stood near the stable. Andrew heard only fragments of words: *sheriff* and *two miles* and *Denchworth*.

Eliot and Jenkins fetched their horses from the stable.

A finger poked Andrew in the back. He turned as Dr. Howard landed a hard blow against the side of Andrew's head. Stunned, Andrew fell. Dr. Howard dropped on top of him, pinning his arms. He shoved a rag into his mouth.

"'Tis for thine own good," Dr. Howard said and was soon busy wrapping heavy twine around Andrew's wrists. "Hadst thou listened, we would be well away from here. Now ... what choice hast thou left me?"

Andrew couldn't think straight. *Why are people always grabbing me or hitting me in the head? I don't think history should be this painful.*

CHAPTER THIRTY-SIX

The question looped in his mind again and again. He felt a burning pain in his wrists and arms along with the sensation of being half dragged and half carried across the courtyard. He was taken behind the outbuildings and dropped to the ground. His arms were pulled up against a splintered post. Something that smelled of old leather was fastened around the rag in his mouth.

Dr. Howard said, "I will return with the stone, with or without Eve. Then thou shalt show me how it works."

37

The Mass ended, and Father Campion stayed on to pray the Divine Office with those who wished to join him. Afterward, Eve followed the crowd to the dining hall. Long tables were adorned with food and drink. Father Campion sat at the head of one table. Eve saw firsthand his good nature and charm. He radiated a kind of holiness that seemed grounded in a good heart that understood what it was to be human. Eve found herself envying Andrew for all of the months he had traveled with the priest.

She looked around and wondered where Andrew was now. She thought she had seen him in the back of the chapel during the Mass. Intuition told her to look for him. She stood just as a young servant rushed in.

"At the gate!" he cried out. "Forty or fifty men at the gate! *Priest hunters!*"

As one, the guests reacted, rising from the tables.

Father Campion also rose. "Fear not! I shall beseech them. If they capture me, they will leave this company in peace."

Mrs. Yate's voice cut through the chaotic reactions. "If the horde doth capture thee, they will know there are others worth taking. The house will be searched all the same. Hear me! There is no time. Good priests, begone into hiding! You know the places."

Father Ford took the lead, summoning Father Campion and Father Collington to follow.

Mrs. Yate called out to Eve and Sister Anne, one of the nuns. "Make haste!" she said. "We shall stall them at the gate."

Eve and Sister Anne followed Mrs. Yate into the hallway.

"You must hold my arms, as if I am too weak to walk in my own strength," Mrs. Yate said.

They reached the stairs to the main door. Suddenly Eve stopped. Dr. Howard was at the bottom of the stairs.

Mrs. Yate tugged at Eve, "Come, child."

With a bow, Dr. Howard allowed them to pass.

Eve was shocked at his appearance. He looked so different—so worn and aged. She thought he had become a man who had spent too much time in very hard places.

"Milady, I beg you to allow me to speak with the child," Dr. Howard said, gesturing to Eve.

"'Tis not the time, sir," Mrs. Yate said.

"'Tis the best time if you value her life," he said.

Mrs. Yate gave him an uncertain look. "All of our lives are valued here, sir. That is why we are going to the gate."

CHAPTER THIRTY-SEVEN

She brushed past him and went to the main door. Richard Buckley came forward to pull it open.

Dr. Howard slipped behind Eve and whispered, "I bid you, hasten to the courtyard. Bring the stone. Andrew is waiting. We must take our leave." Then he moved back into the house.

They took their time walking to the gate. Eve saw the men pressed against the iron bars. Brutus stood inside with his arms folded defiantly.

Eve played her part well. She held Mrs. Yate's arm. She could feel the woman slowing down, dragging her feet a little. She shuffled as if walking was too great an effort for her.

"Is that my good cousin John Fettiplace?" Mrs. Yate called out as she came to the bars.

A man in the very front of the crowd drew closer. He wore purple robes and official chains and medallions around his neck. "'Tis I, good lady. I have come on the business of the queen," he said.

"Thou art the sheriff of Denchworth. What business doth the sheriff or the queen herself have with my humble home?" Mrs. Yate asked. "I am not well. Dost thou not see how fatigued I am?"

"Thy fatigue must be great indeed to have so many guests in thy house," the sheriff quipped. "I have placed men-at-arms all around the walls. Tell thy guests to stay and keep their peace."

"Alas, this is very serious indeed," Mrs. Yate said.

A nasty-looking man pushed in next to the sheriff. He clutched a long black cane with a silver handle in one hand and a piece of paper in the other. He held up the paper. "Good woman, I am George Eliot, and this warrant gives me leave to search your property."

Yet another man squeezed in and announced that he was David Jenkins, there on behalf of the Queen's Privy Council. "My lady, I do believe you delay us so as to hide your guests."

"Guests, sir?" Mrs. Yate asked.

George Eliot grabbed the iron bars and shook them angrily. "Enough! I demand that the gate be opened anon!"

"I shall give thy demand due consideration," Mrs. Yate said.

And so it went for half an hour. The men demanded entrance. Mrs. Yate acted as if she did not understand why so many people desired to search her house.

Finally, George Eliot demanded that the sheriff break down the gates.

The sheriff was reluctant to damage any property.

When Eliot promised to report the sheriff to the queen, the sheriff agreed to cooperate.

Mrs. Yate finally yielded. "The summer heat must be causing you ill humors," she said. "Brutus, allow these poor men to enter. I beseech thee to open the gates."

Brutus scowled but obeyed.

The men flooded in. Mrs. Yate slowly walked back to the house with Eve and Sister Anne helping, as they had before. At the main door, Mrs. Yate said, "Now, dear girls, see to your safety."

"My thanks, good lady," Eve said. The house was now so crowded with men searching the rooms, she went around the outside to the courtyard.

She found Dr. Howard lingering near a grain store. He was clearly pretending to be one of the search party but was half hiding as if he feared that someone would see him. He stepped into full view when he saw Eve.

"What have you done with Andrew?" she demanded.

"Where is the stone?" he asked. "Art thou wearing it? Dost thou keep it in thy pocket?"

"*Where is Andrew?*" she asked again.

"He is *bound* to be at his post," Dr. Howard said with a high-pitched giggle.

"Have you been drinking?" she asked.

He became very serious and said firmly, "The sooner thou deliverest the stone, the sooner we shall be away from this vexing time."

"I do not have it," she said.

Dr. Howard's face twisted into a rage. Eve thought he might attack her. "Where is it?"

"Hidden," she said.

"Get it!"

"'Tis hidden in a place I cannot get to now," Eve said.

Dr. Howard fumed. "Where hast thou hidden the stone that thou cannot collect it now?" As soon as he asked the question, he seemed to know the answer. "'Tis hidden with the priests."

Eve didn't respond.

"I do not care about the priests," Dr. Howard said angrily, stepping forward. "I want the stone!"

The rage in his eyes made her step back.

He clenched his fists. Then his eye caught something behind Eve, and it was as if all of his emotion dissolved.

"'Tis the horse thief," said George Eliot, marching from the house, his cane tapping the dirt. "Wast thou so eager to arrive here before me?" he asked. He didn't break his stride but pushed Eve aside and continued to Dr. Howard.

Eve saw the man's cane rise up and then come down hard on Dr. Howard's shoulder.

She scrambled to get away as the sound of another blow—and another one—thumped around the courtyard. Dr. Howard didn't cry out. He only hissed as if each blow was letting a little air out of him like an old balloon.

Eve didn't look back. She raced to find Andrew.

38

Andrew heard shouts and bangs coming from the house. The foul rag in his mouth kept him from making anything other than a muted grunt. The afternoon sun baked him, giving him hope that his sweat might help him wiggle his hands through the twine. Dr. Howard had bound the twine to an iron ring on a splintered post. Andrew twisted and turned his hands, but they wouldn't come free.

He then stood and pulled at the post. He thought the rotten wood might split away from the ground. The wood held firm.

He also rubbed the leather belt against one shoulder, then the other. If he could move the belt, he'd be able to spit out the foul rag and call for help. It didn't work.

He began to despair.

Then he heard men coming around the outbuilding. They complained loudly that they'd found nothing in the house, save a handful of nuns. Little good that was, since the nuns were given the queen's permission to live there. If Edmund Campion was inside, then he was doing a very good job of hiding.

One of the men cursed George Eliot. He said he resented taking orders from a known murderer. They grumbled and griped. *Now* they were expected to search the grounds, the orchards, the hedges, and the ditches.

A third man laughed as he reminded them about finding two of the Yates' countrymen hiding in a pigeon house.

Andrew stamped his feet and grunted to get the men's attention. They were too busy chatting to hear him.

Just then, he felt a hard tap on his back. He twisted around. Dr. Howard stood over him.

Andrew blinked. Something was wrong with the man. A knot was growing near the man's eye. A patch of his hair looked matted with blood. A purple bruise colored his neck, just beneath the ruff of his collar. His coat was torn at the shoulder. He winced as he worked the leather strap around Andrew's mouth.

"Dost thou grasp why we must flee?" he asked. "By thy troth, thou art in danger of arrest. I shall set thee loose to find Eve and the stone. If thou wilt not, I shall prevail upon the sheriff, George Eliot, and the queen's man to beat from you where the priests are hiding."

The strap fell free.

Andrew tried to spit out the rag, but his mouth was too dry to do it.

CHAPTER THIRTY-EIGHT

"Allow me," Dr. Howard said and pulled the rag away. "Dost thou understand the pain George Eliot will inflict upon thee?"

Andrew gave a sharp nod.

Dr. Howard pulled out a short knife and cut at the twine around Andrew's wrists. "Be thou a good boy and bring me the stone."

Andrew asked, "What kind of man are you?"

"I have been beaten by a man I loathe. Yet here I remain. I am the kind of man who will do anything to go home."

The twine dropped. Andrew rubbed at his wrists.

Dr. Howard lifted the knife as a sure threat. "The girl and the stone," he said.

Eve felt a tiny flicker of hope. The men-at-arms were now openly complaining about wasting a good afternoon for nothing. They hadn't found any priests, and they were tired of searching. They were growing more annoyed at the sheriff and the two strangers for bothering a fragile old woman. They began to leave.

Mrs. Yate stood by the main door as if saying goodbye to departing dinner guests.

With hats off, the men apologized to her.

As an aside, Mrs. Yate told Eve to go to the gate and keep an eye on George Eliot.

Eve easily found him. George Eliot was ranting furiously. He had rushed to the gate and began to berate the men's lack of effort, even calling them cowards. "I shall report all of you to the Privy Council! I will tell them you are in league with the Papists!"

David Jenkins appealed for him to calm down.

Eliot rounded on him. "Didst thou believe Edmund Campion would be a simple catch?" he shouted. "Begone! Find another sheriff and more men. Bring Humphrey Forster. He is the High Sheriff of Berkshire in Aldermaston. He will not shirk this duty!" Eliot glared at Sheriff Fettiplace, who stood nearby.

Jenkins wiped his brow as if thinking. Then he said, "Edmund Wiseman is a justice of the peace in Steventon."

"Summon them all!" Eliot shouted.

Jenkins went through the gate to a horse on the other side. He mounted and rode off.

The departing searchers were now crowded at the gate, looking unsure of themselves.

Eliot turned on them. "Fools to a man! Go back! Break through the walls!"

Sheriff Fettiplace raised his hands. "Nay, nay, sir. We do not have the authority to tear the house apart."

"I do!" Eliot said and pulled a piece of paper from inside his vest. He stood apart and read loudly, "By this warrant doth Her Royal Majesty's Privy Council grant thee, George Eliot, the right to search, destroy, detain, and arrest any known Papist traitors."

Eve had sidled up behind Eliot and looked at the warrant. The paper was a proclamation about taxes in Yorkshire.

She nudged one of the men standing nearby and whispered, "'Tis a tax bill, not a warrant."

The man took a few steps over and pointed to the paper. "He is lying. 'Tis a tax bill!"

The men began to laugh.

Eliot pointed at the man and said to the sheriff, "Arrest him! He supports the Jesuits!"

"'Tis in my power to do," the sheriff said to the man. "I may arrest any I believe are impeding the search."

The man backed away.

"I do not desire this," the sheriff said to his men. "But you must go forth. Search again. Find the hidden priests!"

With a lot of grumbling, the men slowly marched back to the house.

Mrs. Yate was still at the door as the men returned. She swayed where she stood. Sheriff Fettiplace reached out to steady her. She cried, "John, I beg thee. I am not well. Take thy leave in peace!"

The sheriff said, "Jane, if thou hast need to retire, then do. I would ask all of the ladies of the house to retire to their rooms and there remain until we have found our quarry."

"As thou desirest," Mrs. Yate said. She summoned Buckley and told him to send the women to their rooms.

Eve lingered outside, unsure of what to do. She had already searched the house for Andrew. She couldn't imagine what Dr. Howard had done with him—or to him. She assured herself that Dr. Howard wouldn't harm Andrew and risk losing the chance to go back to his own time.

Or would he?

"Am I bleeding?" Andrew asked.

Startled, Eve spun around. He was standing next to her, touching the side of his head. She was relieved to see him. "What did Dr. Howard do to you?"

"He hit me in the head when I wasn't looking. Then he tied me to a post behind the stable. He has lost his mind."

Eve checked Andrew's head. "No blood. Only a bump."

"I have the headache to go with it," he complained. "It will take a week to get the nasty taste of that foul rag out of my mouth."

"What are we going to do?" Eve asked.

"Have you told Dr. Howard where the priests are hiding?"

"No. Have you?" she asked.

"No," he said, "but he believes you've hidden the stone with them."

"He's right."

Andrew frowned at her. "Why did you hide the stone?"

"For safekeeping. Why else?" she said. "And I didn't want to be tempted to use it again."

"Dr. Howard threatened to hand us over to George Eliot if we don't do *something*," Andrew said.

As if on cue, Dr. Howard appeared at the corner of the house and walked their way.

"I'll go with the rest of the women," Eve said suddenly.

Andrew put a hand on her arm to stop her. "No," he said.

Before Dr. Howard could speak, Andrew said, "Threaten us all you want, but Eve cannot get the stone now. Be patient, or I promise you will *never* go home again."

He nudged Eve, and the two of them marched into the house.

When they were just inside the door, Andrew stopped and asked, "Did it work?"

Eve peeked back through the door. "He looks stunned."

Andrew gave a sigh of relief. "Good," he said.

The impasse went well into the night. It reminded Andrew of a game of checkers, where all the pieces were stuck because one more move might allow the opponent to win. It felt as if they were only one move away from the end.

Thomas Cooper announced to the searchers that the good lady of the house bid them welcome to a fine supper in the dining hall.

"All but 'Judas' Eliot," Cooper said and sneered at the man he once considered a friend.

The men laughed at the new name for Eliot.

Eliot was undaunted. "The lady of the house wishes to lull you to sleep!" he shouted at them.

The men ignored him and went to enjoy Mrs. Yate's hospitality.

Eliot wandered the house on his own, tapping the walls, checking for hollows. He tipped over furniture and pulled framed paintings from the walls.

Andrew followed Eliot every step of the way.

At one point, Eliot lifted his cane and threatened to strike the boy dead if he did not go away.

"Would the queen approve?" Andrew asked.

Eliot sneered at him. "Wouldst thou like to find out?"

Andrew wasn't willing to take the chance and left Eliot alone.

Within an hour, Eliot's warning to the men proved to be true. Most of the searchers had eaten their fill and had fallen asleep in and around the dining hall.

Suddenly there was a loud commotion on the second floor. Andrew, who was dozing in a cushioned chair, snapped awake.

"I have seen him! He is here!" a voice shouted.

Eliot bounded up the stairs just ahead of Andrew. Soon, the sounds of the slumbering searchers coming awake echoed throughout the house.

A guard placed on duty outside Mrs. Yate's bedroom said he had heard a noise inside. "A man's voice praying," he said to Eliot. He claimed he had thrown the door open and, by the light of a single candle, had seen a roomful of women on their knees praying. "A man by the window led them."

"What man?" Eliot asked.

"'Twas not a man I have seen at any time this day," the guard said.

Eliot described Campion to him. "Was that whom thou didst see?"

"'Twas him," the guard said.

"Why didst thou not capture him?" Eliot demanded.

The guard looked as if the idea hadn't occurred to him. "I ... I rushed out to raise the alarm," he said.

Eliot ordered that the room be cleared of all except Mrs. Yate. She was allowed to remain in her bed. The searchers brought up lanterns and searched the room.

"Didst thou see a ghost?" the sheriff asked the guard after no one was found.

"Nay! I am sure of what I saw."

Search, poke, and probe as they might, the searchers found nothing.

Andrew caught sight of Eve among the women who had been taken from the room. She rolled her eyes.

The men-at-arms were now even more annoyed with Eliot. They were tired and wanted to go to their homes.

"Donkey-brained fools!" Eliot shouted at them. "I have seen Campion with my own eyes. The guard hath now seen him. He is in this house!"

A new commotion was heard at the main door. David Jenkins had failed to find Justice of the Peace Wiseman. Instead, he returned with another justice of the peace named Christopher Lydcot. Lydcot brought with him an entirely new company of men.

Sheriff Fettiplace and his searchers did not want to be outdone by these newcomers. They put aside their reluctance to use axes, hammers, and spikes to punch holes through the walls. The destruction began in all wings and rooms of the house.

All except Mrs. Yate's bedroom. The woman's faked illness earlier was no longer being faked. She was now genuinely feverish. Though Edmund Campion had been seen in her room, Sheriff Fettiplace would not allow the searchers to destroy it while she rested in her bed.

Andrew drifted from room to room, watching the destruction. He came upon Sheriff Fettiplace and Thomas Cooper.

"What next?" Thomas Cooper asked the sheriff. "Burn it to the ground?"

The sheriff sadly shook his head. "'Tis not a proud moment."

The light of the coming dawn touched the windows with a gray weariness. Andrew rubbed his sleepy eyes. The hammering had ceased. The priests had still not been found.

Please, go away, he prayed.

Eliot, Jenkins, Fettiplace, and Lydcot gathered by the main door to confer.

CHAPTER THIRTY-EIGHT

Andrew noticed Dr. Howard off to the side. He had an odd smirk on his face. He saw Andrew and sauntered over. Andrew braced himself.

"I have been doing some measuring, up *here*." Dr. Howard tapped his temple. "I know where the priests are hidden."

Andrew gave him a skeptical look.

Dr. Howard broke into the circle of men by the door. He whispered something to them.

Just then Thomas Cooper emerged from the kitchen. Rag in hand, he was absentmindedly wiping a plate. "'Tis quiet," he said to Andrew.

Andrew watched as George Eliot went to the stairwell. He climbed up several steps and hit his cane against the wall above the main door.

Thomas Cooper went pale, dropping the plate.

Eliot spun to him. "How now, Thomas?"

Cooper stammered, "Hast thou not knocked into enough walls already?"

Eliot gave him a coy look. "Thou wast never good at keeping secrets."

David Jenkins grabbed a hammer and spike. A chair was dragged over for him to stand upon. He pointed the spike at the space above the door and brought down the hammer. In one stroke, the spike broke through the wall.

Andrew watched with mounting horror.

"'Tis hollow!" Jenkins cried out. He drove the spike in again and again. Some of the men-at-arms joined him in clawing at the plaster and thin timber.

The face of a bleary-eyed Father Ford appeared in a hole in the wall. Then Father Collington looked out of another. Finally, the much-hunted Edmund Campion pushed a piece of loose plaster away and presented himself.

"Have you been looking for me?" he asked.

Father Campion looked cheerful as he was tied up and placed among the other Catholic culprits in the dining hall. Mrs. Yate was told to leave her bed, dress, and await the journey to prison.

Andrew and Eve stood together near the front door and helplessly watched the proceedings. Dr. Howard had found the entrance to the priest's hiding place next to the bedroom window. Andrew could hear him banging around behind the wall.

"Tell me the stone is not there," he whispered to Eve.

She shook her head.

Dr. Howard eventually came out, glaring at them as he walked past.

George Eliot seemed emboldened and now demanded that the prisoners be taken to London right away. Sheriff Fettiplace and Justice Lydcot insisted that before removing the prisoners, they should await Humphrey Forster, Berkshire's High Sheriff from Aldermaston Court.

"He could not be bothered to come last night. Why should we wait for him now?" Eliot snarled.

"'Tis his domain. We must wait," David Jenkins said.

The sudden quiet in the house should have been a relief after so many hours of chaos, but it wasn't. Andrew stood in a sullen silence. Eve looked as if she was about to cry at the mere mention of Father Campion's name. They both expected Dr. Howard to appear and make more demands of them. Instead, he stayed close to George Eliot and the authorities.

"He must be proud of himself," Andrew said.

"Proud of himself for what?" Eve asked.

Andrew told Eve that Dr. Howard was the one who had revealed the priests' hiding place to Eliot.

Eve looked at Andrew with an expression of disbelief. Then she let out a sharp snort and paced furiously. She muttered, "How could he do it? Hath he no honor?" Then she swung around to Andrew and said, "We should go without him."

"We cannot leave him behind," Andrew said. "That would be the same as condemning him to death."

"That is what he hath done to Father Campion," Eve countered.

Andrew shook his head. "We cannot leave him."

Eve said nothing more.

Andrew knew she didn't agree with him now, but she would if they really did leave without Dr. Howard.

The searchers finally departed. George Eliot, Dr. Howard, and the others migrated to the kitchen to wait for the High Sheriff. A guard had been placed outside the dining hall.

"No one is watching us," Andrew whispered to Eve. "We should get the Radiant Stone now?"

Eve hesitated. "We should wait. Just in case."

"What if they take us to London as witnesses or something?" Andrew asked. "If we leave it here, we may not be able to get back to retrieve it."

Eve looked sick. "Do you think they'll take us to London? Will we be imprisoned in the tower?"

Andrew shrugged. "They're not paying attention to us now, but the High Sheriff might show up and arrest everyone in the house."

Eve nodded. "Let's get the stone."

He followed her to the room behind the fireplace. They went through to the small closet with the boxes. Eve stepped into the closet. Andrew squeezed in behind her and closed the door.

"The ladder is gone," Eve said. "There is only a chair."

Andrew looked. Standing on the chair wouldn't get them high enough to reach the panel in the ceiling. "We'll need another couple of boxes to reach it," he said.

The boxes were heavy, as if they were filled with books. Both kids had to lift the boxes together to pile them onto the chair.

"This won't work," Eve said.

"It will," Andrew said and carefully climbed to the top of the boxes. He held out his hand. "Now, you come up and get on my back."

CHAPTER THIRTY-EIGHT

Eve looked at him uneasily. She then leveraged herself between the boxes and the wall to join him at the top. The boxes swayed. He bent over and puffed while she climbed onto his back. He straightened as much as he could, struggling to keep his balance as the boxes and the chair drifted back and forth.

"Is it high enough?" he asked her.

"Perfect," she said. He heard her move the hatch door. Then her weight eased from his shoulders as she pulled herself into the shaft.

Relieved, he looked up at her. She settled herself in the square hatch and reached her arm down.

He guessed that he was just tall enough to grab her arm and pull himself up.

At that moment, he heard voices outside the closet. Dr. Howard and George Eliot had entered the room.

"I told you if we waited, the children would lead us to the other hiding places," Dr. Howard boasted.

Eliot said, "I must give thee thy due. Now, did they slip through a panel in the wall, or are they in that closet?"

Eve gave Andrew a look of panic and waved her outreached arm at him. He grabbed her wrist and jumped up while she pulled. His free hand caught the side of the hatch, and he labored to haul himself into the shaft.

"Come on," Eve gasped. She now had her feet on the edges of the hatch and kept pulling.

Andrew tried to get a foothold on the rough-plastered wall. His foot slipped and kicked one of the boxes on the chair. It fell with a heavy crash.

He heard the closet door open just as he got his upper body into the shaft. Eve stepped back to give him room.

From below, Dr. Howard shouted, "There!"

Andrew kicked wildly. He felt a hand slap against his heel and slide off.

"Use the chair, you fool!" Eliot snapped at Dr. Howard.

There were scrapes and crashes below.

Andrew was trying with all his might to get his lower body into the shaft but was losing strength.

Suddenly, strong hands grabbed him under the shoulders and lifted him into the shaft. Andrew was bewildered until he was face-to-face with Edward Yate, Mrs. Yate's brother-in-law. He was in the shaft alongside Eve.

"Get thee to the top," Edward whispered.

Eve grabbed the rings of the makeshift ladder in the shaft wall and began to climb. Andrew was right behind her. He looked down. Edward was trying to move the hatch door in place to block the men below.

Dr. Howard suddenly appeared in the space and saw Edward. "There is another Catholic in here!" he cried and pushed against the door.

Andrew heard George Eliot shout for help.

Edward said, "I yield!" He knelt and swung his legs into the hatch, kicking Dr. Howard.

Andrew realized that Edward was stalling for time.

"Come down or get out of my way!" Dr. Howard yelled. "I must catch those children!"

CHAPTER THIRTY-EIGHT

Andrew sped up the ladder, almost catching Eve's feet above him. "Faster, faster!" he cried out.

Eve reached the top of the shaft and disappeared over the upper ledge. Andrew arrived only seconds later.

The attic had nothing more than timber beams forming a large A-shape to support the roof.

A bang at the bottom of the shaft caught Andrew's attention. He looked and saw Dr. Howard now struggling to get through the hatch.

"Dr. Howard is coming," Andrew said to Eve. "If we grab him when you touch the stone, we'll go home."

"Right," she said. She had crawled from one rafter to another and was now reaching up to a crossbeam above her. She pulled down a wooden box.

Andrew looked down the shaft again. Dr. Howard must have lost his footing, because he cried out and fell back into the closet.

"Move aside, clumsy fool!" Eliot roared.

Andrew's gaze darted between the shaft and Eve, who was fumbling with the box.

George Eliot was now in the hatchway, not Dr. Howard. Eliot began pulling himself up and grabbing for the rings of the ladder.

"I have it," Eve said.

Andrew turned to her. She held up the locket with the Radiant Stone, then reached up to put the box back in its hiding place.

"George Eliot is coming up first," Andrew said.

Eve gasped. "What'll we do?"

"Is there another way out?" Andrew asked.

They scrambled to search the attic while Eliot's grunts echoed up to them. In a far corner, Andrew saw a cot and a couple of boxes. He assumed Edward Yate had been hiding in the attic while the house was searched.

"There is no way out," Eve said. She sounded frightened. "If George Eliot catches us, he will take us to London."

"I know." Andrew looked back into the shaft. George Eliot was halfway to the top of the ladder.

"Aye, you will go to the Tower of London," Eliot said. "You shall tell the torturers all you know. I was foolish not to arrest you with the others."

Dr. Howard began shouting from farther below. "Wait, Eliot! Leave them to me! I beg thee!"

Andrew moved away from the shaft. He stood next to Eve.

"I cannot be taken to London. I cannot be tortured," Eve said, her voice quivering.

Andrew took hold of her hand. "We have to get out of here."

"What about Dr. Howard?" she asked.

"We will find him another time."

Just then, like a gopher coming out of a hole, George Eliot's head popped up from the shaft. His face was twisted into an expression of victorious rage.

It was the last thing Andrew saw before that world disappeared.

39

Eve didn't usually feel anything when she moved through time. Now she felt a sensation of being bumped in different directions. She and Andrew were still holding hands, and she wondered if he felt the same thing. Suddenly they were in Alfred Virtue's office, as she expected.

Aunt Catherine was there, her mouth was hanging open. She had a deeply confused look on her face.

As quickly as Eve saw her, she was gone.

The next instant, Eve and Andrew were back on Beckery Island. It was daytime, and Anthony Dovedale was in the middle of the ruined chapel shoveling rubble into a pile. It was as if he heard them arrive. He looked up at them. Suddenly he was gone.

Eve and Andrew were then in a narrow passageway. Timbered walls pressed in on two sides of them. Rubbish littered the ground. A black rat gave them a nasty look and scurried into a crack in the wall.

Eve looked at Andrew.

Andrew looked astonished. *"What was that?"*

Eve held up the Radiant Stone, still in her hand. "Can these things malfunction?"

Andrew took a deep breath, as if he was struggling to breathe. "Is this what happened to you before?"

"No," Eve said. "I went back to Beckery Chapel. Ambrosius was there waiting for me."

They looked around. The passageway was open at two ends. Eve saw horses and coaches slowly moving in and out of view on one end. On the other end was a crisscross of iron railings and an open gray sky.

A seagull lighted on one of the railings, squawked at them, then flew off.

Andrew let go of Eve's hand and walked toward the railing. Eve followed. A light snow coated the top of the railing, but the seagull's webbed feet had smudged it. Below the open sky, Eve now saw a wide river filled with masted boats and wide barges. The banks were lined with docks and large warehouse-type buildings.

"'Tis the Thames," Andrew said. "We're on London Bridge."

A blast of wintry wind caught them, and they backed into the passageway again. Eve shivered and hugged herself.

"Why are we here?" Eve asked.

"*When* are we here?" asked Andrew. "It's London, but it's definitely not summertime. We're going to freeze."

"First I'm going to be sick." Eve leaned over and fought the rising feeling.

CHAPTER THIRTY-NINE

Andrew said, "Me, too. No radonite."

"Aha!" Ambrosius said from the busy end of the alleyway. "I hope these fit," he said as walked toward them. He handed them the heavy coats he had draped over his arm.

Still shivering, the kids put on the coats. Eve felt warmer right away. Her coat felt as if it had been made of wool and fur.

Ambrosius pulled out a flask from under his coat. "Drink this. 'Twill ease your travel sickness."

Eve drank first, then handed the flask to Andrew. He took a drink.

"It works fast," Eve said as the nausea faded away.

"A walk will warm you up," Ambrosius said. They followed him to the street. He pointed left. "This way to London."

Eve had never seen anything quite like it. Houses and shops and all the traffic of a busy London road were on the bridge. They passed stalls of merchants selling meat and fish, many with fires blazing in barrels.

"*This* is London Bridge?" she asked.

"The last time I was on this bridge, I was on my way to prison with Father Sherwin," Andrew said, then quickly followed with "How did we get here?"

"The Radiant Stone," Ambrosius said.

"It was supposed to take us back to our time," Andrew said.

"It did, did it not?"

"For a flash, and then we went to Beckery," Eve said.

"Touch points," Ambrosius said. "Places the stone hath recently been."

"The stone hath not been *here*," Andrew said. "*You* brought us here."

Ambrosius gave him a look of innocence.

"How did you do it?" Eve asked.

"'Tis all so complicated and boring to explain," he replied.

"Why did you bring us here?" Andrew asked.

"Unfinished business," Ambrosius said wearily. "One of my tasks is to set things right."

"Like what?" asked Andrew.

"You left someone behind. Vincent Howard."

"We had no choice," Andrew said.

"You did. But your hearts were set upon escape."

Eve said, "We meant to escape *with* him."

"'Tis not an accusation," Ambrosius said. "Though it was not what you intended, 'twas necessary for you to do it."

Andrew and Eve exchanged glances.

"Why was it necessary?" Eve asked.

"It may have been the only way to save his soul," Ambrosius replied.

Eve puzzled over what he meant. "Where is Dr. Howard now?"

"He hath been here and there. We will meet up with him soon."

"How do you know that?" asked Andrew.

"He will not miss the execution."

"Whose execution?" Eve asked.

"Edmund Campion's."

Eve felt her legs go wobbly. She grabbed Andrew's arm.

"Are you all right?" he asked.

Eve swallowed hard. "They are going to kill Father Campion?"

"Aye," Ambrosius said sadly.

"How long have we been gone?" Andrew asked.

"Four months, give or take a fortnight."

"Please tell us what we missed," Eve pleaded.

As they walked into London, Ambrosius explained what had befallen Father Campion after his capture. "He remained calm, even cheerful," he said. "'Twas the same when he and Father Ford and Father Collington were paraded from Lyford Grange to London.

"Others were arrested in the house then, and more were arrested elsewhere as time went on," he said. "George Eliot was declared a Judas by both Catholics and Protestants. Dr. Howard was thought to be in league with Eliot, which did him no favors."

"Was Eliot really a murderer?" Andrew asked.

"A murderer, among many other things," Ambrosius said. "He was bad company for Dr. Howard to fall in with. Though Eliot hath since begged Father Campion for forgiveness—and received it."

"Was he sincere?" Eve asked.

Ambrosius said, "'Tis not for me to judge the man's heart. I know he fears death by Catholic hands for his betrayal. Perhaps he wanted Father Campion to send out a message asking everyone to forgive his betrayer. Father Campion was never given a chance."

Andrew asked, "What did you mean when you said the priests were paraded to London?"

"There were multiple stops along the way from Lyford Grange to London," said Ambrosius. "Abingdon near Oxford, I believe. And Henley, where the queen's treasurer, Sir Thomas Heneage, took over Father Campion's custody. I have been told that the assistant of Father Persons was in the crowd at Henley so Father Campion would know he was thought of and prayed for."

"Father Persons was not there?" Andrew asked.

"'Twas his desire to go, but he was persuaded not to," Ambrosius said. "The queen's spies would have watched for him. What a tragedy if they had captured both priests."

"Where is Father Persons now?" asked Eve.

"He returned to France."

Andrew looked upset. "He ran away?"

Ambrosius shook his head. "He departed England to seek the counsel of his superiors in France and Rome. They forbade his return to England."

Eve thought of Father Campion suffering all of this without his closest friends nearby.

"The three priests were led to Colnbrook," Ambrosius continued. "There they stopped until the Privy Council decided in what manner the prisoners should be brought into the city."

"To show him off," Andrew said.

"Aye. They wanted Father Campion taken into the city at noon on Saturday—a market day." Ambrosius was quiet for a moment as they walked. Snow blew from a roof and dusted his wild hair. "Many Catholics were in the large crowd. Some would have been people he knew. It hath been said that he was much encouraged by their presence."

Eve imagined that he would have been.

"'Twas a humiliating spectacle nonetheless," Ambrosius said. "A sign was put on Father Campion's hat declaring him a 'Seditious Jesuit.' The Privy Council also demanded that the priests' elbows be tied behind them, with their hands tied in front. Their legs were bound by a rope that circled under their horses' bellies. Father Campion was placed on the tallest horse. They were accompanied by fifty guardsmen—lancers. The whole day was spent parading the priests up and down the streets of London. The gentlemen of the city were appalled that one of their own could be treated in such a monstrous way. The mob was entertained."

Ambrosius stopped for a moment and pointed. "They led him down this very road." He gestured to their right. "The Tower of London is that way. 'Tis where the prisoners were taken." He resumed walking and said, "He was placed inside the White Tower, in a cell called *Little Ease*. 'Tis so small that few men can stand up straight or stretch out. The windows are blocked, so the only air and light come from a small tunnel that slants up to the sky. The top and bottom are covered with grates so that nothing can get in or out. Father Campion was not allowed visitors."

"No one was allowed in?" Eve asked. "Nothing could be sent to him?"

Ambrosius shook his head. "Nay. Packages sent to him were searched thoroughly. If anything of value was found, a guard might keep it. For all of the strict rules there, bribery still wins the day."

Andrew asked, "Is that where he hath been all this time?"

"Aye, except when they took him to be interrogated or tortured."

"Nay!" Eve gasped.

Ambrosius glanced at her. "Thou didst fight alongside Robin Hood and Joan of Arc in battle, and now thou art squeamish?"

She frowned at him. "I had hoped they would treat him with more respect."

Ambrosius was not put off. "Know this, my child: Father Campion and the other Catholic prisoners have all had their hands and feet manacled with heavy chains. They have known what it is to spend time in the pit. They have suffered upon a wooden rack and have been tied to rollers that stretched their bodies beyond endurance. They have been hung wearing iron hoops and gauntlets—"

"Stop!" Eve cried out and put her hands over her face.

In a stern voice, Ambrosius said, "Hast thou not been taught about the many saints who have given their lives for the faith, and how most of them were cruelly tortured?"

She nodded her head.

"Thou knowest now what the word *martyr* means."

"I understand," she said, then took her hands away from her eyes. "I understand," she repeated softly.

"The Privy Council inflicted tortures of another kind," Ambrosius said. "Father Campion was taken from the tower and feasted by members of the council. He was given meat and drink while they questioned him, all to lure him to renounce his faith. The queen herself offered him titles and lands and a restored place in her court, if only he would turn away from his Catholic faith. He refused. Back to the tower he went. On feast days and Sundays, the priests were tortured all the more to add insult to injury. Father Campion was racked on the anniversary of the death of Ignatius of Loyola, the founder of his order."

Ambrosius's words clanged like a shrill bell in Eve's ears. She looked at Andrew. He was walking with a grim look on his face. His lips were pressed together, and his eyes were fixed on the ground ahead of them.

"The council lied to him," Ambrosius continued, "promising that nothing terrible would happen to any

Catholics he named. Father Campion heeded them not. He said, 'Come rack, come rope, I shall betray no one.'"

Eve shivered, though she wasn't very cold. But she felt the tears turn icy on her cheeks.

"The council also lied *about* him," said Ambrosius. "They claimed he had recanted his faith. They claimed he had told them everywhere he had been and with whom. He had not." Ambrosius stopped at a corner, waiting as horses and carriages rode past. Then he signaled for the kids to follow him quickly.

Once they were on the other side of the street, he said, "The council dragged him out of the tower to debate their theologians. At times they brought Father Sherwin along, merely for the public spectacle of it. They gave the priests no time to prepare, no papers, no Bible. For hours they were assaulted with opinions and accusations and given little chance to reply. When they did speak, they were more persuasive than their accusers."

Eve glanced at Ambrosius. Was he speaking from his own experiences? Had he been there to see this for himself?

"The council's plan turned on them. The sight of the priests' tortured bodies shocked many in the audience," Ambrosius said. "The Privy Council denied the use of torture. But they quickly ended any further public debates."

"Did they leave Father Campion alone after that?" Andrew asked softly.

CHAPTER THIRTY-NINE

Ambrosius frowned. "In spite of the protests, Father Campion was racked twice more. 'Twas said he sang the 'Te Deum' during the torture."

Eve remembered that the 'Te Deum' was a canticle of praise to God.

"When asked how his hands and feet felt, Father Campion said, 'Not ill, because not at all.' By the time of his trial, he could no longer lift one of his hands. Yet through it all, he remained heroically happy."

"So there was a trial?" Andrew asked.

"A fortnight ago," said Ambrosius. "He and seven other priests were charged with treason. They were accused of having conspired at Rome and Reims to raise sedition and overthrow the queen. They pled not guilty."

Eve groaned. "It was a mockery, not a trial."

Ambrosius agreed. "Father Campion defended them well, though the end was known to all, even before the jury found them guilty. All of the priests were condemned to be hanged, drawn, and quartered. When the sentence was passed, Father Campion and the other priests sang '*Haec est dies quam fecit Dominus. Exultemus et laetemur in ea.*'"

"What doth that mean?" asked Andrew.

"This is the day which the Lord has made. Let us rejoice and exult in it." Ambrosius gestured for them to turn onto a street to the right. "The schemes of the queen did not stop. Father Campion's sister was with him only a day ago. She offered him a lifelong position of wealth if he would recant. He declined. He hath since been fasting from all food, drink, and even sleep to spend his remaining hours in meditation and prayer."

Eve looked up and suddenly realized they had stopped in front of a house. "Where are we?" she asked.

Before Ambrosius answered, the door to the house opened. Both William and Matthew stepped out and bid them hurry inside.

In the entry, they all embraced. Then Eve noticed that Ambrosius wasn't with them. "Where did he go?" she asked.

"Who?" asked William.

"Ambrosius," Andrew said. He looked confused.

William seemed puzzled. "Why would he be with you?"

"He brought us here," Andrew said. "Did you not see him on the road with us when you came out?"

The two priests looked at each other. "You were on the street alone."

Andrew slowly shook his head. "Methinks the man is trying to drive us crazy."

Neither Andrew nor Eve knew the house. When they asked William to whom it belonged, he simply put a finger to his lips.

The modest-sized house seemed to be a series of halls and rooms connected to a single large meeting room on the main floor. The room was now filled with a dozen men and women sitting on chairs and kneeling on the floor. Candles were lit on various tables, bringing a soft yellow light to the room as the winter sun disappeared.

"We are conducting an all-night vigil and prayer service for those in the tower," Matthew explained. "On the morrow, we shall scatter throughout the city to show our love for our priests as they journey to Tyburn."

Andrew felt a pang of anxiety about a dozen Catholics meeting together in one place, especially in a London home. The priest hunters could be at the door at any moment. He prayed that God would protect those gathered and give them peace.

Eve found a spot near the back of the room and knelt down. Andrew knelt next to her. A moment later, Matthew knelt next to them. Someone began to pray from the Divine Office. Afterward, others read from the Psalms. Then prayers were offered for Father Campion, Father Sherwin, Father Ford, Father Collington, Father Bryant, and many others held captive by the Queen's Privy Council.

A delicate-looking man stood up. He had long brown hair brushed back from his oval face. He stroked his well-groomed beard and then signaled with upturned palms to the people to his right. Four men and three boys stood up. They came together in a circle.

"'Tis William Byrd, a court composer," Matthew whispered.

"He works for the queen? Are you not afraid that he is a spy?" Andrew asked.

"He is no spy. He is a faithful Catholic," Matthew explained. "For reasons of her own, the queen tolerates his refusal to attend Anglican services."

Andrew wished she would tolerate letting Father Campion and the other priests go free.

William Byrd raised his right hand only slightly, then brought it down again. The singers began to sing in Latin, in beautiful harmony. Andrew learned the words in English from Matthew:

> *Let us atone for the sins we have committed in our ignorance, lest, suddenly, surprised at the day of our death, we seek time for repentance and cannot find it. Lord, hear us and have mercy, for we have sinned against Thee. Help us, O God of our salvation and, according to the honor of Thy name, deliver us.*

Throughout the night, prayers, Scripture, and songs were intermingled. Andrew expected to become drowsy. But he kept thinking of the disciples who fell asleep in the garden of Gethsemane while Jesus prayed in anguish. Andrew didn't want to let down Father Campion and the other priests on this night before their ordeals.

40

Dawn was hardly dawn at all. A barely noticeable light grew only a little brighter than the night had been. Rain poured down as the gathering broke up. The people went out different doors at different times to go their separate ways.

In the front hall, William asked Andrew and Eve, "Did Ambrosius give you instructions about what you are to do today?"

Both admitted that he hadn't.

"Then you may join Matthew and me," the priest offered. Andrew nodded. William turned and went back to the meeting room.

Eve was sitting on a small chair, her hands tucked between her knees. She rocked back and forth ever so slightly. "I cannot go," she said. "I cannot watch them kill him."

Though Andrew knew how she felt, he said, "But we must find Dr. Howard. Ambrosius said he would be at the execution. This is our chance to take him home."

"Why won't Ambrosius take him home?" Eve complained. "He seems able to do everything else."

Andrew shrugged. "You know the rules better than I do."

"I do not know what the rules are," she said, her mouth turning down into a pout. "He has broken all the rules I thought I knew."

"We should go," Andrew said. "I hope our coats are waterproof."

Andrew was aware that Eve was now staring at him.

"What?" he asked.

"You've changed," she said. "You've become... harder."

"What do you mean?"

"You're worried about your *coat*? You traveled with Father Campion for months. Why aren't you upset about what's happening to him?"

Andrew felt his face turn red. "I'm as angry as I have ever been in my life. It hurts me *here* all the time." He put his hands on his stomach. "I traveled with Father Campion all those months and worried every day that we would be captured. I started to *hate* this queen and all of her hunters and spies and councils. I've had to confess my hatred over and over. Father Campion said I have to let it go and pray for the people I hate. So now I'm trying to be like Father Campion and forgive. If he can do it, then I have to do it too. That's why I need to go. I have to see him. And we have to find Dr. Howard."

Eve's chin quivered. She bit her lower lip.

Andrew took a deep breath and exhaled slowly. "Yesterday was the Feast of Saint Andrew the Apostle."

Eve stared at him with a blank expression.

"It was my birthday," Andrew said.

She looked as if the clouds had suddenly parted. She cleared her throat and said, "Your birthday?"

"I thought you knew."

"Maybe I did in another century."

"It's the second one I've had here. You missed the last one." He held out his hand to her. "We have to be strong. And you don't have to look at anything you don't want to see. We should be watching the crowd anyway, looking for Dr. Howard."

She took his hand.

Andrew's coat was more waterproof than he could have hoped. He guessed the wool and the fur were somehow arranged to keep the rain from soaking in too deeply. He was grateful. The rain was making a miserable day all the more miserable.

Without knowing where they were going, Andrew trudged along behind William and Matthew. Eve walked next to him, her head down. Andrew thought he recognized some of the buildings they had passed. They were going back the way Ambrosius had brought them the day before.

They reached a large intersection. Turning right would take them back to London Bridge. They continued walking straight and were soon in the thick of the crowds heading to the Tower of London.

"Watch for Dr. Howard," Andrew said to Eve.

She nodded but didn't lift her head.

William broke away to move ahead. He came back a moment later and said, "They have taken Father Campion from the White Tower to Cole Harbor and put him with Father Sherwin and Father Bryant. The hurdles are in place."

Eve looked at Andrew. "Hurdles?"

"Large pieces of wood," Andrew explained. "The priests will be tied to them, and horses will drag them to where they will be hanged."

The rain fell harder. The Tower of London itself looked as if it stood behind a giant veil.

A roar came from somewhere closer to the tower gates.

Andrew stood on his tiptoes to look, then dropped down again. "There are too many people," he whispered to Eve. "We will not be able to see anything."

William, the tallest of them, said, "'Tis Father Campion."

The crowd went quiet. Andrew imagined Father Campion alone commanding a crowd this size.

The priest shouted, "God save you all! God bless you and make you all good Catholics!"

The crowd screamed abuse at him.

"He is kneeling," William said. "He is facing east and praying."

Father Campion's voice faded for a moment.

William repeated, "*In manus tuas, Domine, commendo spiritum meum.*"

"Into Thy hands, O Lord, I commend my spirit," Matthew translated.

More abuse came from the crowd.

"Father Sherwin and Father Bryant have been brought out." William then groaned. "They are now bound to the hurdles. Father Campion on one. Father Sherwin and Father Bryant on the other."

The nightmarish procession began as the horses were whipped to move forward. Andrew needed little imagination to know that the mud and filth of the street would make it slow going. They walked at a snail's pace. The spectators grew restless as they followed along the sides of the road. Many people left. Others announced that they would rush ahead to Tyburn, where they would get a better view of the criminals being hanged.

Andrew caught glimpses of the hurdles as gaps opened and closed between the crowds. The three priests were a mess of rain-soaked mud.

The crowds and traffic forced the procession to stop at various points along the route. Andrew heard scattered voices call out to the priests for comfort and blessing. The priests responded with what few kind words they had the strength to offer.

The trek was long and grueling.

At the arch of Newgate, Andrew saw Father Campion try to rise up on the hurdle. "I salute thee!" he cried out. "Be merciful so I may see thee soon!"

"What is he saying?" Andrew asked Matthew.

Matthew pointed to a niche over the gate. In it was an image of the Blessed Virgin that hadn't been destroyed yet. "He was talking to our Holy Mother," Matthew said.

Andrew's next glimpse of the priests shocked him. Through the mud on their faces, he saw smiles.

"How are we supposed to see Dr. Howard?" Eve asked. Andrew knew she had been keeping her eyes away from the scene on the street.

Andrew searched the faces in the mob. "We will find him one way or the other," he said.

In spite of all the pushing and shoving, Andrew was aware of a hand on his shoulder. William and Matthew were farther right. Eve was off to his left. He twisted around and looked into the face of Josiah Stowell.

Andrew recoiled and nearly fell into the mud.

Stowell caught his arm. Andrew jerked it away.

"What are you doing here?" Andrew said. "What do you want?" He noticed a deep scar on the man's forehead and feared Stowell might take revenge. He hooked a thumb at the procession. "Is that not enough?"

"Aye, lad, 'tis enough," Stowell said. The rain dripping down his face made him look all the more like a mangy alley cat. "I have come to pay my respects."

CHAPTER FORTY

Andrew eyed him skeptically.

"'Tis true," Stowell said. "Thou didst fell me like David felled Goliath. Rather than lose my head, I was given a second chance. God is merciful."

Andrew couldn't believe what he was hearing. Was it possible the man was telling the truth?

Stowell slowly backed away, looking like a man rowing against the current. "Vincent Howard is here," he said. "Ahead, at Tyburn. I saw him. He is not himself." And then, as he was swallowed by the crowd, he called out, "Beware of Mr. Nedly."

Eve came up to Andrew and tugged at his arm. "What art thou doing? Thou wilt be trampled if thou dost not keep moving."

Andrew kept pace with her again. "Dr. Howard is at Tyburn," he said.

"I have heard the name Tyburn, but I do not know where it is," she said.

"'Tis where they are taking the priests to be hanged."

Andrew remembered that Tyburn was just beyond the Westgate to the city. It was where Father Campion had once bowed to the triangle of gallows set up there. Today, even with the rain, the crowd had gathered in so close to the place of execution that Andrew, Eve, and the two priests could not get near it.

Even the guards fought to make way for the procession.

Andrew caught another glimpse of the priests, their faces a contrast of rain-soaked mud and pale skin. Then the procession passed. The crowd swarmed in, cutting the priests off from Andrew's view.

"We must get closer," Matthew said and began pushing through the crowd.

"There are thousands of people here," William said. He turned to Andrew and Eve.

Eve shook her head.

Andrew said, "Beware of the priest hunters, William. Mr. Nedly is here."

William gave him a quick nod. Then shouts from the crowd drew his attention away. "The three priests have been cut loose from the hurdles," he said.

After some activity Andrew couldn't see, he caught a glimpse of Father Campion standing on a wagon under the gallows. A noose was placed around his neck.

Andrew looked at Eve. She was standing with her back to the gruesome scene.

Father Campion spoke in Latin for a moment, but Andrew couldn't hear all that was said.

Then the priest cried out in a loud voice, "We are made a spectacle unto God, unto His angels, and unto men. 'Tis verified this day in me, who am here as a spectacle unto my Lord God, unto His angels, and unto you men."

Andrew heard men shouting at the priest, urging him to confess his treason against the queen.

Father Campion called back, "As to the treasons which have been laid to my charge, and for which I am come here to suffer, I desire that all present bear witness with me that I am altogether innocent," he said.

Andrew heard a voice demand that the priest admit what the evidence in court had proven.

"Well, my lord," he said to the speaker, "I am a Catholic man and a priest. In that faith have I lived, and in that faith do I intend to die. If you esteem my religion treason, then am I guilty. As for other treason, I never committed any. God is my Judge. But you have truly been given what you desire on this day."

The mob wasn't satisfied and kept badgering the priest. Father Campion closed his eyes as if praying. Then he spoke again, proclaiming that he forgave all, as he desired to be forgiven. He also asked forgiveness from any whose names he may have given up unwillingly while being tortured.

The Privy Council members continued to push Father Campion for admissions and answers about the queen's authority and a Papal Bull and other things Andrew couldn't hear.

"How long will this go on?" Andrew asked.

Suddenly Eve tugged at his arm.

"What?" he asked.

"'Tis Ambrosius," she said, pointing toward a break in the crowd behind them.

Andrew spun around.

There he was, the man himself, standing a little way off from everyone in the back.

Eve grabbed Andrew's hand, and they worked their way through the crowd. Andrew felt as if they were a couple of swimmers fighting against a flow of giant logs.

As they pushed forward, a loud shout rode like a wave through the multitude. Andrew knew what happened. The wagon had been pulled out from under Father Campion. The priest would hang and, perhaps, by the grace of God, he would die before they began the next round of torture.

Fighting back the pain in his heart, Andrew kept his eyes fixed on what was ahead.

He and Eve finally reached the end of the human obstacle course and broke into the open. Ambrosius wasn't there.

"Where hath he gone now?" Andrew said with a groan. He looked around, and his eye caught men on horseback riding along the edge of the crowd. Mr. Nedly was leading them.

Andrew ducked his head and was about to warn Eve when she said, "Look."

A man was sitting in the mud. His legs were drawn up, his arms were crooked around his knees, and his head hung down. The rain poured over him as if a special bucket was being dumped on him alone.

Andrew turned his back to the hunters and moved to the man.

"Dr. Howard," Eve said.

CHAPTER FORTY

Dr. Howard looked up at them. Andrew was taken aback. The man's face was skeletal. Dark circles had formed under his eyes. His beard hung like torn curtains from his cheeks and chin. Andrew couldn't tell if he was sick, starving, or just plain crazy.

Andrew and Eve knelt next to him.

"Dr. Howard," Andrew said again. "'Tis Andrew and Eve. From Hope Springs."

The man looked at their faces. Then he held out his hands and asked, "Please, help me."

"We must get you away," Andrew said.

The two took his hands and did their best to get him to his feet.

"What happened to you?" Eve asked.

Dr. Howard pointed toward the gallows. "*He* hath destroyed me."

Andrew stole a look at Mr. Nedly and his hunters. They were still checking the crowd and slowly coming their way.

"We have to go," Andrew said to Eve. "Mr. Nedly is here."

Eve's eyes shot to the riders. "Come on," she said.

They each took one of Dr. Howard's arms and began to lead him away from the field.

"Are we going home?" Dr. Howard asked, walking on unsteady legs. "Is this the way home?"

Andrew was lost. A walled park stood in one direction. The gates were closed. In another direction were the remains of a village—or the start of one. He couldn't tell from the few shacks nestled there. He wondered if they should stop where they were and simply use the Radiant Stone then and there.

He was about to suggest the idea when Ambrosius stepped out from behind one of the cottages. He waved them forward.

Andrew tried to push Dr. Howard to move faster.

"I am doomed," the man said softly. "I am forever scarred with the mark of Cain."

"Please stop talking," Eve snapped at him.

Andrew glanced back to check on Mr. Nedly. The hunters were still back at the crowd, but Mr. Nedly was facing his direction. Then their eyes locked.

"Boy!" Mr. Nedly shouted and spurred his horse onward. "Halt there!"

"*Run!*" Andrew yelled.

Dr. Howard groaned as they pushed him forward.

The three of them made a dash for the derelict village.

"Stop!" Mr. Nedly shouted from behind them.

Andrew could hear the horses' hooves beating the mud. Another glance back and Andrew saw not only Mr. Nedly but two other riders coming after them.

"We cannot outrun horses," Eve said, breathless.

They reached the first cottage. Whatever it once was, half of the timber had collapsed into a mere shell. Andrew looked around frantically for another place to go. Then he saw Ambrosius standing outside another cottage a dozen yards away. He beckoned them.

CHAPTER FORTY

What's with the disappearing and reappearing act? Andrew thought as he nudged Dr. Howard in that direction. *Why doesn't Ambrosius help us?*

The three of them slipped on the mud as they scrambled off.

"Go on," Andrew said, pushing Dr. Howard and Eve forward. He then knelt down and searched the ground for a rock, a pebble, or anything he might throw at their pursuers. He clawed at the mud—and found more mud. Then his fingers touched something hard. He wrapped them around a palm-sized stone.

The horses were coming up fast to the first cottage. Andrew shot the rock at a rider who had just passed Mr. Nedly. The rock hit the man hard on the side of the neck, knocking him backward. He lost his balance and pulled the reins to keep from falling. Instead, the horse reared up, slid in the mud and tipped sideways.

Mr. Nedly's horse tried to avoid a collision by abruptly changing course. It also slipped, tossing Mr. Nedly sideways off the saddle.

The third rider pulled at the reins of his horse, attempting to turn, and was thrown against the wall of the first cottage. He crashed through the wall and landed somewhere inside the debris.

Andrew clambered to catch up to the others. He reached the open doorway to the second cottage and threw himself in. It was a single dark room. Rain dripped through the thatched roof. Dr. Howard was holding on to a post and looking as if he might pass out. Eve was hunched over with her hands on her knees, trying to catch her breath. Ambrosius stood between them with an impish look on his face.

"Why did you bring us here?" Dr. Howard asked him. "Now we are trapped."

Andrew looked around and saw that it was true. There was nowhere to go or hide. He stepped back to the doorway and looked out. Mr. Nedly was on his feet, trying to pull the horse off the second rider. The third rider, looking dazed, was climbing out of the wreckage of the first cottage.

"Hurry!" Andrew said to Eve. "They'll be here soon."

Eve pulled out the locket that held the Radiant Stone. Her hands were shaking and wet. She fumbled with the case.

Mr. Nedly's voice was clear and getting closer. "I know where you are hidden. Yield to me now!"

"Help us!" Dr. Howard said to Ambrosius.

Ambrosius stepped forward, spreading his arms wide and wiggling his fingers. "Hasten, children. Gather unto me."

Are we going to have a group hug? Andrew wondered.

Eve gave up on the Radiant Stone and stepped closer to Ambrosius. Dr. Howard let go of the post and moved over to them. Andrew was the last to draw into the tight circle.

CHAPTER FORTY

"How is it your clothes are dry?" Andrew asked Ambrosius.

Mr. Nedly was now at the doorway. Andrew felt Ambrosius place an arm around his shoulder.

Then there was only an echo in his ears of Mr. Nedly shouting, "Stop!"

41

The four of them stood in the ruined chapel on Beckery Island.

"How did you do that?" Andrew asked Ambrosius. "Do the stones move sideways in time?"

"Not all of them," Ambrosius said. He gestured to the Radiant Stone in Eve's hand. "Not that one."

"Show us how it works, then," Andrew said.

"It takes years of practice to master the stones. You do not have the time now. You must take this man home."

Dr. Howard had slumped onto the remains of an old bench.

"How can we take him like this?" Eve asked.

"He cannot stay much longer," Ambrosius said.

"Perhaps I should stay." Dr. Howard spoke softly, almost in a mumble. "How can I teach with any integrity? How can I face Catherine? I am deeply ashamed of what I have done. This *time*—this horrible and loathsome time—has shown me who I truly am."

Ambrosius said sharply to him, "Is this contrition, or are you feeling sorry for yourself?"

Even in the dim light, Andrew could see that Dr. Howard was ashen faced. He squeezed his eyes closed, then dropped his head into his hands. His shoulders shook, but he made no sound.

Andrew looked at Eve, unsure of what to do.

Suddenly, Dr. Howard raised his head again. "I have failed where it really counts—the test of my character."

"You now know what every man and woman must know: our corruption and need of a Savior." Ambrosius knelt next to the man. "What will you do with that knowledge? A betrayer named Judas could not cope and hanged himself. A denier named Peter sought forgiveness and lived. Which one are you?"

At first, Dr. Howard didn't respond. Then he quietly said, "The one who seeks forgiveness."

"Then go home. Find a priest. Confess it all and know God's forgiveness," Ambrosius said.

"I want to confess here," Dr. Howard said.

Ambrosius stood up. "I am not a priest—and this is not your time. Your time here has done you much damage. But it has also done you good, if you mean what you've said."

Dr. Howard nodded.

Andrew suddenly realized that Ambrosius wasn't speaking in Elizabethan English.

Ambrosius motioned to Eve. "Use the Radiant Stone and take him home."

CHAPTER FORTY-ONE

Eve pushed the small pin on the case. The locket opened to reveal the stone.

"Wait," Andrew said. "Tell me how you've done it. You saved me from the burning wagon and came to me in London. You bounced us from Lyford Grange to Alfred Virtue's office to here and then to the London Bridge. Now you've brought us here. It wasn't just practice. What stone do you have?"

"Clever lad," Ambrosius said. He held up his right hand. On his forefinger was a large ring with a stone embedded in it. Though there was little light in the chapel, the stone sparkled with purples and reds.

The two kids came closer.

"What is it?" Andrew asked.

"The most powerful of all the stones we've yet found," he replied. "It is called the Merlyn Stone."

Eve looked unsure. "There's nothing in Alfred Virtue's journals about a Merlyn Stone."

"How could there be?" Ambrosius asked. "The stone hadn't been found in his time."

Andrew thought through what this meant and asked, "How can you know what happens in the future if you're from this time?"

"Why do you think I'm from this time?" Ambrosius asked. Then, with a crafty smile, he drew his hand into a fist and disappeared.

Andrew stood stunned.

Eve gaped at the spot where Ambrosius had been standing.

"Please, take me home," Dr. Howard said, struggling to his feet. "I would be happy if I never saw another Radiant Stone or *any* stone ever again."

Eve reached out for Andrew. He took hold of her free hand, then put a hand on Dr. Howard's arm. Eve wrapped her fingers around the Radiant Stone.

Catherine Drake screamed when the three of them appeared in Alfred Virtue's office. Andrew immediately realized they hadn't changed clothes. The outfits they now wore were not only from another time, but they were drenched from the rain and splattered with mud.

"We forgot our clothes," Eve said to her aunt.

Dr. Howard swayed, then leaned on the desk in front of him.

Aunt Catherine took a step toward him, but held back. She looked distressed at his appearance. "What have they done to you?"

"I'm a mess," he replied, gazing at her with a dull expression.

"I don't understand all this," Aunt Catherine said. She pointed to a crate on the floor next to the desk. "This suddenly showed up right before you did. I was afraid to open it."

CHAPTER FORTY-ONE

Eve lifted the lid. Their modern clothes were inside, clean and neatly folded.

"Ambrosius," she said softly to Andrew.

Dr. Howard suddenly came alive. He rummaged for his clothes, tossing aside anything that wasn't his. Everything he had been wearing when he first touched the Radiant Stone was there—except one thing.

"Where are my boots?" he asked.

"I think Ambrosius kept them," Eve said. "I'm sorry."

Dr. Howard didn't seem to care. He grabbed his clothes and ran out of the office. Andrew heard the telltale scrape of four-hundred-year-old leather shoes on the tile floor.

"Vince!" Aunt Catherine called out, obviously shocked by his sudden departure. She spun on Eve and Andrew. "What have you done to him?" she demanded but didn't wait for an answer. She sprinted out of the office, calling his name as she went.

"Maybe we should keep extra outfits in here, just in case," Eve said.

Andrew picked up his clothes from where Dr. Howard had thrown them. "I have to wash up and change," he said.

"There's a bathroom to the right, just down the hall," Eve said.

The bathroom was an old-fashioned type. It had a wide, ornately carved sink, separate knobs for hot and cold, and a tank above the toilet with a pull chain to make it flush.

Andrew looked in the mirror. Was it the first one he'd seen in hundreds of years? He thought his face looked leaner and more weathered. *My parents will take one look at me and know*, he thought.

He ran his fingers through his shaggier-than-normal hair and winced. The side of his head was still tender from where Dr. Howard had hit him at Lyford Grange.

"He never apologized for that," Andrew said to his reflection.

He carried the bundle of sixteenth-century clothes back to the office. "What should I do with these?" he asked Eve. "I think we should burn them."

Eve shrugged. "I haven't thought that far ahead." She pointed to an empty cardboard box in the corner. "Just throw them in there. I'll figure it out later."

He noticed that Eve had also changed back into her modern clothes. He had forgotten what she looked like as a twenty-first-century girl.

"Look what I found in my pocket." She lifted up a small silver ring. "Reuben gave it to me when we were with Robin Hood. I had forgotten all about it."

"Nice," Andrew said.

"Andrew, we have to figure out what to do with the Valiant Stone," Eve said.

"What about it?" Andrew asked, puzzled that she would bring it up now.

"We used it to come back from the time of Joan of Arc," she said. "So if we brought it back from there *then*

CHAPTER FORTY-ONE

and it's here *now*, how did it wind up under the bridge at Chinon for a worker to find four hundred years later? If it's not there for him to find, then how will it get to Alfred Virtue? And if Alfred Virtue doesn't have it, then Simon Howard can't steal it and go back and ... and ..." She lost her line of thought and looked at Andrew with a comical expression.

He shook his head. "But someone put it under the bridge before we ever came along. If we can't change history, then we have to assume it'll work out somehow."

"How do we know for sure?" she asked. She frowned for a moment, then suddenly brightened up. "The other facets on the Valiant Stone will tell me! If I can find Alfred Virtue's notes, then we can—"

Andrew held up his hand to stop her. "I can't think about that now. I can't think about *anything*. I just want to go home."

"Okay," she said, looking disappointed.

Andrew was unsure about what to do. He wondered, *How do you say goodbye to someone you'd been through three different centuries with?*

Eve seemed to sense his awkwardness. She leveled her gaze at him. Her strange-colored eyes were now stormy, like clouds that were a bruised gray and blue. "If you tell your parents, they'll never let you come here again."

"I have to tell them," he said. He remembered how Eve had gotten upset when they talked about this before. It seemed like such a long time ago.

"I won't see you again," she said. Her hand was on the desk, rubbing nervously on the wooden top.

"That's crazy. We'll see each other." He almost reached out to touch her hand. *Almost.* "We're friends, aren't we?"

"I'm not the kind of friend your parents will want you to have," she said. A flicker of a smile touched her lips. "I mean, what kind of friend takes you back in time?"

"The kind of friend I want to have," he said.

There was nothing else to say. He left her, remembering to grab his coat from the rack stand near the door.

Hope Springs was pretty much the way he'd left it before his time travels began. It was still a pleasant spring day, with just a touch of mountain chill to the breeze.

As he walked home, he wondered, *What am I going to tell my parents?*